Hyde-Chambers, Fredrick.

Lama

LAMA

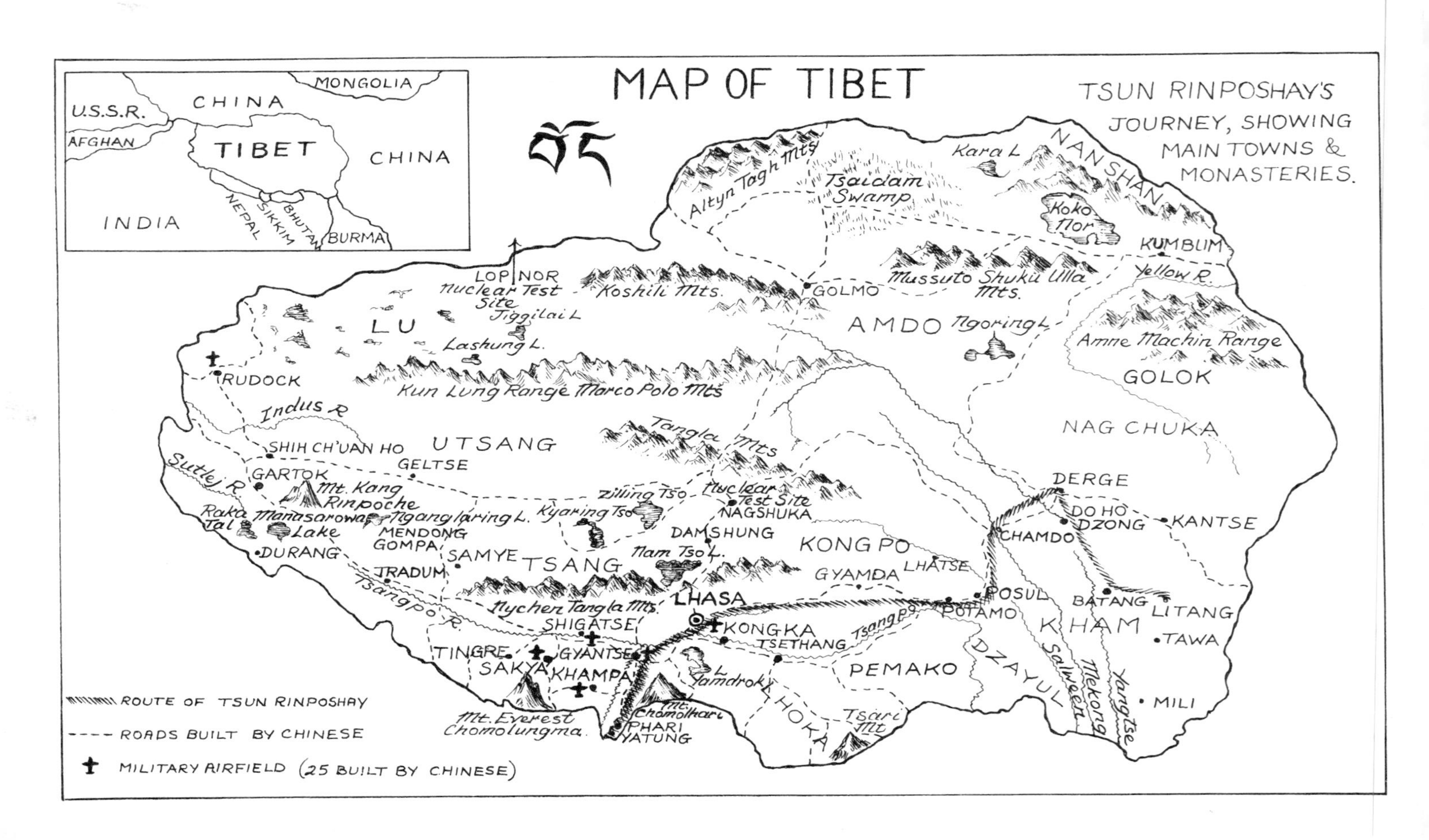
MAP OF TIBET
TSUN RINPOSHAY'S JOURNEY, SHOWING MAIN TOWNS & MONASTERIES.
U.S.S.R.
CHINA
MONGOLIA
AFGHAN
TIBET
CHINA
INDIA
NEPAL
SIKKIM
BHUTAN
BURMA
LOP NOR
Nuclear Test Site
Koshili Mts.
GOLMO
Mussuto Shuku Ulla Mts.
Altyn Tagh Mts
Tsaidam Swamp
Kara L
NANSHAN
Koko Nor
KUMBUM
Yellow R.
Jiggilai L
LU
Lashung L.
AMDO
Ngoring L
Amne Machin Range
GOLOK
RUDOCK
Kun Lung Range Marco Polo Mts
Indus R
NAG CHUKA
Tangla Mts
SHIH CH'UAN HO
UTSANG
GELTSE
Sutlej R.
GARTOK
Mt. Kang Rinpoche
Ziling Tso
Nuclear Test Site
NAGSHUKA
DERGE
DO HO DZONG
KANTSE
Raka Tal
Manasarowar Lake
Ngang laring L.
Kyaring Tso
MENDONG GOMPA
DAMSHUNG
CHAMDO
KONG PO
DURANG
SAMYE
TSANG
Nam Tso L.
TRADUM
GYAMDA
LHATSE
Tsangpo R.
Nycher Tangla Mts.
LHASA
POSUL
POTAMO
BATANG
LITANG
SHIGATSE
KONGKA
Tsangpo
KHAM
TAWA
TINGRE
GYANTSE
TSETHANG
SAKYA
KHAMPA
L Yamdrok
PEMAKO
DZAYUL
Salween
Mekong
Yangtse
MILI
Mt. Everest Chomolungma
Mt. Chomolhari
PHARI
YATUNG
KHOKA
Tsari Mt
ROUTE OF TSUN RINPOSHAY
ROADS BUILT BY CHINESE
MILITARY AIRFIELD (25 BUILT BY CHINESE)

LAMA

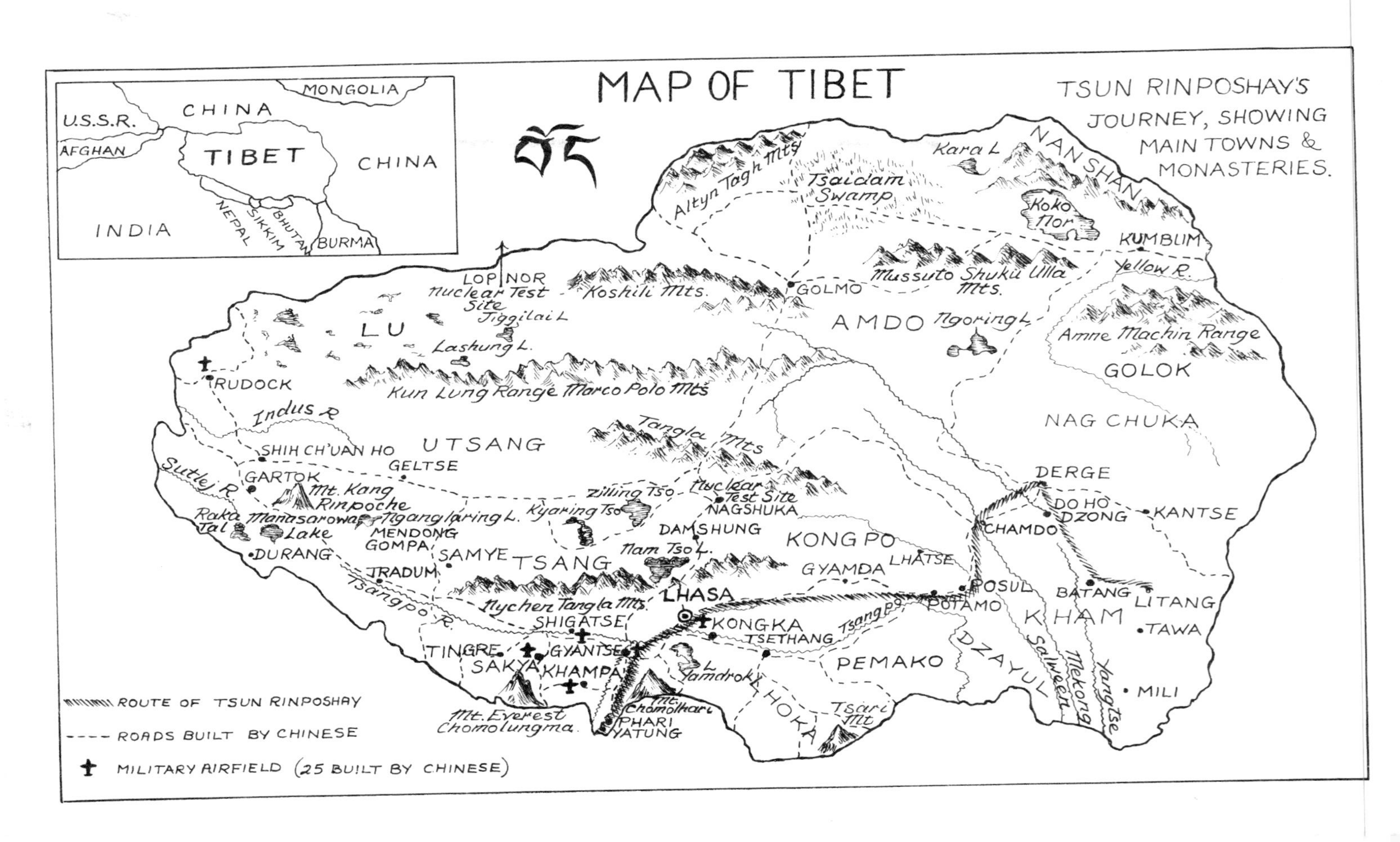
MAP OF TIBET
TSUN RINPOSHAY'S JOURNEY, SHOWING MAIN TOWNS & MONASTERIES.
U.S.S.R.
CHINA
MONGOLIA
AFGHAN
TIBET
CHINA
INDIA
NEPAL
SIKKIM
BHUTAN
BURMA
Altyn Tagh Mts
Tsaidam Swamp
Kara L
NANSHAN
Koko Nor
KUMBUM
Yellow R.
LOP NOR
Nuclear Test Site
Koshili Mts.
GOLMO
Mussuto Shuku Ulla Mts.
Jiggilai L
LU
AMDO
Ngoring L
Amne Machin Range
Lashung L.
GOLOK
RUDOCK
Kun Lung Range
Marco Polo Mts
Indus R
NAG CHUKA
Tangla Mts
SHIH CH'UAN HO
UTSANG
Sutlej R.
GELTSE
DERGE
GARTOK
Mt. Kang Rinpoche
Ziling Tso
Nuclear Test Site
NAGSHUKA
DO HO DZONG
KANTSE
Raka Tal
Manasarowar Lake
Ngang laring L.
Kyaring Tso
CHAMDO
MENDONG GOMPA
DAMSHUNG
KONG PO
DURANG
Nam Tso L.
LHATSE
SAMYE
TSANG
GYAMDA
TRADUM
POSUL
BATANG
LITANG
LHASA
Tsangpo R.
Nycher Tangla Mts.
POTAMO
KHAM
SHIGATSE
KONGKA
Tsangpo
TSETHANG
TAWA
TINGRE
GYANTSE
PEMAKO
DZAYUL
Salween
Mekong
Yangtse
SAKYA
KHAMPA
L Yamdrok
MILI
KHOKA
Mt. Chomolhari
Tsari Mt
Mt. Everest Chomolungma
PHARI
YATUNG
ROUTE OF TSUN RINPOSHAY
ROADS BUILT BY CHINESE
MILITARY AIRFIELD (25 BUILT BY CHINESE)

Dedicated to Derek and Peggy Hyde-Chambers, story tellers in film and written word, to whom I was fortunate enough to be apprenticed.

This is a story to which 100,000 men, women and children have borne witness, by successfully making their escape over the world's highest mountains, the Himalayas. Thousands died in the attempt. A mountain people, they came into a tropical climate with diseases to which they had no immunity. They came, destitute, hungry, having lost country, home, relatives and livelihood, speaking a language few understood. Their belief that their story would be heard was not to be.

With an unshakable faith they have pursued an apparently hopeless cause with seemingly unrealistic methods: using non-violence and moderation to present their case.

Events in Tibet and outside have proved them right.

Acknowledgements

It is almost a trite commonplace for writers to acknowledge the help of their wives. That it *is* so commonplace perhaps indicates the sheer physical labour and long hours in which they are invariably involved!

My gratitude for the help of Audrey, my wife, is certainly not commonplace.

Likewise, my appreciation of Tessa Harrow for her care and courtesy as editor.

To Anne Jennings Brown my thanks for the maps and illustrations drawn on behalf of the Tibetan Institute of Performing Arts.

F.R.H-C.

Contents

'Let China sleep. When she awakens, the world will be sorry.'

Napoleon

'It may happen that here in the centre of Tibet the religion and the secular administration will be similarly attacked from without and within, and the holders of the Faith, the Glorious Rebirths, will be broken down and left without a name. As regards the monasteries and the priesthood, their lands and properties will be destroyed. The officers of state, ecclesiastical and lay, will find their lands seized and their property confiscated, and they themselves made to serve their enemies or wander about the country as beggars do. All beings will be sunk in hardship and fear, and the nights will drag on slowly in suffering . . .'

From the Political Testament of the XIIIth Dalai Lama, died 1933. Sir Charles Bell, Portrait of the Dalai Lama, Collins, *1946, p 380*

List of main characters

NOTE: All Tibetan names and terms are spelt phonetically.

DORJE RI-GON MONASTERY

Tsun Rinposhay – Abbot of Dorje Ri-gon

Kesang – *Dorje Rinposhay*, incarnate lama of Dorje Ri-gon Monastery

Senge – the Shi-tsu dog, Tsun's pet

Champa – } Tsun's three pupils
Jigme – }
Samden – }

Rinchen – Steward of Dorje Ri-gon Monastery

Lopsang – Secretary

Norden – *The Honourable Mother*, Kesang's mother

Ling Tao Yen – Han cadre

ON THE JOURNEY

Genyen Chime – Tsun's former lover. Resistance leader of the Khambas

Tsering Dawa – merchant, Tsun's host

Kalsang – merchant's wife

Jetsun – Tsering's daughter

Tashi – the minstrel – one of Genyen's men

Topden – farmer, one of Genyen's men

Gonpo – one of Genyen's men

AT DERGE

The Queen of Derge

Chopel – silversmith, resistance worker, Tsun's host

Dekyi – Chopel's daughter

Namgyal – Chopel's son

Yangchen – Tsun's sister

Pema – Tsun's younger sister

NOMAD CAMP

Dhondup – keeper of the Queen's herds

Lashee – Dhondup's wife

Norbu – Dhondup's son
Topgay – Dhondup's eldest son
The Garwan – Chief of the nomad clan

WITH THE REFUGEES
Tul-lok – Tsun's cousin, a bandit and resistance leader
Karma – Tul-lok's lieutenant

AT THE LABOUR CAMP
Colonel Liu Ying
Brass Nose – fellow prisoner
Jettie – fellow prisoner and member of Mimang
Khenpo – Master of Studies at Chamdo Monastery

IN LHASA
Tenzing – a ragyapa, disposer of the dead
Pemba – shopkeeper

Glossary

AMBAC — Pocket made by fold of chuba where it wraps over the chest.

AMDO — North East Tibet.

CADRE — Chinese administrator, usually a Communist Party member.

CAIRN — A heap of stones raised as a landmark, particularly at the top of mountain passes, in Tibet surmounted by prayer flags to honour the local dieties.

CHORTEN — Developed, like the pagoda and stupa of India, from the burial mound containing the ashes of the Buddha. In shape like a handbell, Chortens can be anything from a few inches high and made in bronze, crystal or silver for a shrine, up to two hundred feet as wayside shrines, or even as Temples, frequently containing relics. Essentially symbolic of Buddha's Awakening or Enlightenment, it contains a wealth of symbolism.

CHUBA — A wrap-around gown, worn knee length by most men and ankle length by women. Held in place with a woven belt, securing the tucks and pleats at the back, which determine the different styles of each province.

CHUSHI GANG DRUK — 'Four Rivers and Six Ranges' of Amdo and Kham, the eastern part of Tibet. Popular name for the Khamba Resistance.

COUNTER-REVOLUTIONARY	Defined under the Chinese *Act for Punishment of Counter-Revolution* as being anyone 'whose goal is to overthrow the people's democratic regime or to undermine the undertaking of the people's democracy', by such means as 'provoking dissension among the various nationalities, democratic classes, democratic parties and groups, people's organisations or between the people and the government.'
DORJE	Ritual sceptre or thunderbolt, symbolic of the indestructible or Awakened quality of the mind. Generally used with the ritual bell when it also is symbolic of Method or Compassion.
and BELL	Symbol of Wisdom. The Dorje (male) and the Bell (female) are essentially regarded as one.
DORJE RI-GON	The 'Diamond Sceptre Hermitage on the Hill'. The monastery of Tsun Rinposhay and Dorje Rinposhay.
DHARMA	The Teachings of the Buddha.
DRI	A female yak.
FELICITY SCARF	A white scarf exchanged in greeting and offered to teachers, at shrines, and draped over thankas, etc., as a sign of reverence and respect.
GREEN BRAIN	A Tibetan term for someone who clings obstinately to a particular idea. Frequently used by the Chinese in derision of the Tibetans' 'stubbornly' held religious beliefs.

HAN	Majority nationality of China.
KARMA	The Universal Law of Cause and Effect, even to thoughts which can affect the memory, or subtly affect later thought and action. If analysed thoroughly no physical, mental or emotional occurrence is without a cause or an effect in turn causing an effect *ad infinitum* at all levels of being and society: from insect to a nation's karma.
KHAM	East Tibet.
KHAMBA	A person from east Tibet, where there is a strong warrior and clan tradition, the relationship with central Tibet being much like that of Highland Scots and the English.
KUNDUN	'Presence' – a popular Tibetan term for the Dalai Lama, as the presence of the Lord of Compassion.
KUSHO	'Sir'.
INJIS	Tibetan corruption of 'English', learnt during the British invasion of Tibet in 1904 and used for Westerners in general.
LAMA	A recognised spiritual teacher, lay or monastic, and a senior member of the Tibetan Buddhist Order.
MANI MANTRA	OM MANI PADME HUM – the mantra of Chenresi, the Lord of Compassion, Patron of Tibet. The syllables are carved into stones, contained in prayer wheels, printed on prayer flags and constantly being used in conjunction with a rosary. With many layers of meaning, OM refers to the inexpressible Absolute, MANI

to the Buddha Dharma or Teaching, PADME to the world in which the Teaching is expressed and HUM that it is victorious in defeating ignorance and its effects.

MUDRA — Ritual gestures of the hands used in conjunction with mantras as a physical expression of meditation. Images of the Buddha and Buddhist sages have the hands in mudra positions.

PLA — People's Liberation Army of China.

POTALA — 'Place of the gods' – an enormous fortress palace built on a natural hill in the centre of the valley of Lhasa. Nine hundred feet long and six hundred feet high, it was built in the seventeenth century on the site of a previous fortress. It houses the monastery and school of the Civil Service, the National Assembly, the mausoleums of the previous Dalai Lamas, the State Treasury and the nation's archives, as well as the personal treasury of successive Dalai Lamas. It is the official residence of the Dalai Lama and centre of Government.

PRAYER WHEEL — Really the 'Mani Religion Wheel' – a physical metaphor for the setting in motion of Buddha's Teachings. Its use was so widespread as to make it the 'national habit'. Like the rosary, prayer wheels are essentially aids to meditation. All contain the scriptures or mantras. The most popular form is a four-inch metal cylinder on an upright axle with a straight handle; a weight attached to the cylinder by a thin chain makes it like a flywheel, easy to keep in motion with a slight movement of the hand. The largest prayer wheels can be up to several feet high in temples.

RINPOSHAY	'Precious One', title used for incarnate lamas and revered teachers.
SHAPAY	Title given to a member of the Tibetan Kashag (cabinet).
TEACHING	Tibetans refer to Buddhism as the Religion or Teaching.
THAMZING	'Struggle Meeting' devised by the Chinese Communist Party to break old loyalties and social patterns, establishing loyalty only to the Motherland and the Party, using manipulation of emotions, hatred, shame, fear of social ostracism. ('Hatred is a great social leveller' – Chou En-lai.) In Tibet used to rouse the people to denounce landowners, lamas and monks, held by the Chinese to be counter-revolutionary and oppressors. Torture and death are frequently the outcome.
THANKA	A scroll painting.
TRIPLE GEM (KUNJOSUM *when an expletive*)	The Buddha – the Teaching, The Community of Monks and practitioners of Buddhism.
TRIPLE REFUGE	Taking spiritual refuge in the Buddha, His Teaching and the Community of Monks.
TSAMPA	Staple diet made from parched barley flour mixed to a dough with butter tea.

TULKU — Incarnate lama. Someone recognised as being a vehicle for the spiritual influence of a saint or an aspect of the divine. Over a thousand tulkus are recognised in Tibetan Buddhism.

U-TSANG — Tibet's central province.

ULTIMATE REALITY — Buddhism refers to Relative and Absolute Truth. Relative Truth is that which we see to be true from our usual knowledge and experience of life.

or ABSOLUTE REALITY — Absolute Truth is the true nature of man and all phenomena, perceivable by an Awakened man free from all subtle preconceptions, biases, prejudices, knowing the happiness all men seek, and to which, under many names, all religions point.

Introduction

A ninth century poet wrote of his country:

> *The centre of high snow mountains,*
> *The source of great rivers,*
> *A lofty land,*
> *A pure land.*

Written over a thousand years ago, it remains an accurate description of Tibet, the highest country in the world. Covering a million and a half square miles – seven times the size of France – at an average height of sixteen thousand feet above sea level, it is a vast plateau of stony plains and fertile valleys, of pine forested hills, of tortured, stratified cliffs in bare mineral landscapes; and always, on the horizon, glacier-tipped mountains: the massive range of the Himalayas forming its fifteen hundred-mile border with the Indian sub-continent, the Karkorum Mountains to the west and, to the north, the Kuen Lun and Altyn Tagh ranges bordering Russia, Mongolia and China.

Tibet's ice age glaciers are the source of many rivers stretching throughout Asia. Some are legendary, like the Brahmaputra, the Indus, the Yangtse, Salween, Mekong and Yellow Rivers.

More than thirteen hundred years ago, when Oswald, King of Northumbria, was introducing Christianity to his people, before the unification of England, and Mohammed was dictating the material which was to become the Koran, Tibet had built a military empire, encompassing Indian territory as far as the Bay of Bengal, to Turkestan and deep into China. The threat of the Tibetan empire even persuaded Harun al-Rashid, the Caliph of Baghdad (of a 'Thousand and One Nights' fame) into an unlikely defence alliance with the T'ang Dynasty Emperor of China.

Tibet's merchants journeyed far beyond its empire, returning not only with merchandise but with travelling companions who brought with them philosophies and teachings already ancient, from Egypt, Persia, Greece, Rome, India and China, and teachings still comparatively new to men, including those of the Buddha.

The kings of the empire listened to and became adherents of the Buddha's teaching, organising a debate between the proponents of the different approaches that had developed from the Buddha's teaching, that the way for Tibet should be found. Tibet sheathed its sword and picked up the prayer wheel. Within two hundred years, the empire had disappeared.

In time the 'Religious Kings', as they were known, gave way to the dynasty of lamas, and three hundred years ago the dynasty of the Dalai Lama began.

Like all small countries surrounded by powerful neighbours, Tibet, bordered by China, Russia and India, had a sharp awareness of the importance of maintaining good relations with its neighbours. With China there developed a 'priest-patron' relationship between the reigning Dalai Lama and the Chinese Emperors, particularly strong during the time of the Mongol Emperors, as Mongolia had been converted to Buddhism by Tibet.

Then, with the Chinese revolution of 1911 and the establishment of a republic, the relationship ended and for the next thirty-eight years the two countries each went its own way. China suffered invasion, famine and protracted civil war; Tibet remained uninvolved and maintained its neutrality, even during the Second World War, until that day in 1950 when, three months after the Communist victory and Mao Tse-tung's proclamation of the People's Republic of China, the Central People's Government announced the 'Liberation of Tibet' as its next objective for the People's Liberation Army.

After fruitless exchanges of messages, a Tibetan delegation arrived in India for negotiations with the Chinese. The Chinese Government assured the Tibetan and Indian Governments that it had no intention of forcing the issue, but negotiations had to be on Chinese, not on foreign soil. While awaiting instructions from Lhasa, Tibet's capital, the People's Liberation Army (the PLA) invaded Tibet, with a force of a quarter of a million men against a Tibetan army of eight thousand five hundred, eventually taking Chamdo, the capital of Kham, or east Tibet.

Even as Peking announced its intention to advance to 'free three million Tibetans from imperialist oppression and to consolidate the national defences of China's western frontier,' the Tibetan delegation left India for Peking and the Tibetan Government cabled the United Nations for assistance.

A week later, El Salvador's request for a General Assembly debate was postponed indefinitely. No one bothered to reply to the

Tibetan Government. Two days later, on November 17th, 1950, the sixteen year-old Dalai Lama was installed, two years before his majority, as Head of Government.

As the PLA of China advanced into Tibet, there was widespread fear that the Dalai Lama would be captured. He withdrew to a town close to the border with India. Then Peking announced, to the complete surprise of the Tibetan Government, that its delegation had signed an 'agreement for the peaceful liberation of Tibet.' In exchange for accepting the absorption of Tibet into China, China guaranteed that nothing would be forced on the country, that freedom of religion would remain.

In order to reach the Dalai Lama safely, the PLA Commander of the Tibet Military Region had to fly to India to reach South Tibet and so escort the sovereign back to his capital.

By early 1956 there was growing unrest among the Tibetans against the Chinese occupation in east Tibet, which had been effectively cut off from the Tibetan Government, and an extensive, if unco-ordinated, resistance movement developed and took control of much of the countryside.

Men reported many ill omens – earthquakes, the birth of twin-headed animals – as Tibet entered a dark age far beyond even the comprehension of the prophecies.

Prologue: February, 1983

Blood is not the easiest medium with which to write, especially with a split bamboo pen. Which is why the twenty signatures were so badly written – as had been explained to the man who 'whispered the Teachings' as he carefully read the petition addressed to the Indian Premier, Indira Gandhi, as Chairman of the Seventh Summit Meeting of the Heads of State of the Non-aligned Nations. It was dated the fifth day of the first month of the Water Pig Year, the Tibetan Royal Year 2110, or the 18th of February, 1983.

The man rolled the flimsy paper of the petition as tightly as possible round the torch batteries and was just able to re-insert them back into the torch.

That had been last night, when it had become clear that he should leave the country immediately, before information on his identity reached 'higher levels' in the Public Security Office. Neither he, nor those closest to him, were in any doubt that, even under Deng Xiaoping's policy of 'moderation', secretly passing on the Teaching of Buddha was a counter-revolutionary activity and, given his background, he would be liable for a life sentence or execution.

The men and women who had signed the appeal had mostly been born just before or during the occupation. The years of disregarded appeals and petitions were at the back of all their minds, but some day an appeal would be heard and someone would answer. Surely, they tried to convince themselves, the non-aligned nations would not turn away? Not when they were in India and could see and talk to the thousands who had fled across the border. The man with the petition hidden in the torch nodded agreement. But he did not speak. He had seen too much.

Although everyone in the village regretted his going, and many wept, none came to say goodbye. He walked alone. It was safer that way. But it gave a keener edge to their sadness.

It was difficult to place his age, dressed as he was in the ill-fitting and shabby, dull green quilted jacket and shapeless trousers.

His lean, strong face was copper-bronzed, weatherbeaten and very lined, his grey hair close cropped. But he had an ease of stride and manner, making him appear younger than a man in his mid sixties.

He pulled the fur lappets of his green cap over his ears. With the woven cloth bag across his back and the staff he carried, he looked like one of the hundreds of pilgrims who used to pass through Phari every year.

He felt a few delicious moments of exhilaration as he walked northwards through the town, knowing that for the first time in twenty years of living in Phari he could walk on towards the mountain of the Goddess Lady: Chomolhari, third highest peak of the Himalayas; and beyond to the steep ravines and passes to India and Bhutan.

The sun was low in the sky, and as evening approached the bare, round topped hills appeared to stretch to the horizon, Chomolhari rising like a horn, a weather-rounded peak, above a cluster of jagged white mountains. Always unconsciously alive to the grandeur of the mountains, the pilgrim was suddenly vividly aware, as the pink shading of the evening sky spread over Chomolhari, that the mountains lived, ever changing in colour and form.

The intensely cold wind slackened, the massive fort acting as a windbreak; its inward sloping, pyramid-like walls, built of stone, rose from a hillock. The pilgrim looked up at the red flag straining at its pole on the flat roof of the fort a hundred feet from the ground. Despite numerous replacements, the flag was swiftly torn by the full blast of the Himalayan wind, sweeping down from the mountain of the Goddess Lady. The Han never realized the significance the Tibetans placed on this regular defeat. Nevertheless, the pilgrim thought, it flew above them.

The fort had been built to guard the border passes from India and Bhutan, but as the British had seized it in 1904, so had the Han, half a century later. The town was made up of nearly a thousand houses clustered round the fort, each of one or two storeys and with whitewashed walls. Many had their peat-built flat roofs laden with hay to feed the animals in the ground floor stalls, as winter was not yet completely over.

Phari, at four thousand six hundred metres above sea level, was the highest town in the world. Delightful in summer, it was also the coldest place in the world in winter and many of the houses were sunk below ground level as a protection against the wind. Its steadily increasing prosperity had depended on trade with India and the neighbouring states. With the Han occupation the border was closed. A third of the inhabitants had locked up their houses in those first few years after the uprising and fled across the border. Few had succeeded since.

Spumes of dust were picked up from the dirt road by the rising wind; it moaned through a derelict single-storey house as the pilgrim paused, looking through the broken and empty window frames. The door was off its hinges, part of the back wall had caved in and weeds had taken root in the collapsed peat roof.

The pilgrim stooped to clear the low door frame, and looked round into the eyes of a Tibetan in his late thirties, with a fox fur hat, leather boots and the well cut leather jacket of a ranking cadre. He reached into his pocket, as the middle aged woman with him got to her feet. She was dressed in a thick, dirty chuba, a western style jacket and a thick plaid headscarf. Her face was begrimed with years of smoke from yak chip fires. The pilgrim smiled; even with her glasses on, no one would realise she was a Han. It was a good disguise.

'Here are your passes to cross the border as pilgrims'. The man's voice cracked. Very carefully, he took a tightly folded, small white bundle from his pocket, and was surprised that after all this time, he remembered how to handle the six foot long felicity scarf as it cascaded from his hands, the concertina folds yellowed with age.

'Tsun Rinposhay,' he said, bowing very low and draping the scarf across Tsun's outstretched hands. The pilgrim raised Namgyal up with his hand on his shoulder, and as he touched his forehead with his own to bless him and to show his own respect, the silvery light of the evening sun glinted in the younger man's eyes. It had been, the pilgrim thought, a quarter of a century since he had been recognized by his true name. Was it any longer his true name? His mind was flooded with images: Namgyal, the twelve-year-old street thief covered in soot from his father's kiln, stealing so that the family could eat.

It had been snowing, he remembered, when Namgyal's father had insisted he take the boy with him, before he was sent away. That was the last they had heard of the boy's real father; the pilgrim had gradually taken his place. On his release from prison, it had been Namgyal who had ensured that he had the necessary documents to come to Phari. Without them, he would have been retained at the prison as a 'free worker'. To Namgyal he owed his ration book; a job, which gave him enough work points to eat; a home with him, his wife Pasang, and their two children. It had been Namgyal who, because of his adroit use of 'back doorism' – the black market – and his manipulation of the factions among the local administration, had enabled him to consolidate his position over the years and build up a vested interest in his survival among senior local army and party personnel. It was this which had enabled the pilgrim, over twenty years, to whisper the Teachings, and to establish an underground community of monks.

The pilgrim wanted to say that he would be returning, just as Namgyal wanted to say that he would follow with his family. But neither could. There were too many uncertainties. For Namgyal to bring out himself, his wife and his children would be almost impossible.

'Namgyal-la.' The pilgrim used an honorific term of endearment long since banned. 'The Teaching that has been passed on has only been possible through you and, as it has to be whispered, so there are those who are among the greatest of lamas, though never known as such, except by their actions.' The pilgrim draped the scarf over the young man's hands as an equal. 'My heart is here. I'll come back if I can.'

Namgyal nodded. His face strained with emotion, he gave the pilgrim a note. As Tsun read it, the woman felt no offence; caution, even among friends and family, was necessary for survival.

'I may be able to get permission for the children to visit you since the authorities accept you as their grandfather. Pasang and I have thought about it a great deal. If we succeed, it is better that they stay with you. And whatever is said by the Han if they contact you, remember, we have thought about it and the consequences.'

'Tell Pasang and the children . . .' the pilgrim began, but neither could speak, and the pilgrim turned away, stooping under the door lintel. The woman followed him. He did not look back; even had he done so, he would not have seen Namgyal. The woman glanced at him as they walked down the street; the dust picked up by the wind was sticking to his tearstained face. It was as though he were living two lives, he thought, each following the same course; for the second time in his life he had been torn from those he loved most. Again he had to cry out for those who could not speak for themselves; a cry he prayed would not, after everything, go unheeded.

The man and woman pulled scarves up over their faces to

protect them from the biting wind and dust. It was impossible to talk, and each was glad.

A dog was hugging the walls for protection from the wind as it trotted down the street, nose to ground. It was unusual now, the pilgrim thought, to see a dog on the streets. Everything he saw triggered off vivid images of the past; the dog-killing counts; the children spending every afternoon hunting birds. Pasang's public pleasure and private distress that the elder of the two children had, during six weeks, killed more birds than any other child, and the delight of the child at being able to increase the family's rations with the extra work points.

LONG LIVE THE GREAT PROLETARIAN CULTURAL REVOLUTION! LONG LIVE THE RED SUN IN OUR HEARTS, THE GREATEST LEADER, CHAIRMAN MAO, AND LONG LIFE, LONG, LONG LIFE TO HIM!

TIBET AUTONOMOUS REGION PROLETARIAN REVOLUTIONARIES GREAT ALLIANCE REBEL GENERAL COMMAND.

The slogan ran the entire length of a fourteen-foot courtyard wall, now faded and peeling, partly obscured by the swiftly torn-down posters calling for freedom. What else are we to be saved from? the pilgrim thought. Occupied, to save us from 'the Kuomintang and foreign imperialists', from 'the oppressive feudalism of the lamas and the reactionary government', from the 'plots of Deng Xiaoping', Mao's chosen heir Liu Shao-chi, then his close Comrade-in-Arms; Lin Piao, the Gang of Four, Chairman Hua's errors, and now from the errors of the great Chairman Mao himself and the mistakes of the Cultural Revolution.

He smiled as he passed two houses flying prayer flags from the corners of their roofs. It was the twentieth house he had seen with the flags, cut long and narrow like upright planks, and he realized that the dozens of people he taught had, after all, found a way of wishing him well on his journey.

It had been agreed at the last meeting over which he had presided as spiritual teacher that all those present would put up prayer flags on their roofs, on a day to be agreed, to test the reality of the new 'right to freedom of belief', the appearance of the flags throughout the town making it difficult for any one person to be singled out for retribution. He recalled how difficult it had been to obtain the special flimsy cotton cloth used for the flags, and then the problems of printing them in secret with invocations from a wooden block.

A woman carrying a wooden pail of water on her back and a

carefully folded sweater crossed the street a few yards ahead, recognized the pilgrim, but gave no acknowledgement, turning abruptly down a side street. Acknowledgement could compromise. One became conditioned, the pilgrim thought. They had all learnt how to live a double life. And as he and his companion crossed over the side street, they saw that the woman with the water pail had joined a long queue outside the state procurement shop. Most of those in the queue were the elderly and those not fit for work in the fields, instead earning work points by their knitting. The pilgrim was amazed at mankind's ingenuity and determination to survive, whatever the circumstances. How many people, he thought, had struggled to bring up families under the most unimaginable conditions? They cried, but they laughed as well – often with the black humour of those always close to death. He remembered, when he first arrived, the people's amazement and laughter at his ignorance of the 'tide of emptiness'. The constant movement of people walking through the street with empty tsampa bags, to borrow some roasted barley flour from neighbours, or hoping to reclaim that which was borrowed, borrowing to repay, on and on in an endless cycle. In surviving, in livelihood, everyone depended on the decisions of the commune and local party officials. No one could see beyond the day in which they lived. But some had survived for longer than he would have believed possible. And he saw in his mind the faces of those for whom it had not gone on: those arrested; those who killed themselves, sometimes whole families.

The loudspeakers strung throughout the town began the evening broadcast with whistling and wowing, the sound rising and sinking with the wind. It had been exactly the same when he had first walked down the road on his arrival in Phari. It was possible then still to see the foundations of the newly razed monastery. He remembered being able to use them to trace out the rooms and temples, one wall remaining, jagged and broken. Now the foundations were overgrown with weeds and grass and the wall had collapsed, so that it looked a ruin of centuries past.

Between the remains of the monastery and the road was a six foot deep trench. To the pilgrim's surprise, that too had been allowed to become overgrown, but up until only a few months ago it had been part of the town's defences. He had been one of those detailed to dig it for the 'inevitable world war', and although things had changed now, and the world war was not so inevitable, Phari as a border town was still regarded as being in the front line.

As they reached the outskirts of the town, he saw the woman look back anxiously. Three long, bonneted trucks were coming down the road behind them and they moved quickly out of the way, into the shadow of a single storey hut by the roadside. The trucks were full of PLA troops beneath the canvas cover and took the military road towards Chomolhari and the border posts. With his eyes the pilgrim followed the telegraph line from Phari, along the military road and into the mountains, realising that his reaction to Namgyal calling him by his original name had not just been because of the past, but also because of the future; he wondered if they would be able to make it to the Frontier before his name was uttered by those 'higher levels' which could operate the telegraph to the border posts. For a few moments they rested against the wall of the hut, sheltering from the wind. The border had seemed so close; now the trucks had reminded them of the reality.

The woman looked at the man in surprise. He was absorbed in feeling the stones of the hut. She had never seen anything like them before; most were only a few inches long by about an inch in thickness and, she thought, it must have been an enormous amount of work to build what was, after all, only a public lavatory.

The man smiled at the woman's surprised look.

'It was built of all the mani stones in the town.'

Most people, at some time in their lives, carefully worked on the special stones, the mani invocation, adding them to their local mani wall built outside the town to greet visitors and pilgrims. As the man touched his forehead on the stones, the woman murmured, 'I can only weep with you,' and they stepped into the wind and dust, leaving the town and following the military road leading to Chomolhari and beyond.

He wanted to shout for freedom from his memories. He had seen too much, and nothing would take the sights and the memories away. Yet he knew that, while he could not bear to look at them for too long, they were woven into his very being, and had proved to him the saying that, in meditation and religious practice 'one's enemy can be one's best teacher'. To pass on the teachings effectively, he had had to be able to help his pupils to come to terms with the life they all lived.

Suddenly, through icy, howling winds, he heard a familiar sound; after so many years, he still had the instinctive reaction to dive for cover. The woman, her head down against the wind, had walked on quite a few yards before realising that the man had stopped and was watching the 'iron bird' coming in low to land at Phari military airfield outside the town. In those few seconds he was reliving that other, far-off day at his monastery when he had seen the planes . . .

BOOK ONE: February, 1956

It may happen that here in the centre of Tibet, the religion and the secular administration will be similarly attacked from without and within . . .

A shaft of sunlight filtered through the small parchment window in the Litang Monastery and bathed in its mellow light the seventy-six year-old figure of the Lama Ga Nori, ex-Abbot of Litang. Sitting cross-legged, his eyes half closed, the silent unmoving figure was meditating alone in his cell.

Far away along a corridor came the sound of marching feet. They drew nearer. The door of the cell opened. The methodical click of leather boots resounded sharply on the stone floor.

A second's silence. A revolver was pointed at the meditating Lama's face. One shot. The bullet pierced his eye and the Lama Ga Nori died a more merciful death than many of his brothers.

He fell to one side. His blood and brains, 'The flowers in bloom', bespattered the pages of the scriptures that taught the Noble Doctrine of the Sakya-Sage, the way of compassion.

This was the dwelling place of the gods. The roof of the world. Tibet, February 1956.

The death of Lama Ga Nori was placed in evidence before the International Commission of Jurists' Legal Enquiry Committee on the question of genocide in Tibet.

Chapter One

Tsun Rinposhay, the thirty-eight year-old Abbot of Dorje Rigon monastery, stood alone on the balcony of his room which overhung the sheer seven hundred-foot drop to the valley below. The monastery clung to the brown cliff-side, its white walls framed with lush conifer trees. Tsun had decided not to attend the Second Noon Tea Assembly taking place in the great temple above him; instead he listened to the slow, rhythmic, caressing chant of the monks which filled the air. He wanted to be alone to think about the future of the monastery, and stood gazing across the wide valley, his strong, lean face thoughtful beneath the close-cropped hair, copper-tanned by the partially filtered sun of Tibet.

At 15,000 feet, the rarefied atmosphere enabled him to see quite distinctly the sprawling buildings of the Monastic University of Litang, although it was some miles away. In the pure, unclouded blue, the setting sun shot spears of golden red which reflected in the gilded roofs of Litang. It looked, Tsun thought, like a lily: the white walls the petals, the gilded roofs the pistil, set amidst a pool of lush grass which moved imperceptibly in the whispering wind.

Tsun held a pair of field glasses to his eyes, eyes that were deep pools of ebony, focusing them on the entrenchments encircling the massive outer walls of Litang Monastery. For sixty days the monastery had been besieged by the troops of the People's Liberation Army of China. For most of those days they had charged the walls and bombarded the monastery with artillery fire. The monks had defended themselves with muzzle loaders, a few outdated Russian rifles and pistols, and with swords, spears, bows and arrows.

Today there had been no attack. Perhaps, Tsun thought, the rumours about a negotiated peace settlement were true.

Ever since the occupation in 1950 of east Tibet by the Communist Chinese, the Han, he had worked hard to keep his own monastery free and unhampered. He had given the Han no excuse to seize it, but the excuse, he knew, was there. Monks had given their vows into his custody and left the monastery to join the resistance movement, and he had not reported them to the occupation authorities. As a respected and revered personality in the district, he had also pleaded with the Han on behalf of many of the villagers who had been unjustly treated. The Han had listened to him with deference; they were still consolidating their grip on the country. But Tsun knew they would remember, and he would be held to account in the future. He had attempted to be reasonable in his dealings with the occupation authorities and had paid the exorbitant taxes levied on the monastery where other abbots had hidden their monasteries' grain and treasure, only to have it discovered and to be branded as 'hoarders' and 'enemies of the people'. They had been subjected to the 'Thamzing' and their monasteries were taken over and disbanded. But Tsun felt that now, his presence at Dorje Ri-gon was, in a sense, a threat to its existence, and he feared for its safety. Months ago an appeal had been prepared by the resistance for presentation to the United Nations, signed by leading villagers, clan heads, lamas, monks, merchants and ordinary citizens from all parts of Kham, or east Tibet. Many had only the vaguest notion of the United Nations, others had heard that many nations of the world belonged to it, that it believed in justice and peace. All had heard that it had actually sent an army of many nations to defend Korea. They were sure that when the outside world really knew of Tibet's plight, and of the justice of their cause, they would no longer be alone in their struggle.

Tsun had been chosen as the one to take the appeal to the United Nations, because of his knowledge of English and of the world outside Tibet, and because he was a respected religious leader; he would be, it was thought, an ideal person to entrust with the errand. People would listen to him, would know that he spoke the truth. Tsun was in no doubt that the Han knew about the appeal. So many people were involved that its existence was common knowledge. But only a few knew that he was to be the courier.

The distant whining drone of six Russian-built IL28 twin-jet bombers shattered the peace of the valley. They flew over the surrounding blue-grey snow-capped mountains. Circling, the planes banked, then came in low over Litang Monastery, dived and released their bombs.

The first shuddering explosions were followed by a barrage from the Han artillery. The ancient and once beautiful monastery of Litang now looked like a gateway to hell, belching forth yellow and black smoke; billowing waves rolled back on themselves, building up into mushroom clouds.

Tsun clutched the balcony rail. He was witnessing the destruction of friends, of their dwellings, of familiar and irreplaceable books in the monastery libraries, of magnificent works of art . . . part of his life. As the wooden floor vibrated with each explosion, a potted plant overturned, rolled through the railings, then silently fell hundreds of feet before shattering on the valley floor. Tsun watched as if hypnotised, unable to move.

'Tsun!' A young child's voice, shrill and frightened, pierced the spell that bound him. An eight year-old boy with the shaven head and robes of a monk rushed sobbing across the room and flung himself into Tsun's arms, clinging, trying to hide himself in the folds of the Abbot's robe; Tsun dimly aware, as he held the child, that each was clinging on to the reassurance of the other's presence.

Tsun's numbed mind became aware of the clamour of voices around him: from the adjacent balconies, from the flat roofs above and from the corridor outside his room. The heavy cedar door at the end of the room burst open and a tall, well-built woman stood in the doorway. Her long, glossy black hair hung about her shoulders in disarray. She was about forty years old and her face, olive-skinned with high cheekbones, was contorted with fear and anger. In her hand she clutched a prayer wheel.

'We are doomed!' Her anguished cry was an indictment of Tsun. Behind her, a group of agitated monks pushed their way into the room. The Abbot pointed a shaking finger at the woman.

'Take the lady back to her rooms,' he demanded. One of the monks put a tentative hand on the woman's shoulder. She shook herself free and angrily advanced towards the Abbot.

'They are destroying everything.' She thrust the prayer wheel at him accusingly. 'They will destroy us next.' Her face was white with rage and fear. 'This is due to your intrigues. You have brought destruction on us all.' She turned on those trying to crowd in behind her. 'They will kill us all.' She swung round again to point at the Abbot: 'He is to blame.'

'No, Ama-la,' the boy shouted at his mother while still holding tight to Tsun. 'No!'

'Norden!' Tsun shouted at her. 'Control yourself. You are overwrought. Go to your room and stay there, I will speak with you later. I have done nothing to arouse the antagonism of the Han.'

But even as he spoke, he knew that there were many present who did not believe him, and the boy wept at what appeared to him to be the end of the world as his mother showed her bitter antipathy towards his tutor. Norden started to speak, then suddenly burst into tears, while Tsun stroked the boy's head, trying to soothe him.

'Take the Honourable Mother to her room,' he ordered, 'and see that she is not left alone.'

The woman, still crying, allowed herself to be led from the room. The Abbot turned back towards the window. He held the boy's head close. The bombing went on. The monks crowded onto the balconies, at windows, on rooftops, watching the destruction and feeling the agony of helplessness. Litang, the Monastic University of the region, always with 3,000 studying there, was being consumed by flames, while innumerable lips moved, beads were thumbed and prayer wheels turned, invoking compassion, reverence, forgiveness, hope – or, in despair, bitter revenge.

A great pall of smoke built up and hung over the valley until, at last, when all was rubble, the planes flew away. The artillery barrage ceased and the valley was filled with an awful stillness of death.

There was a movement in the corridor outside the Abbot's room, as Rinchen Tsewang, his steward, a short, stocky man, pushed through the crowded doorway.

'Rinposhay?' The word was full of unspoken questions. Tsun turned to him.

'There is nothing we can do,' he said heavily. 'Tell everyone to gather in the Hall of Assemblies. We must decide on our own future. See that there are guards posted to watch for any sign that we might be attacked, and tell them to give warning of any strangers who may approach.'

The steward nodded, motioned everyone outside, bowed to the Abbot and withdrew, closing the door behind him.

Tsun looked down at the child and raised his tear-stained face to his. The boy swallowed a sob and rubbed his reddened eyes.

'Why, Tsun?' he pleaded. 'Why?'

The Abbot sighed and shook his head. 'Ignorance, Kesang, ignorance,' he said. 'Is that not the cause of all suffering?' Echoing the Buddha's words spoken two thousand, five hundred years before. He put his shaking hands on the boy's shoulders and did his best to smile. 'Come, you must compose yourself and change your robes. We will go to the Hall of Assemblies.'

Both noticed the sound of a dog whining pathetically in fright. Forgetting his own fear, the boy ran from the balcony, down two steps into the room and across to a rug-covered mattress in a dark corner. There, Tsun's Shi-tsu, or Lion Dog, a small long-haired terrier, cringed under the rugs in terror. Kesang picked up the dog and, cradling it in his arms, walked slowly to an adjoining room.

The mournful sound of the conch shell called from the temple roof, summoning the monks to the Hall of Assemblies.

'Dress quickly, Kesang,' the Abbot said to the boy. 'I will be close by if you need me.' He left the door between the rooms open and sat down cross legged on the divan, in front of which stood a low carved table. On the table was an ornate painted box. Opening it, Tsun carefully took out a sheet of handmade paper. He removed the cap from an engraved metal pen case hanging from his cloth belt and slipped out a sharpened bamboo pen. He unhooked the copper ink bottle from his belt, put it on the table and unfastened the stopper. Then, carefully, Tsun folded the sheet of paper with its veinlike threads into folds one on top of the other, like a concertina. Supporting the strip of paper with his left hand and holding the pen between his ring finger and little finger, he dipped it into the ink, and with the assured and beautiful strokes of a trained calligrapher began writing, using the folds as guides and unfolding the paper as he needed extra lines.

'Litang has been bombed. Our position is insecure. At midnight be at the Blue Chorten with eight horses, four mules and supplies for a long journey.'

He hesitated before sealing the message. If it fell into the wrong hands, it would be palpable evidence of intrigue against the occupation regime. He put the stopper back on the ink bottle, replaced the pen and fastened both containers back onto his belt. On the folded paper he poured a little melted wax, then impressed it with his silver-mounted seal. He leaned back and struck the brass gong standing by the table. A young novice monk opened the door.

'Champa,' the Abbot spoke quietly. 'Change into lay clothes at once. I want you to take this message to the Blue Chorten. When you get there, circle the chorten three times, no more, then wait. The one who is to receive this message will be watching. Wait for him to approach you. Take all precautions, see that you are not followed, there are spies everywhere. May the gods protect you, for the lives of many depend on the success of your mission.'

The monk took the message from the Abbot's hands, bowed and withdrew. Tsun rose and went into the adjoining room. Kesang was adjusting his brilliantly coloured brocade waistcoat, the insignia of an incarnate lama, and was having difficulty tying his belt over the rest of his long robes. The Abbot tied the knot for him. To both, these moments were precious. The little dog's tail wagged at Tsun's presence and Tsun caressed the woolly head.

'See,' he said to the boy, 'he is better, all is not lost.'

The boy, his face puffy and tearstained, replied softly.

'But nearly all.'

Tsun returned to his room, closing the door behind him. He looked with sadness at the many bookcases which surrounded him. How true it is, he thought, that a scholarly aptitude is a great hindrance to the realisation of the true nature of things. Despite his awareness of the truth of the doctrine of non-attachment, he treasured the hundreds of books in his apartment. All the imported volumes were in English.

For a few moments his mind escaped into kaleidoscopic memories of the past: the six-month-long trading missions with his father, travelling a thousand miles across Tibet with yaks and mules laden with borax and wool; crossing the Himalayas; the truck journey to Calcutta and the visit to the library. For an instant he felt the strange thrill of the touch, the feel, the smell of the books, their binding, their pages. The passionate determination, as he walked down the steps of the library entrance, to learn English; the journey back, the yaks loaded with tilly lamps, and on to China; John Develin, the missionary with the gift and enthusiasm for teaching, who let Tsun stay at the Baptist Mission School at Tatsienlu while his father's caravan meandered on to Peking. How long? Years? No it was months. For a sharp second he saw his father's face, heard his voice, his pleasure as his nineteen-year-old son explained one of his new English language books.

As Tsun fingered the rows of books, the titles reminding him of the carefully prepared lists given to all the monastery trading missions since he had been Abbot of Dorje Ri-gon, he thought of what the Han would make of his library. To them they would be reactionary literature, proof of his connivance with the Western imperialists. Suddenly he thought of all the letters he had sent to his friends abroad. He had not sent any for the last few months. The Han were doing all they could to prevent free communication between east Tibet and the outside world – indeed, even between east and central Tibet, which remained relatively stable and calm. But the fact remained that he had corresponded with a number of people in other lands. Yet, of what use would it be to destroy the correspondence, he thought? The books still remained, and there was so little time.

He walked over to one of the four pillars supporting the ceiling of the spacious room and, stretching up, took from a secret compartment in the pillar a wide-webbed money belt packed with gold dust, which he strapped round his waist under his robes. Attached to the belt was a supple leather package of papers: the petition from the people of the district, addressed to the Dalai Lama and to the United Nations, telling of their oppression and appealing for help. Swiftly, he replaced the secret panel in the pillar and, when he had finished dressing, put on the golden robe of teaching and struck the gong.

Surrounded by the members of his household and officers of the monastery, Tsun and the young incarnate lama, Kesang, walked in procession across the dark paved courtyard towards the façade of the Hall of Assemblies, the main Temple. Tsun glanced up at the two gilded gazelles supporting the Wheel of Law set above the main doors, symbolic of the Wheel of Doctrine which had been set in motion when the Buddha, the Sage of the Sakya Clan, expounded his Four Noble Truths in the Deer Park at Benares in India.

As they drew nearer to the Temple, Tsun could see some of the monks hastily removing their boots before entering the Hall. Their urgent, murmured conversation, against a background of slow, rhythmic chanting from within the Hall, heightened the tension.

It was as Tsun mounted the worn stone steps to the Temple that they heard it: the clear, high-toned bell echoing across the courtyard. All eyes turned to the gallery surrounding the courtyard in which hung one hundred and eight circular wooden prayer wheels, large and barrel shaped. There was nothing unusual in the sound; ever since the wheels had been installed, pious pilgrims and monks had spun them as they walked past, each revolution marked by the striking of a bell. But, this evening, somehow, everyone knew it was not piety that turned the prayer wheel. The yapping of Tsun's little dog broke the silence.

'Who is there? Step into the light.' Tsun's voice was hard. He felt Kesang's hand slip into his. A young Han woman in crumpled blue trousers and tunic stepped from the shadows, her slight smile forced and frightened; but most saw only the uniform, the serviceable, blue plastic-framed glasses: Ling, the cadre, sent the day before by the Han District Committee to persuade the monastery to co-operate in its 'socialisation'.

Instinctively, some of the monks on the Temple steps moved towards her, a focus for their frustrated rage at the atrocities they had recently witnessed.

'Stop! Listen to me,' Tsun shouted. 'Whoever harms this woman, harms the monastery.' He spoke with a threatening emphasis. 'Leave her in peace!'

As he entered the Temple he realized that the cadre was going to follow the procession and turned to one of the monks at the door.

'She is to remain outside the Temple,' he said loudly. The woman heard him, shrugged, and walked slowly away.

The yak hair curtain was held open. Tsun and his entourage entered the Temple vestibule. It was lit only by four mustard lamps resting on slates set into the wall; their flickering flames made the four frescos of the Celestial Kings of the Quarters appear even more fierce than usual. Their background of golden-green sensuous flames appeared to weave in the light, as did the green-white clouds swirling about the heads of the armoured warriors. Tsun walked slowly, his eyes drinking in every detail. Tonight the familiar symbolism became vividly significant.

On one side of the vestibule was the tutelary demon of the ground, a brawny, coal-black creature with hooked fangs, his waist girdled with a living tiger, his feet crushing human victims as he stood astride mountain peaks. To some, he was a real, tangible and objective demon, and they sought to placate him, to woo his favour. To others, like Tsun, he was a personification of an aspect of mind, a support for meditation techniques. His origins, like those of so many of the gods and demons, were rooted in primeval man's attempts to explain the forces of the cosmos, and the forces of the mind. Tsun saw this demon half a dozen times a day and repetition blunted the point of symbolism. Today, he knew that it might be for the last time. Today, each glance was significant.

The cedar doors, embellished with brazen brasses, swung open. Tsun looked down the dimly lit Temple to the altar and the immense statues of delicately sculpted and gilded clay, baked as hard as stone in the dry atmosphere of Tibet. Their turquoise eyes were lowered in contemplation. The placing of the pupils was the final act in the creation of an image, done sacramentally to endow it as a channel of spiritual power.

As he gazed on the personification of Enlightened Peace, Tsun thought of the ferocious, ignorant destruction portrayed in the vestibule, of how both existed potentially in every mind.

The multi-coloured frescos, the silk scroll-framed paintings, the rainbow banners hanging from pillars and ceiling, the statues, all were an externalisation of the participating monks' meditation. Tsun, and all the monks, knew that man was destructive and creative; so there was no incongruity between the demon and the Buddha. Man, inherently, is both.

Slowly, Tsun and his entourage walked down the centre aisle between the twelve supporting pillars, lacquered scarlet, their capitals painted in delicately coloured lotus blossoms. The ranks of seated monks on either side bowed as they passed. Before ascending their thrones, Tsun and Kesang took off their knee-high, white yak-leather boots. The terrier bounded up on to the cushions and curled up in the folds of the Abbot's robes.

As Tsun had ordered, the Precentor began chanting the salutation to the three Holy ones, the Triple Gem: the Buddha, who possesses all excellent virtues and is without fault; the Dharma, which is the understanding of all relative and absolute truth; the Sangha, the assembly of all who tread the path to enlightenment.

The deep bass intoning was followed by the rippling voice of the assembly, interspersed with music. Primordial sounds of a convulsed universe. Huge drums, held aloft like six-foot high handmirrors, rhythmically beaten, mingled with the horns, their calls coming as though from the bowels of the earth. Tiny finger cymbals produced a ravishing crescendo.

As they chanted, the monks meditated. The dog nosed its way from the folds of Tsun's robes, jumped to the floor and scampered into the gloom. The flames from hundreds of copper, silver and gold chalice-shaped butter lamps on side altars, the main altar and the table of lamps in the centre aisle, formed islands of light in the sea of darkness.

The salutation to the Triple Refuge ended. Tsun waited for the assembled monks to ease their bodies and collect themselves. Normally tea would have been served and, in anticipation, some of the monks had taken their wooden bowls from their ambacs, the pocket formed by the fold of their robes across their chests. The atmosphere was tense and apprehensive.

Tsun noticed that the assembly was even smaller than it had been the previous day. For months it had been decreasing. Many of the original inhabitants of the monastery had returned to their families or gone to seek a monastery in central Tibet, where they hoped they could continue their religious life in peace. Others had joined the resistance. There were many strangers from other districts who had sought temporary shelter *en route*. Some, Tsun realised, were probably spies.

'We are meeting here,' he began, 'because we must decide – each one of us – on what our future course will be. There can be little doubt that this monastery and the lives of us all are in jeopardy.' He paused. 'I cannot decide for you what you should do in the present circumstances. That is your responsibility. Whoever wishes to speak should speak now!'

This sudden abdication from authority startled the assembly. Despite the proctors who patrolled the hall looking for the slightest infringement of regulations concerning conduct, the monks began murmured conversations. A stranger rose to speak. Tsun could only just make out the tall figure in the darkness.

'Rinposhay, is there not a possibility that Dorje Ri-gon will be left in peace? Litang defied the Han and suffered the consequences. During my short stay here, I have seen how closely you have co-operated with the Han . . .' he paused, '. . . to ensure the security of the monastery. Why should this count for nothing?'

Tsun was uncertain of the motive behind the barbed words. How committed he was to the Han could be of interest to both collaborator and nationalist. He must be very careful.

'It is true that this monastery has given little cause for offence to the Han. But neither had Litang. Litang defied the Han only after impossible demands were made of it. There is little reason, after today, to suppose that we shall be especially favoured.'

One of Tsun's pupils, a young good-looking novice monk called Jigme, spoke. 'Rinposhay, what do you feel we ought to do? Is there any hope for us?' His open face was deeply troubled.

'I cannot decide for you. I can only give you guidance.' Tsun rocked gently from side to side as he spoke. His voice was unusually full of emotion. 'To many of us this monastery means a very great deal, yet it is impermanent, like all things. This lesson is now being pointed out to us in a very clear manner. As the centre of teaching and instruction we must remember that it, of itself, does not contain the Teaching. It is but a construction of human minds, and those human *minds* contain all the Teaching. For all human minds are capable of realising the Ultimate Truth. So, let each individual realise that he is the true depository of the religion. Let him guard and cultivate it.' The assembly listened in complete silence, appalled at the prophetic quality of his words, for his eyes and attention were focused on his own inner vision as he continued.

'Though our monasteries, our sacred texts, our paintings and sculptures are destroyed, are we not taught that they are, by their nature, perishable, and will pass sooner or later? These are outer manifestations of our faith. The Teaching can only *live* in the minds of men.' A tear stain on the cheek of this man of warriors, as Khambas are known, glistened in the light of the butter lamps. He went on. 'The Buddha, the Sage of the Sakya Clan, taught two things: suffering and release from suffering. These are the foundations. That we suffer, that all things – our families, our loved ones, our homes, our treasured possessions, our very selves – are perishable, is being shown to us this minute. As is the capricious nature of the time of dissolution. It could be a decade hence, it could be ten seconds from now. We have seen this self-evident truth illustrated but an hour ago with the destruction of Litang. So has it always been. We know of mighty empires that have risen and seemed, in the past, to be steadfast for aeons. Yet they have crumbled and are now as dust, memorialised in shattered stone, mentioned in obscure texts understood by few. In a sense, this can hearten us, for surely, the same fate will overcome the occupiers!

'The life of each individual, indeed of every sentient being, of empires, of all that is matter, perishes; even worlds. This is a truth that none can dispute, and which is evident to the most untutored mind.

'The Buddha also taught the second foundation: release from suffering. This can come about through true understanding of the nature of suffering. For it is ignorance that prevents us from seeing things as they truly, really, are. It is an *experience*, a realisation, of the true nature of things that is the knowledge which disperses ignorance, the cause of suffering. We must realise, though, that release is not escape from the world, but realisation that it is we who do not see the world correctly. Yet, despite this suffering, man's situation offers an opportunity denied to other sentient beings. He alone, of beings in all worlds, is fully capable of realising his unique situation and resolving it.

'As in great things, we see suffering in small things. For example, when we are in a field, the sun is setting, all is peace. Lulled, we walk beside a river, we feel an intense harmony, a deep communion with nature, a true happiness. Yet, as we feel this, we are conscious that it will not remain, that it will pass. Inherent in all of us is the desire, the hunger, for contentment of mind, born of true realisation. That this thirst for true knowledge is inherent in man is shown through the fact that, though the teacher remains hidden, away from the multitude, his fame spreads, and many will seek him out as a light for mankind.

'For though the world, and indeed, the universe, is convulsed in historical processes, though empires that seem imperishable vanish beneath the feet of history, though the world is a man tending his sheep on the mountainside, or a man manipulating an "iron bird" – both, with such different mental outlooks, both, and all, have the same basic problem. To both the appeal of Truth is the same.

'It is summed up in the words of the Buddha: "I teach only two things, O disciples, suffering and release from suffering."

'Although I have endeavoured to speak simply, my words will be difficult for many of you to understand. It cannot help but be so. For if words could convey the full meaning of realisation or Enlightenment, then all of us here would now be enlightened.

'Enlightenment has to be individually realised and experienced in each person's mind. Nagarjuna, the great Indian sage, has said: "That I long to speak yet cannot." Such is the inexpressibility of the experience, the realisation. For could one understand the description fully, one would be enlightened.

'Therefore, I can but do as Buddha did – point the way; help you with the means. It is up to each of you to choose whether or not to take the path to attain the goal, and how far you progress. You are all monks and have vowed to follow the path. Remember, that to preach religion and not to practise it is to be like a parrot saying a prayer, and is a grievous failure. Our present circumstances make it incumbent upon us to be aware, not only of the possible nearness of our own death, but of our vows, and so to keep the Teaching in our hearts.

'Remember the words of Marpa: "That which makes one weep is the thought that all creatures could be Buddha, that they know it not, and die in suffering." If that is what you weep about, you should go on weeping without pause.

'Now you must speak.' Tsun opened his hands to the assembly.

Rinchen, the steward, spoke almost coldly. 'It is rumoured, Rinposhay, that you are going to seek help for the monastery and the valley. Are the rumours true? Are you going to leave us?'

The Abbot hesitated, unsure whether to give them the gift of hope and possibly endanger the mission, or not. 'Certainly, if I leave the monastery, and if there is no alternative but to escape to Lhasa, I shall bring the plight of the monastery, and the valley, before the Kundun and anyone who might help us. Whatever happens and wherever I am, I ask you to remember that I shall do my best to alleviate the suffering of our monastery and valley.'

'Rinposhay!' Tsun's secretary, Lopsang, spoke next. 'Surely we should all leave the monastery now?'

'Yes, I believe we should, and we do not have much time, our departure must be swift. Remember that what has been spoken of here will be reported to the Han.' There was a stunned silence in the hall. 'Some of you, I know, have been threatened, or been enticed by material rewards to spy on your neighbour and to sow dissension.' Tsun paused, then said, every word loaded with anger at the destruction of Litang, 'Your odious undertakings will result in your being forever stained with your fellow countrymen's blood. You will be abhorred by your own people and despised by your alien masters. When your usefulness is over, you will be destroyed.'

Some of the monks in the assembly were terrified that they would be revealed. How much did the Lama know? Many believed that he could read minds!

'The suffering that you are promoting will surely come back to you.' Tsun's voice was harsh. One monk, convinced that Tsun was about to expose him, ran from the Assembly Hall. Taken by surprise, no one attempted to stop him. Then, the proctors moved to follow.

'Let him go!' Tsun said. 'The mental torments he will suffer are far greater than any punishment we could administer.' He paused. 'Most people fear to die. The Han ensure that each individual fears for his own security and that of his family. Whether it is the destruction of Litang, or the recording of your class origins, it is inculcated in us that to survive we must follow the dictates of the Han; we must spy on neighbours, even on our own families. The Han are attempting to reduce us to a state of unthinking terror, like a trapped animal, so that we will do anything to escape. This setting of individual against individual serves to forge our own chains of bondage. Though we do not have the forces to overthrow the Han, we must not let them have our minds!'

Another of Tsun's pupils, Samden, spoke. 'Some of our monks, Rinposhay, have joined the resistance. Should we fight?'

'Whether you join the resistance is a matter for your conscience. As a monk, you have taken a solemn vow to abstain from taking life. That vow is solemn because of the possibility of your being faced with a crisis such as we face now. Should the

Chinese wish to seize the monastery, apart from ethical considerations, we do not have the means to defend ourselves.'

'Rinposhay,' the steward asked, 'if we escape, what about the monastery library?'

'We will save what we can, Rinchen. We will hide what we can. Much will be destroyed. But that which we hold in our hearts and minds, we must protect above all.' Then, with a slow emphasis, Tsun said, 'I believe that we should all escape while we have the opportunity. Let us meet at our Trading Agency in Lhasa. Perhaps there we shall find peace.' Tsun paused, then seemed to speak, not so much to the assembly, but to an unseeing, unhearing world. 'This,' he opened his arms, 'is our life! We are impotent while everyone and everything we hold dear is ruthlessly destroyed before our eyes. Now our understanding of the Truths we have been taught is undergoing the supreme test.

'I do not believe that we are totally defeated.' Tears were streaming down his face. 'Nor that the friends we have in neighbouring countries or in the world will let us be totally destroyed. War has devastated our land before. Oppression has brought misery to our households, yet we have overthrown our oppressors. Truth is ours and, according to the law of karma, we shall know peace and vindication.'

No one spoke. Many wept. Kesang cuddled the little terrier and cried unashamedly. Tsun nodded, and the final invocation began.

Chapter Two

Later that evening, Tsun and Kesang visited the holiest sanctuary in the monastery, a dark, cavernous cave, the air heavy and musty from the burning of countless butter lamps. As they made the customary walk of pilgrimage around the cave, automatically spinning the large copper prayer wheels set in a wooden frame running the length of the centre aisle, Senge played hide and seek among the rock crevices, running back and forth to the melancholy couple. His excited yapping only served to emphasise the ancient silence of the cave. A monk, seated alone before the shrine, glanced at them with surprise and then resumed his meditation. For two months, since the siege of Litang had begun, perpetual invocations had been said for the safety of the valley and its people.

Tsun paused to inspect one of the many frescos covering the cave walls. Only a few months earlier he had worked out with the artists of the monastery a series depicting the founding of Dorje Ri-gon. The shrine glowed with hundreds of butter lamps and was piled high with offerings from pilgrims: coins, jewels, flowers and incense. Felicity scarves hung, some rotting and grey with age, like thick cobwebs about the images. Here and there, a blue scarf offered by a pilgrim from far-off Mongolia lay among the heaps of white silk and cotton scarves from the Tibetans.

The monk began a low, rolling invocation. Tsun and Kesang offered their own scarves, draping them with both hands and a silent invocation over the knees of the eight-foot high image of Maitreya, the 'Coming Buddha'. Made of gilded clay and dressed in magnificent brocade robes, the image was modelled with its feet placed firmly on the ground, ready to rise from the Lotus Throne and reveal himself as the future world teacher.

Tsun and Kesang lightly touched the image with their foreheads in reverence and to receive blessing. Beside the 'Coming One' sat the cross-legged, embalmed body of the founder of Dorje Ri-gon. Kesang took a neatly folded white felicity scarf from the folds of his robe. Gently holding each end and releasing the concertina fold, he murmured a prayer of offering before draping the scarf, a symbol of respect, its whiteness personifying a pure, unclouded mind, on the throne of his predecessor. As he looked at the gilded form, Kesang realised that much he used to remember of his previous existence had already gone. He knew, too, that there was nothing unusual in this, it happened to all tulkus as they grew older and their young minds developed anew, but it saddened him that yet another link was fading. He remembered how, when he was about four years old, he had first set eyes on Dorje Ri-gon; he could feel, not just recall, the profound happiness that overwhelmed him. He was sitting on a yak, secured to the bales of wool slung on the animal's broad back. The whitewashed walls of Dorje Ri-gon picked up the sunlight and it looked as though it had been formed out of the cliff, rather than built into it. By early evening they were close enough for his parents to decide to camp below the monastery. They had not been on this particular route on previous trading journeys and so Kesang had never seen Dorje Ri-gon before. He remembered how impatient he had been to visit the monastery and, while his mother, Norden, and their two men saw to the animals, he and his father began the steep climb up the narrow path to Dorje Ri-gon.

Although it was getting quite dark, and normally he would have stayed close to his father, the four year-old Kesang had felt completely at ease, running up the path, looking, touching and laughing, then showing his father where part of the cliff overhanging the path had been worked on to produce two-dimensional figures of dieties chiselled into the rock and carefully coloured. Pennant-like prayer flags were strung across the path from trees, and as they flapped and danced in the cold night breeze, Kesang suddenly caught sight of a chorten which had been built beside the path at the end of a mani wall. He began running towards it, his father calling after him. When his father reached him, he found Kesang beside the chorten with his arms stretched up towards a row of small, canister-like copper prayer wheels set at the base. Begging his father to lift him up, Kesang began turning the wheels, sounding a gentle ripple of bells as each revolution marked a prayer.

His father, though, had felt increasing trepidation. Those boys who entered into a monastery usually began their training at eight years old, and it sometimes happened that one would show a definite determination for the religious life at an early age; but not only did Kesang's father hope to keep the boy with him, having no plans to enter him into a monastery, there was as well something about Kesang's reaction to Dorje Ri-gon that he found disturbing.

Kesang had run ahead through the great main gate and into the courtyard. His father's anger at him for having run off was harsher, he realised, than he would have wished. His troubled face suddenly came into Kesang's mind. He remembered being told, but could not himself remember, that he had taken his father to the temple and shown him the shrines; then, while his father was offering felicity scarves, he had slipped away to the cave.

He vividly remembered the touch of the rough granite, his fingers following the crystals, sparkling from the specks of mica. He had taken a scarf from his ambac, standing then, as now, gazing for a long time at the embalmed and gilded figure of Dorje Rinposhay who had died five years earlier, a year before Kesang's birth. Apparently, when he knew that he was going to die, Dorje Rinposhay had said, when his disciples requested that he leave some guidance as to where he would be reborn, that they need not worry; if they were patient, he would come amongst them.

As Kesang looked at his former body, he remembered, even on that first occasion four years ago, knowing and yet not knowing why he was there. A reason he could not, even now, fully comprehend.

It had been Tsun who eventually found him for his distressed father. The family had stayed for some weeks and his parents often talked with Tsun who himself spent a lot of time with the child. Kesang was aware of an unusual interest in his reactions and remembered playing with some of the monks and being asked to choose a rosary, then a ritual bell and dorje, a bowl and a small ritual drum from about half a dozen of each which were placed before him. He knew now that they had wanted to see if he would pick the ones which had belonged to his former body.

There were to be many other tests before it was explained to him that he was the tulku of Dorje Rinposhay. It didn't surprise Kesang; he was not entirely sure what was being told to him but he knew that he was Dorje Rinposhay even if he couldn't comprehend that tulku meant an emanation body, that he was a human vehicle for the spiritual influence of the first Dorje Rinposhay. But he understood his father's apparent pleasure, and sadness. He remembered the first time they had to leave him, before his mother had returned to spend some time at the monastery. His weeping. Silently, now, the boy began to cry. He looked at Tsun and spoke softly.

'My former body overcame many obstacles to found this monastery. It was his example which inspired its existence. Oh, Tsun! Although I am his emanation, all I can do is watch the destruction of all that he built. I do not have his qualities, Tsun, and they are needed now, more than ever.' The tears streamed down the boy's face as he gazed at his former body, the eyelids lowered in perpetual meditation.

Tsun turned to the boy and gently laid a hand on his closely shaven head.

'Dorje Rinposhay was advanced in years when the monastery was founded. When a tree dies, a sapling grows from its seed. Inherent within it are the qualities of its originator. Yet to what extent, cannot be judged until the sapling is mature. You possess many of his qualities, but you are young. It is enough that you are present.'

'My former body's wisdom was truly shown when he appointed you to be his successor as Abbot and guardian of his eventual incarnation,' Kesang replied. Tsun smiled. 'I am repaying the privilege of being his favoured disciple . . .' His voice faded at vivid memories of the years when, as a younger man, he had sat in this cave, unembellished then, a very simple hermitage for his spiritual mentor. The monastery had not then been built. There was just a man in ragged clothes, whose presence was awe-inspiring, who gave the key to the doors of perception to those who chose to use it.

A mouse ran across the gilded hands of the embalmed body. Tsun was filled with nostalgia and an overwhelming sense that this was the last parting. Silently, he invoked that he be granted steadfastness, wisdom and discernment.

Tsun and Kesang walked slowly down the right-hand side of the cave, spinning mani wheels set in the wall, and then prostrated themselves before the shrine, trying to imprint the cave and its connotations in their memories forever. Senge barked. Tsun picked him up and tucked the little dog into his robe, then they went out into the cold darkness.

According to custom, they should have visited all the other shrines in the monastery in a farewell pilgrimage, but Tsun felt sure it would reveal his plan for departure, and so they returned to his apartment. There, he asked Lopsang, his secretary, to inform the steward, Kesang's mother and his three pupils, that he wished to see them immediately. Kesang watched as he sat down and wrote a letter addressed to the assembly.

'Honourable brothers. When you read this letter, I shall be far away from Dorje Ri-gon, on my way to Lhasa. I know that many of you will feel hurt and resentful that I did not take my proper leave of you. It will seem that I have abandoned you. Yet I have not. I hope you will understand that my action was undertaken with the sincere motive of doing what is best for you and for the people of our valley.

'Many of you, some my dear friends, expected, I know, to accompany me on my journey. Most of you have heard the rumours that I have undertaken a mission for this valley which makes me liable for arrest by the Han. This rumour is true. To travel with me is to make yourselves also liable for arrest. My duty is to do all I can to keep in safety the assembly of monks and our monastery, and to ensure the success of my mission. For this reason, I have kept my purpose secret from you.'

The sharpened bamboo pen paused as Tsun looked across at the boy who was sitting on the divan cuddling the dog.

'Kesang,' he said, 'tonight I shall be leaving the monastery on a very dangerous journey. I want you to go with Lopsang and your mother to Lhasa.' Slowly the boy got up from the divan and walked across the room to stand before Tsun.

'Please . . .' he pleaded, his voice low and filled with emotion. 'Please, Tsun, don't send me away . . . not now . . . *please* . . .'

Tsun frowned to cover his feelings. He took a small jade snuff bottle from his robe, spooned a little onto his thumb and sniffed it up his nostrils. Then he considered. He loved the boy dearly and did not want to be parted from him. Would he, in fact, be safer with another party? Many of the bands of humblest peasants had been attacked. Even so, Tsun thought, with me there is added danger.

Kesang could not keep silent any longer.

'If I am to die,' he said, 'let it be with you.'

Tsun could not resist him. He smiled and nodded his assent. Kesang gave a cry of joy and swooped on the dog. Tsun wrote of Kesang in the letter to the assembly, using the boy's title inherited from his 'former body'.

'Dorje Rinposhay will accompany me. His presence, I feel sure, will be most auspicious for the success of my mission. You know that I will do all in my power to protect him.

'My blessings to you all. My prayers will never cease that, soon, we may again live in security in Dorje Ri-gon.'

Tsun reached for the large seal hanging from his belt. Kesang saw him and heated the wax. When it was ready Tsun impressed the seal at the foot of the letter.

Lopsang, Tsun's secretary, entered the apartment. 'Rinposhay,' he said, 'those you asked to attend are present.'

Lopsang was in his forties, his fine aquiline features marred by a perpetually furrowed brow, as though he were concentrating with great intensity, or was continually worried.

'Have them enter,' Tsun said. 'And we will take tea.'

They came into the room in order of precedence: Norden, the 'Honourable Mother' first, followed by the steward and his three pupils. Tsun glanced at Champa. The youth nodded, he had made contact with the resistance. The Honourable Mother and steward seated themselves on the rug-covered divans set round the room, while Tsun's three pupils placed low tables and cups before each of the guests and prepared the tea in a large brass teapot.

'You are feeling better, Honourable Mother?' Tsun asked.

'Yes thank you, Rinposhay.' She inclined her head and gave him a cold smile.

'Rinchen,' Tsun said to his steward. 'Inform Precentor Sonam that he is to take charge of the distribution of the monastery treasures to those who leave. He is of the valley and will know of the many hiding places both in the monastery and the surrounding countryside.'

'But as steward, Rinposhay,' Rinchen protested, 'I . . .'

'You will not be here,' Tsun said gently, as Samden, second in seniority of his pupils, gently lifted the silver lid of his jade cup and carefully poured in the thick, butter-laced tea. When he had finished, Samden sucked in his breath quickly, as a mark of respect, lest it touch the Rinposhay, then he bowed and turned away to serve the others.

'I have asked you to come here,' Tsun said, 'because I have an obligation to you all. It is my intention to leave the monastery tonight. I cannot tell you where I am going, or what my mission is. To do so, would be to endanger your own lives. It is better that you are ignorant of the facts. I can say that I shall be going first to Derge and then to Lhasa. Once there, I shall decide how best to complete my mission. I can tell you that my journey will be dangerous. To make it less so, I intend taking with me the smallest party and leaving the monastery secretly. Do you wish to accompany me on this journey, Honourable Mother?'

The woman hesitated and looked at her small son.

'Kesang has decided to come with me.' Tsun expected her to

react strongly, but instead she spoke softly. 'I will come, Rinposhay.' She was thinking that the Abbot, for all his protestations about danger, would have the greatest protection against the Han and she was eager to leave the monastery as quickly as possible. Rinchen and Lopsang nodded their assent. Tsun turned to the three young men standing before him.

'Although you are my pupils,' he said, 'I do not expect you to come with me. You must decide.'

At this, Rinchen murmured a protest, just loud enough to let everyone know that he, Rinchen, disapproved of the Abbot's behaviour. Pupils were not asked, they were told!

'Samden?' Tsun waited for his answer.

Samden glanced at Champa and the other pupil, Jigme. Jigme nodded. 'We are honoured that you should ask us, Rinposhay,' Samden said.

Tsun got up and walked over to the pillar containing the secret compartment. Releasing the panel, he removed three Russian Tokareu TT 7–62mm automatic rifles, six mausers, several ammunition belts and boxes of cartridges, and six daggers. One of the mausers and a dagger he laid aside for himself.

His guests were shocked and startled at the sight of the weapons, all except Samden, who looked at Tsun with renewed admiration.

'Our vows forbid us to kill,' Tsun said, 'but our escort will not have taken such vows. We may have to decide whether to keep those vows. These, at least, will ensure we have the choice!'

Lopsang looked sadly at the Abbot. 'Or make the decision for us, Rinposhay.' Tsun gave a grim smile. Norden, the Honourable Mother, picked up a mauser and a box of cartridges and pushed them into her chuba, the wrap-round gown worn by laymen and women. No one else moved.

'It is better that we travel in lay clothes. There will be an escort with horses and mules waiting for us at the Blue Chorten. Take as much food as you can and be discreet in preparing for the journey. First we travel to Derge. I suggest we each take one of these and a pistol.' Tsun pushed an 18-inch dagger through his cloth belt and placed a mauser in the folds of his robe. 'There will be plenty of time to learn how to use it on the journey'. He smiled at Rinchen's evident disapproval. 'Jigme, the rifles and the rest of the ammunition are for our escort, wrap them up with our supplies.' He looked at the small group awaiting his instructions.

'We will meet in an hour at the path to the Blue Chorten. No one must know of our departure. Samden, please fill our cups to the brim. We will leave them untouched so that all may know of our intention to return.'

Silently, the sombre group watched Samden fill the cups, then, bowing, they withdrew and, for a moment, as the door closed, Tsun felt like his own ghost; part of, yet not part of his life. He looked at Kesang.

'I shall need the saddlebags and baling cloth,' he said quietly, and walked over to study the religious texts stacked in pigeon-hole type shelves opposite the shrine. He began sliding the three-foot long xylographed books from the shelves, separating them from their carved wooden covers and wrapping them up in the cloth which Kesang had brought from the large decorated cupboard.

'Kesang, the image of Sakyamuni.' Tsun nodded at the shrine. The boy gently picked up a six-inch high figure in gilded bronze of Sakyamuni, the Sage of the Sakya clan, touched it to his forehead as a sign of reverence, and placed the image of the sage, the Buddha, in its copper and silver travelling container. Then he slipped the precious object into its cloth case and put the strap over his shoulder. He watched as Tsun rolled up two of the most precious scroll paintings.

'Senge, drop it, drop it!' Tsun grabbed the brightly coloured saddle bags from the dog.

'But what of all these?' Kesang pointed to a bookcase full of English volumes.

'The outside world has many copies of these books, but few of our rare texts,' Tsun replied. 'Come, we must change into our lay clothes.'

Low clouds were obscuring the moon as Tsun and Kesang, with Senge tucked into his chuba, silently left the monastery. As they reached the stables, the boy stopped.

'Tsun,' he whispered. 'May I say farewell to . . .'

'Shh! No! We do not . . .' For an instant the clouds parted and Tsun caught a glimpse of a pale hand reflected in the moonlight through the open door of the stables. 'Very well, Kesang,' he said softly. 'But be quiet.'

The boy looked slightly surprised at Tsun's sudden change of mind, but he went into the stables without answering, heading for the stall where his horse was tethered. Tsun followed. Casually he walked past the stalls, inspecting the horses. His hand slipped down to his belt and rested on the handle of the dagger. As he came towards the end of the stables he glimpsed a shadow, darker, steadier than the shadows playing on the unlit wall; he could just make out a figure pressed against the wall. He approached it, apparently oblivious. When he moved next, he moved quickly: in a second his dagger was at the intruder's throat. There was a frightened gasp as it pierced the skin and blood oozed onto the blade. It was only a surface wound, but it was enough. Tsun was looking into the terrified eyes of Ling, the Han cadre. Her Ceska-radom pistol fell to the ground. Tsun knew what he ought to do, and with dispatch. But he could not overcome his deep-rooted aversion to taking life, which his whole way of life during the past thirteen years had embedded so firmly in his being. Some would even consider the thought equal to the deed. To kill her meant the destruction of all he had worked for. He could feel the girl's slender body trembling.

'Do exactly as I tell you or I will kill you.' Tsun turned to see Kesang watching him with big, frightened eyes. 'Get a cord from the stall,' Tsun ordered. 'I will tie her hands.' He pulled a felicity scarf from the fold of his chuba and, when her hands were firmly tied, used it as a gag. Then he went to the door of the stable and listened to hear if anyone else was about. The monastery was silent. With his dagger at the girl's throat, they began walking towards the rendezvous.

'I don't want them to hear a footfall,' Tsun hissed in the girl's ear.

The others were waiting at the foot of the path.

'Rinposhay!' Rinchen cried in alarm. 'What is she doing here?'

'She was watching when we made our escape. There is no alternative but to take her with us.'

No one spoke. Tsun knew they were all considering the obvious alternative.

'We will take her with us,' he repeated quietly, and felt the bitter unspoken resentment at her presence.

Lopsang led the party since he knew the way better than the others. The coarse, grass-covered path grew steeper and steeper. They had to tread carefully in the darkness to avoid sending loose stones hurtling down the rock face, disturbing the sleeping monks in the monastery below. Ling was terrified. She could just make out the sheer drop to the valley floor, hundreds of feet below the path. The heavily laden party made slow progress up the mountainside.

Two hours later they had crossed the summit and were descending into another valley. When they finally reached the

Blue Chorten, it was deserted. There was no sign of the escort. Norden looked at Tsun and spat out, 'Well, Rinposhay, where are the escort, the horses, the mules?'

'I do not know, Honourable Mother,' Tsun replied. He was wondering the same thing, feeling a knot of panic begin to tighten in his stomach. He grunted at the release from the weight of the bale as he heaved the cloth straps from his shoulders and lowered it to the ground. Surely, he thought, it could not be over so soon? The rest of the party also unburdened themselves, piling their cloth packs on the ground, and began talking softly, peering into the darkness. All except Kesang, who was unaware that anything was wrong and was studying the twenty-two-foot high chorten, more by touch than sight.

It consisted of a plinth of steps on which rested a bowl of stone crowned with a golden spire. Its symbolism was profound, expounding the essence of the Teaching.

'Why is it blue?' the boy asked Samden.

'Because, Rinposhay, it is copied from one of the blue chortens of Samye, the first monastery in Tibet,' the youth answered back.

The clouds were banked over the valley, giving the night a deep darkness of uncertainty, without even the glimmer of starlight. Quite some distance away, but clearly heard, was the sound of horses moving at walking pace. It was what Tsun was expecting. Champa's message had asked for an escort from the resistance. But he knew that he couldn't be certain that it was the resistance approaching and suddenly, in the darkness, the slow, steady approach had a sinister quality. Tsun's hand slipped over the butt of the mauser pistol; he was surprised at his familiarity with it, that he knew exactly how to fire it, its reactions. He had used a similar pistol before becoming a monk, but that was many years ago.

The group stood close to one another by the chorten and, as though forming from the night itself, eight horsemen emerged. All were well built, some wearing red fox-fur hats, one a quilted American jacket, but the others were in chubas, Cossack fashion, bloused up at the hips to be knee length. Their weapons spanned a thousand years. All had four-foot long heavy single-edged swords, in heavily ornamented scabbards, thrust through their belts and worn across their stomachs, with foot-long daggers at their hips. One carried a colt revolver and two others had matchlocks or 'prong guns', so called for their forked gun rests. One of the riders was a woman with long black hair.

As they dismounted from their shaggy ponies, Ling noticed in all of them the same bearing she had noticed in Tsun. A dignity, the self-containment of a warrior, or of a Taoist sage. As the Khamba woman stepped towards Tsun, Champa quickly introduced her.

'Rinposhay, this is Genyen Chime. She leads our escort.'

There stood before them a tall, strikingly handsome woman in a sheepskin chuba, hitched up to knee length. Her right arm was bare and her trousers were tucked into black leather Mongolian boots. As well as a matchlock slung over her back, she wore an ammunition bandolier and a reliquary the size of a camera which hung round her neck on a thick yellow strap.

'Thank you, Champa, we know one another.' Her head was slightly lowered in deference and for a moment Tsun reeled, his mind flooded with old memories. Mingled with his pleasure at seeing her unexpectedly after so long was anger at what he knew could be a ploy on her part. He did not see her embarrassment as she bowed low, offering him a felicity scarf which he took in one graceful gesture, draping it over her neck and lightly touching her head in blessing. As Genyen raised her eyes to meet his, he said, 'We are indeed fortunate to have you with us. I have heard of your exploits.' He smiled, and as she turned to offer her scarf to Kesang, the whole escort lined up to present their scarves and receive the two Rinposhays' blessings.

Genyen and her men helped Tsun's party to load their baggage onto the horses and pack mules. Genyen made considerable show of walking round Ling, inspecting her. Ling controlled her anger at being so humiliated by this barbarian woman. She knew that any hope of escape or of turning matters to her advantage depended on her maintaining a keen mental alertness, as unclouded as possible by emotion.

'Tashi!' Genyen looked at one of her men. 'Put her on one of the mules and take the reins.'

Tsun, taking the reins of his horse from Champa, put his hands on the high pommel of the saddle and mounted. They moved off immediately, Tsun riding beside Genyen. A pregnant silence lay between them, both aware of the strength of their memories, a lifetime lived in a moment. Eventually, Tsun spoke.

'We took every precaution with our departure,' he said. 'My hope is that we won't be missed until the morning, but it is possible.'

'Because of her, Rinposhay?' Genyen jerked her head back, indicating Ling.

'Possibly. There are many monks sheltering at Dorje Ri-gon. I cannot be sure of all of them, as was once possible.'

They kept their voices low, half their attention scanning the night, tuned to the slightest suspicious sound or sight.

'Do the Han know of the petition to the United Nations?' she asked.

Tsun laughed. 'Genyen, it would be amazing if they did not know. How many of our own people know about it already? Hundreds? Thousands? I have even been told of it and asked to keep it a secret. The Han know that one is planned.'

'And that you are carrying it?'

'Very few people know that. Not even my party, though some may suspect.'

'And the gold?'

'There are even fewer who know about that, and no one knows my route. In the letter that I've left at the monastery, I've said I'm going to Lhasa. I am, but first, Genyen, I must go to Derge. The Queen Regent has the rest of the petition.'

For the remainder of the night and for much of the following day, they rode, deliberately keeping off the usual trading and pilgrim routes.

Genyen spurred her horse and trotted up beside Tsun. He was taking snuff and she put out a hand to stop him from putting the bottle away when he had finished.

'Rinposhay, you have forgotten?'

'Perhaps,' he handed her the bottle, '. . . but not everything. So much has changed, yet you remain the same.'

The wind caught the snuff as she tapped it onto her thumbnail. Genyen cursed, then looked apologetically at Tsun.

'I hope you have changed,' she said mischievously. 'For it ill befits your robe if you have not!'

They both laughed, each remembering how it had been between them so many years before.

Tsun's short, stocky steward, Rinchen, was leading Kesang's horse beside his own. The boy was asleep, slumped in the saddle. Something woke him. 'Rinchen-la,' he said. 'I had a curious dream. It was so vivid. I was in a great field surrounded by red flowers which I was picking. It was so real. I just walked through the field gathering flowers. Nothing else.' He did not see Rinchen's look of horror as he thought of the disaster the dream foretold.

'What does it mean, Rinchen?' he asked.

'Nothing, Rinposhay,' Rinchen said quickly. 'Nothing. Here, eat this.' He gave the boy a cube of dried cheese to chew.

On the second night they made camp. They were all exhausted. Members of the escort took it in turns to keep watch. The night was cold, even though the sun had not yet sunk beneath the horizon. It hung in the sky, a golden ball suspended just above the distant mountains, shooting darts of gold into the lush green grass of the valley and turning the faces of the mountains a purple red. At the foot of the mountains clustered rich green cedar trees. A densely packed column, the deep green trees, some over eighty feet high, wound their way around the snow-capped peaks. They reminded Tsun of the pilgrims making their long walk around the Potala Palace at Lhasa. He felt their insignificance before unconquered nature.

The next morning, Tsun was the first to awake. As always, he began the day with three prostrations to the Triple Gem and by meditating for some thirty minutes. Then, with the others still asleep or only just stirring, he threw sticks for Senge to retrieve, while he considered what had happened and what might happen. The sky lightened. The false dawn. Shapes appeared vaguely out of the blackness. It was then that Tsun heard the sound of an approaching aeroplane.

'Wake up, wake up!' he shouted, frantically dousing the fire with earth. 'Get under cover.'

Men were pulling the startled horses into the safety of the trees.

'Senge, Senge!' Kesang was urgently calling the dog. His mother grabbed him and pulled him down behind a rock. They all lay still, tensed and waiting as the 'plane flew overhead. It banked and turned to make another run. Tsun's eyes were on the wisps of smoke creeping into the lightening sky from the dying fire. The 'plane was again overhead, and very low. One of the escort raised his rifle. 'No! No!' Tsun shouted at him, his voice nearly drowned by the roar of the engine.

The aeroplane flew on. Senge started yapping. Kesang quietened him. Norden, Samden and Lopsang were rapidly murmuring invocations. The 'plane turned at the far end of the valley and once more came in towards them, flying low. Tsun was sure it had seen them. He tensed, ready for the attack, but the 'plane flew past and continued on until it disappeared over the distant mountains.

'Rinposhay,' Genyen joined Tsun. 'What do you make of that?'

'I do not know,' he answered slowly. 'If they had seen us, I would have expected them to attack, unless they have left us alone to report our position to the PLA. Of course, they might not have seen us; the light is not good and they may have been looking out for resistance camps.' He smiled faintly at Jigme, who was chipping away with his metal toothpick at a flat grey stone, trying to inscribe the words 'Om Mani Padme Hum' on it as a protection against further attacks.

Genyen frowned. 'I do not know of any People's Liberation Army troops in this area. It is the resistance which is in strength here. It would be difficult for the PLA to operate without my knowing.' She sounded worried.

Hastily, they broke camp and resumed their journey. They did not stop for food, so anxious were they to move on. They rode close to the foothills, keeping near to the tall conifer trees for cover. The wide valley, carpeted with lush grass, stretched out before them. The small party was dwarfed by the magnificence of their surroundings.

The moon was high in the sky when they decided to make camp. They had covered many miles that day, with only brief stops for rest, and they were all very tired. The horses and mules were unsaddled, fed and watered. A fire was built and tea was made. Tsun walked over to where the cadre was sitting alone on a rock apart from the others, staring sullenly at her captors. Her round face could have been pretty had it not been marred by a tight, hard look around her mouth, and the fear which burned in her eyes. Her hands were free. She saw Tsun watching her and turned up the collar of her coat in a selfconscious gesture as if to hide her face.

The night was beautiful. The moon hung in the dark sky and the stars shone brightly, but it was cold. Tsun sat down beside the girl. She moved away a few inches and huddled into her quilted coat.

'Do you speak Tibetan well?' Tsun asked.

'Yes!' She turned to glare at him. 'Why do you keep me prisoner? What are you going to do with me?' Tsun looked out over the peaceful valley bathed in moonlight. 'Better to be a prisoner and alive,' he said gently, 'than free and dead.'

Champa, who was the youngest of Tsun's pupils and only eighteen years old, came towards them carrying a large teapot. He served the Abbot first, pouring the tea into Tsun's plain, highly polished wooden bowl. The girl thrust an enamel mug at him. He ignored it and walked back to finish serving the rest of the party, then came back a few minutes later and filled her mug in silence.

One of the men of the escort was playing a Tibetan guitar. Genyen joined the men in a dance. The others sat watching, drinking tea and eating dried mutton and cubes of dried cheese. Then Genyen stopped dancing and sang of clan feuds among the Khambas. Norden was softly reciting her rosary, adding more to the balance sheet of religion. The worn wooden beads slipped through her fingers as, on touching each one, she softly murmured an invocation. Jigme was busy chipping the characters of the Chenresi invocation onto a stone. Kesang was trying to find Senge. Rinchen closed his eyes in meditation.

Tsun was still sitting beside the cadre. She was looking into her now empty mug.

'So you'd like some more tea?' Tsun said.

'It's better than nothing,' she snapped back at him.

'It is most nutritious and suitable for our climate.' Tsun sipped noisily from his bowl. He was interested in this girl, the only Han he had met who could speak Tibetan fluently. Champa came near with the teapot and Tsun motioned to him to fill the girl's mug.

'Tell me what it was you were planning to do at Dorje Ri-gon?' the Abbot asked quietly when Champa had gone. The girl paused and eyed him appraisingly.

'My job was to make known the reforms that are to be instituted in the valley and at the monastery.'

'And by whose order are these so-called reforms to be instituted?'

'By order of the District Committee of the Communist Party.' She sounded slightly surprised by the question.

'Why are they considered necessary?'

'The very asking of that question betrays your reactionary blindness. It was to cure such blindness that I was sent to Dorje Ri-gon. The reforms will better the lot of the people. The monasteries are to be invited to co-operate in the redistribution of their land to the tenant farmers. They are to be compensated.'

'What of Litang?' Tsun sipped his tea slowly and motioned her to drink.

'Litang was plotting a counter-revolution. It harboured rebels and bandits and supplied them with arms. It could have co-operated with the reforms without bloodshed, but refused.'

'Those you call rebels and bandits are the ordinary people your regime boasts it is protecting. Our escort, those people over there by the camp fire, they are weavers and tailors and farmers. Some have families and homes. Do you think they gave them up from choice, to become hunted outlaws, liable to torture and death? They feel that everything they value is threatened by your regime and they have no choice but to fight it.'

'Oh, no!' The girl laughed without humour. She was warming to the argument. 'I do not deny that they believe what they are doing is right. Some of them! But many *are* bandits and reactionaries, who have a vested interest in keeping the social system as it is. Nor do I deny that there are many who are sincere, duped by superstitious attachment to your religion.'

'The opium of the people?' Tsun suggested quietly. She gave him a startled look. 'Yes,' she said, and felt heartened, recalling that this lama had always been considered radical by other members of the priesthood.

Tsun took a small leather pouch from his chuba pocket and shook some of the dried barley it contained into his tea bowl, then mixed it with the remains of the tea into a dough.

'Will you have some?' he asked, offering her the bowl, aware of the consternation this was causing among other members of the party who were watching him. The cadre refused. She was more interested in continuing her conversation with the lama.

'Obviously you know something of Communism,' she said, 'and your radical approach has not gone unnoticed by District Headquarters. It has always been hoped that you would lead the reform of the valley.' Tsun turned to her with a smile. 'Knowing as much as you do about my relations with the District Committee, you must also know that I have declined that bribe many times. The reforms and changes I have made have been in accordance with the genius of our people, and I view them as a development of our civilisation which, like all things, is in a state of change. Of decay and development.'

'Exactly! Decay and development. Communism is the ultimate social evolution. It will supplant your present system. We, who are members of the movement, seek to advance it, for the benefit of mankind.'

'But what right have you to impose this system on an unwilling country?' Tsun continued quietly. 'If what you say is true, this system will come naturally to Tibet, without the dreadful bloodshed that we are now suffering.' He ate some of the tsampa.

'China is a Communist state,' the girl said earnestly. 'Tibet is part of the great Motherland, only recently restored, it is true, but an integral part. China, and that includes Tibet, is on the Communist path.'

Senge came bounding up to Tsun and begged for some of his food. Tsun fed him little bits.

'We believe,' he said, 'that Tibet is independent. We have documents, treaties, some of them recorded in stone, as evidence of our independence. Our ways have never been those of the Han people. Our religion, language and race are different. For many, indeed, countless years, we have been independent, except for the brief occasions when the lust for empire has seized the rulers of China.'

'And *we* have many documents,' the girl said, 'proving that your country is part of the great Motherland. What is race or religion? Is not the Motherland composed of five races? Han, Mongolian, Manchu, Tibetan and Muslim.' The words rolled off her tongue as she continued what must have been an oft repeated and rehearsed speech. 'There are many languages in the Motherland. Does not each province have its own tongue? Tibet has always been part of the Motherland, save for those times when we have been weakened by foreign exploitation.'

'The Tibetan people call you invaders,' Tsun said. 'It is they who fight you.' He spooned snuff onto his thumb and inhaled.

'Because they have been duped by their leaders, in whose interests they make protestations about independence, so that they could continue to rule and exploit the poor.'

'How can you be so convinced of the rightness, the absolute rightness, of your ideology? Please tell me.'

For a moment the girl was taken aback. Despite the hint of irony in his request, she felt that at last she had reached through to him. She was establishing contact, he would surely see that she was right. He would be converted. Again Tsun offered her some tsampa, and this time she took the dough and chewed it thoughtfully.

'I was born in Hunan,' she said. 'Life was very hard. My father tried to earn money by mending kettles and my mother collected firewood to sell. When I was very young there always seemed to be famine. We never had enough to eat. My mother grew old so quickly. One day, when I was about six years old, she went out to collect firewood and to beg for food. By evening she still hadn't returned. In the morning my father and I went to search for her. We found her lying dead beside the road to the village. She was so near home. The firewood she had collected was still on her back and she was carrying some leaves which she had collected for us to eat. That is my most vivid childhood memory. Of my mother lying dead, and of always being hungry. She had died of starvation.' Senge caught hold of the cadre's bootlaces in his mouth and growled playfully. Bending down she stroked his woolly head. 'We ate those leaves she had collected for us,' she continued. 'And we wept. All my life then was concerned with the problem of where we would find our next meal.' Senge rolled on his back and the girl tickled him. 'Then the Red Army came. We were told that we could redistribute the land among ourselves. It was a difficult decision to make. To join or not to join. We knew that if the Kuomintang routed the Red Army we would be held to account and most certainly be beheaded. But when you have been hungry for so long, and clung to life only by willpower, such a risk seems worthwhile. We decided to become farmers.

'It was hard work. But the joy of that first harvest, of at last having enough food to eat! Then I joined the Young Pioneers and spent a little time at basic school. Then suddenly it seemed that the Red Army would be defeated. The Kuomintang entered our village again. We had to flee to the hills, leaving everything. Anyone who was remotely connected with the Communists was ruthlessly punished. What they didn't loot, they destroyed – I suppose to stop the supplies getting into the hands of the Red Army, although I did hear that soldiers took to looting because the officers stole their pay. Fortunately, the Kuomintang were only in the village for a short time before having to retreat from the district. The Red Army took over again, this time permanently. So we went back to the land.

'I began to realise that I was forgetting the awful gnawing ache of hunger, because I was able to eat regularly. My father told me that for generations our people had been starving. Yet now there was food for all. Then, I decided that I wanted to know more of the ideas which had brought about this change, so I joined the Party and eventually became a cadre.

'The Party showed me how the old feudal system was dying, with that of capitalism, and that the new developing process was towards Communism.'

She paused. Tsun gave no sign of not understanding an evolutionary process. 'But I also learned, and this I knew from my own experience, that the peasant classes would never have enough unless they fought for it.'

'A revolution is an insurrection,' Tsun said. 'An act of violence by which one class overthrows another. Is that not what Chairman Mao said?'

The cadre was delighted. For the first time she smiled and her eyes sparkled.

'You know something of our beliefs. You have heard my history. Surely now you can see why I know that Communism is right? And there are millions like me. For otherwise the Party would not have become so securely established.' Tsun looked serious, but in his eyes there was humour.

'Tibet is China. China is Communist,' Ling continued. 'And you have just answered your question yourself, as to why there has to be a violent struggle in Tibet.'

'I do not argue with you,' Tsun said, 'about the overthrow of the social system you had in China. But I do argue that you have no right to force our country to accept your way.'

The girl frowned. She watched him unwind his ivory and coral rosary from his left wrist.

'But Tibet is part of China,' she said tersely.

'So you say,' Tsun answered. 'And no doubt believe, with millions of your countrymen. But surely, it must have occurred to you as strange that the Tibetan people, the ordinary Tibetan people – who have only known the threat of famine during the occupation – have demanded the withdrawal of PLA troops, have fought them in the name of Tibetan independence, and have rejected your way as alien to our own civilisation? As I understand it, the people are the ultimate source of authority in your state? Their will is expressed through the Party and its leadership?'

The cadre nodded.

'Then,' Tsun said, rolling the rosary gently through his fingers, 'you have seen the will of the Tibetan people forcefully expressed. We regard the Han as alien invaders in our land, and their ideology as foreign to our way of life.'

'But the fact remains,' Ling repeated patiently, 'that Tibet is one of the national minorities in China. They are but a small segment of the people. But, even so, they are given special attention. Some of the peoples of the Motherland are more advanced than others, socially and politically. When I was young, I believed that always to be hungry was the natural order of things. Nothing could change it. I honoured the gods, my village was the world. I could not read or write. But, since then, I have learnt. Now I can read and write, I have learnt about science and historical development in the Motherland and other countries. I did not have to seek to learn. Circumstances and conditions were established in which I could learn and the truth was made known. Of course, I do not expect that the Tibetan people, who are part of a centuries-old ecclesiastical, feudal, reactionary system, will immediately desire Communism.'

'The bonds of religion are the hardest to break,' Tsun murmured. The cadre heard, frowned, nodded agreement and continued.

'Unfortunately, Tibetans are imbued with subservience to this system.'

'In short they are green brains?'

'Yes,' she snapped. 'It is our duty to create an environment where they can think for themselves.'

'As long as it accords with your views,' Tsun said. 'Do you not see the danger in your thinking? Men are fallible. Even your leaders. To think that you know what is good for others can often be merely a hidden desire for power.'

'Typically Buddhist!' the cadre jeered. 'So you just sit back as a monk, begging from the poor and doing nothing. Letting hunger and suffering continue.'

'No,' Tsun replied. 'My life is dedicated to the relief of suffering. But my way is different from yours.' He rose slowly to his feet. 'We must sleep now. Perhaps, later, I shall tell you something of my way.'

He walked away from the camp and found a secluded place. He sat cross-legged, his face worn and weary. The pain of the destruction of Litang, the bloodshed, the horror, and the immense sense of responsibility that his mission carried made his heart heavy. The words of the cadre rang in his ears: 'Typically Buddhist'. Tsun closed his eyes and prayed.

'Halt! who is there?' The urgent voice of the sentry awoke everyone. From the darkness a figure moved towards him. 'Jigme,' the youth said apologetically. 'I didn't mean to scare you, I couldn't sleep.'

Cursing Jigme and the sentry for waking them, the party settled down to sleep again. They kept close to one another for comfort against the bitter cold.

Suddenly, one of the horses whinnied restlessly. A moment later the sound of hooves pounding the earth came to them over the still air. Everyone scrambled to their feet. The sound grew nearer. It was almost upon them. The escort fired their rifles into the darkness, and one of the Khambas was yelling 'Demons! Demons!' Norden gripped hold of Kesang and pulled him behind a rock. Senge was yelping and running round and round. 'We are being attacked,' someone shouted. 'Run, Run.' But there was no attack. The sound of pounding hooves faded away as quickly as it had begun. Demons or men, they moved very fast. Tsun was puzzled. Why had the horsemen deliberately risked being shot down? Perhaps they had been demons, and yet . . . ? Rinchen's voice raised in anger broke in on Tsun's thoughts.

'Don't lie! You must have seen them.' Jigme denied Rinchen's accusation with youthful vehemence, barely bothering with the necessary courtesies of speech. Tsun walked over to them.

'Jigme,' he said, 'answer me. I cannot be deceived.'

'Of course not, Rinposhay.' Jigme bowed. He was very frightened.

'Do you know who the riders were?'

'No, Precious One, I did not hear or see anyone.'

'Kunjosum!' Rinchen swore. 'Yet only seconds after you return to camp the horsemen are upon us. Is that not a strange coincidence?' he asked bitterly.

'Indeed it is, sir,' Jigme said. 'But if they were ghosts or demons I might well not have seen them.'

'Triple Gem!' Genyen, who had joined them, exclaimed in exasperation. 'As if we do not have enough to contend with. Now we have ghosts and demons.'

'I do not think they were anything other than men,' Tsun said. 'But why in that case,' he murmured to Genyen, 'would they warn us of their presence?' Genyen shrugged. 'No doubt, Rinposhay, the answer to that will soon be known. For now, let us all try to get some sleep, if that is possible, and leave two people keeping watch. We shall break camp at dawn.' With that she returned to where she had been sleeping and curled up on the hard ground. But, Genyen knew, she would not be getting much more sleep this night.

In the morning, a member of the escort was ordered by Genyen to go ahead and reconnoitre. She picked a man who knew the area well, a young farmer named Topden, recently married, who had joined the resistance because his father had been deported.

It was much later in the day when Genyen reined in beside the cadre.

'You understand Tibetan?' she asked coldly.

'Yes.' The cadre's tone matched Genyen's.

'If you know anything about those riders we heard last night, you had better confess now, because if we *are* attacked, my men will kill you. You are fortunate still to be alive, they all regard your continued existence as an insult to their murdered loved ones.'

The cadre's face tightened. 'I know nothing,' she said. Then after a few moments' pause, she added quietly, 'I have no wish to die.' As if to add emphasis to her denial. Genyen urged her horse on. The cadre was sure that her absence would have been reported to the District Authorities. She was wondering if troops in the area had been alerted and would be looking for her. She wasn't sure now if she wanted them to do so. If only she could find some way of escape, but even if she did, she was completely ignorant of the terrain. Her mule was stamping the ground impatiently. Some of the Khambas had overheard her conversation with Genyen and were crowding round her. The lama and monks were some yards ahead. She spurred on her mule to catch up with them, but one of the younger men leaned across and grabbed the mule's bridle. He grinned, mocking her. She saw the flash of a dagger as he slipped it between the overlap of her jacket. She screamed in terror. The party halted. Tsun turned his horse and came galloping towards her. The knife sliced all the buttons off her jacket. The young man let go of the bridle. No one was laughing now. Tsun waved the cadre forward. 'Ride in front of me,' he ordered.

Later in the day, they were buffeted by a strong wind. The riders muffled their faces, pulled on their fur hats and urged on the horses and mules. There were fears that it might be the prelude to a hailstorm. Tsun was worried. He rode up beside Genyen.

'Why has the scout not returned?' he asked.

'Do not let it worry you, Rinposhay,' she smiled at him reassuringly. 'No doubt we will see him when we make camp tonight.'

They were travelling along the edge of a desolate, stony valley. The sky was grey and there was a lot of low cloud. Suddenly, again, they heard the sound of an approaching aeroplane. The party scattered, desperately seeking what cover they could behind the boulders, pulling and forcing their horses and mules down to give them less chance of being seen. The Khambas unslung their rifles. Glimpses of the 'plane could be seen through the obscuring cloud as it flew past, some distance from them. At the far end of the valley it banked and circled back. The pilot was obviously searching the area. It disappeared into the cloud, then suddenly emerged, flying directly over them.

He must have seen us, Tsun thought. Genyen shouted above the noise of the engine.

'If it comes over again, we must attempt to bring it down.'

This time, the 'plane circled back before reaching the end of the valley. Tsun was now sure. It came in low over them, but just too high for any bullets to be effective. All Han aeroplanes looked much the same to Tsun, but he felt sure that this was the one they had seen two days earlier. Through his binoculars he caught a glimpse of the pilot looking down on the party. Now there could be no doubt that the Han knew of their existence. But do they know who we are, Tsun wondered, and what are their intentions? He saw Norden, Kesang's mother, lying with her arms round the boy, her body shielding him. She is a brave woman, Tsun thought. Senge whimpered, and snuggled against Tsun. He pulled the little dog close and tucked him into his chuba. Grit, blown by the icy wind, bit into his face.

The Khambas had their rifles sighted ready on the 'plane. The horses struggled to rise, trying to free themselves from the monks holding them down. They all waited for the attack. The 'plane seemed to be making a wide circle. The tension mounted as they waited for it to turn and come towards them. But instead it gained height and the noise of the engine faded rapidly as it climbed up into the sky and then disappeared over the mountains.

For a few moments, they waited, hardly daring to move. Tsun stood up. Senge put his head out and licked the Abbot's chin. Tsun pushed him back gently into the folds of his chuba, while he scanned the sky with his binoculars. The party steadied the horses and mules as the animals lurched to their feet. Genyen moved to Tsun's side. She looked worried. Rinchen, the steward, and Lopsang, the secretary, joined them. They too were worried.

'I almost wish it had attacked us,' Genyen said quietly, as she settled the rifle on its strap across her back. 'We would at least know then where we stood.'

'I'm glad it did not,' Lopsang's lanky figure was even more stooped than usual. 'Though the pilot must have seen us.'

'He saw us,' Tsun answered. 'I caught a glimpse of him through my glasses.'

'Then why did he not attack?'

'He could have thought we were only traders, or pilgrims, Rinposhay,' the steward suggested.

'It is possible, Rinchen. Though I think it was the same iron bird we saw a few days ago. It could be a routine patrol, I suppose.' He straightened the beautifully patterned saddle rug which the strong wind had blown back over the saddle, and patted his horse's neck. Genyen caught his eye. Neither had to express their doubts or anxiety. She was worried about the scout's long absence; he should have returned to give a report by now. She slipped her arm into the loose right sleeve of her sheepskin chuba to shield it from the bite of the gravel thrown by the wind, and shivered. Perhaps, she thought, the PLA are waiting to ambush us?

Tsun paused in the act of mounting his horse, left foot in the stirrup, his right hand resting on the high back of the saddle. He turned to Genyen. 'I felt that the pilot of the aeroplane was confident we would be dealt with. There was more than a normal interest, as if . . .' He saw the fear in her eyes and stopped. 'But,' he smiled, and settled into his saddle, 'I could be wrong. Though it might be wise to change our route.' Genyen shook her head. 'It would take us too far out of our way. We would have to cross miles of open ground. If we stay on this route, we should soon reach cover.' She looked up at the black clouds which were scudding across the sky. 'Please, Rinposhay, prevent the dragon from unleashing the storm.'

She swung herself up onto her mount and spurred it into a fast trot. The rest of the party followed behind her across the barren plain, their tiny figures dominated by the surrounding mountains and the lowering clouds. The wind howled, tugging at their garments and making them lean against it, men and animals straining their way forward.

Later, in the afternoon, when they were passing through a ravine, following a path cut out of the side of the rock, with the ice-cold waters of a river roaring only a few feet below, they were all startled by one of the Khambas shouting and pointing up into the sky. Ahead of them, vultures wheeled in a tight circle, their cries drowned by the noise of the river.

Automatically, their pace quickened over the treacherous ground, where one slip on the loose rock would have meant disaster; not speaking, thinking only of what might lie ahead. Rounding a rocky spur they saw a gnarled and twisted tree clinging to the side of the ravine. Something hanging from it was covered in vultures, squabbling with each other as they fought to keep their grip. The whole thing swung in the wind, making the vultures flap their wings to keep their balance.

As the party of travellers drew near, most of the birds reluctantly loosened their grip and ponderously winged their way into the sky or to perch among the rocks higher up the ravine. All except one. Its claws dug deep into flesh, its head inside the ripped-open stomach of a human body, hanging by its feet from the tree. Soft black feathers lightly brushed blood-soaked limbs.

Norden's scream echoed through the ravine. Genyen urged her horse past the older woman. Reaching the tree, she swung her leg over the saddle and slid to the ground, shouting to the rest of the party to take cover in case of ambush. Genyen made to hit the remaining vulture. Her fist struck the bird's body. With entrails trailing from its hooked beak, the bird flew lazily across the ravine. Genyen drew her sword and sliced the rope. The remains of the man's body crumpled sickeningly to the blood-sodden ground.

The rest of the party, having dismounted, watched in silence. Tsun searched both sides of the ravine through his field glasses for any sign of an ambush, but he could see nothing that gave any suspicion of an attack. Genyen knelt down beside the mutilated body and took the eyeless face between her hands. Torn and bloody as it was, she still recognised it. It was the young farmer she had sent ahead to scout. Tears crept down her cheeks. Gently, she laid the head down and picked up the broken pieces of his amulet box lying next to where the body had fallen. His sword and dagger were also on the ground. As she bent to pick up the sword, her eyes flinched away from what she had thought was a large patch of blood, then back again. It was not blood. It was skin. She stepped back in horror.

'He was skinned first.' Her face was white and her voice unsteady. 'They must have skinned him first, then left him for the vultures . . .'

Tsun stood in silence before the torn body. 'Knowing that we would find him,' he said. 'They left him like that knowing that we would find him . . .'

'Who left him?' Genyen demanded. 'What makes you so sure he was left here for us to find?'

Rinchen grimaced. He found the woman's abrasive manner highly offensive. Tsun turned to answer her. 'I am not sure,' he said thoughtfully, as he looked into Ling's frightened eyes, knowing that without his protection, she would certainly be killed.

'You think they are tracking us all the way?' Genyen said.

Tsun sighed. 'The plane, the horsemen, and now this . . .'

'But this isn't the way of the Han. The PLA are no good in the mountains. Tracking, striking quickly, then disappearing, that is the way of the Khambas.'

'The PLA is a big army, big enough for many skills.'

Genyen grunted. 'We've got to know how large a force is in the area. I'll get a message to the local resistance groups.' She swung her leg over the small horse. Jigme hesitated, sure they must be riding into a trap. He called to Genyen a few feet ahead up the narrow path. 'Shouldn't we turn back, Genyen? We cannot be sure of what lies just ahead.'

'If they are going to attack, they'll attack, whichever way we go.'

'We must go forward,' Tsun insisted. 'There is nothing to be gained from turning back.' The rushing waters of the river now made it difficult to hear what else was said, heightening the tension. If the Han were dug in round a bend of the ravine, the group wouldn't stand a chance, nor if a plane attacked.

They rode slowly past the corpse. Kesang looked back. The vultures had returned to their gruesome feast. Numbed with shock, he said a silent prayer for the man whose body was now food for the birds.

For some two hours they travelled. It was growing dark, but they had no desire to camp until they were out of the confines of the ravine. They spoke little, their ears and eyes seeking the slightest sight or sound that would indicate an ambush. The memory of the young farmer's tortured body filled their minds. It was as though his ghost rode with them.

At last they emerged from the ravine into a small fertile valley about two miles wide. Half a mile away, they could see in the dying light a large three-storeyed house. Tsun noticed that it was decorated with many more prayer flags than usual. Then he remembered that it was New Year. Despite the dim light, he could see that the sloping walls had recently been whitewashed. He held his field glasses to his eyes and picked out a small monastery at the far end of the valley, with a hamlet of six or seven houses nestling at its foot. Genyen rode up beside him.

'Rinposhay,' she said. 'I know the owner of that house. He is a merchant. His name is Tsering Dawa and his brothers are in the resistance. He has done much to help us and I'm sure he will give us hospitality.'

'What of the girl, the cadre?' Tsun asked. 'I feel sure that she will not be welcome, especially at the New Year, and I have no wish to compromise your friend.'

'Can she not remain outside? My men will take it in turns to guard her.' Tsun shook his head. 'Somehow,' he smiled cynically, 'I feel an accident might befall her.'

'Then we will say that she is a Han Muslim. She must get rid of her jacket and trousers, we should have enough spare to find her something else to wear. A close watch will be kept. But,' Genyen paused, and her full lips moved in the hint of a smile at Tsun. 'If my men decide to kill her, nothing will save her, even though she be lodged in the Potala itself. Now, I will go ahead and make sure that it is safe for you to follow.'

'But there may be Han . . .'

'If I do not return soon, continue without me.'

She urged her horse into a canter, giving Tsun no chance to stop her. The party watched her lone figure riding towards the house. Tsun looked through his glasses again, but he could see no sign of anyone coming to greet her. She reached the house. He saw her dismount and lead her horse out of sight. He lowered his glasses and prepared to wait.

The party kept close together. If there was to be an attack they preferred to be near to each other. Now and then, someone would start up a conversation, but it faded quickly. They were all tense, ready for the slightest sign of danger.

Tsun was acutely conscious of being entirely at the mercy of events. He felt that it was expected of him to resolve the situation. He wondered if it might be possible to leave Kesang and his mother at the monastery. His pupils could stay with them, but he knew, even as he thought it through, that it was impossible. There was no sanctuary these days. If only he could get them safely to a monastery in Lhasa or western Tibet. It was said that there was peace there, but, though he tried to stifle the thought, Tsun wondered for how long?

He raised his glasses again and focused them on the house. To his delight, he saw Genyen riding out of the main gate, and there was a short, stocky man riding beside her. The others saw her too, and there were murmurs of relief. Two of the Khambas wanted to go and meet her, but the others felt it better to wait.

As she drew nearer they could see that she was smiling. The tension eased. Genyen and her escort reined in beside Tsun and both dismounted.

'Rinposhay,' Genyen said, 'may I introduce our host, Tsering

Dawa.' Tsun nodded and smiled at him. Tsering Dawa, a man in his forties, was dressed in a coat of dark grey broadcloth and black leather boots. A trilby rested on his close-cropped head.

'My wife and I would be honoured, Rinposhay, if you and Dorje Rinposhay and your party would deign to stay with us. We would consider your visit a most auspicious beginning to the New Year.' He handed Tsun a felicity scarf, which Tsun returned with the customary blessing. As he did so, he caught Genyen's eye and glanced towards the cadre. Genyen nodded.

Then Tsering Dawa remounted and led the party down into the valley. They skirted a grove of poplar and willow trees, the branches decorated with fluffy white catkins and prayer flags. Nearby, the river gurgled and rushed on its way.

As they approached the house, six large guard dogs started barking furiously, straining at their chains and foaming at the mouth. Senge, safe in the folds of Tsun's chuba, joined in with a vigorous reply. Reaching the entrance to the house, Tsun waved at a delighted little girl looking through a tear in the glazed rice paper of a window. Colourful window boxes were set into the carved window frames. Hooves clattered on the stones of the courtyard as the party rode through the gateway. The entire household was assembled to meet them. Some of the servants held up hurricane lamps. Others held the horses' bridles to allow the guests to dismount and two men closed the heavy wooden gates behind them.

Tsering Dawa introduced his wife to Tsun, and his young son and daughter and two nephews. Then, the members of the party were escorted up a worn greasy ladder with a rope handrail to the living quarters on the first floor. Genyen stayed with the men to see that the mules were unloaded, the horses well fed and watered. The ground floor of the house, which was built round a courtyard, was given over to stables and storerooms.

The visitors were ushered into a spacious, low-ceilinged room. The walls were freshly painted a pale grey with a vividly painted border running round the room a few inches from the ceiling. Seats piled with rugs and cushions were set against the walls, and two special high seats were being hurriedly prepared by a servant at the far end of the room on either side of the gilded wooden shrine. On it, butter lamps and incense burned before images of Tson-Kha Pa, Chenresi the Patron Saint of Tibet, and Maitreya the Buddha of the future. Beautifully carved, painted tables were set before the seats. The harsh white glare of a tilly lamp filled the room.

Tsun and Kesang bowed before the shrine and then took their places on the high cushioned seats on either side of it. Tsering Dawa's wife, Kalsang, opened a glass-fronted cabinet and removed a pair of jade tea cups on silver and gold stands. She placed them before the two lamas.

'You have had a good journey, Rinposhay?' Tsering asked Tsun.

'Like life,' Tsun smiled. 'Good and bad.'

Kalsang put a bowl of fruit before them. Her husband picked out an orange and began carefully to peel it. Genyen came into the room, followed by the tall Khambas and the servants of the house. The room was full of noise and laughter. Tsering divided the peeled orange into two halves and gave one portion to each of the lamas. As his wife left the room, he leaned towards Tsun.

'I have known Genyen for many years,' he said. 'But little did I know that she would eventually command so many men and all at the same time!'

Genyen heard him, and his roar of laughter brought a redness to her cheeks as she glanced at Tsun.

'What you did not know, Tsering,' she answered sharply, 'is that when my beauty does not enslave men, my wits and agility with the sword conquer them!'

Senge, who had been frightened by the noise and had snuggled down into Tsun's coat, became restive. Tsun lifted him out and put him on the floor. He ran to join the children of the house who were playing in the centre of the room.

'Rinposhay,' Tsering pushed his trilby back on his copper coloured head. 'Genyen told me, when we were riding to meet you, that a member of your party has died?'

Tsun nodded.

'How did it happen, Rinposhay?'

'There was an accident,' Tsun replied. He did not wish to be drawn into conversation about what had happened to the scout. In fact neither man gave a complete answer to the other's queries. It was the custom. One simply did not give too much away too soon.

Kalsang, her daughter and a nursemaid brought in a number of silver-lined wooden bowls containing parched barley flour mixed with fresh butter and cheese. Coloured replicas of the sun and moon, modelled in butter, lay on the top of each bowl in honour of the New Year. As the dishes were placed in front of them, each guest wished his host and family health, prosperity and peace of mind.

'We had forgotten that it is New Year,' Norden said. Tsering's daughter smiled excitedly at her.

'I helped sweep the soot out of the kitchen, then we took it to the crossroads so that the demons will be happy.' She offered the bowl to Norden. 'And I was decorating the kitchen with auspicious signs when we heard you coming.'

Tsun caught Genyen's eye as she came over to sit on a rug beside him.

'I've arranged, Rinposhay . . .' she began haltingly. She found it strange calling him 'Rinposhay', even though she meant it, and hoped that he did not notice her embarrassment as she continued. 'I've arranged with Tsering Dawa to find out the strength of the Han forces in the area. Why don't they just attack? Why are they trying to frighten us?'

'I don't know, Genyen. Perhaps its because we've got the Han woman with us, or maybe it's to weaken our resolve, convince us that we have no hope of succeeding. Maybe they don't have enough men.'

They ate in silence for some moments, each lost in thought, half aware of the excited conversation around them. Genyen looked up at Tsun.

'Could you do the after death ceremony for Topden? He was quick-tempered and some of us feel that his spirit might cling to the place where he was killed and become a vengeful influence.'

Tsun nodded. 'Tomorrow morning.'

'You know that Tsering wants you and Dorje Rinposhay to stay for the picnic and New Year celebrations?'

Tsun took the silver lid off the jade cup and put his hands round the silver stand, pausing before lifting it to his lips.

'Genyen, if the Han know we are here, they don't know yet where we are going. We will go to the celebrations and give every indication that we are staying for the next few days, but tell Tsering Dawa that it must be as laymen. Will you know by tomorrow night the size of the Han forces?' She nodded. Tsun took a deep drink of tea and Tsering's daughter immediately re-filled the cup and replaced the silver lid.

'Then, Genyen,' he whispered, 'tomorrow night we leave.'

'Look what I brought back from my last trading mission to India.' Tsering Dawa went over to a large wind-up gramophone standing on a table. He wound it up very carefully, then placed a record on the turntable. The sound of Glenn Miller's band filled the room.

There were shouts of surprise from some members of the party. Kesang's eyes rounded with childish amazement and fascination. Senge ran round and round the room, barking furiously. Genyen moved closer and stared at the revolving record.

'A magic box,' she murmured. 'But what strange sounds. Why are the little demons it contains so angry?'

Tsering laughed. He stopped the motor and changed the record for one of Tibetan music. The guests crowded round the gramophone to see how it worked.

Barley beer was served in wooden, brass-bound tankards with bamboo straws. The time passed quickly, with much laughter and eating and drinking. The strain of the last few days, the destruction of Litang, the mutilated corpse of the scout, all seemed to fade for a while in the merriment of the New Year celebrations. The guests began to relax until tiredness finally overcame them, and their host, noticing that Kesang could hardly keep his eyes open, asked the group if they would like to retire.

Everyone stood up and bowed respectfully as the two lamas rose and followed Tsering from the room. At the end of the corridor was the shrine room which Tsering had ordered to be prepared for the lamas, with the best rugs and mattresses. Then he showed Kesang to the lavatory. It was a small cubicle built to overhang the outer wall with simply a hole cut in the floorboards. The extreme cold of the climate prevented the waste accumulated on the ground below from causing disease until it could be collected and used as fertiliser in the fields.

'I like the small house,' Kesang said when he returned. 'It's not as dark and frightening as the one in the monastery!'

Tsun smiled at the small boy and watched while Kesang walked round the room, carefully inspecting the many family treasures, the festival clothes, the trading commodities including watches, cigarettes, combs, toothbrushes and bolt upon bolt of cloth. Kesang was disturbed from his fascinated inspection by Senge barking and scratching at the door. The dog had discovered where they were and now demanded to be let in. Kesang opened the door and the little dog bounded in.

In the light of the flickering butter lamps, the two lamas made their prostrations and read from religious texts. Then they untied the belts of their chubas so that the hems of the garments reached the floor, and wrapped themselves up in the loose fitting gowns as they settled down on rugs to sleep.

Tsun was tired, but sleep would not come. He lay staring at the moving shadows thrown by the light from the butter lamps. The wind howled outside causing the flames to flicker wildly, making weird shadows on the walls and ceiling. To extinguish the lamps would have been irreverent.

It was unlike the Han to be subtle. But who else could be playing this cruel game with them? As if knowing every move they would make? He felt trapped. Genyen was in charge of the escort, but they all relied on him for the success of their journey. Finally, exhaustion overcame him and he fell into an uneasy sleep.

Chapter Three

The sharp insistence of rain on the window pane awakened Tsun. The room was dark and very cold. Most of the butter lamps had been extinguished by the draughts. The sound of the rain faded with the ferocious howling of the wind.

Tsun forced himself up, pulling the sheepskin chuba closer round him, and walked to the window. He had not noticed before that the window was glass and not rice paper. He peered out into the valley. The sky was lit by a harsh grey light tinged with purple. He saw an enormous, seething cloud overhead, its heart purple, radiating dark blue, the edges lost in the darkness of the night. The valley was empty. It was as if he stood completely alone, an alien amongst the true inhabitants of the Land of Snows, where the elements, the sky, the water, earth itself and its heaving mountains moved and stretched themselves, man always in their shadow. Tsun had seen many storms but this, he felt, was different, a portent. There was a movement and he glanced round to see Kesang struggling up from his bed and draping a blanket round his shoulders. Tsun put out a hand and the boy came to stand close at his side.

A glaring white light suddenly lit up the valley. The two lamas blinked at its brilliance. The ground beneath them shook with the great crashing roar from the sky.

'The gods are joined in battle,' Kesang whispered in awe as the sound died away.

Once again, lightning flashed across the sky, and again the ground shook with a mighty roar. Tsun remembered the saying that, when the gods were in battle thus, man would soon follow suit. Another thunderous explosion crashed above them. As it faded, Senge's whimper came from a corner of the room.

Gradually the storm passed, leaving the steady downpour of rain distorting their vision as it flooded over the window pane.

'What is to become of us?' Kesang had also realised the portent of the storm. 'You have a plan, can you not tell me?' Tsun smiled reassuringly. 'If I tell you everything, it could be dangerous'.

'You mean that the Han might torture me and that I might reveal the secret?'

Tsun could not answer. He looked down on the solemn little face and prayed for the right words to come.

'I know that the Han hate us, because we are lamas,' Kesang said, 'and have the loyalty of the people. And I know . . .' He glanced up at Tsun with frightened eyes, 'that they will try to kill you. But I am young, they will try to take me to China. Tsun!' He took hold of Tsun's arm. 'Don't let them. Kill me first.'

Tsun looked at the small boy, saying nothing.

'My former body would have withstood them,' Kesang continued. 'He was experienced but I am not. The Han could easily trick me. It is better that I die than betray you, the Triple Refuge . . . everything . . . you must promise me, Tsun,' he pleaded desperately.

Tsun tried to speak, but no sound came. Kesang pulled on his arm.

'I will take the responsibility so that you will not suffer in the hells for breaking your vows,' Kesang insisted.

'I was not thinking of that,' Tsun murmured thickly.

'Then you will do as I ask?'

Tsun was silent for some time. What Kesang asked was in total opposition to Tsun's duties as a guardian and as a monk. But . . .

'Yes,' he said.

'Thank you!' Kesang smiled at Tsun. A smile of relief, but also of the past, Tsun thought, a smile aware of the Abbot's pain.

'Tsun, you know that I have had many strange experiences during the past few months?'

The Abbot nodded. The fact had worried him greatly.

'I keep seeing a strange land,' Kesang went on, 'peopled by gods or demons, I do not know which, but it is not a dream.'

'Describe these beings to me, Kesang.' Tsun and the boy sat down on their rug-covered mattresses.

'They are tall and fair skinned with long noses, and they wear strange clothing. Though it is similar to that worn by the Han.' He spoke softly, as if seeing the things he described. 'They have strange vehicles. There are many of them, and large buildings. There is much movement, and terrible noise.' His voice faded and there was a long pause.

'What you have seen is a country of the Injis,' Tsun said. 'On my own travels to China and India I have seen such places as you describe and seen such people. It means that you will travel, too.'

'No, Tsun.' The boy shook his head. 'I will never leave Tibet. I will die soon.'

Tsun looked into the boy's eyes. His face expressed no alarm, only sadness.

'Why do you believe that?' Tsun asked quietly.

'Perhaps, Tsun-la, perhaps because everything is going to die soon.'

Tsun looked down at the chid and knew that he was not just commenting on the lot of all that lived, but that he had had a glimpse of Tsun's own dark vision. A small boy, he thought, yet also the channel of the continuing influence of Dorje Rinposhay. Kesang, who showed wisdom and insight far beyond his years, and yet was still a child of his age. Kesang rested his hands on the window sill and watched the valley distort, fade and reappear as the rain fell in a sheet across the window pane, then receded. Tsun put a hand round the boy's shoulders as he spoke.

'You've seen many horrors for one so young, Kesang. Your visions are as a result of the abilities of your former body. Yet you are inexperienced and young, and do not have the knowledge to understand completely all that you see.' Kesang was aware of an insistent pawing at his leg. He stooped to pick up Senge and tucked him under his arm, holding him so that his front paws rested on the sill so that he, too, could look out of the window. A paw came out intermittently, trying to touch a rivulet of rain as it struggled across the pane of glass.

'Our country is going through the darkest time of its history,' Tsun continued. 'It will seem that all is dying, and sadly, there is much cruelty and much suffering for our people. Life, Kesang, is going to change, but that shouldn't surprise us. Is there a moment that doesn't change? Is there anything that doesn't change? All that you and I honour, Kesang, may be taken from us, may be destroyed.'

Silently watching the rain through the window, the boy listened to Tsun's words with an aching dread filling his chest like a physical pain. Tsun looked down at him.

'Is Dorje Rinposhay destroyed?'

'No, Tsun-la.'

'Yet he died. But his influence lives on in a changed form. Your form. Our lives are the Teaching, Kesang. However much things change, the Religion will not alter. But the horrors, the visions you have are perhaps to help you, so that when your help is needed, you can give it without fear.'

'Do you think that everything will be destroyed, Tsun-la?'
'We have been destroyed before.'
'But what of our land, Tsun? Everything is being destroyed.'
'We have been invaded before. Our monasteries have been destroyed before, our people terrorised. As people suffer, so nations suffer. We have overthrown the invaders before, and shall do so again.'
'But people will die, Tsun. So nations must die?'
'It can be,' Tsun said. 'Such can be the law of cause and effect – the law of karma. But our duty is to do all that we can to avert it. Truth and justice are with us, Kesang. So, by the law of karma, we must eventually achieve victory.'
Kesang gave him a penetrating look.
'Eventually?' He repeated. 'Aeons?'
He has an understanding, Tsun thought, that is terrible for a child. The wheel of karma could indeed take aeons to turn; the 'victory' could be generations hence, and the nation could suffer the fate of the Buddha's own Sakya Clan, total destruction. He wondered if Kesang knew.
'Tell me, Tsun,' the boy asked quietly. 'What are you going to do?'
'We have friends in the outside world, Kesang. There is a gathering of people, an organisation, that may help us, when they realise how desperate the situation is.'
'So, there is hope?'
'But of course. And remember, that in Lhasa there is still peace.' Tsun found it hard to sound convincing. 'Come now, little one, the storm is passing and we must sleep.'
Tsun tucked blankets round the boy, while Senge struggled to get out of his chuba. Kesang took the little dog and snuggled down with him in his arms. There were tears in the boy's eyes, but he made no sound. It tore at Tsun to see the child's distress.
'Do not weep, Kesang.' He sat beside the boy and stroked his head gently. 'Close your eyes and meditate as I have taught you.'
Gradually, the boy drifted into sleep, but Tsun stayed awake. He had much to occupy his mind.

Further down the corridor from the lama's room, Samden was standing with the shy young daughter of his host, watching the rain pouring down into the valley.
'You are very pretty,' Samden whispered in her ear, and

laughed softly when she blushed. 'But you are.' His lips caressed her ear.

'Sir! Please, no!' She stepped away from him.

Jetsun did not think that a monk should act in this way, but he was so handsome and confident, and there was a strange fascination about the unapproachable. Rumours she had heard whispered concerning the virility of amorous monks arose in her mind, half frightening, half exciting her. And it was flattering for a monk to pay such attention.

'It is inauspicious for the New Year to behave so,' she scolded him.

'Perhaps.' His face was suddenly solemn. There was a moment's silence, then he smiled again.

'But tell me, what do you plan to do on the day of the New Year?'

She smiled back at him, relieved by his change of mood.

'In the morning, I shall collect the Star Water with the rest of the household. Later we will visit our friends and join in the dancing. Pa-la is arranging a big picnic.' She gave a little bubbling laugh of excitement. For a moment Samden's calculating charm gave way to wonder at her vibrant, youthful beauty.

'Why do you have Ling, the Han girl, with you?' she asked suddenly.

'Because she saw us escape . . .' As he spoke, Samden realised that he had said too much. He saw the shocked look on her face. 'But you must not repeat to anyone what I have just told you.' He lowered his voice, and intoned impressively, 'or you will be accursed by demons and . . .'

'I will not say a word, sir, I promise you,' the girl interrupted nervously. 'I only asked because my mother was angered by her presence, saying it would bring us ill-fortune.'

'Empty your mind of all such worrisome thoughts.' Samden stroked her hair with his fingertips, then moved on gently to explore her face.

Chapter Four

Topden's skull was incredibly difficult to break. Tashi, who had ridden with him for five years, brought the half-inch thick blunt edge of his knife down for the fourth time on the cranium. The long black hair, with some beads and coloured thread worked into it, was untouched by the vultures, but made the half eaten face appear even more macabre.

In such a small community there were no professional body-breakers to ensure the complete disposal of Topden's body, so Tashi and Gonpo had taken on the task, riding back at dawn to where his body lay. Practical necessity and spiritual ideal had evolved the 'air burial'. In a land where the ground was often solid rock or frozen hard, to give one's body to satisfy the hunger of other sentient beings was to emulate the compassion of the Buddhas, who so often sacrificed their lives for the benefit of other beings.

So, at daybreak, Tashi and Gonpo, already fortified with barley beer, set about disposing of Topden's body. The vultures were well fed and could afford to be choosy, and Topden's corpse had only been partly devoured. The two men wept. The vultures gathered lazily, unhurried but watching intently, perching on ridges in the cliff face and on branches of the stunted trees by the river, their black wings against their naked heads and necks giving them a sinister, hunched appearance. Topden's skull broke. The vultures shifted and began to move in. The brains were the choicest delicacy. Tashi had even been told by one body-breaker that if given the brains too early, the birds would ignore the rest of the body. The professionals saved them till last, mixing them with the ground-up bones to make sure that nothing remained.

But Tashi and Gonpo were not professional body-breakers. They were friends of Topden. With the vultures starting to cluster around them, snatching at morsels, they hastily did what they could, occasionally laughing as they worked – the laughter Tibetans used when faced with something too awful to express. Both men were conscious that Topden, killed in extreme pain and anger, might seek vengeance, being fixed in his rage at the place of his death.

The two men had to beat the vultures off with sticks in order to reach their horses.

Rinchen's solid figure, accentuated by his maroon robe, moved unhurriedly, every movement deliberate, his mind focused on the task in hand as he stood a small stylized drawing of 'the one whose life had left him' inscribed with Topden's name, on a lotus carefully outlined in white, at the centre of the six symmetrical open petals. The intricately carved wooden shrine with its dozen small niches for bronze images, and large ones for the volumes of foot-long scriptures, was set with fourteen silver bowls containing fresh water and small dishes filled with meat and confectionery as token offerings. Rinchen lit the last of the 108 butter lamps.

Tsering Dawa had arranged for the best rugs to be put in the living room for his guests to sit on during the ceremony, and he and his household had joined Tsun's group. Senge clambered over their legs, weaving in and out of the rugs before making himself comfortable by the brass brazier.

The monks sat at right angles to the shrine, each with a small boxlike table before him bearing the text for the dead, the small brass ritual sceptre, symbol of wisdom, and the matching handbell, symbolic of compassion. Also on the tables were tiny finger cymbals, bowls of offering rice and double faced hand-drums.

Genyen indicated that Ling should sit beside her, and the Han woman decided that in the cramped room she would try sitting cross-legged. As Genyen unwound the string of beads around her wrist and began counting off silent invocations, Ling realised just how nervous she felt. It was not as if she had never seen death, she reasoned, and she had been to ceremonies for the dead before, but at none had she felt such dread. But then, she thought, at the previous ceremonies she had attended she had not been a prisoner, and she had not been troubled by the mixed emotions she now felt about Tsun.

As she glanced at him, Tsun lifted a cup of tea to his lips and caught Ling's eye. She looked away abruptly and he sensed her embarrassment and selfconsciousness.

Ling was startled at the timbre of Tsun's voice as he began intoning the text. The sonorous tones and inflexions were designed to produce sound vibrations with a definite spiritual effect. The other monks accompanied him periodically, their voices equally deep and vibrant, emphasising parts of the text with graceful and intricate movements of the ritual sceptre and handbell, the rattle of the drum and the eerie, high-pitched note of the tiny finger cymbals.

The monks threw some grains of rice into the air with a flick of their fingers, declaring them to be offerings for any spirits of evil and ordering them to be gone. Attention centred on the name card of Topden beneath its little rainbow-coloured canopy. As the dead man was summoned to their presence, Tsun chanted:

'The earthly sojourn is ended, and flesh and bones hitherto inseparable, are parted.

'Birth, old age and death are the origin of all suffering. After death everything decomposes back into the earth. Everything is devoured by birds, dogs, foxes, wolves, worms and flies. There, all religious worship is without purpose. Bones become like stone, flesh becomes earth, blood becomes water and cavities become air; and the spirit is like the emptiness of heaven.'

Although Ling knew this to be true, for it was what scientific materialism had proved, she found the thought of the emptiness of heaven bleak and chilling. But if Tsun's words chilled her, they reassured others for, to everyone in that room except Ling, life, as it appeared, was the shadow of emptiness, 'the foundation of all', impossible to describe rationally, to be experienced only by the mind.

'O Nobly Born Topden, listen. Your present character is really empty, not formed into anything; to be naturally empty is the reality, is the all good.'

Topden's pilgrimage in death was of significance to each person in the room. Death was an opportunity; there was an art to dying and using the opportunity well. Everyone, to a greater or lesser extent, saw life as a preparation for the time.

Genyen loosened her sheepskin chuba and tapped some snuff onto her thumbnail. As she inhaled, specks of the powder clung to the tear stains on her cheeks. Invoking the Lord of Compassion, she watched Tsun. He was immersed in meditation, the visible guide of the dead, an awakened warrior skilfully using his weapons of mind, and she recognised the son untamed of her youth. He was conscious of Topden, and in that consciousness was an awareness of reactions, impressions, thoughts of the dead man's ability to see clearly all those present in the room, his growing realisation of his death and of the surging whirlpool of anger and vengeance which had not yet engulfed him. Tsun's words and presence were designed to reach into Topden's confused mind, urging him to let go of rage, to be calm and to abide by the words of advice; to begin his journey, warning him that he would be subject to sound and light of strange qualities, but that whatever occurred he should remain calm and listen to the words of the text.

Members of Tsering's household picked their way across the crowded floor. Ling tried to ease her legs which had gone to sleep, but it was painful and difficult because of the lack of room. She managed to draw them up underneath her so that she was sitting on her haunches.

As the monks continued chanting, Tsun periodically picked up one of the tiny paintings from the playing card-size pack of miniatures on the table. Each card illustrated aspects of the progress of Topden's stream of consciousness between death and its new state: a journey through the elements of his mind and all that made up his character in life. Tsun was conscious of Topden's attention on the words of the text, of the confusion and conflict of feeling, as he advised the dead man that, with the falling away of the senses and the dissolution of the body, of all the old judgements and preconceptions, with the break up of the subtle structure the mind builds around itself, Topden would be left with the inner essence of his mind and an opportunity just to be aware, to see things as they are. But the ability to remain in this state, to use the opportunity, depended entirely on Topden's karma and understanding.

All in the room murmured invocations, that any merit they might have accrued during this and previous lifetimes be dedicated in Topden's favour. Offerings of food, drink, clothing, a weapon, a bridle, symbols of all desirable things, were laid before Topden's name card by Genyen and each member of the escort. The monks described the offerings as though they were for a king, an echo of the time when the monarchs of pre-Buddhist Tibet were equipped for the lone journey through the underworld, like the pharaohs of Egypt. But now they had become symbols of virtues; the adornment of good conduct, the garment of forbearance, the horse of effort . . .

Ling was acutely conscious of her isolation. She alone was not involved, had nothing to contribute. But her sense of isolation, initially tinged with superiority at being free of such superstitions, now contained a hint of confusion, of a nameless, deep fear.

Halfway through the morning there was a break in the reading while tea and tsampa was served. The children of the house played with Senge; the men and women took the opportunity to stretch their legs, talked, or continued with their invocations. Tsun watched Ling as he mopped up the remaining tea with his tsampa dough. She was studying the scroll paintings of the deities and was working hard at being relaxed. They were both thinking of their conversation during the journey, when Ling had extolled the wonderful scientific achievements of China and Soviet Russia. 'You recognise and have no doubt about the vast power of the mind in all that has been created and developed by individual scientists,' Tsun had said. 'But despite this evidence you dismiss the human mind's potential and power when it looks within and explores itself; the power of those whose very being is to help their fellow man; the power of the mind to *know* contentment, to realise its potential, to bring release from suffering to all beings.' 'Of course,' Ling had replied. 'The mind is doing this through Communism. Your way, though, is a selfish way.'

Today Ling knew her reply had been no answer, that Tsun had spoken of something different. She'd dismissed it before as meaningless, but now, for good or ill, she knew it was a power. She settled herself uneasily as the ceremony continued.

Topden, unable to seize the first opportunity to awaken to his true nature, would now find himself undergoing a pilgrimage of all that made up his character, all that influenced him: the accumulated experiences of generations, the archetypal forms of man's dawn, buried deep in the psyche, combined with his quickness of temper and the broadness of his love. Every aspect of his psyche and character he met on his pilgrimage, some appearing as the deities, wrathful or beneficent according to his reaction. Tsun and the monks, describing them in the text, symbolically illustrated their appearance with the miniature drawings, urging all the time that Topden realise their illusory nature, understand that it was his mind which was the only reality, not the dieties or the experiences he underwent; all were creations of his mind, as a diamond reflects a multitude of light, but in essence remains still and pure.

Again and again, the text called Topden to recognise the great fear, the root of the fear of death, the fear of losing one's self-identity. Tsun and those watching could sense that a turning point had been reached as Topden now faced a review of his life. He had become an observer, witnessing the events he had experienced in the places he had known; seeing all that had gone to make up his short life: his family, his trading, loving, fighting.

Tsun felt the dead man's intense emotion and sense of isolation, a wave of desolation swept over him as Topden lived through his past: his childhood, his wife and children. For Topden, the sensation of barley grains in his hands would seem perfectly real as he heard Tsun explain that death was holding a mirror to his life, so it would be his own understanding of himself which would judge and determine the direction in which his flow of consciousness would be reborn – in the realms of heaven, in purgatory, among life forms unknown, in other dimensions; and of those known, perhaps the animal kingdom or, most precious of all, mankind. And there was still a chance that he would realise the true significance of what was happening to him and awaken to be freed of the round of rebirth.

Genyen was murmering the mantra of Chenresi, *Om Mani Padme Hum*, when Ling leaned across and whispered to her.

'I want to pee.'

Genyen nodded and stood up, waiting for Ling to get up and leave ahead of her. Ling tried to straighten up. She had to hang onto the bales stacked against the wall in order to steady herself; one of her legs had become completely numb and she had difficulty in walking. She stumbled over a Khamba's foot. He looked at her coldly, with hostility. No one offered to help, nor did she expect it. Like Genyen, she regarded herself as the equal of any man and she was not unaware that, as the political vanguard of the Party, any cadre was inevitably in the forefront of the fight against the old feudal society, and that anyone who believed in that order, whether out of self-interest and the privileges they enjoyed, or out of sheer, gullible ignorance, would regard her as a threat, as an enemy. As she felt Genyen's hand on her shoulder, urging her on, she thought that Tibetans were certainly not called 'green brains' without good reason. Indeed, most seemed to be in that category, and this made her task that much more difficult, since, for the most part, they were sincere in their beliefs.

The monks' chanting could still be heard as the two women stepped into the corridor. The cold immediately misted Ling's glasses. Genyen walked slowly beside her, her hand resting on the automatic in the fold of her chuba which hung loosely on her copper-coloured shoulders.

Ling polished her glasses on the sleeve of her woollen chuba, aware that she had by no means mastered the folds and tucks used in wearing it, instinctively comparing herself to Genyen and resenting both the comparison and her own political shortcomings in succumbing to such bourgeois tendencies. She looked at Genyen's hand in her ambac, and then met her eyes.

'Where would I run to in the middle of nowhere?' She struggled to keep the aggression out of her voice.

'If I were you,' Genyen said, 'I would be thinking about running.' She opened the door into a small room with its two crudely-made holes in the floorboards. Genyen leaned against a wall and appeared to be assessing Ling who, turning her back on the Khamba woman, hitched up her chuba, undid her trousers and squatted carefully over one of the holes.

'Why do you speak Tibetan?' Genyen asked quietly.

'I work here in Tibet.' Ling sounded slightly surprised.

'Few of the yellow dogs understand us,' Genyen retorted.

Ling thought it wiser to ignore the remark and buttoned up her trousers, forcing herself to smile at Genyen as she opened the door.

'It is not only Tibetans who are green brained.' Ling kept smiling and hoped that she had not pushed Genyen too far. She had no intention of being cowed, although when she analysed it, her motive had more to do with personal pride than with holding aloft the Great Red Banner – a weakness she thought she might forget at the next Party self-criticism meeting she attended.

Genyen beckoned the cadre to walk ahead of her down the corridor. Ling hesitated by the door of the shrine room, wondering if she could fit herself in near the entrance, but Genyen pointed to the space she had vacated and Ling clambered back over legs and bodies, finally squatting down in her place.

'O Nobly Born Topden, listen,' Tsun was intoning. 'That you are suffering now comes from your own karma. It is not due to anyone else but your own karma. Call on the Buddha, the Teaching and the Assembly of Enlightened Beings that they may protect you. It may be that you will be judged by the Lord of Death. Fear not, whatever happens. Your body is a mental body. The Lord of Death is your own hallucination. In reality, there are no such things existing outside oneself as The Lord of Death, demons or gods. Act that you may recognise this, and if you do not know how to meditate then analyse with great care the real nature of that which is frightening you. In reality it is the void of which you are the void . . .'

Ling was thinking about Genyen's words, wondering whether they were anything more than just a general warning. She tried to drink as much of the tea as possible before it cooled any further and the congealing butter made it unpalatable. She had no doubt as to its nutritional value, but she could never really enjoy it.

Lopsang was moving Topden's name card onto one of the petals of the lotus flower traced out in white on the shrine, as the monks described in their chanting the realms of being. Now Tsun knew that Topden had let go of his feelings of anger and vengeance, had been freed from the place of his death. Unable to take complete advantage of his awakening to his true nature, his stream of consciousness flowed towards a new birth.

Everyone strove to prevent Topden from being swept along into what might be an unfavourable rebirth, praying that he might be able to use his judgement and understanding when choosing where to be reborn. As the little figure was moved into the different realms on the shrine, Tsun and the monks continued advising and counselling Topden on the nature of the mental levels, or realms of existence, and on how to use fully all his propensities for good when he had chosen his rebirth.

While the other monks chanted, Tsun rose and, holding a lighted incense stick to Topden's name card, intoned:

'Listen, Topden. The fire of Body, Speech and Mind of the Lord of Compassion, Chenresi, has consumed the three poisonous evils: greed of all kinds, hatred and anger of all kinds, ignorance of the nature of things.'

It was during those few timeless moments that Tsun felt Topden's sense of well-being leave him. Tsun was aware of himself as thin, his shaven head heavily flecked with grey, the whites of his eyes bloodshot, his face gaunt and lined. The ill-fitting grey cotton shirt and trousers felt strange. Tsun was no longer in Tsering Dawa's house, nor just an observer of some strange future event. He was living it, and a mind-numbing exhaustion swept over him as he filed into the ten-by-fifteen-foot cell and curled up on the sand which formed the inmates' beds on either side of the concrete path running down the centre. The initial moments of relaxing into the sand were delicious after the day's work, and before discomfort set in from the injuries, the bruises, the haunting dreams of hunger, fear and disturbed sleep.

The door slammed and the steel bars rammed home. Little was said. Tsun and three others in the cell employed the few precious night hours in meditation, using the discomfort and pain as part of their contemplation. After so long, their resilience owed much to these silent hours. For a few moments, those gilded bronze figures, broken and melted down in temples and monasteries throughout the land, lived, as they always had, in the minds of men; taking on a form in that cell, created by Tsun's mind as a focus, absorbed into him and into the emptiness which contains all things.

In the blackness, Tsun was aware of movement. A hand touched him. He sat up, unable to see but aware that the others were sitting cross-legged, lotus fashion, waiting for him to begin the after-death rite for one of their number who had died the night before. There was no text, only Tsun's memory. No ritual objects. No shrine or scroll paintings. Nothing, save the desire of those assembled together in the tiny cell to continue their religious tradition in the face of unending despair.

The only sound in the room in Tsering Dawa's house was the crackling of the dying flame in a butter lamp. Senge sat silently beside Tsun as he stood facing the shrine. The name card of Topden was reduced to smoking ashes. Although he had made no sound or movement, the impact of his experience had communicated itself to the entire room. When Tsun turned to face them, it was as if death held up its mirror to them all.

Chapter Five

Only when she was at the edge of the picnic ground did Ling realise that the grassy valley was itself a plateau. The expanse of grass abruptly dropped away and she felt the impact of its awesome beauty as she looked out at a torrential river, diminishing in the distance to a winding, sparkling stream that followed the line of the massive granite mountains; fold upon fold, they stretched into the distance, suddenly thrusting up to spear the blue sky with snow-capped peaks.

Tashi, the minstrel, was close by, watching her every move. In his thirties, he was small and tough, with a typically Mongolian face: snub-nosed, the eyes heavily lidded. He was deeply tanned from travelling over mountains and plains as a professional story-teller and minstrel, rarely stopping for more than a few days in the lonely, scattered villages along his route. Tashi plucked the sheep-gut strings of a yak horn violin and hummed a tune as he walked beside Ling. Already, children were clustering around him, recognising his triangular story-teller's hat of stiff white cloth, decorated with coloured tassels and amber and coral pendants.

Still playing, Tashi sat down on a tree stump by a stream, with Ling beside him. Some of the picnickers were paddling in the icy water. The children clamoured for Tashi to sing them a song. He agreed, and they settled themselves in a circle around him, their eyes full of expectation.

Ling relaxed, breathing on her glasses and polishing them with her sleeve, only half listening to the plaintive melody of Tashi's song as she thought of how she might escape. Replacing her glasses, she gazed out over the valley. Already the air felt chill as the sun slipped behind the distant mountains. Somewhere, not too distant, there had to be a PLA unit. Someone had captured Topden and hung him up. And then there were the horsemen in the night: who were they? Ling wondered. She was puzzled that they had not attempted to capture the party, but she believed she knew why they had not, and it did nothing to hearten her.

As a child she had lived off the land, but never land like this, she thought. The PLA might have control of the air, and they did hold the towns and larger villages, but they certainly had no control of the countryside. If she ever managed to escape, a Han woman on her own in unfamiliar territory would hardly fail to arouse suspicion, and her knowledge of Tibetan might make it seem probable that she was a spy. She realised that, if a resistance group did capture her, they would almost certainly put her to death. She could understand it; if the positions were reversed her reaction would be the same. Any knowledge passed to the PLA was a threat. I am trapped, she thought. Tsun's party was her only safety, and Tsun her only safeguard. But she could not be sure how much longer this situation would last, and she had no doubt that, if Genyen wanted her killed, she would meet with an accident along the way.

Sent, ostensibly, to discuss the setting up of a commune with Tsun, of more significance, Ling knew, was the order she had received to gather all available information on the appeal Tsun was rumoured to be taking to the United Nations. She had no doubt that they were already on that journey, but she could not understand the route they were taking – away from the border and even from Lhasa. Ling was only vaguely aware of Tashi and the music of his guitar and his song as she wondered who it was in Tsun's party who was acting as a spy. An ally would be very useful, but she was more worried about how the spy could use her as a shelter. She was held in such suspicion. What could he, or indeed, she do which would endanger her? She had to get hold of a weapon. Anything, even if it was just a knife.

Her attention was caught by a family of beggars. They were a handsome family beneath the grime and tattered clothing. The man played a flute, while two young girls performed acrobatics and the woman, whom Ling presumed to be the mother, collected money. No one refused. It would be socially dishonourable and against the religion, for giving to those who begged was a basic act of compassion. The beggars, for all their extravagant expressions of humility and gratitude, had an independent arrogance.

The woman was holding out her hand to Ling.

'May the blessings of all the deities be upon you.'

Ling gave her some yen. She had only refused a beggar once since she'd been in Tibet, but never again! Now she knew how she could make her way to a Han garrison in safety. Her skin did not have the copper-gold glint of the Tibetans, but if it was covered in grime, no one would know. And if she were dumb, she thought, no one would notice her Han accent, although she could still make it clear that she understood Tibetan. The removal of her glasses and dishevelling of her clothes would give her a good chance of passing herself off as a beggar on pilgrimage, and she would be granted hospitality wherever she asked for it. One drawback, she thought, would be that without her glasses she would be left short-sighted.

A young girl, with a man in hot pursuit, tripped over Ling's outstretched legs, nearly knocking her from the tree stump. Tashi continued singing. Some of the children had wandered away and were throwing stones and walnuts at a hole in the ground. Tashi had caught the eye of a pretty girl who had stopped to listen to his song. He winked at her. She giggled and lowered her eyes but did not go away. He sang the rest of the song to her alone. When she did decide to leave, he followed her, still singing. She gave a cry as he caught hold of the old, faded silk scarf around her neck and held her prisoner.

'By the walnut trees when the sun goes down,' he sang.

The children giggled. Ling quietly got to her feet. Perhaps this was her chance to get away, she thought, but Tashi saw her and was quick to reach her side and grasp her arm. He glanced back at the girl. Her face was flushed as she tossed her head and angrily walked away, but he knew that she would keep the tryst. He let go of Ling.

'I was only going to pick up a stone,' she said, stooping to grasp a pebble which she threw at the hole. She missed. The children waited for her to try again, but she turned away. Her mind was on other things. She was thinking of Tsun and how she could use him. If she was careful, and clever, perhaps she could make use of the feelings she knew he had for her. She felt his attraction towards her, but he had a quality she couldn't quite understand. Perhaps, she thought, I could play on the attraction. Aware of her own feelings for him, she vaguely realised that she was seeking justification in her training as a cadre. If she could, she would get him to break his vow of celibacy. He could be of great use in the New Tibet.

Tsering and two other prosperous traders had combined their resources for the picnic, erecting two tents, both ten feet square and twelve feet high to the peak of their appliqué-decorated roofs. Above the tents, a sunshade had been stretched between willow trees. Smoke poured through the air vent of the yak-hair kitchen tent as men and women from all three households prepared the food.

Blankets and rugs were spread on the ground and small carved folding tables set up. Every teapot available, from earthenware to enormous crafted pots of brass and copper, were being kept warm on the intricately carved braziers. There were about twenty people in the combined households. Other tents, some larger, some smaller, were scattered throughout the festival ground. Some families had merely erected cotton wind-breaks or were picnicking in the open.

With every family directly affected by the Han occupation, having relatives either at Litang or in the resistance, the very absence of any sign of the Han at the picnic gave it a sense of unreality. A vein of desperation ran through the celebrations.

Despite food shortages, all families had been saving food for the festival. Tsun ate the stuffed apricots and sweet milk with a china spoon, surveying the dozens of dishes set out as appetisers for a leisurely meal that would last into the following day.

'Tsering-la,' Tsun asked, 'have you heard anything about any Han troops in the area?'

His host shook his head. 'You've seen, Rinposhay, how many men from the resistance there are here; many are local, but some have travelled long distances. All of them report a build-up of Han forces in the towns, but none have seen any Han units near the route you have come.'

Tsun slammed the flat of his hand on the table.

'Then it has to be a very small unit, able to hide easily, but too small to attack us.'

'But the whole countryside is held by the resistance!' Tsering sucked at a bamboo straw in a wooden canister of barley beer.

Tsun had to admit that he was puzzled that even a small unit had been able to track them without the knowledge of the resistance.

Some time later Tsering Dawa and Kesang's mother were walking together through the festival ground, discussing trade. Norden's fingers played with the heavy coral and amber necklace she was wearing.

'You look handsome, Norden-la.'

She laughed, slightly coyly. Tsering glanced at the coral studded silver discs that decorated her hair. A ribbon of them hung down her back, representing her life savings.

'Is it true that every disc symbolises a lover?' Tsering Dawa asked.

She laughed again, enjoying the compliments. 'Not quite all, Tsering Dawa.'

He returned to their main interest. In a land where devotion to religion was paralleled by devotion to trade, Norden might have doubts about her attainments in the former, but she had none about them in the latter. Although delighted that Kesang had been discovered to be an emanation body of Dorje Rinposhay, inevitably, her stays at the monastery cut down her trading trips.

'I was thinking of buying a truck, Norden-la,' Tsering Dawa said. 'What do you think?'

'If you bought a truck it would probably be seized by the Han on some excuse. Also, I do not think you would be allowed to use it. I haven't heard of any traders being allowed to use trucks from Lhasa to Kham. I know some traders use them for the journeys from India to Lhasa . . .'

'But there is always a first time. You know, if I could only get the goods through, there would be a fortune to be made. Watches for example. All the Han are after watches or cigarettes.'

'Maybe once there was a fortune to be made, Tsering, but not any more. I destroyed the last consignment of cigarettes I had, rather than sell them to the Han at the price they offered to pay. Last year was good, and the year before that was the best year I've ever had. The Han were treading carefully then. They wanted the things they could not get in China. They paid proper prices for them, too. But now there are many restrictions and it is obvious that the Han want to put us out of business.'

As they talked, they watched a team of novice monks from the local monastery playing 'yak horns' against a team of lay children.

'I am wondering,' Tsering Dawa said, 'if I am going to lose this year's advance to the shepherds. I am not due to have the wool until October and, even now, there is talk of them having to join what the Han call a co-operative. The Han will control it. They will want all the wool to go to China and it will be impossible to get the advance back from the shepherds; I gave it them in tea and utensils. Also, I have had an advance from an Indian in Calcutta. It is very difficult. It will ruin my business if I cannot give him the wool he wants.'

Norden nodded. 'Do you have any transport left?'

'Yes, I have mules and yaks.'

'I lost mine. I had to give some to pay debts. Others the Han took.' The couple watched the children as they talked. Each player was allowed three throws to knock down a pair of yak horns stuck by their tips into the ground. Amongst the onlookers there was much betting and argument on the respective skills of the young monks and the lay boys. Norden stooped and picked up one of the stones used for the game. She tossed it in her hand to estimate the weight.

'Where are your animals?' she asked Tsering Dawa.

'Lhasa.'

Norden took careful aim, threw the stone and knocked down both horns with the one throw. She was loudly cheered by the lay contestants and caused an outcry among the young monks and some of the onlookers.

'I have some watches,' she continued unperturbed, 'in Kalimpong. Perhaps we could come to some arrangement? I use your transport, and you take a share in the profit from the watches?'

She picked up another stone, indicated that she would throw for the novices, and waited for the horns to be set up again.

'What kind of watches are they?'

Norden threw again, but this time she missed, causing howls of dismay from the novices. She put her hand into the pocket formed by the overlap of her chuba and pulled out an expensive-looking Rolex watch. She handed it to Tsering without comment, then threw again and missed.

'Is it Japanese?' he asked, studying the watch.

'Japanese Swiss.'

'Even to the maker's name,' Tsering replied.

They both laughed. 'We must discuss this further,' Tsering grinned. He picked up a large, smooth stone and threw it at the pair of yak horns. Twice he missed, but on his third throw he knocked down one of the horns and was mockingly cheered by the youngsters as he walked back towards his tent.

'Your fortune told, gracious lady?' A shambling figure stepped in front of Norden.

It was a man of about thirty-five. His lean face was tanned and begrimed with dirt, his coat tattered and his naked legs and feet caked in mud. He held out a rosary towards Norden and, bowing, he showed his tongue as he sucked in his breath.

Norden hesitated. The man looked as though he needed the money, and it was festival time . . . She nodded.

The man smiled at her, the whites of his eyes and his perfect teeth gleaming against the skin dark with grime. He concentrated on the turning of the beads between his fingers.

'You have come from far away and suffered much,' he said.

Norden nodded.

'You are a widow, but have children . . . a child. Ah! This child is blessed, indeed. A most remarkable child. He is a tulku?'

Norden nodded, and decided that the man was a fake. He could have learnt it all very easily since they had arrived at the festival.

'You will be travelling again soon. It will not be an easy journey.' The man hesitated, then said, 'It were better that you do not travel. Particularly on the fourth day of the fifth month.'

'Why?' Norden demanded.

'I can not see more.'

Norden felt a shiver of fear. She gave the man a silver coin. He thanked her profusely. As she walked away, he turned to his wife and slipped the coin into the small pouch in his chuba.

'Death is her shadow,' he said quietly.

His wife looked frightened and made her copper prayer wheel spin rapidly. A line of small boys ran in front of Norden.

'Mind, you nearly knocked me down,' she shouted at them irritably, wishing she had not sought to see her fortune.

The children were laughing as, with arms round each other's waists, they pretended to be sheep, singing derisively as they evaded the wolf who tried to seize the last child in the line. Kesang, in lay clothes, lowered his head as the line swung him within a few feet of his mother. Senge fell from his chuba, and Champa was there in an instant to scoop him up, silencing the dog with a hand over his muzzle before Norden could recognise the familiar bark.

Inside the tent, Tsering Dawa stepped over and round the crowd of people who were sitting and lying, eating and gambling, and getting steadily drunker. His young son was with a group playing Mah Jong. He touched his father's arm.

'Pa-la, can I have some money?'

Tsering frowned at him irritably. 'No, it's a man's game.'

His son scowled. The shadows that lurked that day in the back of everyone's mind pushed forward, reminding Tsering that this might be the last festival they would celebrate for a long time. He put his hand into his chuba and pressed three hand-printed, xylographed 100 tranka notes into the boy's hand.

'I expect you to win,' he grunted, and turned away to sit opposite Tsun, bowing slightly as the latter nodded in greeting. The sun was low in the sky, the sharp relief of the mountains already casting deep, chilling shadows over the lower, pine-covered slopes.

The mattress heaved as Genyen sat down heavily beside Tsun. As she put her bowl of barley beer down on the table, she caught sight of Lopsang whose anger at her unseemly familiarity and lack of courtesy towards the lama was obvious. It had the effect of making her pick up her bowl of beer again, which she drank while she talked.

Tsun's eyes followed the lines of dancing men and women while he listened to Genyen's small talk – the colours of their silk blouses and shirts, the brilliant brocade chubas, the long sleeves fluttering in graceful arm movements as they swirled and dipped to the music. He turned to look at Genyen.

'By sunset the feast will be really under way and we will have a better chance of slipping away unnoticed.'

'With a spy in our midst, Rinposhay?' The full lips were set, the look calculating.

'Do you think there are none out there in the crowds? We must slip away unnoticed, so keep your men from the drink.' The force with which he placed his spoon in his bowl before pushing it slightly to one side surprised him.

Genyen bowed and left her bowl of barley beer on the table.

'What was it like when you were in Lhasa, Tsering?' Tsun offered the trader some snuff, and when he accepted, tapped a small quantity onto his thumb.

'I was there about two months ago,' the trader replied. 'It is all happening as it happened here in the east. The Han are slowly tightening their control on everything, trying not to upset the people, so long as they are uncertain of their hold.' He paused to inhale the snuff. While they talked they watched two girls who were turning a skipping rope for the young men to display their acrobatic prowess.

'A good mixture, Rinposhay,' he murmured, referring to the quality of the snuff. 'The people are restive at the size of the Han headquarters, at the requisitioning of the parks for buildings. Prices are constantly rising. For the most part, the Han keep to themselves. Life goes on, but the people have to live while all the time the Han increase their control. The Ministers all have Han jeeps and drivers. Hans have been attached to their households. It is said that even the Kundun is cautious now about what he says in private, knowing that spies are all round him. There is great resentment at the changes the Han are making in the government of the country. Lhasa's control is now limited to parts of central Tibet, and you know, Rinposhay, about the east?'

'It is run by the Chamdo Liberation Committee,' Tsun said.

'Yes, with a few Tibetan collaborators forced to give it respectability, but it is ruled directly by the Han. The same with the west of Tibet – they say it is under the Panchen Lama, but the Han rule there, too.'

The girls increased the speed of the skipping rope, taunting the youths to greater effort. The young men yelled in victory and defeat, one standing on his hands to leap over the rope, another only on one hand. Tsun glanced at Rinchen who had entered the tent and came to sit with the two men, anxious to hear news of Lhasa. Tsering's daughter, Jetsun, cleared away the empty dishes and placed bowls of minced meat dumplings on the carved wooden tables.

'They are clever, the Han,' Tsering continued. 'They do things step by step, subtly, insidiously, like rats, gnawing away at the foundations of the country until we topple, and they can do openly what they want. Tibet is split into three parts now.' He piled some of the crescent-shaped dumplings into Tsun's wooden bowl.

'But what of the people in Lhasa, Tsering?'

'The Han have forced the Government to ban women from singing ribald songs about them.'

'They have no humour,' Rinchen murmured. 'Such grey men.'

'Men who fear, rarely laugh,' Tsun said. 'I hear conflicting reports about the resistance in Lhasa.'

'There is the Mimang, the People's Movement. But mostly they only stick posters on the walls. You know the U-Tsang people, Rinposhay, they are not fighters like us Khambas.'

'And what of our resistance here in the east?' Tsun drank some of the tea left in his cup, and conversation was drowned for a few moments by the cheers of those watching the skipping. Jigme sat down beside Rinchen and was urged by him to join the skipping.

'Go on, Jigme,' Rinchen nudged the youth. 'Show them what you can do.' Jigme stripped off his grey chuba and shirt and self-consciously walked across the grass to join the competitors. He stepped straight into the turning rope and, without causing it to pause, began leaping over it on his side, using one hand and foot. Within minutes a crowd had gathered to shout encouragement.

'All the news I have,' Tsering continued, 'is what I've picked up from wounded men who come to us. They say that the resistance is fighting in scattered, independent groups. Always, they talk of the shortage of weapons, but most of all of the shortage of ammunition and horses. Some of the Lhasa nobles help them secretly, but some, I am told, are lining their pockets by selling the resistance horses and weapons, and ammunition at extortionate prices.'

'It is also said,' Rinchen interrupted, 'that some Khamba clan leaders in Kalimpong are trying to contact friendly countries for weapons.'

'I know, Kusho Rinchen,' Tsering replied. 'But they have no chance. They won't get anything. India will not allow it. Also, some of the clan leaders in Kalimpong are those who plotted to seize Lhasa and replace the Lhasa officials. Many members of the Government have not forgotten that. They distrust the Khambas, and fear the leaders in Kalimpong want not merely to free Tibet of the Chinese occupation, but to seize control of the entire country themselves. So agents have been sent to hamper them.'

'If we are not united now,' Rinchen lamented, 'we shall surely perish.'

Genyen rejoined them and Rinchen leaned over to her.

'Ten trankas to prove that he cannot continue for as long as it takes for this bowl of tea to cool,' he whispered, indicating Jigme who was still performing in the skipping contest.

'You're on!' She turned back to the skipping contest. 'Come on, Jigme-la,' she shouted. 'I will lose a fortune if you stop now.'

The crowd grew. More bets were placed on whether Jigme would be able to sustain his performance. The crowd clapped in time to his every leap.

'You said that India would not allow the resistance leaders to ask for help from friendly countries,' Tsun said. 'Why is that, Tsering Dawa?'

'Have you heard of the treaty that India and China signed?'

'No,' Tsun shook his head slowly. Amidst the laughter, clapping and excitement of the skipping contest, he felt a terrible stab of fear.

'It was signed about two years ago,' Tsering explained. 'I was in India at the time. Some of us tried to warn the Indians what the Han were like. We told newspaper people what we thought about the agreement. The Indian authorities threatened to deport us back to Tibet. In the treaty, the Indians recognised Tibet as part of China.'

The softening effect of the drink evaporated as Tsering Dawa caught the fleeting expression that passed over Tsun's face.

'What else was in the treaty?' he asked, his voice level.

'There were five principles by which China and India would live in harmony. Also, it was agreed to withdraw the Indian troops attached to the legation in Lhasa.'

'What of the legation?'

'It remains, but it is called something different. I cannot remember what, but it's no longer as important as before, and in exchange for the trading agencies the Indians have in this country, the Han are allowed to open some in India.' Rinchen roared with ironical laughter.

'Did no one in India speak for us? India was bound by treaty to guard our independence. They could not just have ignored . . .'

'The majority of the people did not know about the treaty, Rinposhay,' Tsering broke in. 'China has occupied Tibet. Nehru believes that for the peace of Asia, China and India must be brothers, that the treaty with Tibet was something he inherited from the British, and so is best forgotten. When I was in India and they signed the treaty, all the time the mob was calling out "Hindi-Chin brothers". The five principles, the Panch Sila as they call them, are held by Nehru as an example to the world of how disagreements between countries can be resolved.'

'Do they still let Tibetans into India?'

'Yes, if they do not attempt anything political.'

'But the Tibetans in India.' Rinchen's heavy features were set even more severely than usual. 'Surely they speak of our plight, of what is happening in Tibet?'

'The Indians think we are exaggerating, Kusho Rinchen. If they recognise what we say as being true, China becomes a threat to them. It makes a mockery of their peace agreement. They don't want to listen to what we have to say. They fear what we say.'

'They now regard us as part of China?' Tsun mouthed the words, finding it hard to believe. A burst of applause cut him short as Jigme came back to the tent dripping with sweat. Tsering nodded in reply to Tsun.

'Why did we not know of this at Dorje Ri-gon?' Rinchen asked. 'And why is it not common knowledge throughout Tibet?'

'There is so much bad news, Rinchen-la,' Tsun spoke softly. 'It makes men reluctant to bring more.' The little group sat in silence, pondering.

Tsering Dawa broke the melancholy pause, a dark oasis in the laughter all around them.

'How long will it continue, Rinposhay? How far will it go?'

'Long and far,' Tsun sighed, but only Genyen fully realised the impact of the news on him. He had been so sure that India would help him with the presentation of the petition to the United Nations. But now? How would he even get it to the UN? Realisation of life's intrinsic uncertainty did not necessarily reduce the sting, though he could appreciate the irony. It was some minutes before Tsering spoke again.

'Rinposhay, will you tell me if the plan I have to protect my family will succeed?'

'What is the plan?' Tsun grinned wryly. 'Perhaps it will be luckier than my own!'

'At the moment, there is no commune or local Party office here, but it is only a matter of time. I'm not wealthy, but I have tenant farmers and I am respected in the community. We will be attacked and humiliated, if only because of the help I have given to the resistance. I don't want my wife and children to suffer. My brother is steward of the monastery here. He has managed to meet the Han commander of the area and has bought two seats on one of the Han convoys. I want my wife and daughter to have the seats. They should reach Lhasa in six weeks.'

'What of the rest of your family?'

Tsering raised his cup and drank the strong liquor.

'The Han never allow all members of a family to travel together on a convoy, as they would be unlikely to return, and with no one left behind, they would not fear to talk of what is happening here.'

'You could travel with us, Tsering, but . . .'

'I know, Rinposhay, refugee parties are likely to be attacked. I am trying to get Han permission to send a trading mission to Lhasa. Perhaps the boys could travel with that and save something for us.'

'And what of you?'

'My home is here. My parents built our house with their own hands. I cannot leave yet. Not until I must.' He sighed. 'But please, Rinposhay, tell me if my family will be safe on the journey, for the convoy could be attacked by the resistance.'

Tsun nodded. 'Our lives are built on uncertainty,' he murmured.

He unwound his rosary from his wrist, then holding it between his hands, gently rubbing the beads, he held it to his forehead as he murmured an invocation. Tsun's insight, Tsering was sure, would give him the vultures' eyes to see, as it was said, eighteen days' distance. He counted off the beads in threes, odd numbers regarded as favourable, even as unfavourable, until his hands met.

'Twenty-three,' he murmured.

Genyen flicked drops of whisky to the ghosts below, then snapped her fingers, sending globules of the liquid to the gods above, as she and Tsun watched the target practice six of her men had set up. Stripped to the waist, with the arms of their chubas tied round their middle, they galloped in turn across the picnic ground firing matchlocks at the target. Darkness would decide the winner, its onset steadily eliminating the contestants. The growing crowd of spectators were placing bets among themselves.

'Rinchen,' Tsun turned to his steward. 'While the target practice is holding people's attention, I want you, Lopsang, Dorje Rinposhay and Norden and the three boys to go back to the house. Tell no one that you are going. We have weapons – show them, so that anyone seeing you thinks that you're from the resistance.'

'And you, Rinposhay?' Rinchen's brow was heavily creased.

'I will follow within the hour. Prepare for us to leave.'

Tsering Dawa's daughter refilled Tsun's bowl with tea. Genyen watched and, as she lifted her bowl of whisky to her lips, she caught Tsun's gaze and smiled.

'Rinposhay, do you miss it?' she enquired.

She had meant the whisky, but as soon as she had uttered the words, she realised their implication and Tsun's sudden laughter exposed an intimacy both feared to acknowledge. Tsun broke the embarrassed silence which followed.

'Has the resistance any chance of defeating the Han?'

'One Khamba is worth ten Han, Rinposhay. We know the land, the mountains, the valleys, far better than they do. The mountain poisons do not affect us as they do the Han. But if one of our men dies, who will replace him? If one of their men dies, ten men replace him. They have the weapons, we do not! I have even heard it said that they have a vast gun on wheels . . .'

Genyen took a long drink of the whisky. 'Did I tell you of when I was with the Goloks? Such a battle,' she laughed, thinking of the warlike nomad clan of Amdo. 'The Han had arrested Hou Wan Sieling, their leader. The clans threatened to revolt. They seized a patrol, and . . .' Genyen was convulsed with uninhibited laughter, 'cut off their noses, then sent them back to their masters. The Han were so enraged that the clans had to fight. We killed thousands.

Kunjosum! If we had the weapons, we could drive the Han from this land of snows.' She downed another large quantity of whisky and her voice grew louder. She never could hold her liquor, Tsun remembered.

'We shall never drive the Han from this land without careful planning and co-ordination,' he said.

'Rinposhay, you should be one of our lama generals. It is in your blood. You are a Khamba warrior.' She looked at him laughing. In that instant they were reliving their old days together, and both recognised that no matter what the present situation, or how spiritually committed Tsun might be, there was an indissoluble link between them.

Night had come swiftly, and with it a severe drop in temperature. Camp fires burned throughout the festival ground. Only two of Genyen's men remained in the target contest. The clouds hung low across the mountains, shrouding the light from the moon, and the target itself was barely visible until the contestants were almost upon it.

'See, Rinposhay, how good they are?' Genyen shouted. She took another drink. 'But I could beat them all,' she boasted belligerently, and loudly enough to ensure that those around heard and urged her to take part. Unsteadily, she rose to her feet and walked out of the tent. She put her foot into the high stirrup and swung her leg over the rug-covered saddle. Responding to the slightest touch, her horse cantered out of sight in the fire-lit darkness to the far side of the festival ground.

An expectant hush fell over the crowded ground as the wild nomad woman galloped through the camp with a war cry on her lips. Guiding the horse with her legs, she unslung the polished wood and horn bow and loosed an arrow at the vague outline of the target. She hit the bull at eighty yards.

A roar of approval reverberated through the crowd. Swiftly, she drew another arrow, waited until she was forty yards past the target which hung from a gibbet, turned in the saddle, loosed the arrow and hit the target dead centre on the other side. Then, with a yell, she wheeled her horse round, spurred it into a gallop and notched another arrow in her bow. She dropped down beside the horse's neck and from sixty yards hit the target again. Genyen personified the great warrior, whose skills had brought the capitulation of the Chinese Emperor, and even those who realised that that time was long past, and that this was 1956, still let themselves be carried along in the wave of euphoria that belief in certain victory brings. The excitement was tangible as it spread through the camp. Only Tsun carried within him an inexpressible grief, a deep aching well of pain filling his whole being.

Genyen reined in hard, causing her mount to spray a cloud of dust over a finely dressed young girl. She was wearing a bright green blouse and brocade dress, and her hair was carefully plaited with multicoloured strands of wool and decorated with coral and silver disc ornaments. Delicate and carefully made up, she pouted at a young man standing near her as she angrily brushed the dust from her clothes. Genyen caught the young man's eye, laughed, then swooped down and snatched the silk scarf from the girl's neck. She shouted at Genyen and tried to grab the scarf back. The young man made a feeble attempt to catch hold of Genyen's horse, but she was far too quick for either of them and galloped across the ground to throw the scarf down in front of Tsering's tent, cantering on into the camp.

She turned, let out a Khamba warrior cry and galloped back through the night. As she reached the tent, she swung down from the saddle and caught the scarf up in her teeth. The crowd roared with delight. Genyen reined in, dismounted and presented the scarf to Tsun. Smiling, he blessed her.

Genyen exchanged her bow for a matchlock 'prong gun', named after the forked support used when hunting, and, slinging it over her shoulder, vaulted over her horse's hindquarters into the saddle and trotted back down the field. When she reached the far side of the festival ground, she opened the powder horn and tipped a little into the gun, ramming the lead ball home with a rod fitted beneath the barrel. Again, she urged her horse into a gallop. It snorted and tossed its head, foam flecking from its mouth. Genyen felt as one with the compact rhythm, aware of the immense flow of energy as she sped across the ground, her black hair streaming behind her.

As she neared the target, she brought the gun up to her shoulder, aimed and pulled the trigger. There was a tremendous explosion. The horse reared, screaming in terror as it, and Genyen, were enveloped in a great cloud of thick black smoke. Thrown from the saddle, she hit the ground with a sickening thud; her terrified horse, nearly trampling her as she lay motionless, careered into the crowd before someone grabbed at the loose reins and gradually managed to bring the animal under control.

People were crowding in on Genyen, her men pushing them aside as they struggled to get near her. Tashi, the minstrel, picked her up and carried her to Tsering Dawa's tent, where he laid her gently on a mattress. One of her men was crying. All thought she was dying. The concerned and the merely curious pushed their way into the tent.

'She must have used too much powder,' Tashi said.

Tsun looked at Genyen's soot-blackened face, her eyes wide and frightened as she struggled to catch her breath. He put a hand gently on her forehead, then expertly felt her body.

'You're winded,' he murmured to her. 'Don't be frightened, you're not badly hurt.'

Her men gave great cries of delight. Tsering Dawa dabbed at the blood running down her cheek from a cut near her eye. Gradually, her breathing grew easier, her eyes constantly seeking reassurance in Tsun's face.

'Son untamed,' he whispered. Genyen smiled.

Chapter Six

When Tsun, Genyen and her men reached Tsering Dawa's house, they found the others ready to leave. Tsering Dawa had wanted to accompany Tsun back to the house, but he had insisted that the party leave quickly, and alone. Genyen was still feeling stunned by the explosion, but more difficult for her to bear was her embarrassment at having put too much powder in her matchlock. She tried to make light of the incident while her men were relating the event to members of Tsun's party.

The courtyard was lit by the harsh glare of tilly lamps and the horses stamped and snorted, their breath vaporising in the freezing air. Genyen had decided that the bells usually attached to the horses' harnesses should not be worn, but the scarlet tassels and plumed headdresses remained, together with delicately woven pile skull caps. Samden, Champa and Jigme helped the Khamba escort tie sacking over the horses' hooves so that their departure would be as quiet as possible. While Tsun did not think that the Han would expect them to be leaving the New Year celebrations so quickly, the less attention they drew to their departure, the better.

The tilly lamps were extinguished. The only noise in the blackness of the night was the frenzied bark of a mastiff. Kesang tucked Senge into his chuba, and the party slowly and quietly left the courtyard, each silent, absorbed in his own private thoughts. Genyen was examining the events of the evening, conscious of the difficulties and strains in her relationship with Tsun. His remoteness seemed to her to become more pronounced whenever she attempted to release the tension and break down the barriers which the years had created between them. She felt unsure, aware of her own vulnerability and that her hatred of the Han woman was based on more than nationalistic pride.

Tsun's own thoughts were almost too painful for him to acknowledge. Tsering Dawa's news of the treaty signed by China and India was a hard blow, and what confidence he had had in the success of his mission was sadly diminished. Many questions invaded his mind. Why had he not heard of the treaty? He had contacts outside Tibet and news spread like wildfire in the country itself, even though the natural barriers to communication, such as the sheer distance between towns and villages, made any sort of interchange difficult. He thought of Derge. The Queen Regent could not know of the treaty. If she did, surely she would have sent word. Although Derge was a principality, with its own royal family, it was still part of Tibet, involved in its affairs and accepting the supreme rule of the Kundun. Bad news, Tsun reflected, can so easily be put to the back of one's mind if there is still hope. And the petition represented that hope.

Lost in thought, he was unaware of the distance they travelled, of the soft, muffled sound of his horse's hooves as the party made its way from the valley. He pondered over his other mission, the mission which represented the basis of his life. It was the vocation of every lama, of every monk of learning, and Tsun wondered what would happen if he ever had to make a choice between serving the people of his land by delivering the petition, or by serving the mission of his heart, to pass on the unique teachings of Dorje Rinposhay; to protect and develop the religion in Tibet. More and more, he felt that he was abandoning the latter in favour of the former.

Overhead loomed the grey faces of the mountains. Roused from his reverie by the cursing of Norden as her horse missed its footing on the stony ground, Tsun spurred his horse to ride up beside Ling.

'Why did you not leave me at Tsering Dawa's house or the village?' she asked.

'Our hosts would have had to keep you prisoner while we escaped. Then, if they had let you go, you would have told the Han and they would have suffered. So, instead of letting you go, you would have been killed.'

'You are always saving my life,' she said sardonically.

'Storing up merit for my future lives.' Tsun sounded equally sardonic. He paused. 'Yet do not think,' his voice was now genuinely sad, 'that you will not be killed if you do not do as you are told.'

'But what of your vows! It would be against your religion. You could no longer be a monk.'

Normally such a barb would not have affected him, but suddenly Tsun felt intense rage seethe within him at the memories of many friends, distracted by the sufferings of their families, who had eventually been unable to resist the temptation to strike back.

Each had been acutely aware of and tormented by the fact that he, in a sense, betrayed that for which they all fought.

Tsun had become a monk quite late in life. He had lived in the world and had been very much part of it. He was a Khamba, with warrior blood running in his veins, and with each moment he was now becoming increasingly aware of the demands made on him by his conflicting loyalties.

Ling was worried by his silence. She knew that if she was to survive, then just like the bamboo, she must bend with the wind, she must not destroy the rapport that was developing between them.

'You are a threat to our lives.' He looked at her with cold, piercing eyes and both, for an instant, saw the vulture-cloaked figure of the farmer, Topden, swinging from the tree.

'Many here would kill you now if I were to allow it,' Tsun continued. 'I have the power to stop them. If I relax that power, I shall be just as responsible for your death as the man whose hand drives the dagger into your body.'

Despite the firmness in his voice, Ling felt his indecision and knew that she could not rely on him to keep her alive. Somehow she had to escape.

The party rode throughout the night and the following day, stopping only for short breaks to rest the animals and take refreshment. The brief rest at Tsering Dawa's house had only served to increase the tension in the company. There was little humour, only weariness and intense dissatisfaction borne of exhaustion. This general feeling was taking its toll of the party, and progress was slow. Norden, never able to conceal her true feelings, was grumbling to anyone who would listen. Kesang, frightened and uncertain, hid his disquiet in silence, and Tsun's three students tried to relieve their own sense of despair by discussing amongst themselves what they would do on reaching Lhasa. Genyen, in an attempt to regain her self-confidence, was morosely retelling stories of her exploits. All were waiting for the next incident which would confirm that the Han were still on their trail.

It was nearing sundown when they first saw the cave. The entrance had been blocked with clay bricks and a small wooden door set in it. At first they thought it was a hermit's cave, although it was not facing in the prescribed direction, ancient custom dictating that a hermitage should overlook a lake as an aid to meditation and should enable the hermit to watch the sun's rising and setting.

Further along the valley, tall sugar pine trees fanned down the cliffs. Two of the Khambas rode ahead to reconnoitre. The rest unslung their rifles, removed the safety catches, checked the chambers of their revolvers to ensure that they were loaded, spun prayer wheels and fingered the pommels of their swords.

When the two Khambas were within a few yards of the cave, a short man with an enormous coil of false black hair perched lopsidedly on his head, rushed out and, bowing low, with much indrawing of breath, greeted his visitors. He had a large heavy nose and thick-lidded eyes. A few white hairs on his upper lip and chin served as an apology for a moustache and beard.

After talking with the man for some minutes, the two Khambas rode back down the narrow path. One of the men dismounted and walked over to Tsun and Genyen. He bowed.

'The man is called Gyatso, the weathermaker. He would be honoured if we would spend the night in his cave. He has not heard of any Han in the area, but he saw some members of the resistance a few days ago.'

Tsun, Genyen and Rinchen exchanged glances, each seeking an answer. It could be a trap. Genyen shrugged and laughed. It was decided. Slowly they made their way to the cave.

Tsun thought the weathermaker's accent strange and difficult to understand. 'Where do you come from?' he asked.

'Szchewan, Kusho.'

He was obsequious, bowing and sucking in his breath all the time. He had an intelligent face, but Tsun was suspicious of the man's servility. Yet, he knew that the weathermaker might fear them as brigands, and so ingratiate himself.

After the horses and mules had been unsaddled and fed with the fodder they had brought with them, the party crowded into the tiny cave. It was pitch black inside from the soot of years. The weathermaker had already peeled some of the yak chips off the outside wall, where they had been drying, to build up the feeble fire which provided the only light and filled the cave with smoke. He poured weak tea, with little butter content, into his guests' bowls, apologising all the while for the inadequacy of his hospitality, while his guests praised him for it.

Norden gave him some of her tsampa to mix with his tea, for which he thanked her profusely. He smiled at her, showing a mouth of yellow teeth in his podgy face. It was unusual to see anyone with such bad teeth. Tsun wondered what illness he suffered from.

Glancing at the implements of the weathermaker's trade, Rinchen asked him, 'Has business been good?' He nodded towards the thigh bone trumpets, drums, and thread crosses.

'Unfortunately not! So I do not get my share of the harvest. Times are bad, the gods are very angry, Kusho.' He shook his head.

'How do you make weather?' Kesang asked.

The man laughed and chucked the boy's chin. 'It is too hard for you to understand, little one,' and knew he had made a mistake as he looked into Kesang's shrewd eyes.

'Tell *us* how you make weather,' Tsun requested. 'We are all interested.' He noticed the flicker of emotion in Gyatso's eyes.

'But, good sirs, if I told you my secrets, I would have no trade. All men would be weathermakers, and then what would become of me?' He laughed and changed the subject.

'From where do you come, Kusho?'

'Yonder.' Tsun slowly poured some barley flour into his bowl from the small leather pouch he carried. The weathermaker laughed again, politely.

'You are on pilgrimage?'

'And trading.'

Outside, the wind began to howl. The horses bunched together against the bleakness of the elements. Tashi, the minstrel, began strumming his guitar and singing softly in a deep voice of the exploits of Gesar, born a thousand years ago to save his principality in east Tibet from oppressive rule and persecution of the Religion. To the riders it was not just the immediate relevance of his life which was significant, but that Gesar lives still; his song when travelling, is as an invocation for protection.

'Kunjosum!' Genyen swore softly. 'This cave must be the birthplace of all fleas.' Desperately her fingers sought out the tiny pests that were sucking her blood, then scurrying, gorged, into the seams of her sheepskin jacket. Those she caught she threw into the fire, while the more pious Norden flicked hers to the floor.

Tsun was assiduously but cautiously questioning the weathermaker. He replied readily. Too readily, Tsun thought. But, it was easy to have one's judgement distorted under stress, to suspect everyone, everything.

Already some of the party had fallen asleep and were snoring. Genyen had a watch posted outside. Tashi still sang his warlike songs, but as a lullaby. An owl hooted mournfully.

Kesang picked his way over his sleeping companions, hovered near the door, then clambered back to his place. After a few minutes, he struggled back to the door, awakening almost everyone in the cave.

'What are you doing?' His mother complained.

'I want to wee, but . . .' he hesitated, his eyes reflecting conflicting emotions and indignation at having to explain. 'I want someone to go with me.' There was much laughter, and eventually half the party accompanied him outside. It was very dark. Low-lying clouds obscured the stars and moon. Rinchen remonstrated heatedly with Kesang for standing whilst urinating.

'You know that the stream might enter a female demon and give her a child, causing you much misery later.'

Kesang stared at him, the shrewdness absent from the big round eyes of the child, and squatted.

Genyen stumbled over something in the dark and cursed. It was solid, yet yielding. Suddenly apprehensive, she felt round with her hands. They touched something soft and cold. Her mouth went dry and she broke out into a sweat. She fumbled for her tinderbox, then struck the flint on the metal at the base of the leather pouch. It flared for a few seconds, reflecting in the glazed eyes.

The body was naked. It was not the sight of death that frightened Genyen. It was the implications of the nude body. The hooked weathermaker's staff caught and dragged by a foot, as if an attempt had been made to hide the body in the undergrowth, told her the man in the cave was an impostor. Her voice cracked as she shouted a warning.

'We are betrayed!'

Those outside reached for their weapons, startled by the piercing shout. Those in the cave woke to find Gyatso threatening them with a pistol. He motioned to those lying near the door to move aside. When they had done so, he slipped out into the night. One of the Khambas fired, but missed. Gyatso pressed the trigger of his automatic pistol and sprayed the surrounding darkness with bullets as he untied one of the horses. The company flung themselves to the ground and tried to pinpoint the source of rapid fire. The resounding thunderous explosion of prong guns was interspersed with the tight staccato of an automatic weapon as the Khambas tried to reach Gyatso in the pitch blackness.

Senge was barking with frightened fury. Kesang caught hold of him. Gyatso fired another round as he swung up into the saddle, then urged the horse down the slope. It stumbled and slid, carried by the cascading shale; the Khambas fired into the darkness, but were inhibited by lack of ammunition.

'He has a Han pistol.'

'Are we surrounded?'

'Surely they would have attacked.'

'Rinposhay,' Genyen called, 'we must leave at once.'

'Yes,' Tsun answered, 'and at dawn we should go to ground.'

'If we leave now, we can cover many miles before daybreak,' said Lopsang. 'The Han will not know where we are.'

'They should not,' said Tsun but, he thought, they have up until now. Could the spy in their midst be leaving signs? He looked at Ling, the cadre. She was cursing herself for not having taken advantage of the confusion to escape.

'We are cursed,' Norden murmured, as her horse, its hooves still bound with sacking to muffle the sound, stumbled through the bitterly cold night. They rode close together. Genyen watched the sky, but the clouds obscured the stars.

'It would not take much experience to track us,' one of her men grunted.

'I know,' was her terse reply.

They struggled on through the night, whenever the ground was easier urging their horses to a faster pace; sometimes having to dismount and walk; travelling in virtual silence, each trying to understand a situation in which they never seemed able to elude the enemy.

Tsun felt sure that it was the petition the Han were after, but he could not understand why they did not attack. And what, he thought, of the spy in their midst? Someone must be betraying them and until they could find out who it was there would be little chance of eluding the Han. He had watched Ling carefully; the thought of her leaving signs for the Han to follow has crossed his mind quite early in the journey, and it was certain that the others in the party laid the blame on her shoulders. But he had seen nothing to arouse his suspicion that she might be responsible. Whoever was marking their route for the Han must be one of the Tibetans. The Han were probably using some great pressure on one of them, and who, Tsun thought, was without some weakness through which he or she could be blackmailed by the Han, be it through family, friends or relatives? The Han were not known for their compassion. No matter which way he looked at it, Tsun could find no pattern, no answers to satisfy him fully.

On the fourth day after leaving Tsering Dawa's house they decided to travel by daylight only and, two days later, the party turned westward, leaving the Litang river and travelling as far as possible parallel with the Batang-Derge trade route that followed the course of the Ba-Chai river. Fed by ice-age glaciers, the rivers had forced their way through the great mountains of Tibet. As they climbed steadily, a carpet of rhododendron bushes receded, leaving grey, unyielding rock. Near the summit of the Haragu La Pass, at 15,000 feet, every step became an agony for Norden, making her gasp for breath.

'The poisonous vapours of the mountains,' she explained breathlessly to her son, but few of the others were affected by the lack of oxygen.

At the summit, each member of the party wearily added a stone to the cairn, crowned by tattered prayer flags, with a murmured, 'The gods are victorious.'

It took them a day to negotiate the bare, treacherous expanse of the pass, the struggling line of horses, men and mules standing out starkly against the glaring white snow.

Suddenly Lopsang's horse began to sink under him. His anguished cry echoed again and again as he desperately tried to stop it sinking deeper. Snow covered everything and it was difficult for the others to know whether or not they, too, were stepping into the crevasse as they tried to help Lopsang rescue the horse. He had slid out of the saddle and was on firmer ground. The quick, terrified breath of the horse's whinnying vaporised. Twisting and turning, it sank deeper and deeper until, despite their efforts, Lopsang was left holding a pair of reins, biting into his palms as they pulled into the snow. He opened his fingers and the rope reins, greasy with the sweat of many rides, slid out of his hands.

It was a day and a half later when they sighted the village of Gaji or Kayu. From the cliffs, Tsun focused his field glasses on the tiny hamlet of ten houses. He couldn't see any sign of Han activity. Most of the people were working in the fields, men and women, stripped to the waist, using pebbles from their slings to urge on the pairs of dri – hybrids from yak and cattle – drawing their wooden hoes. Three women were carrying empty wooden pails down to the river and, while the rest of the party remained hidden, Genyen and one of her men rode down towards them.

Tsun watched them through his field glasses. The women had

filled their buckets by the time Genyen and the Khamba rode up. The rest of the villagers had also seen the two riders and stopped work to watch them approach. Genyen spoke to the women. They became angry, gesticulating wildly. One stooped to pick up a stone and flung it at Genyen. Another seized her and tried to pull her from her horse. The horse shied.

Some of the villagers had left the fields and were running towards the group at the river's edge. Genyen and the Khamba appeared to be trying to reason with the women. Then, as the rest of the villagers drew near, they wheeled their horses round and galloped away.

Making a detour, in case they were being followed, Genyen and her companion did not rejoin the rest of the party until nearly an hour later. She sat slumped in her saddle, resting her arms across the pommel, as she reported on her meeting with the villagers.

'They told us Khamba resistance fighters entered the village a few days ago. They took all the stores, brutally beat up one of the men who protested and raped two of the women.'

'Are you sure they didn't mean bandits?' Rinchen asked.

'No, Kusho,' Genyen replied. 'The raiders said they were resistance fighters and had a right to the food they took.'

'Have you any knowledge of who they could have been?' Tsun asked.

'No, Rinposhay, I don't understand. There is something wrong . . . very wrong.'

Resuming their journey, the party skirted the village where they had hoped to supplement their supplies and, instead, added nettle soup to their diet.

Coming down from the mountains into a valley, they found the air warm. The trees were vivid shades of green, casting deep shadows across the undulating yellow-green grass-covered slopes. The sky was a wonderful translucent blue. The great dominating cliffs mellowed in the diffusing haze until the snow-shrouded peaks appeared ethereal and intangible.

Tsun and Ling sat on a tree trunk, absorbing the beauty of the empty valley, unspoilt by man. The only sounds were the birds singing and the insects rustling in the grass, nothing more in those shimmering moments. A word could have broken the enchantment. It was such a fragile beauty, that their delight was tinged with poignant awareness of its impermanence.

They looked at each other and smiled, both wanting to share

their pleasure, and in that intense, exquisite communication, they saw one another for the first time. Both Tsun and Ling were shaken and frightened by the strength of their attraction for each other. When they looked back at the valley, it was not the same.

Each one was filled with the sense of the other's presence. There was now a vibrant tension between them that neither was prepared for, nor wanted to acknowledge. They had revealed their innermost being to each other, and each had become far too vulnerable. They remained still for a few moments, but the silence and the nearness became unbearable. Tsun rose abruptly. He glanced at Ling, gave her a tight smile, then side by side they walked briskly back to the camp.

In the late afternoon of the following day, the party were riding across a wide stony plain, surrounded by mountains. There was no cover of any kind, but as they drew nearer to the rocks at the foot of the mountains, they saw the ruins of a castle. The broken and crumbling terraced walls followed the contours of the rocks.

Tsun wondered why it had been built in such an infertile area. Then he heard the aeroplane. All their experience of iron birds was that they laid iron eggs.

'Race for the castle!' Tsun shouted.

They spurred their horses up the sloping rock. The aeroplane flew over them; its shadow blanketed them for an instant as it roared overhead, frightening the horses. Norden's and Kesang's horses had hurled themselves up the slope, so they were the first to reach the ruins. The others followed, pulling the reluctant mules after them.

The aeroplane turned and came back towards them. The mule that Samden was leading sat down.

'Kick him!' Tsun yelled at the youth. The mule's head snaked out to bite Samden as he tried to pull the animal to its feet.

'Run! Run!' Tsun bellowed at his pupil.

The very ground seemed to reverberate as the aeroplane reached them. They threw themselves to the ground. Spurts of dust and stones erupted around them. The Khambas rolled onto their backs and fired repeatedly at the exposed belly of the 'plane but, apparently, without hitting it.

No one had been hit. They all ran for the cover of the ruins. All except the mule, which stayed sitting half way up the slope braying wildly, and one other mule which was wandering loose.

The aeroplane came down at them again. Kesang put his hands

over his ears to try and shut out the clatter of machine gun bullets and the screaming roar of the oncoming 'plane. One bullet hit the sitting mule in the side. It clambered to its feet in shock, braying with fright and pain. Then another bullet tore into its neck and it collapsed dying, blood gushing from the wound. Bullets dug into the ruined walls, sending slivers of clay flying in all directions. The loose mule, sensing death, bolted down the slope, lost its footing and rolled sprawling and twisted down the rocks, breaking its neck.

Genyen aimed her rifle at the 'plane. Nothing happened.

'Holy Tara, the magazine has jammed!' She shouted at one of her men, who was kneeling and levelling at the 'plane. 'Now! Now!' The Khamba pressed the trigger. They all saw the bullets rip into the belly of the aeroplane as it passed over them. They ran to the other side of the ruins, expecting the sight of the 'plane crashing, but it flew on and disappeared over the mountains. They remained under cover. Weapons were rapidly reloaded.

'Rinposhay.' Genyen worked the jammed magazine free and fed bullets into the repeating rifle. 'Do you think it will return?'

Tsun smiled at her expectancy of some oracular pronouncement. 'No,' he said. He was right.

'Do they attack anyone?' Rinchen asked Genyen.

'Only when they think they are trying to escape, or are resistance.'

Tsun sent Lopsang to check that no one had been injured. 'I think it was the same 'plane we have seen before,' he said quietly to Genyen after Rinchen had moved away.

'Could it not be a normal patrol?'

'Yes, maybe . . .' Tsun's voice was devoid of conviction. He was sure that it was just another part of the web in which they found themselves.

'It is astonishing! We must indeed be protected by the Triple Gem,' Lopsang, the secretary, reported. 'No one was hit. We have lost only two mules.'

'We can distribute their loads among the others,' Genyen said, turning as a sudden uproar broke out behind her. Members of the escort were shouting angrily at Ling.

'We are betrayed, she must be killed.' Ling looked at them defiantly.

'If I am harmed, you will be held to account!' Her voice was resolute, but held more than a trace of apprehension.

Tsun hurried towards the group. Genyen had to run to keep up with him. Tashi, the minstrel, grinned at Ling. She backed away.

'Rinposhay,' Genyen pleaded, 'let us leave her here. We cannot afford to have her with us. It is too dangerous. We will give her food, she will be able to find her way to a village.'

'I know she is a danger,' Tsun answered, 'but she does not know this country. She will never find her way anywhere. She will simply die. We cannot leave her to die.'

'We cannot leave her to die?' Genyen's voice rose with anger. 'But she would see us burn in hell if she could!'

Tsun could not see Ling, she was hidden by the Khambas. 'No!' The anger and fear in her voice was drowned by the cheer of the Khambas. They fell silent as Tsun approached. Tashi let Ling's snapped glasses fall from his hands. 'Rinposhay, she is a danger to us,' he said, quietly. 'It will be difficult for her to signal to the Han without her glasses. See!' He put out his foot and crushed the shattered glasses further. Tsun's face showed no flicker of emotion as he looked at the terrified figure of the woman before him.

Ling was now really frightened. She had known from the beginning of the journey how hated she was by most of her captors, but with each strike of the Han she had felt the increase of resentment towards her and knew that the time would come when even Tsun would not be able to stop them taking their revenge on her. She tried to control her trembling, determined not to let them see that she was frightened. She narrowed her eyes in an effort to see clearly. Without her glasses, everything was slightly out of focus. But she could see well enough, although she had no intention of letting anyone else know that.

As he looked at the faces surrounding him, Tsun could see that the resentment and fear of the cadre was all too obvious. These men were risking their lives to protect him and his party; how much greater was their risk of death with a Han cadre in their midst? She was becoming an unbearable symbol of all that they feared.

'I am a monk,' he said slowly. 'I have vowed not to take life. I know that I have no right to place you in danger because of my vows. Especially as you have undertaken to protect Dorje Rinposhay and myself during our journey. So, I am asking you to leave us. Go back to your homes.'

'But this is madness!' Norden shrieked.

'Rinposhay, please!' Genyen slung her rifle across her shoulder. 'You know that we could not leave you now, knowing of the danger that you are in. It would be as wrong as you breaking your vow. There must be some way . . .' She held out her hands, pleading with him.

If there was some other way, Tsun did not know it. A conscience, he thought, can often be a tiresome thing. He looked at the circle of waiting faces, their eyes echoing Genyen's plea. When he looked at Ling, her eyes alone were turned away.

'We shall keep her under strict watch,' he said. 'We shall leave her at the next village we reach.' Ling was grateful for the reprieve, but for how long? Tibetan villagers, she knew, did not like the Han.

Tsun walked over to the castle wall and looked out across the plain. Visions of a burning Litang rose before him, of the pursuing aeroplane that they could not escape, of the traitor in their midst, of Ling, of her fear and dignity. He doubted his motive for saving her. Had it really been because of his vow? He turned to find himself facing the nomad woman.

'Rinposhay, I am used to fighting the Han.' She came up beside him and rested her back against the wall, easing her long hair free of her sheepskin chuba. 'I am used to them pursuing me, of being shot at. Used to my men being killed. But this is different. For days and days they have been after us. They have found us, but how? How have they been able to track us down without our knowing? Why are they wasting their time? Why, when they fire at us, do they always miss? Why, when they have us in their sights, and have gone to such trouble to find us, do they not attack us? Why are they playing with us?'

Tsun looked at her.

'You know why, Genyen.'

'Because of the petition?' she snapped. 'Because they are afraid that it might be destroyed?' Tsun did not reply. In his silence she had his answer.

'But, why, Rinposhay, do they even bother to make their presence known? Why not follow us secretly to our destination?'

'I do not know, Genyen.'

'Do you know why they are always able to find us?'

'No!'

'There is someone in our party who is letting the Han know where we are. There must be! There have been too many coincidences.' Her voice had lost its respectfulness, she was talking now to her former lover.

'We are taking them with us,' she said more quietly. 'To Derge. To the Queen Regent. If they get to know about her involvement in the petition, we shall surely be signing her death warrant.' Genyen walked away. Tsun gazed after her, a plan forming in his mind.

'Do we stay, Rinposhay?' Rinchen approached the Abbot. 'That 'plane might radio for help. If we are caught on the plain, we would stand no chance.' Tsun did not answer. He turned away abruptly and walked into the solitude of the castle keep. Roofless, its walls were eroded by battle and time. Tsun sat down on a piece of fallen masonry and closed his eyes. He wanted to clear his mind of the myriad thoughts and possibilities which invaded it; to be alone and let a little space into his life for a few moments. He knew that his decision at this time must be the right one and, yet, he had the feeling that the decision was already made. He was being guided. He did not have to think too long or too hard. He returned to the group.

'We go on,' he said.

By nightfall, they had crossed the plain, but they continued into the night. No one talked much. The minstrel sang softly to himself.

'Surely we can stop now,' Norden grumbled to Rinchen who was riding beside her. 'I do not think my horse or I can keep awake any longer.'

Genyen was scanning the surrounding hills. She rode with her rifle across her saddle. They could easily be seen tonight, she thought, with the moon shining so brightly.

Kesang had long since fallen asleep in Champa's arms. The horses' hooves clinked against the stony ground, sounding loudly through the crystal silence.

'You are surrounded . . . surrounded . . . surrounded . . .' The voice, distorted through the blaring loudspeakers, came from at least four points, Tsun realised, and echoed around the valley.

'This is it,' Champa thought as, clutching Kesang, he rode behind a rock.

'What is wrong?' Kesang cried, waking up. 'What is that noise?'

One of the Khambas pulled Ling down behind another rock. They all unslung their rifles. All the monks, with the exception of Rinchen and Jigme, took pistols from their chubas.

They were being fired at. The bullets came from all directions, pinning them down behind a cluster of boulders, yet no one was hit.

Norden caressed Kesang's head. She had worked her way over

to her son where he crouched beside Champa. Quietly she drew a revolver from within her chuba and murmured the invocation of Chenresi, over and over again, 'Om Mani Padme Hum,' so quickly that the words of the mantra mingled together as one long, sonorous sound. Senge ran out of the shadow and crouched in Kesang's arms.

Tsun Lama, the loudspeakers blared in Tibetan, *We have your party surrounded. We meant to miss. We do not wish to kill you. Do not jeopardise the lives of Dorje Rinposhay and the rest of your party any further. Give yourself up.*

Genyen grabbed Ling's hand, pulled her to her feet and stepped into the moonlight, holding a revolver to the girl's head.

'If you do not let us go,' Genyen shouted, 'your comrade dies. Tell them who you are.' She jabbed painfully at the girl's ear with her revolver.

'I am Ling Tao Yen of the Public Security Ministry,' the cadre shouted in Chinese. 'I am here in connection with Vice-Premier Chen-Yi's visit.' Ling had no wish to die and she did not delude herself that a member of the Kanze District Committee was likely to receive as much consideration as someone connected with the Vice-Premier.

There was a few seconds' pause. Then the Han opened fire again. Bullets ricocheted from the rocks around them as Genyen, pulling Ling with her, dived for cover. Ling caught the look in Genyen's eye, now that she realised that the cadre was not even useful as a hostage. Genyen pulled back the hammer of her revolver. There was a pause in the firing. With her eyes fixed on Genyen, Ling shouted desperately.

'I am here on Comrade Hsishe's instructions to assist Comrade Chen-Yi. If I am killed as a result of your negligence, Comrade Hsishe will hold you to account for it.'

Even Genyen believed her. 'Who is Hsishe?' she asked.

'Minister of Public Security,' Ling answered curtly.

This meant nothing to Genyen, although the Ministry of Public Security directed much of the campaign against the resistance.

Release Comrade Ling and surrender. You will not be harmed, the loudspeakers stated.

Derisive laughter filled the valley.

You cannot escape, the voice crackled. *You are completely surrounded. If you surrender, you will be dealt with leniently.*

The words were followed by another burst of rifle and machine gun fire. Genyen and Ling ducked.

'We shall shoot Comrade Ling,' Genyen shouted again, 'if you do not let us go.'

If any harm comes to Comrade Ling, you will all be killed, the voice responded. *It is impossible for you to leave the valley. If you surrender now, you will not be harmed. We shall not detain you for long.*

Ling felt the sweat running down from her armpits; she realised that she was becoming increasingly expendable.

'Tsun! Tsun!' The lama looked across to see why Kesang was calling him. 'Do not forget your promise, please!'

Tsun frowned, not remembering at first, then he nodded at the boy. Some of the horses had been dragged to the ground as cover, others pulled at the reins, neighing in fear.

There was a sharp exchange of fire. Genyen left Ling in the charge of one of her men and rolled across a space of open ground to Tsun. Bullets hit the soil around her.

'They must want to take us alive,' she said to Tsun. 'They could have hit some of us by now. They are bad shots, but not that bad.' She took Tsun's field glasses and searched the valley for the Han positions. 'I am sure that there are not as many of them as they would have us think.'

'Perhaps that is why they do not attack us,' Rinchen suggested. 'There are too few to ensure success.'

'Genyen,' Tsun murmured, 'do you think you can find a way through their lines, if I manage to hold their attention for long enough?'

'You mean, alone?'

'No, with the rest of the party.'

'Possibly, but in this moonlight it will be difficult. They will see and hear the horses.'

'Then we shall have to leave them.'

'No!' Lopsang protested loudly. The bullets kicked up the dirt at his feet.

'Keep down and keep quiet!' Genyen ordered.

'I will not!' Lopsang insisted. 'The horses are carrying all that remains of our monastery, also, many precious books. Rinposhay, do not abandon them.' Genyen reloaded her rifle from the ammunition belt slung over her shoulder.

'I could take some of my men and get behind them to draw their fire while you escape, Rinposhay,' she said.

'You cannot be sure. They seem to be all around us.'

'Shall I scout round and try to find out where they are?'

They all started nervously as the minstrel fired his flintlock unexpectedly, then began methodically ramming another shot down the barrel.

'Leave me two of your men,' Tsun said, 'to draw their fire while you and the others escape. We shall join you later. Leave some of the horses. Go quietly and quickly, for cloud will cover the light of the moon very soon.' After a moment's hesitation, Genyen spoke.

'Hurry, get the packs loaded onto as few horses as possible, and muffle their hooves.'

When Kesang realised that they were moving out and Tsun was not going with them, he ran towards the lama, but Genyen stopped him.

'He wanted us to do this, Rinposhay. He wanted you to come with us,' she said gently, as the child, still clutching the little dog, gazed sadly up into her face. 'He said that he would join us soon.'

Norden took her son's hand and led him away. They waited. In a very short time, clouds had dimmed the light of the moon. They started off in single file, working their way up the slope, seeking what cover they could and leading the horses. Genyen could just make out the figure of Tsun, sitting in meditation. 'Kunjosum!' she swore. 'Meditating at a time like this!'

Three men from her escort had stayed behind with Tsun. They returned the fire from the Han continuously, two firing and a third reloading.

Genyen grabbed at her horse's mouth to stifle a neigh. The rest of the party were over the crest of the hill, except for Norden who, a few feet from the nomad girl, whispered to her: 'Look, it is Tsun!' She was pointing down the rocks to where they had left Tsun. His tall figure was silhouetted against the sky. 'No! No!' Genyen murmured. Tsun was making a perfect target, and she could not understand why he had not been hit.

He stepped out into the open and was holding a scroll in his hand as he walked slowly towards the Han position. The firing on both sides stopped. The loudspeaker crackled into life again.

You must all surrender. Take the example of Tsun Lama, or we shall kill him.

'Oh . . .' Genyen stifled another curse and held her hand to her mouth in terror.

There was a burst of machine gun fire. Even from a distance, Genyen could see the bullets ripping a bush to shreds only a few feet from Tsun's erect figure. A twig cracked near her. She swung round, aiming her revolver and pulling back the hammer.

'Don't move, or I shall blow your head off.'

'It is I.'

Genyen recognised the voice of one of the men she had left behind, but she did not release the hammer until she could see all three of them. Then she saw the fourth.

'Rinposhay!' She could not believe her eyes. She looked down at the valley. The tall figure was still standing there. 'Who. . . ? she stammered.

'Hush,' Tsun smiled at her. 'It will keep them amused for a while. Let us move quickly.' He became serious. 'You are not to mention this to anyone.' Genyen nodded. Her mind was benumbed, unable to take in what had happened. They hurried after the others, who were taking it in turns to ride the remaining horses.

Much of the following day was spent travelling under the cover of a vast pine forest. Despite Genyen's wish to keep it secret, everyone was soon talking about Tsun's 'wonder-working'. She discussed it with Samden.

'I have heard before,' the monk said, 'of lamas who can create phantom bodies, but I have never known Tsun Rinposhay to do it before. What was it like? Did it look real?

'Completely,' Genyen answered, with awe. 'It even moved like him. As far as I was concerned, it was him.' Samden laughed. 'And, luckily, as far as the Han are concerned!'

They were resting for a short while during the late afternoon. Ling walked to Tsun's side.

'It is said that you performed some kind of miracle,' she said.

Tsun chuckled. 'What is a miracle to some, is commonplace to others. An iron bird is a miracle to those who know nothing about iron birds. It depends on the level of perception, the degree of knowledge. We are all magicians. We all create our own universe. The people who built that iron bird which attacked us, they are magicians. They altered events. They did it from outside, we do it from inside. That's the difference.' He tapped his head.

Ling sat down on a rock. 'I do not understand,' she said. 'But then there is much that I do not understand, nor would I begin to try and understand such things.' She looked at him for a long time. Neither spoke. There was a certain weariness about her now, Tsun thought. It must be really hard for her to comprehend such an alien culture. To Tibetans, brought up to accept that there is more to life than mere appearances, such miracles are taken for granted, but to a Han cadre? We must seem a very strange people, he mused, very strange indeed.

Ling sighed. 'Will you release me at the next village?' she asked.

'If it is possible.'

'If you do, I will tell the authorities that you have protected me, and do all I can to make sure that no harm comes to you.'

Tsun smiled slightly. 'I have learnt not to trust the promises of Han people. Their ethics are those of expediency. Is this not, in fact, what Communism teaches?'

Ling's face flushed. 'I am sincere. I do not want to die. I do not want . . .' she hesitated, 'any harm to come to you.'

'Before the face of death all artificialities pale and wither away. Only the reality remains. Yes, I am sure you are sincere. Today, you ride with death. Today, you are sincere. But what of when you are with your comrades? What then? You will be able to brush away the cold touch of death. Of what necessity to be sincere then?'

Ling opened her mouth to speak, then closed it again. She shook her head helplessly.

They kept on the move constantly, remaining well clear of the known tracks, stopping only for brief rests and to eat. Food was running short. They conserved it as much as possible. It took them almost a day to climb through the twisted lime and sandstone rocks to the Me-La pass, some 15,000 feet above sea level.

They were all cheered by the auspicious sight of two eagles, which they had disturbed, wheeling overhead. Wearily, stones were cast onto the snow-covered cairn. A vast mineral, lunar landscape stretched away on all sides. Man, Tsun thought, was as nothing here, dominated by a nature that had no place for him. No shelter. No sustenance. The earth's crust frozen in primeval convulsions.

No mist obscured the intense clarity of the turquoise sky. All of them wore snow goggles and masked their faces with cloth against the fierce snow glare and burning ultra-violet rays of the sun. Tsun paused to gaze around him, and smiled in wonderment, although he knew that for many hours they would be completely vulnerable to air attack as they made the descent.

During the next two days of travelling they twice had to endanger themselves by crossing the tempestuous Ba-Chu river at comparatively well known fording places. Like most Tibetans, none of them knew how to swim, and the river was particularly dangerous at this time of year, swollen by the mountain glaciers melting in the spring sun.

Life became the journey. The survival of the day, against the elements and the Han, natural and unnatural enemies; the eking out of the food; the constant watch for the Han. The minstrel sang as they sat round the camp fire, talking, reminiscing, boasting of how the resistance would drive the invaders from the country. Or how the invasion was a passing evil. How Tibet had been occupied before, and had regained its freedom. Tsun had a growing conviction that the invasion and occupation were part of a vast, almost incomprehensible change in the history of Tibet. But it would be of no use to express these views to his companions. They were fighting, suffering and dying for their families, homes and country. What he could tell them would not lift their spirits and fill their hearts with joy. Best that he keep his own counsel.

Champa and one of the escort went ahead to reconnoitre the hamlet of Beyu. When they came back they reported that it had a sizeable Han garrison. They were very short of food now and had been hoping to purchase fresh supplies from the village. Also, Tsun thought, there was Ling!

'Rinposhay,' Genyen said. 'Beyu is the last village before Derge. We cannot let the cadre go to Beyu now. She would let the garrison know immediately.'

'I know,' Tsun said wearily. 'I know.'

'Why don't we tie her up and leave her here?'

'Say what you mean. To tie her up and leave her is to kill her as surely as putting a blade in her belly.' Tsun urged on his horse, but he knew that he could not ride away from the decision.

It was almost exactly noon when they heard the sound of the aeroplane again. They pulled the horses down among clusters of boulders and crouched there, remaining absolutely still as the 'plane flew over.

'No! No!' Genyen hissed at one of her men who was levelling his rifle at the 'plane. 'Let it go. You could never hit at this range. It is too high.'

It was just possible that it was a routine patrol. At the height it was flying she thought it surely could not see much detail, but it turned and flew back towards them.

Senge, by now reduced to abject horror at the sound of the aeroplane, had a fit. He foamed at the mouth and screamed and struggled. Kesang could not hold him. The little dog flung himself out of the boy's arms and ran out into the open, just as the 'plane came in low towards them. Tsun waited for it to attack. Kesang was crying for Senge to come back. Champa moved like a flash as the 'plane roared overhead.

'No! Champa, no!' Norden screamed and tried to grab him as he moved from the cover of the boulders, grabbed the snapping dog and brought it quickly back to Kesang. 'They could have shot you,' Norden took the dog from his arms. 'If they saw you . . .' 'They could have done.' Champa smiled. 'But the iron bird was above me as I ran out. They could not possibly have seen me.'

'Scatter,' Genyen shouted. 'Scatter and take what cover you can.' The cover was sparse and she knew that when the 'plane attacked it was going to hit them hard. But the 'plane did not come back. They watched it fly away and waited for some minutes after it had disappeared over the silent hills before resuming their journey.

'It will report our position,' Tsun said, as he urged his horse to its feet.

'We must go on,' said Genyen. 'But we must keep under cover as much as possible.'

Tsun shrugged expressively and looked about him. They were at least three miles from the cover of the rocks and hills. For the next day and night, they saw no sign of the Han, but from past experience, it gave no reassurance.

It was late the following day when they entered a small and beautiful valley. Broad fans of sugar pine trees swept down the snow-crowned, lichen-covered slopes of rock. A marmot bounded out of the woods a few yards ahead of Kesang and Norden, delighting the little boy as it stared at them for a moment, then darted away. Senge, completely recovered from his fit and barking wildly, ran after the little animal.

Laughing at him for a moment, the group forgot their constant watch, releasing a little of the tension which had held them in its tight grip for so many days. Genyen had stopped some fifty yards ahead of the rest of the party. She held up her hand in warning. The Khambas unslung their rifles.

'There is someone in the woods,' she passed the message back. One of the Khambas took the reins from Kesang and Norden and led their horses under the cover of the pines.

They all waited. As they watched, a party of Khambas rode out of the forest. One of them, apparently the leader, waved to Genyen. She did not respond. Some of the men released the safety catches on their rifles. Silently, they watched and waited. Genyen felt that something was very wrong. She noticed the way the newcomers held their weapons, as if on the alert, and she remembered the villagers' tales.

'Han!' she shouted, firing at the same time, and spurring her horse towards the cover of the trees.

Her bullet grazed the neck of the leader's horse. It reared, throwing him against his companions. In the few vital moments of confusion, Tsun's party dashed after Genyen. The clatter of automatic rifle fire rasped on Tsun's ears. A bullet plucked his fur hat from his head. He could hear the angry shouts, Norden's cry, the whinnying of the horses and the terrified yelping of the little dog, as instinctively he ducked and spurred his horse to go faster. They reached the shelter of the trees, and the Khambas dismounted and prepared for attack. They returned the Han fire, the crack of their rifles interspersed with the loud explosion of the minstrel's flintlock followed by a cloud of smoke.

Tsun dismounted and reached into his pocket for his revolver. If he used it, it meant the repudiation of the cornerstone of his life. Yet, it was not just to save himself. He searched the area round him, looking for Kesang, Genyen, Lopsang, Rinchen and the others, and for Ling. A bullet dug into a tree beside him, spitting bark into his face. He was holding the revolver with hammer released.

He could see Genyen now. She was kneeling and bracing an automatic rifle on her knee. She fired it repeatedly, her body hardly moving with the recoil.

'Where is Tsun?' Kesang was crouched down beside his mother.

She shook her head. Her eyes were following a movement in the bushes a few yards away. She gripped her revolver with both hands and pressed the trigger. There was a pause, then the body of one of the Han fell face forward out of a bush. Norden's face was white and shocked. The minstrel winked at her and smiled, then he glanced at the boy.

'Take him up there,' he said, pointing up the densely wooded hillside. 'It would give you more of a chance.' He swung Kesang up onto his horse. 'Go on.' He slapped the horse's rump to persuade it to move quickly through the undergrowth and up the sharply sloping ground.

Kesang's eyes were wide, his face pale. He was absorbing everything. Norden saw him looking at the revolver she still held in her hand. The eyes were no longer the eyes of her child. She urged her horse on.

'Come on Kesang, hurry,' she called softly.

'Samden!' Jigme clasped his friend's arm to stop him sighting a rifle.

'It is done,' Samden smiled and pulled the trigger.

The Han were moving among the trees, trying to work round behind them. Suddenly, Tsun caught a glimpse of Ling's blue quilted jacket. She was darting from tree to tree in an effort to escape deeper into the forest. Tsun levelled his revolver at her and followed her for a few seconds. Then he lowered it slowly, knowing that he could not pull the trigger.

He worked his way over to Genyen. 'We should move back up the hill,' he said.

'There are only fifteen of them,' she laughed. 'We shall get them all.'

'Here, give that to me.' Tsun took the ammunition belt from her and loaded the Chinese .32 automatic. He felt inadequate. His training had enabled him to see the futility of war, of fighting, but he remained a Khamba, a warrior descendant from the hordes of Ghengis Khan. Buddhism had pacified the Khambas, but a Khamba still duelled to the death, where another man would argue and pass on.

'Tashi! Tashi!' Genyen called to the minstrel, who was now firing arrows from a bamboo bow. She took a hand grenade out of her pocket and held it up for him to see. 'After me!' she shouted, and darted off through the bushes. The minstrel followed her.

Smoke and flame erupted from the explosion. Branches ripped from the trees and scattered over a wide area. A horse screamed with pain, hit by a piece of shrapnel. A bullet sliced past Tsun's cheek, drawing blood. He flung himself to the ground and rolled towards a rock. Bullets ripped his chuba. He caught a glimpse of a Han firing at him from behind a rock farther up the slope.

'Rinposhay, get under cover!' Samden aimed his rifle at the sniper.

'No!' Tsun shouted as he fired.

The bullet hit the Han in the chest. He tipped to one side, his finger still on the trigger, spraying them with a hail of bullets. Tsun saw three black holes appear in Samden's chuba across his belly. He gasped, knocked from his feet by the impact. Tsun pulled him into the cover of the rocks, untied his belt and gently opened the sheepskin chuba to see the wound. Samden was fighting for breath. Tsun laughed and Samden, in his desperate struggle for breath, thought the Abbot must have lost his senses. 'Oh, Kunjosum!' His hands clawed across his stomach, seeking to stem the flow of blood, terrified by what they might find. But there was no blood. He felt cautiously; his fingers went through the bullet holes in his chuba and touched the silver filigree reliquary box that he kept in his ambac. Tsun eased Samden to a sitting position, with his back against a rock. He had only been winded. As he felt the reliquary box, he was a little overawed at being the beneficiary of the protective powers of a small bronze buddha statuette contained in the box, which had prevented the bullets from entering his flesh. Samden praised the gods, and his uncle, who had given him the consecrated buddha statue when he had first entered the monastery, telling him many stories about its history. It was very special. Now Samden would add his own tale to the many already surrounding the image.

Another explosion tore through the trees, then another. The firing dwindled. There was a thud of hoofbeats. The Han were fleeing.

For some minutes, the party remained under cover, waiting to see if it was a trap. Tsun, using his field glasses, caught a glimpse of the escaping Han and Ling riding with them. There was a sound behind him. He swung round to see the Khambas coming out from their positions. Their cries of victory echoed through the forest.

'The cadre was with them.' Genyen's voice was without expression as she spoke to Tsun. He did not answer. 'Have you seen Dorje Rinposhay and the Honourable Mother?' she asked.

'Yes.' It was Tashi who answered. 'They're hiding up among the trees.'

Tsun took the reins of his horse and began leading it up the hillside. The others followed him. Samden was excitedly telling everyone of his miraculous escape.

'We must get away quickly,' Lopsang interrupted him. 'It won't take the Han very long to contact headquarters.'

'They have taken so much trouble trying to capture us,' Genyen replied. 'I doubt they will give up now.'

Tsun hardly heard them. He was weighing the alternatives open to them and thinking further on the plan which he had already begun to formulate.

Genyen and Rinchen were behind him. Tsun beckoned them to follow and quickened his pace. He stopped when they were well ahead of the others.

'You're right, Genyen. They won't stop hunting us, but now at least we know how we have been followed, and can make it more difficult for them.'

Rinchen looked puzzled. 'How, Rinposhay?'

'Those men disguised as Khambas are not the usual PLA troopers. They're skilled fighters, used to mountains, used to living off the land, and some at least must have been able to speak Tibetan. They've passed themselves off as one of the hundreds of resistance groups in the mountains. I'd be surprised if at least one or two of them weren't at the New Year Festival.'

'I think I saw a radio pack' Genyen said. 'It was that which made me suspicious, as I know all the groups with radio transmitters, they're so few and precious.'

Tsun nodded 'You did. That's how they were able to keep in touch with the iron birds, and to summon help.'

'So after all the suspicion,' Rinchen rubbed the stubble on his face, 'we don't have a spy?'

'Yes, of course we do. How easy it must have been for him just to leave a sign as we journeyed.'

Genyen's reply was cold. 'It was the Han woman.'

'No! It is one of our number.'

'But who?' The steward sounded shocked at the suggestion.

'That I do not know,' said Tsun. 'But, Genyen, you were right about us leading the Han to Derge. It would be foolish to do so and dangerous for the Queen. The only way is for you to take the party on and for me to make the journey to Derge alone. I shall meet you in the Valley of Giants. I have given this much thought,' he said solemnly. 'It is the right thing to do. Genyen, you can lead the party safely. You have evaded the Han many times, you can do so again.'

'If anyone can.' Genyen shrugged and smiled. 'When will you meet us?'

'I should be able to attend to my business in Derge and make the Valley of Giants in ten days' time. If I have not arrived by the fifteenth day from now, go on to Lhasa without me.'

'But, Rinposhay, this is madness!' Rinchen protested. 'At least take someone with you. Do not go completely alone.'

'It will be safer. Who is going to know that a lone traveller is Lama Tsun? You will have the more difficult journey, and will need protection more than I.'

'If there is a spy among us, who in some way is able to communicate with the Han, will not he or she report your leaving the party?' Genyen asked.

'Yes, that is probable, but if the Han do follow me, it will be easier to evade them on my own.'

'No, Rinposhay,' Rinchen protested. 'Because they want you, and because if there is a spy in our midst, your movements will be reported, it is even more reason for you to take someone with you.'

Tsun brushed the suggestion aside. 'You will need all your wits. They are very clever. They may try to seize Dorje Rinposhay as a hostage. The boy must be protected above all.'

They both looked at him with troubled faces.

'Do you know who the spy is?' asked Genyen.

'I am not certain.'

'But while he is with us, we are in certain danger,' Rinchen insisted.

Norden and Kesang appeared above them. Now that the fighting had stopped they had ventured out, seeing Tsun and the others coming to meet them. Tsun answered their shouts of greeting then, turning to his steward, said:

'Yes, the spy, whether he or she, is a threat to us all. Trust no one. Do not mention my suspicions of a spy in our midst to anyone else. They have all believed that it was the cadre who betrayed us. Just observe and be cautious.'

'Tsun! Tsun!' Kesang came tumbling down the hill with Senge yapping at his heels, to fling himself into his tutor's arms and hug him. Smiling, Tsun took him by the hand and led him a short way from the others.

'I am going away for a few days, Kesang.'

The fear returned to the boy's face. 'You aren't going alone to Derge, are you?'

'Yes, but I shall be all right. You are not to worry. We shall meet again very soon.' He placed his hands on the boy's shoulders. 'Do all that your mother, Lama Rinchen and Genyen tell you. Take no heed of any other.' Kesang looked at Tsun with puzzled eyes, frowning in his effort to reach behind Tsun's words and grasp the real situation.

'Let me come with you.' For the first time he became conscious of the slight wound on Tsun's cheek where the bullet had grazed him. 'You are hurt . . .'

'It is nothing.' Tsun dabbed at the wound with a handkerchief. 'You cannot come with me, Kesang. I am sorry, but it is impossible. But remember, whatever happens, I am with you. Remember that always, my little one.'

Kesang looked into his guardian's eyes and was conscious of the feeling burnt into the words. Tsun led him back to the others and gave his hand to his mother's care. Then he turned away abruptly.

Tsun mounted his horse and rode on up the mountain. Just before he was lost from sight among the trees, he turned and waved a white felicity scarf.

BOOK TWO: March, 1956

'As regards the monasteries and the priesthood, their lands and properties will be destroyed . . .'

Chapter Seven

It was dark when Tsun reached the outskirts of Derge. From behind an outcrop of rocks on the surrounding hills, he focused his field glasses on the Han quarter, dating from Imperial China, a mile down the river away from the town. There were lights, but he could not make out any detailed movement. Above him an owl hooted. Clouds scudded across the night sky. He focused the glasses on the town. Many of the houses were in darkness, but the streets were lit dimly by street lamps, a recent innovation. A jeep was patrolling the streets. He could see a machine gun mounted at the back and the four men sitting in it. Then he swung his glasses to focus on another jeep making its way over the rough ground round the perimeter of the town.

He wondered how often they patrolled this area. He wanted to slip into town under cover of darkness as, from what he had heard, the Han were checking on all visitors. The jeeps met, then drove their separate ways.

Tsun waited until they had gone. Then he took pieces of sacking from his saddle bag and bound them round his horse's hooves. He checked to see that there were no other Han patrols in sight. Leading the horse, he made his way quickly and silently down the hill towards a narrow alley which led into town. It was just wide enough to accommodate his horse. Despite his efforts to move silently, the muffled hooves, even, it seemed to him, his own breath, proclaimed his presence. He stumbled over a stone and stopped, waiting for the guard dogs to start barking. Not one did.

Cautiously, he moved on. There was an eerie silence about the town. Usually there was some movement, some sign of life, however late, even if only among the animals. Tonight there was nothing.

He reached the end of the alley and peered round the corner. There was a deserted dirt road intersection to cross. He listened for the slightest warning sound but there was only the distant purr of the jeep engines. He led his horse across the intersection.

A sharp crack sent a chill of fear through Tsun's body and he whipped round to see what it was. A torn poster fluttered in the wind. He steadied his nervous horse as he reached up to tear the poster from the wall. In the dim light he read the announcement of a dusk to dawn curfew, and that curfew breakers would be shot on sight. Now Tsun understood why the streets were so deserted.

Holding the horse by its bridle, he padded softly along the narrow street, at every step expecting the dogs to bark, for they were trained to give warning at the slightest sound of an approaching stranger. But there was no sound from them as he passed by the shuttered windows of the houses. Tsun could feel the tense atmosphere of the sleeping town.

Turning into a side street, he heard an approaching jeep and pulled his horse quickly down a passage beside a house. He tied the reins to a post, then climbed onto a windowsill and worked his way along a ledge of the single storey house until he could pull himself over the parapet onto the roof. As he crouched down, he knew that every movement he made on the roof would disturb the occupants, for although they were town dwellers, they still had the 'ears of the night' of country people. He heard the jeep drive slowly past.

Tsun raised his head to look over the parapet. Like the jeeps he had seen earlier, this one had four PLA men in it and a machine gun mounted at the rear. He realised that not a dog had barked at the jeep. The silence was extraordinary; it was like a dead town. It depressed him to find how much one of the major towns of east Tibet was in the grip of the occupation forces.

He waited until the patrol had disappeared from sight, then climbed down from the roof, untied his horse and started off again through the narrow streets. The dim bulbs of the lamps swung in the wind from their wooden gibbets. Loudspeakers were placed at intervals on standards along the streets. Red flags flew where once prayer flags had decorated the rooftops of buildings. Tsun's eye was caught by another large poster pasted on the wall of a house. It showed a muscular youth with a rifle in one hand and a red flag in the other, and bore slogans in Han and Tibetan urging the people to greater productivity.

Suddenly, he heard the sound of footsteps. There was more than one person, and they would turn the corner of the street ahead of him at any moment. He pulled his horse into the deep shadow cast by a tree at the side of a house, and flattened himself against the wall. The footsteps drew nearer. Tsun watched the four-man patrol walk briskly past and stroked his horse's muzzle, praying that it would not betray his presence. Do they move everywhere in fours? he thought, while he waited for their footsteps to fade away, then crept round to the front of the house and knocked softly on the door. The battered sign on the doorpost read 'Chopel Dakpa – Silversmith'. Tsun knocked again. There was no reply. They must have heard, Tsun thought. Something was very wrong. Was it a trap? He remembered how well the Han had planned their attacks during the escape from Litang. They were always one move ahead. Was it so this time? He decided to spend the rest of the night on the roof and see who came out of the house in the morning. A knock on the door then would not seem so unusual. He began to climb the tree beside the house, as this seemed the best way of gaining access to the roof. He was only a few feet up when he froze, hearing the creak of the door. Glancing down, Tsun could see that it was slowly opening.

'Namgyal?' A voice whispered hoarsely. 'Is that you?'

A bald head appeared cautiously round the door. The man's eye was caught by a movement. He saw Tsun among the lower branches of the tree and started back with a gasp of fear. Then a look of amazement and recognition came over his face.

'Rinpo. . . ?'

Tsun put up a warning hand, and dropped down from the tree. 'My horse is at the side of the house.'

Chopel beckoned. 'Quickly!' he whispered, glancing anxiously up and down the street and, as he darted past Tsun, hissed, 'Get in quickly and bolt the door.'

Tsun entered the house and closed the door behind him. There was total darkness inside, and he was still feeling for the bolt when a paraffin lamp flickered to life. A short, stocky girl dressed in a flowered shirt and denims and wearing her long black hair in pigtails, blew out the match she was holding and stared coldly at Tsun. For a startled moment he thought she was a Han.

'Chopel's seeing to my horse . . .' He began to doubt the attempt to reassure even as he spoke.

'This is Dekyi, my daughter.' Chopel emerged from the darkness at the back of the shop, then turned to his daughter. 'And this is Tsun, a very old and respected friend of mine. I have known him for many years and owe him a great deal.'

He picked up a grubby felicity scarf and gave it to his daughter, who draped it over Tsun's arms with an indifferent attempt at a smile. He returned it, placing it over her arms.

'I used to help your father in his smithy,' he said. 'He taught me some of the art of silversmithing.'

The girl nodded politely and adjusted the flame of the lamp.
'Will the horse cause problems?' Tsun asked.
'No, Rinposhay,' Chopel answered, saw Tsun's reaction and smiled apologetically.
'Did you see a young boy anywhere outside in the street?'
'No,' Tsun answered. 'I only saw the patrols.'
Chopel offered Tsun the best rug in front of the clay stove.
'I am worried about my son,' he said. 'He should have been home from school hours ago.'
Tsun took out his bowl and placed it on a leather case which served as a table.
'Do you know why he might be so late?'
The girl filled the bowl with weak tea from a copper and silver teapot.
'No, I . . .'
'Yes you do, Pa-la,' Chopel's daughter interrupted. 'He steals from the Han,' she told Tsun, 'and my father encourages him.' Angrily, she raked the fire into activity. 'I knew this would happen. I knew they would catch him one day. I warned you, Pa-la.'
'Be quiet, girl,' Chopel scolded her for her disrespect, but his voice carried little conviction.
Tsun rose to his feet. 'I must tend to my horse,' he said.
'No, I will do it.' Dekyi said.
'But, the curfew. . . ?' He broke off as the girl slipped into the darkness.
'Please excuse our poor tea, Rinposhay,' Chopel said, pushing the lama's bowl nearer to him.
Tsun drank some. 'It is excellent tea, Chopel,' he said. 'But we must be cautious. We knew one another long before I took the Robe and then I was called Jigme. Call me that now. It is not safe to call me Rinposhay. You are endangering yourself and your family by giving me hospitality, do not add to the danger by acknowledging my true identity.'
Chopel nodded. 'Very well,' he said. 'My daughter is right . . . er . . . Jigme. It is so difficult now. The Han take everything. Namgyal, my son, and some of his friends, have become very clever at taking things back from the Han. It is not really stealing. I do not want you to think that we have become thieves.'
Tsun smiled. 'I do not think that.'
Chopel offered him a jar of tsampa. Tsun refused. 'I have enough,' he said. He shook the last of the barley flour from his

pouch into his wooden bowl and mixed it with the remains of his tea.

'If he has been captured by the Han,' he asked, 'what would they do with him?' He immediately regretted his question as he saw the anguish in Chopel's eyes. Then Dekyi came back into the room and extinguished the lamp.

'We must save fuel,' she said.

So the three of them sat huddled by the fire, with the reflection of the flames flickering on their faces. Chopel broke the long silence.

'Things are not good,' he said. 'Our children are being deported.'

'Deported! Where to?'

'China.'

'Why, what children are they taking?'

'Any child.'

'You mean they take them from the streets?' Tsun said, stunned by Chopel's news. He was aware that the Han might well take young incarnate lamas such as Kesang – those who would have some great influence among the people. But any child? Chopel saw Tsun's shocked look.

'No, not exactly.' Chopel rubbed a weary hand across his grimy face. 'Usually, they call us to a meeting. All those living in a certain street are called to the meeting. There, members of the District Committee tell us that our children should be given the chance of a fine education in China.' He paused. 'It is very difficult.'

Dekyi poured them both more tea then crossed to the window. She wetted her finger and made a small hole by softening the rice paper glazing, so that she could look out onto the street.

'But,' Tsun asked, 'if the children don't want to go, what then?'

'You get shot if you refuse,' Chopel said numbly. 'I, myself, saw it happen a few months ago. At one of these meetings a woman protested that she was a widow and that her son was her only child. He must have been about fifteen years old. The boy told the Han that he did not want to go. The Han argued with the woman and her son, but she was a strong and forceful character and unafraid. Her resistance somehow gave strength to those whose children had been taken. The crowd became more and more restive. The Han grew apprehensive. The tension was high. The crowd drew strength from her and she seemed to draw strength from them.

'The Han ordered her to stop protesting, but she continued. She was shot and killed. It was terrible. We all knew her. She was old and used to help with the birth of babies.'

Chopel gulped his tea, then refilled Tsun's bowl from the copper and silver teapot. 'Something in all of us died with her. A pride. She had stood up to the Han, we had not. Now she lay dead, and we had just been spectators.' Tsun offered his snuff bottle. Chopel took some before continuing.

'It was that which made me join the resistance.' He glanced towards his daughter, a black outline against the surrounding darkness, at her vigil by the window, then turned his anxious eyes on Tsun and whispered, 'Rinposhay . . . please, is my son safe?'

Tsun unwrapped the amber and coral rosary from his wrist and lowered his eyes in meditation as he counted the beads. The time went slowly. Chopel joined his daughter at the window.

'I suppose, Pa-la,' she said softly, 'he might have found it impossible to reach home before curfew and is staying the night with a friend.' Chopel grunted, and wandered back to the fire. He unwrapped his own rosary from his wrist and began murmuring invocations.

Tsun's eyelids rose. Chopel gazed at him with fearful anticipation. Tsun smiled and nodded. Chopel smiled broadly, then bowed his head. 'Thank you, Rinposhay.' He silently mouthed the words.

'Continue with your story,' Tsun requested. 'I wish to know what happens to those children who are deported to China.'

'It is not easy to say. So many have gone from Derge, and none have returned. Some of the children of my friends send letters. They are strange letters. They say very little, but mention that they labour as well as learn. They are silent about so much. They rarely answer their parents' questions. Sometimes they ask for things, like watches that they can sell, as they have no money . . .' He broke off. His mind fixed on the fate of his son. 'Even if the Han have not captured him for stealing, they are bound to send him away for education soon.'

'Is there no way of stopping the Han from taking him?'

'Only if he leaves the town, and that is a difficult thing to arrange now. I might be able to get a friend, a merchant, to take him to Lhasa, but it would be hard to send him away from the family, and we can't go.' For some minutes there was silence.

'Kusho,' Dekyi whispered urgently from the window, 'are you staying long in Derge?'

'No, only for two or three days,' Tsun answered.

'Take Namgyal with you, please!' She came over to Tsun's side. 'I work for the Han. I know how thorough they are. He will not remain free for long.'

Tsun frowned. 'If your brother comes with me, he will be in even more danger.'

'But we are the only people who know you are in Derge, is that not so?'

'Yes.'

'Then you can leave as secretly as you came. If my father, or I, should leave the town, my father's clients and our neighbours would know at once. There are even street informers now.'

'If I leave,' Chopel said, 'I lose my house, my business, everything. We shall become fugitives. The Han are already suspicious of me.' He shrugged. 'People talk of going to Lhasa, but what can they do there?'

'Do not be foolish, father, you have a trade. You will get clients in Lhasa,' Dekyi insisted.

'It takes time to build a business,' Chopel answered, 'and I am well known here.'

'But your business is dying.' Her voice rose.

'Perhaps,' Chopel nodded sadly. 'But how do we know that it is better in Lhasa? I have heard that there is a food shortage even there. No! It is better that we stay and send the boy to safety.'

Dekyi went and knelt beside her father, putting an arm around his shoulders and looking up at Tsun.

'Tell him,' she pleaded with Tsun. 'Tell him that it will not be wise to stay.'

Tsun swallowed a lump of tsampa that he had been chewing. 'Your daughter is right, Chopel,' he said. 'It is not as it was when the Han invaded before, and I do not feel that it will improve. If you have the opportunity to escape, do so!'

The old man's brow was furrowed. He slapped his hand on his bald head and grunted. Then he sat silent, gazing into the fire. Tsun heard a slight sound. 'There is someone outside,' he whispered.

They scrambled to their feet. Dekyi was already at the window, peering through the tiny hole she had made with her finger. She gave a gasp. 'It is he! It is Namgyal!'

Chopel hurried to unlock the door. He reached out, grabbed the boy by his chuba and pulled him inside, bolting the door again behind him.

'Where have you been?' he demanded angrily of the frightened boy, shaking him. Dekyi ran forward. 'No, Pa-la!' She pulled the tousled and grubby boy away from his troubled father, led him over to the fire, put a bowl on the case and poured him tea.

'Did anyone see you come in?' she asked him.

He shook his head. 'No, Dekyi-la.'

'Where have you been?' his father insisted.

For answer, he took from his ragged and dirty chuba a bunch of enormous radishes the size of plums, then six turnips. Dekyi's eyes widened in horror.

'Where did you get them?' She grasped him by the shoulders and shook him. 'Where did you get them?'

'You are hurting me,' he complained. 'They fell out of one of the trucks.'

'Liar!'

'Children, children,' Chopel interrupted. 'Remember we have a guest.' He gave a scarf to Namgyal to give to Tsun, which he did with shy courtesy.

'Now, Namgyal,' his father continued, 'tell us the truth. How did you get those vegetables?'

Namgyal rubbed his lips with the back of his finger, and looked stubbornly at his sister.

'Namgyal . . .' His father's voice carried a note that did not brook defiance.

'We, some of the other boys and me, were climbing trees. We waited for the trucks from the Han depot. The road was beneath the trees. There was a pile of rubbish across it. The trucks travelled slowly and we were able to drop into the back. We took what we could, then jumped out.'

'But why are you so late?' Chopel demanded.

'Well . . .' the boy hesitated.

'Come on, boy, tell us!'

'Well, one of the drivers saw us and raised the alarm. We had to hide. We waited until it was dark before we came home.'

'You might have been shot,' his sister said, shocked.

The boy shrugged.

'You are sure you were not followed?'

'Yes, Pa-la.'

'What about the other boys?' Dekyi asked sharply. 'Were any of them caught?'

'No! None of us got caught.' He lost interest in the conversation. 'Dekyi-la, will you make some soup with these turnips? I am hungry.'

'Namgyal,' Chopel said sternly, 'you must not do such things. It is wrong to steal. You will bring misery to yourself and your family.'

'But, Pa-la, the Han take grain from us, we are hungry. I only take back a little of what is ours.'

Chopel put an arm round the boy's shoulders. 'I would rather that we were hungry,' he said, 'and have you safe. Now, do as I say. Swear by the Triple Gem.' Namgyal protested and squirmed.

'Swear!'

'Yes, Pa-la,' he said wearily. 'I swear.'

'Come now,' Dekyi said. 'It is time for you to eat and then go to sleep.' She gave him a piece of dried meat and some peas. The boy ate quickly and intently, then, as Dekyi poured more tea for the men and herself, Namgyal curled up by the fire and she covered him with a blanket.

'So food is very short?' Tsun inquired. He offered Chopel his snuff bottle. The old man took it and shook some of the powder onto his thumb.

'Now, we live on green herbs and peas. Peas! Peas that we used to feed to our horses. Everything is changed. I used to be a silversmith. You remember, Kusho, what fine pieces I made? Real craftmanship. Now, no one has the silver. And to order a religious item would brand you as a hoarder for having the money to have it made, and an upper class reactionary for desiring a religious item. So now I have to make these.' He sounded bitter as he pointed to a pile of tin saucepans.

Tsun turned to the girl. 'And what do you do, Dekyi?' he asked.

Her father answered for her. 'She works as a clerk for the Han. I do not like it, but then, she is right, we need the money. And she is young. It is easier for her to adapt to their ways. But what of the resistance? What news do you have, Kusho?'

'They seem to hold much of the country between here and Litang. But most of the villages are under the control of the Han. The Han are disguising themselves as Khambas and raiding villages, taking the food and the women and saying that they are the resistance.'

'They are clever,' Chopel muttered sourly.

'What of the Prince and Queen?' Tsun asked.

'It is difficult for them. They are virtually prisoners. The Queen is a member of the local Han District Committee. She tries to make things easier for us, but there is little she can do.'

Tsun moved closer to Chopel. Dekyi took the hint and lay down in front of the fire, pulling a blanket over herself.

'I have to see the Queen, Chopel.'

'What?' Chopel was shocked. 'It would be madness.' But even as he spoke he changed his mind. 'I suppose it could be arranged,' he agreed reluctantly, 'I have done a lot of work for Her Majesty in the past.'

'But it was always easy to see her.'

'I told you, everything is different now. There are spies everywhere.' Chopel was studying Tsun's face as he spoke. 'Why are you here, Kusho?' he asked softly.

'To see my family.'

'No! There is more to your visit than that. You did not work for me for all that time without my learning to know when you are . . .' He stopped himself.

Tsun chuckled and slapped him on the shoulder. 'You are right,' he said. 'But the less you know, the better, and the safer it will be for your family.'

'But, what of your monastery?'

Tsun held his finger to his lips and glanced at the boy and girl sleeping by the fire. 'Later, Chopel, later I will tell you. Now, perhaps you will tell me something. Do you know where my family are staying?'

Chopel looked uncomfortable. 'Your sister is working with the Han.'

Tsun frowned.

'So many people have to work for the Han now,' Chopel said. 'Look at Dekyi.' He paused to gaze at her recumbent body. 'Such ugly clothes. It shames me that you should see her dressed so.'

Tsun chuckled, then asked, 'Do you see much of my sisters?'

'Yangchen has come to call on me twice, when she needed some work done. Did you know that she has not been back in Derge very long?'

Tsun nodded.

'Dekyi has met your sisters at the PLA garrison.'

'They know one another well?'

'No.'

'And my mother?'

'I have heard nothing.'

'Do you know where I might find my sisters?'

'Dekyi might. I will ask her in the morning.'

'I am awake,' Dekyi murmured softly, in the darkness. Tsun

wondered how much she had heard. She turned her face into the light of the fire and looked up at him.

'I am trying to find my sisters', he said. 'Can you help me?'

'They live in the Han garrison,' Dekyi answered dryly. She saw the flicker of disbelief in his eyes.

'Can you help me to see them?' he asked.

'Unless you work there it is difficult.'

'But, surely relatives are allowed in?'

'I do not know. It will be difficult. I shall have to enquire.' Her voice became slightly querulous.

'Dekyi-la!' Her father reprimanded her.

'Pa-la, it is going to be difficult,' she said with barely concealed irritability. 'And, well . . .' her voice trailed off.

'Dekyi,' said Tsun, 'you are right to be anxious for the safety of your own family.'

She looked at him, startled and slightly frightened.

'Pa-la doesn't understand,' she said. 'Every day that I go shopping, it is harder to find food, and every day I see our neighbours' children being sent to China. It is so hard to keep the family together . . .' She stopped abruptly as the tears welled up in her eyes.

Late next morning Tsun went out into the narrow streets. Dekyi had already contacted his sister Yangchen, who had said that she would expect him and would warn the guards at the gates. Tsun walked slowly along the streets which ran down towards the valley floor. He needed to buy supplies for the journey. There was a long queue at the State Food Shop. It was a single-storeyed, corrugated iron-roofed building. Tsun looked through the window. There was very little food inside. Most of it had been snapped up by those who had been in the queue at dawn and, anyway, he did not have a ration book. He walked slowly away. The Tibetans laughed at the Han love of bureaucracy and couldn't understand why they should have to have ration books and identity cards. But Tsun began to realise fully the implications, the means it gave of controlling each individual.

From the walls of the inns, smithies, teashops, warehouses, shops and houses, beamed full-face portraits of Chairman Mao, with exhortations to increase productivity and crush counter-revolutionaries. He felt oppressed by the posters. Tibetans still thought, he realised, according to the old customs. Disguise was easy, as everyone assumed you still dressed according to position.

Tsun couldn't help but think how fortunate it was that no photographs of him existed for the Han to use, and that he had not yet been issued with any form of identity card that would put him on record.

He stopped by a wooden lamp standard to look up at the still-dominating ruins of the ancient castle of the kings of Derge, a dynasty that could trace its ancestry back a thousand years. No, nothing had changed about the ruins, he thought. It was as he remembered. Nor had the monastery changed, its predominant feature still the gilded roofs of the printing press, famed for its printing of religious texts. The town cascaded in a jumble of buildings down the hillside to the valley floor. Tsun thought of Derge as he had known it: a crossroads of Asia – China, Tibet and Mongolia. Centre of fashion, finance, gossip, culture, the finest silversmiths. A shell remained. The life was gone. The rhythm was gone. The Derge Tsun had known was, he realised, already part of history; an overwhelming depression came on him.

Yangchen had said he should come to the camp after noon. He realised he was too early and wandered into a shop. It was dark despite the open door and window shutters. Busts of Chairman Mao were displayed on crude tables, together with beautifully bound works on Marxism-Leninism and the Chairman's writings. On another table were displayed paraffin lamps and wicks.

A short, stout man in grey cotton trousers and plaid shirt was arguing with the owner of the shop.

'But, surely you must have *some* paraffin,' he demanded.

'It is in short supply,' the owner answered curtly, 'I have none.'

'But why sell lamps if you can't get fuel?' The owner shrugged his shoulders at the stupidity of the situation.

Tsun picked up a volume of Chairman Mao's writings. Outside, in the street, loudspeakers were broadcasting Han music, interspersed with political news and warnings to the population to be on their guard for reactionary counter-revolutionaries. The shop was filling up. A toothless old woman came out to help serve. She approached Tsun.

'It is very cheap, Kusho,' she said, indicating the book in his hands.

'What does it cost in Tibetan money?' Tsun asked.

The woman frowned. 'Yuan only are used in Derge, Kusho.'

'It does not matter,' Tsun said.

As he was about to leave the shop, his eye was caught by some coloured photographs pinned to the wall. They were of the

Kundun during his visit to China in 1954. One photograph was of the Kundun with Chairman Mao Tse-tung. It had a white scarf pinned over it. A woman waiting to be served touched the picture with her forehead in reverence and to bless herself.

Tsun left the shop and continued to walk down the narrow, dusty streets. He had to push his way past a mule train, the animals' neck bells ringing in disunity, their hooves kicking dust over the wares spread on the ground. Fewer people were in the streets than usual. Some were playing dice, but there was nothing like the old crowds placing side bets. Tsun noticed the sullen looks of the young Khambas when Han patrols passed them, how their eyes would follow the Han. He noticed, too, that a number of houses in the town were unoccupied and falling into disrepair, the rice paper windows torn and fluttering in the breeze. The occupants had fled to Lhasa or been deported.

Many of the shops were run by Han. Tsun turned at an unfamiliar sound, and had to step aside as two Tibetan boys sped by on bicycles, ringing their bells for everyone to get out of their way. There used to be so many beggars in the streets. And the dogs? He had not seen any dogs since arriving in Derge.

A monk was buying some cloth from a woman who had some poor quality bales laid out on the ground. Tsun realised that he was the only monk he had seen in the town that day. What had happened to all the monks? Derge was a monastery town. Life had become very serious and it was reflected in the faces of those he passed in the streets.

The loudspeakers had stopped for a few minutes, and Tsun became aware of another silence. The complete lack of birdsong. He glanced up at the flat roofs, expecting to see the usual collection of wild birds perched there. But there were none. Childhood memories of the magpies filled his mind. There used to be swarms of them on the roof of his home. They were so tame that they would sit on the hand to eat. He had been fascinated by their sturdy, purple black bodies, white plumage, and twinkling, beady-black eyes. Now, there were no magpies.

A few yards down the street, Tsun noticed another poster, which seemed to carry more implications than the usual slogans. It called for the destruction of parasites.

A blast on a horn shattered his thoughts. He stepped quickly aside as a Han truck carrying bags of cement drove past him, making for a large construction site near the outskirts of the town.

The Han have invaded our country before, Tsun thought, and

we have thrown them out. But they, like the Tibetans, have long memories, and this time, he realised, they meant to stay. This time it was more than kow-towing to the Emperor.

There were still areas administered by the Tibetan Government in the central and western provinces, and resistance was growing. Tibet had its friends in the outside world. When they knew what was happening, surely they would react favourably? Yet, there was growing within him a gnawing suspicion, a feeling too awful to entertain, that the Tibetan civilisation was dying. Everything that gave it identity, family, nation, religion, everything . . .

Was it really the end of the world? Philosophically, he thought, it was inevitable that the civilisation should pass, but it did not make it any easier.

The loudspeakers were pounding at his ears again. It took Buddha to give his body to the tigress, so that she could feed her cubs. At the moment, Tsun did not feel himself to be a Buddha. Only a mere human, he felt that he, and everything that he held dear, was being devoured by the tiger. It may be, he thought, that Tibet's time has come. But in the meantime, he intended to do everything within his power to avert such a catastrophe.

He was at the edge of the town where the Han were erecting dozens of barrack-like buildings, with corrugated iron roofs. The old Chinese quarter, which had been a squalid collection of ramshackle huts by the river, just outside town, had been cleaned up, and beside it was the District Military and Administrative Headquarters in a well-guarded encampment.

A long military convoy, carrying personnel and equipment, was entering the camp when Tsun arrived at the main gate. For the first time in his life, he saw a tank. It was being carried in through the main gate on a tank transporter. He stared at it fascinated.

'What do you want here?' one of the sentries shouted at him in Chinese.

'I have business with comrade Yangchen Thondup,' Tsun answered in the same language. 'She is my sister.'

The sentry remained suspicious. You could never trust these Khambas. They were devious and ruthless. Only a few days ago, he had heard of how a small party of them had slipped into the garrison and killed half the sleeping men with their daggers. He kept his finger on the trigger of his rifle.

'Watch this fellow,' he ordered his companion, who was checking the convoy from a paper on a clip board. Then he walked over to the sentry hut and made a call on the internal telephone.

How unreal time is, Tsun thought. How relative. It seemed he had been waiting hours, yet he knew without looking at his watch that he had been waiting only a few minutes. He could see the sentry talking on the telephone through the window of the hut, and watched him put down the receiver, stamp a card and come out of the hut. He handed the card to Tsun. 'This is your pass,' he snapped. 'Your sister is in the officers' quarters over there.'

He pointed to a long low barracks on the far side of the square. Tsun walked through the gate with the roar of motors in his ears as the convoy moved slowly past him. He walked round the edge of the square in which the trucks, troop and armoured carriers were unloading. The sight and sound of the tanks rumbling off the carriers riveted Tsun's attention, so that he stopped and stared. Eventually, the sentry at the gate noticed him standing and watching and shouted at him: 'Hey! You! Green brain, move on!'

Startled, Tsun did as he was told, aware how easy it was to get oneself arrested. He appeared to be the only Tibetan in the camp wearing national dress and felt very conspicuous. The few Tibetans he saw were wearing shapeless, crumpled blue shirts and trousers.

A woman in grey tunic and trousers, with a soft cap perched on her head, was walking towards Tsun in the wide avenue between the buildings. The sun was shining in his eyes. He couldn't be certain, but he thought she was Tibetan, and there was something familiar about her. Then, he saw that it was his sister, Yangchen. His step quickened. Neither ran, but Tsun thought her step, too, became faster. It had been a long time. Much had happened. How changed they would seem to each other.

When they were within speaking distance, Tsun held out his arms. She glanced at him with a tense smile and turned aside to lead the way to the officers' quarters. She led the way into a room, waited until he was inside, then closed the door behind them.

When she turned to face him, Tsun saw that tears glistened in her eyes. 'Rinposhay,' she whispered caressingly, and bowed.

He grasped her by the shoulders. 'I am your brother today, nothing more,' he said, as they hugged one another. 'How long has it been?' Their hands clasped. They sat beside one another on the bed in the plain white-painted room. The sun shone through the large glass-paned window onto the wooden floor.

'Seven years,' Yangchen murmured.

Tsun wiped away a tear from her cheek with his finger. For a few moments they looked at one another, smiling, each absorbing the other's presence.

She has aged, Tsun thought. And she looks weary beyond her years. Her round face was deeply tanned from working in the open, the skin still showing pock marks left by the illness she had had as a child. She was pretty, with a small, pert nose and a small round mouth. But her black hair, no longer glossy from applications of butter, was parted severely in the middle, drawn back with the plait wound round her head.

She patted his hand, then got up from the bed, filled an iron kettle with water from a bucket and put it on the oil stove. Tsun glanced round the bare room, focusing on the framed colour photograph of Mao Tse-tung hung at the head of the double iron bedstead. Yangchen broke off some tea from a brick and crumbled the coarse fibres into a white enamel pot.

'Dekyi told me you were in Derge, and wanted to see me,' she said, realising how inane the comment was as she took two enamel mugs and some biscuits from a cupboard and put them on a little table which she moved beside the bed. She sat down beside her brother.

'You know Litang was bombed?' he said quietly. 'It is only a matter of time before Dorje Ri-gon is taken too. So, we escaped while we could. But I'm alone now. I had to come and see how you and Pema-la are managing.'

Her eyes were brimming with tears again. 'Oh, Rinposhay,' she sobbed. Tsun put his arms around her and held her close. 'Will it ever end? I've heard rumours of the siege at Litang, and I have been so worried about you. It is months since I received a letter.'

'I wrote to you, through Chopel, whenever someone was coming to Derge.'

'So little mail gets through now.' She dried her eyes and sat up. 'And one has to be so careful, it is hard to know what to say. A letter could so easily get into the wrong hands.'

The kettle started to boil. She got up and poured water into the teapot. In silence she waited for it to brew.

'What are you doing here, Yangchen?' Tsun asked after a few minutes. She filled the two mugs with tea and handed one to him, sucking in her breath and bowing politely.

'We are brother and sister,' he reminded her gently.

'Oh, Jigme-la,' she called him by his childhood name. 'So much has happened that I have been unable to mention in my letters.'

'What of your husband, Gyalo? Have you no news of him?'

She shook her head. 'I don't know where to begin . . . everything has changed so . . .'

Tsun drank some tea. 'Tell me, Yangchen, tell me everything,' he said. 'It might help a little . . .'

She looked at him with a faint, strained smile. Then she took a sip of tea and sat silent for a few moments. Tsun waited. In the square outside they could hear the sounds of the convoy being unloaded and the shouts of the Han troops.

'You know that, when I married Gyalo,' Yangchen began, 'Mother and Pema came with us to Amdo to live on his farm in Doi village. Though I could not write about what happened there and why we came to Derge. We moved just before the beginning of winter in the Iron Tiger year. The Communists had taken over in China. Not that we thought about that, although some in the village told us of the ravages the Communist guerrillas had inflicted on them during their Long March to Yenan.

'It was a bitter winter. The snow was higher than I had ever known. Then a courier came from Sinning. He had walked for miles, after losing his horse in a blizzard, and was suffering from frostbite. It had taken him three days to cross Amdo. He had been sent by the local Tibetan leaders to warn Lhasa that convoys of military personnel and equipment were being moved by the Han and converging on the border. He told us that as soon as the weather improved, our village would be occupied and the attack on Tibet would begin.

'Of course, we were frightened, and the old ones told us of the horrors the Butcher, Chao Feng, had brought to Tibet with his invasion of 1905. But still we did not really appreciate the full significance of the danger. Though I can remember still, the look of fear on the face of the courier when we told him that the telegraph lines were down.

'The next day, the weather improved and the courier left for Chamdo, and a few families abandoned their farms and decided to go with him.

'We decided to stay and see what happened. After all, we reasoned, it might not be so bad. Who could say? It was told by some that the Communists were much more reasonable than the Kuomintang. Then someone came and warned us that the Han were on their way to the village.

'Ever since we had heard of the impending invasion, assemblies had been held to try and find a way to stop them. The District Governor, village heads, abbots, everyone attended them and talked and talked, but little came of it. Except that we all agreed to hide our food stores, and all our weapons and ammunition.

'We also sent a message to Lhasa, appealing for guidance. We had hoped that the Tibetan army might reach us in time to stop the invasion, but we heard that the army had not even reached Chamdo. So we were virtually defenceless.

'The Governor set off to meet the Han to see if he could negotiate with them. Members of his party arrived back at the village a few days later. They said he had been arrested and deported to China. We never heard of him again. His staff had been allowed to come back so that they could give us the ultimatum from Chang Kuo-hua himself. It stated that Doi Gyatsan had always been part of China, and that resistance from reactionary foreign elements would not be allowed to stand in the way of the People's Liberation Army which meant to free the entire area and all Tibet from the oppressors. So, now we had to choose. To fight or surrender?'

Yangchen paused to pour Tsun and herself more tea. Then she glanced nervously at her watch, moved to the window to look out across the square, and came back to sit beside Tsun.

'We decided to fight,' she went on. 'If the Han believed us to be part of China, we had to show them that we did not agree. I remember it so well. A still winter's day. Parts of the streets knee-deep in melting snow. The sky dark and overcast. It was bitterly cold. All the lower windows of the houses were shuttered and, at most of the upper windows, armed villagers waited. Some of us stayed in the streets so that the village would look normal when the Han arrived.

'They came like an army of grey locusts. An endless column. No bands. Nothing but the muffled tramp of their feet. At their head, great portraits of Chairman Mao, Chou and Chang Ching-wu.

'Those of us in the street began throwing mud at the portraits. We got pushed aside as we knew we would be. Those in hiding opened fire. There was complete confusion for a few minutes. The portraits fell and were trampled underfoot. The Han were taken by surprise. Fortunately, most of us managed to reach cover before they began returning our fire with machine guns and automatic rifles. For the first time, we saw hand grenades.

'Some of our men rode out of the village to try and draw their fire and let others escape to the mountains. But it was useless. It did not take long for the Han to crush the resistance. Our weapons were old and powerless against their might. Some of the villagers escaped, but very few.

'Every building was searched for weapons. Armoured cars patrolled the village, shooting indiscriminately. Then thousands, or so it seemed, of troops marched through the main street before setting up camp on the outskirts of the village.

'All the best houses were requisitioned for the officers and military departments. Within hours we found our lives controlled by the Communist Party Work Committee and the Security Committee, both of which were virtually run by the local Military Commanders.

'It was incredible how quickly they stripped us of everything. I found my ordinary cooking utensils requisitioned. Our horses, the village grain stores, just disappeared to feed the vast army. Then, after a few days, the greater part of the army left to march deeper into Tibet.

'But those who were left made sure that we had no hope of rising against them again. A number of our people were shot. The Han ordered them to their Headquarters for questioning, and they did not return. It was announced that they had been executed as Kuomintang agents, as hoarders, or for resisting the PLA. All the village leaders disappeared in this way. It was terrifying.

'Some of us tried to escape, but it was difficult. The village was closely patrolled, and one needed a pass before leaving, which was issued by the Security Committee, stating where you were going and when you would return. Still, some did get away.

'Gyalo planned how we could escape. Every day we feared that one of us might be taken to the Han Headquarters and not return. We had all participated in the resistance against the Han, even Mother, and she was ill, so it was not possible for her to travel. I begged Gyalo to try and escape with Pema-la, and I would follow with Mother when she had recovered sufficiently, but he refused.

'A few weeks after the occupation, it was announced through the loudspeakers that Mao had assured the Indian Prime Minister, Nehru, that force would not be used against Tibet. It was extraordinary how they could broadcast this lie. I do not know what they hoped to achieve, for it only served to convince us of their duplicity. We were also told of the invitation for a Tibetan delegation to go to Peking to discuss peace terms.

'It was impossible for us to know what was true and what was not. However, we did hear from a trader who had returned from Lhasa, that just before the invasion the Kundun had been asked to take over the Government from the Regent, even though he was two years short of his majority. This news cheered us, for had we not defeated the Han when the Great Thirteenth Kundun governed? The trader also told us that the Tibetan Government and the Kundun had retreated to the Indian border, to strengthen their bargaining power and prevent the capture of the Kundun.

'Still, we had to live from day to day and adapt ourselves to the terrible conditions. We tried with great difficulty to nurse Mother back to health. Then the Han opened a clinic. Mother was not improving so we thought we should try their medicines. Many of the others would not, because they thought they might be poisoned, and Mother did not want to go but she was in such pain that she almost gave up caring what happened to her. So we took her there, and the treatment they gave her worked and she started to improve, which made us wonder if, perhaps, things would not be so bad after all.

'Then the weeks went by and the Han did not arrest anyone, and the security restrictions were eased. We were allowed greater freedom to go about our business, although the requisitioning still continued. Then we heard of the complete destruction of our army by the PLA!

'The details of the Seventeen-Point Agreement between Tibet and China was broadcast over the loudspeakers. It was horrifying to listen to. We could not imagine how such an agreement could have been signed by our delegates, except under duress. There seemed to be no hope. We were at the complete mercy of the Han.

'For a few months things still continued quietly. Political lectures began, which all the villagers were expected to attend after a hard day's work in the fields. A local Socialist Party was formed, and it was announced that everyone would be dealt with according to their class. The first class was what the Han called capitalists, though at that time none of us knew what they were talking about. The second class were landlords. The third, traders, craftsmen. The fourth, the poorer peasants. The fifth, servants and agricultural workers. We were in the third class.

'Some of the villagers had been talked into working for the Han who were lavish with their payments. These villagers were made the new leaders of the people, and were called upon to accuse those members of the first three upper classes. I honestly don't think they realised what would happen.

'Every day now, people were being arrested. Dozens of them. Then we would be forced to attend mass assemblies, the

Thamzings. The Han went from house to house to see that everyone did attend. Not to go made you liable for arrest. Even the children had to go. I used to hold Pema's face against me so that she would not see, and Gyalo tried to stand in front of us to block the view.

'The accused people were tortured for their confession and often executed in front of us. The terror of the Thamzing had begun. We saw many people killed in that field outside the town – usually, no more than ten at a time, men and women. The Han would accuse their victims of being exploiters of the masses, counter-revolutionaries, but we all realised that it was because they either represented Tibetan Nationalism as leaders, or because they were devout and closely connected to the Religion. There could only be one loyalty, we learned, and that was to China. Day after day, the same people would be brought out to be "struggled against", each time with increasing violence.

'I can remember so well, one old man. He lived next to us in the village and used to tell stories to Pema-la. His name was Dawa, and the Han must have learnt from someone that he had hoarded money. Anyway, they demanded three thousand yuan from him. He didn't have anything like that amount. So all of us who knew of his difficulty helped him to make up the sum. No sooner had he paid the money to the Han, when they promptly demanded another three thousand to be paid in five days. Of course, none of us could raise that amount. We couldn't help him.

'He was arrested, and at the Thamzing, his family had to stand on the platform while he was hanged.

'You know, Tsun-la, I think all our senses were blunted by the horror. We tried to shut it out of our minds. To do anything else would have sent us mad. That poor old man, whom we knew so well, having his family stand there . . . I shall never forget it.

'Then they came and stripped his house of everything, distributing part of his possessions among the collaborators. His family were thrown out of their home. The house was taken over, and his widow and elder daughter were allowed to live in the stable.

'The taxes were increasing all the time. There was a shirt and a furniture tax, and it was even harder to get out of the town, let alone the district, security was so tight. We thought it must be bad in all parts of the country. We had no news. We didn't know how others were faring. It was said things were better in Lhasa, but how could we be sure? It was impossible to communicate.

'All the local monasteries were desecrated, and we were forced to watch them burning scriptures and paintings. It was even regarded as an offence to burn incense or a butter lamp at our shrines. The monks who were not broken physically by torture or killed, were forced to do the most menial tasks, like collecting the manure.

'The Local Working Committee had broken up all the land holdings and redistributed them, telling us where to work and what to harvest. At first, we had enough left over from the previous year's harvests to allow two meals a day, but this went and we began to eat wheat husks and wild plants, as more and more of the harvests were collected as "voluntary" gifts to the State.

'There were many suicides. I often thought of killing myself. But what would have happened to our Ama-la, and to Pema-la and Gyalo, if I were not there to help them?

'We were made to join the co-operatives under the direction of the CCP Working Committee. We received no payment for the harvest, but were given provision of wheat husks, oil-cake, chopped leaves, and an endless diet of re-education classes.'

She got up, poured more tea for them both and offered Tsun a biscuit. He took one.

'Some escaped,' she continued, 'in spite of the tight security, and formed resistance groups. Many times, Gyalo and I talked about how to escape, but Ama-la was still weak because of poor food. She wasn't fit to travel, and we couldn't leave her behind. She was always begging us to go without her. She said that she had had a good life, and that if we stayed we would all die. But, Tsun-la, how could we leave her? I pleaded with Gyalo again to escape with Pema-la, but she didn't want to leave Ama-la and he would not leave me.

'The yaks and the mules died off one by one of exhaustion and starvation, and the people were dying of starvation, too, especially the old ones. So, those whom the Han had taken as prisoners were made to pull the ploughs, particularly the lamas.

'I had seen children who were ill before the occupation, but never like this. They were starving, their bones showing through their flesh, their bellies blown out. It was terrible to watch them dying. None of us had known anything like it in our lives.

'Deputations of villagers demanded from the Working Committee that adequate food be given them, but all we were told was that we should send our children to China, where they would be properly fed and receive a good education. Many of the members of the deputation were arrested. Some of the parents, not being able to bear the sight of their children suffering, and feeling that there was no hope for them if they stayed, let them go. But Pema insisted that she would rather stay, and die if she must; she would not leave us, and we had no wish to force her to go.'

Yangchen sipped her tea as she relived the past, but it was an unconscious action.

'Then one day, in the Autumn of 1953, a Han patrol knocked at our door. It was after sunset and we had just returned from working in the fields. They informed us that more volunteers were needed to work on the new Chamdo-to-Lhasa road and that Gyalo was to be one of the "volunteers". We protested, telling them that he was the only man in the family, and that we women were not strong enough to support ourselves without his help. But they didn't even bother to listen. They said we could write to him and that we could send him supplies. Send supplies! When we had not even got enough for ourselves!

'They spoke of our patriotic duty to the Motherland. Oh, Kunjosum, I could have killed them. The corporal in charge of the patrol said that the Great Motherland would look after us. When he realised that we were not impressed, he reminded us that we were of the third class in society. We were the ones who traded, who had our own herds.

'He didn't have to say more. We knew what happened to "reactionary landlords" and their relatives. We were helpless. Pema-la was at the back of the house with Ama-la. She kept calling out, wanting to know what was happening. Gyalo and I stayed quite calm. They gave us no time. He was to leave with them. I gave him all the food I could find, I knew he would need it more than us. Then . . . he was taken from me . . .'

Tears welled up in her eyes and spilled down her cheeks. 'I am sorry,' she said. 'I should not cry. I thought I was empty of tears. It is seeing you again. The memories that I've shut out come crowding back.

'So, Gyalo was sent away. I used to send him pathetically small food packages, through traders who were travelling along the new Chamdo-to-Lhasa road, but I doubt if he ever received them. Sometimes, a trader would bring a message from him. They didn't tell us much, for he was never very good at writing, but they meant that he was still alive. Then there was silence.

'All I have left of him are those little scraps of paper. The last one mentioned an uprising of the road workers. He knew that he was going to be arrested, but he said that, some day, somewhere, we would be together again, and that he would never rest until this was made possible.'

Yangchen's eyes closed. She dropped her head into her hands and quietly sobbed. Tsun gently stroked her head. She quickly wiped away the tears and sat staring unseeingly at the floor as she continued.

'Some weeks later, I was told that extra help was needed at the laundry in the local garrison. The money was quite good and I could still work in the fields when I had finished there. I had to collect and deliver the officers' laundry, and one of them, who spoke Tibetan, seemed to like me. After a few visits, he asked me to sit down and we talked for a short while. This went on for a few weeks. Then I discovered that I was down on the list of men and women, aged between fifteen and forty, who were to go to the special clinic that had been opened. No one knew why we were going, and I was scared and did not want to go, but I didn't dwell on it. The work at the laundry left little time for thought.

'Then, rumours started trickling through to us. It was whispered that some of the patients had been bed-ridden after attending the clinic and were in great pain, that the Han were experimenting on us. Of course, this made all those on the list very frightened. So I mentioned to the Han officer who talked with me that I was going to the clinic, to try and find out from him what it was they were doing there. He didn't answer my questions, but seemed concerned. He asked me what day I was due to go and that was all.

'When the day came, a truck arrived to collect those who had to attend from the laundry. It was in the evening. I suppose I must have looked as frightened as I felt, for one of the soldiers helped me to climb into the truck and whispered to me that I would be all right and wasn't to worry.

'There was a curfew in force that night, owing to recent attacks from the resistance on soldiers in the village. It was eerie driving through the silent village, it seemed empty except for the patrols. There were about twenty of us in the truck, all women, some very young girls, and so scared that they couldn't stop crying. The older women sat quiet, silently praying. Then, as we drew near to the clinic, one of the girls became hysterical. The strain must have been too much. She tried to throw herself out of the back of the truck. We grabbed her and tried to quieten her, but she was so strong, and fought us like a wild animal.

'Then the corporal in charge got up and slapped her hard across the face, and shouted at her to keep quiet. But it only made her worse, so that she wrenched herself out of our grip and threw herself from the truck.

'She fell heavily and lay in a heap. We thought that she must have injured herself, but she started to get up. The corporal hammered on the roof of the driver's cab to make him stop. Then the girl scrambled to her feet and ran. The corporal drew his pistol and aimed it at her. We all flung ourselves at him, but the soldiers pulled us back. In the confusion the girl got away. The corporal swore at us, then shouted to the driver to move on.

'As he accelerated, we heard shouts, then a burst of gunfire followed by a scream, then silence. None of us spoke. We were numb with horror.

'The clinic was a bleak square building, and even as we climbed out of the truck, the smell of disinfectant hung on the night air. Many of the women had never smelt the sharp smell of disinfectant before and it frightened them. We were taken into a cold, bare waiting room and told to sit on the wooden benches. The walls and ceiling were painted white, as were the entrance and corridors. The impersonal cleanliness of the place did nothing to calm our fears. A few of the women said their rosaries openly, and the guards didn't attempt to stop them. This made me even more worried. I was very frightened, and terrified of what might happen to Pema and Ama-la if I became bed-ridden.

'Then, a woman in a white coat came to fetch us. We were led away one by one, with quite long intervals in between. No one came back.

'I had learnt a little Chinese while working at the laundry, so I was able to ask the guard what was happening. He said that he didn't know, but he had heard one of the doctors say that the operation would make us more intelligent. By now, I was sick with fear, for I had been clinging to the hope that we would only be going to have something simple done, like . . . oh, Jigme, I shouldn't be telling you this . . .'

Tsun tried to soothe her. He stroked her hand. 'Yangchen,' he said gently, 'I am going to see the Kundun. He should be told of these terrible things. The outside world must be told of them.' His eyes were full of grief and concern for her. He knew, also, of the risk he was taking in even hinting that he intended to make contact with the outside world. But Yangchen hardly heard him. She was reliving again the horrors of the past. She pulled her hand away.

'But, Jigme-la, you are a monk. It is not suitable. I cannot, I would be too embarrassed.'

'Yangchen, you are my sister. I want to know what happened to you.' She was twisting the bottom of her jacket with her fingers. Gently, he placed his hand over hers. 'Tell me, Yangchen,' he said, quietly.

'I have never told anyone this . . .'

'Tell me,' he repeated. 'Then you will be free of it.'

She did not fully understand him, but she knew that she must tell, despite an overwhelming aversion to telling anyone, especially a lama, of what had occurred. She looked down at her hands held in his. Then in a low voice she began.

'By the time the Han woman came to call me, I was almost too weak with fear to stand, but she took a firm grip on my arm and helped me through the door and down a corridor into another large whitewashed room. The windows were shuttered, but it was the most brilliantly lit room I have ever been in. It was like a nightmare room, quite unlike the other clinic Ama-la had been to. It was filled with the stench of disinfectant. Very powerful lights hung low over a strangely tilted couch. The couch was standing in the centre of the room, surrounded by glass-topped trolleys with strange instruments on them.

'A male doctor was in charge, and there were three women nurses with him. One of them ordered me to undress, I didn't move quickly enough, so she started to help me. I pushed her away.

'They spoke in low voices to one another in Han. I couldn't understand what they were saying. One of the nurses put instruments into a container in which boiling water bubbled constantly. The noise was filling the room. There was a coloured photograph of Mao on the wall, but nothing else. One of the nurses told me I was to have a blood test. I thought they would empty me of blood, they took so much. I had to take all my clothes off. It was so humiliating. I was cold and shivering.

'One of the nurses was studying my blood at a bench covered with instruments and equipment. Another nurse asked me my name and age, and wrote this information on a form. I took courage and asked the doctor what would happen to me. He waved my question away irritably, and one of the nurses said that he didn't speak Tibetan and that I did not have to worry, as it would only hurt for a short while. Then the doctor pointed to a bowl and spoke angrily to the nurse standing near it. She covered it quickly with a cloth, but not before I saw a revolting piece of yellow flesh in it. I was nearly sick. The nurse carried the enamel bowl from the room.

'Then the nurse who had been examining my blood led me to the couch. She was about my age and spoke Tibetan. I pleaded with her to tell me what was going to happen to me, but she only tried to soothe me with meaningless words. Then they were strapping me to the couch, and I began to struggle and kick. But they were well practised and strong. My head and arms were held so firmly that I couldn't move. My legs were strapped wide apart and my body thrust up by a hump in the middle of the couch.

'The doctor was wearing rubber gloves . . . oh, Jigme-la . . .' Yangchen looked at her brother despairingly, but she did not stop. 'He fingered my . . . my private parts, and investigated them with a tiny torch. A nurse passed him a rubber tube. He pushed it into me. It was cold and hurt, there was so much of it. I began to scream. With all the energy I had left, I screamed. But no one took any notice. One of the nurses attempted to put a hand to my head to reassure me, but I tried to bite her. I could still feel the tube going inside me. I thought I would faint or die. I could feel its cold knifing my belly. I had exhausted myself with screaming. I longed for unconsciousness, for madness, for some escape. As I watched, the doctor pressed on a balloon which was at the end of the tube. I felt the tube inside me grow. I was in agony. I begged them to stop, pleaded with them. Then the pain was so intense that I could not speak.

'Tears streamed down my face. I could see the picture of Mao over the doctor's shoulder. I pleaded with it, begged it to stop them hurting me. It felt as though my whole body was being blown up. I thought I was going to burst . . . then I must have fainted.

'I don't know for how long I was unconscious, but when I regained my senses I was being unstrapped from the couch. There was blood and something being carried away in a bowl. I was very sick. Then someone gave me an injection with a needle in my buttock. The nurse who spoke Tibetan gave me ten pills. One to take in the morning and one at night for five days. As she helped me to get dressed, she said I was to tell no one of what had happened. Only that I had been given an injection to protect me from venereal disease.

'We were taken back to our homes in the truck. None of us talked. We felt too ill and frightened. When I got out of the truck I could scarcely walk. Pema-la was very frightened, too, by the way I looked, but I told her nothing for I knew she would never be able to keep it to herself.

'The following day, I was too ill to go to the laundry and was so worried about where we would get the money to buy food that Pema-la said she would go to the laundry in my place. On the next day, the captain came to see me, saying that he had heard from Pema of my illness. He was very kind and brought some food as a gift and we talked of our families.

'He visited me every day for a week. Life was dull for the troops; mostly they were confined to barracks and there were very few girls who would have anything to do with them. He said that he loved me. I told him that I liked him as a friend and was deeply grateful for all that he had done for me, but that I was waiting for my husband to come back. I was crying. He comforted me and told me that he was being sent to Derge. He said I would be bed-ridden for some days, but if I agreed to go with him to Derge, I could take Ama-la and Pema-la with me, and that they would get proper care and food. He spoke sincerely. He agreed to let me think his offer over for a few days.

'I didn't know what to do. My mind wandered. Poor Pema-la thought I must be going mad. My strength didn't return and gradually I realised that I would have to accept the captain's offer. I wrote a note for Gyalo and hid it where he would find it if he returned. I did not tell him of the captain, only that we had gone to Derge and Chopel would know where to find us. Pema-la understood why I had agreed, but Ama-la was furious. She refused, at first, to come. We had some terrible arguments, but she, too, was too weak to look after herself and finally had to give in.

'Our neighbours agreed to look after the house for us. Not that it was worth anything. A Han jeep came to collect us at dawn. I knew what concern it would cause Gyalo if the neighbours told him when he returned that we had been taken away in a jeep, but neither Ama-la nor I could walk and we couldn't expect the neighbours to help us get to the garrison.

'It was a long journey from Doi to Derge. Twice we were attacked by the resistance. I felt a traitor then, having to take cover from the bullets fired by my own people. The journey was too much for Ama-la and, despite my hopes, she could not reconcile herself to being under the protection of the Han. She lost the will to live. I tried to explain, but she would not listen. I knew she was dying because I had forced her to make the journey. I prayed that she would live long enough to reach Derge, but she died a few miles from the town. It was my fault for bringing her. If she was to die, it should have been in her own home, not in the company of our enemies. I shall never forgive myself.'

'Yangchen,' Tsun said gently, 'you did what you could. She had her family with her. Many were not so fortunate.' There was an ache in his chest. His mind was flooded with childhood memories of his mother. 'Go on with your story, Yangchen.'

'We cremated Ama-la. The captain had troops cut the wood. She had a noble's funeral, but not a religious one. Tsun, please make sure that she is protected. I have been unable to persuade the monks at the Derge Gonchen monastery to do anything for her. Not that there are many of them there now. I am privileged now, Tsun-la, we do not suffer hunger, but I cannot leave the camp without an escort. Partly, it is funny, but . . . for my own protection. To the townspeople I am a traitor. They know that I eat well while they starve. Li, the captain, is good to me. I have asked him many times what happened to me when I was at the clinic, but he would never tell me. Then, during the journey, the first time he made love to me, suddenly, I knew.

'I felt sorry for Li. He loves me and he was gentle. He loved me then ardently, but I felt nothing. It was not only because I did not love him, I could not react. My body was in a sleep from which his kisses and caresses could not waken it. It was as if something within me had died. I knew then that I had been made barren.' She paused, then continued.

'About a month ago, in the town, I met our cousin, Tul-lok. He was pleased to see me and told me that he had learnt that I had access to some useful information. He asked me to pass this information to the resistance. I have done this, but I do not know how long I can continue. It also distresses me to deceive Li and to use him in this way, for he has been so very good to me. I don't know how long I shall be safe here, but I must get Pema-la away.

'She has been attending Han schools for so long now that she has changed. She is becoming like them. She was only ten years old when Tibet was invaded. Please, Tsun-la, take her away with you.' She got up and stood looking out of the window. 'So many children are being sent to China, I'm sure they will want Pema-la to go.' She turned to face Tsun. 'Please say you will take her with you.'

Tsun tried to smile. 'Of course, Yangchen, and you must come too.'

She ran to him and clasped him tightly. 'Oh, Tsun-la, it is so good to see you. Perhaps there is some hope left, but I cannot come, for if I leave here I am sure that Gyalo will never find me. I must stay in Derge.'

Tsun was silent for a moment, stroking her head. 'For how long will you stay?' he asked. 'The Han are clever, they will find out before long that you are deceiving them.'

She raised her head slightly and gazed into his dark eyes. Then moved away to fill the kettle with water.

'I do not know what to do,' she said. 'I have already promised to get some very important information for Tul-lok which he says will affect the whole future of Tibet. Hope had died in me, Tsun-la. Working for Tul-lok brings some back, not just for myself, but for our country. I cannot leave now. It is important that I stay for a few more weeks.'

She lit the stove and put the kettle on it.

'Is that because of the visit of Chen-Yi?' Tsun asked. Yangchen spun round. Her brother's face was stern.

'Yes,' she answered nervously.

'Tell me about it, Yangchen.'

'I cannot Tsun-la, please do not ask me. I promised Tul-lok I would tell no one.'

Tsun frowned deeply. 'Tul-lok is planning to kill Marshal Chen-Yi on his way to the inauguration of the Preparatory Committee. You are to give him the information on his route and the timing of his visit.'

Yangchen stared at him wide eyed. 'No . . .' she said, but by the inflection in her voice Tsun knew he was right.

'It is madness,' he insisted. 'If the Han Defence Minister is killed by the resistance, the Han will have no mercy in taking reprisals and nothing will be gained.'

'But the world will know of . . .'

'Who told you that? Tul-lok? Our cousin knows nothing of the outside world! For a few days, the eyes of the world will look with interest on our agony, but that is all. While innocent Tibetans will die as a result of this folly.'

'But innocent men and women are dying all the time,' Yangchen replied angrily.

'This will only add to their number. The Kundun has little enough power to stave off the Han. This will destroy what is left.'

'How can you be sure?'

'Reason, Yangchen. Chen-Yi is a member of the Politbureau. His killing would be just the excuse the Han are looking for. And what will it achieve? There is only one thing you can be certain of achieving: reprisals! The destruction of the little that is left of our independence.'

Yangchen moved restlessly round the room, picking things up and putting them down again.

'Rinposhay, you are a holy lama. You do not believe in violence. I know that, ultimately, you are right, but Tul-lok and I have to fight for our country.'

'Fighting for your country should make it even more necessary for you to have unclouded reasoning. A clear perception of the situation. This is stupidity.'

Yangchen shook her head. She did not wish to go against her brother, neither did she want to go against the promises she had given her cousin. She crumbled tea into the teapot.

'I would like to meet Tul-lok,' Tsun said.

'He will not be in Derge for another nine days.' Tsun could not wait that long. He had to meet Kesang, Genyen and the others in three days' time.

'Where is he?' he asked.

'I do not know.'

'Is there any way in which I could get a message to him?'

Yangchen shook her head again. 'No! I have to wait for him to contact me.'

'Then when he does contact you, tell him that I am eager to speak to him. Tell him it is most urgent.'

'Where will he find you?'

Tsun was silent, then he said, 'Tell him when you see him that I know of his mission and that it is doomed to failure. Say that I beg him to relinquish it. Remember that, and now repeat it back to me.'

Yangchen repeated his message. Tsun stood up and took his sister by the shoulders. 'Yangchen, please come with me.'

'I want to,' she murmured, 'but I cannot, not yet.'

'It is said that the chance of being born a human being is rarer than the success of a turtle leaping from the seas through a golden yoke. It is true, Yangchen. Do not sacrifice your life for a mission that can only fail.'

'My life finished a long time ago, Tsun-la.' Yangchen turned abruptly away and busied herself with pouring tea. 'When are you leaving Derge? I have talked so much that you have not been able to tell me where you are going.'

'It would be safer if you did not know, Yangchen.' He was aware of his sister's hurt feelings. 'The Han want me. They are hunting me. It will be dangerous to take Pema-la with me, but I will try to get her to safety.'

'With you,' Yangchen said, 'she has a chance. Here, she has nothing.' She sipped the scalding hot tea.

Tsun shook his head. 'Here, she is among the favoured. The Han nurture the young, re-educate them for the new Tibet. She is more sure of her life than you or I. We are irremediably chained to the past; one way or another, we will die with that past.'

Yangchen did not understand. 'You mean,' she asked in shocked tones, 'that everything is lost forever?'

'No, not everything,' he murmured sadly. 'But the terrible trials of our country are not yet over. We must consider Pema-la's future carefully.'

'That is what I am doing, Rinposhay,' Yangchen said. 'So please take her with you. If she is sent to China we shall never see her again.'

Tsun considered for a moment, then nodded his head.

'Very well,' he said. 'I will do as you ask.' He frowned. 'I am worried for you, Yangchen. There is the poison of hatred working strongly in you. I want you to come with me also. You know that, by the law of karma, the Han will eventually receive exactly what they have forced on others. Revenge is unnecessary, and hatred will destroy you more surely than our enemy.'

'I try not to hate,' Yangchen answered quietly. 'I do not have control over my feelings any more.'

'We should stay together as a family,' Tsun insisted. 'In this way we can help each other.'

'I want to come with you,' she said. 'You have brought hope and sanity back into my life. But I am needed here by the resistance, and I always hope that Gyalo will come looking for me. For Pema it is different.'

Tsun tapped out snuff onto the side of his thumb from a jade bottle.

'Yangchen,' he said, 'when it is possible for you to get away from here, go to the Dorje Ri-gon house in Lhasa.'

She smiled faintly. 'I will, Rinposhay,' she said, and came to sit down once more beside him. 'We are allowed nothing of the Dharma here. Please, give me something.'

'Do you remember Grandmother's image of Chenresi? It stood on the shrine in her room.'

'Yes. It was my favourite as a child.'

'Can you visualise it? Picture it in your mind?' Yangchen nodded.

'Then,' Tsun said, 'regularly, during each day, take refuge in the Triple Gem and beseech the blessing of the Triple Gem, as we were taught as children. Concentrate on that image of Chenresi. See it as a solid object, but do not strain. At first, let it be only for a few minutes. But be sure that you persevere, Yangchen. It will serve to quieten your mind, to give it a one-pointed concentration. Constant thoughts will arise. Whatever their content, let them float by as clouds in the sky, being unmoved by them and not giving them any attention.'

As he spoke, Tsun could see an unease in her eyes that made him pause. 'Yangchen, what I am saying troubles you?'

Her eyes reflected guilt and surprise that he should see so much. She hesitated in answering and, to her, the seconds of silence grew oppressive and imprisoning. She wound the corner of her faded shirt round her fingers and tilted her head like a nervous child about to make a confession.

'For so many years, Tsun . . . it is not that I don't believe . . . but for so long they have spoken to me only of Communism, questioned the Religion . . . I do not believe them, but it seems to have . . . to have . . .'

She burst into tears and buried her face in her hands. Gently, Tsun stroked her head, and soothingly murmured her name.

'I doubt, Tsun. I doubt . . . what is left?' She raised her head and looked at him with tortured eyes. 'I no longer have faith in that which I have always believed to be the basis of my life . . .' Tears welled up in her eyes and flowed down her cheeks. Tsun smiled as he brushed away the tears.

'Yangchen,' he said softly, 'doubt is a path. You know as well as I do that every person is different in his or her capacity to learn and understand.' He moved over to the window and looked out at the long, low barracks.

'Out there, I see the horses of the Han cavalry being groomed, and in the distance one of the iron guns that I believe they call . . . tanks. Tell me, Yangchen, is it likely that a soldier who could ride the horses could also drive one of the tanks?' He turned to look at her, waiting for an answer. She sniffed and shook her head slowly. 'No.'

Tsun nodded. 'So it is with the Religion, Yangchen. It has many paths at different levels; someone on one path cannot understand another path, and so we have what are called 'hidden teachings'. Hidden, because people will not see!' He moved to the centre of the room. 'Now if the resistance attack somewhere in Derge, how would the PLA soldiers get to the area under attack?'

Yangchen looked puzzled. 'By truck, some I suppose would march, some would travel in armoured cars or jeeps . . .'

'Exactly!' Tsun emphasised his words with slightly stylized gestures, as a result of participating in so many monastic debates. 'Many different ways to the same destination. So it is with our Religion.'

Yangchen shook her head in bewilderment. 'I know there are many paths, Tsun, but I doubt the reality of these paths, so what is left for me?'

'Doubt, Yangchen, doubt! That is *your* path. Now the choice is up to you. Do you choose ignorance, or do you use your doubt to question and explore?'

'But, Tsun,' Yangchen looked at him imploringly, 'I have no teacher . . .'

'When you need a teacher, one will come, but you will find you have all you need within yourself. Let me show you where doubt can lead you, just a glimpse . . .' He paused. 'Just a glimpse . . .'

Sitting on the couch, Yangchen was aware of the presence that emanated from her brother, that made his words appear as symbols of knowledge impossible to impart. She found it hard to believe that the brother she had played with as a child, and this man, were the same person.

'Just before he died,' Tsun went on, 'the Buddha himself called upon his followers to *doubt* and to accept nothing that they could not *themselves* prove! Remember that, Yangchen. Realise its significance.'

The sunlight streamed through the window onto his tanned face, and Yangchen felt almost frightened at the way he seemed to retreat from her gaze. Tsun did not look at her, but into her, and there was a quality of joy in his eyes.

'That glimpse that doubt can give you,' he said. 'So we doubt the Religion . . . that is nothing.' Yangchen was lost now. 'Tell me, Yangchen, what is the nature of Reality?' But he did not wait for her answer. 'Everything you can describe as being yourself, everything, is subject to the same laws of change.'

Yangchen got up and added more water to the kettle, replacing it on the paraffin stove. She seemed perplexed and was frowning as Tsun continued.

'A Han scientist will tell you that your body is basically emptiness, yet it is energy-filled emptiness. An indefinable emptiness. You must use your doubts, Yangchen. Question what I have said, test its validity.'

Yangchen pulled thoughtfully at her pigtail, then got up to pour the now boiling water onto the fresh tea she had crumbled into the enamel teapot. She stood waiting for the tea to brew, silently reflecting on what her brother had said.

'I can see what you mean, Jigme-la . . . I think . . . but what can *I* do?'

'Each person has individual circumstances; yours are such that I have spoken to you of things which, although you cannot fully comprehend now, you will. Visualise Grandmother's bronze image of Chenresi. It has been consecrated with powerful thoughts of men of great vision. It is as though those men were a mirror and reflected the light of the sun into the image. Just think on the image, and think on what I have said. There are two truths, Yangchen. The relative truth, relative reality, of how you perceive yourself and the world, and the absolute truth, the ultimate reality, that the Buddha discovered when he became enlightened. We all have that same power of discovery within ourselves, if we follow the advice of the Buddha, to seek, to question, to experience for ourselves what is real.'

Yangchen poured the tea into the two enamel mugs and handed one to her brother, sucking in her breath as she did so. Tsun took the tea in one hand and grasped her hand with the other. 'Yangchen, he said, 'you cannot doubt too much or you would not grant me the courtesy of respect as you do.'

Yangchen laughed. The atmosphere was suddenly lighter. She hugged her brother and clung to him, his hand stroking her hair.

'I have tried, Yangchen, to show you ways to use your doubts creatively. To question what people commonly call reality, and to find a source of comfort on which to draw in your hours of pain, and to realise, too, that you are not alone. Use and cling to Chenresi and use his mantra, for the force is very great and will sustain you. At first, little will seem to happen, but persevere and you will see glimpses that will keep your feet on the path.'

'Jigme-la.' She swallowed to clear the constriction in her throat. 'I wish you were not going . . .'

Yangchen bowed her head, and in that austere little room, Tsun laid his hands on her head and murmured an invocation.

'As I impart this blessing,' he said, 'be assured that it will strengthen you for all things. Through it you will draw on the courage of the awakened, by it you will find refuge in the Triple Gem that is enshrined in your heart.'

For a few moments, they stood looking into each other's eyes. Then at last Yangchen said:

'Where shall Pema-la meet you?'

'In the Square, tomorrow, by the chorten.' He noticed she was wearing a watch. 'At four o'clock.'

'She has grown, Rinposhay, you will not recognise her.'

'Will she be wearing Han clothing?'

'Yes.'

'Tell her to carry her cap in her left hand.'

Yangchen glanced at her watch. 'Li will be back soon, do you want to meet him?'

'No,' Tsun moved towards the door. He took some silver coins from his pocket. 'Take these,' he said, offering them to her.

'No, Jigme.' Yangchen refused to take them. 'You will need money.'

'Please, Yangchen.' Tsun pressed the coins into her hand and folded her fingers over them. Yangchen reluctantly held on to the coins, then took some biscuits and gave them to Tsun.

'It is so little.' She gazed at him with tear-filled eyes. 'Oh, Jigme-la, there is so much more to be said.' She clung to him and wept.

'Whatever happens,' he tilted her chin up and looked down into her face, 'we shall be together.'

He put her back from him and gently opened the door, leaving her alone. As he walked to the main gate, his mind was filled with all that Yangchen had told him. He wished that he had been able to see his mother before she had died. He would conduct the after death ceremony for her. So much of his life had gone. So much that made up his identity. It was as though the mental techniques he used, in an attempt to destroy his imagined ego, were being enacted in the physical realm.

The main gates were closed. Tsun looked for the sentry who had let him in, but another had taken his place. He glanced round the square. A troop of soldiers were being marched across it. Another troop, in vests and shorts, were being taken in PT. Tsun walked up to the round-faced corporal leaning against the door frame of the sentry hut. His hand rested on the butt of his gun. He looked at Tsun with sardonic eyes.

'I have been visiting my sister,' Tsun said politely. 'Now I wish to leave.'

'You have a pass?' the corporal asked in very bad Tibetan.

Tsun put his hand into his pocket. The pass was not there. He searched through the rest of his pockets, but could not find it.

'I must have dropped it.'

The corporal waved him aside and stepped into the hut. 'Come and interpret,' he ordered a trooper inside. The man came out, carrying his rifle. The corporal indicated with an imperious wave of his hand that Tsun should repeat what he had said.

'I have been visiting my sister,' Tsun explained.

The trooper interpreted.

'Why have you no pass?' the corporal demanded. He looked bored. He called to another soldier in the hut. 'Telephone through and check up on his sister,' and turning to Tsun, asked, 'What is her name?'

'Yangchen Li.'

'Yangchen Li,' the corporal repeated. He sized Tsun up lazily. 'Live in Derge?'

'No.'

'Where?'

'In a small village called Baje.'

'Never heard of it. What brings you to Derge?'

'To see relatives. To buy things.'

'Who came with you?'

'I came alone.'

The corporal frowned. Here was a man who could well be in the resistance. Tall, strong, and with an impudent inflexion in his voice.

'Where are your papers?' The corporal's words struck Tsun like a blow. It was impossible to make a dash for freedom, the barbed wire-topped fence was at least eight foot high. He must try and bluff his way out.

'We haven't been given papers in Baje,' he said. 'We are as one family, why should we need papers?'

'Everyone needs papers.' The soldier interpreting seemed slightly surprised at such ignorance.

'Our cadre,' Tsun spoke in a low tone, his face showing no sign of emotion, 'our cadre asked me to buy Chairman Mao's *Selected*

Works, Volume III: Some questions concerning leadership.' Tsun repeated the title he had read in the shop earlier.

This is a clever fellow, the corporal thought. He distrusted clever Tibetans.

'We need the book,' Tsun continued, 'for the special night classes we are holding.'

The telephone call had been made, the second soldier mumbled something into the corporal's ear. The corporal gave a slight sneer. He jerked his head towards the gate.

'You can go,' he said derisively. 'Your sister's here.'

Tsun smiled, bowed, and walked towards the gate without any sign of haste.

'Open up!' the corporal shouted at the gate keeper, who unlocked the tall metal gates and swung them just wide enough for Tsun to get through. Tsun felt the corporal's eyes boring into his back as he walked out of the camp and then the gates clanged shut behind him.

Chapter Eight

A hint of spring was in the air as Tsun walked back to Chopel's house through the streets of Derge. His mind worked constantly on how he might persuade Yangchen to travel with him. He stopped occasionally to browse round the stalls and shops without really seeing anything clearly. At one stall, he picked up some turnips and weighed them in his hand.

'How much?' he asked the old woman in charge.

'Three yuan.'

'Kunjosum!'

'You will not find finer in Derge, Kusho,' the old woman assured him.

Tsun paid the price without haggling, which surprised the woman, but he was in no mood for it. He tucked the turnips into the fold of his chuba.

Some children were playing in the street. One ragged, muddy little girl nearly bumped into him as she tried to keep a shuttlecock in the air with her bare feet. She was laughing. Tsun paused for a few moments to watch the game. It was good to hear the children's uninhibited laughter as they leaped, ran and deftly kicked the little copper ball of the shuttlecock, shouting their score to one another. For a brief moment Tsun was able to forget the constant quiver of the web in which he was caught, as the spider advanced towards its prey.

As he turned away, he caught sight of Ling looking at some cloth on the other side of the road. She was dressed in the same blue tunic and trousers, but was not wearing a cap. Apparently, she had not seen him. Surely he had not been tracked down; he walked quickly along the street. The sight of her caused shimmering memories to boil up in his mind, memories of much that he wanted to forget. He paused and appeared to be looking at a carpet stall. Out of the corner of his eye he saw Ling coming nearer. Tsun was still not used to being hunted and felt a physical stab of fear. He walked casually on down the street, heading for a crowd of Tibetan and Han civilians clustered round a dice game. He pushed his way through them. People shouted at him for barging, as they placed side bets on the players. Ducking into a narrow alleyway, Tsun looked back; he could see no sign of Ling, so ran as fast as he could, nearly knocking over an old woman who was standing quietly relieving herself beneath her thick, ankle-length skirt.

At the end of the alley, Tsun turned to look back again. There was still no sign of Ling. He had lost her. Over and over in his mind he turned the reasons why she should be there at that moment. She could have been following him, but there was also a curious empathy between them which ensured that they would meet again.

Tsun eased himself down another alley, crowded with the clientele of the craftsmen whose workshops were there. If she had seen him, Ling would alert the authorities that he was in Derge; he was sure of that. Patrols would be on the lookout for him. Derge was not that large, he thought, and the Han were very efficient. He knew that he must leave the town quickly, but realised that this would make him even more vulnerable since the patrols at the exits of the town would be particularly watchful. He wondered if his presence in the camp that afternoon would be discovered. He was tired and depressed. Perhaps he would know tomorrow at his meeting with his sister, Pema.

Tsun bought some raw yak meat from one of the stalls and became conscious of the envious glances of the passersby. They were envious because he had enough money to pay the exorbitant prices.

He was quite near Chopel's house when he heard the jeeps and motorcycles. People scattered instantly, herding their children into doorways and alleys away from the street. A motor cycle roared past. Tsun's immediate thought was that Ling had informed the occupation authorities, and that all this was to bring about his capture. He slipped into a dark and dingy inn packed with men drinking barley beer, and slammed the door shut behind him. People were crowding to the small windows. All around Tsun, anxious voices were debating the reason for the Han blocking off the street. He saw beside him a middle-aged man quietly loading bullets into a pistol.

Jeeps with four-man crews and mounted machine guns had sealed off all exits from the street. The officer commanding the operation consulted a list as he walked slowly down the mud street with some of his men, and indicated certain houses. Troops were detailed to each side of the street and, starting at the far end, began hammering on doors shouting for them to be opened.

Tsun could see nothing, but every action of the troops was reported by those at the windows for the benefit of those unable to see. Tsun pushed his way towards the back of the inn to find if he could slip through a back door, but there was none.

'It's a deportation squad. They are taking the young ones,' someone shouted.

Tsun could hear the loud protestations of a man and woman in the street, as soldiers led away their daughter, a girl of about thirteen. He forced his way to the window. The rice paper panes had been torn out. A few yards away he saw a soldier manning the machine gun on a jeep, panning it slowly in readiness. The grey-haired parents were gesticulating wildly as they argued with the soldiers; the girl was crying hysterically. The parents rushed up to the officer, the woman's hands tugging at his sleeve as if attempting by physical contact to emphasise her pleas. One of the soldiers lifted the girl onto the truck and climbed up after her, keeping his Russian-made Sten gun ready in his hands as he sat on a bench. The girl leaned over the side of the truck, looking at her parents. Tsun saw her lips moving, her arms stretched out to them. Rage welled up within him, but as he looked at the troops lining the street, the machine guns mounted on the jeeps, he realised that they would have no chance if they resisted.

Other children were being taken from their homes. Someone brushed past him and he looked into the frightened face of the innkeeper's wife; she was carrying her baby tucked into the fold of her dress and was rushing to hide him in an empty cask. Outside the officer ticked off names as the children, ranging from about ten to sixteen years old, were helped into the truck. An argument had developed in the doorway of the house opposite the inn, while inside the inn itself, the innkeeper and some of his customers were attempting to hide his ten year-old daughter by crowding round her.

Farther down the street, the Han were hammering with their rifle butts on a barricaded door. Opposite, an old man was remonstrating with the Han and with his son, a strapping youth of about sixteen. The old man grabbed him, but the youth shook him off and they argued. Tsun saw the Han soldiers laugh. The old man was furious; he grabbed hold of the boy again and began to drag him back into the house, but the youth violently shook himself free, so that the old man fell back into the dust of the street. As the boy jumped up into the truck, Tsun saw him look anxiously at his father when he saw he had fallen and as the old man climbed to his feet, he gazed back at his son for a few seconds. Other children and young people were being loaded onto the truck and a Han soldier came to move the old man on, waving him away with the barrel of his rifle. The old man grabbed at the rifle. It happened in a second! Tsun was not sure if the old man pulled the trigger, but it fired, the shot reverberating through the street. The Han automatically moved into cover, thinking that it heralded an attack.

The old man was sent sprawling against the side of his house. Blood covered his clothes and a thick red puddle formed in the dust. Tsun saw the old man's son start to get down from the truck, but he was pushed back by a soldier. He struggled to get past the soldier but was threatened with a rifle. He slumped onto a bench and wept. A small child, a girl, sitting beside him, also cried. One of the soldiers in the truck put her on his knee and tried to soothe her. Meanwhile two soldiers were coming towards the door of the inn.

'Keep close together. Do not let them part us, then we can hide her in the middle,' one of the men said tensely.

There was a hammering on the door. The innkeeper opened it.

'The time has come,' one of the soldiers said in a thick accent, 'for your daughter to go to school.'

'But she is not here. She is away with relatives in Chamdo,' the innkeeper protested. The soldiers pushed their way into the inn. It was so crowded it was difficult for them to move. The closeness of the Tibetans made the soldiers back up against a wall.

'Out! Come on, all of you, out!'

Keeping the Tibetans covered, they motioned with their rifles, and did not notice a burly farmer lift the little girl up against his bare chest, then fold his bulky, knee-length sheepskin chuba around her body so that it completely covered her. The innkeeper and his customers, including Tsun, crowded in close to the farmer, jostling him as they ducked out of the low doorway of the inn, and stood together by the wall, keeping the farmer well covered.

Tsun watched as, on either side of the narrow dusty street of single and two storeyed, flat roofed houses, families were destroyed. Parents wept. Some had barricaded themselves in: soldiers hammered down the doors. From one house came the hysterical screams subsiding into moans of a woman abandoned to her grief. The younger children were screaming as they were lifted onto the truck, each adding to the fear of the others. Tsun heard the slow clicking of the empty chamber of a revolver, as it was surreptitiously loaded. He wondered how much longer it would be before there was an outburst of violence; how long the Tibetans would be deterred by the threat of the machine guns at either end of the street and the open truck of children in the middle. The atmosphere was as taut as a bow string. The Han knew that at any moment the Tibetans might attack them, which made them frightened and brutal.

'Out! Out!' Fear for her daughter's safety had brought the innkeeper's wife out of hiding, only to be bundled through the doorway by the two soldiers searching the inn. She clutched at her husband who put his arm around her. Her hands were shaking. She saw Tsun looking at them and quickly shook down the long sleeves of her blouse to cover them.

Tsun invoked protection for the baby left alone in the cask and the little girl hidden against the farmer's breast, and for all the other children he knew must be hidden close by. The officer picked up a megaphone from the front seat of the truck and put it to his mouth.

'Listen, all of you. Your children will come to no harm. If you were not so stubborn, we would not have to take them from you by force. They need schooling in the ways of the new Tibet. No harm will come to them. You can write to them, the Work Committee Office will forward your letters.'

He lowered the megaphone and walked briskly back to the jeep. Some of those in the street began to jeer. The soldiers came out of the inn. 'We will be back,' one of them warned the innkeeper.

The roar of the motor cycle engines filled the street. Their wheels sent spumes of dust into the air.

'Praise be to the Triple Gem, they did not find my babies,' the innkeeper's wife sobbed with relief. Her husband urged her to be quiet and to get back into the inn quickly before anyone realised what had happened. The engine of the truck roared to life. The children in it waved to their parents, and called and cried as the truck moved off. They kept calling and waving until the truck disappeared from sight.

'We will have to get her away quickly,' the innkeeper muttered to Tsun, as the farmer carried his daughter, still hidden, back into the inn. As he spoke, the jeep bringing up the rear of the column swept past, covering them with dust and making the tethered horses rear.

'Where will the children be taken?' Tsun asked a man who was spinning a hand-held prayer wheel.

'Who knows?' was his anxious reply.

Tsun remained looking down the road after the convoy had gone. Neighbours were commiserating with one another; the sound of weeping filled the street. Some of the men from the inn mounted their horses and urged them into the brisk trot peculiar to Tibetan ponies.

Tsun continued his walk up the steep streets back to Chopel's house. For a moment he hesitated, thinking of Ling and wondering if perhaps the Han were waiting. It was almost sunset when he arrived. He entered the back way, past the lean-to stable where Namgyal was bedding down Tsun's horse. He slapped the animal's rump.

'It is the fastest animal in Derge, Kusho,' he told Tsun. 'You will have to be careful that someone doesn't steal it for food.'

'A protective spell was put on that horse by a powerful magician,' Tsun smiled. 'Anyone who steals it will forever have to ride it across the icy wastes of the Chang Tang Plateau.'

The boy frowned, undecided whether he should believe Tsun or not. Tsun smiled to himself, for he knew that if anyone was likely to steal his horse, it would be Namgyal.

Inside the small dark house, Dekyi was stirring a mixture in a copper saucepan, while Chopel sat cross-legged on a rug saying his rosary. He rose when Tsun entered and made a place for him to sit, then continued to finger his rosary.

'Did you see your sister, Kusho?' Dekyi asked.

'Yes,' replied Tsun, 'and I am grateful to you for arranging it.' He brought the turnips and yak meat out from his ambac and handed them to the girl.

'Pa-la, look, meat! The Rinposhay has brought meat! Namgyal-la! Namgyal-la!' The boy came running in from the stable, his eyes alight. Any pleasure Tsun felt at their happiness was lost in awareness of the days ahead. Where would their meals come from then?

As Dekyi began cooking the meat, Tsun looked at Chopel.

'On my way back I saw some children being taken by the Han.'

'Where, what part of town?'

'The Knot of Eternity Street.'

Chopel looked up from his rosary. 'I must visit my cousin. Her child will have been taken. Oh, Kunjosum! Will it never stop?' His bald head was creased with anxiety. 'How long ago was this, Kusho?'

'A pipeful's time.'

'Too late to ambush the truck,' Chopel sighed. 'They will be at the garrison by now.'

'What happens to them then?'

'They will be taken in one of the large convoys to China.'

'Is there any way of getting them out of the garrison?'

'The camp is well fortified. It is too big. We have not been able to get in so far. Anyway, I couldn't get the men together in time.'

Tsun was thinking of the newly arrived tanks. 'You've been able to rescue some children, then?'

'Yes, Kusho, when we have known in time that they were being taken. I tell my friends and we ambush the truck before it reaches the garrison. But it is harder now that the Han expect to be ambushed. They are more careful.'

'What happens to the children when you've rescued them?'

'We keep them hidden until we can find someone who will take them to Lhasa.'

Dekyi offered Tsun some greenish watery soup.

'My apologies for the poorness of our food,' she said, ladling it into his bowl. 'The meat will be ready soon.'

'Ah, Dekyi,' Tsun said. 'Did not our most famous poet saint, Milarepa, eat nettle soup? I wonder if we shall turn green like him?' They escaped into laughter for a brief instant, their humour naive and unsubtle.

'Chopel, what happened to the beggars and the dogs and the birds?' Tsun asked. 'The pigeons and magpies? There used to be scores of them in the city.'

'They were considered harmful to the people. There is a word they use . . .' He could not remember. 'You know what I mean.'

'Parasites.' Dekyi said.

Her father nodded as he packed tobacco into his clay pipe with its twelve inch arched stem.

'We had to kill . . .' He hesitated to tell a Holder of the Dharma that he had killed anything, for it was to break one of the fundamental precepts. After all, it appeared that one was cursed enough in this life without compromising one's position in the next, and a Rinposhay had influence in both realms.

'The Han tried to use the beggars at first. Told them to seize the property of those better placed. But they refused, so then they were offered money. Some have become collaborators, but most have been taken to work on the roads. We had to kill the dogs, the birds . . .' he shrugged in remembered pain.

'It was strange walking through the town without the birds. It was as though they had all stopped singing and were waiting with apprehension, just as they do before a storm approaches.'

Chopel frowned. He did not like to hear such things from a Rinposhay. They could be taken as a prophecy or, even worse, disaster.

'What news of the Queen, Chopel? I must leave by tomorrow night at the latest.'

The old man slipped a piece of flint out of a brass-studded leather purse and struck it on the curving metal blade forming the bottom of the pouch. The sparks caught the edelweiss grass. As it flared, Chopel applied it to the bowl of his pipe and sucked hard to make it draw.

'Kusho,' he said, 'I told her secretary that I had some business with her concerning an order which she placed with me. In fact, I had not, but I knew that Her Majesty would realise that I had something important to tell her. Anyway, she saw me. It was difficult, Kusho, for many members of her court are Han spies now. We talked of the "job" and I mentioned "Jigme" while we talked. Her Majesty said she would give further instructions to my assistant in the morning.'

'Excellent, Chopel. I congratulate you. So I am to pose as your assistant to see Her Majesty. Excellent.' Tsun smiled at his friend. 'Do you know of any way I can get supplies for the journey?' He did not miss the quick look Dekyi gave her father.

'You have money?' Chopel asked.

'Yes.'

'Then Namgyal and I shall get your supplies.'

'Pa-la!'

'Be quiet, Dekyi,' Chopel said sharply.

'Chopel, what does it involve? How will you get this food?' Tsun asked, concerned at Dekyi's growing agitation. Namgyal, crouched by the fire, looked on in silence.

'If you are found out they will punish you,' she burst out at her father. 'Do you want your family to suffer? Every day you do something more . . .'

Chopel looked at Tsun. There was no way of appeasing his daughter. She was frightened and lived constantly in fear of her life and that of her father and brother.

'It is true, Chopel,' Tsun said quietly. 'You must not risk your own safety and that of your family for mine.'

'I will judge the risk, Kusho,' Chopel insisted.

'Where does the food come from? I mean, who supplies it?'

'Some from people who have hidden it from the Han. Those who prefer money to food. They gamble on a good harvest, or on things getting better, and that one can always use money, so they sell their food and forget that when you are starving you cannot eat money. But most of the food is stolen from Han warehouses.' Chopel coughed. 'Have you the money with you?'

'Yes.' Tsun handed him some Han dollar bills. 'Is that enough? I shall need as much as I can carry.'

'That will be enough,' Chopel answered.

'Buy what you need for the family, too, Chopel.'

'Kusho, paraffin is so scarce . . .' Dekyi sounded apologetic as she blew out the lamp. 'Even mustard oil . . .'

For some minutes they drank their soup in silence. Dekyi rose and, lifting the pan of meat from the fire, helped them all to the unaccustomed treat. Namgyal was aware of his father's and his sister's troubled minds as they mentally turned over the events of the last few hours, and Tsun's news about the deportation party. Thoughts, questions, echoed in their brains, with no answer.

Eventually, Chopel, reminded by the food they were eating, said:

'Do you remember, Dekyi, when you first ate Han food?'

Dekyi smiled and nodded.

'We had an enormous meal, Kusho, and she couldn't finish all of it. We were at the door on the way out, when we heard Dekyi arguing with the Han waitress. She had filled her hat with all the noodles she had left from the meal and wanted to take them home. She thought they were like tsampa and could be kept in a pouch.' Chopel roared with laughter.

'Pa-la, I was very young.' Dekyi protested.

Their laughter broke the black spell of Tsun's news. After the soup and meat they had tea and chewed tough, dried cheese cubes, while Namgyal asked them riddles. Tsun encouraged the boy, for in their laughter, as they struggled for the answers, Tsun felt the re-awakened spontaneous enjoyment of life that is the reaction of every Tibetan, but which he had seen extinguished across the land just as the flames of a butter lamp are blown out by a mighty wind.

Chapter Nine

The castle of Derge was built high up the side of the valley overshadowing monastery and town. Fanning out from the central complex were turreted walls that followed the contours of the hillside down to the valley floor, a patchwork of fields interlaced with streams. Part of the castle, higher than the rest and older, had fallen into disrepair, the walls and square turrets crumbling.

As Tsun climbed the streets, so narrow and steep that no motor vehicle could negotiate them, he escaped the noise of the loudspeakers. They were exhorting the Tibetans to be politically conscious, to beware of reactionary, counter-revolutionary elements and to implement the policies of the Party.

On either side of him, in irregular tiers, Tsun could see the monastery buildings, painted white with a vertical red stripe beside the windows to indicate that the monastery was of the nine hundred year-old Sakya Order, whose dynasty of Grand Lamas had at one time sat upon the Lion Throne of Tibet.

Tsun looked at the tattered prayer flags on the flat, faggot-edged roofs. Flower pots on the window sills of the monks' apartments held withered plants. The haunting sound of the conch shell filled the air with an infinite sadness as it called the few remaining monks to the temple. The monastery was falling into decay. Chapel doors banged loosely on their hinges in the wind. Tsun walked round a three-foot high incense vase that lay across the path, broken. Weeds were growing in it, earth mingling with the ash of incense. Tsun felt that he was walking through a corpse showing the first signs of decomposition.

'Kusho! Kusho! Blessings upon you, Kusho.'

A man in his thirties, with long, unkempt hair was sitting on the ground holding out his hands to Tsun. Around his neck was a three-foot wide wooden collar. 'Help a hungry man, Kusho, and gain merit.'

Tsun handed the man part of a string of cheese cubes.

'Blessings on you, Kusho,' the man said. 'There is little food about these days, people do not give as before.'

Tsun was trying to read the notice nailed on a board, giving details of his crime, but rain had made the ink run and it was impossible to read.

'I killed a member of our enemy's family,' the man said.

'In a feud?'

'Yes, Kusho. Our families have been feuding for twenty years. I am the only one of the family left.' He lifted the wooden collar up to ease his shoulders. 'My enemy is waiting for when I am released to kill me. So I will have to kill him first.'

'How long have you to remain here?'

'I have been like this for six months. The Governor has probably forgotten that I exist, so who can tell when I shall be free? It is not too bad, though. I stay with a palace official. He sees that I am given some food, so I do not starve. I was fortunate not to be lashed, for I had no money to pay the life money to the family of the man I killed.'

'If I were to obtain your release, would you swear not to seek out and kill your enemy?'

'But he will kill me!' the man protested.

'You could leave the district, start a new life somewhere else, where he could not find you.'

'But that would leave the death of my brothers, my sisters, my father, and my grandfather all unavenged.'

'Today,' Tsun said, 'revenge is sweet. But tomorrow, when we face the Lord of Death, it is very bitter.'

'I shall be born in one of the hells?' He looked questioningly at Tsun. 'You think that?'

Tsun sat on the wall near to him. 'Who can say in what realm of existence you will be born? Any action you take now will have an effect in a moment, in an aeon, but every action, whether a mental thought or a physical deed, will have its effect in your future.'

'You are a monk?'

'I have practised a little religion.'

The man shook his head. 'I know I shall suffer for what I have done, but it is my duty to seek revenge for the wrongs committed against my family. Even if I cannot return a favour, at least I can return evil done to me.'

'And if you kill your enemy, what will become of you?'

'Perhaps I shall escape,' he shrugged. 'Perhaps I shall be caught and punished.'

'You may be lashed to death next time.'

'*If* I am caught,' he laughed.

'Of what use revenge then? Your family will cease to exist when you, the last member, die. Compassion and wisdom are the attributes of a Bodhisattva. Have the wisdom to have compassion on yourself, on your future family.'

The man listened then. He respected Tsun. Obviously he knew what he was talking about and he was gentry, probably with influence.

'I shall bring your release if you swear by the Triple Gem to do as I ask.'

'I swear,' the man said.

Tsun nodded, then got off the wall and walked away.

The Han sentries in their wooden hut at the entrance to the palace were too bored by their ceremonial duty to question as he walked through the open gate. The activity about the courtyard seemed normal enough. The big guard dogs strained at their rusty chains and barked furiously at him. Some of the women, in long serge chubas, were carrying empty pails for water. Goats were being milked. A long-legged, scrawny chicken squawked, running across Tsun's path as he crossed the large stone courtyard towards the wide wooden verandah.

Khamba guards, their hair plaited with coloured threads, squatted on the verandah. They looked up from their game of dice as Tsun approached.

'I have come from Chopel the silversmith, to see Her Majesty.'

One of them pulled himself up with the aid of his Russian-made rifle. He weighed Tsun up thoughtfully, chewing on a cheese cube. The quality of Tsun's clothes, his manner and his bearing, made him more than a silversmith's apprentice, of that he was sure. He beckoned lazily to Tsun and led the way into the palace, to the Chamberlain's office.

It was small, but lighter than most Tibetan rooms, the whole of the large window frame having been removed to allow sunlight to pour in. From the pillars and high walls hung bundle upon bundle of scrolls of letters and documents.

The Chamberlain did not look up as Tsun entered the room. He was bent over a low table, writing. After a few minutes, he replaced his pen in its case, took off his small steel-rimmed spectacles and looked up at Tsun while he breathed on the document to dry the ink. Tsun bowed slightly, sucking in his breath and presenting the Chamberlain, a man in his fifties, with a felicity scarf. The Chamberlain returned it.

'Sit down!' He fingered the symbol of his rank, a long turquoise and gold earring so heavy that it was supported by a leather thong over the left ear, as he looked at Tsun who bowed again, sucking in his breath.

'Your business?' he demanded.

'I have come from Chopel, the silversmith. I have an appointment with Her Majesty.'

The Chamberlain slipped his arm through the loose sleeve of his well-worn, brown serge chuba. He remained silent as he pulled on his black boots with their multicoloured cloth insets and turned-up toes, binding them just below the knee with woven straps. He stood up and indicated for Tsun to follow him.

'The Queen is expecting you.'

They walked along a wide, windowless corridor, the walls covered with intricate frescoes depicting the history of the Derge dynasty. The brilliant colours were muted in the light of the mustard lamps flickering dimly from slates set in the walls. The Chamberlain opened double doors leading into the audience chamber. A slim, slight figure stood against the light of the window.

'Silversmith Chopel's assistant, Majesty,' the Chamberlain said, then bowed and withdrew.

Tsun walked down the avenue of red wooden pillars. When he was near to her, the Queen Regent of Derge stepped forward towards him and, bowing her head slightly, took a panelled white silk scarf, six feet long, from a table and presented it to him. 'Rinposhay, I am honoured.'

She was in her late fifties and would have looked much younger but for the tension in her pale, untanned face. Deftly, Tsun accepted her scarf, then draped his own silk scarf round her neck, lightly touching her head with both hands in blessing. Her long black hair set off her soft pink skin, and the high cheekboned, delicately made-up face.

'Your Majesty is very good to see me.'

'Come, let us go outside.'

Her figure-fitting brocade chuba rustled as she led the way out onto the flat roof of the lower storey overlooking the town and the valley. Her hair was parted in the middle and plaited into a thick waist-length pigtail ending in golden and red tassels which she pulled over her shoulder in respect to Tsun.

'There are spies everywhere, I cannot risk being overheard,' she said quietly.

The roof had been turned into an attractive patio with potted plants, rug-covered mattresses and box-shaped tables beneath a canvas awning. Like great steps, the roofs of the lower storeys led down to the gilded roofs of the printing press, below which stretched the town. They sat down at one of the tables and, with some difficulty, the Queen lifted the heavy brass and silver teapot from its brazier and carefully poured tea for them both. Tsun sucked in his breath and thanked her.

'I have told my servants that we are not to be disturbed,' she explained.

'Will that not cause suspicion, Majesty?'

'Suspicion is my shadow, Rinposhay,' she smiled wearily as she offered him a bowl of apricots. 'Food is scarce, I wish I could offer you more.'

Tsun demurred.

'I had hoped one day to be able to visit your monastery.'

'I fear that by now it has been seized by the Han. We were fortunate to escape. Litang is in ruins.'

'So is Derge, spiritually.' She looked down at the town and monastery. 'But what news of the resistance?'

'The co-ordinated rising that we had hoped for did not take place. The tension became too much, and eventually some, especially the Golok clansmen, acted on their own. The wandering story-tellers now speak of when the Goloks captured some Han soldiers, cut off their noses and sent them back to their garrisons. Litang is completely under the control of the Han. But much of the surrounding country is held by the resistance.'

'It is the same here. You have seen the town for yourself. But there must be co-ordinated action. So many of the resistance groups are acting on their own, only thinking of their own interests. To fight the Han effectively, there must be a co-ordinated national movement. Tul-lok, your cousin, who leads the resistance in this area, agrees. There is talk of a headquarters being established in the south.'

'It must be done quickly.' Tsun drank some of the hot tea.

'But they lack arms and equipment, Rinposhay, and ammunition. More than anything else, they lack ammunition. It is so very important that you reach India safely. That gold is desperately needed.'

Tsun nodded, and did not express his fear that, when he gave the money to the resistance representatives in Kalimpong, they might not be able to buy the arms.

'Rinposhay,' her voice was anxious. 'Is there any hope of our being able to regain our independence?'

'I believe so, your Majesty. Anything is possible if we have the will and determination.'

The Queen poured him some more tea and then both ate from the bowl of dried apricots.

'They are as determined as we are,' she said. 'If they cannot achieve their objective one way, they will try another. It makes no difference, so long as they gain the result they desire. I remember when they first came, how careful they were to give a good impression. I think it was genuine. The troops were well behaved, they worked very hard. Even their commanders joined in humble tasks. They were disappointed that we did not welcome them as liberators, but nevertheless, we were impressed during those first months. They opened clinics and gave smallpox vaccinations. They kept to themselves, but how carefully we were wooed. I was invited to receptions to see films on the new China, to see sports and demonstrations, new clinics, the new roads they were building, schools they were opening. I was asked to advise on so many projects for the new Tibet. Of course, people felt an underlying anxiety at having the country occupied, but then it had been occupied in the past and we had managed to come through relatively unharmed. Perhaps it would be so this time.'

'It was the same in Litang,' Tsun said. 'Because I had initiated some reforms, the Han decided that I should actively participate in their schemes for the development of our area. They were most solicitous.'

'Yes,' the Queen agreed. 'But food became scarce. Prices doubled, trebled. Some became wealthy overnight, because the Han paid, no matter what the price. But the Tibetans did not have such amounts of money. Lamas and members of my Government Council were taken to China and shown the wonders that would come to Tibet. But I think by then most of us realised what was involved in the creation of a new Tibet!

'Now I am used. No more am I wooed. Now, I am given directives from the Han Headquarters to attend various meetings and so give a semblance of Tibetan participation to their plans for this State. As each day passes and their hold on the country strengthens, I become less useful. The day will come when I will be disposed of and . . .' her voice faltered. 'I do not think I have the courage to face the Thamzing, to be beaten, tortured and humiliated before my people.'

'They would not risk . . .'

'If they can risk our people's anger at the humiliation of our most revered Lamas, I would not be an obstacle.' She drank some tea, her sad eyes gazing at Tsun.

'All is perishable, an ever dancing play of shadows which, grasped at, bring only sorrow. Yet, though a thousand years are but a second in the aeons and kalpas of creation . . . I mourn, Rinposhay. What throne of glory will my son succeed to? I am mortal. For a thousand years our dynasty has looked after the welfare of Derge. All passes, Rinposhay, and unless we are awakened, we grieve in our ignorance, but it is no less painful.'

Tsun did not answer, because there was no answer, and she knew it.

'You must forgive me for talking so much about my own problems, but there are so few now whom I can trust.'

'I am honoured that you should confide in me.'

The Queen leaned over and grasped his hand. 'Warn the Kundun, Rinposhay! Warn him! He is also being used. Warn him that as each day passes he is being bound with invisible, indestructible bonds, until he and the nation will be helpless. I have seen it all happening.'

Slowly, and in silence, Tsun stood up and looked down at the town. He thought how normal it all looked. The Queen came up beside him. He could not hear the loudspeakers, could not distinguish the Han from the Tibetans. The houses were like little white models in a beautiful valley interlaced with winding streams. Too far to see that the flags fluttering in the breeze were not those of Buddhism but of Communism. Too far to see that the monastery was empty and dying. The sun shone gloriously in the limpid sky.

'I am helpless, Rinposhay,' the Queen said. 'I protest, but it has no effect. My dignity is enhanced by Han bodyguards, by a car brought specially from China. Yet it all serves to isolate me, to imprison me. I act as Queen, but I'm no longer Queen. Our throne is in Peking. I have heard that life is easier in Lhasa, that the Kundun still has some authority. Warn him, Rinposhay, please!'

'I will,' Tsun said quietly. He raised her hands to his forehead in reverence and to bless her. They went back to their seats and she poured more tea.

'I have studied the Han ideals carefully. They talk of a people's democracy in which everyone participates. Yet when I attended meetings of the District Committee it did not take long for me to realise that while we could advise, the power of decision-making lay in Peking. Often I have to read speeches which the Han have prepared for me. They speak of the people having decided this or that. But it is a lie. Our people have not decided. Peking has decided. Faceless, nameless men, they decide our destinies.

'I see them taking taxes for the Motherland, issuing documents, ration books, in the name of the Motherland State. There are passes, licences for this, licences for that . . . all in the name of the Motherland. My trading agents have to get passes to leave the city and if they want to travel to India for goods, their request is forwarded from the local Han Area Command to the Chamdo Liberation Committee, and then from one department to another. Is this progress, Rinposhay? When our people wanted to go to India, they just went. Our family was the highest authority in Derge. People knew us, recognised us. If they had a grievance they could come to us and see us. Life was simple. People were individuals. But now . . .'

Tsun nodded. 'Even had we not been invaded, greater complexity in our life was inevitable, Majesty,' he said. 'It is part of the modern way of life.'

But the Queen did not appear to hear him. 'How ironic karma is. It is our very desire for independence that prevents the Han from conquering us, yet that same desire is being used by the Han to conquer us.'

Tsun looked at her tense face, her burning eyes.

'You know of the plots of the Khamba families?' she asked.

'Yes,' he replied quietly. 'Some clan chiefs were planning to seize power from the nobles in Lhasa.'

The Queen nodded. 'I was informed of the scheme,' she said. 'Indeed, I was asked to participate, but I declined. For generations, our dynasty has sought to guard the independence of our state while acknowledging the Kundun as the supreme Sovereign of Tibet, yet not acknowledging the power of Lhasa government officials over us, nor the power of the Han. Ours is a tiny state. Our independence has been achieved by diplomacy. For us to enter into a conspiracy against Lhasa at such a time would have damaged the trust of years. As it was, enough damage was done. Various nobles in Lhasa learned that I knew of the plot and that was enough for them to think of me henceforth with suspicion. Some of my officials joined the conspiracy and so I was held in increasing suspicion. The Han, too, became aware of the plot, and indeed, deluded some Khambas into helping them with the invasion. The

Han have told me that they will ensure Derge's independence. And they have made sure that Lhasa has heard of this too, thus driving the wedge between us even deeper.'

'Is there no way of explaining these things?' Tsun asked.

'I have sent couriers to Lhasa. Most have been intercepted, and those who have got through have been of little use. I have had to word my messages so carefully, lest they fall into the wrong hands, that their content became meaningless. Our only hope lies in co-ordinated resistance and more weapons. Good weapons. We must get help from outside.' She stopped at the sound of approaching footsteps. A servant came in with freshly made tea. She waited until the man had withdrawn, leaving them alone together again.

'Rinposhay, there is a rumour that Marshal Chen-Yi will be assassinated on his way to the inauguration of the Preparatory Committee.'

'I know, it is madness.'

'It must be stopped. Chen-Yi can be replaced. What they will destroy in retaliation cannot be.'

'You know who is planning this?'

'I think your cousin, Tul-lok, is involved.'

'Have you spoken to him about it?' asked Tsun.

'No. Increasingly I am losing contact with the resistance as the Han restrict me and watch me.'

'We must prevent it. Can you warn the Han? Say that there is a rumour?'

'They would demand to know how I had heard the rumour. They would tighten security in the town even more, arrest suspects, until they were satisfied that they had found the potential assassins. They would not defer Chen-Yi's visit.'

'I am hoping to see my cousin, but I cannot be certain that I shall. There must be a way in which we can stop them.'

'When Tul-lok is in Derge he usually contacts Chopel. Chopel will pass on my views.'

'And if Tul-lok doesn't come to Derge before Chen-Yi arrives in the country?'

'Then I shall have to risk sending another messenger. For I am a coward, Rinposhay. I know what the Han can do, and I fear it. What is to become of us?'

Tsun did not answer immediately, and in his hesitation she read an answer.

'Perhaps you are right, it is better not to know. Did not the Han philosopher, Lao Tsu, say that we assume the knowledge we seek will be what we want to know, yet it can be what we fear most?'

'Yet, what we fear most, the dread of our innermost being from which so many flee without realising it, can be the gate of liberation, if we would but turn and face it.'

The Queen did not understand him, but still the words comforted her. Changing the subject, she asked him about himself. 'Do you need anything for your journey?'

'Yes, we need horses, Majesty. We lost most of ours during the attacks by the Han.'

'They know of your mission?'

He nodded. Her eyes widened slightly. 'Fortunately,' she said, 'my best horses are with the nomads on the plains, for it would be difficult for you to take even a small number out of Derge without arousing suspicion. How many do you want?'

'Twelve, and four mules.'

'I shall give you authorisation to take them.' She hesitated, then began to speak more intensely. 'Rinposhay, could you help me by warning the nomads of a decision made by the local Working Committee of the Chinese Communist Party?' As Tsun listened he wondered how he could possibly convey the ramifications of the decision to the nomads.

'I'll give them the message . . .'

'You *must* make them understand,' said the Queen, aware of his unspoken doubt, and he nodded to reassure her. Then, raising her hands, she unclasped the amulet from her neck and handed it to Tsun. It was of silver and gilt with turquoise studs and in the shape of a pentagram.

'This contains that for which you have come,' she murmured. 'The petition from Derge.' It had been signed by representatives of all sectors of society from far beyond Derge. Tsun took it and slipped it into his ambac, then he followed the Queen back into the audience chamber. She stopped suddenly and he heard her quick, low gasp. Her small hands were clenched by her sides.

'Phuntsog, how long have you been here?'

The man servant was slowly skating round the poorly lit audience chamber on pads of cloth tied to his feet, as he silently polished the floor.

'A little while, Majesty,' he said.

'Go now,' she ordered him icily.

He bowed and, picking up his feet as though stepping through mud, began walking down the pillared length of the room.

'What do you know of him?' Tsun asked softly.

She clasped her face and looked at him with agitated eyes. 'Little. He could easily have heard us talking. I don't know if he is a spy or not. One of my most trusted advisers was forced by the Han to spy on me.'

'Call him back!'

'Phuntsog!'

The man turned.

'Come back here.'

Slowly and clumsily, with the polishing pads still on his feet, he walked back, bowed, and looked apprehensively at the Queen. She turned to Tsun for guidance.

'Who asked you to polish the floor at this time?' he enquired.

'The Chamberlain.'

'But I told him we were not to be disturbed,' the Queen said.

'I'm sorry, Majesty, but he did tell me, and I did not know that you were near.'

'Do not lie, Phuntsog,' Tsun said. 'You must have seen the Queen was on the balcony.'

The man looked worried. 'Only as I drew near the window and heard voices.'

'What . . .'

Tsun coughed and caught the Queen's eye and she did not press the question, instead looking at him interrogatively. He nodded.

'Very well, you may go, Phuntsog!' she said.

For a few moments after he had left the room, neither of them spoke. Then the Queen murmured, 'He will tell everyone of my strange behaviour.'

'It is natural for you to be careful these days.'

'Carefulness is suspicious to the Han,' she replied. 'Why, they have sown suspicion in the hearts of many, Kusho, and it flourishes. I find myself wondering whether my Chamberlain did ask Phuntsog to polish the floor at this time?'

She sat on a divan and wrote an authorisation for Tsun to take twelve horses and four mules from her herds. As she sealed the document, she pointed to a large, ornate jade seal on a chest, delicately painted with flowers and creepers.

'The Han Emperor presented that to our forefathers. Today, I am given this,' she indicated the telephone. 'Both were given with the same design.'

'I prefer the former, Majesty. It is more beautiful and has a less direct connection with the bestower!'

The Queen smiled and handed him the authorisation.

'We have not decided on a price for the animals,' Tsun said.

She shrugged. 'What use have I for money now? I cannot entertain you as I would wish, forced as we are to hide your identity, but at least I can give you these horses with my ever constant prayer that your mission is successful.' She got up and, this time in farewell, presented Tsun with a long silk felicity scarf which he took, then draped over her neck, bestowing a blessing.

'I have one further favour to ask,' he said.

She nodded.

'Outside the palace there is a man in the stocks. He killed someone in a feud. He has sworn to me that if he is released he will not continue the feud. Will you release him?'

'It shall be done today.' She looked at Tsun with anxious eyes. 'Pray for me, Rinposhay. I am not a courageous woman. I fear what will happen to me.'

'I shall keep you in my heart.'

There was a knock on the door and the Queen called to the person to enter. The Chamberlain came into the room.

'Majesty,' he bowed. 'You are expected at a meeting of the League of Women in an hour.'

'Yes, yes, thank you, Dorji,' and to no one in particular, complained, 'Now I am a slave to clocks and telephones. Life was better without them.'

For the Chamberlain's ears, she was talking to the silversmith's assistant when she said to Tsun, 'Goodbye. Give my greetings to Chopel and, remember, I want the stones in the amulet to match exactly.'

Tsun bowed and left her. Before he closed the double doors he heard the Chamberlain say to the Queen, 'The car is ready, Majesty.'

'What are we to talk of this afternoon?'

'It is to do with the nurseries for the children. I have put the papers on your desk and . . .'

Chapter Ten

Tsun was anxious to use the opportunity of his visit to Derge to obtain copies of two key meditational texts, and a copy of the Great Thirteenth Kundun's Political Testament to accompany the petition.

He entered the monastery's printing press by the side door and asked to see the director. A young man in monk's robes with ink-stained hands and wearing a dirty leather apron, led Tsun through dark corridors and rooms lined with shelves stacked with thousands of wooden printing blocks. The director of the printing press was sitting by an open window studying proofs. He did not recognise Tsun at first, then put on his steel-rimmed spectacles. At once, he got to his feet, bowed, and presented Tsun with a felicity scarf.

'It is good to see you again,' Tsun said. 'I am here privately on a visit.' The old man nodded and told the printer to bring tea. An old monk was sitting cross-legged opposite the director with a two-foot long plank of wood placed against a table, on which he was carefully chiselling out letters, in reverse, perfectly practising the art of xylography which the Tibetans had learnt from the Chinese in the thirteenth century. The oblong shape of the blocks and printed papers reflected the appearance of the original Indian palm leaf manuscripts of Buddhist Teaching.

After an exchange of news, Tsun and the director walked together through the immense, silent building. Tsun asked about the texts he wanted. 'I cannot wait to have them printed. I have to take them with me.'

'That will be difficult, Kusho, but I think there may be some old copies of what you want, though they will not be in good condition.'

'That doesn't matter. I also want a copy of the Political Testament of the Great Thirteenth Kundun.'

They were walking past row after row of empty printers' benches. At the far end of the vast room, with its large rice paper glazed windows, eight printers were working in pairs. The director stopped by the first.

'A dangerous document to have,' he said. 'The occupation authorities have issued a decree against its distribution.'

The printers, who worked facing each other across the bench, hesitated and glanced at the director. He nodded for them to continue. They worked with practised skill and rhythm, one taking the printing block from the stack behind him, the second inking it, while the first picked up a sheet of handmade paper and laid it on the inked block, his partner running a heavy leather roller over it. When the paper had been peeled off the wooden block, the director took it and showed it to Tsun.

'The Thirteenth's testament. It is in great demand these days!' He smiled at Tsun, then led him up a slippery ladder to one of the upper floors. He lit a paraffin lamp in the windowless store room which was lined from floor to ceiling with numbered and coded pigeon holes, stacked with printed volumes carefully wrapped in cloth, most measuring two to three feet in length and up to a foot in width. The director was able to find copies of the texts that Tsun wanted. Short, and containing only the essential elements, they were known as 'pith teachings', needing a commentary by a religious teacher.

Tsun decided against taking the wooden covers as they made the books heavy to carry; instead, the texts were carefully packed into a cloth bag.

After leaving the printing press, Tsun walked only a few yards to a saddle shop.

'You are the only customer I have had today,' the owner complained. 'The Han have their saddles made in China. They want me to join a co-operative, but I am a craftsman. I have my own business.' He talked on as he lifted saddles from their stands to show Tsun. 'These bicycles and trucks will ruin my business . . .'

Tsun was assessing the size of the saddles, unchanged in style since the Tibetans joined with the Mongolian hordes sweeping through Arabia and Europe a thousand years before, their trees two short wooden planks with a high pommel and cantle. He chose a well made one of good strong birchwood, well padded, with silver filigree work on pommel and cantle. The saddler showed him saddle rugs of varying qualities.

'Even some of the traders have trucks now,' he grumbled. 'If this goes on, Kusho, I shall be ruined.'

Tsun chose a good quality rug with a design of dragons, carefully cut round to give an embossed appearance, and a felt rug to go beneath the saddle.

'100 yuan.' The saddler held out his hand.

'Ridiculous! I'll give you fifty.'

'Kusho! Prices are rising. Things are scarce. This is a fine saddle, you won't find another like it in town.'

The saddler grasped Tsun's hand and, out of habit, for there was no one else in the shop to hear, bargained with Tsun by touch as had been done for hundreds of years.

'I'll take your watch,' the saddler said finally, knowing that he could get a good deal on a Rolleiflex watch, with the Han or the Tibetans. Tsun had been given the watch some years back. He thought for a moment, then slowly undid the strap and handed it over. The saddler asked him where he should deliver the saddle, but Tsun picked it up and slung the rugs over his arm. 'I'll take it with me,' he said.

'Good fortune, Kusho.' The saddler, cheered by the sale, sounded as though he meant it. 'May that saddle see you through many safe journeys.'

'May the watch bring you much prosperity,' Tsun responded, then left the shop.

It had been raining. The loudspeakers were playing Tibetan music.

Chapter Eleven

The breeze blew crisp leaves across the square and billowed the white cloth of the square umbrellas shading the stall holders' wares: enamel mugs, rugs, umbrellas, watches, toothbrushes, prayer flags, charms, bales of wool, cloth, sheepskins, chopsticks – but hardly anything edible. What food there had been had gone earlier in the day.

A Han civilian, in blue tunic and trousers, cycled into the square and began distributing copies of the broadsheet, *Tibet News*, published by the occupation authorities. A Tibetan girl, wearing blue quilted jacket, red plaid shirt and grey trousers, with a soft cap perched on the back of her head, took a sheet from the cyclist and walked slowly, reading as she went, to the Great Chorten in the square. Tsun had taken a copy of the paper too, and was leaning against a wall by the stalls, apparently reading the bulletin, though in fact he was watching the girl.

When she reached the chorten, she took off her cap and held it in her left hand. She glanced round the square, then continued reading the paper. An old woman was walking round the chorten, spinning a squeaking prayer wheel. Tsun moved away from the wall and walked round the stalls, passing off-duty groups of Han soldiers, wandering curiously through the market. His eyes flickered over every rooftop, every face, every doorway, searching for any sign of a trap. Finding none, he walked slowly across the square towards his sister.

She had changed beyond recognition. He had last seen her when she was a little girl, with a slight cast in her left eye. Now she was an attractive young woman. Her eyes and mouth had a sensual maturity, but there was something of the determination and character of the child he remembered in the firm and regular features. When he was a few feet away, she glanced up, looked at him, down at her paper, then up again as she realised that it was her brother. Now he would know if it was a trap.

'Rinposhay . . .'

As she spoke he held his finger to his mouth, took her arm and led her down a side street. He glanced back; no one appeared to be following them. Pema was looking at him. She was uncertain what to say and felt embarrassed. She was confused by the secrecy and by seeing him in lay clothes. Moreover, it had been seven years since they had last seen one another and each had been through a great deal.

Tsun noticed her red kerchief, of the Communist Youth League movement, and the badges on her shirt. Evidently, he thought, she has established herself in her new world.

'You are a fine looking young woman, Pema,' he said, and chuckled when she blushed.

They spoke little during the few minutes' walk to Chopel's house. In some respects, Pema was surprised how little Tsun had changed, but there was a weariness about his eyes, and a quality about him which she did not recognise.

Chopel, stripped to the waist, his body streaked with soot and covered with the sheen of sweat, stood up as they entered the tiny, smoke-blackened smithy. His perfect white teeth gleamed in a face made ebony with ingrained soot.

'No, Chopel,' Tsun motioned to him to sit down. 'Do not let us disturb you.' He made the introductions.

'This is my sister, Pema. You remember Chopel?' he asked her. 'You met him when you were very small. I used to work for him.' She did not remember, but smiled politely, wiping her eyes which were smarting from the thick smoke.

Namgyal was sitting completely naked while he worked the wood and leather piston of the hollow log bellows, keeping the sheep dung fire at the right intensity. On seeing Pema, he quickly slipped on his sheepskin chuba.

'Make some tea for our guests,' Chopel ordered his son, and put some more dung on the fire.

'We will go onto the roof, Chopel,' Tsun said.

'Yes, Kusho.'

Pema missed her footing on the greasy notched pole and nearly fell. Tsun caught her. They both laughed, and it broke the ice.

On the roof, Pema fiddled with the wooden shuttle of a loom on which Dekyi had been weaving some cloth for the family's clothes, from a pile of grey wool.

'Yangchen told me of what happened in Doi, and of Ama-la dying,' Tsun said.

'Yes!' She spoke abruptly, wanting to turn away from those memories. The shuttle clicked back and forth.

'But what about you, Rinposhay? We have thought about you a lot. I have kept your letters. Ama-la liked me to read them to her.'

'We are brother and sister, Pema, please, forget that I am a lama.'

She smiled. 'It is difficult.'

'It is very important if we are going to be truthful to one another.'

'I don't understand.'

'You will.'

There was a pause. The shuttle moved back and forth on the wooden loom.

'Kusho-la,' Pema said, 'why did your letters stop coming?'

'I wrote regularly until we had to leave Dorje Ri-gon.'

'I wonder why we didn't get them. But then, one can put so little in a letter.'

'Sometimes,' Tsun said, 'it is not what is written in a letter which is most important, it is what is left unsaid, and *that* one can occasionally read.' Pema did not understand him. She made designs with the point of the shuttle in the dust on the roof. The loudspeakers were broadcasting Han music.

'Why are you here, Kusho-la?' she asked.

'To see you and Yangchen.'

'Will you be going back to Dorje Ri-gon?'

'Yes,' Tsun said. 'One day.'

'Why are you without your household? What has happened, Kusho-la?'

'It is better that you do not know at the moment.'

Namgyal brought up the tea. As Tsun held out his bowl, Pema said, 'I do not have a bowl. We do not use them.'

The words seemed to reverberate in the moment's silence. She blushed. Namgyal dug around in the bulging fold of his chuba and produced a battered wooden bowl which he filled from an earthenware pot.

'Where is your sister?' Tsun asked him.

'Sowing our field, Kusho.'

Pema was trying to make out what the liquid could be. It was certainly not tea.

'It is made from a redwood shrub,' Tsun told her after the boy had gone. 'Tea is scarce outside the Han garrison.' She looked at him sharply.

'Why have you decided not to come with me?' he asked.

'What do you mean?' Pema sounded startled, but knew exactly what he meant and was a little frightened.

'Yangchen has told you that I am going to Lhasa and that she hopes you will come with me?'

'Yes. I came to the square because I wanted to see you after so long, but . . .' She hesitated. 'I cannot go with you, Kusho. I would like to but I cannot.'

'Why?'

'It is better that I go to the Minorities Institute in Peking. I am progressing well and the institute will give me a wonderful opportunity. The new Tibet will need well educated young people, trained in modern techniques.'

'You told Yangchen this?' Pema nodded. 'What did she say?'

'She didn't agree. I don't want to go against her, but she does not understand.' Pema knew that if Tsun really exerted his authority as head of the family, it would be difficult for her to refuse, quite apart from his being a lama.

'What else did she say?'

'That those who have gone to China for training have not returned, that they labour in the fields, and learn about politics. But what is so wrong with that?'

'Does she say nothing else?'

'Well, she said that we are taught to despise our religion and independence, but surely that depends on the person? Both are always in my heart.'

From the background noise of the people in the street, the bicycle bells, the jeeps, the horses and mules, one familiar sound had caught Tsun's attention, nagging at his mind. Abruptly, he stood up and walked over to the parapet. The old woman he had seen walking round the chorten in the square was in front of the house, head down, still spinning the squeaking prayer wheel as she walked. He watched her for a few moments, then went back to his seat.

He took out his tsampa pouch and shook some of the rich barley flour into Pema's bowl, then into his own. She picked up the teapot and added a little liquid to each bowl. With their fingers, they kneaded the mixture into a brown, doughy ball as they talked.

'Pema, the Han way in Tibet is wrong. Certainly, let us develop our schools, but let *us* do it, not they.' Tsun saw the eager response, stifled by an innate courtesy to a lama.

'We must be frank with one another', he said. 'You must speak out even when you don't agree.'

'You say that I do not understand,' Pema said, blushing slightly at the anger in her voice. 'Meaning, I suppose, that I am too influenced by my surroundings, my new way of life, that I am a "green brain".'

'Yes. Think, Pema! Almost all Tibetans know that everything about everyday life – this bowl I am holding, this house, the prayer flags and incense vases on the roof, those trees, the clothes I wear, the very person I am – is all passing, ever changing. Is the reflection of the moon in the lake, the moon? So we know that this life is but a passing reflection, is not, in fact, reality. Is this not so? You understand me?' She nodded, chewing on the dough.

'I do not say that everyone can realise this, but it is there within them, for so much in life shows them this. Do you understand me?'

'I think so,' she said. 'I'm not sure.'

'The Han believe that the ultimate reality is their Communist State.'

'But . . .' Pema lapsed into silence.

'Please speak, Pema. Say what your thoughts are.' He chewed on the tsampa.

'Why is their way less likely to be true than ours?'

'The Han speak of the "people", the "masses" making the decisions, but these are words used to mesmerise the people. The people never rule. Individuals rule. Individuals with human failings. And the greatest of their weaknesses, the greatest of their temptations is, that once they have power they are reluctant to relinquish it, no matter how wrongly or how badly they rule.'

'In school,' Pema said, 'we discussed people who think like you. They are called idealists.'

Tsun laughed. 'No, Pema,' he said. 'I am a realist.'

Pema was staring into her bowl, thinking of what Tsun had said.

'Come, come,' he coaxed her. 'Speak openly. We have so little time, there can be no evasions.'

'I wonder,' she said reluctantly, 'if you *are* a realist. What you say is true, to a degree, yet it is not. You know more of these things than I, Kusho-la, I only know what I have seen, what I have lived through. When I was in Doi, and I had to attend the Thamzings, where the lamas were tortured and told to use their powers to save themselves, I expected them to. I wanted them to, so much. So that the suffering would end. Ama-la and Yangchen did not seem to expect them to – I do not know, for I did not talk of it. But none did. I couldn't understand *why* they didn't use their powers! I still don't understand. Then, I thought, well perhaps the Han are right, and the only way to shake us out of our stubborn clinging to our mistaken belief is brutality. Yet, I knew this wasn't right, that there was much I just didn't understand. But there was no one to tell me, Kusho-la.

'Now that is past. Many opportunities have been shown to me, undreamt of by our parents. As you know much of what I do not understand, Kusho, I know something which you do not understand. I believe that I am a realist. Because the Han are here and are likely to stay. We have to live with them, and that is what I am doing.'

She shrugged as she spoke, opening her hands, taking the edge off the blunt words. Tsun undid the brass ball button at the collar of his shirt and slipped his arms from the sleeves of his chuba. His attention was caught by the cry of a lone raven in the sky.

'You remember the birds, Pema? How they used to come to the roof to be fed?' She nodded. She missed them too, yet . . . 'I understand why they had to be got rid of, Kusho.'

'Then, indeed, Pema,' Tsun said, 'you understand far more than I. But to return to what you were saying. You are right! You can only really decide from your own experience. Come with me to Lhasa and you will learn a little more of what I mean, and I can learn more from you. Then *you* must decide what to do.'

'I should like to, Kusho-la.' She felt acutely embarrassed by her obduracy. 'But I shall miss so many months' training on the journey. There are so many exciting things about to happen in Tibet. I want to participate in them. Please understand. I do not want to go against you.' She poured more of the redwood shrub liquid into their bowls.

Tsun looked into her troubled eyes. 'I have to travel tonight. I shall not see you again.'

'Kusho-la!' she gasped, her eyes wide with fright. 'Why?'

'As you are part of the new Tibet, so I am part of the old Tibet. You should have learnt from your lessons with the Han, that there will only be one loyalty in the new Tibet. Remember the lamas at Doi? I am a lama, Pema-la.'

'No!' She clenched her hands. 'It will not happen to you. It need not. You know it need not.' Her voice was angry. 'You want me to be free to choose then leave me no choice.'

'Have you not wondered,' Tsun's voice hardened slightly, 'why I am dressed as I am?' He spread his hands. 'Why I ask you not to treat me as a monk? Why I asked you to meet me at the chorten in the square? Have you not thought this strange?'

'Yes, I suppose so,' she murmured reluctantly.

'The Han are hunting me,' said Tsun. 'And if I am captured, I will suffer as the lamas of Doi suffered.'

'No!' She stood up, refusing to acknowledge his words. 'I shall speak to Yangchen. Captain Li has considerable influence.'

'Pema-la!' His voice was harsh. 'Swear to me, by the Triple Refuge, that you will tell no one of my presence here.'

From his voice, Pema knew that her brother was wanted by the Han for far more than just being a lama. She looked at him for a few seconds, then nodded slowly.

'I swear by the Triple Refuge,' she said softly. 'What have you done, Kusho-la? What have you done?'

'What had the lamas at Doi done?'

'Kusho-la, you said we should speak frankly.'

'Already I have endangered myself,' said Tsun, 'by making myself known to you. If I tell you more, it will further endanger us *both*.'

'But . . .'

'Yes! Pema, without you knowing what my mission is, I still want you to come with me. You are my sister. You speak of the new Tibet. Of the changes. Yet they are greater than you realise.'

'I can do nothing to stop it, Kusho-la. It is useless to fight . . .'

'I want to be able to show you what these changes really involve, then return to your studies with the Han if you wish.'

'But, Kusho-la, I shall not get permission to leave Derge. I am expected to go to China.'

'If you just disappear?'

'It will be held against me in the future.' She frowned, conscious that her brother was not listening. His concentration was fixed on the sound of a motorcycle coming up the street with loudly revving engine. He got up and walked over to the parapet. The Han motorcycle and sidecar continued on past the house. Tsun glanced up and down the street. Pema now began really to appreciate that he was a fugitive. The implications frightened her.

'Kusho-la,' she said. 'You know I want to go with you, but you are making me give up everything to go with you.'

Tsun turned to face her and leaned his back against the parapet.

'How can I refuse?' Pema continued. 'You are the head of the family, my brother and a Rinposhay, but you ask so much. If I go with you, I lose so many opportunities.'

It was true, Tsun thought. Not only had she passed the rigorous if arbitrary classifications of class origin, but found herself placed in the heart of the ruling elite. With him she could be a fugitive enemy of the people, damned as a counter-revolutionary. She pleaded with him. 'Please do not ask me to choose . . .'

He did not reply. 'Kusho-la, please . . .' She moaned the words. She was, he thought, still very young. He opened his arms. Pema held onto him and wept and it was as it used to be when she could always find comfort with her elder brother.

'You are right, Pema. You could have a great deal to lose, which is why it has to be your choice. I can understand your wanting to stay, I would not blame you for not coming with me.'

'But you're forcing me to choose!' Her voice was angry and resentful.

'Aieee . . .' Namgyal's shout filled the street. Tsun spun round and looked down. The sun glinted in the tear stain on Pema's cheek as she peered nervously over the parapet. In the street a small crowd had gathered to watch as the grubby twelve year-old boy took a smooth stone from his chuba, slipped it into the woollen sling, then swiftly whirled it round his head before loosing at a rat scrambling desperately up the rough wall of a house. The stone hit the rat. As it fell there was a rush to catch it, but Namgyal managed to grab it and ran into the shop to tell his father that tonight they would eat well.

Pema walked slowly towards the trapdoor in the roof. Tsun watched her.

'Kusho-la, I can't. I can't . . . forgive me, please?'

She could not look at him as he came up to her and laid his hand on her head in blessing.

'You have chosen. I am content.'

'But, you wanted me to come?'

'I want you to be happy.'

'I want to come.' She wiped her eyes. 'I should, but I cannot . . . perhaps, because I am frightened, I do not know . . .'

'Pema-la, you have decided. It is enough.'

She walked aimlessly about the roof. 'I do not know what to do. You frightened me when you said that I shall not see you again.'

'Not as we are today, but we will always be together.'

'What is going to happen, Kusho-la, do you know?'

'Everything changes. A child is born and every day of its life it grows slightly and changes. From one day to the next, it is changing, altering, never quite the same person. Growing old and eventually dying, to be reborn, and so it begins again. So it is with nations.'

'Is that bad, Rinposhay?'

'It is ultimately neither good nor bad. It is just life, and being human, we grow attached to our way of life, to what is about us. So, its changing causes us sadness. It is our grasping at life which causes suffering, which causes us to lose life.'

'I do not know that I understand you, Kusho. How, then, can you be against the Han, when you say that it is inevitable, that to resist is attachment, grasping?'

'A child is born, he matures, develops and dies. If someone tried to smother that child, we would endeavour to stop him.'

Pema toyed with the teapot, then poured more 'tea', but it had grown cold and neither of them drank it.

'Why do you go to Lhasa?' asked Pema.

'I have business there on behalf of Dorje Ri-gon.'

She knew these moments to be precious. Tsun had told her that they would not see one another again; perhaps these were the last moments they would have together and she felt that she wanted to collect and preserve each one. There was so much to say, yet Tsun seemed unmoved and unconcerned, despite his efforts to persuade her to accompany him. Her confusion of mind increased.

'You assume too much,' he said quietly.

'Kusho-la!' she stared at him. 'You talk to me in riddles!' He smiled.

'Write to me,' she pleaded.

Tsun nodded. But both knew that letters rarely got through from Lhasa these days.

'You should have ordered me to come,' she said after a few minutes' silence.

'You would have been even more resentful.' She looked at him quickly.

'You will stay and see me off?'

'You do not trust me! You think I will report to the Han that I have seen you.' Her voice hardened.

'I would be foolish if I didn't take precautions,' he chuckled and ran his finger down the line of badges on her lapel, given to her as a member of the Communist Youth League.

'But I am your sister.'

'Today, Pema-la, I saw a boy publicly humiliate his father when he tried to stop the Han from taking his son for education in China. The father felt so disgraced that he killed himself in front of all who watched.' So, she thought, he did not trust her.

'You think I might betray you, Kusho?' All courtesy evaporated in the heat of her anger. 'You can read minds!' She spat the words at him.

'People can be forced to betray.'

But she was hurt and wounded. Tsun walked towards her, then stopped. She saw him struggling with his anger, then she realised how little she knew and it frightened her. Slowly, Tsun climbed down the notched pole into the darkness of the house.

Chapter Twelve

'It is not good for you to travel during darkness, Kusho.' Chopel warmed his hands in front of the clay stove. 'The weather will be bad tonight, already it is cold. I think it will snow. It is not safe.'

His daughter was serving turnip soup from an iron pot.

'Kusho-la.' Dekyi smiled at him as she poured the soup. 'Stay longer. Pa-la is right. At least wait until morning.'

Tsun shook his head. 'The longer I am here, the more I endanger you. Also, friends are waiting for me. I must not delay for they are anxious for my safety.'

'You are going with the Kusho?' Dekyi asked as she leaned across to pour out Pema's soup. Her attention was caught by the flames reflecting in the enamel Communist Youth League badges. Dekyi's smile froze on her lips and Pema noticed the flicker of fear in her eyes. One did not have such badges without earning them.

'No! I have just come to say goodbye to my brother.' Pema's face was taut as she licked her dry lips.

'I work in the ration office,' Dekyi explained, to show that she, too, was trusted by the Han. 'I thought I had seen you at the Area Command.'

'I don't work,' Pema said. 'I live there. I am training.'

'Really,' Dekyi said huskily, as she struggled not to show her fear and suspicion. Her mind was full of Pema's words and their implications. She offered more soup to her father, though his bowl was still full.

'No, no, thank you. Later.' Dekyi bent closer to Chopel. 'Father, I must speak with you for a moment outside,' she whispered.

Chopel frowned. 'Not now.'

'Pa-la, it is really urgent. Please, now!'

The note in her voice convinced him. He excused himself to Tsun and followed Dekyi into the tiny dark workroom.

'What is it?' he whispered.

'Pa-la, that girl. She lives in the Area Command. She is a member of the Communist Youth League.'

'Yes, well. She is the Kusho's sister.'

'That does not mean she is not a spy. She must have realised from our conversation this evening that we help the resistance.'

'But she would not betray her brother, and she knows that the Han are hunting him.'

'It is not for him I am worried. As you say, he is her brother and will soon be many miles away. We are not her relatives, and we shall be here in Derge. She has only to say the wrong word to the wrong person and we are finished.'

'No! No!' But Chopel was beginning to feel worried too.

'I know the Han, Pa-la. I work for them. They are thorough. How do you think they manage to keep such strict control? To know of those who plot against them? I warned you, Pa-la, what your helping the resistance would lead to, I warned you.'

'All right!' His voice was sharp. 'You must go with the Rinposhay.'

'And you?'

'I must remain here. Everything I have is here.'

'And of what use is it all to a dead man?' she said bitterly.

Chopel looked at his daughter angrily, as though she had put a curse on him.

'Oh, Pa-la.' She clung to him and wept. 'What are we going to do?'

'We will ask the Kusho.'

'How can you, Pa-la? She is his sister. He is unlikely to say that she would be a danger to us.'

'Dekyi, have you not noticed that there is something different about him from other men?'

'Perhaps, something. I don't know . . . why?'

'He is a very holy man.'

Dekyi was unconvinced as she followed her father back to join their guests.

'Would you show me where the lavatory is, Dekyi?' Pema asked when she and her father came back into the room. The girl nodded and led Pema through a low door into the yard at the back of the house.

Tsun's and Chopel's horses were lying down in the lean-to stable. The air had a bite to it and the sky was darkening rapidly. Chopel was right, Pema thought, it does look like snow.

Dekyi closed the wooden door after them and leaned against it. Pema looked around the bare yard. For a moment she was disconcerted; since living with the Han she had become used to an earth closet.

She undid her trousers. As she lowered them and squatted beside a wall, she thought how useful the voluminous Tibetan chuba was in such situations.

'I suppose you know,' Dekyi said, 'that my father has given shelter to your brother because he knew him as a young man. He does not usually do such things.' Pema smiled slightly, but did not reply.

'You must be very highly thought of to have such badges?'

'You should join the League. It is very interesting.'

Dekyi felt a surge of resentment that she should have to curry favour with this arrogant collaborator, but struggled to subdue it as she could hardly afford to offend her.

'Perhaps I should,' she replied instead.

Pema did up her trousers and they returned to the others. Chopel was rubbing his bald head with his hand. He drew Tsun aside and spoke softly to him.

'Kusho . . . Rinposhay . . . it is difficult, but my daughter, she is worried about your sister, that she might tell the Han that we help the resistance.'

'Do not worry, Chopel. She will not have the opportunity to betray you.'

Chopel did not understand Tsun, who was looking without expression into the flames of the fire.

'Dekyi,' he called to his daughter. 'Cook the meat Namgyal brought us.'

'No, Chopel,' Tsun said. 'Keep it for when I am gone.'

Chopel was about to protest, but Tsun was emphatic. 'I insist!'

Chopel moved closer to Tsun and spoke in a low voice. 'Kusho . . .'

He watched Dekyi light the paraffin lamps, then sit down next to Pema. Namgyal settled himself to listen to the women talking.

'Kusho-la . . .' Chopel continued. 'I have a great favour to ask you.'

'You have risked everything for me, Chopel. Your family, your home, everything. I can never repay you. So, tell me what favour can I do for you?'

'It is Namgyal. You know he takes such risks stealing food, which is going to get more scarce, not more plentiful. Sooner or later, he will be caught by the Han. Please take him with you.'

'But, Chopel, I told you before, he will be in danger with me.' Though speaking to Chopel, he was looking at Pema as he said, 'The Han are hunting me, I cannot guarantee his safety.'

'What is safety today, Kusho? Please, take him with you. We have relatives in Lhasa, they will look after him.'

Tsun was not worried about what would happen to the boy in Lhasa. He was thinking of the two thousand-mile journey to the Holy City. But he knew that Chopel was right, the boy had no future in Derge, neither had the rest of the family.

'Why don't you and Dekyi come too, Chopel?' he asked.

'Later, Kusho. My business is here, my home. If I leave, I lose everything. The Han take the belongings of those who flee. Anyway, it will not cause so much comment in the street if just the boy goes. But if they awake to find us all gone, the gossip will spread and soon the Han will know about it. Also, I am doing useful work with the resistance and am needed here.'

'And Dekyi?'

'I have asked her to go, but she won't leave me.'

Dekyi handed round a small bowl of apricots and walnuts. The apricots were dry and shrivelled with age. Tsun declined, he knew how precious such food was, but Chopel insisted so he took an apricot.

'Namgyal,' Chopel called, 'come here.'

Namgyal came and sat beside his father.

'Namgyal, I want you to go with the Kusho to Lhasa.'

'Pa-la, really?' The thought of the adventure excited the boy, but quickly receded.

'Are you and Dekyi coming?'

'We will come later. We must stay for a while.'

The boy was silent for a few moments. 'Let me stay too, Pa-la.'

'No, Namgyal.' Chopel's concern made him sound sterner than he intended. 'You must go. It is safer. The Han will want to send you to China if you stay.'

'Is it because I have taken things? I promise I will not take anything more.'

'It is for your own safety, Namgyal. The Han will want you to go to school in China, even if they don't catch you stealing.'

Namgyal was young and had spent most of his life under the occupation, but he was not too young to understand that under such conditions, when families parted, as often as not it was forever.

'I want to stay with you, Pa-la, but I will do as you say.' His usually bright eyes, mischievous, yet with inborn wisdom, were sad.

'It will be an exciting journey, Namgyal,' said Tsun quietly.

'Through all Tibet, then the Holy City itself. You will see many wonders and have much excitement. Perhaps,' he smiled, 'too much excitement.'

'You remember when you worked for me, Kusho?' Chopel said to Tsun. 'How I used to say that one day I would make the pilgrimage to Lhasa to see the Great Temple and receive the blessing of the Kundun.' He ruffled his son's hair. 'Make the pilgrimage for me, Namgyal . . . make it for me . . .'

'He will see the Kundun,' Tsun assured his host.

Pema sat thinking of all that she wanted to say to her brother, and yet could not. He did not even look at her. She thought of the opportunity she had missed when they had been alone. Soon he would be gone. He said, for ever!

'Chopel, we must go shortly,' Tsun said.

'Namgyal, saddle both horses,' Chopel ordered his son.

'Kusho,' Dekyi spoke softly. 'Please bless us before you go, and advise us.'

Chapter Thirteen

Tsun pushed his arms into the sleeves of his chuba, adjusting it across his chest and knotting tight his gaily coloured woven belt. He took a red-fox fur hat out of his ambac. Dekyi was fussing around Namgyal as he dressed in his warmest serge chuba and trousers and a knitted woollen hat. She looked startled when Tsun pressed strings of cheese and silver yuan on her.

'Oh, no, Kusho. I cannot take all this, you will need it for the journey.'

'It is yours,' Tsun insisted. 'To show my gratitude for all the hospitality Chopel's family have given me.'

Dekyi and Chopel both offered Tsun grubby and crumpled felicity scarves and, to their embarrassment, Tsun, in recognition of his former mentor, bowed his head so that after some moments' hesitation they placed their scarves on his neck. No one spoke as Chopel and Dekyi draped scarves over Namgyal's neck to wish him luck. As they went outside, Dekyi handed Pema a scarf to give to her brother, realising that she was unlikely to have one. Chopel held Tsun's stirrup while he mounted. The wind was bitter. Tsun pulled on the fur hat. Pema stepped forward to hand the scarf to Tsun. The wind tore it out of her hand. He looked at his sister and smiled.

'I'm coming with you.' She almost mouthed the words, shivering in the biting wind.

'Chopel,' Tsun asked his host, 'have you a chuba I could buy for my sister?'

'I will see what I can find, Kusho,' Dekyi said, and Pema followed her into the cramped, dark shop.

The horses whinnied and stamped impatiently. Pema came back wearing thick serge trousers, a battered and filthy sheepskin chuba and a fur hat.

'You are too good to us.' Tsun pressed more silver yuan on Chopel. The silversmith lifted his son onto the hindquarters of the horse Pema had already mounted. Dekyi stretched up and Namgyal bent down to hear her above the wind.

'Take care,' Dekyi entreated her brother.

'And mind you do all the Kusho tells you,' Chopel warned him. 'Remember, this is your pilgrimage for me.'

'Yes, Pa-la,' answered the boy, his voice low and full of emotion.

Tsun urged his horse into a walk. Chopel and Dekyi walked along beside the horses.

'Chopel,' said Tsun gently. 'If you accompany us, it will bring more notice of our departure.'

Chopel hesitated, then nodded and stopped, putting out a hand to his daughter to do the same.

The street was almost empty as they rode. Flakes of snow were beginning to appear on the wind. They turned back before reaching the corner of the street to wave a final goodbye to Chopel and Dekyi. As they did so, Tsun caught sight of a huddled figure in a doorway. For a moment, he thought it was the old woman with the squeaking prayer wheel.

The snow came quickly. Pema pulled down the corduroy ear flaps of her hat and flicked off a flea that had ventured out of the sheepskin chuba and was tickling her neck. The wind roared in their ears, striking them physically like a blow, taking their breath away. The snow surged and twisted on the wind before carpeting the street and houses and trees. Tsun glanced at the branches of a tree against the darkened sky. It stood black and bare, one side striped with snow driven by the wind. People were scurrying for shelter. The curfew had not yet begun. The two horses leaned against the wind and lowered their heads. The three riders pulled up their scarves to muffle their faces.

The dim street lamps had been turned on early. The loudspeakers had stopped broadcasting. Tsun found that the biting wind on his face, the snowflakes clinging to his skin and melting on his cheeks, exhilarated him. The snow covered the traces of Han occupation, the posters, the loudspeakers. The snow was a part of Tibet, and the town became as he had known it during his childhood. It made him feel more optimistic.

They rode towards the new bridge spanning the river. The Han had let the old wooden one fall into disrepair, replacing it with a steel bridge that could carry military vehicles. It had sentry boxes at both ends.

A guard in quilted jacket, thick shapeless trousers and fur hat pulled right down over his eyebrows, stepped out of the box and motioned with his rifle for them to stop.

'Where are you going? Where is your pass?' He shouted in broken Tibetan against the wind.

'To visit relatives.'

Tsun did not want to show the document he had received from the Queen, as he knew that if later he was caught, it would have repercussions on her.

'I am from the Communist Youth League,' Pema shouted at the guard. 'My brother and I are going to return our nephew to our sister in Baji.'

For a few moments she struggled beneath the sheepskin chuba, then held out an identity card. The guard took it over to the light of the sentry box, holding his automatic rifle casually, but ready, and studied it carefully. After a few minutes he returned, gave the card back to Pema and waved them on, then went back to the warmth of the hut.

They rode slowly over the bridge, through the surging snow and past the sentry box at the far end. Tsun glanced back across the river at the dim yellow light in the windows of the houses of the town of his childhood, and then at the brighter electric lights in the windows of the Han Military Command further down the river.

The snow clung to their coats and settled over the horses. It was twenty degrees below freezing. The cold began to gnaw at their bodies despite their thick clothes and fur hats. Visibility was barely six feet. The snow caked their eyebrows and the wind roared so loudly that they had to shout to be heard.

Namgyal's horse stumbled, sending the boy to the ground. The wind threatened to knock him off his feet, and he had great difficulty in remounting.

'Please, Rinposhay, it is madness to continue,' Pema shouted at her brother. 'Let us make camp now.' But Tsun shook his head in refusal.

They made only a mile an hour as they climbed steadily up the side of the valley away from the normal route. After three miles, horses and riders were exhausted, but they had reached the rim of the valley. They found shelter among a cluster of rocks and made camp, lying close together for warmth, wrapping themselves in their chubas and pulling blankets over their faces to protect themselves from the biting wind.

'We shall be frozen to death,' Pema grumbled.

'Living with the Han has made you soft, little sister,' said Tsun. 'When we were children we often used to sleep like this.'

Pema grunted and tried to get to sleep. But despite her association with the Han, she still had an innate fear of the night – the time when witches and demons are abroad and bandits attack the traveller.

The wind had dropped slightly, letting the snow fall more thickly. One of the horses lay down. The other remained standing, shaggy head drooping. Tiredness overcame Pema's fears and she too fell asleep.

Tsun awoke at sunrise. It had stopped snowing and the wind had dropped considerably. He shook the blankets free of snow and laid them back over the still sleeping boy and girl. With his gloved hand, he brushed snow off the horses. Then he made a triple prostration and sat in meditation. After about half an hour, Pema and Namgyal awoke.

'I'll find some fuel,' said Namgyal.

'No,' Tsun told him. 'We are still too close to Derge. There are many Han patrols, we don't want to attract their attention by making smoke.'

So they ate snow for liquid, Namgyal and Pema squealing at its agonizing coldness. Tsun cut them off strips of dried meat and gave them some cheese cubes. Then he poured some parched barley flour into his bowl and gave it to the horses, but he knew that he would have to find something more substantial for them soon or they would not survive. They nosed in the snow trying to find grass.

The ground sloped, then rose as they climbed another hill. It was a vast, undulating expanse of snow while, in the distance, groups of snow-covered trees stood out like clusters of skeletons.

They travelled during the day, stopping only to make tea and give the horses a rest. The snow melted rapidly in the heat of the sun. They slipped their arms out of their chubas and tied the sleeves around their waists. Tsun pulled out the lappet of his fur hat to shade his eyes against snow blindness and Pema tried to wind her short 'revolutionary' pigtails around her head, remembering how useful the old style of long pigtails was, and made do with her cap. The temperature rose swiftly and it was hard to believe that it had been so cold just a few hours before.

'Jigme-la,' Pema said, 'you knew that I was going to come with you didn't you?'

'Perhaps.'

'Why do we cause ourselves so much trouble?' she mumbled aloud.

She still did not quite know what had decided her to come and she half suspected that he had used some power to influence her. All her opportunities were at Derge. I am respected there, she thought. My sister is there. Now I am little better than a bandit. Hunted. A criminal. More and more she realised what she had given up. All because Tsun had impressed her. She had acted on an impulse that she was already regretting.

They would walk for a while, then ride, and always, steadily, they climbed. The trees receded as they gained height, the ground becoming more barren and rocky, alleviated by the clumps of vividly coloured mountain flowers and lichens in the melting snow.

Tsun kept scanning the surrounding countryside through his binoculars, but he saw no one. They did not talk much. Tsun kept them going all the time; he was thinking of Kesang and the others and wondering if they would reach the rendezvous in time.

With her increasing tiredness, Pema's resentment grew and she wondered if there was still time for her to escape and get back to Derge. Namgyal looked about him, enjoying his new surroundings and, occasionally, when Tsun was not looking, using his sling to launch a stone at a bird or marmot.

The only sounds were the creak of the saddles, the horses' hooves on the rough ground and now and then a bird call or the sudden whirring of an insect darting close to investigate. Sometimes they would exchange a few words, but against the vast stillness, the soundlessness, their voices seemed almost an interruption. Pema felt it more than the others, because she had been used to the noise of the Han camp with its ever-present activity, even at night. The crowds of people, the constant hum of the electricity generator, the convoys of trucks entering and leaving the camp. The stillness awed and troubled her; indefinable memories mingled with impressions of the present.

Chapter Fourteen

It was late in the afternoon of the third day when they rode slowly over the crest of a hill. A grass-covered plain stretched before them. In the waning sunlight, the distant, encircling blue mountains were no more tangible than the clouds in the turquoise sky.

Tsun felt his horse brace to urinate. He eased himself up in the stirrups to take the weight off its kidneys. His nostrils were filled with the tang of ammonia as he assessed the encampment of black circular yak-hair tents some half a mile away. Scattered over the plain he could see the distant herds of yaks, horses, sheep and goats.

'Tsun-la,' Pema asked nervously, 'are they brigands or nomads?'

Tsun did not reply. He counted twenty widely separated tents which meant over a hundred people. It was a large encampment. To his right, a herd of goats were grazing, the boys tending them staring solemn-faced at the travellers. Even from a distance, Tsun recognised the tenseness of their bodies, like animals smelling danger, poised for flight. They were probably trying to decide whether the strangers were the scouts for a raiding party from a neighbouring clan, the Han, or friends. One of the boys remained sitting on a rock, playing a flute while gazing intently at the strangers.

'Though they are the country's ornaments, the rich die first when hunger's knife through famine comes,' Namgyal said, and watched eagerly for Pema's reaction. She glanced at him quickly, then away, knowing that he told the truth, and in these times, she thought, you did not have to be rich to merit the knife.

'Rinposhay!' Namgyal pointed at a group of five men who had ridden to the edge of the camp and were waiting for them to approach. They carried their rifles cradled in their arms and wore double bandoliers. Pema looked questioningly at Tsun. He nodded, and the three of them urged their horses down the steep slope, then walked them towards the camp and the tall mahogany-skinned nomads, whose aquiline features remained impassive. All five of them wore their winter sheepskin chubas. Two of the men had on wide-rimmed hats with red tassels falling from the high crown. Their horses shifted restlessly beneath them, but the men did not move, their steady, suspicious eyes fixed on the strangers approaching them from across the plain.

Tsun realised that the occupation had changed a natural caution of strangers into a feeling of suspicion that all strangers were a threat.

Namgyal cried out in delight at the sight of marmots suddenly appearing from the ground, shrieking then chasing one another through the grass. He reached into the fold of his chuba to remove his sling, then, remembering Tsun's presence, left the sling untouched in his chuba.

'Greetings!' Tsun called out. 'I have business with the Queen of Derge's herdsman.'

The men stared unsmilingly at him for a few seconds, then one of them gestured to him and the rest of the party to follow. The five men urged their horses into a rapid trot through the camp, then two of them swung away and rode off, back to the rim of the valley from which Tsun and the others had come, so that they could be certain the strangers were alone.

Most of the men were out tending the herds, but those who were left in the camp, as well as the women working at the looms or tanning hides and spinning wool, stopped what they were doing to look at the strangers as they rode past.

Tsun's guide stopped outside one of the large black tents. A woman with a squint was adjusting the shuttle on a wooden loom. The guide spoke to her.

'These people say that they have come from the Queen of Derge and have business with your husband.'

Tsun could hardly understand the man's thick, nomadic accent. The woman smiled up at Tsun.

'Come,' she said, and led them round to the rear of the tent where a man was tending a horse. It shied with pain as an acupuncture needle was stuck into its belly. The herdsman replaced the needle in a leather bag.

'Dhondup,' said the woman, 'these people have business with you.'

The man patted the horse's neck and made soothing sounds, holding onto the bridle and moving with it as it danced and tried to shake itself free. It was some minutes before the animal quietened and Dhondup was able to tether it.

Tsun slipped his left leg out of his stirrup, swung the other over his mount's neck and dropped to the ground. He took the letter the Queen had given him out of his ambac and handed it, wrapped in a felicity scarf, to the herdsman, a tall, well built man of middle years.

Dhondup frowned at it, then took off his red-banded trilby hat and rubbed his hand agitatedly over his close-cropped head. He walked across to the mounted nomad and handed the letter to him.

'I cannot read,' he said. 'Tell me, what does it say?'

The nomad split the large envelope with his thumbnail, opened the sheet of paper and read haltingly.

'The bearer of this letter is to be given every respect and is to have any twelve horses and four mules he chooses.' The nomad handed the letter back to the herdsman who looked at the seal and said, 'It is from the Queen.'

He took a silk felicity scarf from his sheepskin chuba. It was covered in dirt and crumpled from many years of use. He handed it to Tsun who took out of his saddle bag some needles and tsampa and gave them to Dhondup with a felicity scarf. Their contract was now sealed.

'Kusho, I am honoured to have you as my guest. Come, eat at my fireside.' All the suspicion and tension had gone. Dhondup settled his trilby back on his head. The nomads uncocked their Mauser rifles and slung them across their shoulders. Dhondup called to his eight year-old son.

'Boy, tie the horses.'

The grubby, tousled child, dressed only in breeches and a tattered sheepskin jacket which he had tied round his waist, tethered the horses to pegs in the ground and loosened their girths, while his father led his guests past the windbreak, a wall built with yak dung, and shouted at the large mastiff guarding the tent entrance to move aside. The dog glared at the strangers with blood-flecked eyes, straining at the chain round its neck, foam at its snarling lips. The men stopped. Then the squint-eyed woman flung a cloak over the mastiff's head and the guests were quickly ushered past it.

The tent was large, some twenty feet long and twelve feet wide. The only light came from the flames of the clay stove, the butter lamps on the altars and the smoke vent in the roof.

Although Pema had often lived in a tent when her family had camped in the summer with their herds, she had been much younger and now it seemed strange as her nostrils were filled with the sharp bitter smell of burning yak chips and the stale odour of animals and people.

Lashee, Dhondup's wife, was shooing some newly born lambs out of the way so that she could stoop and rake up the fire, beside which a toothless old woman was squatting chopping up a lump of cheese into cubes and threading them on a string. She looked up and smiled at the strangers, showing pink gums against a wrinkled, blackened face.

Tsun's gifts were given place of honour on the gaily painted wooden chest that served as the family altar.

While the nomads stacked their weapons with those of the family, Dhondup, using his flint pouch, lit an extra butter lamp, a singular honour for his guest.

They sat on sheepskins beside the stove which was giving off blue flames as Lashee worked a pair of crude bellows made of goat's skin. Another woman emerged from the darkness of the tent to see who the strangers were. She picked the teapot off the stove, swirled it round twice then offered it to Tsun who held his maple wood bowl for her to fill. The old woman offered them some cheese.

Tsun blew the film of butter to one side and drank some tea. His bowl was immediately refilled. They all drank and ate, saying little except for the customary pleasantries on the excellence of the tea. Everyone in the tent was gathered around the fireplace and sipping scalding-hot tea. The women kept on spinning and carding wool while they listened. It was only through travellers that the nomads kept in touch with the outside world.

'What news from Derge?' Dhondup asked. His youngest son carried in the visitors' saddles one at a time and leaned them against the tent poles. Dhondup picked up a brass prayer wheel, rested the end of its long handle on the ground, and began spinning it. Pema, noticing his close-cropped hair, wondered if he was a lapsed monk.

'Derge is not a good place to be,' Tsun said. 'There are too many Han there. It is no longer free. They question you when you enter and when you leave. There are street patrols and loudspeakers.'

'What are they, Kusho?' Lashee asked.

Tsun tried to explain to his intrigued hosts, but as he had only the vaguest idea of the principles of radio waves and electricity, everyone came to the conclusion that it was probably magic. This impressed the nomads. To be a sorcerer one had to be accomplished.

The two other women asked Pema questions, but she feigned shyness and was noncommittal. To the nomads, the Han were enemies who had invaded their homeland to make good ancient pretensions of conquest. She knew that the nomads would regard anyone who had the remotest connection with the Han as a traitor.

When Tsun spoke of the deportation of the children and of why Namgyal was with them, everyone fell silent and thought of their own children.

'Do they not fight?' Norbu, Dhondup's younger son, asked as he stood cleaning his flintlock.

'Of course,' Tsun replied. 'Often there is fighting, but it is unorganised. They do not have enough weapons.'

'If the Han have weapons, our people should take them,' said Norbu.

'It is not as it used to be when the Han came. If the people attacked their garrisons, the Han would send their metal flying machines to bomb and destroy the town.'

'How can it be?' The old woman continued cutting the cheese with practised movements. 'That they have such great magical powers? Surely ours will be greater than theirs?'

She did not ask anyone in particular and so Tsun did not answer her, for he agreed that their magic should be greater than that of the Han.

'But what of the wool, meat and butter prices in Derge?' Dhondup asked, as Lashee gave her guests some yoghurt. 'We shall be taking our wool to the market there soon.'

'Trade is not good.' Tsun took some snuff which Dhondup offered him. 'Because of the higher price of food and the extra taxes. People don't have the money or the goods they used to.'

'What about the Han? They paid good prices last year.'

'No longer! Derge is their town. They pay what they want to pay.'

'Here, try this.' Dhondup's son gave a pipe made of a sheep's thigh bone to Namgyal. Namgyal took one suck on it, then spluttered and coughed violently.

'You will kill the boy!' Pema snatched the pipe away violently. 'He is too young.'

Dhondup's son grinned at her. 'I was going to give you some,' he laughed.

Pema flushed slightly with embarrassment and her anger faded.

'Norbu!' his father scolded. 'Do not tease the girl.'

Pema smiled at the young man, then put the pipe to her lips. She drew the smoke into her lungs and was caught up in a spasm of coughing. Everyone laughed. Norbu patted her back with a heavy hand. He was about nineteen years old, with broad shoulders and the short stocky legs of a peasant. He had taken off his sheepskin coat, baring the upper part of his body, and Pema became irritatingly conscious of his delight in his muscular, copper-tanned torso. She moved away from him and sat behind him so that she could not see his grinning face, but her eyes kept being drawn to the jet-black pigtail which hung down his back to his waist.

'Perhaps we could take our wool to Jykundo, or Chamdo,' Dhondup's wife said. 'We must get a good price for it. We need barley and rice and many more things.'

'We shall not starve,' Dhondup said. 'We have everything we need. Maybe life won't be so easy, but that is good. We should not have to depend on the Han for everything. If we do not, we are still free.'

'But for how long?' Lashee asked.

'For as long as we fight for our freedom. If we give in, we lose everything.'

Lashee gave Tsun a strip of dried meat. 'The Garwan ought to know the news our guests have brought with them,' she said. She was wearing a large part of the family wealth in a coral studded belt and silver and coral hair ornaments. Many of the merchants who travelled to India and China brought back coral and semi-precious stones. Her teeth flashed white against her face, tanned almost black by the scorching sun of the plains.

Tsun chewed on a piece of leathery meat and flicked a flea off his neck. He nodded his head in agreement, for he had planned to see the Garwan, the head of the clan.

Norbu reached out and touched Pema's hair. 'You are very pretty,' he said. 'But why is your hair so short? It is like the Han.'

Pema glared at him, then mixed some butter with her tsampa. Norbu was intrigued by her. She did not have the fluttering shyness of the nomad girls. He eased himself closer to her. When she looked up, his face was inches from hers. He offered her the arak bottle. As she took it she smelt his sweat and it was sweet.

Just before dusk, Dhondup, Tsun, Pema, Norbu and Namgyal stood outside the tent and watched the herds being rounded up.

'Has the Han occupation affected you at all?' Tsun asked Dhondup.

'They have been to see us a few times, to talk. They took some of our horses but they paid a good price for them. Otherwise, we have seen little of them, except for their metal birds which sometimes fly overhead.'

The mastiffs started barking in anticipation as chunks of raw meat were thrown to them. The women and children of the camp were carrying leather pails in readiness for the milking and were checking the tethering posts. A blacksmith's hammer echoed through the air as he pounded a sword blade into shape. A group of young men were practising with their swords, cleaving a ball of wool thrown into the air in two.

'My eldest son,' Dhondup pointed.

Tsun saw a man on horseback about half a mile away. He was whirling a sling above his head, then unleashing a stone at the family's herd of yak. The fifty or so yaks and dris did not need the biting sting of the stones on their rumps to remind them that it was time to return to camp. With bellowing roars and tails erect, they thundered down the sloping plain to the herdsmen's tents.

Pema and Namgyal were frightened and moved away from the path of the animals, but Tsun, Dhondup and Norbu stood their ground. The snorting animals stopped a few feet in front of them. A mastiff tethered nearby was barking hysterically.

Lashee and two other women came out of her tent carrying three-gallon, wooden milking pails and began to help Dhondup's youngest son to tether and hobble the animals before starting to work on milking the dris.

Tsun spent some time going through the lines of tethered horses and mules, checking their backs for sores, their eyes, teeth and legs. Dhondup tied a thread of red wool on the bridles of the twelve horses and four mules that he had selected. Tsun bought as much feed for the horses and mules as they could carry, also butter, yoghurt and meat.

'I shall need the help of at least two men to take these goods to my companions.'

'My sons will accompany you,' Dhondup insisted.

'It may be a dangerous journey, Dhondup. And what about your own herds?'

'My neighbours will help me with them,' Dhondup said.

Darkness was falling by the time they finished and the mountains were a black silhouette against the grey-green sky. The sun flared like a dying fire. Already Tsun felt the biting cold and slipped his arm into the sleeve of his chuba.

Lashee was singing soothingly to the goat she was straddling as she milked it. Dhondup's young nephew nearly tripped Tsun as he ran past him trying to catch a lamb to take back to the tent for the night.

The evening passed pleasantly. Norbu played his guitar, and everyone joined in the songs of love, hunting and war. Dhondup offered snuff to his guests from a cream-coloured yak horn. The chickens murmured in a corner of the tent. The lambs bleated, disturbed by the movement. The men and women played dice, while Dhondup discussed with Tsun the current price of wool and the condition of trade generally.

'Aye, Dhondup,' a middle-aged man called across from the game. 'You fuss like an old woman.' The others laughed. 'We have horses and weapons. A Khamba is worth ten Han. If all the clans were to unite, we could sweep the Han from our country.'

'It is no longer as simple as that,' Tsun murmured.

Although the temperature was below freezing, all except the old woman slept outside the tent covered in felt blankets. They did this because it kept them tough and able to bear the extremes of temperature. Removing their felt boots to prevent frostbite, they loosened their belts and lay in a circle with their feet touching, for, it is said, if the feet are warm, the body is also warm.

Pema lay on her back, unable to sleep, and shivered. She gazed up at the moon and listened to the heavy breathing and snores of her companions, interlaced with the lowing and grunting of the animals. Namgyal, lying beside her, was fast asleep. She heard the dogs baying; a horse whinnied. She picked a flea from her arm and carefully placed it on the ground.

'Here!' someone whispered. A ragged, dirty sheepskin was thrown over her. She turned her head to find Norbu lying beside her, his head propped in his hand as he smiled down at her. Pema smiled back. Then his hand reached out to touch her face, feeling every feature with exquisite tenderness. She lay still, keeping her eyes on the moon. Then she felt him slide under the sheepskin and press his body close to hers. His heart beats filled her ears. As a person, she did not like him, but she was aroused by his raw virility. She thought of her brother sleeping a few feet away and was embarrassed. But then, the moon vanished and his mouth was seeking hers, his tongue thrusting deep, his hand caressing her breast.

She responded with expert, subtle caresses; but he was younger than she realised. His body was heavy. It reacted urgently. Only moments later, she murmured for him to wait, but he ignored her. She dug her fingers into his buttocks and hissed at him to wait. But it was too late. He lay limp on top of her. She grasped his ears and raised his head so that she could look into his eyes.

'You are a boy!'

His lips tightened. She let him go and turned over, curling up under the sheepskin. He is a boy, she thought again. I am younger than him in years alone.

Suddenly, the sheepskin was pulled from her. It was Norbu's elder brother. She cried out in alarm. Norbu leaped up, made a grab at the coat and missed. Some of the others woke up, saw what had happened and laughed. Pema reached desperately for the coat, but Norbu snatched it from her and held it to him. He grabbed his dagger and advanced on his brother. Pema clumsily adjusted her clothes and rolled onto her stomach to try and hide her embarrassment. One of the women threw a blanket over her.

The two young men circled each other, both with daggers drawn, their heavy breathing vaporising in the freezing air. Norbu was growling like an angry animal, his heavy dagger cleaving the air towards his brother's head. Dhondup separated them.

'You humiliate me in front of my guests,' he said angrily.

The two young men let their daggers fall to their sides, their bodies relaxed and they both looked ashamed as their father berated them and ordered them to return to the circle and sleep.

Everyone settled down again, except for Norbu. He lay on his back, seething with rage. Pema lay with her eyes wide, staring up at the moon.

Some two hours later, she eased herself to her feet and picked up her boots. She gasped as a hand circled her ankle. It was Norbu. His teeth flashed white in the darkness. Pema wrenched her ankle from his grip and moved away swiftly.

Shivering, she tugged her chuba round her and pulled on her boots. She made her way to where the horses were tethered, listening for the slightest sound, frightened that Norbu might be following or had aroused some of the others. She half expected the mastiffs to start barking, but the only sound was the rustling grass and the whine of the wind to remind her of the demons that roamed abroad in the night. She approached the line of horses, murmuring soothingly so as not to startle them, and made for the one at the end of the line. It pawed the ground nervously then whinnied.

A low, guttural growl came from behind the horse. Pema caught sight of a sandy brown body. Kunjosum, she thought, a mastiff, and it's loose!

Her fingers struggled with the rope tethering the horse. Her first thought was to mount and ride away as fast as she could, for although the mastiff might spring, she would stand more chance on horseback than on foot. She was agonisingly aware of the brown body sinking to the ground in readiness to pounce.

'No!' she cried aloud.

A movement to her side made her turn to see the light from the moon glitter momentarily in the eyes of another dog.

'Help me!' Her voice cut the silence of the night. 'Tsun, help me . . .'

Almost immediately, there was a babble of voices.

'Pema!' A tall figure was running towards her. One of the mastiffs saw Tsun. Snarling, its ears went back.

'Down! Down!' Dhondup's voice rose above the others. Pema screamed as one of the dogs pounced, knocking her off her feet. The yellow fangs strained at her face and throat, and she pushed her hands against the thick neck with all her strength. Tsun ignored the dog threatening him and drove his dagger into the back of the neck of the mastiff attacking Pema. It yelped, then twisted convulsively and collapsed limply on top of her. She felt its warm blood on her arm. Tsun pushed the body aside and pulled her to her feet. She was white and shaken. Tears, dirt and saliva smeared her face and chest.

'Are you hurt?' Tsun asked gently. She shook her head, unable to speak. He took her back to the tent and sat her by the smouldering fire while he rubbed her frozen hands. The old woman snored peacefully.

Dhondup had the body of the mastiff wrapped in an old blanket and brought into the tent to prevent the other dogs from eating it.

'At night, all the mastiffs are set loose to guard the camp,' he explained. 'I should have warned you.' He told the two men carrying the dog to set it down at the back of the tent. 'Tomorrow we will skin it,' he said. 'The hide will be useful.'

Pema's head dropped onto Tsun's shoulder. She felt safe and warm with his arm around her. He didn't ask her why she was among the horses. He did not have to and she knew it. Exhausted, she fell into a doze. Taking care not to wake her, Tsun felt in his ambac and handed some silver to Dhondup.

'The dog was valuable,' he said. 'I must recompense you for my sister's foolishness.'

Dhondup took the coins and thanked him. 'I have lost a valuable dog,' he said. 'But, I think, Kusho, you have lost something of greater value.' Tsun did not answer. He cradled Pema's head in his arms. It was true that he had broken one of the fundamental precepts of his order. Not to kill.

'I dreamed last night,' Dhondup said, 'that we would be visited by a lama.'

'It is better that no one knows,' Tsun interrupted him.

'Kusho, I am past my youth and advanced in age,' Dhondup said heavily. 'In my life I have killed, been intoxicated, loved many women. I have broken all the precepts. Now, I spin my prayer wheel, invoke the blessed Chenresi and hope that his compassion will ensure that I am born into a religious land.'

Chapter Fifteen

Tsun plunged his hands through the film of ice and splashed his face with the bitingly cold water in the wooden pail. It was an hour before dawn, and in the expectant stillness emphasised by the lone song of a bird, Dhondup, his family and guests made the morning offering to the Triple Gem, tossing grains of tsampa into an incense fire of smoking rhododendron leaves on a small stone altar.

Pema shivered in the cold darkness of the plain. She looked at the stunted trees in the distance, black silhouettes marking not only the edge of the plain, but of darkness. Beyond were drifting clouds in which appeared to float a superbly beautiful mountain, its outline sharp in the lightening sky of dawn, its granite rock and glaciers tinged with mauve by the rising sun. It was, Pema thought, as though the world of reality had ended and given way to the land of dreams, of legends, of harmonious contradictions.

They rode the three miles to the tent of the chief of the clan, the Garwan, the largest in the encampment. The Garwan greeted Tsun with a scarf, draping it over his hands and bowing. Tsun smiled. Dhondup had evidently told the Garwan of his dream and the visiting lama.

The Garwan was a stocky, broad faced man with a powerful presence. There were flecks of grey in his well buttered hair, which was plaited with red wool into a pigtail and wound round his head. He took his seat in front of an ornately carved and gilded wooden altar. A number of men, mostly middle-aged with a scattering of old and very young, sat resting their backs against the leather storage sacks lining the walls of the large tent.

Tsun and Dhondup were shown to seats on either side of the Garwan. Tsun's seat was slightly higher than the Garwan's, a mark of respect and honour. The women and children poured tea for the guests and set it before them on plain painted tables.

The Garwan leaned towards Tsun. 'Dhondup says you are a holy lama, Kusho.'

Tsun smiled. 'But I'm not even dressed as a monk,' he said.

'My wife,' the Garwan answered slowly, 'though dressed in her finest silks and jewels, is not the most beautiful woman in Tibet.' But he understood the implication in Tsun's words and did not press the point.

'Kusho, I have asked you here to meet the camp council so that you can explain to them yourself the message you bring from the Queen of Derge.'

Tsun took a long sip of tea. He knew that telling the nomads of the Queen's message would inflame the situation between them and the Han. To be the bearer of the news of death was not easy, but Tsun knew that this was much more.

'The Queen of Derge has asked me to tell you of a decision made by the Local Working Party of the Communist Party.'

'What is the Communist Party?' A tall, wrinkled old man with a livid scar running from his temple across the empty socket of his right eye to his split lips asked the question testily.

'They are the Red People that the Great Thirteenth Kundun warned about in his Testament.' The Garwan twisted the red tassel falling from the end of his pigtail. 'They believe that all property, livestock, all possessions should be held in common,' Tsun explained.

'Like the ideas of Muni Tsonpo.' The man with the scar spoke scathingly of the eighth-century Tibetan king who divided the wealth of his realm equally among his people.

'Three times, Muni Tsonpo's ideas were put into practice, and three times they failed.'

'People are people.' The Garwan stuffed tobacco into his long-stemmed pipe, made from a sheep's thigh bone.

'Some use their assets, some waste them,' he said. 'And we have all created our karma. One year my herds breed well. There are few blizzards. I lose few young ones. The pasture is good. I am a rich man. The next year, my herds may be stolen by another clan, or they may die in a blizzard. I am a poor man. Life is the toss of a dice.'

He shredded some edelweiss grass onto the table in front of him and struck the piece of flint on the curved blade of his flint pouch. The grass caught on the first spark and the Garwan applied it to his pipe, puffing vigorously. Tsun's bowl was refilled with tea. The Garwan's wife threw some sweet smelling herbs onto the fire. A bald headed man was cleaning out his ears with a silver ear spoon.

'It is more than that,' Tsun continued. 'The Han say that

religion and the nobles must be overthrown. They must be destroyed, because they oppress the people.'

'If they mean to overthrow the Lhasa nobles, I agree with them.' The young man who spoke grinned at some of his companions who laughed in agreement. The Garwan sucked on his pipe.

'Kusho, what is the decision which will affect us?' he asked.

'The Han are linking the trade of Tibet with that of China,' Tsun said. 'They have many methods which they say will help grow more crops.' He looked at the Garwan. 'They will toss the dice and the odds will always be high. Your herds will be stronger. You will lose fewer in winter.' They were all giving him their complete attention.

'To do this,' he smiled, 'the Han have to control everything. They . . .' The rest of his words were lost in laughter.

'They have decided,' Tsun continued when the laughter had died down, 'that pasturing, the sale of wool, butter, yoghurt, cheese, hides . . . everything, should be state controlled. That you should have a base camp, with houses which they will help you to build. There your children will have schooling. Your sick can go to a medical clinic. Your animals will be treated by an animal doctor. Special storage buildings will be built for winter fodder, so that the animals will not go hungry during the winter months, and will be in better condition throughout the rest of the year. In summer, the men will take the animals out to pasture as it is now. But your wives will remain at the base camp and your children at school.'

For a few moments there was silence. Then everyone started asking questions and voicing opinions.

'If we do not agree?' an old man asked.

'That is rebellion.'

'The sugar on the sharp knife.'

'Why should our children have to go to school? We have a monk with us who teaches them to read and write.'

'Why do they need to go to school? Will that teach them how to help a cow have her calf?'

'Perhaps it will,' Tsun answered. 'The Han say that they will give your children many opportunities. They might even learn how to fly iron birds.'

'And would they also learn how to lay their iron eggs on their parents who rebel?'

'Yes! That they would learn too.' Tsun lifted the lid of the copper filigree-worked tsampa container on the table, took out a handful of barley flour and put it into his bowl, then mixed it into a dough with the dregs of his tea.

'They would learn that they are Chinese, not Tibetan. Instead of invoking the Lord of Compassion when they wake up, they would honour Chairman Mao Tse-tung and the Chinese Communist Party.'

The Garwan looked at Tsun.

'Did the Queen have any suggestions?'

'Your plight is her plight, Derge's plight – indeed, Tibet's plight. All she can do is warn you that the Han will be here in a few days. Can you move from this area?'

'Not for many days,' one of the older men insisted.

'The animals have no fat on them after the winter. Some are already carrying their young. A long journey will kill them.'

'But surely,' Tsun asked, 'it will soon be time for you to move to new pasturage?'

'Not for a few more weeks, when the winds and snows have gone. Even then, we could only travel for short periods. The animals are very weak.'

'The Han would soon find us,' said a heavy-featured man. 'We must fight. We are free. We move when *we* wish. We have food and do not starve. We have shelter, clothes. We work and ride, sing and dance, make love, hunt and fight. We honour the religion. What else do we need? Life is short and full of suffering. The Han would stop all joy.'

'If you fight,' Tsun explained, although he agreed with the man, 'you will be rebels and will lose everything.'

'It is better to fight now.'

'Is it? Who will say what the future will bring? The colour of the sky changes with the rise and fall of the sun and the moon, but always there is sky. So it is with the Han. Over the centuries, the weapons change, the dynasties change, but always they are the celestial kingdom, the "centre of the civilised world".'

'We must fight!'

'Things are not as they used to be.' Tsun paused to drink some tea. 'You have seen the Han iron birds. They will lay their iron eggs on your herds, your tents. Nothing will remain. It will be as though a dragon has breathed on you.'

'This is our ground.' A young man fixed Tsun with the intense eyes of a Khamba warrior. 'My grandfather was killed fighting for this land. Even today that feud still continues. Better that I die honouring my ancestors, than live in dishonour.'

'You choose the easy way. What of your family, who have to live under the Han? What merit is there in your death, when by your action you will make the Han take revenge on your family, and you will not be there to protect them?'

'Then let us send the herds away with a few men and the women and children. The rest of us will stay and fight.' The young man's face was hidden by his long black hair. He sat bent over the silver lined wooden bowl which he turned continuously, swirling his tea round and round.

'But,' Tsun reasoned, 'if you fight, you have to win or be completely destroyed. You cannot win. I have seen Litang reduced to a rubble because it fought. The Queen of Derge is virtually a prisoner of the Han. The city is in chaos.'

'But we are not monks or city dwellers.'

'You talk from ignorance,' Tsun said sharply. 'Namgyal, the boy with me, was placed in my care by his father, because the Han are sending children to China to be educated, without their parents' permission. His father, and many like him, have rescued children and smuggled them out of the city.'

'You believe, Kusho,' Dhondup said, 'that we shouldn't fight the Han?'

'It will happen, that either you will, or will not, have to fight. If you fight, fight to win, with weapons that will match those of the Han. When that time comes, everyone should fight. Not just a handful, but the nation, because then, there will be no alternative.'

'Then what can we do?' the young man with the burning eyes asked Tsun. The lama spoke sadly.

'You know your situation better than I do. I can only tell you that I know from experience and suggest that only when every other alternative has been tried, should you resort to violence.'

'We could gather all the clans!'

'That would take weeks.'

'We should consult the oracle.'

'We *must* fight!'

'You have never fought.' The scarred man stabbed a finger at the young man on the other side of the tent. 'So you can be eager to fight.'

'My brother died in my arms with his throat slit.'

'It was not your throat,' the old man growled. 'The blade was not slashed at your throat. You have never thrust a blade into someone's belly and watched him die. The blood on your hands. When you have done this, you are different. Life, death, mean much more. You know what it means to fight, to risk your life, to face death. You realise the value of life. There are experiences which are always with you. It is like making love to a woman. I can tell you what that is like . . .' His words were drowned in a burst of laughter. He waited until it had died down. 'I can describe the feelings to you, so that you have a good idea of it, but it will not change you. Only when you have experienced it will you be changed.'

'Unless I fight, how can I know that this is true?'

'The snake doesn't go after its enemies. It waits. In time they will come and it will strike.'

'Old men grow cautious when death is their shadow and life precious,' the young man murmured to one of his companions.

'I think we should move,' said the Garwan. 'The Han will be here in a few days. There is a chance that they will not find us.'

'But they will have come far, they . . .'

'We can make it difficult for them.'

'They will have iron birds.'

'It will take time.'

'The Han control very little of the country,' said Tsun. 'Their greatest strength is in the villages and towns.'

After a further half hour of indecisive discussion, Tsun turned to the Garwan. 'I must leave now, I have far to travel.'

The Garwan tried to dissuade Tsun, but he could not, and after a final drink, he escorted Dhondup and Tsun outside. It was so warm that Tsun slipped his arms from the sleeves of his chuba. The three men stood and watched as an excited crowd gathered round a yak which was bellowing, sensing danger. Placing bets with the onlookers was a middle-aged man who was stripped to his plump waist. Some of the onlookers shook their heads and spun their prayer wheels.

'One of my horses, that he will succeed, Dhondup,' the Garwan said.

'Of course he will succeed, Garwan.'

'You grow clever in your old age, Dhondup.' He tapped his teeth with his pipe and glanced at Tsun. 'Or is it just that you grow pious?'

Dhondup did not answer. He too looked at Tsun and made to move away, but Tsun remained where he was. The crowd had fallen silent. The middle-aged man picked up a long double edged sword. He weighed it in his hands, his eyes on the yak. Tsun noticed Namgyal, leaping and whip-cracking his sling in the air as

he ran excitedly towards them with a bunch of nomad children.
The yak side-stepped away as the man approached. Its deep-throated roar filled the silence. The animal's moist black nostrils worked constantly as it smelt danger.

The man stopped beside the yak. He held the sword high above his head, closed his eyes in concentration and invoked the aid of his tutelary diety, and that the thousand eyes of Chenresi looked mercifully upon the yak. He forced the energy from every part of his body into his arms. The yak bellowed once, mingling anger and pain, as the blade sliced through the centre of its spine. It staggered then collapsed, cleaved in two. Blood fountained. It covered the yak, the swordsman and many of the crowd, gushing so high and free that for a few moments Tsun could not see what had happened.

The crowd retreated rapidly before the crimson spouts. Tsun murmured a prayer for the yak. Nothing had changed, he thought, not for a thousand years, since the forefathers of the nomads had conquered Nepal, Burma and north-eastern China. Nothing had changed, except the enemy.

'It is not enough,' he said aloud, looking at the Garwan.

It was several hours later. Seated beside the painted wooden altar in Dhondup's tent, his eyes lowered, Tsun sat in meditation, while the family and their neighbours said their rosaries and spun their prayer wheels.

Dhondup had asked Tsun to bless the household before his departure. The lama began chanting, his voice unrecognisable in its depth, impersonal, mighty as the roaring of the wind across the plain. It was as if his chanting had, indeed, conjured up the gods. The silence, when he stopped, was not just absence of sound, it was a living silence, charged with energy.

Pema was suddenly afraid of the charged atmosphere. On Tsun's copper-tanned face the afternoon light splashed brightly through the roof vent. She remembered, as a child, having seen faces like that of her brother when she was taken to receive the blessing of revered lamas. Glancing round at the totally absorbed people in the tent, she wanted to see something, to grasp something, that would break the spell, that would deny what she felt. She tried hard to be aloof, detached; it was impossible. She was part of it, and she knew that it was not just her conditioned responses.

Dhondup was bowing very low and sucking in his breath as he

laid his felicity scarf on the rug-covered divan on which Tsun was sitting. He kept his eyes lowered as Tsun laid his hands on his host's head in blessing.

Pema waited until most of the others had been blessed before picking her way around a small tea table, over saddles, hides, and constantly pecking and scrabbling chickens. Her stomach tightened with increasing anxiety and apprehension as she approached her brother. She had been a child when she had last paid her respects to a lama and she felt awkward as she bent double and laid her scarf with the others in front of Tsun. Surreptitiously, she glanced up at her brother. His eyes remained shaded by lowered lids. There was not the slightest reaction on his impersonal, motionless face. She saw his hands rise and lowered her head further.

As his hand touched her, a bolt of energy raced through her body, her mind like a stunned bird with faltering wings falling through the sky. She had no idea how long it was that she lost consciousness, but no one else seemed to have noticed. Tsun's hands rested on his lap in the ritual gesture of meditation. Pema felt weak and staggered slightly as she moved to a rug near her brother. She sat as the others came forward to be blessed.

She wondered if they, too, were having the same experience. Her whole body felt torn apart, yet beneath the fear was an exhilaration. Perhaps, she thought, he used magic to impress me and make sure of my loyalty. Looking at him, though, she was convinced that he did have the power to make one aware of the energy received during blessing.

Chapter Sixteen

'Namgyal, hurry, we are leaving,' Pema called to the boy, as Topgay, the eldest of Dhondup's sons, helped her to mount.

Barefooted and even grubbier than usual, Namgyal abandoned his sling competition with the nomad boys and leapfrogged over the hindquarters of his horse, causing it to shy nervously and the boys to laugh as he landed clumsily in the saddle, almost losing his balance and badly wrenching the muscles in his groin.

As Tsun received the felicity scarf from Dhondup, he felt the leather pouch, heavy with silver coins, in its folds.

'The hospitality of the pastoral ones is legendary, Dhondup,' Tsun murmured to him, as Lashee bowed, sucking in her breath. Tsun blessed her, laying his hand on her head.

The Garwan rode up with a dozen men while Dhondup was holding Tsun's stirrup for him to mount.

'Kusho, we will escort you,' the Garwan said. And with that, the party urged their horses forward across the plain, waving and calling their farewells as they rode.

'What has the council decided?' Tsun asked the Garwan.

'We shall move during the next few days. The oracle is divining the most auspicious day. I have sent messengers to the other clans to warn them, and to tell them that I want to call a meeting of all clan leaders.' His broad face was creased with worry. 'This time it is different, Kusho?' Tsun nodded. They trotted towards the edge of the plain.

'The barley in the field is barley. The barley flour I add to my tea is the same barley. Yet, had I not harvested it, winnowed and parched that barley myself, I would not know the barley of the field and the barley of the bowl to be the same. So it will be with Tibet.'

Tsun was first to reach the ridge. He stiffened as he saw a flash of reflected sunlight on the barely perceivable ribbon of a track that wove among the mountains. He focused his field glasses on the point where he had seen the flash.

'Han!'

His horse reared, startled by his shout. Tsun reckoned that there were at least a hundred men, and they were equipped for a long journey with spare horses and pack mules. He focused the glasses again. At the head of the column, among the olive-green military tunics, there was one blue civilian uniform. Tsun tried to focus on the face. It was impossible to see clearly, they were at such a distance, yet there was a dread in his heart, as he thought it might be Ling who was riding with the PLA column. He was tormented with thoughts of what he might have brought on those he'd been with at Derge.

'I am the one they're after,' Tsun said to the Garwan as he handed him the glasses.

The Garwan looked at the point Tsun indicated, then shouted to one of his men. 'Warn the camp. Tell them not to fire one shot until I give the order.'

'Ramdaramda!' The man yelled the alarm cry as he rode back towards the camp. Within moments, men came running, mounted their horses, and rode to join the Garwan.

'This way!' Norbu, Dhondup's son, pointed towards the north and drove his heels into his horse's flanks. Pema and Namgyal cantered after Norbu and his brother Topgay, keeping below the ridge and out of sight of the approaching Han, shouting at the horses and mules as they fought to keep control of the lead reins.

Tsun turned in his saddle to look back, fearful of the harm that his visit might have brought to the encampment. The Garwan was spinning the chamber of his revolver as he and his escort waited on the crest of the ridge.

Pema was dropping behind. Tsun reined in and waited for her to catch up. He realised how tempting it could be for her to rejoin the Han.

Topgay took a path leading down from the ridge. The ground was rocky and precipitous, sloping as it did for some hundred feet, then rising sharply.

Three hours later, Tsun stood looking down at a narrow surging river flowing beneath a tall glacier that cloaked the side of a mountain. The edge of the glacier was a massive wall of serrated blue ice poised inches above the rushing water. For a few moments, Pema and Namgyal stood and looked in wonder at the awful beauty of it all.

Tsun shaded his eyes against the sun's glare and searched the sky as he had done so many times during their ride. Memories of the aeroplane which had haunted them since the flight from Dorje Ri-gon filled his mind.

Topgay, of the silent face – for he smiled little and his large dark eyes always looked slightly troubled – paused by the side of the turbulent river and invoked the protection of Tara, the goddess of mercy. Then, shouting and kicking, he forced his horse, and the two on either side of him, into the water, their lead reins attached to his saddle. The rope tied round his waist was looped round a tree and held by Tsun, Norbu and Namgyal. They let it out slowly, straining against the unrelenting pull of the river as it threatened to sweep Topgay and the horses away. Swimming frantically, the horses appeared to be held stationary in the ice cold water. Topgay, unable to swim, was relying entirely on the horses to get him to the other side. Their terror kept them paddling, but he could feel his own horse faltering as they reached the bank and scrambled ashore.

Untying the rope from his waist, Topgay attached it to the bole of a tree, then he gave the signal for the others to attempt the crossing.

Pema was next to go. She had taken off her sheepskin chuba, realising that wet, its weight would pull her down. Namgyal held her horse, while Tsun and Norbu tied a second rope around her waist with a running loop over the line stretched across the river.

'Hold onto the rope,' Tsun told her. 'Don't panic. Even if you fall from the horse, you can keep hold of the rope and we shall pull you ashore.'

Pema nodded curtly. She was afraid. 'Fetch two horses,' she said.

'No! It is better that you go alone.'

'Nonsense! How can you, Namgyal and Norbu take all of them. Please, Tsun.'

Tsun hesitated, but she was right. Without her help they would have to leave them behind, but it was a risk he did not like her taking. He nodded at Norbu, who brought two of the horses forward. Again, they had to be forced into the river, trying to evade all attempts to get them into the cold water.

The roar of the river pounded in Pema's ears; it battered and clutched at her with icy fingers as though the very demons of the cold hells sought to drag her down to their midst. The pull of the reins in her left hand increased as one of the horses, weakening fast, began to succumb to the drag of the current. Desperately, she urged it on as the other horses, feeling the drag, slowed down. The reins bit tightly into her numbed flesh as she struggled to keep the animals moving. The current surged, pulling the horses away so violently that she cried out at the wrenching on her arms. She tried to open her hands to release the reins but they were wound so tightly that her fingers could not move. She became conscious of nothing but the searing pain and the water, dragging, beating her down, filling her mouth and nose.

Topgay grasped the bridles of the horses and dragged them onto the bank, catching Pema as she fell from the saddle. He held her and unclasped her fingers from the reins. As she lay gasping on the ground, she was aware that she was alive, that the earth, the air, life, had never seemed so good.

'It is auspicious!' Norbu said, tying the rope and loop to Namgyal's waist. The boy looked towards the rainbow that had formed in the spume below the glacier and hoped that he was right.

'It'll be easier,' said Tsun, 'with the second rope across the river.'

Namgyal's horse backed and sidestepped to avoid entering the river, but eventually, Norbu and Tsun forced it in. The pain in Namgyal's groin was intense; his legs had lost the strength to control the horse and it swam vigorously in a circle and straight back to the bank. Norbu pulled it out of the river and began telling Namgyal how to control it better.

'Give him another horse,' said Tsun.

'Kusho!' Namgyal was thoroughly humiliated. 'Please, I will take him across this time.'

Tsun shook his head. 'The horse is tired, the current is strong.'

Namgyal dismounted, undid the girth of his wooden-framed saddle and carried it to a horse Norbu picked out for him. He was beginning to wish he hadn't shown off by leaping onto his horse when they were leaving the camp; the pulled muscle in his groin was becoming increasingly painful.

He was small and light, so the water hit him with even greater effect. The spray stung his face, taking his breath away, and he, too, felt the dreadful grasping hands of the river. The horse lost its impulsion to swim when they were three quarters of the way across and, in that instant, the river took control. Norbu, Tsun, Pema and Topgay felt the strain on the rope. In his efforts to get the horse moving again, the boy's grip with his legs slackened and he lost his balance. Pema screamed as Namgyal vanished beneath the water. He paddled desperately, sucking in water-laced breaths, but he was exhausted and was quickly swept away from the bank. The rope entangled round his arm and he felt its bite as Pema and Topgay pulled him in as quickly as possible. Topgay lifted the limp, sodden, but still breathing boy from the water. Down river, his exhausted horse struggled to the bank.

Tsun and Norbu lessened the mules' burden by strapping some of the supplies onto the horses. With two reluctant horses on one side of him and two mules on the other, Tsun entered the river.

The current pushed the animals close together so that they jostled one another and Tsun's mount snapped at the horse next to it. Tsun cried out in pain as a desperately paddling hoof caught his shin bone.

They were some twenty yards from the shore when he heard a loud cracking. The terrified horses plunged forward, their heads tautly erect. Tsun struggled to keep them together, for they pulled in all directions. Through the spray he saw Pema and Topgay shouting and pointing.

He turned to see an enormous block of ice slide into the water. The river surged as it received the ice into its depths. The animals snorted and whinnied with fear as they jostled and lunged. Tsun had to let go of the leading reins or his arms would have been torn from their sockets.

The river settled, and Tsun saw the block of ice bearing down on him. He felt the sympathetic lift and push of the river. He shouted and pushed his horse into a further effort to get clear. Norbu was untying the stretched ropes from the tree before the ice block hit them. A horse screamed as the ice caught it in the hindquarters and bore the wounded animal before it like some glacial juggernaut.

Tsun's horse swam for its life. The ice slid past, barely two feet from them. The wake threw horse and rider violently upwards, unseating Tsun. He grabbed at the horse's mane as the waters enveloped him. The rope from his saddle to his waist held him and he struggled to remount, but it was impossible in the turbid water. They were being sucked alongside the ice.

Like the others, unable to swim, Tsun pulled himself up half over the saddle. The horse was tiring and only struggled weakly against the pull of the ice. All Tsun's energy was concentrated in urging the animal forward. He shouted, encouraging the horse into action, clinging to his saddle and kicking out with his feet as the two of them fought their way slowly and painfully to the bank.

Topgay was at the river's edge to grab the bridle. Tsun's grip on the saddle loosened and he fell face down into the shallow water. Pema and Namgyal helped him to his feet and Topgay untied the rope attached to the saddle from Tsun's waist. Pema stayed with Tsun while Topgay tethered the horse and ran along the rocky bank with Namgyal to round up the remaining horses and mules struggling ashore. They saw the wounded animal being swept out of sight round a bend in the river.

'Tsun-la?' Pema leaned over her brother.

He smiled at her anxious face, then doubled up with cramp in his legs. When it had subsided, he sat on a rock and watched Norbu enter the water from the opposite bank with the remaining four animals. Without the ropes to hold him, he was swept steadily downstream by the current. Tsun glanced at the wedge-shaped ice-age glacier waiting, it seemed, like some predatory animal, to slip into the river to devour another victim. He knew that imperceptibly, it was moving from the hidden heights of the mountain to feed the rivers of Tibet. Like a mother feeding her child, the mountains of the Land of Snows fed the Brahmaputra, the Indus, the sacred Ganges, the Yangtse and the Salween.

Tsun rose, his clothes heavy and sodden, and walked to the river's edge. The youth's sheer physical strength kept the horses swimming, in an ever-increasing diagonal as the river pulled Norbu away from the bank. But eventually, with the aid of a rope thrown to him, he reached it.

'Can we rest here?' Pema asked when they were all safely ashore. Tsun shook his head.

'We could be trapped too easily. Up there,' he pointed to the cliff top, 'we shall be safer.'

Pema dried her hair in front of the fire and listened to the roar of the river a hundred feet below. There were chubas and shirts propped up around the fire on sticks. Topgay poured boiling water into the teapot. Norbu lay on his back and stared up at the strange world he could see in the clouds which hung a few yards above him. Namgyal padded his groin carefully with the medicinal leaves that Tsun had collected for him, and tried to ignore the laughter at his expense.

'Can we spend the night here, Kusho?' Norbu asked.

Tsun shook his head.

'But, Kusho, the horses and mules are too tired to go on.'

'It will kill them,' Pema entreated.

'The Han have hunted my party all the way from Litang,' Tsun said. 'They are not going to stop now. The only way is to keep moving.'

Pema turned on him, exasperated. 'None of us have the strength to go on.'

'Yes we have, little sister.' He ruffled her hair teasingly. She looked at him angrily, and remembered that this man, her brother, was the person who had blessed her in the tent. She shrugged with ill grace.

Unable to speak over the howling wind, they crossed the plain. Their legs moved slowly against the wind, their breath freezing on their faces and eyebrows. The animals, with their ears pressed against their drooping heads, were too exhausted for the party to attempt to ride them.

It was Tsun who first heard the familiar sound, plucking it like a fish from the deep river of the wind's dirge. At first, he could only just make out the pinpoints of light like glowing embers in the darkness. Then, suddenly, in the light of the moon, they saw the Mig flying towards them from over the mountains.

Tsun shouted, and they pulled the animals down and crouched in their shadows. The 'plane flew nearer. It was just possible, Tsun thought, that the pilot would identify the dark irregular shapes on the plain as a group of rocks. The 'plane was so close now that Norbu sighted his rifle on it.

'It's too high', Tsun shouted at him, although he was only a foot away. He shouted at Pema and Namgyal, who just heard him above the roar of the 'plane's engine and the wind.

'Keep well down behind the horses.'

They struggled to keep the frightened animals still. Pema's tongue touched her iced, cracked lips.

The 'plane flew over and they stayed still until the sound of its engine died away.

As they continued their journey, Tsun's mind was filled with memories of the escape from Dorje Ri-gon. Each time they had sighted the 'plane it had apparently reported their position. They were all ill with exhaustion. Tsun, who was beginning to hallucinate with tiredness, did not know whether he was awake or asleep when he dreamed of the Han capturing them and seizing the petition.

It was late afternoon of the tenth day since Tsun had left his party for Derge. He stood on the brim of the valley and focused his field glasses on the rows of enormous uniform shapes standing one on top of the other, eroded from the rock by a curious quirk of the winds, snows and rains, into a canyon of legendary giants.

'Move, or I'll see your guts!'

Tsun froze as he felt the prick of a blade in his side, but the voice was familiar. He turned.

'Genyen!'

They laughed and clasped one another. In that spontaneous embrace, relief, ghosts of the past, and of the future, were resurrected. They saw the implications in one another's eyes and moved apart.

'Genyen?' Pema sounded surprised to see the nomad girl she remembered from her childhood. Genyen looked at Tsun.

'It is Pema,' he answered her unspoken question.

Genyen laughed and held the girl's pink face in her tough, copper-coloured hands. 'You have grown beautiful, Pema-la.'

The girl blushed, then reddened more deeply because she had blushed, and caught sight of Tsun's smile.

Genyen turned back to Tsun. He realised she had aged in the short time since they had parted. Her face was gaunt.

'You have more horses, Rinposhay.' The relief in her voice was evident as she caught sight of Topgay and Norbu coming up the path.

'Yes, but they are weak.'

Tsun signalled to the two brothers to wait with the horses and mules, while Genyen led him, Pema and Namgyal along a narrow, crumbling ledge 500 feet above the valley floor, to a row of caves that honeycombed the sides of the cliffs.

Suddenly, a barking ball of black and white fur darted out of a cave and leaped into Tsun's arms. It nuzzled at his chin and licked his face.

'Senge! Senge!' Kesang ran out of the cave, stopped in disbelief, then ran back into the cave shouting at the top of his voice.

'Tsun Rinposhay is back! He is back, quick, come!' Then he hurled himself towards the lama.

Tsun tucked the ecstatic dog in his chuba and swung Kesang off his feet as he reached him, hugging and holding him close. In those moments he realised yet again just how much the small boy meant to him and how truly vulnerable love had made him. He set the boy down and held his hand as they walked towards the cave. Kesang talked excitedly, asking questions and not waiting for answers, telling of the adventures they had had since they had been apart.

'You've become thin, Kesang.'

'So have we all, Rinposhay, there has not been much to eat.'

Lopsang, as he came out of the cave, looked even more stooped than usual, Tsun thought. Rinchen, the steward, his three pupils and Norden crowded with the Khamba escort on the narrow ledge outside the cave.

Tsun was welcomed with tattered felicity scarves and plied with questions about his journey. He was distressed to see how worn they all looked and as a bowl of weak soup, little more than coloured water, was pressed on him, he realised why. Turning to Genyen, he asked her to send some men to relieve Topgay and Norbu and to ask them to bring the supplies.

'Rinposhay, you have brought food?' Norden could hardly believe it. Tsun was struck both by the warmth of her welcome and by how shrunken her face had become. Her thick black hair was matted and lank.

'And horses and mules,' Genyen was laughing with pleasure.

'Truly, the Rinposhay has the siddhas,' Rinchen murmured with mock piety, referring to holy powers, and laughing as he caught Tsun's eye.

Tsun sipped the scalding liquid and looked round the cave. It had evidently been a retreat for an artistic hermit at some time. The walls were covered with peeling and faded frescoes. Some were still beautiful. Norden was helping one of the Khambas, who was lying at the back of the cave, to drink.

'What is wrong with him?'

'He was shot, Rinposhay,' Lopsang replied.

'Is he badly hurt?' The secretary shook his head.

'We thought he was going to die,' Kesang said. 'But Kusho Lopsang healed him with herbs.'

'He is quite a magician,' Tsun smiled. Lopsang smiled in acknowledgement, but the smile was empty, his face lined and tired.

'Tell me of *your* journey?' Tsun looked at Genyen.

'After we left you, Rinposhay, we saw the Han cavalry a few times, but we didn't let them see us, we kept off the usual tracks.'

'And the iron bird?' Genyen shook her head. Then there was excited confusion as Norbu and Topgay, with two of Genyen's men, arrived with leather sacks of barley flour, butter and bricks of tea.

'Did you meet anyone?' Tsun asked as he mixed the tsampa and butter into a dough. Samden, his eyes watering, raked the fire with a knife to try and dispel the smoke which was filling the cave.

'We met a trader,' Lopsang said, relishing the chewing of a piece of dried meat. 'We said we were pilgrims.'

'He believed you?' Tsun was incredulous. 'With all your weapons?' Rinchen laughed. 'I think he thought we were brigands.'

Tsun nodded towards the injured man lying at the back of the cave. 'How was he wounded?' he asked Genyen.

'We were short of food, so we stopped at a village to buy some supplies.' One of her men refilled her bowl with tea. 'There were Han in the village. They asked questions, we had to run. He was shot.' She watched Norden breaking off a handful of compacted tea leaves from the brick.

'Was it a trap? Did the Han expect you?'

'No. I think they were only suspicious, Rinposhay, and guessed that we were resistance fighters.'

'And how long have you been here?'

'Two days.'

Tsun wondered if he ought to go on alone, for he was sure that the spy was still amongst them. He thought of Ling and of the Han cavalry and of how near they might be now. He had brought fear back into the lives of his friends. Once again he could see them being mercilessly hunted. He spoke softly to Genyen, so that the others would not hear, but even as they spoke, their attention was on Norden, as she added butter, salt and soda, amid a chorus of instructions, to the thin soup-like liquid.

'A day and a half ago, I think I saw cadre Ling riding with the Han cavalry. I think that they were looking for me. And last night an iron bird flew over us.'

Genyen thoughtfully rubbed the side of her face and frowned. 'They could be close, then?'

'Possibly very close, Genyen. I must go on alone. Without me the party is much safer. That is proven.'

'I will leave some of my men with the party, but I and the rest of them will go with you,' Genyen said firmly.

'But there is a spy among us,' Tsun insisted. 'There are so few we can trust, and you are needed with the party. Who else will lead them?'

She turned to look at him, about to protest, but he had moved to sit with Rinchen and Lopsang. For some moments the three men sat in silence. Then Tsun said:

'The Han, as you know, are after me and little Dorje Rinposhay especially, but not the rest of the party. Therefore it is better that

I go on separately to Lhasa and meet you all there at the Dorje Rigon house.'

Rinchen's heavy features were set more deeply than usual. His sloping forehead heavily creased, his fingers working over his rosary.

'Who is to go with you, Rinposhay?' he asked.

'One of the escort, Rinchen-la, no one else.'

'But why, Rinposhay?'

'You are safer without me,' Tsun answered, but he knew that was not the question that Rinchen was asking.

'But for how long are we safer without you, Rinposhay?' Lopsang asked. 'The Han are clever. If we are captured, if Dorje Rinposhay is caught, they will make sure that you learn of it.' He did not bother to say more. Tsun rested his head in his hands. There was no escape. Lopsang's words would make sense to the spy too. He was right. It was obvious. Whether he was away from them or with them would make no difference in the end. They already knew that the way to capture Tsun would be to capture Dorje Rinposhay.

Their silence was heavy in the laughter and commotion that greeted Norden's pouring of the tea. Tsun watched Kesang and Namgyal romping with Senge, and was glad he did not have to leave them all again. He looked across at Genyen, at her gaunt face and dirt-stained hair, long and wild.

'Is he well enough to be moved?' Tsun asked, nodding towards the wounded man.

'Yes Rinposhay,' she smiled.

Rinchen offered his small round silver snuff bottle to Tsun who took out the thin stopper, tapped some of the mixture onto his thumb nail and inhaled. Like a cool draught it went through his head.

As they ate and drank, the lama told them something of his visit to Derge. Norden looked at her child, Kesang, his pale face, his dirty chuba which was too big for him, and yet the Dorje Rinposhay had a resilient quality about him that far outweighed his eight years. He was leaning against Tsun, silently listening.

The strengthening wind was blowing snow spume from the mountain peaks, their mantles of snow and glaciers reflected in the pale sulphur yellow of the evening light. Tsun found their impersonal beauty chilling. Truly they are, he thought, the abode of the gods. The hermitage and its decaying frescoes, the barren canyon, being worked into dust by nature's remorseless hands, the dying sun . . . each spoke to Tsun of the ephemeral nature of all things, of nature, beast, man and country. He was exhausted and despaired of what lay ahead.

Kesang, walking later beside his guardian with Senge at their heels, pulled at his hand.

'Has the sun never risen, Tsun-la?' the boy said, chuckling.

Chapter Seventeen

Tsun stopped to pick up the mani stone that Jigme had thrown aside.

'Jigme,' he called to the youth who was leading his horse a few paces ahead of him. 'Will you never finish one of these?'

Jigme turned; it was almost a habit of travel to inscribe the mani invocation on large flat pebbles to add to the mani walls. He laughed.

'I make many mistakes, Rinposhay.'

How many stones had the boy begun, never finished, and discarded since they had left Dorje Ri-gon? Tsun felt a vague suspicion. If the Han knew what to look for, it would not be difficult for them to find the mani stones. The suspicion strengthened. Someone had to be the spy! But it was ridiculous! Jigme had entered the monastery when he was ten years old. His uncle, who had been his guardian in the monastery, had died in 1955. So Tsun had had the boy as his own pupil for the past year. He was not brilliant, but intelligent, hard working at his studies and reliable. Tsun knew that Jigme could erupt in anger, but his character was not one of calculation, of maintained duplicity. Perhaps though, he argued, the other side of reliability, hard work. . . ? He realised how surprised he had been at Jigme's instinct for trading. Could he be sure of anyone?

They travelled through the night and made camp just before dawn. Too exhausted to talk much, they lay or sat around the fire eating. Genyen was one of the three to take the first watch.

Tsun leaned over to speak quietly with his steward.

'Rinchen-la, can you tell Jigme I wish to speak with him.' Rinchen passed on the instruction to Samden, who went to fetch his fellow pupil. Jigme was feeding his horse with the dregs of tea and butter from his bowl.

'Rinposhay?'

Tsun motioned for the youth to sit beside him. Jigme felt uncomfortable under Tsun's intense gaze.

'Where is your family, Jigme? What was the last news you heard from them?'

'Heard from them?' Jigme frowned. 'I heard that my brother had to join the PLA and go to China.'

'Have the Han ever talked to you?' Tsun let Senge work his way out from his chuba. The dog, his alert eyes hidden by a mop of black and white hair, padded off towards Kesang who was playing dominoes with his mother and two of the Khambas.

'I do not understand, Rinposhay.' Jigme felt nervous. 'In shops, markets, and sometimes patrols. They have questioned me.'

'When was the last time?'

'The last time? I think it was about three months ago, Rinposhay. I was visiting my parents.'

'What did the Han ask you?'

'Get away, Senge!' Samden let out a shout as the dog cocked a leg at his saddle which he was using as a pillow. 'Get away!'

Jigme hesitated. 'They asked me what I did, Rinposhay . . . about . . . Dorje Ri-gon.'

'Yes?'

'They asked about you, Rinposhay.'

'What did they ask about me?'

'They asked about the resistance, whether you were connected with it, but I did not know anything about you, Rinposhay.'

The flames of the fire danced in Tsun's black, unblinking eyes. 'And what did you tell them?'

'I told them that you only spoke of spiritual matters, and told us to co-operate with the Han in what was good.'

'Yes?'

Senge ran up to Tsun and pawed at him. Tsun opened his chuba for the dog to jump in. Jigme looked away for a few seconds, unable to bear the intensity of Tsun's gaze, and realised that in doing so, he revealed himself.

Norden was singing a lullaby to Kesang, who had fallen asleep against her. Silently, she continued playing dominoes, using traders' finger signs to indicate her bets.

'Rinposhay,' Jigme murmured. 'I am sorry.'

'Tell me.' Tsun's voice was quiet, but it frightened the novice.

'I should have spoken of it before.' He hesitated again. 'Two Han cadres . . . they took me to a restaurant and invited me to eat with them. They gave me something to drink. They said it was harmless. They lied. It confused my mind, Rinposhay, I broke the precepts!'

'You break them again,' said Tsun, 'in trying to deceive me.' The words hit the youth like a physical blow. His mouth formed words without sound. He cleared his throat.

'They . . . they talked to me constantly,' he said, 'of the opportunities I was missing by being a monk. Always, they were asking me questions. Asking me to prove how much better my way of life was than theirs. Rinposhay, you know dialectics is not my best subject, and soon, though I did not agree with them, I had no answers. But they wouldn't let me rest. All the time they wanted to get me involved. A young Han woman was introduced to me . . .' his voice faltered.

'Go on.'

'They talked to me of what I was missing by being celibate, and the woman touched me. I was in great confusion. But when I tried to leave they pushed me back into my chair. They told me, asked me, to get information for them. I refused. They said we would go into a back room where we would be more comfortable and private. As we crossed a passage, I saw a door which was slightly open, and I escaped through it into the darkness. I ran faster than I have ever run in my life.' He paused.

'Some weeks later, I went with steward Rinchen to Litang. The same two Han found me, after I had only been there a day. They would not leave me alone, and again they asked for information about you, Rinposhay, and about Dorje Ri-gon.'

'What did you tell them?'

'I said that I was just your pupil, that the monks at the monastery led a spiritual life.'

'Was it enough?'

Jigme shook his head. 'They asked me to supply them regularly with information. To spy, Rinposhay, on you. I refused. They said that my parents were going to be labelled as serf owners and subjected to Thamzing. When I protested that it was nonsense, and that trading had been so difficult my father still didn't know how he was going to meet his loans, one of them agreed with me, but far from encouraging me, it frightened me more. He said my parents had the minds of serf owners, this is what had to be watched and struggled against, but that if I gave them the information they wanted, I could protect them.'

Tsun did not say a word. He kept his eyes on Jigme and waited for him to continue.

'They wanted me to report on what you were doing. Some things, I told them, that seemed safe. Some things I made up. They only wanted me to give information on the present, Rinposhay.

'Sometimes, I was frightened by what they knew about you, as they could only have got their information from someone close to you.' He hesitated. 'That is the reason I have not spoken before, Rinposhay. I did not know who might learn of it.'

Tsun looked thoughtfully at the boy for a few moments. 'If anyone tries to get you to spy again, tell me at once. Otherwise I cannot protect you or any of us.'

The youth sucked in his breath respectfully and nodded.

'Sho! Sho! Sho! Come! Come! Come!' The riders shouted at the reluctant animals, feeling their uncertainty and urging them on with their bodies along the narrow ledge. In the dust of erosion whipped into swirling clouds by the deafening night winds, it was easy to become separated, and no one would hear if help was needed. Weakened by hunger and exhaustion, struggling against the wind, they made only a mile an hour. It was 50 degrees below freezing.

Rinchen's horse staggered as a hind leg slipped on the crumbling ledge. The steward shouted and Namgyal, seeing what was happening, grabbed the horse's tail and pulled it back, giving the animal time to recover itself while the stones which its hoof had dislodged plummeted over a thousand feet to the valley below.

The party rode in single file. On all sides stretched a petrified, rolling sea of granite and limestone. Riding through damp clouds, they heard the roar of an aeroplane engine. It set the horses dancing with fear, for the sound, through the mists, seemed to be almost level with them.

A few hours after dawn they came out of the clouds onto a high wide path and decided to look for a place to camp. It was then that they saw the smoke. It was coming from behind a ridge, as if someone had built a fire. The party took cover while Tsun and Genyen crawled up the ridge and peered carefully over the top.

For some minutes they lay silent, staring at the scene before them. Then Tsun waved for the others to join them.

'Kunjosum!' Norden gasped as she gazed at the sea of thousands of men, women, children, sheep, yaks, donkeys, horses and mules, filling the vast plain as far as the eye could see.

It was a great convoy. Part of the company had camped, but most of them were moving slowly, their yaks, mules, donkeys, even their sheep, loaded with supplies, produce and furniture.

'Is it a caravan?' Kesang asked.

'No,' Tsun replied. 'I think they must be fleeing from the Han.'

They watched in silence, awed by the significance of that long river of people.

'We need supplies . . .' Rinchen looked at Tsun. 'And to rest . . .' His heavy features were accentuated by exhaustion and loss of weight.

'Rinposhay, we must avoid them,' Genyen said. 'A party that size will attract the Han. It could never escape them.'

Tsun laughed. 'A party of our size hasn't had much success either.' He was scanning the plain with his field glasses. 'Always the Han manage to find us. There are thousands down there. Enough people to make it difficult for the Han to find us.'

'You don't think, Rinposhay, . . . that we have lost the Han?' Norden murmured.

'Do you, Genyen?' Tsun was still scanning the valley.

She shook her head. 'And, we do need supplies,' she said.

Chapter Eighteen

'Could I have your sling, Namgyal?' Tsun beckoned. The boy handed it to him. Tsun bent low from his horse and picked up a smooth, round stone. Then fitting it into the pocket of the sling, he whirled it round his head and launched the missile. With a pistol-shot crack from the tassel at the end of the cord, the sling let loose the stone, hurling it towards a stocky man riding a little ahead of a group not far from the travellers.

The man's startled shout as his hat flew from his head was drowned in the laughter of Tsun's companions. The man swung his horse round to confront his attacker and cantered towards Tsun, who was grinning broadly. As the man drew a long-barrelled Chinese automatic pistol from his ambac, the Khambas moved up close to Tsun. Genyen, too, rode up beside him, holding her rifle across her saddle, her finger on the trigger.

The man pulled up a few feet from Tsun. Genyen recognised him and relaxed. The man took rapid aim and fired at Tsun. Norden and Pema screamed. The bullet tore a hole straight through Tsun's fur hat. He felt the bullet brush his hair. The Khamba escort drew their swords, but Genyen put out a hand to stop them.

'You are lazy Genyen-la,' the man said as he came up to them. 'You should not relax for a moment.' Genyen was not amused. The man turned to Tsun.

'I have ruined your hat, Rinposhay. But it was nearly your head, cousin, I didn't recognise you in lay clothes.'

'And I nearly ruined your reputation, cousin Tul-lok!'

The two men looked at one another for a few moments, then burst out laughing. They rode side by side through the crowds of slowly moving refugees. There was almost a festive air about them. Many sang pilgrims' songs as they travelled, each adding a few verses. Others bartered as they rode. Some had stopped for a meal, or to milk their dris and cows, to adjust harnesses or redistribute loads. Children darted back and forth through animals and people.

Tsun felt the leather of his cousin's saddle and smiled appreciatively. 'English?' he asked.

Tul-lok nodded and grinned, his teeth glistening white against his brown, deeply lined face.

'How did you get it?'

Tul-lok lifted his shoulders in a heavy shrug and smiled slightly without answering.

Kesang and Namgyal rode together, watching the two men. Tul-lok, the former brigand, had become a legend in Kham. Many of the story-tellers told of his exploits.

'Look at his ear,' Namgyal whispered to Kesang who eased his horse closer and saw that Tul-lok's right ear was just a few irregular, jagged bits of flesh around a black hole. Tul-lok noticed them and beckoned.

'Come here.'

Nervously the boys urged their horses forward. Kesang took a scarf from his ambac, looped his reins around the high pommel of his saddle and held the scarf out to Tul-lok.

'This,' said Tsun, 'is Dorje Rinposhay of Dorje Ri-gon.'

Tul-lok accepted the scarf and held it while he studied the pale, wide-eyed, intelligent face of the boy. The breeze took hold of the scarf and flapped it in the face of Kesang's horse, causing it to shy nervously. Stroking the neck of the unsettled animal, and speaking in awed tones, Kesang asked Tul-lok: 'Is it true that you are also a tulku, Kusho?'

'So it is said.' Tul-lok smiled.

Then Namgyal presented a gauze scarf while Tsun introduced him to his cousin.

'Namgyal,' Tsun said, 'is the son of Chopel, the silversmith of Derge.'

'I know him well,' Tul-lok said. 'He has helped us many times. How is your father? Is he with you?'

'No, he stayed in Derge,' Namgyal answered.

'And your sister, Dekyi?'

'She also stayed. We shall meet in Lhasa.'

Tul-lok was silent for a few moments, thinking how unlikely this was. Then he smiled.

'This boy will be a brigand,' he said, laying a hand on Namgyal's tousled head. 'And this boy will be a great lama.' He looked at Kesang and then at Tsun and chuckled. Namgyal was delighted. Kesang was not. Being a brigand seemed far more exciting than being a great lama. The two boys moved their horses away, and

Kesang took a stick from his belt and threw it for Senge, who dodged between groups of refugees and pounded through the grass of the plain in search of it.

The two men looked at each other, assessing the changes which the years had made, and relaxing as their horses followed the direction of the herd of people and animals.

'You grow older and more tired, cousin,' Tul-lok said. 'It is the spiritual life.'

'While you grow fat on brigandage!' Tsun poked his cousin's stomach, and they both laughed. Senge ran up beside Tsun's horse, carrying the stick. He bent down to take it from the dog's slavering jaws and threw it for him. Tul-lok looked at Tsun, his face suddenly solemn. 'You are fleeing?'

The lama nodded and told his cousin of the bombing of Litang and their flight, his voice muffled by the surrounding babble of laughter and shouting, the braying, bellowing and whinnying of the animals, and the endless, rippling ring of the harness bells as the exodus moved slowly across the plain. In the far distance, black shapes floated on currents of air, circling, slipping to fall sideways, then straightening and rising.

'Vultures are an ill-omen for us all,' Tul-lok murmured.

'Are all these people fleeing?' Tsun asked.

Tul-lok nodded.

'Where to?'

'Some, like you, say to Lhasa. Others that they are going on pilgrimage to Mount Kailash. Some are just going somewhere – somewhere where there is peace.'

'So many,' Tsun said. 'Why, cousin?'

'You saw what happened at Litang, at Derge. It is the same throughout Kham.' Tul-lok pushed the trilby back on his head.

'But the Han will not allow them to escape,' Tsun said. 'They can easily find a great mass of people like this.'

Tul-lok shrugged and took an aluminium flask from his pocket. He offered it to Tsun, who shook his head.

'You should give up the robe,' Tul-lok grinned, downing the whisky so that it dribbled from the sides of his mouth. 'I recommend it.' He wiped his mouth with his hand.

Tsun was not listening. 'The Han do not fight like brigands,' he said. 'The people will get no protection by forming large caravans. It will just make them an easy target for the Han iron birds.'

'You know, cousin! I know! But try explaining it to them! I have.' Tul-lok pushed the flask back into his ambac and gently eased his horse round the large, rolling body of a heavily laden yak.

'They have travelled this way for centuries. They will not suddenly change. I cannot change them. I don't control them. No one does. Each group makes its own way.'

'Have you seen the Han?'

'I have been with these people for two weeks, and the first sign of the Han was yesterday when an iron bird flew overhead.'

It could have been the same plane which had been shadowing them for so long, Tsun thought. Why was yesterday the first time the refugees had seen the Han? Perhaps it was only coincidence, but Tsun began to feel like someone who finds that he has brought a fatal disease to his household.

'One iron bird is enough,' he said. 'Were the people frightened?'

'Yes, they were frightened, but it did nothing, so they forget. They believe that their number gives them strength. The passes are blocked with people. Many of the valleys ahead are full of people. They couldn't disperse now if they wanted to!'

The plane had been ahead of them, which encouraged Tsun, but he knew that Ling would not give up the search; he wondered whether she and the Han cavalry had picked up their trail yet.

'Why are you here, Tul-lok? The Queen of Derge said you were leading the resistance there.'

Tul-lok smiled as he tapped a long-stemmed pipe against the heel of his leather boot.

'I am going south of Lhasa. A headquarters has been established in Kongpo. All the resistance groups are trying to work together.'

Tsun knew his cousin well enough to dispense with the usual courtesies, the indirect allusions. 'The Queen says that there is a plan to kill the Han Defence Minister, Chen-Yi, when he comes to inaugurate the Preparatory Committee.'

Tul-lok sucked on his pipe to make it draw.

'We are both agreed,' Tsun continued, 'that to kill Chen-Yi would bring about terrible reprisals. What good would that do, Tul-lok?'

'Through the Preparatory Committee, the Han will rule Tibet.'

'They rule now. The Preparatory Committee is the honey on the sharp knife. If we do not accept that – there is the knife!'

'More reason to prove to the Han that we can strike at their heart.'

'The heart beats in Peking, not in Chen-Yi. He can be killed by the resistance, but can the resistance protect their families who will suffer as a result of the assassination? The Han will use it as the excuse they have been waiting for.'

'Open resistance is coming. If not today, then tomorrow. Can you not smell it, cousin?' Tul-lok waved his pipe over the people filling the valley. 'They can. They do not realise it perhaps, but they know.' He laughed.

'And they think that by staying together they are safe from Han attack,' Tsun murmured.

'About you, cousin,' Tul-lok continued. 'It is said that you carry a petition to the United Nations.'

'If you know that, how many others know? Keeping a secret in Kham is like trying to keep water in a sieve.'

'Will the United Nations help our land?'

'I do not know, but we have to try. What makes me think the petition is of value is the trouble the Han are taking to capture it. If they wanted to, they could have killed our party, but they did not. No, they want their hands on the petition and are concerned for its safety. They cannot steal what is in our minds. Dorje Rinposhay and I will be far more useful to them alive than dead. What chance *has* the resistance, Tul-lok? In India, the Injis will want to know.'

'We are short of everything.'

'But with supplies?'

'With supplies we could do anything. For two, three years, thousands of Khambas have been fighting. My men have used daggers and swords to save ammunition. The Han have tanks, armoured cars, automatic rifles, iron birds. They have not defeated us. The gods are with us. Think what we could do if we had supplies!'

'How many do you think are in the resistance?'

Tul-lok shrugged, his eyes following Pema as she rode with Norden. 'She has grown into a fine looking woman.'

Tsun nodded. 'She did not want to come with me. She wanted to go to the Minorities Institute in China, to complete her education. Even now I wonder whether she will try to get away and go back to Derge.'

'You should have left her there. She will be a danger you can ill afford.' Tul-lok moved his horse away from some ill-tempered, heavily laden mules. What his cousin said was true, Tsun thought. But Pema was his sister and he wanted to believe that the bond of blood was stronger than her desire for Han learning.

'I saw Yangchen while I was in Derge,' he said.

'How is she? She has helped with the resistance.'

'I know. I tried to persuade her to come with me. She didn't tell me, but I know she stayed on to get information about the visit of

Chen-Yi. Does she know you have left Derge, Tul-lok? It was only for you that she stayed.'

'I only decided to go to Kongpo a couple of weeks ago. I have sent a messenger to Derge to make contact with her. But you know, cousin, she stays for other reasons also. She still hopes that her husband will find her there if he ever escapes the Han.'

'She should have come with me,' Tsun murmured.

'She should have come with you,' echoed his cousin. His words had a heavy finality about them, like a salvo of bullets.

'Where is your wife?' asked Tsun.

'Dead, cousin.' Tul-lok smiled grimly and drew on his pipe. 'You remember how, as a child, I was always the strongest, always the bravest, the most certain, the master of his destiny? And even when, as a child, I was enthroned as a tulku, how religious I was? Was I not religious, cousin?' He laughed. Tsun smiled and nodded.

'Well,' Tul-lok shrugged. 'Perhaps I was a little wild, but even so . . . And then when I left the order, it took courage to do that, knowing the distress it would cause our family, my tutor and the monastery. It is easier for a monk than for a tulku to leave the order.' He shook his head. 'Now, as a brigand, my name is famous throughout Kham . . . master of my destiny . . . vanity, Tsun, vanity!' He sighed, then went on: 'There was nothing I could do but watch my wife die in agony. I think the child had turned inside her. I could do nothing. I didn't even have any liquor to ease the pain. We were high in the mountains, the nearest village was three days' ride away. It took her all night to die. She died as the sun rose. That was auspicious!' He paused. 'What a curious thing the mind is, cousin. How often I have killed. How often I have seen death. Yet her death demented me with grief. What difference is there between her death and the death of those I have killed? All the difference, and yet no difference.'

Chapter Nineteen

That night they made camp early, to give themselves time to buy in supplies. The vast gathering, with its hundreds of dung fires and its background of human and animal movement and sound, engendered a feeling of security. For the first time in days, Tsun's party felt able to relax.

Pema cursed herself as she tried unsuccessfully to force a bone needle through her sheepskin chuba. Samden sat down opposite her. She looked up and smiled slightly at the fine featured young man, then returned to her labours.

Samden laughed, taking the needle and sheepskin from her, and with deft, practised movements, began to sew.

'Where did you learn to do that?' Pema asked as she watched.

'In the monastery. Who will repair my robes if I don't?'

'When did you become a monk, Samden?' she enquired.

'When I was six years old.'

'You are different from the others,' she said. 'The way you talk to me.'

'I am a tantric yogi in search of a consort,' he leered at her and laughed.

'You will not be a monk for long,' Pema smiled, and Samden was conscious of the sensual quality of her face. The slight cast in her eye did nothing to detract from her attractions. He continued sewing for a few moments, and neither spoke. Then he looked up at her.

'You are different from the other girls I've met, too,' he said. 'You are direct.'

Again, they sat in silence with their thoughts. Each had touched a sensitive spot in the other's character. Looking up, Pema noticed a barely discernible glimmer of light among the black mountains, far away on the other side of the plain.

'What's that, Samden?'

The young monk stopped what he was doing and followed Pema's line of sight. 'It must be pilgrims going to see the nun.'

'Who is she?'

'Many of the people here are talking about her. Apparently she has lived alone in these parts for years. It is said that she has strong powers. Many people set out to take her gifts and to seek her blessing, but few manage to find her.'

'I would like to try,' Pema said thoughtfully.

'Tomorrow, we will go,' Samden said. But he knew that it was most unlikely that Tsun would allow them to wander off from the rest of the party.

As if catching Samden's thoughts, Pema asked, 'What is my brother really like, Samden?'

Samden chuckled. 'What do you mean? He is *your* brother.'

'It is many years since I have seen him. He has changed.'

'What was he like as a young man?' Samden was re-threading the needle. 'There is some mystery about his early life.'

'He was like any young Khamba.'

'Son untamed?'

'Yes. He worked with my father and went on long trading trips to India, China and Afghanistan. I gather that he was a very intelligent boy, though much of what I know about him is what I have heard from my mother and sister.' She laughed. 'The feuds the family were involved in because of his women! He was a marvellous swordsman.'

'Why have I never seen you or any of Tsun's relatives at Dorje Ri-gon?'

'We came when he was first Abbot, when I was very young. But it was difficult after the occupation. We could not move so freely. My father died and things became very difficult . . .' Her voice trailed off, she laughed with embarrassment, shrugged, and asked, 'What is he like with you?'

'By some he is considered revolutionary.' Samden sewed while he talked, repairing the rent in the sheepskin chuba. 'Most of the people in our valley are devoted to him. He is a fine teacher and concerned for their welfare. But some are quick to criticise him.' He paused.

'I was left an orphan in the monastery,' he went on after a moment, 'with no relations to pay towards my keep or education. The Rinposhay has treated me like a son and has given me a good education.'

Pema studied him for a moment. 'Do you want to be a monk?'

Samden put down the needle, looked at her and laughed. He could think of no other girl who would ask such a direct question.

'No, Pema, I do not think I want to be a monk. In fact, I'm not a monk any more.'

'But . . .'

'Swear not to tell anyone. Only Tsun Rinposhay knows.'

'How. . . ?'

'A girl . . .'

Pema smiled wryly. Samden grinned back, then frowned. 'I have broken my vows, so am no longer a novice. In a way, I was glad. Tsun Rinposhay told me that I need only re-take my vows if I wanted, but . . .' he laughed. 'I am still a monk in my mind. I still think like a monk, react like a monk.'

Pema raised her eyebrows. 'Perhaps not entirely like a monk!' Then, without thinking she added, 'There are too many monks, it . . .' She looked at him quickly, and in her hesitation rather than her words, Samden caught the significance.

'You sound like the Han,' he said.

'Perhaps it is because I went to a Han school.' She looked at him directly to catch the slightest reaction.

'You are like me.'

'In what way?'

'I am still a monk, you are still a pupil.' He grinned at her broadly. Her eyes widened.

'I shall keep your secret if you will keep mine,' he said.

'By the Triple Refuge,' she said quickly and softly, then turned away and began greasing her harness. 'Why is my brother so involved with the resistance?' she asked, changing the subject to cover her embarrassment.

'He is not involved with the resistance.' Samden looked up from his sewing and smiled at her. 'No more than we all are.'

She was irritated by his smooth and patronising evasion. 'It is said that he carries a petition.'

'So I have heard.'

Pema unrolled her sleeve so that it covered her hand and used it to take the lid off the boiling pot on the fire, then poured the liquid through a bamboo strainer into the butter churn.

'Who is the petition for?'

Samden shrugged. 'I do not know. Why do you want to know?' He looked up at her.

'We are being hunted because of it. My brother has done something to make the Han hunt him as though he were a deadly enemy.' Steadily she worked the wooden plunger up and down in the churn, mixing the butter with the boiling tea.

'You have been to a Han school. You should know that, to the Han, the religion and the lamas are enemies.'

His tone infuriated her so much that she swung the plunger at him. He dodged it, laughing, enjoying teasing her, then returned to his sewing. When he had finished, he bit the thread and tied it. He held the large earthenware teapot steady as Pema poured tea into it from the churn.

'I did not want to come with my brother, Samden. He and my sister forced me to accompany him. I had no choice.'

'Why?' Samden took his bowl from his ambac.

'They said that Derge was unsafe. That I might have to go to China for education.' She poured tea into his wooden bowl.

'Would you have minded going to China?'

'No,' she said definitely. 'I would have had good opportunities. What opportunity lies ahead of me now? I hardly know my brother, he has changed so.'

Samden looked at her long as he drank his tea, and she held his eyes, finally relinquishing them and turning away to offer tea to the others.

Karma dropped the string weighted with an iron seal down the barrel of his Russian-made 7.62 mm rifle. He pulled the butter-soaked felt cloth to and fro through the barrel to clean it, accompanying the rhythmic movement with a housebuilder's song, sung to emphasise the rhythm of the clay being tamped down. Formerly a member of the monastic guard at Drebung Monastic University in Lhasa, he had now left the order and become Tul-lok's lieutenant. At the sound of a footfall, his hand reached into his chuba for his pistol. He looked up.

'Tsun Rinposhay!'

Karma got up and bowed, embarrassed. Tsun chuckled and beckoned for him to sit. Karma added dung to the fire. His wide, full-lipped mouth and large nose were accentuated by his heavily lidded and narrow eyes. His hair was close cropped, like that of many former monks.

'Rinchen, my steward, tells me that when he was arranging to buy supplies from you, you told him news of Dorje Ri-gon.'

Karma frowned and nodded. The wind was becoming sharper, howling from the mountains. Tsun pulled down the flaps of his fur hat and tucked his hands into the sleeves of his plum-coloured chuba. It was well below freezing. He sat down beside Karma, who went on cleaning his gun.

'Please tell me!'

'No one knows of this, but I met a monk from Dorje Ri-gon a few days ago.' Karma did not look at Tsun as he spoke; he found the dark, seeing eyes unsettling.

'He had escaped from the monastery. He said that PLA troops had entered Dorje Ri-gon and searched for you. When you could not be found, the Han . . . Rinposhay?' Karma hesitated.

'Go on Karma. I want the complete story.'

'When they couldn't find you, the Han assembled everyone in the Temple and told them you were an agent of . . . of . . .'

'Imperialists?'

'Yes, Rinposhay, and that you were trying to contact foreign governments. They showed the monks foreign books and letters they had found in your library. The Han said that many of the monks from Dorje Ri-gon had joined the resistance with your approval and that . . .'

'Karma, the discourtesy is not yours.'

'. . . that you were an enemy of the people. The monks were told to reveal your hiding place and they could go unharmed.'

'But none knew!' There was a slight note of desperation in Tsun's voice, as though he feared Karma's news. During the journey, although he had thought often of Litang and Dorje Ri-gon, he had forced his mind not to dwell on the fate of his monastery, hoping that the monks had taken his advice to leave.

'So the monks told the Han,' Karma continued. 'Although the monk who told me this said that he and many of his friends believed you were hidden somewhere in Dorje Ri-gon. The Han ransacked the monastery in their search for you. A monk was taken and forced to stand before the others in the Temple. The Han shot him. First in the feet and then in the calves. Explaining between each shot that they would continue the punishment until the monks confessed their knowledge of your whereabouts. They continued shooting until they finally reached the man's head. Then some of the monks tried to break loose from the temple. Many were killed. Some escaped. Among them the monk I met.'

'Did he tell you his name?'

'No.'

'What happened then?'

'The Han set fire to the building. The monk told me that only the walls remained afterwards.'

'And the monks?'

'They were taken by the Han, I suppose. He did not say.'

'I left a letter!' The howling wind was stronger. Tsun raised his voice. 'Did the monk mention it?'

'He didn't mention a letter.'

'So they had no idea what had happened to me?'

'No.'

'Some thought,' said Tsun, his voice without emotion, 'that I was warned that the Han were coming and had escaped without giving them the opportunity. But I had spoken to them in the Hall of Assemblies.' He stood up and wished Karma goodnight. Walking back to the camp fire, the roar of the wind filled his ears and tears froze on his cheeks as the flying grit bit stingingly into his face.

Rinchen sat close to the fire so that the blue flames illuminated the pages of the book resting on his knees, each page some twelve lines deep and a foot in width. A few yards away, the three students were feeding the horses and mules. Although it wasn't unusual for a monk to wear lay clothes on long journeys, Rinchen always felt uncomfortable in them. Lopsang sat beside him tapping snuff onto his thumb nail. He offered the bottle to Rinchen. The steward shook his head. Picking up a thin yak-dung pat, Lopsang threw it onto the fire which flared as it accepted new fuel. Both men were thinking of the fate of Dorje Ri-gon.

'Rinchen-la, do you think that anyone will take notice of the petition Tsun Rinposhay carries?'

The monk's severe face creased in a frown. 'I do not know about such things. India is our friend. It is the land of the Buddha.' He replaced the leaves of the book in a wallet-shaped container. 'The Han think the petition important.'

Lopsang stared into the fire. 'But what good will it do? Will India fight for us?'

'It is not good that India should fight for us. But she might be able to persuade the Han that they are being unreasonable.' Rinchen began unwrapping the woven garters of his boots. 'But why ask such questions? Do you think that Rinposhay should not take the petition?' He pulled off one red boot easily, but the other clung.

'No!' Lopsang said with such vehemence that Rinchen looked at him in surprise. 'We have had to flee for our lives, always being hunted by the Han because of that petition.'

He helped the steward remove his left boot and Rinchen began pulling out the old straw which lined them both.

'But, Lopsang, what of Litang and the people in this valley? They haven't *all* got petitions, why should they need to flee?' He shook the loose bits of straw from his left boot.

'As the enemies of the Han, we are doomed,' Lopsang said. 'We should have learned from Litang to co-operate with them. We might have had some influence then, Tsun Rinposhay was respected by the Han.'

'What do you mean?' Rinchen frowned.

'The Kundun wants us to work with the Han. Did he not send the Gyalwa Karmapa Lama to try and stop the fighting in Kham?'

'Tsun Rinposhay is not fighting.'

'The petition is to the people the Han call enemies.'

'If our friends are the enemies of the Han, what are we? The petition is just that our friends may know what is happening.'

'It will make no difference, it will only cause more suffering.'

Rinchen began wrapping fresh straw round his feet. The secretary sat staring at the flames of the fire, warming his hands. The news of Dorje Ri-gon has depressed him, Rinchen thought. But it can hurt none of us more than Tsun Rinposhay, he whispered inaudibly.

'It is like an avalanche,' Lopsang continued. 'A strong gust of wind dislodges a pebble, it dislodges other pebbles, then stones and, gathering snow and rocks, it grows in speed and strength as it sweeps down the mountainside, until it becomes an avalanche. The Han thought we would welcome them. We did not. We resented their presence. They reacted and became oppressive. We reacted and became determined to resist . . . and so, like an avalanche, it grows. Now, no Han trusts a Tibetan, and . . . the avalanche will soon destroy us all.'

'May the Triple Gem protect us,' Rinchen murmured, padding the soles of his boots with fresh straw. 'It is karma, Lopsang.'

'How far can men be driven by fear?' Lopsang threw another yak-chip onto the fire.

'Too far!' Rinchen struggled to put his boots on.

'How man loves to delude himself. His life is based on the delusion that he has a self. From the womb of delusion, fathered by ignorance, is born fear. Han or Tibetan, we are all shackled by fear and we lock the padlock on ourselves.'

Lopsang paused. Rinchen had never seen him so bitter and angry, but he understood his feelings. Although it had always been a possibility, he himself still could not take in the destruction of Dorje Ri-gon. Very methodically he pushed the bottoms of his trouser legs into the long cloth boots, binding them below the knee with woven straps.

'Sometimes,' said Lopsang, 'it is better that we kill ourselves.'

'To take any life, including one's own, is wrong.' Rinchen spoke softly.

'It is a brave man who commits suicide. A braver man than he who kills another,' Lopsang replied. 'How ridiculous man is. He tries to tell himself that he is guided by high ideals, but in reality, it is fear. Fear leads him like a rider leading a horse. We are ruled by fear, live by fear. Fear of losing something we do not, in reality, possess. Indeed, we are the sport of the gods, Brahma's playthings . . .'

The steward was about to speak, but Lopsang continued. 'How many days, weeks, months, years, or even lifetimes, before we realise the true nature of our being and are liberated from our ignorance? Of what use is all this to us now?'

Rinchen looked into the dark, haunted eyes of his companion. 'But now is all we have, Lopsang. We do not live yesterday, or tomorrow, but *now*! Is it not said that our place in life is determined by our past actions, but our honourable deeds are the result of our own effort?'

'And our evil ones!' Lopsang murmured. 'Indeed, we are victims of our own karma.' His eyes still searched over the changing flames of the fire. 'I fear, Rinchen, what will become of us. The Han have spared no effort to keep track of us. Now we are trapped. There is no escape. We cannot get away and the Han will surely find us.'

'The escaped horse is easily seen on the plain. But in a herd of wild horses, who can tell which he is? If the Han find us, it will be because someone has betrayed us.'

'Who?'

Rinchen shrugged. 'A fishbone in the throat, drink water. A chicken bone in the throat, dig your grave,' he said. 'If we are fated to die at home, we shall die on our mother's lap. If we are to escape, we shall. Even in the face of our enemies.' His voice cracked. Lopsang looked up. The steward was crying.

Genyen was playing a game of Mah Jong with Tashi, Norden and Gonpo when Senge began pawing at her. It was her move and she was losing. She pushed the dog away without looking at him, but the pulling at her leg continued and as she looked round to see if Kesang could take him, she realised that the boy was nowhere to be seen. The others were too engrossed in their game to notice.

Saying she had to relieve herself, and wondering why she knew that she shouldn't tell them the truth, Genyen followed the little dog away from the light and noise of the camp fires, into the cold darkness.

In the moonlight, beside a large rock, she made out the silhouette of the small, lonely figure of Kesang. He was standing quite still, watching something. He looked up as she reached him, his face full of concern. Taking her hand, he led her forward to where Tsun, lying spreadeagled, face down, was weeping in the black shadow of the rock.

Chapter Twenty

High on the mountain, a figure crouched in the shadow of the rocks, forming a windbreak as he swiftly brushed away stones and pebbles, smoothing the ground. Rapid, shallow breaths of tension accompanied the drawing, with sprinkled powdered chalk, of a magic circle. Close by, the twigs of a little fire crackled as the flames licked them. Poisoned leaves, lying outside the circle, were laid carefully and skilfully within it, forming the silhouette of a lama, their edges held down with small pebbles to prevent the tugging breeze from taking them. The remaining leaves were spread out to form a dish. The white sandalwood resin hissed as it was poured from a pouch into the dish of leaves. Silently, a split bamboo pen was drawn from a pen case. A globule of spittle hung by a thread between dry lips and was carefully deposited on the resin. The hands trembled as they used the nib of the pen to mix the spittle with the resin. The pen hovered for a few moments, uncertain, then wrote shakily on the silhouette of leaves three characters – Dorje Ri-gon – and below that the simple characters for Tsun Rinposhay.

A small brown lump of flesh, giving off a faint aroma of pork meat, was laid beside the fire. It was dirty and dried, having been kept for some months, for it was not easy to obtain human fat.

A slender hand shook as it held a bronze, six-inch long triple bladed dagger, the hilt of which was a six-armed god whose serpent body entwined the three blades of a weapon used only in the psychic realms. The fat was dropped carefully onto the fire. It smoked acridly for a few seconds and then began to splutter and spit. The silhouette was held with twigs over the thin, wind-plucked ribbon of smoke from the burning fat. There was a soft intoning of a mantra. The head of the silhouette was touched by the dagger. Then the figure was laid carefully back within the circle and the fire suffocated with handfuls of dust.

For a moment, the caster of spells stood in the bright moonlight, looking down at the magic circle, then turned away to return down the mountain.

During the night, the wind gathered strength, tugging at the edges of the leaf silhouette of Tsun Rinposhay, plucking at the granules of powdered chalk, diffusing the edges of the circle. Eventually, the wind worked beneath the figure, suddenly tearing it apart, lifting it and carrying it away.

The night breeze caught the snuff Genyen had tapped onto her thumb. She cursed and, half listening to Tashi's songs, sat down beside her companions at the camp fire. The scouts hadn't seen any sign of Han troops. Genyen wondered if they really had managed to shake them off. Perhaps, she thought, the very size of the refugee caravan would deter them from attacking. Tashi was urging the men to dance. Genyen needed to forget.

She danced with wild grace, executing a constrained stamping step, her arms linked with a line of her men dancing parallel to Tul-lok and a line of his men. Their lines broke as they whirled round the fire. Genyen felt a hand grab her cloth belt and pull it from her waist. The sheepskin chuba fell open, revealing her brown, sweat-glistening breasts. The men were used to seeing women stripped to the waist working in the fields, but because it was Genyen they roared with approval. Tul-lok stood looking at her for a few moments with a broad grin on his face. He tucked her belt into his chuba and walked unsteadily into the darkness. His men laughed at his show of interest in the woman. If Genyen felt the same way, when everyone was asleep, she would go to reclaim the belt.

But Genyen stood, her legs apart, glaring after Tul-lok. Her men, seeing her anger, stopped dancing. The music faded. Genyen enjoyed being admired, but her relationships were always on her terms, and she realised that Tul-lok would compromise her in the eyes of the men she led.

'Tul-lok.' She growled the name slow and long.

He turned. She was crouched, dagger in hand. Tul-lok looked surprised. A Khamba's dagger was never drawn except to wound or kill! He laughed and, grinning broadly, walked back towards her. Her black hair, shiny with sweat, fell loose about her taut face, lips slightly parted, eyes quick as an animal's, watching for an opportunity to pounce. Tul-lok knew from her eyes the moment that she sprang, and turned just in time for the blade to lunge past his stomach. He laughed again, nervously, as he realised just how serious and enraged she was. Genyen growled. Their men gathered around them and passed a clay bottle of arak from hand to hand while they placed bets on the outcome.

As Tul-lok drew his dagger Genyen swung her weapon at him; he parried the blow, but she managed to slide the side of her dagger against Tul-lok's temple. He staggered. It was traditional in duels and fights for daggers to be used in slicing blows, a direct thrust being left to the last. Tul-lok side-stepped another blow and swung his dagger at Genyen's head. She dodged and brought her blade down on his arm. For an instant, his face registered acute pain, but he made no sound and his grip on his dagger did not slacken.

He closed in on her. The quick, gasping breaths, the crackling of the fire and the murmur of the onlookers, heightened the tension. They grappled. Tul-lok grabbed the girl's hair and pulled her off balance. He saw the anger in her eyes as she hit the ground. Her dagger slit his chuba, scratching his belly. He threw himself on top of her. Her nails dug into his wrist as she struggled to keep his blade away from her throat. Their feet kicked up the dirt as each attempted to counter the other's move.

The salt of sweat stung in the cuts on their faces and hands. Each gasping and grunting with exertion, their faces only inches apart. He felt her try to get the blade into his gut. He forced her hand up and the blade sliced his chest. The blood dropped into her eyes so that she could hardly see. Through a bloody haze she saw his face, closer now, and his smile, and she knew what he was thinking. His mouth was on hers, his tongue thrusting deep. She bit hard.

With an agonised cry, Tul-lok leapt from her. For a moment she thought she had bitten his tongue off. With relentless fury she came at him. Tul-lok deflected her blade and thrust his own at her belly. It bit into her breast. Her men immediately moved in to stop the fight. Genyen stuck the nearest man across the head with the side of her dagger.

'Get back!'

She advanced on Tul-lok with death in her eyes. Her left hand clasped her cut breast, the blood threading through her fingers, down her belly and dribbling to the ground.

Tul-lok hesitated a moment, then held out her belt. She had started the fight because, as a woman, she refused to acknowledge his domination over her. Because she was a woman she would not accept his peace. She shook her head. He threw the belt at her, turned and walked away. Her soft footsteps came up behind him. He side-stepped swiftly, but she knew all the moves and anticipated him. He staggered from the blow to his head, and only just parried the thrust to his throat.

There were no smiles now. Genyen and Tul-lok circled one another. For an hour they fought, grappling, kicking, tripping, slicing, thrusting with their daggers. Each knew all the devious moves and each knew all the countering moves.

Eventually they were so exhausted that their movements were like those of a drunkard. They looked at one another, bleeding and bruised, clothes torn, hair matted with dirt and sweat, barely able to stand, and both roared with laughter.

'Is it the convulsive disease?' Rinchen asked Tsun as he and Champa held Jigme down. The young monk appeared to be unconscious; his eyes were closed, his breath gasping, his body racked by spasms during which his hands clawed at the earth.

Tsun looked at the change coming over Jigme's face and shook his head.

'I don't think so,' he replied as he sat down beside the youth and began chanting.

Lopsang was rapidly searching the trays of round herbal pills in a wooden medicine box. With extraordinary strength, Jigme reared up, throwing off Champa and Rinchen.

'Samden!' Pema held the youth's arm tightly. 'What has happened to him?'

Jigme sat cross-legged, his hands resting on his knees, his body rocking gently. His whole demeanour emanated a great strength; his face appeared larger, older, with heavy angry features. The skin had a faintly bluish hue.

Tsun continued chanting and slowly Jigme turned his head. His eyes were still closed, yet seemed to be surveying his frightened companions. The change in his face was enough for Samden to know that he'd seen the look before: it was the face of an image at Dorje Ri-gon.

'It's our protective deity,' Samden murmured.

'He must have come to take revenge for the destruction of the monastery,' said Norden, just loud enough for everyone to hear.

'No!' Kesang ran to sit beside Tsun and joined in the invocation. Lopsang and Rinchen steadied Jigme as he rose to his feet, moving unsteadily like a new-born creature just learning to walk. His breath was harsh and rasping against the sonorous tones of the invocation. Suddenly, Jigme stepped swiftly over to Samden and pulled his two-foot long steel dagger from its scabbard. He moved round the fire, taking large, ponderous steps, yet with a curious lightness and swiftness, whirling the dagger in his right hand;

Lopsang and Rinchen had difficulty keeping up with him. Then, with the hilt of the dagger in one hand and the tip of the steel blade in the other, with two quick movements he twisted the half-inch steel blade like a corkscrew.

'It is a test of a true oracle of a deity,' Samden murmured to Pema. Jigme no longer resisted the attempts of Lopsang and Rinchen to get him to sit down. Now they all knew that it really was the 'Haughty One.'

Senge lay on his stomach close to Tsun, his attention fixed on the oracle. Tsun leant towards Jigme and spoke to him quietly. Lopsang and Rinchen, standing at the youth's shoulders, could not make out his replies. The conversation was short; Jigme's breathing became harsher, the rocking more violent, then gradually subsiding.

'Samden, his face! His face!' Pema turned her head, unable to look. Jigme's face, reacting to a force from the most distant beginnings of man, began to shrink, the skin tightening so that the cheek and chin bones protruded, taking on the colour of parchment. Then the youth collapsed.

A few minutes later, when Pema brought him over a cup of tea, the open-faced Jigme she knew smiled weakly up at her as he lay exhausted by the fire.

Kesang saw the look of concern on the faces of Lopsang and Rinchen as Tsun spoke to them. When they had finished, he took Tsun's hand.

'Why did the Haughty One come, Tsun-la?'

Tsun looked at the boy. He knew too much for him to be able to soften the reply.

'To warn me that I've been cursed.'

Kesang was confused and concerned. His face creased into a frown.

'Why? What will happen to you, Tsun-la?'

'Kesang, if . . .' Tsun stopped to stroke Senge as he spoke. 'If I was truly awakened to my true nature, and no longer divided by my ego, nothing! But sadly such is not the case.'

'Do you think the curse will work?' Kesang's eyes were wide and full of dread.

'That the Haughty One manifests through Jigme makes me think that I should prepare my mind.'

Kesang was silent for some moments, looking into the fire. He made to speak, but stopped short.

'What is it, Kesang?' Tsun spoke gently, his attention

apparently on Senge who had rolled onto his back to have his stomach rubbed.

'Could it be Ama-la who has cursed you?'

'I do not think so, Kesang. Norden has a temper, but her temper is like the fire – something fuels it and the flames leap, but they soon die down.' Tsun hoped that he sounded convincing.

'How can I help you?' Kesang asked.

'You can join Lopsang and Rinchen-la when they perform the protection ceremony for me.'

Kesang thought for a few moments. Tsun could see that he was struggling to comprehend what was happening.

'How can it be, Tsun-la,' asked Kesang, 'that in meditation we can create beings, deities, and dissolve them in our minds? That we can tell Topden in the after death ceremony that all he sees is illusion, and yet the Haughty One takes over Jigme and appears before us? That was certainly not an illusion.'

'It is just as we say, that all life is illusion, Kesang. That to be enlightened is like waking from a dream. Although we understand it to be illusory, it still appears real to us – solid. So, with those insubstantial things, the deities we create with our minds. They are as real as you or I and sometimes they manifest in solid form, through a human being who is particularly sensitive and able to act as a channel. These people are oracles. It would seem that the protector of Dorje Ri-gon is able to manifest through Jigme.'

'What did you tell your men?'

'That I would sleep with the stock tonight and keep watch,' Tul-lok murmured as his lips caressed the cuts his blade had inflicted on Genyen's breasts.

She laughed. 'Everyone will know why.'

'So you win the fight, and me,' he said mockingly.

They lay near the tethered horses in the darkness, covered by a blanket and their sheepskin chubas. Genyen giggled.

'We wouldn't be much use if we were attacked now!'

Tul-lok gazed at the glistening stars and the brilliant moon. If it had been a few years ago, he would have been pleased by the unclouded moon making it difficult for a surprise attack by raiders; but tonight, he thought, is ideal weather for an attack by the iron birds.

He kissed Genyen's neck through the strands of black hair. His hands caressed her body, moulding, following every contour, every hollow, every rise, gently touching her skin as though assessing the texture of a piece of jade. For, like jade, Tul-lok thought, each woman has a different texture.

She turned her head and looked at him, her large, impenetrable dark eyes always wistful, her strong, dark beauty reminding him . . .

'You remind me of the dakinis,' he said.

She smiled slightly. 'How?' Her strong hands ran down his back, pressing his body to hers.

'When I used to meditate,' he said, nibbling and sucking at her breast, 'I would conjure up my dakini, my special goddess.'

'What was she like?'

'A ferocious, great-breasted woman.'

He chuckled as Genyen pouted.

'Why did you conjure her up?'

'Because she was the symbol of my awakening. She was a key to the depths of my mind that normally I could never reach.'

Genyen did not understand a word.

'And what did you do with this key?' she said, arching her back to receive him.

'We became united, absorbed into one another, and so the knowledge she represented was awakened within me.'

'If I am a dakini,' Genyen said sardonically, 'let us see what knowledge I can awaken in you.'

'Now I know why you are a lama,' she said after a while. 'The proverb is true.'

'And for you, we should make a new proverb.'

With gentle kisses and touches they communicated in the fragile way of lovers.

'Come with me.'

'I cannot, Tul-lok. I have to escort your cousin to Lhasa.'

'I could send some of my men with him.'

'No!' She turned her back on him. 'The Rinposhay is under my protection. I cannot just leave him, you know that, Tul-lok.'

She looked over her shoulder and smiled. 'Come with us. After we reach Lhasa, we could go on to . . .' Her voice faded as he gave her a long look, his face solemn. She caressed him to distract the searchings of his mind.

'You still love him,' he said.

She looked at him with shocked eyes. Her hands were still, and for a few moments neither spoke.

'It was seeing him again,' she whispered. Then she clasped Tul-lok, her mouth seeking his as she cried.

'Love me . . . love me . . .' and her eyes filled with tears.

Chapter Twenty-One

The party had kept a good pace during the morning, passing dozens of refugee groups. At noon, they stopped to eat and rest the horses. Tul-lok and Genyen had scouts out for any sign of the Han.

The men around Tul-lok's camp fire rose as Tsun walked over to his cousin. He sat down beside Tul-lok, who was honing the blade of his three-foot-long sword. Tsun sighed. From the courtesy paid to him, it was evident that many more people knew of his identity. Tul-lok spat on the whetstone to keep it moist. One of Tul-lok's men, bowing and sucking in his breath, offered Tsun tea. Irritably Tsun waved him away.

'Wait! Before you go, tell me how you know who I am?'

The man frowned at the question, then smiled and pointed to another man on the far side of the fire.

'He told me, Rinposhay.'

'Everyone must know who you are by now,' said Tul-lok. 'That woman, Norden, has been telling everyone who will listen about the destruction of Dorje Ri-gon.'

'Too much food is poison, too much talk is alloy,' said Tsun acidly. 'No doubt she blames me, and I can understand it.'

'She does!'

For some moments they sat in silence, listening to the rapid scraping of blade against stone.

'Too many people know your identity, cousin. You must put on a disguise and lose yourself out there.'

Tsun laughed, but Tul-lok was serious as he pointed at the slowly moving flow of people and animals. 'One of my men can dress in your clothes and pretend to be you, so that you are not missed. We can say that you have taken a vow of silence for a period,' he added.

'But Kesang, Rinchen, even the dog . . . they would know it wasn't me.'

Tul-lok sighed heavily. 'Cousin, you have no vision. It would be natural for the person disguised as you to keep away from the others, for you would be meditating. He could keep his head covered. It would not be difficult.'

'But for how long could such a pretence be kept up?' Tsun selected an ear scoop from the set of silver toilet instruments hanging from his belt, and began excavating his left ear. 'Eventually, someone would expose the impostor.'

'Of course they would, cousin, but how long do you need to lose yourself in that crowd? A few hours? Maybe less. Any time that we gain by such a pretence makes the plan that much more sure.'

'It would make me safe, but what of the others? I have a responsibility to all in my party, Tul-lok. They are all that is left of Dorje Ri-gon.'

'You have a greater responsibility. As you told me, the assassination of the Defence Minister would endanger not only your mission, but Tibet. So, I tell you again, that unless you disappear tonight, your mission will never be completed. Yours is not the only spy in the encampment.' Tul-lok spat on the whetstone and continued honing his blade.

'No, the Han will always find us, Tul-lok. They must be really worried by the petition, the lengths they will go to get hold of it.' Tsun thought for a moment. 'There is another way,' he said, flicking the wax from his ear scoop. 'You could take the petition. What benefit is there in my carrying it? There are hundreds of Tibetans who know I have it, and certainly the Han know that I carry it. I shall say that I am going to travel separately to Lhasa so that the Han will continue to believe that I have the petition. In fact, I shall go into retreat which will make it even more difficult to find me, and you will be carrying the petition. None but us will know.'

Tul-lok shook his head and ran the blade of his sword between his fingers to clean it of the yellow whetstone dust.

'You know foreigners, I do not.'

'There are Tibetan merchants and nobles in Kalimpong who will help you.'

Tul-lok did not answer. He removed the remaining clinging wet dust with a cloth.

'Also,' Tsun continued, 'you are no longer a monk. You can guard the petition with greater freedom. Perhaps I have put the petition above everything else. Norden is right, too, in that one does not change one's character when one puts on the robe. Why else would I carry gold for ammunition and weapons? When I took my vows, I swore to abstain from taking life.'

'What harm are you doing by carrying gold?' Tul-lok winked and smiled, but he knew that Tsun was not naive enough to accept this easy answer. He looked at his cousin with concern.

'Do you believe in what the resistance is doing? I do not delude myself. I know what will happen because I kill, but I also remember that it is no less than those who rid the country of King Lang Dharma. They saved the religion from the persecution of the Apostate. Hundreds of years afterwards, we still honour those who killed the king. The good outweighed the evil. Does the resistance do less now? Now that it is not only the religion, but the nation which is in peril?'

'I honour the resistance, Tul-lok. If I did not believe in what it was doing, I would not have agreed to carry the petition in the first place. But you know well enough that the vows taken as a monk are easily compromised. I received from Dorje Rinposhay sacred teachings, and my primary duty is to hand on those teachings. Especially now that Dorje Ri-gon is destroyed. The responsibility is even greater. Is it not said that every village has its own dialect and every lama his own teachings? So, Dorje Rinposhay's teaching is unique. If I do not live it, I make a mockery of passing it on. No, Tul-lok, for many reasons it is right that you take the petition.'

Tul-lok sheathed his sword. 'And Genyen?'

Tsun laughed. They could always follow each other's train of thought.

'She is part of it, but not the whole. Whatever happens during the coming time, it is not going to be easy. The people look to the lamas for spiritual help in their distress. I must do what I can to give it to them, but to do that I need to retreat, to prepare myself. After pursuing me so long and so far, after spending so much on my capture, the Han are not going to treat me as an honoured guest.' He smiled.

They sat in silence while Tul-lok filled his bone pipe with tobacco. Both knew that, if captured, they would be publicly tortured at the Thamzings.

'All that you say is true, cousin,' said Tul-lok. Tsun waited for the qualification, but none came. He continued working away at his ears with the ear scoop.

'The Han seek not only me, Tul-lok, but Kesang. Because he is the tulku of Dorje Rinposhay, and because he is young, they will hope to use his influence as they have that of the Panchen Lama. Also, they know that if he were a hostage I would give myself up.'

Tsun paused. Both men watched, without really seeing, four of Tul-lok's men playing dice at the far side of the fire.

Tsun finally broke the silence. 'Have you decided about Chen-Yi?'

Tul-lok shook his head. 'I have not been able to talk to those concerned.' He held a glowing twig from the fire to the bowl of his pipe. Tsun looked at him sharply.

'Do not play games with me, cousin.'

Tul-lok took the pipe from his mouth and murmured, with a hint of mockery, 'I would not play with you, cousin.'

He sucked at the pipe for some minutes, then turned his strong, brown face to his cousin.

'Tsun, you were chosen to carry the petition for many reasons. You have experienced all that the petition speaks of. This will mean something to the Injis.'

'You have lived through as much.'

'Cousin, I am a renegade ex-monk. A brigand who has never left Tibet. You are the respected head of a monastery, a lama, honoured wherever you go. You know the Injis' language, their ways. Tell me, cousin, which of us is the more fit to deliver the petition? It is for you to decide.'

Tsun reached for the teapot on the hobstone, waving back one of the Khambas who moved to get it for him. He filled Tul-lok's bowl, then his own. He took a long drink, and smiled.

'I will take the petition, Tul-lok.'

Lopsang weighed the small hairy skin pouches in his left hand. The other rested on the pommel of his saddle.

'The scent is strong.' The party had slowed to walking pace as the caravan of refugees approached a gorge leading from the plain.

'They were taken in winter when the deer is ripe,' Norden said. Lopsang fingered each pouch as they rode, weighing and sniffing each.

'What did you give in exchange?'

'Oh, very little, a few supplies.'

He sucked in his breath doubtfully.

'They were a bargain,' Norden insisted. 'The musk is of the best quality. We could get a good price for it in Calcutta, and probably a better price for it in Lhasa with all the Han there.'

'Are these modern Han like their forefathers? Do they still believe that musk is an aphrodisiac, or indeed, do they want one?'

Lopsang smiled, Norden laughed.

'They are still Han, and still men!'

Pema came up beside them. Realising that she was interrupting, she was about to turn away, but Lopsang motioned her to stay. He nodded to Norden and left the two women alone, riding on to join Tsun and Rinchen.

Norden had looped her reins round the pommel of her saddle and carefully wrapped each pod, replacing it in its leather pouch.

'Musk?' Pema asked.

Norden nodded and handed her the pouches. Pema sniffed the pods which had been cut from the penis of the musk deer.

'Do you sell them as they are?'

'It is in fine condition. If I leave the powder in the pods, I shall get the best price.'

'What will it be used for?'

Norden smiled, slightly surprised at the question.

'As an aphrodisiac. It is said that one grain makes a man an insatiable lover.'

'Does it?'

Norden shrugged. 'If you believe, perhaps? I can also sell some for incense.'

Pema wondered at the amazing ingenuity of man where his appetites were concerned, and at the fate of the poor musk deer, seeking only to attract its mate and instead attracting the hunter's arrow.

'Are you going on a trading mission, Honourable Mother?'

The woman looked at her with shrewd eyes.

'I should like to, but who can say in these troubled times? What will you do in Lhasa?'

'I do not know,' answered Pema. 'It is up to my brother, he leads us.'

'He leads us to hell!' The words were involuntarily angry, but Norden watched Pema's reaction.

'Why are we hunted all the time? Is it true that he carries a petition?'

Norden nodded. 'For that petition, everything has been sacrificed. I have heard what your brother was like before he was ordained. He was reckless and wild. He has not changed during all the years he has been in the Order. You cannot tame a man like that. He has tasted blood, wine and women. You do not lose these tastes easily.'

'He has been a good monk?'

'Yes,' Norden answered reluctantly. 'Although . . .' She was seething over the news she had heard of Dorje Ri-gon. 'Have you seen the way he looks at Genyen?'

Pema nodded and wondered if their past relationship had survived the years.

Norden frowned. 'If he had to join the Order so late in life, at least he should not have been made an Abbot. His clothes have changed but his character has not,' she said bitterly.

In her emotional and volatile state, Pema thought that it might be the time to learn something.

'What is in the petition that the Han hunt him for?'

'It is an appeal and a report on the situation in Kham for the United Nations.'

'What is that?'

'All the countries of the world belong to it and are meant to help one another keep peace. I heard something about it when I was in India.' Pema remembered vaguely hearing about it at school as an Imperialist Front Organisation.

'Is it so important to the Han?'

'They destroyed Dorje Ri-gon for it.'

She took the musk from Pema and tucked the leather pouches into her ambac.

'I cannot speak of it. My son has nothing now because of your brother. I warned him of the disaster he would bring on us. We have had enough signs on this journey. But no! He had to go on!'

'Tsun, look!' Kesang pointed to a twenty-foot high, part painted figure of Chenresi chiselled in the rock. By it was a cairn of mani stones. They walked over to take a closer look, and Kesang pointed again to a rough canopy of branches over the mouth of a small cave beside the sculpture. A figure, swathed in a tattered maroon robe, came from the mouth of the cave.

'I would be honoured, Rinposhay, if you would have tea with me.' As they entered the cave, the brown, lined face of an old woman, with shaven head and a mouth empty of teeth, smiled at the two lamas. She picked up a battered clay teapot from the hobstone as they sat down, and poured tea into their wooden bowls. Neither showed surprise that she should know them. It merely indicated she had advanced on the spiritual path.

'Tsun-la.' Kesang nodded toward an antelope nestled at the back of the cave in a patch of sunlight. The antelope looked at the strangers with black, liquid eyes, full of curiosity.

'It is good tea,' Tsun said. 'Especially after such a climb.'

'No, no!' The old woman pulled her cloak over her shaven head. 'The tea is very poor.'

And so it is, Tsun chuckled to himself.

'The quality of the giving is good,' he said.

The old woman laughed at his compliment which she could not demur in the customary way.

'Where did you come from, Rinposhay?'

'From Litang.'

'All these people, Rinposhay?' She opened her arms at the thousands stretching back across the plain. 'For so long I have been alone, now it seems that the whole world has come to dwell with me. Why is this, Rinposhay?'

'They flee the Han.'

The old woman shook her head sadly.

'How long have you been here?' Kesang asked.

She shrugged and laughed. 'Since long before he was born.' She patted the antelope, which licked her hand.

'Where do you come from?'

'From the north.'

'Where have you been?' Kesang persisted with his questioning.

'East, west and south. With the winds of the four directions.'

'You have no home?'

'My home is where I am, Rinposhay.'

Kesang frowned. 'Are you a witch?'

The old woman rocked with laughter; then tears filled her eyes and the laughter ebbed away. She reached out a hand, blackened by sun and dirt, to touch him, then withdrew it, thinking it not right to touch one of such exalted rank, but Kesang clasped her hand in his.

'That I were a witch,' she murmured, and though she smiled at the boy, her eyes met Tsun's and he saw the infinite sadness which filled him with dread.

'I am just a pilgrim, Rinposhay, a nun.'

'Why are you painting Chenresi here?'

'But why not, Rinposhay?'

'It's so lonely here, no one will see it.' The boy sipped his tea noisily.

'I just painted it, Rinposhay, where it was necessary for me to paint it.' She laughed, but Kesang did not understand that it did not matter who saw the image, or indeed, if *anyone* did, or whether it was poor or good. It was an unselfconscious, genuine act of creation. But something responded in Kesang, for he put his bowl of tea down, took a felicity scarf from his ambac and went into the sunlight to lay it at the feet of the thousand-armed sculpture. He shivered at the touch of the cold rock as he bowed in reverence. The wind quickly snatched the muslin scarf away. It seemed to Kesang that the painting had been plucked from the night, the womb of demons, fairies, gods and goddesses, and impaled on the rock.

The antelope jumped when he returned to the cave, unused to strangers.

'You have been to the holy places?' Tsun asked the nun.

'Yes, Rinposhay.'

Tsun offered her some tsampa, which she accepted with a murmured thanks.

They talked for some time. Kesang plied her with questions about her pilgrimages and she answered, reliving her experiences as she described the holy places. She had a great simplicity about her – no guile, no façade – she was completely natural and spontaneous in all that she said and did. She encouraged Kesang to stroke the antelope, and gradually it accepted his caresses. It was while his attention was completely held by the antelope, that the nun said to Tsun, 'Rinposhay, I must speak with you.' She moved away from Kesang so that he could not hear.

As Tsun rose to follow her, the nun looked at him with an anxiety in her eyes which cut deep. The silence was long.

'Do not be afraid to speak, I have already looked in death's mirror.'

'Rinposhay . . .' But she could not find the words to tell him, and in her very anguish and hesitation Tsun learned more than she could ever put into words.

'Rinposhay, whatever happens to you, your destiny is to pass on the Teaching.'

Tsun was puzzled. This had been so since he had been ordained a monk.

'Whatever defeat you suffer, Rinposhay, when the time comes hear these words and know that yours is a specially blessed destiny. Your name will be as the whispering wind in the forest, imperceptibly moving countless leaves.'

Norden pulled the fur lappets of her hat down over her ears and threw two yak chips onto the fire. The demand for fuel created by the heavy concentration of refugees was beginning to make even these scarce. She watched the light from the flames flickering over

Tsun's impassive face as he sat meditating. He had persuaded Lopsang and Rinchen that it was better for him to meditate alone and that after a good night's rest they could conduct the protection ceremony to alleviate the curse the following evening. The tension had eased, since nothing had happened during the previous night and there was no indication during the day that the curse was taking effect. But Lopsang and Rinchen had agreed to take turns in watching over Tsun as he sat in deep contemplation.

As Norden poured tea into Rinchen's bowl, the steward gently removed Tsun's own wooden bowl from his ambac so that the lama would know that tea was poured if he wanted it. Rinchen thanked the Honourable Mother and she nodded back, smiling. Then suddenly her smile faded. Rinchen followed Norden's gaze. Beads of sweat had appeared on Tsun's face, despite the cold. Rinchen was frightened, but Tsun had been adamant that he should prepare himself alone.

Lopsang, Rinchen and Norden sat by the fire for over an hour, watching and meditating. Tsun remained sitting with no movement; only his steady, rhythmic breathing, the beads of sweat rolling down his face. Every now and then, others of the party would come to the fire, to drink tea in silence and watch the lama in his silent struggle. On seeing him, most of them stayed to help, for Tsun's face, although superficially impassive, was visibly if indefinably reflecting his inner fight for survival.

'Om Mani Padme Hum, Om Mani Padme Hum'. The invocation of Chenresi was low and rippling, enveloping Tsun in the cold darkness. Pema counted off the invocations on her rosary; Norden's mani wheel turned steadily; Kesang and the other monks, their rosary beads slipping through their fingers, each focused their minds on Tsun.

Norden was the first to see the alteration in Tsun's face. Automatically she gripped Kesang's arm. 'Look!' Tsun's eyes slowly opened and the murmured invocations ceased. In the tense silence the Abbot smiled gently and wiped the perspiration from his face. Genyen's shout of delight acted as a catalyst and everyone relaxed and began talking, asking questions. Pema handed her brother a bowl of tea, looking at him shyly, awed by the mental struggle etched on his face. As she looked into his deep, warm eyes, she murmured, 'Is it over?' His eyes changed, appearing troubled for a moment, then he nodded slowly.

'Namgyal, look!' Kesang was pointing in the direction of a tiny white light in the darkness which appeared to be coming from the tree-covered hill above them. Even as they saw the light flashing, they heard the lookouts raising the alarm and, on the other side of the valley, more pinpoints of light bloomed and winked in reply.

Within moments the refugees realised that they were encircled. As they began shooting at the lights, the Han opened fire, lobbing mortar shells into the camp from positions in the hills surrounding the valley.

Chapter Twenty-Two

All over the plain there was turmoil as the thousands tried to defend themselves and find some way out of the valley, while the Han steadily and devastatingly bombarded them with mortar fire.

'Samden!' Genyen yelled as she broke her revolver and spun the chamber to check that it was fully loaded. 'Douse the fire!'

'There must be thousands of them,' Pema shouted at the nomad woman, swinging her high pommelled saddle onto her horse and tying the girth over the saddle rug.

'Aye! Aye! Come on, get up!' shouted Jigme, slapping the two supply mules to get them to their feet. Norden ran with two teapots which she began strapping to the mules as Samden threw handfuls of earth onto the flames of the fire.

'Namgyal!' called Lopsang. 'Look out behind you!' Strapping on his horse's bridle, he had caught sight of a bolting horse careering towards the boy, who was carrying the butter churn. He turned suddenly, hearing the racing hooves and stood as though mesmerised. Champa just managed to pull him to safety. Norden yelled with fright as a bullet nicked the sole of her red embroidered felt boot. Two hundred yards away, the ground erupted in a great ball of fire and smoke.

'Hold onto him!' Samden shouted as Pema's horse reared in fright, almost pulling the reins from her grasp. Pema tried to keep clear of the flying hooves. Samden grabbed the reins and urged her horse towards some rocks where the rest of the party were gathered. People were shouting and running in all directions; throughout the valley the ground trembled with the explosions of mortar bombs.

'Ama-la! Ama-la!' A little girl of about six years old was shouting for her mother as she wandered, distraught and lost. Bullets whined as a man grabbed her, pulling her back behind the shelter of a boulder. Tsun crawled over to Genyen.

'Look!' he pointed. 'There is quite a distance between those lights. The trees between them would give us cover.'

'It may be just what the Han are waiting for.'

Tsun grinned, his perfect white teeth brilliant against his deeply tanned face.

'What chance have we down here?'

Genyen shrugged. The Han were using medium mortars, submachine guns and machine guns against the Tibetans' recoilless and automatic rifles, barely half a dozen machine guns and a good many matchlocks. Pinned down with little cover, the refugees would soon be forced to surrender or be massacred.

'Tul-lok?'

Tsun saw his cousin sitting with his back to a rock lighting his pipe. He cursed softly as the tobacco failed to ignite from the flint spark.

'Get down under cover!' Tsun shouted, and pushed a curious Kesang down from peering over the rocks.

'Have you a match?' Tul-lok called to Tsun.

The Abbot threw a box to his cousin. Tul-lok lit his pipe, then, taking careful aim, he sighted his rifle. He fired a single shot at the nearest lamp a few hundred yards up the hillside. His men cheered as it smashed and went out. The Han opened up on them with intense automatic fire. Tul-lok used the binoculars to search for the tell-tale barrel flashes; they crouched close to the rocks, bullets and rock splinters flying in all directions.

'Did you see that?' Tul-lok called above the din.

'Clearly!' Tsun replied.

'You've brought a hornets' nest down on us,' Genyen shouted angrily.

'Nothing came from between the lights, from the trees.' Tul-lok pointed. 'There is a machine gun to our left, and to our right there is a mortar, but they don't have as many men as they would have us believe. My men will keep you covered and draw their fire, while you make for the trees.'

'And you?'

'We are needed here, there are few of the resistance with the refugees.'

'It is safer here,' Genyen murmured, then shouted, 'Get ready to move out! Keep close together and take the bells off the mules!'

Kesang pushed Senge into his chuba. Tsun grasped his cousin's hand.

'We will meet in Lhasa.'

Tul-lok nodded. 'Give me your sling, Namgyal.'

He fitted a hand grenade into the sling, pulled out the pin, whirled the sling around his head, then launched the grenade towards the Han position.

It fell short of the PLA troops, mushrooming in flame and smoke, but gave Tsun and his party a chance to start up the steep scrub- and shale-covered hillside.

They climbed in silence, slowed down by the horses and mules which were struggling to keep their feet. At some points they had to zig-zag across the slope. Below them, Tul-lok's men kept up a steady fire and threw more grenades to keep the Hans' attention. It was difficult to see what was happening, apart from the mortar explosions in the valley, but they heard well enough. The explosions, the screams and shouts of men, women and children. The rattle of the Han automatic weapons, the irregular answering fire of rifles, revolvers and matchlocks.

Norden heard the startled indrawn breath of her horse as it stumbled and she leaned forward to stroke its neck, anticipating a neigh, while praying that the noise of the shale clinking beneath the hooves would not be heard by the Han. Pema, riding close behind, looked up towards the pine trees looming high above them, and thought that they seemed as far away as ever. She grasped the stark branches of a stunted bush to help her horse up the hillside. A few feet away, she saw the hind feet of Rinchen's horse slipping on the stones. Desperately, the horse tried to keep its balance as the loose ground moved, then its legs started to buckle. Pema leaned as far forward as she dared and grabbed the struggling horse's tail.

'Jigme,' she hissed at the young man nearby, 'push on its flank or it will slide.'

Between them they managed to hold the horse steady long enough for it to regain its footing and get onto firmer ground.

The horses shied nervously at a mortar bomb exploding in the valley, close to the rocks behind which Tul-lok and his men were hiding.

'I think it's hit them,' Genyen murmured, but looking back as they struggled up the hillside she could not see anything clearly through the smoke. Then a grenade exploded away to their left, thrown by Tul-lok or one of his men. The Han machine gun opened up again.

'What are those red lights they are firing? Kesang asked the Abbot.

'Tracer bullets. To help them with aiming. Come on, Kesang,' he urged the boy. 'Keep up.'

Another mortar bomb exploded near the rocks. Tsun glanced at Genyen riding beside him.

'The mortar is firing over us,' he said.

Genyen glanced up at the clouded moon. 'Rinposhay,' she said, 'use your powers to keep the moon veiled.'

In unwelcome moonlight the Han would easily see them and, with virtually no cover until the trees, they wouldn't stand a chance. Kesang lurched forward on top of Senge and gave a small cry. The little dog let out a muffled yelp. Norden pulled at the back of the boy's clothes to help him straighten up, then she grabbed at the bridle of his horse, while the boy fumbled to get Senge back into his chuba.

'Put him down,' she hissed.

Kesang shook his head firmly.

'Kesang!'

'No, Ama-la.'

Tsun reached over to Kesang and lifted the dog by the scruff of its neck. He pushed Senge down into the folds of his own chuba and felt the little body trembling against him.

Stones the horses had dislodged gathered momentum. Genyen signalled the group to halt. Tensely, they waited to see if the tumbling stones would attract the attention of the PLA troops. Then, as nothing happened, they dismounted and, grunting with exertion, pulled their horses upwards towards the trees. They were close now.

'Lord of Mercy!' Norden murmured. She glanced back to the valley, its darkness blooming with the tight crimson clouds of exploding mortar bombs.

'The moon!' Genyen called in warning, as loudly as she dared. They made a scrambling dash for the shadow of the trees as the clouds parted, leaving Norden struggling behind them, crying in desperation as she fought for a foothold on the loose shale. There were shouts from the Han, then they opened fire with their machine guns, the bullets hitting the stones around them. Kesang looked back and saw his mother trying to get up the slope.

'Ama-la!' he cried out to her.

Jigme's horse screamed as the bullets ripped its flanks. The youth was almost jerked off his feet by the pull of the reins as the animal collapsed and rolled down the hill.

Crouching, with bullets ricocheting off the shale at his feet, Jigme ran for the shelter of the trees. One of the Khamba escort fell and his wounded horse slid down the hillside, dragging him with it. Senge yelped as Tsun flung himself down in the undergrowth at the foot of the trees. Genyen fired at the barrel flashes from the Han weapons.

'Grab the horses,' Tsun shouted to Champa. They tugged at the frightened animals' reins, pulling them into the cover of trees. Branches tore and cracked above them. For an instant, Pema saw the dark shape of a mortar bomb before it fell to the ground and exploded. Jigme pushed Lopsang aside as a massive branch crashed down where he had been standing. Another bomb fell. Tsun felt his legs bathed in warm liquid; the little dog, tucked into his chuba, was urinating with fear. The black smoke from the bombs hung low, allowing them to take advantage of its cover.

'Come on!' Tsun shouted to the others.

Crouching and leading their horses, they moved quickly through the tall trees. Rinchen's face was peppered with slivers of bark as the bullets chipped the trees.

'Rinposhay!' Samden shouted urgently.

Tsun turned, and saw the silhouetted figures of PLA troops moving among the trees.

'Keep down!' Genyen shouted.

She fired her revolver at the Han. They returned her fire and one of the bullets nicked her clothing. Norden saw Namgyal fitting a grenade into his sling.

'Where did you get that,' she asked automatically, thinking that he might get hurt.

'From Tul-lok, look! There!'

Namgyal pointed to a stealthily moving figure coming towards them. Norden took careful aim on the Han and pulled the trigger. She screamed as the revolver exploded. Tsun thought, on seeing the flame and smoke, that a grenade had exploded among them.

'Ama-la! Ama-la!' Kesang ran through the smoke to his mother. Pema grabbed the reins of his frightened horse.

Norden lay doubled up, covered in her own blood and that of the horse beside her, its neck ripped open, pumping an ocean of blood onto the ground.

'Ama-la . . .'

'No . . . keep back . . .' Norden gasped chokingly at the boy.

Tsun ran, bent low, as bullets hammered into the trees around him. He grabbed Kesang.

'Don't let my blood touch him or it will be his,' Norden cried.

'Ama-la . . .' Kesang's despairing voice carried the realisation of the extent of his mother's wounds. Tsun swung the boy over to Pema.

'Get him away from here.'

'No!' the boy screamed. 'No! Ama-la, Tsun, let me stay.' But Pema lifted the boy up into the saddle of his horse and ran through the trees, leading her own horse, together with those of Kesang and Tsun.

Tsun winced as he bent over Norden and saw her shattered face. An eyeball was hanging by a thread. Beneath her, he saw the massive pink ball of her intestines. She groaned in agony. Tsun threw himself to the ground as the Han Norden had tried to kill opened fire on him.

'Go back, Namgyal, Go back!' Tsun could see the boy darting from tree to tree. Namgyal pulled the pin from a grenade, whirled it in his sling around his head, and released the missile. It exploded within a yard of the Han, killing him.

Tsun looked helplessly at Norden. He wished she were dead. She could not live, but only linger. He could not just leave her. Genyen and her men were trying to hold off the advancing Han. Tsun looked again at Norden; she was losing consciousness. He laid his hand on her head in blessing and, amid the loud hail of bullets, said a prayer to transfer her consciousness and ensure her favourable rebirth.

Norden, the Honourable Mother, was dead.

Namgyal pulled at Tsun's chuba, and pointed towards a group of figures moving up the hill to their right.

'Rinposhay, the Han!'

They ran then, into the trees, having only a vague idea of the direction the others had taken. The Han opened fire and bullets ripped through the trees.

'Tsun-la!' Pema called to her brother. Kesang, holding her hand, did not ask about his mother but his face was streaked with tears.

'Where are the others?'

'Just ahead of us I think.'

Tsun was untying his money belt with the pouches of gold dust and the wallet containing the petition. He winced as he took it off, pulling out the pubic hairs to which he had tied it so that he would be wakened if anyone tried to steal it while he slept.

'Pema,' he said, holding the belt towards his sister, 'you know what this is?'

'Yes.' She sounded surprised.

'Keep it safely for me,' he said hurriedly. 'If anything happens to me, or if we get separated, try to get it to Genyen or Tul-lok. Many have given much for it to reach its destination.'

Pema nodded uncertainly, took the belt and pushed it under the fold of her chuba, tying it around her waist.

'If you are captured,' he said, 'hide the belt, bury it, burn it. Do anything, but do not let the Han get it.'

'Why do you ask *me* to do this?'

Tsun smiled in the darkness.

Keeping low and leading the horses, they steadily climbed the hillside, hugging the cover of the trees. The pines were dense and tall, obscuring the moon and stars. Tsun heard something moving through the undergrowth towards them. He slipped his long dagger from its sheath. The little dog inside his chuba trembled and whimpered. Then Tsun caught a few words whispered in Tibetan and a woman, holding two small, twin girls aged about eight, by either hand, emerged from the darkness in front of him. She stifled a cry of fear on seeing Tsun, then realising that he was Tibetan, she stepped nearer.

'Please help us, Kusho, we are lost.'

She looked at Tsun with desperate eyes.

'I do not know the way,' Tsun answered low. 'We, too, are lost.'

'*Please*, Kusho,' the woman pleaded. One of the little girls reached out and touched Tsun's hand.

'Very well,' he said.

Silently, he groaned. It was hard enough looking after what remained of his party without adding to it. As they moved on, the woman and her two children fell in beside him. Then Tsun became aware of women and children converging on him from all sides, all looking at him expectantly.

'Where have they come from?'

'We are together, Kusho. Our husbands told us to take the children and find a safe place while they fought the Han.'

Tsun reckoned there were about twenty women and children surrounding him. To slip through the Han lines with such a large unmounted party would be almost impossible.

'Hide,' Tsun told them. 'Keep under cover. I cannot help you. I, too, do not know where to go.'

They looked at him with frightened, despairing faces, but did not move. Tsun sighed and realised that it was to be his karma that he should lead them.

'Keep close together and keep quiet! If I signal, hide!' he said.

'Whatever happens,' the woman beside him told her two children, 'keep hold of each other's hand.'

'Keep quiet!' Tsun scolded some children who were beginning to chatter.

The darkness caused by the high trees obscuring the moon would make it harder for them to be seen by the Han, Tsun thought, but equally, it made the going that much more difficult. The scrub- and leaf-covered ground was full of treacherous dips and hollows. Twigs whipped and scratched at their faces. Roots seemed to reach out and deliberately ensnare their feet.

The battle had spread from the valley, so that the party could hear Han and Tibetans shouting and fighting only yards away. As he could not get a bearing from the stars, Tsun was not certain that he was, in fact, moving away from the valley.

Suddenly he became aware of someone very, very close, and signalled for the others to take cover. Even as his arm was raised, he felt the pressure of a gun barrel in his ribs, and heard the click of the safety catch.

'Move, and you're dead!'

Tsun turned and found himself looking into the dark eyes of a young Khamba. The man lowered his gun when he realised Tsun was a Tibetan. The women and children re-emerged from the shadows.

'Is it safe ahead?'

The man shrugged.

'Have you seen Tul-lok or Genyen?'

The man shook his head and disappeared into the darkness. The party walked on, throwing themselves to the ground as a mortar bomb exploded nearby. Sometimes they heard Tibetan voices, sometimes Han, and occasionally a lost child crying for its parents. Senge, still trembling, pushed his head out of Tsun's chuba. Suddenly, Tsun heard Han talking a few yards away.

'Ama-la . . .' One of the children cried out as she tripped.

'Hush!' The child's mother, who was carrying a baby, picked her up. 'Come on.'

'I cannot, Ama-la, my foot hurts.'

'Come, Tsering, you must.'

'Keep quiet!' Tsun hissed.

Pema took the child in her arms and carried her. Tsun glanced down at Kesang. The boy sniffed and wiped tears away from his face with the back of his hand. Tsun gave him Senge to hold, and as the boy took the dog in his arms, he hugged him close and wept silently.

The Han voices were moving closer. The temperature had dropped sharply, but Tsun still sweated. One of the babies started to cry and struggled violently as a hand was clamped over its mouth.

'You will smother him,' the mother wept as she and another woman tried to soothe the child.

A middle-aged woman close to Pema tripped and fell. She and Namgyal both helped her and, as she pushed herself up, she became conscious of cloth, not earth, beneath her hands. She found herself looking into the cold dead eyes of the body she had tripped over. Pema clapped her hand over the woman's open mouth.

They came across some ten dead bodies, all of them men. Many of the women wept as they thought of their husbands fighting, perhaps only a few yards away. The trees thinned ahead. Tsun signalled for the party to halt while he went to look over the slight rise. Kesang sat down and stroked Senge.

'Ama-la, I have a stone in my shoe,' one of the twin girls cried.

'Then take it out,' her mother snapped.

'Help me, Ama-la.'

The woman undid the laces on the back of her daughter's felt shoe. Feverishly she searched for the stone, as the other women and children crept past her, following Tsun. She re-tied the shoe laces, and leant against a tree for a moment to rest. Her eyes focused, without her mind registering, on a sliver of moonlight reflecting from a bayonet held only a foot from her chest. She gasped and clutched tightly at her children's hands as she edged away, her mind numbed. She saw the Han's face more clearly in the moonlight. For a few moments, she did not register the contorted face, then she realised it was a dead man who held the rifle, standing petrified in a cadaveric pose. Before her screams died away, Tsun was running back through the women and children, pushing them to cover beneath the bushes. Sobbing, still holding the hands of her two terrified children, she stumbled towards Tsun.

'I am sorry, Kusho.'

A flashlight blazed into Tsun's eyes.

'Stand exactly where you are!' The voice spoke in a thick Han accent. PLA troops surrounded him. As his dagger was taken from him and his hands tied, Tsun watched the Han searching the bushes. An infantryman led past him the horses belonging to Namgyal, Kesang and Pema, but Tsun could see no sign of his sister or the boys. It was impossible to see in the darkness whether or not they had been captured.

The five-year-old boy looked up at the moon, the colour of the milk he had seen his mother take from the cow just before they were attacked. He settled his head back on the shoulder of the PLA infantryman who was carrying him. His troubled mind wondered where his mother could be. She was not among the Tibetans roped together who were being marched through the freezing night. He wondered where she was . . .

The Lieutenant of the PLA unit shouted at an old man who had collapsed with exhaustion, bringing the column of thirty-five prisoners to a halt. He looked up at the Lieutenant uncomprehendingly. Again the Lieutenant shouted at him, gesticulating.

'He does not understand Chinese,' Tsun said to the Lieutenant. 'I will tell him.'

'The Lieutenant says that he cannot release any prisoners.' At first the old man did not understand. Then he let his body sink to the ground, but his fellow prisoners reached down, lifted him up, and carried him, with his feet dragging on the ground.

'Do you know where they are taking us?' Tsun asked the man next to him. The man shook his head.

BOOK THREE: March, 1956 to March, 1959

'. . . and the holders of the Faith, the Glorious Rebirths, will be broken down and left without a name . . .'

Chapter Twenty-Three

Colonel Liu Ying watched his knee-high, black leather boots crush the frost-covered grass as he rocked back and forth on his heels. Of medium build, with only one arm, he wore a thick quilted jacket and a cap.

From outside his tent, he looked across at the eight hundred and sixty-three prisoners being assembled in the middle of the narrow green valley. As soon as his men got the Tibetans into a semblance of a line, it immediately disappeared as prisoners moved to other lines, looking for relatives and friends. The Colonel turned to the Captain beside him.

'I'm not waiting any longer,' he said angrily. 'I want these people ready for inspection in five minutes. They are like milling sheep.'

Like all the prisoners, Tsun was weak from exhaustion and hunger. He tried to sit down but a guard ordered him to stand ready for inspection. He took deep breaths of the icy, bracing morning air, but it carried with it the smell of his own foul body. Increasingly, his skin was being irritated by Senge's stale urine, but at least, Tsun thought, it had solved the flea problem for him.

Like the other prisoners, his eyes constantly searched the sea of faces, but no one did he recognise.

'Attention! Attention!'

Voices subsided as people listened to the loud hailer, distorted by the wind.

'Anyone who moves out of place will be shot! Anyone who moves out of place will be shot!'

The ever-changing pattern of movement ceased. The Colonel and his party began their inspection. Some of the prisoners, hoping to win his favour, sucked in their breath and bowed, but most just looked at him sullenly. The young man next to Tsun suddenly shouted.

'Chokyi!'

A woman a few yards away in the front row, turned and raised her hands in acknowledgement.

'My wife,' the man exclaimed with delight, smiling at Tsun. 'I thought we had lost one another for good.'

Another woman, beside Tsun, squatted, arranged her ankle-length chuba and urinated. Weak from marching and hunger, and unable to balance herself with tied hands, she found it difficult to get up from her squatting position. Laughing, Tsun and the young man helped her to stand.

Then Tsun saw a small boy, bare bottomed, wearing only a tiny battered sheepskin chuba, sitting on the grass between his row and that of the prisoners in front. He was building a cairn of pebbles and planting prayer flags of twigs and blades of grass. The Abbot joined in the boy's total involvement and absorption in the moment . . . all that was . . . is . . . and could be . . .

The concentration of them both was broken when a hand reached down and pulled the boy back into line.

Tsun could see the Colonel's party slowly moving down the line, carefully scrutinising each male prisoner, but no questions were asked, or orders given. He glanced up and down his line to see if any of the guards were looking his way, then reached down, dug a handful of dirt, and smeared it over his face. The young man next to him thought he had gone mad.

'Can I borrow your hat?' Tsun asked him, for his shaven head marked him as a monk.

The man laughed and gave it to him. Then, as the inspection party moved down Tsun's line, he lowered his eyes and stilled his mind in an attempt to render his presence invisible.

The Colonel paused for only a moment before Tsun and was already looking at the young man when a hand touched his arm. Tsun felt his hat being lifted from his head. He looked up. In front of him, beside the Colonel, stood a tall figure in PLA uniform, his face covered by a dust mask and a pair of anti-snow goggles. Through the tinted glass of the goggles, Tsun saw the eyes of Lopsang.

'Bring him,' the Colonel ordered.

Two soldiers grabbed Tsun and marched him behind the briskly walking Colonel. 'Hi, that's my hat!' the young man called after them.

When they reached his tent, Colonel Liu sat down heavily in a canvas chair.

'Tell the men and the prisoners they can eat,' he ordered.

Then he drank some hot water from an enamel mug and looked up at Tsun who was standing in front of the table.

'Strip him and search him,' he said. 'Lopsang, you know what we are looking for.'

A soldier pushed past the guards and put a plate of rice and dried meat on the table. One of the guards poked Tsun with the barrel of his gun.

'Get undressed!'

'Not in here, you fool,' the Colonel said. 'The man stinks, take him outside.'

Colonel Liu took his chopsticks out of an inner pocket and placed them carefully on the table, slightly apart, so that his one hand could pick them up and adjust them easily. But he disliked eating with a glove on, and mentally cursed this bleak and inhospitable land with its treacherous, ignorant people. It was impossible to trust them. Any one of them might stick a knife in you.

'Comrade,' he said to a young captain, 'what news of the fighting?'

'Field HQ say it is over.'

The Colonel grunted. At least they could now go back to Chamdo, which bore a faint resemblance to civilisation.

'The one they are searching, and the children, are to go to Chamdo,' he said. 'The rest of the prisoners can go to the road camp. Remind me to have interrogation units sent here when we get back to Chamdo.'

'Comrade Colonel, there are not enough trucks to take all the prisoners to the road camp.'

'Radio Field HQ for some more trucks, and if they haven't got them, radio Chamdo.'

Tsun was brought back into the tent.

'He does not have it on him,' Lopsang said, removing the goggles and dust mask.

'Where is it?' the Colonel asked Tsun briskly.

'I have nothing,' Tsun said. 'I was travelling to Lhasa to seek sanctuary with the other refugees.'

'The petition,' Colonel Liu's voice was professionally hard.

'I only had a message from our people to His Holiness.'

The Colonel shook his head and smiled at Tsun.

'You are an intelligent man.' He leant back in his chair. 'Unless you tell me what has happened to the petition, I shall order one of those prisoners to be shot every minute, until you do tell me.'

Tsun knew he was not bluffing.

'I destroyed it before I was captured. When the PLA started to attack the refugee camp.'

'And where is the young lama?'

The Colonel looked at Lopsang inquiringly.

'He was not among the prisoners,' Lopsang said.

'I doubt,' Colonel Liu lit a cigarette, 'that you tell us the whole truth, but partly perhaps. However, at Chamdo, we shall have the whole truth. We shall leave immediately.' He looked again at Lopsang. 'You will come with us.'

He took a pair of handcuffs off the table and tossed them to a guard.

'Put these on the prisoner.'

'May I have something to eat and drink,' Tsun asked.

The Colonel looked at the Abbot's haggard face and parched lips.

'Give him a little water,' he said.

As Tsun walked past the rows of long-nosed, Russian-built trucks drawn up beside the Chamdo road, he watched bewildered children being loaded into one of the eight-wheeled vehicles, one of the thousands supplied to Chiang Kai-Shek during the Japanese war.

The Colonel was sitting in the front of a jeep beside the driver. As Tsun held onto the side of the jeep to pull himself up, he felt sharp pains in his wrists. He sat down between Lopsang and a guard and studied his handcuffs. They were equipped with small metal teeth which tightened, digging into the flesh, if any strain was put upon them. He turned in his seat to watch the children being loaded aboard two more of the trucks, half hoping to see Kesang and Namgyal, half hoping that he would not. He caught Lopsang's eye. The monk knew what he was thinking.

'What became of the others?' he asked with genuine concern.

'I do not know, Lopsang.' Tsun spoke slowly, feeling a wave of bitter resentment at the question. 'We became separated during the fighting. They may be alive, they may be dead.'

They heard shots being fired among the prisoners, as parents protested at their children being taken away. An armoured car passed, bouncing wildly as it drove up onto the road ahead of the jeep. Tsun cried out with pain as the jeep moved off with a jerk and the handcuffs bit into his wrists. He cushioned his hands between his legs against the bouncing, swaying vehicle.

As the convoy gathered speed, he had a last glimpse of the valley, of the prisoners being herded into trucks, before his vision was obliterated by a dust cloud.

It was years since Tsun had been in a motor vehicle, and then never at such speed. For some time he sat watching the dominating mountains, ever changing in shape and colour, as they sped along the road which snaked before them, climbing back and forth across mountain faces at what Tsun felt was an incredibly exhilarating speed.

Lopsang tried to tap some snuff onto his thumb, but each time he tried, the wind whipped it away. He caught Tsun's eye, made as if to speak, and then fell silent.

'Why did the Han attack the refugees?' Tsun asked.

He felt Lopsang's mental defences go up.

'Because there were counter-revolutionaries among the group.'

Both knew that the secretary did not use the term in the Han pejorative sense, but as the Tibetans used it, to mean the resistance.

'Why, Lopsang? Why did you betray us?'

The secretary pulled his dust mask down and adopted his habitual bland, impenetrable expression.

'Was it *I* who did the betraying?' he asked.

'You have just betrayed me,' said Tsun, 'and all that you, as a monk, stand for.'

The Abbot had touched a raw nerve. Lopsang looked away. There was a long pause.

'You remember the last trading mission?' he said.

Tsun nodded.

'Some officers of the PLA garrison in Litang suggested that I get them a large quantity of cigarettes. I agreed, but had to borrow the money to buy them. When the mission arrived back in Litang from India, the Han offered me a price that barely covered transport costs, let alone the cost of the cigarettes.'

He paused, and Tsun was about to ask him to continue, when he decided not to. He had a feeling that there was a purpose in his explanation, and if there was, he would need no prompting.

'It ruined me,' Lopsang continued. 'I couldn't pay the money back, nor find a buyer for the quantity of cigarettes I had . . .'

The Colonel turned round in the front seat. He was wearing dark glasses and a dust mask.

'What are you talking about?' he asked Lopsang.

'I am explaining how I learned that the only way for Tibet is the way of the Great Motherland.'

The Colonel did not believe Lopsang, but he liked to keep everyone on their toes. He turned back in his seat.

'Then, when I was on business in Litang,' Lopsang continued, 'I saw the person I had borrowed the money from. He said it had to be repaid immediately. He said, if I did not repay the debt, he would report me to you, Rinposhay.'

Remembering Lopsang's resentment at his rapid elevation to the Abbatial throne, Tsun could well understand just how humiliating that would have been for Lopsang.

'The Security Committee Office said they would repay my debt for me, if I succeeded in persuading you to co-operate with the Han.'

Tsun watched a whole colony of marmots dashing for their burrows as the vehicles sped past them.

'And without success?' he asked.

Lopsang hesitated. 'I agreed to help stop your mission. I saw it as the only way of saving Dorje Ri-gon.'

'You betrayed us, Lopsang.' Tsun rolled his words out slowly as the memories of their flight filled his mind.

'What is betrayal? Yesterday I was the betrayer . . . today . . .' Lopsang looked long at Tsun's handcuffs, 'it is you.' He frowned. 'I warned you of the danger of taking the petition, of assisting the reactionaries.'

Tsun smiled slightly. Lopsang's frown deepened.

'Rinposhay, you remember what is said about the little rabbit?'

'It is impossible for him to place his hands on the beautiful horns of the deer.' Tsun completed the proverb for him, and got the point. His stomach began to revolt against the petrol fumes, the dust and the swaying jeep. In an effort to distract his mind from his physical discomfort, he raised his eyes to the road ahead, which climbed in curve upon curve across a mountain. Tsun realised they would arrive in Chamdo in a few hours, whereas before the Han had built the road it had taken days to complete the journey they were now making. The roads, indeed, Tsun thought, bound Tibet as ropes.

'Rinposhay, there is time yet for you to co-operate with the authorities. They will be lenient with you. Is it any less than the Kundun is doing?'

'No, Lopsang, it is a great deal more.'

'The horse, remember, does not come to the calling of a bird.'

Tsun grinned at his impassive secretary, and then was flung against him as the jeep swung round a sharp bend. His violently protesting stomach suddenly heaved, and he leaned across Lopsang and retched over the side of the jeep, his handcuffs biting unmercifully into his wrists with every convulsion.

The soldiers were used to travelling by truck, although a few still got travel sick. But none of the Tibetan children had travelled by truck before and all were sick during the journey. They were packed so closely in the seatless trucks that those in the middle had to vomit in their hats.

In the jeep, Tsun sat exhausted, his head up, trying to gasp some unpolluted air. He saw a bird lazily weaving on the currents of air, past swiftly scudding wisps of clouds. Then they drove through a valley of wheat and barley, and he thought he would tear his inside apart with the sickness.

When the convoy halted at a village, Tsun gratefully breathed great gulps of fresh air. He noticed that the occupants of the armoured car remained on duty and that soldiers patrolled the road.

'Bring him,' the colonel ordered, nodding at Tsun as he climbed out of the jeep. 'The children can relieve themselves. I'll have some food and water sent out.' A PLA corporal saluted.

Tsun was so weak that Lopsang and the guard had to help him out of the jeep and over to the corrugated-roofed Han eating house. There were two other single storeyed buildings with bunk beds in them for travellers. In all, the village consisted of six square, flat-roofed houses.

A group of poor villagers, mostly old or very young, watched the Han sullenly from the doors of their homes. The able bodied men and women were out in the fields. From their alertness, it was evident that the Han feared an attack, and Tsun realised that their speed along the highway had also been dictated by fear of an attack by the resistance. He was mildly encouraged as he drank tea in the bare room, sitting on a bench at a table with the Colonel and Lopsang. Some of the troops sat at another table.

The Han civilian and his wife who ran the place, were told to take water and rice to the children. A Tibetan girl, who also worked there, offered Tsun some more tea.

'Thank you,' Tsun said. 'Do you have some tsampa . . .?

'Lopsang!' the Colonel said sharply.

'Comrade Colonel?'

'Watch him!' The Colonel nodded at Tsun.

The girl put a pouch of tsampa on the table and winced as she saw the blood on Tsun's wrists from the biting of the handcuffs. The Abbot found it impossible to open the bag of tsampa. Blood dripped onto the table.

'If they get any tighter,' he said to the Colonel. 'I shall probably die from loss of blood before we reach Chamdo.'

'I doubt it,' the Colonel said sardonically.

But he took a key from his pocket, inserted it in the handcuffs and released the pressure. Lopsang opened the bag of tsampa and pushed it across the table to Tsun.

'Rin . . .' Lopsang stopped himself as he caught the Colonel's eye.

Chapter Twenty-Four

CONFESS YOUR CRIME AND YOU LIVE
HIDE IT AND YOU DIE!
THIS IS SUPPRESSION AND LENIENCY COMBINED

Tsun read the Chinese and Tibetan characters painted in gold on the red banner hung on the wall behind his interrogators. A large sepia portrait of Mao Tse-tung hung on the opposite wall of the spacious, whitewashed room. It smelt, Tsun thought, as though the sun had never penetrated the boarded window. Exhausted and hungry, a wave of dizziness hit him. Still handcuffed, he had to cling to the tiny stool to keep his balance.

'Read the slogan and understand it, for in it lies your only hope.'

Tsun forced his swimming mind to concentrate on the icily firm voice of the officer. His serge uniform indicated that he was above the rank of Captain, but like all PLA officers, he wore no insignia. Bald, with a lean olive face, heavily creased round the lips, he had a habit of pulling at his bushy black moustache and the tiny tuft of black hair growing beneath his lower lip. To his right sat a younger PLA officer, earnest and attentive, and Lopsang, repeatedly stifling a yawn as he struggled to keep awake.

On the interrogator's left sat a small taciturn man with jug-handle ears and cynical eyes behind steel-rimmed spectacles. He was dressed in a plain blue tunic and soft cap, which he kept on, although the two officers had laid theirs on the black cloth covering the table.

'Keep still!' the senior officer ordered Tsun, speaking in fractured Tibetan. 'We know everything about your counter-revolutionary activities.' He tugged gently at the hairs of his moustache. 'As a reactionary and counter-revolutionary who has conspired to commit crimes against the people, you know . . .' he paused to emphasise each word, 'that there is no hope for you. The mercy of the people can only be obtained by co-operating and confessing.'

Tsun forced his bleary eyes to focus on his interrogator, and wondered why, if all the 'crimes' were known, he had to confess?

'I know your sister, Yangchen, wants you to co-operate.'

For a few moments, Tsun was stunned, yet now wide awake as if a bucket of cold water had been thrown over him. A hundred questions were born in his mind. Was it a trick?

As though aware of his thoughts, the officer continued.

'If you care for her, you will tell us who has the petition.'

To admit anything, Tsun knew was dangerous, to deny everything was equally dangerous.

'Who?' The officer took an ivory cigarette case from his jacket pocket. His eyes holding Tsun's, assessing.

Tsun realised that he was valuable only so long as he had information to impart, and the more time he gained, the more was gained for Kesang, Rinchen and Pema . . . if they were alive . . .

His fevered thoughts were distracted by the clicking of the officer's lighter, breaking the tense silence.

'Answer! Who has the petition?'

Tsun's head began to loll as he sought the warm, dark escape of sleep. The man in the blue suit leaned across the table and murmured to the officer.

'We know of your visit to Yangchen in Derge.'

The officer drew deeply on his cigarette, then tapped ash onto the floor. Tsun struggled to reason and yet to sink into the oblivion of sleep. Each remark, he realised, was carefully calculated to give the minimum of definite information, but to be loaded with implications to arouse his emotions, to confuse his mind. The officer drew again on his cigarette.

'If necessary,' he said, 'we shall sit here for a week waiting for you to answer. Wake up!'

Tsun's head stopped rolling and his eyes jerked open.

'Who has the petition?'

Tsun's eyelids began to droop. The officer nodded to his younger comrade.

'We know of your correspondence with foreign imperialist agents,' the younger man said.

'By not co-operating,' the officer exhaled smoke through his nose, 'you affect not only yourself, but your family.'

Tsun lurched awake so violently that he slipped forward off the stool onto his hands and knees. The bleeding started again as the handcuffs bit deeper. The two guards lifted him back onto the stool. The two officers relentlessly hammered out the questions.

'Your only hope is to co-operate.'

'Each moment of non-co-operation confirms your guilt.'

'Who has the petition?'

'We know the signatories!'

Tsun's reeling mind was filled with a sea of echoing and re-echoing questions.

'We know of your visit to the Queen of Derge.'

This statement touched him as though on a raw nerve, but still he had no answer. Just observing, not grasping at the multitude of thoughts spawned by each harsh sentence. Barely conscious, his lolling head was quickly checked by the cold steel barrels of the guards' sten guns. He lost track of time completely as his mind swung like a pendulum from consciousness to unconsciousness. He was dimly aware of Lopsang and the interrogators leaving the room, presumably to rest. Two new interrogators took up the questioning with barely a pause, delivered, like their predecessors, in exactly the same tone of distaste. Increasingly, he wanted to urinate. He murmured something to this effect though dry, cracked lips.

'Who has the petition?'

'I must go and piss.'

'Who has the petition?'

'You must be tired.' The interrogator sounded almost solicitous as he poured some water from a china jug into a tumbler 'Tell us, then we can all rest and end this uncomfortable interview.'

The pain in Tsun's bladder was becoming unbearable. He slumped forward on the stool in an attempt to relieve the pressure. A guard grabbed his shoulder and pulled him up straight, keeping his hand on his shoulder to steady the ashen-faced Abbot. Tsun hovered, like a moth by a flame, on the brink of consciousness.

'Just tell us who has the petition.' The officer drank a little of the water.

'I . . .' Tsun spoke in a hesitant whisper. 'Gave it to one of my escort . . . when we were attacked . . .'

He closed his eyes to escape the violent rocking of the room, but it was even worse in the multicoloured darkness of his mind. Nausea welled up.

'His name?'

'Dawa . . .' Tsun spat the word in desperation. 'Now can I go and piss?'

'Where is he now?'

'I do not know,' Tsun groaned. 'I lost him during the fighting.'

He was aware of a pause and a murmured conversation as the

officer with the moustache, the younger officer and the man in blue returned to continue the interrogation, with Lopsang following on their heels.

'Where was this man, Dawa, to take the petition?' The officer pulled on the wisp of hair below his lip.

'Let me go and piss . . .' Tsun slipped off the stool and lay on the floor. A guard jabbed him in the kidneys with the barrel of his gun. Tsun cried out in pain.

'Let me go . . . then I will tell you . . .'

'Get back on that stool!'

The senior officer took another cigarette from his ivory case and offered the case to his two companions. He worked his lighter and they lit their cigarettes from the flame as they watched Tsun struggle to grasp the stool and pull himself up onto it. The blood trickled down his arms as the handcuffs bit still deeper into the wounds on his wrists. He was delirious and weak, and as he eased himself up onto the stool, it moved across the stone floor. Urged on by the prodding gun of the guard, he crawled after the stool and again attempted to sit on it.

The man in blue let the smoke escape through his pursed lips and thought it was like watching a child, his movements awkward, unco-ordinated and weak. He tapped ash into the ashtray. If they kept up this pressure, there was a chance they would break him.

The stool slipped away. Tsun fell to the floor. The pain in his bladder was agony. The guard prodded him harder. He almost blacked out. Blissfully aware of the relief from the pain, he felt the warm liquid pouring down his leg.

The senior officer nodded at the guard who lifted Tsun back onto the stool and held him there. Tsun's trouser leg was sodden with urine. The younger officer looked at the puddle on the floor.

'You are disgusting!'

The senior officer stretched his legs to avoid cramp and shifted his chair.

'Where is the petition to be taken?'

Tsun knew that he was delirious and that it was better to give some sort of answer while he still had a certain amount of control over what he said.

'To the Kundun.'

'Why?'

The man in blue poured some water for himself and his two colleagues. To Tsun the sound of water splashing into the glasses filled the room. He looked at the man through his bloodshot eyes and kept silent. The man in blue drank slowly, his cynical eyes fixed on Tsun. Then he repeated his question in excellent Tibetan.

'Why was the petition being taken to the Dalai Lama?'

He poured another glass of water and pushed it across the table.

'Here, take a drink.'

Tsun started to rise, but he was too weak. The man gestured to one of the guards to give Tsun the glass. Taking it, Tsun's hands shook so much that he spilled some of the water, but he managed to raise it to his lips and had to stop himself from gulping it down. He took small sips of the cold liquid and felt it run down his parched throat, cooling, healing. He pushed from his mind the nagging question of why the man in blue had spoken of the petition being taken to the Kundun in the past tense. A trap? Had Pema been caught? If so, surely they would have no need to question him, as they would have the petition? But Pema could have destroyed it, or buried it, as he had instructed her.

On and on, the questions spiralled. Tsun struggled against becoming his own tormentor, a far more effective torturer than anyone else.

'Tell us why the petition was being taken to the Dalai Lama?'

Smoke drifted lazily from the nostrils of the man in blue.

'To ask him . . .' Tsun licked his dry lips and felt the restraining hand of the guard as he began to sway off the stool. 'To ask . . .'

'Yes?'

'To ask him to intercede with Mao Tse-tung . . . the people of Kham asked . . .' Tsun tried to withdraw his mind into unconsciousness. 'Let me . . . rest.'

The man in blue slammed his hand down on the table.

'Where else was the petition to go!'

'Where . . .?' Tsun's eyes closed. 'Where . . . nowhere . . .'

'You lie!'

The senior officer stubbed his cigarette out in the ashtray. Tsun shook his head.

'Why did you go to Derge?' The younger officer leant forward to put his question.

'To see my sister.'

'Why?'

'Because she is my sister.'

'Why do you lie so much?' The senior officer sounded incredulous.

Tsun shook his head. He was acutely aware of the dangers of answering their questions, he also knew that they would keep him awake until they were satisfied. Even now he found it difficult to reason, to think about his answers. Later, he would find it impossible.

'Who has the gold?'

The words, spoken softly by the man in blue, clove through Tsun's mind. Slowly he opened his eyes, desperately working out his reply. He noticed the faintest hint of a smile on the lips of the man in blue.

'What gold?'

Tsun's words were but formed breaths. Devoid of substance. The senior officer slammed the table hard with the flat of his hand.

'The gold you were to use to buy weapons for the counter-revolutionaries.'

The man in blue held Tsun's eyes with his as he took off his steel-rimmed glasses and sucked one of the wire arms. His lips parted in a humourless smile.

'I never agreed to buy weapons . . .' Tsun murmured. 'The gold . . . was . . . was for the Kundun . . .'

'Why?' The officer asked, turning to look at his companions.

'It is our custom.' Tsun paused, his angry eyes black in his haggard face. 'When we seek the . . .' he struggled with the words, 'blessing of a High Lama . . . we offer him a gift . . . of homage . . . Thousands . . .' Tsun emphasised the word. 'As in the petition for the help of the . . . the Kundun . . . thousands contributed to the gift.'

Tsun's head dropped to his chest, his eyes almost closed. The senior officer glanced at Lopsang, who gave a curt nod.

'Who has the gold?' the younger officer asked.

'The Honourable Mother.'

'Who?'

'The mother of Dorje Rinposhay,' Lopsang explained.

'He,' the young officer jabbed his finger in Tsun's direction, 'is the one being interrogated.'

'Where is she?' the senior officer asked.

'I do not know.' Tsun increased the desperation in his voice. 'We were . . . separated . . . during the attack . . .'

'Where did you arrange to meet?'

'We . . . did not . . .'

'You had time,' said the younger officer, 'to give the petition to this man, Dawa, and the gold to the woman, but not time to arrange a rendezvous?'

Tsun forced his eyes open.

'We were under attack.' He spat the words.

'Obviously,' the younger officer continued, 'you do not understand the seriousness of your position.' He sounded concerned. 'As a counter-revolutionary you are an enemy of the people. As such, you have no rights, not even to existence, unless you make amends. You may not be concerned for yourself, but what of your family and friends? You have involved them in counter-revolutionary activities, as you involved your monastery, Dorje Ri-gon. Your monks paid for your evil. Are you going to let your family suffer for your reactionary plotting?'

Tsun's eyes were closed. His head rolled. Although on the edge of sleep, he heard, but could not speak.

'We have been patient enough.' The senior officer sighed and looked at his companion in blue, who nodded.

'Take him!'

The two guards lifted Tsun from the stool. They half carried, half dragged him out of the room and down a dark corridor. A blast of cold air hit him. He groaned. His eyes flickered open.

Brilliant silver stars shone in the black void, bringing memories of another life, a lost life.

With the guards supporting him, he stumbled across a high-walled courtyard, empty except for the three wooden posts set a few feet from the wall. It only occurred to him when he saw the chipped and bullet-marked wall, that the posts were for executions. Fear thrilled through him, and he attempted to clear his mind for the end.

The guards stopped by the outside post and leaned Tsun's limp body against it. Then came the darkness of unconsciousness, split by vivid images.

'Tsun-la! Tsun-la!'

Tsun winced at the white light searing his eyeballs. His shoulder was being shaken. He turned his aching head and found himself looking into the concerned eyes of Lopsang.

'I have brought you something to eat.'

The secretary helped Tsun to sit up on the trestle and plank bed. Soundlessly, the Abbot opened his mouth in pain and looked at the handcuffs. Blood spotted his filthy, urine-stained chuba. Lopsang took a key from his pocket and loosened the handcuffs. For a moment he caught Tsun's eye, then he looked away and gave him a tin plate on which was some boiled rice and steamed bread. He put the plate on Tsun's lap and held an enamel mug of hot water to his lips. Tsun began to gulp the water but Lopsang stopped him. The Abbot, realising that it must have been his Secretary who attempted to curse him, leaned his head back against the wall and laughed. A hollow laugh which reflected the irony of the situation. Then, with dirty, bloodstained fingers, he tore at the bread. Never had eating been such ecstasy.

'How long have I been asleep?' He spooned down the rice. Lopsang shrugged. Within minutes the food was gone, but Tsun still felt hungry.

'More?' he asked in a tone of doubt.

Lopsang shook his head. In the silence that followed, Tsun studied the small cell, lit by a flaring, hissing tilly lamp hung from the ceiling. The only furniture, the plank bed.

From somewhere outside the building, a loudspeaker crackled and whistled into life. Tsun thought it must be the beginning of a day, but he had no idea which day. China's national song, 'The East is Red', was being broadcast.

'Why did you lie about the gold, Lopsang?'

'I am a realist, but also a Tibetan.'

Lopsang's face creased in an enormous, insincere grin, his lean form bowing slightly. Tsun did not believe him, and wondered why Lopsang had come into his cell.

'Have you any news of the others?'

'Only of Kesang, that is why I came to see you.'

'Well?' Tsun's voice was crisp and urgent.

'I was with the Colonel when he was given a radio message saying that Kesang had been found.'

'Alive?'

'Alive.'

'What of Rinchen, Pema and the rest of the party?'

'None have been identified.'

Tsun picked up the tin plate and handed it to Lopsang; he needed to hear no more. But Lopsang tossed the plate back onto the bed.

'They will, if they have to, use Kesang to force you to co-operate!' There was a look of desperation in Lopsang's eyes which Tsun almost believed could be genuine.

'It is true,' Lopsang insisted. 'Whatever you think of me, *this* is true.'

'Let me see him.'

'You want him to see you here?'

'I saw his mother . . .' Tsun paused only a moment, 'disappear in the horror of the attack . . . men, women and children killed . . .' He attempted to cover the slip.

The secretary involuntarily looked away from his piercing dark eyes. He picked up the chopsticks and mug and put them carefully on the tin plate. Tsun's legs were chapped from the rubbing of his urine-stained trousers.

'Can you get me another pair of trousers and a chuba?'

Lopsang was not listening.

'They will come soon,' he said. 'If you co-operate I can save you.'

'And what is co-operation?'

'Tell them everything, the truth. Do you think they believe that lie about the petition?'

'It is no lie,' Tsun grinned. 'And *you* know everything.'

'Not everything. Co-operate for your own sake, and for Kesang's.'

Tsun's face tightened, but he kept his voice level.

'I tell them the truth, Lopsang, and they trust me no more than they trust you.'

He saw a responsive flicker of apprehension in Lopsang's face. The secretary was acutely aware of his precarious position. He unlocked the door of the cell.

'You will tell them, Tsun. It is only time to them.' He went out, locking the door behind him.

Tsun shifted his body lower so that he was lying flat on the wooden bed. He closed his eyes and listened to the slow, heavy footsteps of the sentries in the corridor. His mind was filled with ever-recurring questions, scenes, of Kesang, Pema, Rinchen, Tullok and Genyen. The battle, the interrogation, the questions, the answers, the future . . .

He let go of them. Let them just come and go and come again. The music from the loudspeakers outside his cell grew louder. A Tibetan girl announced that Marshal Chen-Yi was on his way to Tibet from Peking. Tsun listened intently.

The Vice Premier and Foreign Minister of the Central People's Government is leading a delegation of eight hundred representatives from all parts of the Motherland, to celebrate the inauguration of the Preparatory Committee for the Autonomous Region of Tibet. Lhasa is in a ferment of excitement, with people coming from all over the region to join in the celebration. Red flags and banners of welcome fly from the rooftops. The Lhasa Great Hall, with seating for a thousand, has been finished, through the enthusiasm of the workers, in record time for the inauguration. Comrade

Chen-Yi's vast convoy has been slowed down during its journey from Peking to Lhasa by the hospitality and enthusiasm of the villagers and farmers.

The convoy frequently stops at villages as the people have insisted on holding day-long celebrations for the delegates, and have plied them with endless questions on the New China. The delegation often show films on the proposed work of the Preparatory Committee for the Autonomous Region of Tibet, which are enthusiastically greeted by the audiences. Thousands of colour pictures of our Great Helmsman, Mao Tse-tung, have been distributed to delighted villagers. The people are making sure that this first visit to the Tibet region by a Comrade of the Central People's Government will not be forgotten.

The announcement was followed by suitably uplifting patriotic and revolutionary songs.

If his efforts and those of the Queen of Derge to prevent the assassination of Chen-Yi had not succeeded, and there was an attempt on the Marshal's life, the visit, Tsun thought, would, indeed, not be forgotten!

He wondered if his interrogators knew of the plot? They knew of his visit to the Queen! What had happened to Tul-lok? He knew that Lopsang was right. It was only a matter of time before they broke him. He contemplated both escape and suicide, and decided to explore the possibilities of the former first.

He held up his aching hands and knew that it was probable that the wounds would soon turn septic. He looked round the cell, trying to work out ways to escape, and thought of what was likely to happen to him. He found himself drifting into a doze where vivid scenes were re-lived. His eyes jerked open as the door of the cell opened.

He recognised the guards who motioned to him to get off the bed and leave the cell. With their fingers on the triggers of their sten guns, they made him walk in front of them. Tsun glanced into the other cells lining the corridor. Outside stood a covered jeep. They made him get into it. The guards sat at the back of the vehicle, and another Tibetan, an elderly monk, sat opposite Tsun, his bound hands in the lap of his russet robe, counting off the beads of his rosary.

Tsun recognised the lean, pale face with its wispy, white beard. The monk opened his eyes from meditation and looked at Tsun with a quizzical smile, but without recognising him.

'Khenpo . . . I am lama Tsun of . . .'

'Silence!' one of the guards shouted.

'Aha!'

The old man reached forward in delight to clasp Tsun's hands, then frowned on seeing his wounded wrists. He looked up. Each had much to ask of the other. The Khenpo was a much revered master of studies at the monastery of Chamdo. The two men had first met when they were both on pilgrimage to the Holy places of India. When Tsun was still a layman, he had received spiritual instruction from the Khenpo, so both felt a special bond with one another.

The two prisoners, with their guards on either side of them, were violently bounced as the jeep, its horn blaring, drove through the muddy, rutted Chamdo streets. Through the windscreen and the yellowed celluloid windows of the canvas hood, Tsun caught glimpses of another world. People were going about their business, working, talking, queuing at the state shops. Life, sun, sky, light, food, water, puddles in the muddy road. A mangy dog urinating against a wall. Normality.

The handcuffs bit deep into Tsun's wrists as the jeep jerked to a halt. Awkwardly, he jumped down from the vehicle. Few of the troops, smoking and talking as they lounged against the row of parked army trucks, even glanced at the two prisoners being marched towards the enormous canvas-covered wooden stage of the People's Ground.

The proscenium, flanked with brightly decorated Tibetan-style wooden pillars, bore the slogan 'Revolution is Class Struggle!'

Tsun and the Khenpo were marched to the centre of the brilliantly lit stage, at the back of which hung huge colour portraits of Mao Tse-tung, General Chang Ching-wu, political representative of the Central People's Government, and General Kua-hua, Commander of the PLA in Tibet. A male cadre in a crumpled blue suit and soft cap was passionately addressing the crowd of some five hundred men, women and children gathered in the People's Ground, around which PLA troops were positioned.

Chamdo was situated on a triangular peninsula bordered by the 'East' and 'West' rivers. The People's Ground was close to their confluence, the birth of the great Mekong River.

From the high stage, Tsun could see over the heads of the crowds to the sprawling monastery on a flat-topped hill rising above the town of square, dun-coloured houses. Encircling the monastery, hill, town and peninsula, were scrub-covered mountains, blue-grey in the shadow of clustering rain clouds. Over there, he thought, it is raining, but the People's Ground was sunlit. The vast blue sky was full of swiftly moving clouds forming faces, houses, animals. To Tsun they told a story reflecting life; as soon as a pattern formed, it melted away, reforming, dissolving, reforming . . .

'These people . . .' The cadre, his voice full of emotion, pointed at a group of Tibetans sitting to one side of the stage. 'These serfs have told you of their sufferings before the Liberation by the Motherland. They have shown you the reason why there must be a class struggle, to overthrow the landlords and oppressors, before there can be happiness and freedom for the people. As Comrade Mao said: the enemy will not perish of himself, there must be a struggle between the peasant and the landlord classes, if you want your freedom. It is no good always talking about a fight. To win a fight you have to fight!'

The cadre wiped his face with a large white handkerchief. Tsun saw a rainbow form across the mountains behind the monastery.

'So it is,' the cadre continued, 'with the class struggle. To defeat the oppressive classes, you must fight them, confront them!' He turned abruptly and beckoned the guards to bring Tsun forward. It was then that Tsun recognised the cadre as the taciturn interrogator. 'This is the reactionary landlord Tsun of Dorje Rigon monastery. Let his former secretary tell you of his wickedness.'

From the wings, Lopsang stepped forward, wearing dark glasses and dressed in a grey tunic, trousers and cap. The cadre walked towards him.

'We won't be needing the glasses.' He looked at Lopsang with the cynical, practised eyes of power. 'It is going to rain.'

Lopsang hesitated, then removed the glasses. The cadre walked to the wings and sat down, while Lopsang's mind worked on the reason for making him remove his glasses. He had wanted to hide behind them and dark glasses were a symbol of high rank in Tibetan society; also, to be recognised was to be committed. He coughed nervously as he adjusted the height of the microphone. Tsun glanced at the Khenpo who stood with his eyes lowered in meditation.

'The reactionary lama Tsun' – Lopsang's voice was soft and tense. The soldier operating the loudspeaker system had to adjust the amplifier – 'was the favoured disciple of the famous Dorje Rinposhay. When the Rinposhay died, the reactionary Tsun seized control of the monastery.' Lopsang cleared his throat, strengthened his voice, and tried to put feeling into his words. The cadre shook his head, sighed and sipped at a mug of tea.

'The reactionary Tsun pretended to be a friend of the peopl bring reforms, while, in fact, he worked desperately against far-reaching reforms of the local Chinese Communist Party W Committee which were demanded by the people. He urged monks of the monastery to join the counter-revolution terrorists. He pretended to lead a holy life, yet was tryi frantically to keep his oppressive hold over the monastery and tenants.' Lopsang was getting into the rhythm of the situation a endeavouring to emulate the cadre in his passion.

'When he was about to be arrested, he fled secretly, leaving tl monks he had tricked and used to face the consequences of his ev deeds. I was among . . .'

Lopsang's voice was drowned in the threshold howl from th microphone. Nervously he tapped it and glanced across the stag at the soldier operating the amplification system.

'I was among those tricked and used. I was on that secret . . . The microphone whistled loudly. Lopsang tried to speak over it, 'That secret flight. I saw the reactionary Tsun distribute the weapons he had hoarded in his apartment.' He began coughing with the strain of the shouting. 'Is this . . .?' Again his voice was drowned by the surging whine of the microphone.

The cadre walked briskly across the stage and handed Lopsang a megaphone.

'Is this,' Lopsang continued, 'how a lama should act? Also, I have seen with my own eyes the letters he has had from imperialist agents.'

Lopsang watched two soldiers with a ladder shouldering their way towards the loudspeaker pole in the centre of the crowd.

'During our journey from Dorje Ri-gon, the reactionary Tsun contacted counter-revolutionary bandits, and it was arranged that he should obtain arms from the Imperialists who threatened our great Motherland.'

Lopsang stopped abruptly. His mind had gone blank. He could think of nothing more to say. He lowered the megaphone in his hand, raised it to his lips, then lowered it again.

'You have heard from an eyewitness,' the cadre said, 'of the crime of the oppressor, Tsun. You have heard from someone who was involved with the counter-revolutionary in his crimes against the people.'

Tsun glanced at his former secretary standing a few feet away from him, but Lopsang gave no reaction. He had not missed the implication, though, and as he watched the two soldiers with the

stepladder adjusting the loudspeaker on the pole, he thought how the cadre's power-filled delivery and confident manipulation of words showed up the inadequacy of his own performance.

'But realising the evil of this enemy of the people, Comrade Lopsang Nyima came over to the people. The people are merciful to those who come over to them. Comrade Mao Tse-tung has said: 'Whoever sides with the revolutionary people is a revolutionary. Whoever sides with imperialism and with feudalism . . .' The cadre realised that the term meant nothing to his audience. 'With the landlords and oppressors of the poor. These are counter-revolutionary!'

The loudspeaker had been adjusted so that it was not directly facing the microphone. The soldiers carrying the ladder pushed their way back through the crowd. The cadre caught sight of a signal from the amplification operator and flicked the microphone switch.

'This reactionary,' the cadre pointed at Tsun, 'has made it clear which side he stands on. Look how arrogant he is.' The cadre took off his steel-rimmed spectacles and waved them at Tsun. 'So sure of his position.' He wiped the sweat-stained lenses with the corner of his jacket, then slipped the springy steel arms over his jug-handle ears. 'For long enough he has ridden on the back of the poor.'

The tension of the crowd, partly self-induced by all that a Thamzing had come to imply, was being steadily increased through the cadre's careful manipulation. Yangchen's story of the Thamzing at Doi and a dozen other Thamzings he had been told of filled Tsun's mind. He was aware of everything going on about him, but not reacting to it physically or mentally.

'Well! What is to be done to this counter-revolutionary?'

The tense faces spread out before the cadre showed no sign of answering. Some glanced at each other, some bowed their heads, but no one responded and, in that, there was a certain strength. The cadre rocked on his heels, just once, and pointed to a woman a few feet away in the front of the crowd.

'What do *you* think should be done with him?'

The woman shook her head, opening and closing her mouth in mute terror. The cadre looked amazed.

'But he is a counter-revolutionary! You have heard of his crimes . . .'

All heads in the crowd strained to see the woman.

'He should be punished.'

The words were mouthed and barely audible. The cadre

beckoned her onto the stage. She did not move, praying that his attention would move to someone else, but it did not. Everyone was waiting for her. She undid the blanket holding her infant on her back and slowly handed the baby to the woman next to her. Slowly, she walked across to the stairs which led up to the stage. Perched on her head was a large Y-shaped headdress, gaunt and severe without the hairpieces and seed pearls it was designed to carry. She lifted her skirt to climb the steps and wiped a tear from her eye with the other hand. The cadre stepped forward and helped her onto the stage. She glanced quickly at Tsun with wet eyes, then as quickly looked away.

'We did not hear you down there,' the cadre said.

He led her over to the microphone so that she could speak.

'Do not do it,' someone shouted from the crowd.

'Long live Tibet!'

The woman caught sight of the man as he ducked down and moved through the crowd to evade the troops who were already pushing their way in to find him. She felt her arm being tightly gripped by the cadre as he led her closer to the microphone.

'You see, even in our midst there are counter-revolutionary agitators. We must prove to these bandits . . .' For a moment his eyes held hers. 'We must prove to these bandits that the people ruthlessly crush counter-revolutionary terrorists. Those that do not denounce the reactionaries and reveal their misdeeds are as guilty as they.'

He pushed her so that her mouth was level with the microphone.

'I said . . .' her voice was soft and flat, 'that the reactionary should be punished.'

'Punished? This . . .' the cadre looked at Tsun, 'this is not just an ordinary counter-revolutionary terrorist. This is an upper-strata reactionary. Someone of power who, had his plan succeeded, would have obtained arms for the bandits to ravage the people.'

The cadre's body shook with indignation.

'I, myself, have attended the meeting, lasting many hours, where every effort was made to persuade him to come over to the people. But, stubbornly, he refused. Such wicked elements are a danger to the people and have to be eliminated. He has been given his chance.'

The cadre turned to the group of Tibetans sitting on a bench at the side of the stage.

'What should be done with him?'

A wall-eyed woman in a tattered, dirty dress jumped to her feet.

'Kill him! Kill him!' she yelled.

The chorus was taken up by the others who advanced across the stage shaking their fists at Tsun. The cadre looked at the audience. Scattered shouts from 'plants' joined in the chanting of those on stage. Like pebbles dropped in a still pool, their effect spread through the crowd, as fear of being seen 'not to be of the people' spurred them on. Soon, almost everyone was shouting. When all were silent, they were strong. When all shouted, they were safe. And having committed themselves, the crowd was easily whipped into a frenzy, determined to prove to the cadre that they were 'of the people'.

'Kill him! Kill him! Kill him!'

Rhythmically it surged through the gathering, increasing the tension off which it fed. One of the men on stage raised his handless arm like a club to hit Tsun in the face. Others beat him about the body and head. He staggered and fell.

'For long enough,' the cadre shouted above the din, 'he has ridden on the backs of the poor. Now let's see how *he* likes it.'

The wall-eyed woman dropped heavily onto Tsun's back, her hands clawing at his head and face. He struggled to keep his eyes clear of the gouging fingers. The cadre moved quickly to the young woman from the audience, who stood watching silently. Tears fell silently down her face. She knew what was wanted of her even as the cadre approached. She moved to join the group beating Tsun. Everyone had to be involved.

Threads of blood formed a network across Tsun's face. Rage welled up in him and he struggled to throw off the woman on his back who was screaming obscenities in his ear. He cried out in pain and collapsed, but was dragged up onto his knees so that the screaming audience could see him ridden. Desperately, he tried to commit suicide through meditation as he was driven slowly across the stage on his knees by the blows and kicks of the clustering tormentors. His hands were slippery with blood as each move made the handcuffs dig deeper.

'Kill him! Kill him! Kill him!'

The chant was like the cry of a demonic force which had taken possession of the crowd.

Tsun cried out again and again when someone stepped on his hands. His anguished eyes caught sight of the girl from the crowd. She was crying as she moved her foot which had accidentally touched his hands. Silently, she mouthed the words 'I'm sorry', then feigned a blow at his head. Tsun collapsed again, and this time, despite the blows and kicks, remained inert.

The cadre moved in and pushed the group aside. He gripped Tsun's bloody hair and turned his face towards the crowd. Tsun's eyes were closed. For a moment the cadre thought he was dead, but then caught sight of a slight movement of his nostrils.

'Take him away,' he shouted at the guards. 'And wake him up!'

The group on stage walked silently back to their places.

'Now,' the cadre shouted above the waning chant, 'is not the time for him to die. That would be too easy.'

The girl who had been the first to speak out against Tsun slipped furtively down the steps from the stage, took her baby from her friend and tried to hide herself in the crowd. The cadre flung out an arm to point at the Khenpo.

'What of this yellow robber?' He beckoned to the Khenpo's guards to bring him to the front of the stage which they had steadily piled high with religious paintings, images, scriptures, carpets, silver teacup stands and lids, teapots, and brocade costumes used for the monastic plays.

'Yesterday,' the cadre continued, 'the people struggled against and accused this yellow robber, who has used the cloak of religion to hide his ruthless exploitation of the people. See how well he lives? How well he has lived off the people?'

The cadre took in the contents of the table with a sweep of his arm. As he spoke, a rope was thrown over a thick beam and then tied to a ten-foot high bronze image of Lord Buddha.

'For centuries such people have lived off the poor.'

Tsun, sprawled on a chair at the side of the stage, was having cold water flung in his face. Gradually, he became conscious of the cadre's words.

'Thousands of people have come to this yellow robber for his blessing, a touch of his hand, a magic pill. And each one that came gave an offering. Indeed, his power must be great, that so many should give so much.'

It was taking six soldiers to haul the heavy bronze statue from the floor.

'If I am to buy a horse and the price is expensive, I want to see the horse. I want to see it run, to see what qualities it has that makes it so expensive . . .'

The bronze image was being steadied as it was carefully lowered onto a strong table, which groaned and protested under its weight.

'But how can people test such as this yellow robber? When it is thought that even to look at him disrespectfully is blasphemy, that he could curse you, relieve you of your sickness, even arrange that your dead be reborn in heavenly realms. He has used you, and your fear of him, to keep you in bondage!'

The cadre took off his glasses and mopped his face with his handkerchief.

'Chairman Mao has said: 'Everything reactionary is the same. If you do not hit it, it will not fall. Like sweeping the floor, where the broom does not reach, the dust will not vanish of itself . . .'

Tsun could hardly hold the mug of water he was given to drink as his handcuffs were loosened by one of the guards.

'Yesterday, we struck down a reactionary!' The cadre pointed an accusing finger at the Khenpo. 'Today we struck down a reactionary!' The cadre turned to look at Tsun. 'Nothing has happened to us, yet it is said that lamas are like magicians with their powers. These lamas, it is believed, must not work. Yet they enjoy the fruits of the labour of the people.'

The cadre picked up the microphone and walked over to the trestle table.

'Why should you . . .?' He pointed to the group of Tibetans on the bench at the side of the stage – 'Why should you wear rags, when the reactionary Khenpo has enough clothes in his cupboards to clothe a whole village? Here!' He threw the Khenpo's robe of instruction towards those on the bench. 'Take what is rightly yours, and return this plunder to the people from whom it was stolen.'

The five Tibetans stuffed their ambacs with choice items from the table and then carried what remained to the edge of the stage and threw it at the audience.

'As the reactionary Khenpo and lama Tsun have sold their so-called blessings like wares in the market, let us see the quality of the wares, as we would in the market.'

As he spoke, he took a rolled thanka from the one-handed man who was about to throw it into the crowd, and switched the microphone off.

'They are of no use to anyone,' he said, tossing the thanka into the wings.

The man looked startled, and the cadre did not miss the thought held for just a moment in the man's eyes. Indeed, these people are green brains, he thought. He switched the microphone on again and beckoned Tsun's guards to bring him over to the table. They had to support him beneath his armpits to prevent him from collapsing. The cadre nodded at one of the soldiers by the table, who slung his rifle over his shoulder and tied the end of the rope hanging from the beam to form a noose.

'For years,' the cadre pointed at the ten-foot high statue of the Buddha, 'pilgrims have given gold and jewels to adorn this image. Wealth that was much needed to improve the country, and the life of the people. But, instead, this reactionary Khenpo extracted what wealth there was from the people, and so kept them poor and subservient. Well! Let the Buddha decide!'

Tsun's guards took off his handcuffs. He held onto the edge of the table for support.

'Let us see,' the cadre continued, 'the powers of these two yellow robbers.'

The soldier with the noose dropped it over the Khenpo's head and tightened it round his neck. The Khenpo did not give the slightest reaction as he remained meditating. The cadre picked up the microphone and carried it to one side of the stage, so that the audience's view would not be obstructed.

Tsun looked with horror at the Khenpo as he realised that the image of Maitreya, the coming Buddha, attached to the other end of the rope, was being pushed towards him by four soldiers. Already the edge was pushing on his chest. Three soldiers were holding down the other end of the table to prevent it from suddenly tipping.

There was a total and terrible silence.

A few feet away, behind the stage, some soldiers laughed. They were lost in conversation, unaware of what was happening on stage. Automatically, Tsun's hands gripped the wide bronze base of the image as he attempted to push it back onto the table. But he did not have the strength against the pressure of the four soldiers.

'Now we will see,' the cadre shouted through the microphone, 'whether these reactionary robbers have any powers, or are just deceiving bandits who have plundered the people.'

Tsun's bloodied hands worked their way along the base of the image as, grunting with exertion, the four soldiers pushed it inch by inch off the table. On reaching the point of balance on the table edge, the image tilted and his legs started to buckle. He staggered and settled his feet slightly apart to take the strain. His breathing slowed and he concentrated his mind and body, bracing himself. Then the soldiers pushed the image right off the table.

Tsun rocked, sweat pouring down his face and arms, but he held it. Incredibly he held it, while he stood swaying like a tree in a gentle breeze, each second an eternity, but he held the image.

The crowd began to murmur.

The cadre was surprised at Tsun's amazing strength; he would not have thought it possible for one man even to move the image, let alone hold it. He wondered for one awful moment if he was going to be confronted with a miracle.

Apprehensively, he glanced at the crowd. If he intervened now, the whole purpose of the Thamzing would be ruined. Tsun's legs and body began to give way beneath the weight, agonisingly slowly, as he fought to prevent his body from succumbing. The rope tightened round the neck of the Khenpo, making him cough and fight for breath. His eyes met Tsun's. Tsun let go of the image.

It crashed to the floor, splintering the boards. As Tsun collapsed, he saw the robed body of the Khenpo swinging wildly across the arc lights, his neck stretched, head lolling, swinging back and forth, back and forth . . .

As he was driven back to the local Security Committee Office in Chamdo, the cadre drew on a cigarette and came to the conclusion that, while not an ideal Thamzing, he had handled it well. According to the textbooks, his job was to prepare and educate the masses for the class struggle, and then to act as a catalyst of the people's spontaneous condemnation of the upper-strata reactionaries. In this way, the masses themselves make the traumatic break with the old way of life, old loyalties.

The danger, as Mao pointed out, was that if the people were just passive onlookers, uninvolved, they might begin to sympathise with the person being punished. The cadre had yet to attend a Thamzing in Tibet where the people reacted spontaneously. He never ceased to be amazed at their incredible, stubborn faithfulness to their religion. In such cases, terror was the only way.

He was pleased with his subtle use of it and, unlike many meetings, he had got the people to chant for Tsun's death. The worms of recrimination and self-recrimination would eat away at their loyalty to the old way of life. The mere fact of being helpless observers of Tsun's humiliation and the Khenpo's execution would undermine their morale.

He wondered about the effect it would have on Tsun. It was, he thought, tapping the ash of his cigarette onto the floor of the jeep, one of the potentially most effective Thamzings of all the dozens he had organised since his posting to Tibet in 1954.

Chapter Twenty-five

The white light burned into Tsun's eyes as he drifted back into consciousness. Still he saw the swinging body of the Khenpo. He groaned and turned his aching head, keeping his eyes tightly shut, but nothing obliterated the burning light, the swinging body . . . like driftwood on the raging waves of a river, he felt himself being lifted and spun. His stomach heaved and his eyes opened as he thought he was about to vomit. He grasped the sides of the soft straw mattress, vainly trying to steady himself as he was swirled about in a sea of colours and shapes.

He felt a hand holding his right arm reassuringly, and a warm damp cloth dabbed gently at his temple. Slowly, his surroundings, his nausea, settled. The shapes and colours became defined. Tsun was aware of the luxurious feeling of a sheet beneath his naked body. His eyes focused on the girl sitting beside him. It was Ling. She was cleaning a cut on his neck. She smiled when she saw Tsun looking at her, then bent down to rinse out the cloth she was using in an enamel bowl set on the floor. She wondered what his reaction would be when he realised that he was naked in the presence of a woman. She had been long enough with the Tibetans to know that some monks in a similar situation would have made a grab at anything with which to cover their nakedness. But Tsun seemed oblivious as he gazed blankly at Ling, then round the room.

He was finding it very difficult to gather himself together and he was becoming increasingly aware of the tenderness of his bruised body. He drew in his breath sharply as Ling applied antiseptic to the cut on his neck and covered it with a plaster, but even his breath hurt him, and his right hand explored the bandage wound round his chest.

'The doctor says nothing is broken,' Ling said gently. 'But you've been badly bruised and you've had some stitches put in the cut above your eye.'

Tsun winced as she smoothed down the plaster on his neck.

'How considerate,' he croaked through cracked lips.

His throat was sore and swollen. Waves of nausea rose again, then receded. His yell made Ling giggle. She had been cleaning and bandaging an area of raw skin on his stomach. She glanced up at him with a faintly mocking smile.

'And you were so brave at the . . . Thamzing.'

Tsun did not move or speak, but his eyes held hers. She wished she had not mentioned it and felt compelled to add: 'Someone told me, I was not there.'

Tsun turned his aching, spinning head to look round the room. There was a chair on which his clothes had been neatly folded, and a table covered with propaganda magazines. In one corner stood a galvanised bucket topped with a wooden lid. The room smelt clean and had a low window. On the glass he could see sparkling droplets of rain, splashing and merging with one another.

Tsun felt good. He realised that he was almost certainly meant to, but still, he felt good.

He studied Ling as she bathed his stomach, her small full lips slightly parted, showing the tips of glistening teeth. Her long hair, unplaited, fell framing her face and emphasising her delicate features. Tsun thought they reflected a strength and intelligence, and in that intangible depth he found great beauty. He knew that it was not by chance that she was there. He sighed. Nothing was by chance.

'What happened?' he asked hoarsely. 'After Khenpo . . .?'

'You collapsed,' Ling put in quickly. You have been unconscious for hours.' Noisily, she rinsed out the cloth in the bowl. 'Would you like something to eat or drink?'

'Ling!'

Her eyes came up slowly to his bruised, drawn face.

'I wish you were not here,' Tsun said slowly.

Ling smiled quickly, tightly, opened her mouth to speak, hesitated, then decided to say something different.

'It is because I am here that you are having this treatment.'

'Just so,' he murmured and raised an eyebrow slightly. Ling frowned and stopped bathing his stomach.

'Trust me, Tsun.' Then, as though in explanation, 'You saved my life once.' Tsun did not reply, and after a while she found his steady gaze disconcerting and lowered her eyes to his wounds. Tsun thought he would try and extract what information he could from her while he had the opportunity.

'Where did you go after you escaped,' he asked.

'Derge District Committee.'

'Once I saw you . . .'

'I know.'

She emptied the bloodstained water into a bucket and poured fresh water from a jug into the bowl. 'And again at the nomad camp.'

Already it has begun, he thought.

'I do not remember any nomads,' he said.

Ling looked at him and grinned. He wanted so much to ask her what had happened when the cavalry detachment reached the nomads' encampment, but to do so would mean admitting that he was there.

'Do you know anything of the . . .' He was convulsed by a fit of coughing. Ling poured him a mug of water and supported his head while he drank.

'Don't talk,' she said. 'Wait until you are more rested.'

'Do you know anything of the other members of my party?'

Ling moved down to bathe his legs. She screwed up her face. 'Don't you Tibetans ever wash?'

'Your friends wouldn't let me go and piss.'

Ling shrugged. 'You have read the writings of Comrade Mao,' she said. 'You must have read his description of a revolution – it is not a dinner party, a writing of an essay, the painting of a picture or the stitching of embroidery, it cannot be so refined' – Ling continued to wash his legs '– so leisurely and gentle, so temperate, kind, courteous, restrained and magnanimous. A revolution is an act of violence by which one class overthrows another.'

'Are you getting me ready for my next session?'

'I am giving you a chance.' Ling's face was set and determined. 'This . . .' she indicated the room with a swift movement of her hand, 'was my idea.'

'A different approach.' For the first time there was a trace of bitterness in his voice. 'And you start from a stronger position than your friends.'

Ling flung the cloth into the bowl.

'All right, I'll tell you. You have only had a glimpse of your future.' She paced the room, her voice shaking with barely controlled rage. 'Do you realise what it means to be accused of being a counter-revolutionary? There is no worse crime. Under the Organic Law, all your rights are suspended. You have no future.' She struggled with a sudden surge of emotion. 'Not even . . .' she stabbed a finger at him '. . . the right to kill yourself!'

She pulled out a packet of cigarettes from her pocket and fumbled with it so that three of them fell out onto the floor.

'Why are you so concerned?' Tsun asked mildly.

As she bent to pick up the cigarettes, Tsun saw her face and neck grow red. He could feel her anger. She straightened up and leaned against the table. Carefully, she replaced two cigarettes in the packet and lit the other with a plain steel lighter. Then she looked at him through the smoke. Her hand was shaking as she lifted the cigarette to her lips again. She avoided his eyes. Acutely conscious of the colour in her cheeks, she felt humiliated and angry.

'It complicates matters,' Tsun murmured.

Ling stared at him coldly. He had a faint smile on his lips, and his eyes . . . she felt herself redden again. She dropped the cigarette on the floor and stepped on it, working hard to control her emotions. She took up the cloth again and gently bathed his legs and feet. Gradually, the tension between them eased.

'What news of the others?' Tsun asked again.

Ling looked straight into his eyes. 'Nothing, Tsun. I have heard nothing.'

'Was it your job to find and capture me?'

Ling smiled nervously, and lit another cigarette. She inhaled deeply and watched the smoke rise to the ceiling. There was a long pause. Then Tsun grunted:

'Well?'

Ling tapped the ash from her cigarette with her finger, then balanced it on the window ledge and went back to bathing Tsun's legs.

'It's up to you, Tsun,' she said. 'I cannot protect you forever. It is known that you visited your sister in Derge.'

She dropped the cloth into the bowl, wiped her hand on the seat of her trousers and picked up her cigarette. 'It could go badly for her.'

Tsun laughed. 'Now you sound like your friends.'

Ling turned on him angrily.

'It does not matter what I sound like. I tell you of facts!' Her hand shook and the cigarette dropped to the floor. She stepped on it without seeing it.

'You understand the position. Don't you care?'

For a moment she thought he was going to pull himself up and strike her. Then, suddenly, he grinned.

'I was just wondering,' he looked down at his legs, 'if you were going to wash everything?'

Ling followed the line of his eyes, felt her face redden again, picked up the cloth and threw it at him.

From outside, Tsun faintly heard voices talking in Tibetan, then the broadcast from the loudspeaker drowned them, but it gave him the idea that his prison might well be in the town and not in the Han garrison. The town offered more opportunities for escape.

He decided that the window was too small for him to get through. It was long and low but far too narrow, and the door was very solidly built. He wondered if Ling had the key.

Ling was lighting another cigarette. Then she wiped the sheen of sweat from her forehead with the index finger of her right hand as if brushing away strands of hair from her face. She let the smoke out of her nostrils and it wove up through the air, iridescent in the sunlight, reminding him of the smoke from a censer in the temple at Dorje Ri-gon. Ling looked at him lying on the iron bedstead.

'Trust me,' she said.

He moved his eyes until they were on her, but unseeing, focused on the past.

'May I have some water?' he asked politely.

Ling put her cigarette between her lips while she poured water into a china mug.

'We shall never think the same, I know that,' she said, sitting down on the bed beside him and noticing that the dust had already spread a film over the water in the mug. 'You are a reactionary, and a counter-revolutionary, but . . .' Tsun found her puzzlement very attractive. 'I wonder why? At some point our ideas meet. You were known in Litang for your progressive policies . . .' She realised that they had had a conversation like this before. If only she could make him understand.

Tsun was murmuring to himself, smiling.

'Progressive policies – progressive policies . . .' He used the words like one would a stone, for its feel.

'You could be of great service in the New Tibet.' Ling caught his familiar, mocking smile. 'I do not agree with everything that is being done in Tibet, no thinking Communist would, but Comrade Mao says, revolution is not a dinner party. People are people.' She raised his head with one hand and held the mug with the other, holding it so that he was able to sip the water slowly.

'As one of the new leaders of Tibet, you could obviously influence its progress.'

Tsun tried to hold the mug for himself, but his hand shook so that she had to help him keep it steady. He took small sips of the water.

'In 1952, here in Kham, some of my friends believed offers similar to the ones you are making to me.' He coughed, then sipped more water to soothe his dry throat. 'Today, most are imprisoned, dead, or in the resistance.'

'Not all,' Ling said quietly. 'What of the Kundun? The Panchen Lama? They understand the situation.'

Tsun could smell her hair. It was sweet.

'Yes,' he sighed. 'They do!'

She ran a hand nervously over her face and tapped ash onto the floor.

'Very well, Tsun.' She put the mug down on the floor and dropped her cigarette into the bucket. 'Do not lead, but at least *live* in the New Tibet. Otherwise . . .' Her eyes were glistening with unshed tears. 'There is nothing.'

Tsun frowned and put a hand gently on her head. He felt her body go rigid, but she did not move away.

'Please, Tsun . . . Please . . .'

He reached up and pulled her head down. Their lips touched, then his tongue was thrusting deep into her mouth, finding an instant response. He pushed her head back, holding it so that he could see her face, and caught an expression of apprehension in Ling's eyes. It vanished as he kissed her eyelids, her nose, and gazed at her. Lifting her hair, he let it run through his fingers; he moved to touch her ear, but her hand came up to stop him.

'No, Tsun.'

'Why?' He pushed her hand aside, raised her hair and saw that her ear lobe was only a fringe of ragged flesh. Gently he touched it.

'What happened?'

'Do not talk.'

Ling swung her legs up onto the bed so that she lay beside Tsun, and ran her hand caressingly along his side. Her head dropped to rest on his chest. He winced at the pain of her touch. They both laughed. He stroked her hair, her lips touched his bare flesh.

'Tell me!' Tsun said.

Ling gave a reluctant groan.

'It was eight years ago,' she said. 'There was a boy who wanted to marry me.' She moved her body closer to his. Slowly, he caressed her. 'I thought that we should wait until we were thirty, as the party recommended. One night we were making love, we discussed marriage and began arguing. I told him I wanted to wait.' She paused. 'He bit off the lobe of my ear and swallowed it. I thought I was going to die, there was so much blood.'

Tsun started to laugh, then began coughing and moaning with pain. Ling found herself laughing as she raised herself on one elbow, and his anguished cries only made them both laugh more.

Then their eyes caught and held. Ling felt her heart thumping. This was real, something she could not control. Tsun was quiet now and breathing quickly, his eyes showing the pain of conflict. For an instant, both of them remembered that moment in the valley, a lifetime ago. Then Tsun's hand reached slowly towards her. As it touched her cheek she felt it trembling. Then, with both hands, he ripped open her checked shirt and pulled her down to him. Her olive breasts, like ripe fruit, her hard nipples brushing his chest. She lay still. Gently his hand covered her breast.

Ling was disconcerted and completely unsure of herself and Tsun. Yet with every kiss, every caress, he expressed the intensity of his desire. The world had vanished, the room, the voices, light, darkness, in their complete absorption in each other. Tsun's mouth was on Ling's shoulders and her neck. She felt him pressing hard against her body and put a hand down to unbuckle the belt of her trousers. Tsun felt the coldness of the metal on his stomach. He looked into Ling's eyes, then their lips touched.

'Khup Tho!' Ling shouted the curse as she was flung to the floor. Tsun swung his legs off the bed and stood up, his desire still incongruously apparent. He glared at her angrily.

'How much did they offer you? he demanded.

'They didn't! They didn't!' Ling was shaking, her words broken by sobs.

'No? Not money? Promotion? A medal?' His grin was a sneer. 'For Comrade Mao? Or just part of your work?'

Ling rose to her feet, weeping silently as she adjusted her trousers and buckled her belt. Then she picked up her shirt from the floor and started to put it on. Tsun grabbed her by the hair and stared at the tear-stained face of a woman humiliated by love.

'You can tell them,' he jerked her head so that she had to look at him, 'that you were very, very good!'

Ling grabbed at his hand and wrenched it so that it came away with strands of her hair pulled out at the roots.

'All right!' she shouted at him. 'Everything you say is right! If that is what you want to believe, you believe it! You are so sure.'

She struggled into her shirt, tried to button it, realised that most of the buttons had been torn off, and tucked it impatiently into her trousers.

'You are satisfied. You know you are right. I should have left you at the Thamzing. You have not got the guts to admit your own feelings, let alone express them.' She brushed away the tears with the back of her hand. 'I must be mad,' she muttered. 'Well,' she snapped. 'Now we owe each other nothing. You saved me, and I offered you a chance of saving yourself. Don't take it.' She spat the words at him.

Tsun stood watching her. He did not move, just watched and listened as every word hit him like a physical blow.

Ling flung her head back and fought to control her rage.

'I should have known,' she said bitterly, 'but I fell right into the trap.' She started to walk up and down, parodying herself. 'Remember, in every class society, everyone lives as a member of a particular class. And every kind of thinking, without exception, is stamped with the brand of each class. I thought . . .' she waved a despairing hand at Tsun. 'I do not know what I thought . . .' She turned and stood with her back to him, staring out of the window.

'By limiting a profound truth' – Tsun's voice was quiet and calm – 'you talk only of the visible lotus floating on the water. What of its roots lurking in the murky depths of the water, in the mud and the slime at the bottom of the pond? Pluck the flower and its root remains to give life to another. It is that basic conditioning, that ignorance of our true natures with which I am concerned. You, I, everyone, suffers from that, not just those in a class society.'

Ling turned to face him. 'I talk of practicalities,' she said. 'You . . .' She stopped on seeing the pain in Tsun's face, shocked by the tear stains on his cheeks.

He moved towards her and she did not stir. He put his arms gently around her and she lifted her fingers to touch the wetness of his cheek. She, too, wept.

'I am sorry,' she murmured.

Their tears, the gentle gestures of love, expressed their regret not only for their own actions, but for so much more.

'Ling,' Tsun said, 'I love you.'

Ling pulled her hand back and stared at him with almost childlike amazement in her eyes. Tsun laughed, and the moment was lost. He let go of her and moved away to pick up his trousers, then dropped them in disgust.

'Can you get me a clean pair, these stink.'

Ling, fumbling a cigarette out of her packet, did not take in what he said.

'Umm?'

She blinked her eyes dry.

'Clean trousers? And chuba?'

'Oh yes, I'll try.'

Tsun slipped on his shirt, sat down on the bed and reached out to catch hold of Ling's arm as she passed him. Her face was white and tense as she sat beside him, like an obedient child.

'You're shaking.' He placed an arm around her waist. 'Why?'

'Because . . .' She gave him a weak smile. 'Because . . .'

Her mind seethed with thoughts of what might have happened, should have happened. Tsun was absorbed in tracing the outline of her features with his finger.

'Well,' she murmured softly, 'what do we do now?'

Her eyes pleaded with him for an answer. The calmness of his look did nothing to soothe her troubled mind.

'If the situation were different . . .' he said.

She stared at him unbelievingly. 'What do you mean – different?'

Tsun indicated the room with a wave of his hand. 'The circumstances . . .'

'There could be a way,' Ling cut in. Then catching the disbelief in Tsun's eyes, added, 'I have influence. It would be impossible in Chamdo, but if you were in Lhasa where you have not been publicly denounced . . .' She looked thoughtful. 'And then I could get posted there . . .'

'How could you do your work and be with me?'

'I would give it up. We could find other work to do.'

She did not look at him and there was no need for him to reply. No one stopped working for the Party, unless the Party wished them to.

'At least,' Ling said desperately, 'we would have some time together, that is better than nothing.' She paused. Tsun watched and waited. Ling lit the cigarette she had been holding and looked at the glowing tip.

'Tsun, if . . . if only you could give me something that I could use on your behalf.' She glanced at him nervously, anxiously awaiting his reaction, but his face was impassive.

'For example, you could say that you realised you had been wrong in the past and that you wanted the New Tibet.'

Tsun laughed. 'That is what your friends are waiting to hear.'

'It is something. Tsun, please, however little . . .'

'The head of the worm is insignificant when it emerges from the ground, yet it is what the bird seeks, for when it is seized and pulled, it all comes.'

Ling shook her head in irritable disagreement.

'I was tortured at the Thamzing,' Tsun said. 'Because I mean something to the people, because I represent the religion and because, like them, I believe that the Motherland is *not* China, but Tibet! Because of that respect and my influence, the Han have tried every means to discredit me.' His words were slow and ominous to Ling, as though he wanted her fully to appreciate their significance.

'The ordinary Tibetans, the laymen and women, are enduring far greater hardships than I, a lama, in their struggle to save our religion and our nation. It is better that my neck is stretched a foot before the people of Chamdo, than that I live and break the trust and responsibility they have given me.'

'Tsun, how can you be so blind? Can't you see that, whether you like it or not, Tibet *is* now part of China.'

She put a hand on the side of his face as though the physical contact would emphasise her words.

'This is reality. If all the Tibetans in Tibet rose up today, they would be crushed. Face it, Tsun, please. Not just for yourself, but for your followers. Don't you see that your resistance and your counter-revolutionary activities will lead not only to your own death, but to the death of many who, you say, trust you. It is a vicious circle doomed to destruction, because it feeds off the respect given to you and your own stubborn determination to be heroic no matter what the cost to others. There is already a New Tibet. Please, Tsun, please understand. It is time for you to join the New Tibet. Meet me half way. Do you believe that the Kundun and the Panchen Lama are wrong to work for the peaceful liberation of Tibet? Should they join the terrorists and kill people?'

'Ling, Ling, Ling . . .' Tsun carried her name on a sigh. 'You ask me to understand, but what of you? I know what I must do. Of course the Kundun and Panchen Rinposhay are right to counsel peace, as many of us have in Kham. But Lhasa is not yet Kham. Your friends will decide if it is to be so.' He paused, then said: 'Tell me Ling, would you come with me to fight for the resistance . . . would you?'

Ling stared at the floor. 'I don't know . . .' She looked up at him with unhappy eyes. 'I could not fight, Tsun . . .'

'You see,' said Tsun. 'You and I are like the snake in the proverb: if you beat a snake, can it show forth hands and feet?'

A faint smile crossed Ling's face and she gave the proverb straight back to him.

'You have left out the first line – If you beat a Han can he speak Tibetan?'

Tsun chuckled. They were both silent for some minutes.

'Oh, Tsun,' Ling murmured.

'You could help me escape,' Tsun said lightly, his mind working to find a way.

'No! Escape is impossible, there is no way I could get you through the security checks.'

She tossed her head and some strands of hair fell over the lighted end of her cigarette. There was smoke and the smell of singed hair. Ling put out the tiny flame with her fingers.

'I'm not used to wearing my hair like this, it's dangerous.'

She smoothed it back, close to her head, and Tsun thought how cleverly she had managed to conceal her deformed ear throughout the time she had been with the party, by carefully plaiting her hair so as to cover the damaged lobe. He put up a hand to touch her head. 'Your hair is beautiful,' he said.

'Perhaps,' Ling muttered, 'perhaps I could *lose* you . . . maybe there is a chance, Tsun. It will not be easy, though . . .' Her eyes were sad and worried. 'But it could not be any worse that what has already happened and what *will* happen here.' She dropped her cigarette on the floor and ground it out with her heel. 'You must have a different name,' she said briskly.

'How about Yeshi Norbu?' Tsun asked.

'Yes,' Ling nodded. 'That is good. I shall put that on the forms.'

'Do you know what is going to happen to me?'

'You are being sent to a rehabilitation camp. It is for reactionaries who show signs of wanting to reform. Remember that, Tsun!' She saw his smile, and frowned. 'It is your only chance, please don't throw it away. It will not be easy, but from there I might be able to arrange your escape to Lhasa . . .'

Tsun's gaze made her falter. He raised a hand to touch his bruised face and flinched. Ling's face showed her concern.

'It may not be for a few weeks,' she said. 'Tsun . . . please . . . be careful, and try to co-operate . . . otherwise . . .'

Again there was silence between them.

'Why are you crying?' Tsun whispered.

'Everything is so uncertain . . . time is so short.'

Suddenly, his arms were around her and she was weeping unrestrainedly, her face pressed against his neck. He held her close, but her tears flowed faster. There was no passion in his caresses. She drew back to look at him with tear-filled eyes.

'Love me . . . please . . .' She saw the answer in his face, but would not accept it.

Tsun ran a hand gently over her head, held her close and kissed her lips. For a moment she felt the renewal of his desire.

'Tsun, please . . .'

'No!' The words were breathed through dry lips.

'But we have so little time together.'

'Not now, not here!' He held her face between his hands. 'I want to so much, but where and when, we shall choose, with no one to gain from it.'

'Please . . .'

'No, Ling!' His refusal carried the same desperation as her pleadings. He put her aside firmly. 'How much longer do we have?'

Ling glanced at the Omega watch on her wrist, a concession to capitalism, bought from a Tibetan merchant. 'An hour,' she said.

'Could we have something to eat?'

'I'll get some food and some clothes,' she said.

She looked at him in surprise as he pulled his shirt across himself and sat down cross-legged on the bed.

'What are you doing?'

'I am going to meditate.'

Ling was annoyed at this intrusion of a world she did not understand and her ignorance fed her suspicion, but she said nothing. The sight of the lama sitting silently, with his eyes closed in meditation, made her feel ill at ease and yet unwilling to leave him. She stood with her back to him and looked out of the window. Then, growing restive, she turned and walked over to the bed and, feeling a little embarrassed, sat down beside him.

Tsun's eyes opened slowly, then he reached out his right hand and touched her lightly on the head.

Ling did not know if she cried out or not. Indeed, she was too confused even to think properly, for how long after she did not know – a second, a minute, an hour? For, as Tsun's hand touched her, a bolt of energy tore through her mind and body.

When she did begin to realise what had happened, Tsun was meditating again, hands linked, the fingers forming a mudra, a symbolic pattern, reflecting his mental state. As if in a dream, she sat on the bed looking at him, aware of a reality of which he had often spoken but which she had never before understood. Slowly, she rose and walked towards the cell door. Standing there, she took a key from her pocket, slipped it into the keyhole and turned it. As she opened the door she watched Tsun, her mind filled with a confusion of thoughts, questions and emotions; a sense of loss, of attraction, a need to know more about her experience, a fear of what would befall him. Gently she closed the door behind her.

Chapter Twenty-Six

The click of a key turning and the sound of the opening door made Tsun look up, expecting to see Ling returning, but a PLA trooper, in green uniform and soft cap, threw in trousers and a chuba, dumped a plate of rice and a mug of hot water on the floor, then slammed the door shut.

'Ling!' Tsun shouted her name with more anger than he had ever known as he stood there, hands gripping the door frame. His anger changed to laughter as he realised the irony of his reaction, when his whole training had been to awaken the mind and dispel internal darkness and emotional afflictions.

He dressed in the clean chuba and trousers. The rice was still warm, and as he lifted the plate something caught the palm of his hand. Underneath he found an identity card stuck to the bottom of the plate, made out in the name of Yeshi Norbu, metal worker's assistant.

Tsun smiled, realising just how glad he was that Ling had not tricked him. He wondered if she had got the information about his being a former metal worker from Lopsang. Certainly, his work with the silversmith, Chopel, would stand him in good stead if he ever needed to prove his background.

An hour later the door opened again and the same guard, keeping Tsun covered with an automatic, moved him quickly down the passage way and through a door into a courtyard, packed with men being loaded onto trucks bound for the labour camps. Some faces he recognised from the refugee camp, but everyone by then was wary of the dangers of mutual recognition.

Tsun became one of the thousands working on the network of roads being built throughout Tibet. The Han considered the work a priority, for when the PLA entered the country they had found a land virtually devoid of roads fit for motor traffic. Apart from the thousands, like Tsun, who were under detention as 'bad elements', whole villages were ordered to work on building the road system, designed to ensure that the PLA could effectively control the whole country and bind it to China.

Tsun knew that it might be some weeks before he would hear from Ling, but somehow he was sure that he would. Even after three months, he still clung to the hope that she would work something out for him. Had she not said it could be some time before she would be able to contact him? After six months without word, he no longer expected to hear.

Of Kesang, Pema, Rinchen and the boys, he knew nothing. His only source of hope was that they had not been captured. It was after he had been in the camp for almost a year that he accidentally heard that Tul-lok and Genyen were alive and active in the resistance in the Lhasa area. Then he broke the survival rules he had learnt so well over the past months, and when a tailor he knew was being released, he asked him to get a message to Tul-lok or Genyen, saying simply that 'the son untamed' was at the camp. He could not risk any more; to do so would have meant jeopardising his cover. He hoped they would understand. The tailor agreed to do what he could, but Tsun knew that even if the message did reach them, it would probably be some months hence.

His training had been directed towards living each day to the full, to being in the present moment as the only one which really exists. The camp life ensured it. It was the best way he knew to combat despair.

At dawn, for nine hundred and eighty-two mornings, Tsun and the other twenty-four men in the bunk house mentally tried to block out the clanging of the rod rattled between two pieces of iron railing, trying to remain in the sleep of forgetfulness; but always they had to wake up. Unless they were dead.

Today, Tsun thought, staring at the small window made blind with a thick coating of frost, is different. Today, there was no demanding clanging to get him up. Wild, wonderful thoughts arose. Perhaps the reistance had overcome the guards and they were free . . . but what of the silence? The silence that had woken him in a way that countless clangings of the iron railings had never achieved. He smiled. How quickly and easily one is conditioned.

A freezing blast of air filled the cabin as someone quickly opened and closed the door, pushing past the sackcloth curtain.

'What is happening, Brass Nose?'

The newcomer had taken the lid off the iron stove to warm his hands. The quivering, dancing flames reflected on the origin of the man's nickname, his brass nose.

'The guard has dropped the rod in the snow and can't find it.'

Brass Nose looked up at Tsun lying on the top row of the four-tier bunks, took off his fur hat and stamped his feet to get warm. Tsun laughed. 'Perhaps it is an omen?'

He was aware of a bed bug pushing its way through the hairs on his arm, then biting.

'Kunjosum!' Brass Nose cursed softly as he lowered the lid back onto the stove. 'Cooking, warming myself, it is always the same. My nose becomes afire before I even begin to feel the heat.'

Tentatively, he felt the well modelled brass nose which hung from his ears on leather thongs. A guard flung open the door and shouted in fractured Tibetan:

'Wake up! Wake up!'

He went out and Brass Nose slammed the door shut after him as, groaning and cursing, the men of the Twenty-Second Unit climbed out of their bunks.

Tsun pulled up his sleeve, seized the bed bug and pushed it through a crack in the plank wall. Hardly any of the prisoners killed bugs. Even with himself, Tsun was never quite sure how much was due to piety and how much to the appalling smell the bugs emitted when crushed.

The dark, cramped cabin was full of milling figures, shapeless in bulky, tattered chubas, collecting their boots from the vast pile around the stove. An eighteen year-old, snub-nosed youth was wrapping straw round his feet. In the darkness, a man stumbled over the youth's red and black felt boots. Some of the other prisoners laughed and the youth giggled, his mouth splitting in an enormous wide grin. The man turned and seized the boy's boots, holding them high.

'Look at these fine boots. Who is going to have them?'

As the youth made a grab for the boots, they were tossed into the jostling crowd of prisoners. The youth, laughing, reached for them, only for another hand to take them and pass them on. The guard had found his rod and, above their laughter, the men heard it clanging the signal for breakfast. Some left the hut, others stayed, struggling with their boots or teasing the youth.

'Come, you have only been in the camp one day,' an old man said. 'You must have something on you. What will you give for the boots?'

He spoke just loudly enough for the others to hear, and the game immediately ceased to be a game, the laughter became hard, and with a businesslike determination the boots were whisked from hand to hand.

'Leave the boy alone!' Brass Nose shouted. 'Give him back his boots.' The men stopped, reluctantly, then with murmured complaints the boots were handed over.

'Thanks.' The youth looked at Brass Nose questioningly as he pulled on his boots.

'What is your name?' Brass Nose demanded.

'Jigme Tsering, they call me Jettie.'

'Well, Jettie, I am the leader of the Twenty-Second Unit.' Brass Nose waved a hand towards the men surrounding them. I am the leader because I know my way around better than most here.'

Tsun laughed, then cursed as the string broke with which he was tying his boot. Brass Nose ignored him and looked the youth up and down. He frowned.

'I think we had better get you on light duties my boy, or else you will not last four weeks. You will not be used to the hard work here.'

Tsun glanced at them. 'Unless the young bird leaps from the nest, how does he know whether or not he can fly?' he said.

Jettie grinned. Tsun laughed again and pulled the shortened string round his boot.

'The young bird is pushed by his parent.' Brass Nose laid an affectionate hand on the youth's shoulder as the three of them left the hut for the mess hall.

'Now, for the packet of cigarettes in your pocket . . .' Jettie looked at Brass Nose sharply. '. . . I could get you on light duties for a month.'

'What does that mean?' Jettie asked as, with head down, he watched the snow crunching beneath his boots.

'Making granite chippings for the road surface. A lot of old people do it. You will come to me eventually to help you, so why not take my advice? Yeshi Norbu!' Brass Nose turned to Tsun who was pulling his woollen hat over his ears. 'Is it not true that I was here before you came three years ago? Indeed, I was one of the first here.'

'I thought,' Tsun chuckled, 'that you built the place. It is good business you have got.'

Brass Nose spat angrily. 'My business is to keep myself and my unit alive.' He looked at Jettie. 'Well?'

'What do you think?' Jettie asked Tsun as they pushed their way through the crush in the corrugated iron-roofed mess hall. Jettie felt drawn to Tsun. He was as ragged as the other prisoners; his body slightly more skeletal than most, the flaking brown, leathery skin shrinking more tightly each day round the bone structure of his head; his hair was grey, yet, Jettie thought, he was probably only thirty or forty years old. Tsun always kept his hair close-cropped, and something in his manner told Jettie that he must once have been a monk. But it was Tsun's eyes which attracted him. Like those of all the prisoners, they had the look of a hunted animal, a blend of exhaustion, pain and desperate hope. Yet, unlike the others, Tsun's eyes had an indefinable quality, reflecting something other than the life of the camp.

'I think that you should make a friend of Brass Nose,' Tsun yelled at Jettie above the din as he thrust his bowl into the serving hatch. 'Come on, stir it, take it from the bottom,' he shouted through the hatch.

Jettie could see a vast monastery tea cauldron from which a gruel of tsampa and vegetables was being ladled into the bowls crowded in the hatch, amid a chorus of angry shouts as the precious food was slopped.

Brass Nose stopped Jettie as he started down the mess hall, looking for a place at one of the trestle tables. He caught the eye of a prisoner who had finished his meal and indicated with a jerk of his head for him to make room. The prisoner and his two companions reluctantly gave up their seats. Brass Nose sat down and cupped his hands round the steaming bowl to warm them.

'Always sit as close as you can to the kitchen,' he said. 'For the warmth.' Tsun's lips moved in prayer for a few moments, then he probed the watery gruel with wooden chopsticks. He turned to Jettie.

'Yes, make a friend of Brass Nose, because his friends always get his services a little cheaper. But remember, he is a businessman and, like all good businessmen, he will try to get the best of a bargain. You must argue with him as you would in the market place. Remember, too, that the value of your cigarettes is always high here. The value of the privileges they can buy depends on how badly you need them, and even then, like your cigarettes, they will only last a short time.'

'You are no friend of mine,' Brass Nose muttered noisily, sipping his gruel. 'All right!' He waved an admonishing finger at Jettie. 'Today you work like us and see for yourself.'

Tsun laughed, then, with the look of one totally absorbed in what he is doing, he carefully and with great relish ate a piece of turnip. He had learnt to make the most of these few precious moments, all that a prisoner had to himself, to savour and delight in every single morsel of food. To enjoy the feel of the hot liquid running through his body. The hunger not totally, but partly abated, its ravages held off for a short while.

Jettie lifted his bowl to his lips. The greasy fluid tasted foul. His first inclination was to spit it out but, instead, he returned his bowl to the table and sat looking at it with disgust. As he stared at it, an indeterminate piece of vegetable bobbed to the surface.

'Do not worry,' said Tsun. 'Everyone feels like you to begin with. You will soon come to tolerate it.' He reached for the bowl and looked questioningly at Jettie, who nodded agreement. Tsun drank half then passed the remainder to Brass Nose.

'Kunjosum! I have lost another tooth!' Brass Nose stared with horror at the tooth, a glistening white island in the small pool of greasy fluid, flecked with blood and lying at the bottom of the bowl.

Jettie saw apprehension in Brass Nose's eyes as he opened his mouth for Tsun to inspect. Jettie had never seen anything like it. Half his front teeth were missing and those that remained were distorted into buck teeth by blackened gums. Jettie felt his stomach heave. A combination of the greasy mess he had been served for breakfast, Brass Nose's foul teeth and the sight of the rotten, blood-streaked tooth lying in the bowl of grey fluid, made his mouth water with nausea, but he controlled it. He was starving, but not so hungry as to eat that muck, he thought.

'Brass Nose, use your influence to see the medical officer,' said Tsun flatly, 'or I shall soon be wearing those fine boots of yours.'

Brass Nose grunted. 'I shall be wearing them to carry *you* to the body breakers.' He paused. 'After so long . . .' His murmured words were lost in the noise from the loudspeakers. 'Fall in! Fall in!'

Tsun could hear snatches of martial music being pumped through the broadcasting system before it was swamped by the loud wind. Dogs barked hoarsely at one another, waiting beside their handlers during the roll call of the one thousand, three hundred and twenty-six prisoners assembled on the parade ground.

The duty officer, checking that the members of each unit were accounted for, stopped in front of Tsun. It had happened before, but rarely, and each time Tsun wondered if his real identity had been discovered, or perhaps – wild ridiculous hope – Ling had arranged for his release. He wondered what had happened to her? Perhaps she had just forgotten? No, perhaps she was dead? Three years! Still, in his dreams, he was at Dorje Ri-gon, heard the laughter of Kesang, of his pupils, fought with Norden, played with Senge . . . and, sometimes, the wild, exciting beauty of Genyen . . . another world, an illusion, a dream. But dreams can be painful.

The lieutenant was frowning at the dirt-covered white label sewn on Tsun's coat.

'What is your number?'

'G6846, lieutenant.'

'Get it repainted.'

The sergeant with him made a note on his clip board. Brass Nose was arguing with the work allocation officer.

'But the man cannot work for ten minutes without shitting. You have seen him.'

'He has been passed as fit by the medical officer.'

Brass Nose laughed emptily. 'Let him do light work for today,' he suggested. 'The Chief Engineer said only yesterday that he needed more granite chippings.'

'When I get a request for more chippings, I will assign more people to the work.'

'A quarter rice.'

'Three quarters.'

'Half.'

The officer nodded.

'Scavenging bastard!' Brass Nose muttered as he stepped back into line beside Tsun. 'And for that lazy Rindak who has been ill ever since he arrived.'

The wooden gates swung open. The men formed fours and marched out onto the snow covered plain, accompanied by four hundred guards and their dogs. Once outside the camp, they ignored the order prohibiting talking during the march.

'What was Brass Nose doing back there?' Jettie asked Tsun.

'Each unit has a quota to fill.' Jettie had to move closer to Tsun in order to hear him above the low rush of the wind. 'Rindak is too weak to do much work, but by getting him officially registered as sick and assigned to other work, our quota will be lowered accordingly. Of course, we shall all have to contribute to the bribe, but it is the unit leader's job to see that the bribe works out less than we would lose if we could not fill the quota with Rindak on the team.'

Some of the men began verbal singing contests, in which one group would try to exhaust the other's repertoire. It helped with the monotony, Tsun thought, the dull, gruelling routine of the camp. He pulled down from beneath his hat the fringed rag which he used to protect his eyes from snow glare. In the grey dawn light, he saw the head of the column curve across the wide plain, patches of yellow stones revealed by the morning light, the only feature in the bleak magnificence of the white plain. Tsun grabbed Jettie as he made to leave the column.

'They will shoot you!'

'I want to pee.'

'Get the guard's permission.'

The song contest carried on and Tsun added his own voice to the unfolding verses. Brass Nose thought on his own fate; he had seen enough men in his condition to know the likely progress of the disease.

Tsun pulled his coat collar up around his neck. Already his feet were numb with cold. Each day they seemed to become colder quicker. Somehow, he thought, I must get a new pair of boots. He raised his voice against the wind and the singing to speak to Jettie.

'Why are you here?'

'I was with the People's Resistance Movement, the Mimang, in Lhasa, and was arrested for sticking up anti-Han posters. But where is this camp? I was driven here during the night.'

'It is one hundred and thirty-eight miles from Lhasa. We are here to build the road leading from the Chamdo-Lhasa highway to the Indian border. What news of Lhasa? Occasionally we hear rumours from the guards, but they know little more than we do.'

Jettie was silent.

'It is good,' Tsun continued, 'that you have been warned of informers, but I talk openly to you although I know that the Han have told you to spy on me . . .'

'No!' Jettie looked shocked. He looked round to see if Brass Nose or any of the others had heard Tsun. 'I did not agree.'

Already, thought Tsun, his eyes could have been those of any of the prisoners. He grinned at the youth. 'Good!' he said. 'Then tell me of Lhasa.'

For a few moments Jettie did not answer. Tsun had confused and frightened him. There was a saying in the camp that informers woke up to find their throats cut. The men still sang of the impermanence of all things; of the waterfowl seeking food at the bottom of streams, liable to be drowned; of that which is thrown away today, only to be needed tomorrow. Tsun was not listening to the songs; he wanted to hear whatever Jettie could be persuaded to tell him about Lhasa.

'There are thousands of refugees from the north and east camped round Lhasa,' Jettie began. 'The news they have brought of what the Han are doing in the east has frightened everyone. At first people would not believe it, then each day more and more people came and told the same stories, so they had to believe. The Han tried to buy up copies of the *People's Daily* which contained an attack on the religion. About two weeks ago, just before I was arrested, the Han began making a list of the refugees. This frightened them and many have fled to join the Chushi-Gang-Druk at Lhargeri.'

'What is the Government's attitude?'

Jettie grinned. 'One mouth, two tongues. One for the Han, one for us. They had to issue a decree suppressing the Mimang, but we exist.'

'And the Kundun?'

'As always, he seeks peace, but . . .' Jettie shrugged. 'Did you hear about his invitation to the Indian Prime Minister, Nehru?'

Tsun shook his head.

'In 1956, when the Kundun and Panchen Rinposhay went to India for the Buddha Jayanti celebrations, the Kundun invited Nehru to Lhasa. Later, the Han cancelled the invitation, because they said they were worried about Nehru being harmed by the Khamba terrorists. So . . .' Jettie shrugged again.

'Is there no help from the outside?' asked Tsun.

'I do not know! Perhaps. Some of the Chushi-Gang-Druk leaders are in Kalimpong and the resistance are doing well. The day I was arrested we heard that a PLA garrison only thirty miles from Lhasa had been wiped out.'

Tsun was still conscious of reticence in the youth.

'What is this "no reforms for six years" campaign?' he asked.

'Have you no knowledge of that?'

Tsun shook his head. 'We do not get much news. Even the Han magazines are out of date. You are the first prisoner from Lhasa for months.'

'When the Kundun went to India, he met Chou-en-lai and told him of the people's horror at what the Han were doing in the east. Anyway, Mao Tse-tung himself announced that there would be no reforms for six years as the Tibetan people did not want them. There were speeches in Lhasa by the Generals, saying that most of the Han cadres were being sent back to China and warning the PLA and cadres against "Great Hanism".'

Tsun roared with laughter. 'Has it made much difference?'

Jettie grinned his wide grin. It was all the answer Tsun needed. 'Where do you come from?' he asked.

'Chamdo.'

Perhaps, Tsun thought, if Mao himself had had to back down, it meant that Tibet had something to bargain with? Then there was hope? Hope! That elusive bird, so long ago it had flown over the horizon out of sight. But no one forgot it!

'Were you a monk?' asked Jettie.

Tsun nodded. 'Where do you live in Lhasa?' he asked.

'Sho.'

'I have some friends in the street of the Golden Fish, off the Barkor. Do you know that area at all?'

'No.'

Tsun had hoped to find out if some of his party were at the Dorje Ri-gon house in the street of the Golden Fish, but he dared not ask specifically. Even a friend could be made to talk.

The bazaars are a market place of gold,
The bazaar drinks are of turquoise hue.

The song contest continued. Tsun, again, added his voice to the rejoinder, that love, like water, although precious, cannot be grasped as gold.

Suddenly, he was at the festivals and picnics of his youth, singing with Genyen. Laughter, food, drink. The mountains and horses and freedom. 'Memories are for old men,' he grumbled to himself.

The noise of the column descending into the three-mile long valley disturbed some vultures. They rose with harsh cries from beneath the crest of the ridge, their wings slowly beating. Tsun watched them, fascinated. The awesome beauty of the valley never failed to make its impact on him. For those few moments walking along the ridge, he was not looking up at the leaking roof of the bunk house, at gruel, at scurvy-ridden faces, at his battered boots, at his pick striking sparks off the rock. For those few moments, he was looking at life, at freedom.

The sun had risen in the limpid blue sky. A single sheet of cloud was driven swiftly by the sharp north wind behind the chiselled glacier-wrapped peaks. Tsun could just make out tiny figures and an irregular string of yaks using the frozen river as a road, twisting through the rugged, narrow valley.

A clump of snow fell, like ripe fruit, from the snow-laden

branches of a tree. As spring approached, the snow was receding up the mountains, leaving the road to stand out sharply like a cream-coloured ribbon, snaking back and forth as it climbed the green-brown mountain side. It was such a contrast to the stark plain. Tsun thought of some words of Milarepa, the cotton-clad saint:

> That all the wealth revealed within my mind,
> And all the circling threefold worlds contain,
> Unreal as it is, can yet be seen – that is the miracle.

'Kusho . . .' Jettie had quickly learnt to respect Brass Nose's position. 'What is the story, Kusho, behind . . .?'

As the heavy-featured man looked up from his bowl of gruel, the youth hesitated, uncertain of the man's reaction. Tsun laughed.

'Go on, Brass Nose, tell the boy about your nose.'

The three men were eating their lunch, sitting on a rock overlooking the valley.

'Every good storyteller gets paid,' said Brass Nose. 'What about one of your cigarettes?'

Jettie grinned, took a packet of Wills Whiffs from his ambac and gave one to Brass Nose.

'Got any matches?' Tsun asked the youth.

Jettie shook his head. Tsun struggled to get the kusha grass to light from his flint. The other two drank their gruel while they watched. At last the grass flared. Brass Nose stopped eating and held the end of the cigarette to the flame. He drew the intoxicating smoke deep into his lungs, then sat back, relishing the feel of the cigarette between his fingers, enjoying every puff as if it were the last. Tsun trod out the tiny fire.

'I was fighting with the resistance in Batang in 1956,' Brass Nose began. 'I split a Han's skull with my sword. At first I thought he was dead, then I saw him trying to get at his revolver, so I started to dismount to finish him off. My stirrup broke and I hit the ground so hard that my rifle discharged its only shot. It nearly blew my head off. I've still got the burn mark, but it missed me and killed my horse.'

Jettie was convulsed with laughter.

'I had a great struggle with the Han, during which he managed to cut off my nose!' Brass Nose grinned. 'I killed him in the end, though, and had this nose made from the brass buttons off the uniforms of all the Han I killed.'

Tsun laughed. 'I believe none of it, Jettie. Knowing Brass Nose, it is more likely that his nose dropped off from the Han's disease.'

'If anyone else said that . . .' Brass Nose's voice was without humour, 'I would kill him . . .' He grinned. 'And I might just kill you some time.'

Tsun chuckled. 'I have one thing which Brass Nose wants from me, Jettie.' The youth still could not bring himself to finish the bowl of gruel and handed it to Brass Nose.

'One thing which if I'm not alive, he cannot have, and which he can only have once.'

Brass Nose offered the cigarette to Jettie who drew on it, offered it in turn to Tsun who shook his head, then gave it back to Brass Nose.

'He believes that I can see him through the realms of bardo if he dies here. Lead him on the road to a favourable re-birth.'

'Can you, Yeshi?' Jettie asked. He wound his long plait around his head and tucked it in at the end. But Tsun was not looking at him. He was looking at the sixteen-foot high chorten standing a few yards away from the mountain side. He smiled.

'Listen!' he murmured, just loud enough for them to hear. Almost inaudible, so as to seem a trick of the mind, they could hear, above the shouts and laughter of the men, the gentle tinkling in the wind of the little bells, hung like precious stones on a necklace, one end attached to the spire of the chorten, the other end dangling loose, having broken away from the ruins of another chorten nearby. The sound of the bells, the chorten, always delighted Tsun, because it represented everything – man, and his eternal quest.

'What does it mean, Kusho?' Jettie knew that a chorten was of profound significance and often contained holy relics, and that it was a meritorious act to build one, for it reminded the traveller of the eternal truths, but that was all he knew.

Tsun chuckled, then caught his breath which turned into a hacking cough he had difficulty in controlling.

'When Buddha was dying . . .' he managed at last, 'there was much grief among his disciples over his approaching death, but the Buddha chided them saying:

> Everything comes to an end, though it may last for an aeon. The hour of parting is bound to come in the end. N[illegible] have done what I could do, both for myself and for others. To stay here from now on would be without any purpose. In the hour of joy it is not proper to grieve. The goal, so hard to win, which for

many aeons I have wished for, now, at last, is no longer far away, when that is won, unchanging bliss, which none can take away . . .

'He instructed his pupils to place his bones and ashes in funeral mounds, knowing that they would become centres of pilgrimage. So this made the funeral mound of great significance, and this is what the chorten represents.'

Brass Nose uprooted a stunted weed growing near a rock and chewed on it thoughtfully.

'The funeral mound tells us one sure fact,' said Tsun. 'The fact of death, of his death and impermanence, of the world's impermanence. We, with the Buddha's disciples, weep and feel afraid, but only because we do not see the world as the Buddha saw it, rendering death meaningless, giving him cause to be joyous.'

Brass Nose pulled up some more weeds and offered them to his companions. Jettie refused, but Tsun took some and chewed on the wiry stems.

'So you see, Jettie,' Tsun said, 'the Buddha's funeral mound also serves to remind us of the goal of Buddhism, the awakening to reality, and so in all Buddhist countries, it has been adopted as the symbol of man's quest for fulfilment, built in a different style in each country – the pagodas of China, the chortens of Tibet.'

'Quickly, Yeshi,' said Brass Nose, looking at Tsun. 'If we do not hurry they will have us for slacking.'

For weeks, Tsun had been assigned to a group carrying two hundred buckets of rock a day down the mountain side. The running sores on his back were so bad that Brass Nose had managed to get him reassigned to digging. Jettie, his partner that day, worked the rope attached to the spade.

'Yeshi,' Jettie grunted with exertion, 'is this easy work or hard work?'

Tsun laughed. 'You will see,' he said.

By late afternoon, the men were working in silence, too exhausted to talk or sing the mournful songs with which they had begun the day. Tsun's mind lusted after the night-time gruel and then rest, sleep, the escape. Each moment of his three-year imprisonment he had had to struggle to retain something of his mental freedom, but now it was only glimpsed beyond the enveloping, dehumanising struggle for existence.

Chapter Twenty-Seven

The reaction to the distant shots and shouts, like ripples expanding from a pebble thrown in a pool, took a few seconds to reach the section of the road on which Tsun was working high up the mountainside.

'The resistance!' Jettie shouted, dropping his pick.

Prisoners and guards looked down into the valley, from the spiralling road, cut like steps into the mountain, to the horsemen charging out of the snow-covered woods to attack the camp below.

'Fall in! Fall in!' The sergeant in charge of Tsun's unit drew his automatic.

'Get them down there,' he shouted to the guards, and pointed to the camp.

'Use them as a shield.'

Even as he spoke there was a burst of sub-machine gun fire as fighting broke out between prisoners and guards on one of the lower levels of the road.

Brass Nose tripped the guard nearest him and grabbed at the gun he carried. A chain reaction was unleashed as the prisoners smelt freedom and set upon their guards, venting months of pent up hatred. The sergeant, his back against the mountain side, shot at Brass Nose but missed. The prisoners advanced. Someone hurled a stone, hitting the sergeant on the head. He fell, and immediately disappeared beneath the prisoners' flaying pickaxes and shovels. Realising they were in a hopeless position, the guards started shooting. They were caught unawares, outnumbered by the prisoners whose ferocity made up for their lack of weapons. With no cover, and with the mountain too steep to afford a tenable position, the guards tried to shoot their way out, but now their fire was being returned by those prisoners who had taken weapons from the guards they had killed.

Tsun pulled Jettie down behind some baskets of rubble which were being rocked by bullets ricocheting off the stones. Within a few feet of Tsun, Brass Nose and a guard were wrestling on the ground for possession of a sub-machine gun. As Tsun crawled forward to help his friend, Brass Nose brought his knee up into the man's groin. Screaming and writhing in pain, the guard rolled off the road and over the sheer side of the mountain. Tsun flung himself forward and grabbed hold of Brass Nose's legs to prevent him from being dragged over by the guard. But Brass Nose was clinging to the gun and the guard was doing the same, holding onto the strap by which he was hanging, suspended, over the thousand-foot drop. Brass Nose, his face contorted with strain, stared into the terrified eyes of the guard whose hands were moving up, one of them reaching for the clothing of the man above him, trying to weave itself into the very fabric. Brass Nose jerked the gun suddenly, the strap twisted, the guard lost his hold on Brass Nose and his hands slipped on the strap.

'Hold on!' Brass Nose shouted to Tsun who was having difficulty in stopping them both being dragged over the edge, while Brass Nose swung the man round like a pendulum, trying to dislodge him. He did not understand Chinese, but he got the meaning of the man's tone, pleading, screaming, as he swung back and forth, his fingers slipping.

Tsun felt the jerk as the man fell away. Brass Nose fell back onto the road, then sprang up, steadied the gun, and opened fire at the other guards.

Lying close to the edge of the road, Tsun saw mortar shells explode in the midst of a group of horsemen. They were using grenades on the base camp. On a lower level of the road, he saw a guard being beaten to death with spades. Another was lifted high to be hurled down the side of the mountain. Near him, one of the guards was using the dead and dying as cover while he carefully picked off prisoners with his gun. Brass Nose crouched behind a wheelbarrow, the magazine of his sub-machine gun nearly empty. Tsun crawled across the road towards a dead guard. A bullet nicked his woollen hat. He reached the guard and unhooked the grenade from the man's belt. He reached for the pin . . .

'Yeshi, no!' Jettie shouted. 'Over here!'

The youth, crouched behind the baskets of rubble, cupped his hands to receive the grenade. Tsun threw it to him. Jettie caught it and grinned. It was good to help a monk to keep his vow not to kill. Pulling the pin, he tossed the grenade at the mound of bodies shielding the guard. The blinding white glow became a fire ball, blooming into black smoke and raining parts of dismembered corpses. A hand and part of a forearm hit Tsun in the face. The sleeve was bloodsoaked, the hand open, barely scratched, the nails bitten. Tsun threw the dismembered arm down the mountain side.

The firing had stopped. Prisoners were shouting, cheering and dancing for joy. Others lay wounded and groaning. One of the buildings at the base camp was burning fiercely. Five horsemen were riding up the road, pausing often to give instructions. There were still some isolated shots.

Brass Nose came up beside Tsun, rested his arm on his shoulder and watched the slow progress of the horsemen.

'Twelve of the unit are dead,' he said, 'and four are wounded, one badly.' They walked over to where the seriously wounded man was lying and knelt beside him. They looked wordlessly at each other. The man, in his thirties, had been shot twice in the stomach. He clutched at his ripped abdomen, gasping with pain, his head rolling from side to side.

The sound of the approaching horsemen made Tsun look up. For a moment he thought he must be dreaming. Slowly, he rose to his feet. The leader was mounted on a white horse and was wearing a high red fox fur hat and sheepskin chuba. The right arm was bare. The hand held a revolver. Tsun moved closer.

'Genyen . . .'

The girl looked down at him without recognition, surprised that he should know her name. She started to speak, then suddenly stopped short, staring at him, the anguish and horror in her eyes reflecting his condition more honestly than any mirror. She bent down, and her trembling hand touched his face. Gently, she brushed aside the ragged fringe of cloth over his head to look at his red, swollen eyes. She mouthed his name as softly as a breath. Then she laughed.

'I knew I'd find you alive. We only got your message a few weeks ago. Tonight we shall sing and dance.' And she put out a hand to swing Tsun up onto the back of her horse.

'The men of my unit,' he said, holding back. 'My friends?'

'They can come with us.'

The cries of the mortally wounded man startled her horse. It shied and snorted. Haunting, dreadful cries from every man were given voice through him.

'The wounded . . .' Tsun said.

'Those that can walk, can walk. Those that can be carried, can be carried.'

Tsun looked down at the tormented man. 'And those that can do neither?'

'There is only one thing we can do for them.' Genyen slid off her horse and lifted her revolver. She glanced at Tsun and saw the look in his eyes.

'What do you think I was doing back there?' She pointed briefly down the twisting road. 'If there is no hope, it is kinder. My men want it that way.' She held the revolver steady. 'And I want it that way.'

As she moved closer to the man, Brass Nose pushed in front of her. Genyen paused and looked at him, frowning.

'He is the unit leader,' Tsun said.

Genyen nodded, handed Brass Nose her revolver and stepped back. The man opened his eyes and looked straight at Brass Nose as he pumped a shot into his head.

Brass Nose handed the revolver back to Genyen. She broke it open and reloaded. A Han guard, lying face down at their feet, moaned. The revolver, now loaded, snapped shut. Genyen tucked it into her chuba.

'Bullets are as rare as wish-fulfilling gems,' she murmured and, slipping her foot under the guard's body, she deftly tipped him over the edge of the road. His screams echoed through the cold crisp air.

A horse was found for Tsun, and he and Genyen rode together as the party made its way from the mountain side and the carnage on the road. There was so much he wanted to ask.

'What news do you have of Kesang, and of Rinchen and Pema?' he began. 'I heard that Kesang had been captured.'

'Captured?' Genyen looked puzzled. 'I have had news that Dorje Rinposhay is safe and well and is studying. They are all in Lhasa.'

Tsun could hardly believe it. So, after all, it had been a trick of the Han to try and make him talk. For so long he had hoped that they might have escaped, but always with the fear that they were dead or in prison.

'What of the others?'

'About nine months ago,' said Genyen, 'I went to Lhasa. On the surface, life goes on as before, and although the Han are everywhere, they tread softly, treating the Kundun publicly with great respect, because of their fear of the people's loyalty to him. Yet, as always, they offer the honey on a sharp knife. The Han are suspicious of all Khambas in Lhasa, and I soon realised that I was being followed. So, I had to be careful. Dorje Rinposhay is safe and, like your pupils Jigme and Champa, is studying at Sera monastery. Your steward, Rinchen, is working as a teacher and Pema and the boy, Namgyal, were at one of the Han schools in Lhasa. So far, Samden told me, the Han have not discovered their identities. I heard of the death of the Honourable Mother.'

'She died very valiantly, Genyen. A truly Honourable Mother.'

One of Genyen's men came galloping towards them. He had been sent on ahead to scout for the party. As he drew near, he slowed his horse down to a trot and came up beside them.

He spoke in a murmured voice to Genyen. She was frowning.

'Go and join the other men,' she said to him. 'We will go on ahead to look for ourselves. Beckoning to Tsun to follow, she urged her horse into a gallop.

'It's a trap! Genyen shouted, reaching into her chuba for her revolver. 'It must be.' She raised her arm and made a wide slow sweep, encompassing all the thousands of pack animals. 'Look!'

There were yaks, donkeys, mules and sheep grazing and wandering among the scattered bales of wool, sacks of grain, painted chests and cupboards, lacquered tables, rugs and mattresses, copper pans and teapots, clay pots, wooden-bound scriptures, a child's carved wooden horse . . . people's lives abandoned among the camp fires on a carpet of budding yellow flowers.

Tsun scanned the distant foothills with Genyen's field glasses.

'If it is a trap,' he said. 'It is well concealed.'

'The best traps are.'

Tsun closed his heels on his mare's flanks, urging the animal on into the mysterious valley. Reluctantly, Genyen followed.

'I did not rescue you, Rinposhay, to have you captured again,' she grumbled, her eyes searching for the slightest sign of Han.

Tsun laughed. 'If you are frightened,' he said teasingly, 'go back.'

Genyen grunted. 'No one leaves all their possessions without reason.' She slipped her right leg over her horse's back, dropped to the ground, and picked up a four-foot long amber-studded sword. 'And it has to be a bad reason,' she continued.

She turned over the ashes of the camp fire with her foot, then bent down and felt them. She looked up at Tsun.

'Can you see anyone?'

Tsun shook his head. There was no sign of any other human being in the valley, alive or dead. Genyen looked into a clay cooking pot; the stew was covered with dust. Angrily, she knocked the pot off the hobstone and stood up.

'Tsun,' she said tensely. 'Someone has got their eyes on me . . . I know it!' Tsun laughed and pointed at the milling animals.

'There are your eyes,' he said. He walked his horse over to a line of tethered sheep with long curly fleeces, some black, some white.

'Whoever was here must have been about to break camp,' he murmured thoughtfully. 'Most of the animals are already loaded, but still tethered.'

Genyen walked over to the plaintively bleating sheep. As she sliced through their tethering ropes with a knife, she studied the grass round the sheep; there was still much to be cropped.

'They can only have been gone a few hours,' she said, cutting loose the leather packs of salt on the sheep's backs. Some were startled and tried to get away from her. Tsun showed her how it should be done by riding slowly along a line of tethered donkeys, freeing them from their loads, then cutting the tethering ropes. For a few moments he watched Genyen struggling with one of the sheep. She saw his mocking smile and made a rude gesture at him. He laughed, slid from his saddle and helped to hold the sheep while she cut the pack ropes.

They cantered on up the valley, scattering the frightened animals. Tsun smiled at the woman beside him.

'Genyen, to be free, after so long . . . to be free!' He almost sang the words. 'If you only knew how it feels to have a horse beneath me again, to ride where I want.'

They slowed down to a walk. A cloud of twittering sparrows rose from a torn grain sack as they approached.

'Sometimes I used to see a sparrow – not often, because we had to kill them as parasites – but sometimes I would see one winging up, flying this way, then that . . .' His face reflected the delight he had felt. 'Undecided, or just basking in the movements of the air. That was life, living. I was a dead man. I knew envy, really knew it, for the first time then.'

Genyen held his eyes with hers, but he was not seeing her as he re-lived the past.

'And . . . I knew despair.' He stopped suddenly, conscious of her. Genyen in that moment, realised that his tormented body was only a shadow of his mind.

'Look!' Tsun slowed his horse as they approached hundreds of saddled horses grazing at the end of the valley.

'Tsun, I tell you this valley is cursed!'

Genyen started to turn her horse, but Tsun rode on,

manoeuvring his way through the scattered bales of wool, lambskins, silk, brocade and satins.

'It reminds me,' she said, 'of the refugees we met so long ago, when . . .' She paused. 'It reminds me of what happened to us when the Han attacked. No one leaves their horses, all their possessions, like this, unless disaster has overtaken them.'

Tsun handed her the field glasses as they were jostled by the milling horses all around them.

'Look up there,' he said, pointing to the track leading from the alpine meadows as it wound high above the snow line. 'See how narrow the track is. Too narrow for animals. If the people were being pursued they would have to leave everything behind.'

'But why is there no sign of fighting? Surely someone, or some of the animals, would have been killed or wounded?'

'Perhaps there was no fight. They are refugees, Genyen. For refugees there is no way back.'

Genyen took off her fur hat, tucked it into her chuba and shook free her long black hair. The implications of what Tsun said only added to her unease.

'Well!' She spat into a yak chip fire. 'I don't like it. It isn't natural. If hundreds of people can be driven away, to leave their tea still warming on their fires, from the very saddles of their horses . . . what will happen to us, a handful?'

They sat together on a rock aflame with scarlet-coloured lichen; and in the pallid light of the watery yellow moon which hung like a melon slice in the sky, they watched Genyen's men and the freed prisoners get drunk on the barrels of arak and chang left lying about the valley.

'You have no confidence in my powers to protect you?' Tsun said with a grin.

'Of course, Rinposhay.' Genyen inclined her head in faintly mocking respect and sucked in her breath. 'So much, that I do not need to put it to the test.' She frowned as Brass Nose dropped his wooden tumbler and ran behind a rock.

'What is the matter with him, Tsun? That is the fifth time he has gone in an hour.'

Tsun drank some of the scalding tea, exulting in the richness and warmth of it. He had almost forgotten what real tea tasted like.

'Have you seen his gums and teeth? It is the disease of the camp. The food they gave us was unfit for animals. Perhaps, if we reach Lhasa in time, I can get some herbs there which will help him.'

Genyen inhaled some snuff, then handed the small jade snuff bottle to Tsun as she exhaled the fine powder through her mouth. Tsun took some snuff and, unused to it after three years, found it made his eyes water and his mind rock. For a moment he held his head, waiting for the effects to clear. Genyen chuckled and poured more tea into Tsun's bowl. One of the Khambas was playing a sad melody of lost love on a wooden flute.

'Tell me what happened after the Han attack,' Tsun said. 'We tried to find you but it was impossible.'

Genyen took some butter from a leather sack and rubbed it into a rag.

'After we were all separated,' she said, 'Tul-lok and I tried to find you, but there were Han everywhere and we ourselves only just managed to escape. Thousands were captured . . .'

'I know, I was among them.' Tsun shook some barley flour into his tsampa bowl and, with his fingers, mixed it with the dregs of his tea into a dough.

'I did not know if you were alive or dead,' Genyen continued, 'until I heard of you being a Thamzing victim at Chamdo.' She pushed the butter-soaked cloth into the hollow ramrod and worked it up and down the barrel of her musket.

'Here!' She put down the gun and, from a tiny cloth bag, sprinkled the rare delicacy of sugar into Tsun's bowl. He smiled his appreciation and their eyes lingered on each other as she said:

'I went to Chamdo to try and rescue you.'

Tsun chuckled. 'Genyen . . .' he murmured. The word was soft and loving as he reached out to stroke her head. Hers was a strong, wild beauty.

'But I could not find anyone who knew what had happened to you after the Thamzing.' Genyen went back to cleaning her musket and Tsun chewed his tsampa. He thought of telling her how Ling had saved his life, but decided against it.

'The Han knew that members of the resistance were hiding in Chamdo,' she said. 'And they were searching the houses. I had to leave, so I went to join my men at Lhargeri. Then Tul-lok got a message that the "son untamed" was alive, and we knew it must be you. Though it was difficult finding the camp.' She pulled the cloth out of the ramrod.

'Rinposhay?' Jettie sucked in his breath and bowed. 'Mo Mo!' With a wide grin he held out a clay dish of steaming hot dumplings. It took a few minutes for Tsun to emerge from so many memories. He reached to pick up some of the dumplings, but

Jettie produced a cylindrical silver and leather chopstick and knife case from his ambac. He handed it to Tsun.

'I found it in the valley, Rinposhay.' His voice faded. Tsun had crammed a dumpling into his mouth; hunger had so conditioned his mind, that his whole being was suffused in its richness. His fingers worked round his lips, ensuring not a morsel was wasted. When he had finished, he looked confused and angry at his reactions, the abandoned camp only adding to his sense of unreality. He lifted a second dumpling into his bowl with the ivory chopsticks, saying, 'Take some to Brass Nose. See that he has arak. Tend to him as you do to me, for I owe him much. And, Jettie' – the youth looked at him – 'You did not call me Rinposhay in the camp. I appreciate why you do it, but there is no need to now.' Jettie, his face serious, nodded at Tsun as he served Genyen and then Brass Nose on the other side of the fire.

'What of the petition?' Tsun asked after some minutes. 'And the gold?' He was aware of Genyen watching him thoughtfully as he sucked at the juicy meat-filled dumplings.

'I heard nothing of them after the attack,' said Genyen, slotting the ramrod back into the barrel of her gun. 'We thought the Han got them when they captured you.' Then she realised the implication of Tsun's question. 'Who did you give them to, Rinposhay?'

Tsun continued eating for a few minutes in bitter silence. 'How vain man is, Genyen.' His voice was low, but heavy with self-accusation. 'Of all the words uttered around our camp fires, Lopsang's alone have proved right.' He took another bite of dumpling. 'He warned me what the petition would cost. Even when his words were borne out during our escape, even when I heard of the destruction of Dorje Ri-gon, still, even then, I believed the petition was important, because so many people put their trust in it.'

'It was, and perhaps still is . . .'

'It has achieved nothing, as Lopsang prophesied. It has brought only suffering . . .' Why, he kept asking himself, had Pema not passed on the petition? Samden must have told her that Tul-lok and Genyen were at Lhargeri? She had had nine months to send a message to them. Why? Among the questions, one ever-recurring thought, like a heart beat, invaded his mind. Had Pema betrayed them and given the petition to the Han?

'Tsun . . .' Genyen's tone caught his attention. 'Who did you give the petition to?'

Tsun looked at her without speaking.

'Look!' Brass Nose yelled at Tsun as he came staggering out of the darkness followed by a group of former prisoners and Genyen's men, drunk and loaded with loot from the abandoned valley. 'I'm a Shapay!'

He had wrapped himself in gold brocade, which trailed out into the night and back to the bale. Brass Nose sat down heavily and tipped the contents of his ambac onto the ground. Laughing, he lifted up a leather bag of silver yuan and shook it over his head so that the coins rained down on him.

'It is all cursed.' Genyen picked over the jewelry and pouches of musk. She lifted the lid of a small cardboard box. 'Where did you get these?' she asked, holding up a bullet from the box of ammunition.

Brass Nose waved a bottle of whisky vaguely towards the darkness. Genyen pulled the bottle from his lips.

'Are there any more?' she demanded.

Brass Nose jerked his hand free, staggered with half closed eyes, and pointed to the boxes on the ground.

'Out there,' Genyen shouted, trying to reach his fuddled brain. 'Have you left any boxes behind?'

Almost unconscious, Brass Nose shrugged. Genyen growled curses at him as she undid the bandoliers around her waist and across her chest, and began loading them with bullets from the boxes of ammunition.

'There is probably enough wealth in this valley to make us the richest people in Tibet,' she mused. 'More than I have ever stolen in my whole life.' She sat hunched, not looking at Tsun as she spoke. 'Life has a lovely mouth, but a cold heart.' She looked across at him and grinned. 'Here is a lesson in the truth of the religion, Tsun.'

She watched him pick up one of the bandoliers and slip bullets into the narrow leather loops.

'O, ironic karma,' she said. 'Here am I, a bandit, given more treasures than I could imagine, yet what can I do with them? Where can I take them?'

Tsun laughed. 'For me, and for my friends from the camp,' he said, 'life has a warm heart . . . food, drink, horses . . .'

'Yes,' said Genyen. 'We need those horses, and, Kunjosum, how we need ammunition.'

'The musk and the gold and silver will buy it.'

'The wealth of the world will not buy us ammunition.'

'Why?' Tsun put down the full bandolier and tossed some yak chips onto the fire.

'Wangyal!' Genyen called.

The man, sitting a few feet away, answered by tossing a bag of popped barley into her hands.

'No one wants to know about us, Tsun. Seven months ago we sent an appeal, not for arms, just for people to listen to our plight. We sent it to many people like Prime Minister Nehru of India, the Queen of the Injis and . . .' Her brow furrowed. 'That place you were going to . . . the United Nations. Leaders of all provinces signed it. We sent out three hundred copies!' She handed the bag of popped barley to Tsun, who took some.

'What happened?'

'Nothing! Except India ordered our representatives in India to stop all political activity, with the threat of being handed over to the Han if they didn't obey.'

She threw some of the popped barley into her mouth and waved the bag at the valley. 'It is like the treasure out there. Victory is ours for the taking. We have a national resistance now – the Chushi-Gang-Druk – with proper headquarters at Lhargeri. From all over Tibet people are joining us. We still hold much of Kham, and most of Kongpo, U-Tsang and western Tibet, except for the cities. Even in Lhasa, there is now the Mimang Resistance Movement. We have stopped the building of the railway from China.' She held out the bag to Tsun again, and he took more of the popped barley. 'The Han have to move in massive convoys now, and even then we strike them, even garrisons, and now a labour camp! We've just blown up the Chamdo-Lhasa highway . . .' She laughed. 'A bridge! It will take them weeks to repair it. It was a waste of ammunition rescuing you all, but . . .' She grinned. 'I suppose we gained something.'

'So victory is within our grasp, if we had enough ammunition?'

Genyen nodded, then picked up a diamond ring from Brass Nose's loot.

'Anxiety destroys the Han . . .' Tsun quoted the old proverb. 'And hope destroys the Tibetans! The Han must be worried.'

'They arrest people and send them to China. So far, though, there have not been any attacks on monasteries or any Thamzings, in U-Tsang.' She chewed the barley. 'The Han are indeed worried. They have arrested a lot of the Tibetan cadres trained in China and replaced many of the Han officials.' She laughed. 'A few days ago we came across a group of Han civilians. They had no arms or food and were trying to walk back to China!'

'What did you do with them?'

'Gave them food and directions,' she grinned, showing her perfect white teeth. 'I do not mind helping the Han to leave Tibet.' She paused. 'A few weeks ago the Generals denounced the Tibetan Government at a meeting of the Women's Patriotic Association. They called the Shapays traitors to the Motherland, and said they would be publicly tortured.' She snorted disbelievingly and answered Tsun's look of reproach. 'Well, look at Shapay Ngabo. He makes no secret of his collaboration, few of the nobles do. Some of those vultures have got arms from India through their trading agents and are selling them to us at extortionate prices.'

Tsun pulled his sheepskin collar round his neck.

'They are as blind as you are, Genyen. The Han are clever, they feed on people's weaknesses, use them as weapons of self-destruction. Remember how, when they invaded, they promised the Panchen Rinposhay's followers and the Khamba clan princes greater freedom from Lhasa? And what happened? They used those wedges to cut Tibet in three . . . that was using our own provincial mistrust against ourselves. They will try and make the Tibetan Government distrust the resistance and the resistance mistrust the Tibetan Government.'

Genyen grunted, got up and walked over to a pile of loot her men had gathered from the valley. She returned with a pair of white and black felt boots.

'Try these, Tsun,' she said dryly.

'Only the Kundun is left,' Tsun said. 'And how long before the Han attack him? The Kundun is our weakest point at this moment.' Automatically, he untied the string round his tattered boots.

'Genyen?' His voice was urgent with the sudden realisation that all Tibet was poised on the edge of destruction.

Genyen looked at him with hard, bitter eyes. 'I know, we all know!' She took a bottle of whisky from Brass Nose's limp hand. 'It has gone too far, Tsun. There is no turning back now. My men, the thousands of men and women in the resistance, have nothing left now. Nothing left . . . but to fight.' She held out her hand and studied the effect of the diamond ring on her finger. 'A few weeks ago, the Kundun sent a delegation with a promise of amnesty from the Han if we stopped fighting.'

'What happened?'

There was a yell from the other side of the fire as Jettie held up a squirming three-foot long snake above the heads of the others around the camp fire. It was mottled green. He dropped it among them. With the flat of their daggers they tossed the snake back and forth, avoiding its lunging mouth.

'What happened?' Tsun repeated.

'We called off our attacks and talked. But most of us no longer have any homes to return to, and Han promises are like piecrusts.' Genyen threw a yak chip on the fire, it spluttered and flamed. 'Their promises are made to be broken. At the end of our talks . . .' she smiled emptily at Tsun, '. . . the delegation joined the resistance.'

The snake had at last managed to bite one of its tormentors. Tsun and Genyen watched as it was thrown away into the darkness and the man's wound attended to.

'What have *you* been during the last three years?' he asked.

Genyen grinned again. 'Fighting!' She poured him more tea. 'I went to India a few months ago for the Chul-Ka-Sum meeting.' She shook her head. 'Calcutta! So hot! And so many people, all rushing here and there.' Her grin widened. 'Tell no one of this?' Tsun shook his head.

'I was only in Calcutta for about two hours when all my baggage was stolen! I did not even see it go!' Not appreciating Tsun's laughter, she quickly changed the subject.

'I suggested at the meeting we had in Kalimpong with the Chul-Ka-Sum representatives, that we take over Kalimpong and Darjeeling and invade Bhutan and Sikkim. Then the world would have to take notice of us. We could have got fresh supplies of food and ammunition. Many agreed with me. But the U-Tsang people, the Mimang leaders, thought we should do it only as a last resort, and that at first we should send out the three hundred appeals.'

'Has there been *any* response?'

Genyen shook her head. 'No . . . and India has made it difficult for us even to have contact with any foreigners.'

'So?' Tsun drank from his bowl.

'Perhaps, Bhutan and Sikkim . . . I don't know . . . Tul-lok has gone to Lhasa to make plans with the Mimang.' She clenched her fist. 'We're so near to victory, Tsun. If only we had the ammunition. Thousands of Han civilians have been sent back home to China. Those that remain are discontented and want to return to their homeland.'

'The fleas! The fleas!' Brass Nose was kneeling on the ground, pulling off his sheepskin chuba and desperately searching the four-inch long wool. 'Yeshi Norbu!' He looked at Tsun. 'They have gone! There is not a flea in my coat, yet it was alive with them when I picked it up in the valley.'

Genyen stared at him as if he had gone mad.

'Do not worry, my friend.' Tsun took the bottle of whisky from Genyen and handed it back to Brass Nose. 'Tomorrow we shall ride to Lhasa and I shall get some herbs to help you.'

He turned to Genyen, and spoke softly. 'When even the fleas and bugs desert you, only Shensi, the Lord of Death, will receive you.' He looked at her for a long time. 'I learned much at the labour camp.' His voice had a gentle concern that chilled her. 'During my training under Dorje Rinposhay, I was in retreat for many months, entirely alone. My hermitage was built in such a way that all I could see was the sky through a small hole in the roof. Twice a week, food was pushed through a flap to me, and from that I could tell the number of days that passed. At first, they seemed never to pass – each minute was an hour – though I had a great deal of mental work and prostrations to do, to exercise my body and concentrate it on my meditation practice. Twice I thought I was going insane, for though Dorje Rinposhay said that my training would make use of the experience of the world I had gained as a layman, still, coming so late to the spiritual life, I did not have the discipline of one who has been brought up in a monastery, and I found it very difficult. But I was blessed in having the guidance of Dorje Rinposhay.' He paused. His gaze on Genyen's eyes was so penetrating that she wanted to look away but could not.

'In the labour camp, our only privacy was our minds, and the Han worked as hard on that as we did on their roads, to try to enter that last refuge. Yet I am grateful for the experience, for in a sense I was truly alone, nothing save the Guru in my heart. Remember what the Buddha said: "What is not useful to you, put aside." Tomorrow, Genyen, I shall choose the best horse I can find for our journey to Lhasa. But it is only through the actual journey that I shall know whether or not I have chosen the horse wisely. Only then will the horse be tried, as I was tried in that camp, as the teaching that has been entrusted to me has been tried, and worked. Lopsang used to say that I had entered the Robe with my body, but not my mind. Many said I was too old to cast off my old ways. Tullok . . .' He paused and smiled. 'You . . .'

Genyen opened her mouth to answer, but he continued talking.

'In small ways, I was able to help some of the people in the camp. The teaching I communicated brought some light into the darkness of their lives. That, Genyen, is what is important, more than a million petitions. All we have is ourselves and time. This life is such a rare opportunity.'

He had answered the question she had not asked. Genyen wrenched her eyes away and looked up at the weeping moon.

BOOK FOUR: March, 1959

'The officers of state, ecclesiastical and lay, will find their lands seized and their property confiscated and they themselves made to serve their enemies, or wander about the country as beggars do.'

POTALA PALACE AND THE GREAT CHORTEN FORMING THE WESTERN GATE TO LHASA

Chapter Twenty-Eight

The young Han pilot of the Yun-5 reconnaissance bi-plane had been instructed to ascertain the disposition of the thousands of refugees from east Tibet who were encamped around Lhasa, doubling the population. Many were known to be active in the resistance and the Han feared demonstrations during the Kundun's religious examinations. He banked and crossed the Happy River which cut straight through the wide vale of Lhasa, to circle the close-packed town of adobe and stone two- and three-storeyed houses. Most had been freshly whitewashed for the New Year and had new prayer flags fixed at the corners of the flat roofs.

The narrow lanes of the market, most of the town's streets, and the refugee camp, were deserted. Virtually the entire population was attending the Kundun's examinations. Thousands were in the courtyard of the Jo-Khang, the oldest and holiest temple in Tibet. Thousands more were in the square outside the four-storeyed, gilt-roofed building and lined the route to the summer palace.

The pilot followed the processional route from the city, as it crossed the turquoise-roofed bridge of a tributary of the Happy River into New Lhasa. High walls surrounded the new Han barracks, hospital and administrative offices, the only buildings with high-pitched roofs. The new Han section of the city steadily encroached on the meadow land between the old city and the Potala.

The Potala Palace never failed to impress the pilot. In a country where nature dominated man with the vast beauty of mountain, plain and valley, man, he thought, had contrived to produce something as awesome, but which did not compete with nature. Indeed, it seemed almost part of it. With its sloping granite walls, the Potala appeared to grow from the hill on which it was built in the centre of the valley. Tier upon tier of sweeping white walls; at each end of the nine hundred-foot building great defensive turrets, each of the flat-roofed tiers leading subtly to the highest at the centre, the Red Palace, surmounted by golden pagoda roofs. The village of Sho, as the buildings at the foot of the Potala were known, was a traditional site for public gatherings, and the pilot had been warned that this was the most probable starting point for any demonstration. As instructed, he studied the crowd with field glasses, but all looked peaceful, he thought, as he flew over the Great Chorten, with its gilded spire, forming the city's main gate. He remembered the first time he had walked through it: the impact of the Potala rising above him and the distant golden roofs of the temple in the heart of the city. He knew nothing of Buddhism, but could understand the feelings of the pilgrims who had walked with him.

The crowds were even greater for the last mile leading to the Norbulinka Park where the Kundun had his summer palace. The pilot straightened up and prepared for his approach to the airstrip close to the Han Army Administrative Headquarters of the Tibet Military Area Command. In his unarmed reconnaissance plane, carefully chosen not to give an impression of an armed patrol, the pilot would have been astonished at the wake of anger and resentment left by his flight over Lhasa, which was seen as a calculated insult to Tibet. For it was the custom that, out of respect, none should be higher than the Kundun, and whenever he passed in procession people left the upper floors of their houses so as not to overlook him.

Tsun watched the clouds of yellow butterflies as they hovered, then settled, on the clumps of anemones and primulas. All the time he was aware of how much the labour camp had conditioned its inmates, of the narrowing of perspectives. No one but Jettie and Brass Nose could really understand how he felt about being able to watch butterflies for as long as he chose. A lark, its crest raised in anticipation, moved cautiously forward to seize an insect from the potted plants, but was startled by the low flight of the bi-plane. It flew from the five-hundred foot balustrade of one of the Potala's flat roofs, into the translucent blue sky where swifts curved and wove an invisible web. For an instant, Tsun remembered again the longing with which he had watched the free flight of birds when he was in the labour camp. He still found freedom strange, fascinating, as almost his every action and thought served to underline it. He felt reborn, as if in a new life, and yet it was like stepping back in time. For though Han convoys of trucks, jeeps with mounted machine guns, and armoured cars were constantly entering and leaving the enormous compound of the Tibet Area Military Command, it was still Lhasa, the Holy City.

Brass Nose was going through his sheepskin chuba which he had laid out on the balustrade, but the fleas had not returned.

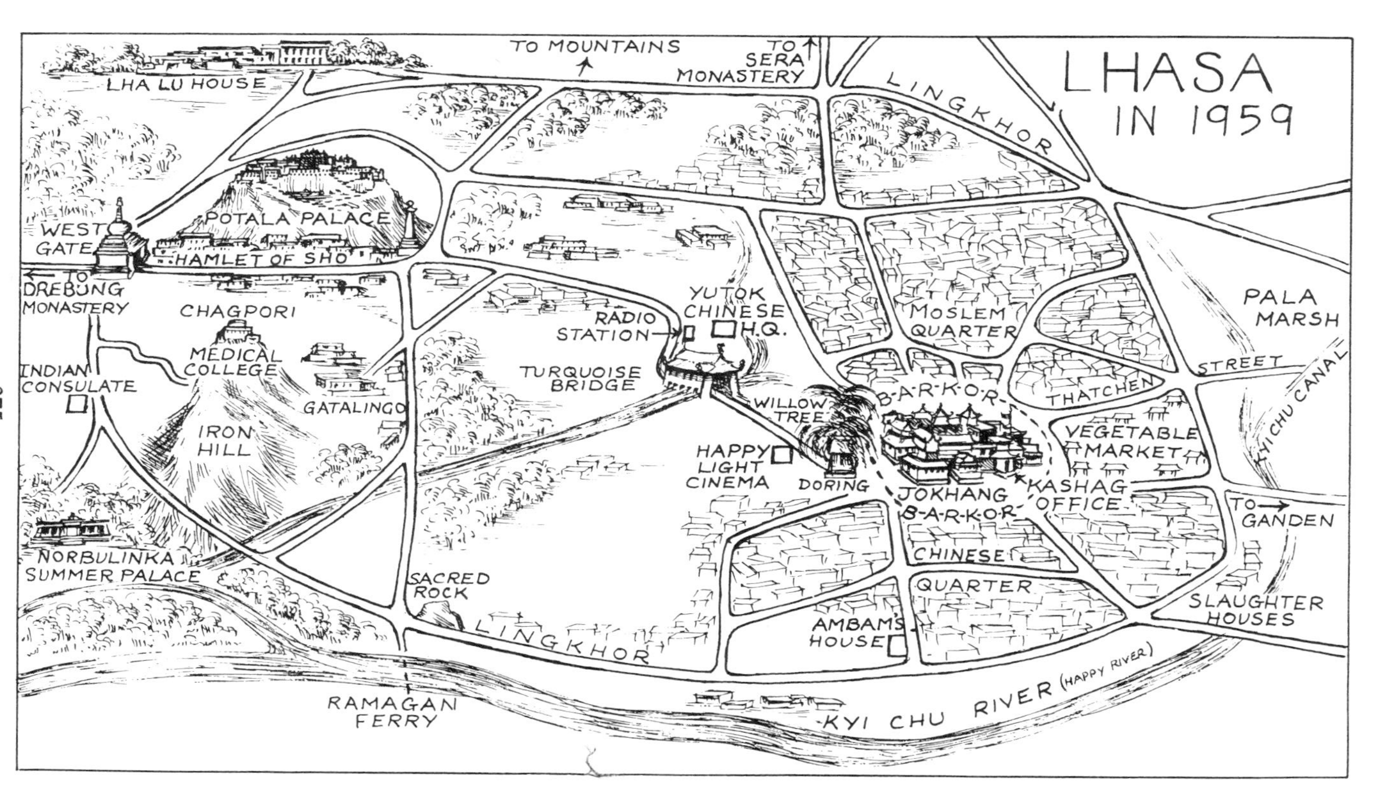
LHASA IN 1959
TO MOUNTAINS
TO SERA MONASTERY
LINGKHOR
LHA LU HOUSE
POTALA PALACE
WEST GATE
HAMLET OF SHO
TO DREBUNG MONASTERY
CHAGPORI
MEDICAL COLLEGE
INDIAN CONSULATE
GATALINGO
IRON HILL
NORBULINKA SUMMER PALACE
RADIO STATION
YUTOK
CHINESE H.Q.
TURQUOISE BRIDGE
WILLOW TREE
HAPPY LIGHT CINEMA
DORING
MOSLEM QUARTER
B-A-R-K-O-R
THATCHEN
PALA MARSH
STREET
KYICHU CANAL
VEGETABLE MARKET
JOKHANG
B-A-R-K-O-R
KASHAG OFFICE
TO GANDEN
CHINESE QUARTER
SLAUGHTER HOUSES
SACRED ROCK
LINGKHOR
AMBAM'S HOUSE
RAMAGAN FERRY
KYI CHU RIVER (HAPPY RIVER)

Clouds of incense rose from bonfires of fragrant-smelling leaves lit by the crowds lining the two-mile route from the Jo-Khang Cathedral, waiting to pay homage to the Kundun. For although the outside world knew him as the Dalai Lama, Sovereign of Tibet, those lining the route essentially revered him as the Presence, the Kundun, of the Lord of Compassion, Chenresi, Patron of Tibet.

Tsun focused the field glasses on the head of the procession as it left the Jo-Khang. The monks, with clashing cymbals and deep throbbing drums, the melody sustained by trumpets and oboes; the twelve-foot long drone trumpets, their bell-shaped ends supported by young novice monks, coming in at the climax with their deep, reverberating notes. Genyen joined Tsun and Brass Nose.

'Why are we here, Genyen?' Tsun asked. She had insisted as soon as they came through the western gate of the city that Tsun should go with her to the Potala and had immediately disappeared into the vast building, having despatched Jettie on a secret mission to the city.

Genyen leaned on the balustrade next to him. She was wearing crossed cartridge belts over her fleece-lined satin-figured chuba that only just covered her copper-gold shoulders.

'There is someone I want you to meet,' she said. 'It is safe here.'

'Safe?' Brass Nose looked up from his sheepskin chuba and grunted. 'I don't like it.'

Genyen ignored him, but she, too, felt uneasy at the apparent discourtesy to the Kundun, sharpened by her anger at the Han plane flying over his procession.

Tsun did not hear the soft footsteps behind him. Then every nerve tensed as he felt a gun barrel pressed into his back. His hand slipped towards his ambac for the revolver which Genyen had given him, then stopped. Slowly, he lowered his field glasses and turned his head.

'You are no Khamba, cousin,' Tul-lok grinned as he slipped the Mauser into his chuba. 'I made enough noise to wake a whole camp.'

'Tul-lok!' The two men wept openly as they clasped one another. Tul-lok looked much the same, except that his close-cropped hair was greying and his copper-tanned face even more lined. He was still wearing his trilby and long turquoise and gold earring. Kesang was with him, and Tsun recognised him immediately, even though three years in a boy's life can change him beyond recognition. His delight on seeing Tsun faded momentarily, and in his eyes Tsun saw mirrored what three years in a labour camp had done to him. Kesang flushed with embarrassment as he realised that Tsun had noticed his reaction. The boy took his outstretched hands and burst into tears. Tsun was aware that the almost physical pain of bereavement, which had been with him since his capture some three years before, had gone.

Kesang was balancing on an incense jar so that he could see over the balustrade to watch the procession.

'Genyen has told me of your successes against the Han,' Tsun said over the boy's head to Tul-lok. 'I have heard some of the songs telling of your exploits!' He adjusted the field glasses for Kesang.

'To have heard this from Genyen is indeed a compliment,' Tul-lok smiled mockingly at the girl.

'What news do you have, Tul-lok?' Tsun asked his cousin.

'My exploits make many legends, but they seem to do little else. That . . .' Tul-lok pointed towards the Kundun's procession making its way through New Lhasa from the Turquoise Bridge, '. . . is where the fate of our country lies.'

'What is happening at the religious examinations?' Kesang asked Tsun.

'It will be like those you watched with me at Dorje Ri-gon and Litang,' said Tsun. 'Every year debates are held at the Jo-Khang for three weeks. Only this year's debates are of vital importance to the nation.'

'Because the Kundun is being examined?'

'Yes,' Tsun said. 'For though we revere him as the presence of Chenresi, he is still a man.'

Somehow, to the others, the word seemed slightly blasphemous. It was hard to think of the Kundun as being an ordinary mortal. Brass Nose polished his nose with his thumb and forefinger as he listened to Tsun.

'As an ordinary monk,' Tsun continued, 'he steps down from his throne and joins in dialectical debate with the country's leading minds, for hours and days.'

'They are the same as my practice sessions?' asked the boy.

Tsun chuckled. 'Just like you, he has had to learn the same stylised gestures of emphasis, to memorise the texts, to train his reasoning. But while you practised with a few dozen watching, the Kundun is surrounded by his examiners, watched by the entire Government and thousands of monks and laymen. Both for the country's temporal and spiritual welfare, much depends on the outcome of the examination, especially at this critical time in our history.'

Tul-lok put an arm round the boy's shoulder.

'There are those,' he said conspiratorially, '. . . in the Kundun's Court, who watch to see how he will withstand the pressure of the arguments. Whether he is decisive or not could be of importance to an official seeking to influence the Kundun.'

'To have the lama's ear . . .' Kesang murmured the old proverb. Tul-lok laughed.

'The Han, too,' he added, 'are well aware of the importance of the result of the examination for their own plans.'

Tsun realised how much Tul-lok had changed. The brigand was of long ago. He had all the weariness of a resistance leader.

The head of the procession reached the hamlet of Sho at the foot of the Potala. It reflected the structure of power, before the occupation, being led by the Monastic Civil Service in ascending order of rank.

Kesang looked in wonder on the procession as it moved, at walking pace, beneath them; in the distance shone the golden palanquin.

'Have you heard about the Han broadcast?' Tul-lok looked at Tsun, who shook his head and handed the field glasses back to Kesang so that he could get a better view. The spontaneous smile of affection in the boy's eyes told him that the shock and embarrassment, the barrier of the years, was gone. They were at ease again.

'Peking Radio,' Tul-lok pulled at his earlobe, 'has been broadcasting that the Kundun will be attending the People's Consultative Congress in Peking.'

'Kunjosum! They must be mad!' Genyen said disbelievingly.

'But the Kundun,' Tul-lok continued, 'has not accepted the invitation.' They looked at one another as they thought of the implications, but it was Tsun who voiced their fears.

'To announce publicly that the Kundun is going, the Han must be sure that they can make him attend the Congress, or they want an excuse to bring about the final confrontation.'

'For the Kundun not to attend after announcing that he would, would be a terrible loss of face,' Tul-lok murmured, offering Tsun some snuff.

'Too terrible,' replied his cousin, taking some of the powder. He helped Kesang to focus the glasses.

'Perhaps the Han are just stupid,' said Genyen. She was slumped on the balustrade with her chin resting on her folded arms.

'In Tibet, yes,' said Tsun. 'But in Peking, no!' He paused. 'Although the generals here tell Peking what they think it wants to hear.'

'What is the difference?' Genyen snapped irritably.

'Perhaps none. Perhaps all the difference,' said Tsun.

Tsun helped Kesang up onto the wide balustrade so that he could have a better view of the procession now moving past the Potala. Genyen came up beside him and handed Tsun her field glasses.

'Have you noticed anything?'

Tsun took the glasses and after a few minutes, handed them back to Genyen.

'There are no Han in the procession.'

Brass Nose looked at her enquiringly.

'For the past eight years,' Genyen explained, 'the Han have taken part in the procession, ever since the occupation.'

'Why not this year?' asked Tsun without looking up. Genyen shrugged. Like most of the Han actions, it could mean much or little.

'Look! There is Ngabo!' Tul-lok seized the glasses from Genyen and focused them on the gold-robed Cabinet Minister who had become notorious throughout Tibet for his collaboration. He rode beside the Kundun's palanquin.

'Tsun,' Tul-lok spoke while still looking through the field glasses. 'I have been talking to members of the Assembly and they feel that you should talk with the Kundun as soon as possible.' He realised that Tsun was not listening.

'Look, Tul-lok!' Tsun pointed and Tul-lok followed the direction with his glasses. Amongst the senior members of the Monastic Civil Service was the lanky, slightly stooping figure of Lopsang. Genyen took the glasses from Tul-lok and swiftly focused them on Tsun's former secretary.

'He has been useful to the Han,' she said bitterly. 'I've heard it said that he's been made a member of the Preparatory Committee for the Autonomous Region of Tibet.'

'A man of influence,' Tsun murmured.

Tul-lok grunted. 'Genyen told me that it was Lopsang who betrayed you. Now he rides with the Kundun, and Ngabo, the Cabinet Minister, is now a General in the People's Liberation Army.'

'What good is it going to do, my seeing the Kundun?' asked Tsun.

'The Court hasn't changed. Politics lie behind a morning's greeting,' said Tul-lok. 'I remember being warned that, at Court, one should keep a blank face and tell little, for the walls have ears to listen. Some of the nobles continue their games. They accept Han positions, and then sell bullets to the resistance at high prices. They tell the Kundun what they think he wants to hear. From you he will learn something of the truth.'

Tsun could understand the Khambas' mistrust of the nobles. 'But surely,' he looked at Genyen, 'others have told him? Thousands of refugees have camped in Lhasa.'

'Of course, Rinposhay,' Genyen agreed. 'But you are well known, your mission is well known.'

Tsun laughed. 'Too well known as it proved.'

They fell silent as the Kundun's palanquin, small and toylike from their vantage point, drew level with the Potala. No one focused their field glasses on the smiling youth within the palanquin. Like the thousands lining the route, they had their heads bent in veneration before the embodiment of the Lord of Compassion, the Gentle Glory, the Kundun.

'Rinposhay, what happened to the petition?' Tul-lok enquired. 'What happened to the gold?'

Tsun caught Genyen's eye and looked away.

'Before I was captured,' he replied, 'I gave both to someone.'

'Who?' Tul-lok sensed Tsun's hesitation. 'We need that gold desperately. Is there any chance of getting it back?'

Tsun sighed as he watched the procession moving through the Great Chorten forming the city's main gate.

'Perhaps,' he said. 'Give me a day or two.'

'We have so little time.' Tul-lok gripped Tsun's arm. The Abbot could not remember ever seeing him so anxious.

'Up here we have the best vantage point for seeing everything of the procession but we miss what everyone is talking about down there,' Genyen frowned.

Tul-lok was still looking anxiously at Tsun. 'During the Kundun's examinations at the Jo-Khang, two junior Han officers forced their way into his presence to give him an invitation to a show in the Military Compound.'

'What else is there that we have not heard about yet,' Genyen said angrily, but not at Tul-lok.

'You see, Tsun, why we must be ready?'

'Yes, but I must have a day or two. I believe the gold is safe, but I cannot be sure.'

'Who did you give it to, Rinposhay?' Genyen pleaded, then wished she had not spoken as he turned to look at her. Then the expression in his eyes changed. Genyen's hand moved towards the gun in her ambac, but Tsun put out a hand to restrain her.

'What are you doing here?' The sharp, heavily accented voice shot fear through them all and they turned to see a PLA officer standing a few feet away.

'Like you,' Tsun spoke in his best Chinese, and with equal authority, 'we have been watching the procession. And you? Do you have an invitation? I am sure General Chang Ching-wu would not be pleased to learn that one of his officers had been discourteous enough to wander into the palace of the Kundun as if it were a public place. Especially . . .' he went on, as the man began to speak, 'at such a delicate time as the eve of the Kundun's departure for Peking.'

The officer hesitated, and his hand dropped to rest on his holster.

'How is it that the greatest families in the land move to their ground floors out of respect for the Kundun, and yet you . . .' he eyed the disreputable group around him, 'can stay up here?'

The pause was too long.

'They are here at my request,' said a firm, assured voice. A man stepped forward from the shadow of a carved wooden doorway. His maroon robe was edged with the brocade of a member of the Monastic Civil Service. The officer knew that their monastery was in the middle of the Potala and recognised the old man with the large goitre overlapping the neck of his robe, as a member of one of the administrative committees. He hesitated, then nodded curtly and turned and walked away. They watched his receding figure, conscious of his disbelief.

'Come!' The lama beckoned the group to follow him through the dark passages of the Potala, lit only by the occasional butter or mustard lamp.

The outside of the Potala was built with wide, simple lines, but inside it was a maze of thousands of rooms, chapels and halls, the decorations similarly contrasting in their brilliance and complexity, whether a wall fresco or the carved and painted capital of a wooden pillar. The brilliant colours were muted by the poor lighting.

Tsun took Kesang's hand and stopped opposite the glass-covered imprint of two hands in the plaster of the walls.

'The hands of the Great Thirteenth Kundun,' he whispered.

The entire party stopped to touch the case reverently with their foreheads, then they went on down the steep, worn wooden steps of the largest palace in the world, into a reception hall, part in shadow and part in sunlight, one end of the hall forming a shrine-cum-balcony round the high mausoleum chorten of the former Dalai Lama.

The lama motioned Tsun and Tul-lok to a rug-covered divan with a long, low table set before it, while Kesang explained to Genyen and Brass Nose the scroll paintings, frescoes and magnificent hangings covering the red lacquered pillars. The elderly lama had a habit of fingering his goitre, as though to relieve the discomfort it caused. Tsun waited for the introductions.

'It is better for the moment if you do not know my name,' the lama said. 'In time you will learn.'

'You put me at a disadvantage . . .' Tsun caught Genyen's eye as she nodded to vouch for the lama's integrity. They watched as he took a cloth and lifted a copper and silver teapot from a brass filigree brazier, pouring tea into three jade teacups.

'Rinposhay,' he said, 'you must try the Inji tea. I have made it especially for you.'

He poured milk into each cup and offered a bowl of sugar cubes to the two men. Tul-lok followed Tsun's example and took two. The three men drank. Tul-lok winced at the taste. The lama dispensed with the usual polite enquiries, which meant that his business was very serious.

'As you know, Rinposhay, when our country is faced with an emergency, the National Assembly is convened. To do this now would be impossible, so we do what we can. I have been asked by some of the leading members to see you, because we have heard of your mission for Kham.' He paused for Tsun to speak but the Abbot remained impassive.

'Also,' the lama continued, 'we know that you have knowledge of India, of the Injis, and speak their language. We all work at different levels,' he continued. 'The great heights, Rinposhay, are for the birds of heaven, while the rock crevices are the hiding places of the grouse. Which are we?' He sipped his tea noisily, looked at Tsun, and laughed. 'Good?'

Tsun nodded and smiled. 'Excellent.'

The lama was pleased. The tea tasted only vaguely like English tea, but to have said so would have been grossly rude.

'Who can say,' Tsun said, 'whether we can be like the birds who have the whole of heaven as their limit, or whether we are to be like the scuttling grouse, ill-equipped for flight, searching for rocky clefts?'

The lama re-filled Tsun's teacup. 'From the State Archives, we are preparing a dossier of documents which make our claim to independence irrefutable. We have had scholars working on the manuscripts for months.'

Tsun shook some snuff onto his thumbnail from the silver bottle he had borrowed from Genyen.

'The manuscript must be taken to India for safe-keeping, and must be shown to the rest of the world,' the lama said.

Tsun inhaled the snuff and exhaled a thin cloud of smoke through his mouth. Far away they could hear the music of the procession, and the scuttling rustle of a mouse made Brass Nose reach for his gun. Tsun realised the risk the lama was taking. If the Han knew that the National Assembly was preparing evidence for another appeal to the United Nations, it would be enough excuse for them to take over completely.

'You are trusted and highly regarded by both the Khamba resistance and the Mimang, so if you consented to take the documents, it would ensure maximum co-operation among our people, and that you spoke for all Tibet.'

'There are others,' Tsun said wearily.

'Who, Rinposhay?' the lama demanded. 'We have so little time. The Han have been constantly urging us during the last few months to loan the Central People's Government all our documents relating to the borders with Ladakh, Nepal, Sikkim, Bhutan and India. They say they want them for an exhibition.'

Tul-lok laughed. 'They would never return to Tibet!'

'Chang Ching-wu,' the lama continued, nodding in agreement, 'tells us that the lost territories on our borders will be returned to the Motherland. For this, he only needs his army, but the documents could be used to substantiate their claim, and even more, they are aware that the documents also substantiate our independence and power to make treaties.'

'Is there no way of hiding them?' Tsun asked.

Tul-lok was surprised at his cousin's apparent lack of enthusiasm.

'Some of the early records weigh eighty pounds each, and apart from the physical difficulties of moving them, everyone is watched now.' The lama shrugged helplessly. 'I do not even know what spies there are among those sorting the documents. It is difficult. Yesterday, a directive from the State Council itself was given to the National Assembly.'

Tsun put down his teacup and replaced the lid. 'The original documents are to be sent to Peking?'

'They will not accept copies.'

'Can you not say that they are too valuable to be moved?'

'The Kundun himself could not get the directive altered. Quite openly, Chang Ching-wu has had an inventory made of the gold reserves at the Jo-Khang. He says that it is in case of war with India, but already the Kundun has been virtually forced to make "patriotic" gifts from his own treasury towards China's foreign aid programme, whatever that means.'

'Will the documents be in manuscript?'

'Yes, Rinposhay, and some of the very important ones will be originals.'

'One man can carry them?'

The lama nodded. 'You will take them for us?'

'Yes.'

A spider dropped down from the darkness of the rafters, slipped on the edge of Tul-lok's cup and fell into the dregs. Carefully Tul-lok lifted the drowning insect onto the table.

Chapter Twenty-Nine

Lhasa City

The thousands of monks coming out of the Jo-Khang Cathedral joined with the milling crowds of laymen in the square and side streets containing the market and bazaar of the small capital city. If religion was the first subject of national interest, commerce was the second. Despite the crush, every purchase, from apples, meat, vegetables, a thermos flask, to coral, turquoise and fox pelts, was bargained for by monk and layman alike.

The owner of a small shop, just off the Barkor Square, outside the Jo-Khang, was doing well with his plastic toothbrushes. Like all the buildings, the shop had the same inward-sloping walls and narrowing windows, which helped to retain the heat and catch the sun, and the same deep-set window frames outlined in black, their sills laden with flowers in pots and tins.

Pemba, the shop-keeper, had a perfectly bald head. His face, deeply tanned and lined, with a wispy, irregular white beard, was unusually animated as he discussed with a customer the Han invitation to the Kundun, while selling him a bunch of radishes the size of turnips from the hammock-style shelf.

Tsun looked through the torches, cigarettes, shoes, and other sundry items heaped on the trestle table and, picking up a toothbrush, let the bristles run across the ball of his thumb as he indicated to Pemba that he wanted to buy it. Putting his hand into his ambac, Tsun realised that he had no money whatsoever. Nor had he anything he could barter with. Kesang emerged from the crowd of people offering Pemba Han yen. Pemba was embarrassed that he had not recognised his guests and didn't want to take the money Kesang offered for Tsun's toothbrush.

Tul-lok put his arm round the man's shoulders and, ducking under the shirts and green and blue caps strung across the door lintel, swiftly manoeuvred him inside so that his welcome was not too public.

'Pemba, here are Tsun Rinposhay and Brass Nose, about whom Jettie will have told you.'

The man nodded and, bowing, offered Tsun a felicity scarf.

'Dorje Rinposhay you know, and Genyen.'

Pemba greeted them, hesitating only at Brass Nose.

'Did Jettie arrange for the others to be here?'

Pemba nodded. He was about to speak when he heard a scrabbling on the steep ladder which led to the roof, and Tsun was almost knocked off his feet as Senge hurled himself at the Abbot. The dog did not bark, merely nuzzling and licking him in excitement as Tsun lifted the dog up in his arms. He could hardly believe that the little dog had survived the Han attack. He had hoped, but never really thought, that he would see Senge again.

Kesang stroked the dog in Tsun's arms. 'Always, when I lost hope that I would ever see you again . . . Senge always told me we would.'

Tsun saw the figure of a monk silhouetted in the shaft of light slanting down from the trapdoor to the roof. As the figure descended the steep ladder, without having to see his face, he knew that it was Rinchen. The steward clasped his hands. Rinchen's emotional and delighted welcome surprised and moved Tsun deeply.

Pemba's wife and his son, Thubten, were setting out sweet-breads on the low tables which had been placed before the rugs carefully laid on the flat roof. A wisp of smoke snaked into the sunlit sky from the smouldering juniper leaves in the incense vase. Two of the men on the roof wore robes, a third a Han grey cotton jacket and trousers, well cut and well pressed. All three looked uneasy and tense.

As the newcomers emerged onto the roof of the small shop in the heart of the noisy Lhasa bazaar, the young men's greetings to Tul-lok, Genyen and Kesang were formal and nervous and, in the silence as he too stepped onto the roof, Tsun was aware of the strength of emotion; of a solemnity as deep as anything he had ever experienced at Dorje Ri-gon. His three pupils all felt the same mixture of delight and pain on seeing the evident effect of the labour camp. Tsun was struck by how much they had matured in three years. They were all now men.

Offering felicity scarves in greeting, the three pupils bowed in reverence, not looking at Tsun. Rinchen conducted him to one of the rugs, with Kesang beside him. Pemba's wife could not stop crying as she poured them all tea. Samden, Jigme and Champa sat on rugs with their eyes down. Tsun sipped his tea, settled Senge on his crossed legs, and began chanting the invocation of Chenresi:

'Om Mani Padme Hum . . . Om Mani Padme Hum . . .' Everyone joined in the invocation and meditation as he sought to tap and release the energy in the emotionally charged group. When he concluded there was a noticeable relaxation and a sudden ability to weep and laugh. He looked at his three pupils.

'You are at Sera Monastery with Dorje Rinposhay and Rinchen?'

'Except for Samden,' the steward answered for them.

Samden's lips tightened. 'I am a non-party cadre,' he said. 'I am trained in administration. I do not belong to the Party.'

Tsun noticed Samden's obvious embarrassment and, as Pemba's wife poured more tea, he turned the conversation away.

'Thank you for your hospitality,' he said. 'It cannot be easy.' He saw that she seemed nervous of Brass Nose who was smiling, showing his two remaining front teeth which stuck out in macabre fashion from his blackened gums. Tsun put an arm round his shoulders.

'To Brass Nose,' he said, 'I owe my life. When you care for him you care for me.'

Brass Nose looked at Tsun with sly eyes.

'I only stay with you,' he said, 'to make sure that our bargain is fulfilled.' Tsun laughed and slapped him on the back, and Pemba's wife made a point of offering him tea with all the subtle movements and words accorded to an honoured guest.

'We thought you must be dead, Rinposhay,' said Rinchen. 'I couldn't believe it when I received the message.' He nodded at Jettie. 'He told us something of the labour camp.'

'His telling will have been far better than mine,' sighed Tsun. Samden offered biscuits and fruit and Tsun took some of the food.

'What has happened to Dorje Ri-gon House?' he enquired.

'When we arrived, we found it had been requisitioned.' Rinchen spoke in a low voice. 'Very few people know that Dorje Rinposhay is here. It seemed safer that way.'

'And my sister, Pema?'

Rinchen drank some tea. 'She works at the new radio station. She announces.'

Tsun nodded, but made no comment. 'And Namgyal?'

'He is at the Han school. All youngsters have to go unless they are registered at a monastery.'

'Namgyal is perhaps not cut out for the monastic life,' Tsun chuckled. 'What do they teach at this school?'

Rinchen shrugged. 'Pemba's wife would know. Namgyal stays with her, as does Pema.'

Tsun looked at the woman.

'Yesterday we were talking, Rinposhay, and he said that in the morning they had a class on . . .' she struggled to remember the words. 'On the historical inevitability of Communism, and in the afternoon they had to kill flies, which was to help them be part of the working masses.'

'Kill flies!' Rinchen sounded incredulous.

'The Han,' she continued, '. . . said they were harmful, and the children had to see who could kill the most.'

Rinchen could not conceal his horror. Automatically one avoided killing any insect, as it was a sentient being which had its own particular karma to live out, and the thought of training the youth of the country systematically to wipe out such beings horrified him. He was angrier than Tsun had ever known him.

Rinchen was one monk. In the streets of Lhasa were some seventeen thousand monks from the three monastic universities, come into the city for the great Annual New Year Prayer Festival and the religious examination of the Kundun. Their resentment at the Han occupation had grown into a dangerous anger with the news the Khamba refugees brought of the atrocities in east Tibet.

Samden leaned across the table to speak to Genyen and Tul-lok.

'Have you heard the news,' he said, 'of the Chushi-Gang-Druk butter lamp?'

They shook their heads. Tul-lok was trying to light his pipe from the brazier. Genyen chuckled at his ineffectual attempts and tried to help him.

'What butter lamp is this? she asked.

'It is very special,' Samden continued. 'Most of the members of the Chushi-Gang-Druk helped to pay for this special lamp for the Jo-Khang, to be a perpetual reminder of their fight. It had to have the largest bowl – ' Samden illustrated the size of the goblet with his hands ' – and the thinnest stem, and to be of the purest gold.'

'Well?' Genyen said.

'So one day it leans one way, and the next the other,' he chuckled. 'Because it is top heavy.'

Tul-lok pulled thoughtfully at his pipe and shook his head.

'It is very inauspicious,' he said. Samden began to wish that he hadn't bothered to tell the story. He fell silent and looked over the edge of the roof.

'Tul-lok, look!' He pointed down at the street. Tul-lok followed the young man's gaze in time to see a Han officer lean his bicycle against the shop and go inside. Pemba shouted up the stairs to his wife.

'It is Captain Chan.'

Pemba's wife hurried to the steps and disappeared down them. Tsun looked enquiringly at Samden.

'The Captain is very helpful and friendly,' he said. 'He may have brought some news.'

'Tul-lok,' Tsun pointed to the adjoining roof separated from them by a narrow alley, 'if you have to escape . . . I'm going down into the shop.' He went swiftly down the ladder, followed, before he could be stopped, by Kesang.

Inside the shop, the Captain was talking to Pemba and his wife. He pointed to some packs of English cigarettes.

'Are these really aphrodisiac?' he asked.

'Who told you that?' Pemba asked, then frowned at his son. 'Thubten!' The boy looked acutely embarrassed.

'How much are they?' the Captain asked.

Pemba told him the price and the Captain took some money from his wallet, paid for the cigarettes and gave the change to Thubten.

'No! No!' Pemba insisted. 'It will only encourage him.'

'I have children of my own,' the Captain smiled.

Tsun and Kesang entered the shop, followed by Samden.

'When is Thubten going back to school?' the Captain asked.

'Next week.'

'And the younger one?' The Captain looked at Kesang.

'He is going to Sera,' Pemba replied.

The Captain bought some Indian sweets and gave them to the boys, then he put his hand on Kesang's shoulder.

'It would be good for the boy to go to school in Kalimpong, too,' he said, his words heavy with meaning. 'It would be good if you could *all* go on pilgrimage to India, do you not agree?'

'Yes . . .' Pemba murmured shakily.

'Then, my friend,' the Captain said in his heavily accented Tibetan. 'Go now!'

There was a shocked silence. The Captain looked at his watch, picked up the cigarettes and walked to the shop entrance. He looked back.

'Tashi Deleg.' He murmured the Tibetan words used in greeting and farewell.

They all watched him duck under the curtain of shirts over the doorway and be lost to view as he pushed his bicycle into the milling crowd.

'Kunjosum! what are we going to do?' Pemba's wife cried.

Pemba motioned to her to be silent, and led the group back onto the roof where they joined Tul-lok, Genyen and Brass Nose. Pemba glanced round at the neighbouring roofs to make sure that he would not be overheard.

'A Han officer we know very well,' he said quietly, 'has just warned us to leave Tibet for India immediately.'

His wife groaned, shaking her head in anxiety.

'Is this officer to be trusted?' snapped Genyen.

'Completely,' Pemba answered. 'He must know something is going to happen.'

'It was a tremendous risk for him to take,' said Tul-lok. 'You could be informers.'

'He likes my boy, Thubten,' said Pemba. 'He reminds him of his own son.' He turned to his wife. 'We must leave as soon as possible.'

'But what of the shop?' she said.

'We'll just have to close it. I'll ask a neighbour to watch it for us. I shall tell him we are taking Thubten back to school in Kalimpong and may continue on pilgrimage.'

'Kunjosum!' his wife moaned again. 'How can we leave everything? What if we cannot come back? We shall have nothing.'

'We shall have our lives,' Pemba said. 'And we shall take money.' His wife put her hands to her face and began to cry.

'Pemba-la! Pemba-la!' Tsun recognised his sister's voice immediately. He turned to see her come through the trap door onto the roof. She was wearing a flowered shirt and denim trousers, her hair braided in the Han style of two plaits. The boy, Namgyal, was with her. She stopped short on seeing Tsun, then walked slowly towards him.

'Tsun,' she said huskily. 'It is you?'

Tsun nodded. Pema burst into tears and ran from him to the end of the roof. Tsun got up. The others started to rise, but Tsun motioned them to remain seated.

'Namgyal . . .' he said, smiling. The boy had grown into a youth. Tsun touched his head in blessing, then walked over to where his sister was standing. He laid a hand on her shoulder. She turned to look at him with tear-stained eyes.

'I thought you were dead,' she said. 'I thought I had lost

everyone . . . and look at you. What have they done to you?'

'I was in a labour camp, Pema. It was not easy. But tell me about yourself. What happened to you?'

'At first,' she said, 'I wanted to go back to Derge, but the stories told about what it was like there by those who came to Lhasa made me unsure.'

Senge was whining for Tsun to pick him up. He took the dog in his arms and let him settle in his chuba.

'I wrote to Yangchen,' Pema said despairingly. 'So many letters, but none were answered. I don't know whether or not she received them. Tsun, what could have become of her?'

The fears expressed in Pema's face were reflected in his heart, but she did not wait for an answer.

'I thought at first that it was just because they took a long time to arrive. Then I got frightened that she might have written to me at Dorje Ri-gon House. The Han have seized the house. If it had not been for Pemba, I don't know what we should have done.'

She sniffed and wiped her eyes. In the street below, small groups of people had gathered to discuss the latest rumours and the anti-Han posters on some of the walls. Pema's eyes followed them without seeing.

'I thought,' she went on, 'that you would never find us. I didn't know where to leave a message, although Rinchen tried. How did you find us?'

'Fortunately, Tul-lok and Genyen know Pemba well.'

The mention of the resistance leader made her remember.

'Tsun,' she lowered her voice. 'I still have the gold.' She paused. 'And the petition. I didn't know what to do with them and I was too frightened to trust anyone, even Rinchen. I was going to speak to Genyen, but it was months before she came back to Lhasa, and by that time I was working for the radio station and it seemed better to wait . . .'

'Does anyone know you are my sister?'

Pema shook her head, frightened at the very thought, and Tsun sighed, both that he should be the cause of such anxiety, and at the insidious fear the Han successfully inculcated in individual hearts.

'Where is the gold now?' he asked quietly.

'Come with me, I will show you.' Pema walked swiftly across the roof without looking at the others who remained seated, watching sister and brother. She went down the steps which led onto the roof and took him to a room that was filled with trunks containing the family's stock and festive clothing. She closed the door behind them and turned the key in the lock. Then she pulled her mattress away from the wall. Tsun looked at the Han propaganda magazines and text books arranged neatly along the window sill and wondered.

Pema was on her hands and knees. She started digging at the tamped earth with a penknife. Tsun found shovels and they dug further, lower and lower, until a dreadful uncertainty filled her mind.

Tsun held up the remains of the petition, which had been almost entirely eaten away, and from the disintegrated cloth Pema handed him the gold.

The pigeons were flying back in their thousands from the square to their roosting places on the pagoda-style roofs of the cathedral, on which the gilding was turning red-gold in the setting sun.

In the square, Genyen stopped and looked doubtfully at a man seated on a rug with a small crowd around him. He had matted shoulder-length hair and tattered clothing. Hung on a thong around his neck was a dried, dismembered hand, and he brushed his greasy hair from his eyes with the stump of his right arm. Realising that his hand must have been amputated as a punishment for repeated theft, Genyen was about to move on to find a more reputable diviner.

'Why hesitate?' the man called to her. And in his eyes she saw his recognition that she, too, was little better than a thief. Perhaps, she thought, moving closer, he might be a good diviner. He was filthy, but he sat on a thick pile rug that only a good thief could steal, or a good diviner afford.

The man waved the crowd aside to make room for Genyen to sit down in front of him. For a moment, they considered one another.

'What is your question?' the man asked.

Genyen was so acutely embarrassed that her laugh cracked.

'If you are a good diviner, I need not tell you.'

The man grinned, then brushed the street dust from a small square of red cloth spread out on the carpet in front of him. The crowd clustered round, pressing closer. With his only hand, the man took a leather pouch of barley seeds from his ambac and shook them into the middle of the cloth. The chatter of the crowd stilled as the diviner lowered his eyelids and murmured an invocation to his guardian deity. Then he picked up some of the seeds and held them to his forehead, concentrating deeply for a few moments, then threw them to the winds. He blew the lazily burning pile of juniper leaves beside him to greater activity, gathered up the corners of the cloth, and after touching his forehead with it, passed it three times over the incense smoke. Without looking at her, the diviner touched Genyen's head with the cloth.

'Concentrate on your question,' he murmured.

After another invocation, he laid the cloth out carefully on the carpet and examined the pattern of the seeds.

Watching him, Genyen felt her stomach knot with anxiety as she waited for him to speak, but he said nothing. He picked up the cloth carefully and again held it to her forehead, invoking the answer from his guardian deity. Then he sucked in breath at the corner of his mouth and Genyen knew that the answer was not good. In a fury, she took her revolver from her chuba and levelled it at the man's chest. A murmur went up from the crowd.

'I want it done again,' she snapped angrily.

The man laughed. 'Three times the seeds are cast and if each time they give the same decision . . .' He shrugged.

'Cast them again,' Genyen demanded icily. 'Properly!'

The man smiled, gathered up the sides of the cloth, held it to her head and murmured the invocation. The crowd watched in silence. Then he opened the cloth in front of him and studied the seeds. There was a long pause.

'All the castings match,' he said.

Genyen would not believe him. She cocked the hammer of the revolver.

'You will not get him,' the man said quietly.

'Cast again!' Genyen ordered him, pushing the revolver at his chest. He grasped the dried-up amputated hand and thrust it at her face.

'Kill me,' he mocked, 'but you will not kill this, and one night you will be sleeping and it will come for you, it . . .'

'The Han are coming! The Han are coming!' someone cried urgently.

Genyen's eyes remained locked with the diviner's.

'My friend,' the diviner jerked his head in the direction of a shop behind him, 'will give you a potion.'

Genyen hesitated, then as the crowd scattered before the approaching Han patrol, she thrust her revolver back into her chuba, threw some coins on the rug and darted into the covering darkness of an alleyway. She would wait until it was safer before venturing into the shop.

Chapter Thirty

Next morning, Tsun and Tul-lok received the news explaining the Han Captain's anxiety that Pemba and his family should leave the city as soon as possible. While Pemba and his wife and son were packing and closing up the shop, in a back room the Abbot and his cousin conferred with the lama official they had met at the Potala the day before. Tul-lok pulled at his long turquoise earring, then rubbed a hand over his close-cropped hair as he listened.

'We have just heard that the Han want the Kundun to go to the Tibet Military Area Command tomorrow, without any of the usual officials or a bodyguard,' said the lama. 'Just six of the most senior Government members, and no announcement is to be made.'

'But why?' asked Tsun.

'They say that if it is announced and the Kundun goes in the usual procession, it will spark off trouble.'

'What purpose do they think this secrecy will serve?' Tsun shook his head.

'The Kundun has never been to the Han camp.' The lama sat hunched on a trunk in the tiny, dark room, his hands agitatedly fingering the beads of his rosary. 'The people will never allow it. The Han want the Kundun to see a theatrical show.'

Tul-lok grinned wryly at Tsun. 'Do you remember what happened in Kham?'

Tsun remembered, as did most of the Khamba refugees in Lhasa. It had been a practice of the officials to invite the province's most senior lamas to an apparently innocuous social occasion. The lamas had either disappeared, 'gone to China', or were known to have been put to death.

'The Kundun cannot go,' Tsun said.

'The Han have put him in an impossible position,' sighed the lama. 'They would regard his not going as an unacceptable loss of face. Equally, he cannot go.'

'What do you want me to do?'

'Two things,' said the lama, looking intently at Tsun. 'We have to try and pacify the people and not give the Han an excuse to take over completely. You are well respected and known for your work for freedom. We need your help with the Mimang at the Norbulinka, to help prevent the situation deteriorating when the news of the Kundun's visit to the camp gets out – as it surely will . . . has,' he reflected. 'Secondly, we must be ready very shortly to take the documents to India.'

Tsun nodded. He got up and took leave of the two men, agreeing to meet them later at the Norbulinka. First, he wanted to see Kesang.

A stiff breeze sent ripples across the lake, distorting the reflection of the Potala, whipping up puffs of sand from the plain of Lhasa, unsettling the four horses halted by the milling crowd at the foot of the Potala. The wind tugged at Tsun's fur and brocade summer riding hat. Senge poked his head out from the Abbot's plum-coloured layman's chuba when the horses stopped, then catching the cold wind in his face, buried himself deep down against Tsun's stomach.

Kesang and Rinchen pulled the hoods of their maroon cloaks over their heads. Genyen stroked her pony's neck to quieten its uneasy stamping. It had not been an easy ride from the city centre, across the Turquoise Bridge spanning the Happy River and through the Han quarter of New Lhasa. Everywhere, knots of people were gathered to discuss the latest rumours; shopkeepers were boarding up their shops; armed riders galloped through narrow, muddy streets. A large, militant crowd of ill-armed men and women were barricading themselves into the Jo-Khang Cathedral.

The ponies were nervous of the people shouting for Tibetan independence as they streamed through the enormous gilt-spired chorten forming the Western Gate, toward the Norbulinka Park, the Kundun's summer palace, at the end of a straight processional road.

Senge pushed his wet nose against Tsun's throat, and he fondled the little dog's head, caressing his ear. Without looking at the dog, he was aware of the affection between them, and wondered if he knew that they were going to be abruptly parted.

Genyen glanced back at Rinchen. The steward looked anxious and drawn. Suddenly, his pony reared and nearly lost its footing, startled by a man prostrating himself full length along the road at the edge of the crowd. Tsun reached out and grasped the pony's bridle as it regained its feet. They saw the man continuing his prostrations while the yelling crowd flowed past him.

'This is the pilgrims' way, Kesang,' said Tsun. 'Whatever happens, the pilgrims' way does not alter.'

The boy nodded, his eyes fixed on the man measuring his lengths. It would take him hours to complete the circuit of the road encompassing the Holy City, which for centuries had received the prostrations of princes and peasants.

Tsun, still fondling the dog's ears, was looking past the Norbulinka Garden of Jewels across the plain at the largest monastery in the world: the Monastic University of Drebung, the heap of rice. Apt, he thought, looking at the heap of white buildings piled against the sandstone mountains.

Senge whined as Tsun lifted him out from his chuba, looked into the brown wondering eyes, smiled and handed him to Kesang. Senge snuggled against the boy's warm body.

'Learn from Senge, Kesang,' he said. 'Learn to love as he loves, without expecting anything in return. And learn from his ability to see beyond man's imperfections, for he accepts all. From that, learn wisdom.'

The boy looked at Tsun and tears filled his eyes.

'Rinchen will take you to Drebung,' said Tsun in clipped tones. 'The Han patrols will not suspect a monk and his servant. From Drebung you can escape to India.'

He turned his pony, looked deep into the boy's eyes for a moment, then reached out and touched his head in blessing.

'I shall join you later,' he said. His knees closed on the pony's flanks and he flicked its rump with the end of the reins. Senge barked from Kesang's robe as he realised the lama was leaving. Kesang cried out above the heads of the milling crowd:

'Tsun!'

Rinchen grabbed the reins of the boy's pony and urged it on through the crowds. Tsun did not look back at the sound of the boy's cry. Genyen, riding with him, wanted to comfort him, but always there was the barrier, and instead she found herself shouting above the noise.

'Everyone is going to the Norbulinka, Rinposhay!' Her arm spanned the crowd closing in around them.

Tsun glanced at the woman beside him and saw her worried frown. She looked into his dark eyes and held them. Instinctively, he reached out to grasp her hand. Perhaps – Genyen dared not think in case it broke the spell – perhaps the aphrodisiac was working? It needed so little.

Chapter Thirty-One

The Norbulinka

Far across the plain, at the foot of the grass-covered sandstone hills, Tsun saw a long convoy of trucks and armoured cars spewing up dust as they made their way towards the Tibet Military Area Command. Genyen, too, saw the significance of the Han reinforcements as she and Tsun rode with the crowd to the Norbulinka.

'Tsun, look over there!' She pointed to a group of Khambas setting up an elderly First World War Lewis machine gun at the side of the road. Just then, a PLA armoured car drew up beside one of the telegraph poles carrying the telephone link between the Norbulinka and the Military Area Command. From this vantage point, a soldier was spotting for a Han Field Battery.

A few yards ahead of them stretched the largest crowd ever to assemble in Lhasa. Men, women and children, shouting slogans, waving banners, sticks, swords and rifles. Some had camped on the outskirts of the Norbulinka, smoke rising from their fires, as though they were waiting to hear one of the Kundun's sermons.

'We shall never be able to get through this crowd.' But even as Genyen spoke, the surging crowd parted to make way for the Ragyapas, the body breakers, their matted hair and tattered clothes smelling of their profession. They were dragging a battered and bleeding corpse by felicity scarves tied round its ankles.

'Who is it?' Tsun asked a young woman with a two year-old child in her arms.

'Phakpala Khenchung . . . he was caught trying to enter the Norbulinka with a revolver. It is believed he had come to kill the Kundun.'

Tsun and Genyen had great difficulty controlling their horses as the body was dragged past by the running Ragyapas like a grotesque dummy, spewing up the dust from the road, arms stretched out, bouncing on the uneven surface. Although a notorious collaborator, Phakpala Khenchung was also a highly respected lama. That the body breakers should refuse even to carry his remains was an unprecedented humiliation.

Tsun and Genyen managed to force their way through the crowd in the wake of the body breakers. He glanced up at the clean spring sky, hearing the familiar cry of the wheeling vultures waiting for the corpse to be taken to the top of a small hill and, as for centuries past, dismembered on a stone slab on which had lain the highest and the lowest in the land, before being fed to the voracious birds, so that nothing remained.

They had to stop in front of the main gate. The crowd was angrily encircling a Han limousine, its curtains drawn, but were being held back by members of the Mimang.

The gold-robed Premier of Tibet stood beside the car with two of his government colleagues, trying to make himself heard above the shouting crowd, while Mimang leaders searched the vehicle in case the Kundun was being smuggled into the Military Area Command. The Premier was explaining that he, and other ministers, were only going to the Han headquarters to inform the Generals why the Kundun could not attend their theatre programme. Tsun listened to him pleading with the crowd to disperse and pointing out the anger and possible retaliation from the Han that their continued presence round the Norbulinka would bring, but this served only to make the people more determined to stay.

'You see,' Genyen said to Tsun, 'even the government are frightened of the Han. If these people were crowded round the Han headquarters they might have the right to complain. Tsun . . .' She looked at him with eager eyes – how often had he seen her look like that before she attacked a caravan. 'They are trying to protect the Kundun. The Han will rule unless we fight!'

The ministers climbed back into the limousine and it nosed its way slowly through the throng. Tsun and Genyen felt the pressure of the crowd closing in on them while they explained their business to the Mimang leader who had been appointed to be in charge of the gate. The mastiffs chained on either side of the gate were beside themselves with fury, snapping and snarling at anyone who came near them. The guards swung open one of the gates a little way, allowing Tsun and Genyen to pass through into the Norbulinka.

Government officials and other members of the Mimang Committee greeted them and, as their horses were stabled, discussed news of the National Assembly which had convened in emergency session. Tsun persuaded the Mimang Committee to show the Han that they were willing to talk rather than fight, by dismantling one of the most visible machine gun posts and a barricade.

The park, with its lush grass and groves of willow trees, government villas and chapels, instilled a quietness in everyone within its walls. Groups of Lhasa civilian irregulars and Khambas guarded the gates or clustered in groups, intensely discussing the situation with government and religious officials. Lay officers, wearing ankle-length chubas, long turquoise earrings and tiny turquoise amulet boxes on the crowns of their heads, walked swiftly along the gravel paths carrying documents to and from the villas of the Government, the Lord Chamberlain, and the Commander of the Royal Bodyguard. Tsun and Genyen walked towards a flat-roofed, two-storeyed villa, its canvas appliqué sun shades pulled out. Tul-lok and the resistance leaders were meeting there with a Cabinet Minister.

'So . . .' said Genyen, 'the National Assembly have declared independence.'

'To declare,' said Tsun, 'and to achieve, are as the reflection of a bird in the lake, and the bird itself.'

'Tsun!' called Tul-lok. 'You have no imagination, cousin, that is why you are a lama and I am a bandit.'

Tsun turned to see his cousin. He was standing behind him, chuba hitched up Khamba fashion, showing his knee-high boots, his right hand resting on the strap of an amulet box and his left hand holding the strap of his rifle slung across his back.

'Cousin!' Tsun walked towards Tul-lok and poked a derisive finger at him. 'It is because I *have* imagination that I am a lama.'

Tul-lok chuckled and linked arms with Tsun, leading him away from the villa. Genyen joined them, walking on the other side of Tul-lok. He clasped her round the waist.

'Hasn't she grown more beautiful, Tsun?'

As the lama looked at the blue-black-haired woman her eyes caught his and, for the first time in his life, Tsun saw her blush. She was indeed beautiful!

In silence they listened to their footsteps on the neatly laid out gravel path, bordered by carefully tended flower beds.

'I have never been here before,' said Genyen, peering through the arbour work. 'There are flowers everywhere.'

'There is even a collection of wild animals,' said Tul-lok,

watching a duck waddle slowly across their path. Tsun reached up and touched the branch of a budding willow tree.

'So many birds,' said Genyen, and they paused to listen to the incessant twitters and calls rising above the shouts of the crowd outside the walls.

Tsun sat down on the thick, neatly cut grass, and leaned against a poplar tree. Genyen sat down beside him.

'It *is* beautiful,' she murmured.

She looked out over the small lake. Brilliantly coloured ducks were already sending out gentle wakes as they swam expectantly towards the group. A stone bridge arched across the water from the bank to the tree-shaded island on which stood a small, plain pavilion.

'It is said that the Kundun spends much of his time there when he is in the Norbulinka,' she said softly.

Tsun found himself slightly surprised by Genyen's reaction. He detected more of a woman in her than he had ever known before. Tul-lok was sitting on the grass facing them, his head bent. He broke off a piece of grass and sucked at the hard, stringy stalk.

'Have you been able to persuade the Mimang leaders?' he asked quietly.

'At the moment, only to take down a barricade and dismantle the most obvious machine gun post, and to try and stop any more going up.'

'We may need it,' Genyen murmured.

Tsun grunted. Tul-lok looked up, still chewing on the stalk of grass. Tsun took off his fur hat and scratched his closely cropped head.

'My men have seen the Han taking artillery sightings,' said Tul-lok. He offered his snuff box to Tsun who took some, then offered the box to Genyen. She shook her head.

They all fell silent, listening to the soft gulping of the enormous goldfish in the lake as they raised their heads to the surface. One of the ducks, frustrated at not being fed, snapped angrily at the darting fish.

'What is happening here, Tul-lok?' said Tsun. 'What is the Kundun going to do?'

Tul-lok looked suddenly haggard.

'No one knows what is happening. They . . .' Tul-lok waved his arm as though to encompass the whole park, 'they scurry like marmots to their burrows, looking for shelter, for an answer . . .' He flicked the stalk of grass at Tsun. 'But there is none!'

Genyen looked at him in disbelief. 'But the whole city has risen against the Han. They cannot kill everyone! The world must hear!'

'And who is to tell them?'

'The Consulates,' she said triumphantly. 'They will . . .'

'Genyen,' Tul-lok shook his head and dropped a small pebble into the lake, sending the goldfish darting away as the ripples spread over the water's surface. 'Neither India nor Nepal will send troops. Did they help us when we were invaded? Or in 1956, when the Kundun himself asked for help?'

'But they will have to recognise that the whole people are against the occupation . . .' But even as she spoke, she knew that it was useless to hope for aid from their neighbours. 'All right!' she said irritably. 'I agree, it is an unorganised rising, that the people are not properly armed . . . but they *have* risen, Tul-lok, and we shall not have another chance.'

'I know that as well as you! Why do you think we have the Mimang Committee?'

'Tul-lok, why can't some of the Khambas seize Bhutan and Sikkim? There are enough Khambas near the border. The Tibetans living there would rise, we know that.'

'No, Genyen,' said Tsun. 'The Indians are already unsympathetic. If we take Sikkim and Bhutan it is more than probable that they will become actively hostile.'

'He is right,' Tul-lok agreed. 'And even so, we do not have enough ammunition.'

Genyen's eyes were bright. 'The Han have,' she said. 'We *could* attack.'

'It would be suicide,' said Tul-lok. 'Even now, it is all we can do to keep the crowd under control. Most of them are unarmed and inexperienced in fighting. The Han may well attack us. Certainly they would retaliate if we attacked the Garrison. It would be the excuse they have been waiting for to crush us completely.'

Genyen ran an agitated hand through her hair. Tul-lok looked down on hearing a strange gulping sound. The goldfish had clustered beneath the bank, lips opening and closing on the surface of the water, waiting to be fed.

'A small group of us could do it tonight, Tul-lok.' Genyen spoke his name cajolingly. 'You and I have killed six times as many men as we have had with us.'

Tul-lok dipped his hands in the water. 'Perhaps. But remember, this time there are thousands of Han, not hundreds.'

'If I could raid their arms dump and get away without killing a single Han, I should be satisfied. I shall try tonight.'

'No!' Tul-lok said sharply. 'Not until I have discussed it with the others. This is not like any other fight we have had with the Han. The crowds are stopping them from entering the Norbulinka and taking the Kundun, but they cannot stop them from radioing China for the iron birds. You have seen what they can do; imagine what would happen if the iron birds should attack the Norbulinka.'

'He is right, Genyen,' said Tsun. 'Any action we take will have repercussions on the Kundun.'

'Ever cautious . . .' Genyen looked with faintly mocking eyes at the lama. 'Ever cautious, Tsun.'

Tsun smiled at her but said nothing. For some minutes they all sat, listening to the gulping fish, the birds, the crowd. There was so much to be done, and yet, Tsun thought, what *could* be done? Genyen became increasingly impatient. She frowned at the two men absorbed in their thoughts and sighed. Her eyes followed Tsun's to a cawing crow above them. It circled, then settled on a string of prayer flags. Swinging in the wind, it kept cawing softly. Tul-lok looked up at it. The prayer flags were green, the Kundun's personal colour.

'An omen,' he murmured.

Genyen took the sling from her ambac and picked a pebble from the path. She swung the sling and loosed the pebble at the bird. The stone hit one of the flags, startling the crow which cawed louder, spread its wings and flew away.

'An omen!' she cried vehemently, thinking of the divination she had had done concerning Tsun. 'Omens are what you make of them!'

Tul-lok rose to his feet, shaking his head. 'You are foolish, Genyen.'

'No,' said Tsun, 'she is right.' He had an idea.

Genyen grinned at him broadly as they both got up and walked down the path to a small villa.

The building was crowded with government officials. Tsun caught sight of Jettie and asked him to get a message urgently to Samden. The portly figure of the lama they had talked with at the Potala approached. He greeted Tsun, then took him by the arm and led him into a small room overlooking the Garden of Jewels. He gestured to Tsun to be seated, then eased himself onto a carved wooden seat with the carefulness of the stout. A manservant placed a dish of sweetcakes before them and then poured tea into a pair of Chinese porcelain cups.

'Have some sweetcakes, please, Rinposhay.'

As the lama offered Tsun the dish, he watched him with alert, shrewd brown eyes. The manservant closed the door quietly behind him.

'May I know my host's name now?' Tsun asked politely.

The lama laughed, causing the goitre on his neck to wobble.

'What is a name?' he chuckled. Then, continuing on a more sombre note, 'It is dangerous, Rinposhay.'

'For everyone.'

'You know of the independence declaration of the National Assembly?' Tsun nodded and drank some tea.

'Others have been asked to add their names to it, including the Cabinet. It is all we can do to keep the crowd under control. The Kundun is deeply concerned that they will attack the Han and provoke them into destroying everything. The Generals are already furious!'

The lama added more tea to Tsun's cup. Tsun found himself almost agreeing with Genyen.

'It was inevitable that it should happen.'

'Perhaps! But little can be gained and much can be lost.' The lama smiled thinly and offered Tsun another sweetcake. Tsun took one.

'Please use your influence with the Mimang Committee, Rinposhay, to calm the people, and stop them trying to do anything dangerous.' His face became very grave. 'They must disperse as quickly as possible,' he said. 'The Kundun has given them his assurance that he will not go to the Military Area Command.'

'I shall do what I can.'

Tsun was thinking of Genyen's plan to raid the Han garrison that night. He drank his tea and refused more. The lama was eating a biscuit, his eyes totally absorbed in assessing Tsun. Tsun's eyes were expressionless.

'How,' he smiled apologetically, 'can I trust someone I don't know?'

The lama fingered his goitre and chuckled.

'If I tell you my name and my rank in the Government, does it make me more trustworthy than the person you are judging now?'

'No.' Tsun inclined his head, indicating that the lama had won the argument, or almost. 'But it helps to know who one is talking to.'

The two men laughed. The lama was not going to yield. Tsun got the impression that he was telling the truth, and yet . . . he was astute and manipulative . . . Tsun did not like being manipulated.

The lama sipped his tea slowly and shifted his gaze over the rim of his cup to the window. There was no one in sight. He lowered the cup onto its silver stand.

'The documents . . .'

'Yes?'

'They are almost ready. They must leave Lhasa as soon as possible.'

'How soon?'

'It is a matter of hours.' The lama drank more tea. 'Treat this as your house, Rinposhay, until you have to leave.'

'I have to go back to the city before I leave for India.'

'But that is madness! Already firing has broken out. Who can say what will happen? No! You cannot jeopardise the whole mission. You must stay here, Rinposhay.'

Tsun decided not to debate the point. 'Does the Kundun know of these documents?'

'There are some things it is safer not to know.'

They were interrupted by a hurried knock at the door, which was suddenly opened by the manservant.

'Kusho . . .' He hurried forward and murmured in the lama's ear.

'Very well!' The lama held out his arm irritably to obtain support from the servant as he heaved himself to his feet. 'You must excuse me, Rinposhay, but I must leave. I will return shortly.'

Tsun watched the plump figure hurry out of the room, followed by his servant.

Chapter Thirty-Two

The guard eyed Tsun suspiciously, but he could see from the Abbot's bearing that he was a man of rank and hesitated to challenge him. Tsun used the moments of doubt to unbolt the door, slip through and close it behind him. The Norbulinka was protected by its high walls, and granules of sand bit into his cheeks, carried by the rising wind which was growing chill as the sun set. He hunched his body against the blast as he made his way through the crowd. The mass of people were outside the main gate, so by leaving through a side door he was able to make his way fairly easily through the crowd. Not knowing what to expect, he had decided to walk the four miles back to the city. Dotted along the road were small fires, with clusters of people crouched round them trying to keep warm. Some were leaving, while farther along the road he met others who were coming to join the vigil.

A heavy twilight hung over the city, pierced at regular intervals by the spill-over of the harsh lighting from the Military Area Command. For some reason the dim street lighting had not been switched on, which gave Tsun more cover. As he walked through New Lhasa's walled compounds, he heard an engine and saw lights bounce out of the enclosed turquoise-tiled bridge spanning the Happy River. Tsun ran across the now deserted road and flung himself into the long grass. The armoured car roared past.

He crossed the bridge quickly, listening to the rushing waters of the Happy River overflowing from the spring thaw. Nearing the city, the sound of water receded and he could hear sporadic gunfire. Only a few of the houses had lighted windows and twilight was giving way to velvet blackness.

He walked down the narrow muddy streets towards the Cathedral and city centre and the firing grew louder. Dogs were barking, frightened by the shooting. As he entered the street containing Pemba's shop, a bullet whined over his head to splinter the woodwork of a window above him. Answering shots came from the rooftops. He edged down the street, keeping close to the wall and dodging in and out of doorways. More shots were exchanged. For a moment, Tsun thought he had passed Pemba's shop, then remembered that it was close to the Barkor Square. He inched himself along the last few yards.

The frightened householders had barricaded themselves into their homes without waiting to pull up the sun awnings, leaving them to flap in the strong wind, sounding like great bats as they pulled on their ropes.

Tsun came at last to the door which he thought he recognised as belonging to Pemba's shop. He wrapped his knuckles on the door, hoping to be heard above the shooting. On a flat roof down the street, he could just make out the shape of a man levelling his gun, black against blackness.

There was no answer to his knock; he tried again, a little louder this time, but still there was no response. He fumbled for the handle and turned it, but the door was firmly locked and the windows shuttered. He rapped again, and once, during a lull in the shooting, his knocks sounded like drum beats echoing in the night.

Then, after what seemed like hours, Tsun thought he heard a movement behind the door; he tapped again, and heard a bolt being drawn back. The door inched open and the barrel of a flintlock was thrust through the small aperture.

'Who is it?' came a hoarse whisper.

Tsun recognised Samden's voice. 'Khenpo Tsun,' he whispered back.

The door opened wider and Samden thrust his head out. His hair was long and parted at the side in Western fashion. He peered at Tsun through the darkness, then, recognising him, opened the door to let him enter. Tsun stepped inside and Samden locked the door after him. He led Tsun in silence through the dark shop to the kitchen which was one floor above.

Pema, Champa and Jigme were sitting alone together round the clay stove drinking tea. When they saw Tsun, they all rose to their feet and greeted him. Pema poured him some tea.

'How long has the shooting been going on?' Tsun asked Samden.

The youth sat down on the floor by the stove and fingered his faint moustache.

'Since the afternoon,' he answered.

'Where is Brass Nose?' Tsun asked sharply.

'He is with those fighting at the Cathedral.' Pema handed Tsun a piece of thick creamy paper, veined with thread. 'He left this note for you.'

Tsun took the note, unfolded the paper slowly and read the contents.

'Rinposhay, I have found a better way of dying than waiting for death to take me slowly, hour by hour. For how long did I protect you so that you could guide me through the after death state when I die? Now, I think you will know when I die, and remember me still. Look after your family. Journey in peace.'

Tsun leaned forward and gently dropped the paper onto the flames. It was the first time he had known Brass Nose to be wholly serious. He turned to Pema.

'You must leave here in the morning. Go to Drebung and see if Kesang and Rinchen are there, then you must go to India. I shall give you a note to help you get horses at Drebung.'

'What is happening in Lhasa?' Pema sounded as though Tsun had prompted the question, yet, in effect, she ignored his instructions. She handed him a string of dried cheese cubes.

'No one knows,' Tsun answered, 'but whatever happens, it will be a long time before Lhasa is at peace.' He took a cube of cheese from the string.

'But why must we leave?' Pema's voice had a defensive note in it, and she sounded as if she was about to be angry with her brother. 'Why, Tsun?'

Her attitude to the lama caused the three youths to move away in embarrassment and start a conversation among themselves.

'Because now you can escape. You can always return,' said Tsun. 'But if you wait much longer even the *chance* to escape will be lost.'

'What are you going to do?' Pema nervously fingered one of her thick plaits, drawing his attention to her typically Han hair-style. She had grown, he thought, into a strikingly beautiful woman.

'I shall follow you as soon as possible,' he said, 'but first I must return to the Norbulinka.'

Pema played with the plait, pulling at the end of it.

'What will become of us in India?' she asked frowning. 'What will become of us? . . . We do not know anyone . . .'

'I shall give you some money, so that if you have to stay for a while you can pay for further studies and, Pema, you should use the opportunity to go on pilgrimage to the holy places. You will learn much from the visit.'

Pema was silent, with lowered eyes. Tsun felt the unspoken resistance, but it was not so strong as when he had virtually forced her to leave Derge. This time the air was heavy with her embarrassment. Both brother and sister found themselves acutely uncomfortable about the atmosphere between them.

'Do you remember,' said Tsun, 'how reluctant you were to come to Lhasa?'

Pema nodded.

'Was it such a mistake? he asked.

'No . . .' She looked up at him with a shy smile and put out her hand. 'No, my brother. I am grateful, and perhaps I understand more . . .' There was a long pause. 'It's just that . . .'

'Yes?'

Tsun's quick response disarmed her. She withdrew her hand from his and was on the defensive again.

'It is because our situations are . . . do not be angry, Tsun, but they are different . . .'

'You mean you have no reason to fear the Han as I have,' Tsun said slowly.

'I have been here three years now. I have made a life for myself. Why should . . .' She stopped short. Her pearl-white teeth bit into her lower lip.

'Why should the Han harm you?' Tsun finished the question. Pema nodded curtly with embarrassment.

'Nobody knows,' said Tsun, 'what is going to happen after this rising. Life will never be the same again. We fight! We march! We declare our independence, but we both know that there can only be one victor in this battle . . . the Han! After this rising, it could be that *everyone* will have reason to fear the Han! Remember what it was like in Kham? It will be worse here.' He paused. 'It could be that you will have even more to fear from Tibetans . . . look at Phakpala Khenchung.'

'He was stoned to death.'

'Exactly!' Tsun nodded. 'There may be a chance for you to escape tomorrow morning, but even that is not certain. Pema . . .' His expression showed his concern. 'It would be madness to miss that chance, you . . .'

'Holy Tara!' Pema pulled angrily at her plait. 'For how many more years is this going to go on? Most of my life there has been fighting, running, losing my family, my friends . . .' Her eyes filled with tears. 'Tsun . . . I do not want to be homeless in a strange country.'

'No . . .' he put out a hand and tenderly stroked her head. 'But you did not want to come with me to Lhasa.'

'I know . . .' she sighed deeply. 'But I want to stop running.' She looked defiantly into his deep brown eyes. 'Tsun-la . . . Tsun-la, I like my work at the radio station. I do it well. *Why* should I have anything to fear?' Tsun looked at her thoughtfully.

'I know that what you say is probably true,' she went on, 'but afterwards people will still have to make lives for themselves. Perhaps I can help. I don't agree with everything that goes out on the radio, of course I don't . . . but isn't it better to try and influence the Han . . .' her voice grew louder with nervousness. 'We've got to live with them. You're saying that yourself.'

Tsun nodded. 'Pema-la, I do understand what you are saying, and indeed, there is truth in it. You are now a woman, and well able to make your own decisions. Make the decision you believe in.'

Pema overcame her inhibition at his status as a lama and took his hand, seeking refuge in his arms as she wept.

'I wish, Pema-la,' Tsun whispered, 'that you had been born in a better time.'

'Rinposhay.'

'Samden?' The man bent his head close to Tsun's ear.

'I succeeded in passing on your message. It was not as difficult as I thought it would be. So few Han speak Tibetan. I have found out that there is a Ling Tao Yen who works for the Public Security Office. She is quite senior.'

'Have you been able to contact her?' Tsun's voice was low. The others worked at being absorbed in their conversation. Samden nodded.

'Yes, I've managed to speak with her and she would like to see you.'

'Where are we to meet?'

'I am to bring her here as soon as you arrive.'

'But can you? You are liable to be shot in the streets tonight. Will she come?'

Samden nodded. 'I won't be long, Rinposhay.' He disappeared up the ladder and through the roof trapdoor, carefully closing it behind him. The others watched for a few moments, wondering where he was going.

'Pemba has sent his wife and child away,' said Pema, breaking the silence. 'But he has stayed to go to the Norbulinka to help protect the Kundun. He said to use whatever we wish.'

'Pemba is a man of good heart,' Tsun murmured.

Outside they heard a sudden burst of firing, some dogs barking, then silence. They sat in a tight group round the stove, its flames providing the only light. Tsun looked at his two pupils.

'Champa, Jigme . . . before dawn, please go to Drebung. If during the day you have news of fighting, then leave at once for India. Please, do not delay. Go with Rinchen and Dorje Rinposhay.'

Tsun's anxiety frightened them both.

'You don't think it will improve, Rinposhay?' Champa poured some barley flour into Tsun's bowl, adding a little tea.

'No, Champa.' Tsun kneaded the flour and tea into a dough with his fingers. 'I believe that none of us fully realises what is going to happen.'

'But why India, Rinposhay?' Jigme asked. 'Couldn't we go to a monastery in west Tibet?'

'If the Han take over completely, it will be as it is in Kham all over Tibet.'

The two boys found it difficult to conceive. Champa's words were heavy as he asked:

'What do you want us to do if we reach India?'

'Realise the Teachings.' Tsun smiled. 'I think you will find there will be more than enough for you to do.'

'Rinposhay . . .' Jigme looked more earnest than usual. 'What will happen to our country?'

I do not know, Jigme,' Tsun sighed. 'But I do know that much which we hold dear in our way of life is going forever. Who can say how much of what is left will remain?'

'But the Religion, the teachers,' Champa asked. 'What will become of them? How can our religion be practised in the new Tibet?'

'Maybe it can only be practised in the heart, Champa. The Great Thirteenth Kundun foretold what would happen in our country. He urged us to be prepared for an event such as this.'

'Then it is the end,' Champa muttered thickly. 'Nothing will be left.'

'We do not know that, Champa. For some time there will be those who will keep the Religion alive.'

'But if they are not allowed to practise it?'

'That is why I believe you should escape. For those who escape, though they will be impoverished, will have skills and crafts and will be free to practise and pass on the Religion.

'When I was in the labour camp, I had a dream. I believe now that the meaning of that dream was that Tibet is undergoing a tremendous change, entering a new era of history; so, too, is the world. The prophecies of our forefathers tell this.'

'Then what is there to hope for, Rinposhay?' Jigme asked. 'I remember the prophecies telling of the end of the Order, so we shall be like the Sakya Clan of the Buddha, completely destroyed. Or the pathetic remnants of the world, lost forever. Exiles, waiting for death as the only state where we can be ourselves.

'What is happening is momentous, Jigme. You are too pessimistic. Remember, although your vision of the future may seem black and empty, in fact, the wheel of life is turning. What appears lost, dead, is being transmuted into yet another form as we, ourselves, will be.

'During the reign of King Lang Dharma, our temples and monasteries were destroyed. Our monks and lamas were forced to abandon the robe, or flee. The scriptures were burnt. It seemed that nothing remained. For nearly seventy years, although nothing of the Religion was to be seen, men practised it and kept it alive in their hearts. They were the true guardians of the ancient wisdom. They nurtured it, sometimes on foreign soil, but the flames lived on.

'And it is told in the prophecies that India, the birthplace of the Buddha, and Tibet, will come together. Many will leave the Land of Snows and will fulfil the prophecy by keeping alive the essence of the Religion.

'It is for this that I have prepared you. This is why I have given you both many initiations and teachings far ahead of your capabilities and understanding, so that the seed of wisdom and spontaneous love is sown.'

'But, Rinposhay, I am not special. Why should I escape?' Champa protested.

'You will,' Tsun said quietly.

'But it will take so many . . .'

'If it is the time, and all the indications show that it is, enough will escape to keep alive the traditions. But I ask you to remember this, both of you. Here in this room, the simple design on the teapot speaks to you of religion, the eternal truths. Everywhere you look you can see reminders of the faith. In India, there will be few reminders. India is not a land of Buddhism. You will find that although there may not be open attacks on the Religion, as there are in Tibet, the people's lives have different aims. There will be subtle ways in which you will be tempted to forget.

'Remember always, that all mankind, all beings, seek peace, security, happiness. Man so endowed, so blessed, can frequently in his search follow selfish, brutal ways, causing suffering to others. Nevertheless, always remember that common quest.

'Here, in our Land of Snows, we are all prisoners. Our time, our movements, our work, our clothing, our very expression, are all under someone else's control. Our minds, too, are sought. But those, we have kept free. That is the greatest freedom. Realise the vast space, the freedom of the mind, the greater understanding, peace and awareness, beyond that which we generally accept as our mind. You all know of what I speak. And if, in the dark times, you despair and cannot see how your awakened mind can change matters, think of the profound teaching of karma, of the countless effects we can cause for good or ill.'

Jigme looked very worried and kept tapping his teeth with his fingers. Tsun asked him to come and talk to him in a cramped corner of the room.

'We should take supplies, Rinposhay?'

'From Drebung. Travel lightly from Lhasa. You may have to move quickly and do not want to attract attention.'

'Rinposhay . . .' he began quietly, but couldn't say what he felt. 'It is a great honour to be chosen by the Haughty One as his oracle . . .'

'Yes?' Tsun waited for the youth to continue, to say what was really on his mind. 'It is also,' he tried to help Jigme, '. . . a great strain on the one who is chosen.'

Jigme's dull eyes opened wider. He looked at Tsun intently, debating whether he could tell, then decided.

'Rinposhay, I know it is a great honour, and since being at Sera, I have learned much as an oracle.' He paused. 'Oracles do not live long.'

'No.'

'It is not that so much . . . it's just that I feel no satisfaction. I feel that I should not be the oracle! Somehow, although at Sera I have learned how to make the possession easier each time, each time it is . . . harder . . .'

'Do you know what it is you want to do, Jigme?'

The youth hesitated.

'Well, when I went on trading journeys for the monastery, I was really happy.'

'You want to become a trader?'

Jigme nodded. 'My mother is a trader, and before I joined the monastery I would help her. It is in my blood. But surely the Haughty One would be angry that I say such things? Also, I don't want to disappoint you, Rinposhay.'

'Why not ask the Haughty One if he will choose another mouthpiece, as you are unsuited?'

Jigme looked shocked. 'But, my tutors at Sera . . .'

Tsun smiled at him. 'You will not be going back there for some time. Use the opportunity. Ask the Haughty One and see what is the result. You are not the first oracle to feel as you do, and you will disappoint no one, Jigme.'

He took a pouch of gold and silver Han coins from his chuba and handed it to Jigme.

'You will need money. If you can get a message to Namgyal without endangering yourself, do so. Tell him that I think it best that he escape, but the choice is his.'

He thought of his own journey earlier that evening, from the Norbulinka to the shop, and wondered what it would be like in the morning. For a brief moment, Tsun doubted his wisdom in urging them on an escape which held so many uncertainties.

Chapter Thirty-Three

Tsun explained Samden's mission as they sat round the fire. Even when he explained the purpose, neither of the monks could readily understand why he had done it, and Jigme slipped his revolver into his robe. Amongst Pemba's small but diverse stock, Champa had discovered a clock. Knowing that three hours had passed since Samden had left them did not make it any easier. They found themselves watching the minutes passing, it seemed, incredibly slowly.

'Rinposhay, will you join us tomorrow at Drebung?'

'I expect to, but if I am not there when the day is advanced, you should not wait for me. It may be that we shall have to make our separate ways.'

'You talk,' Pema said, 'as though you were uncertain.'

He chuckled. 'Pema, listen to the shooting. How can we be certain of anything? Are you, that you will be going with Champa and Jigme?'

He was quite right, she thought, pulling a face at herself.

'Listen!' Tsun was already up the ladder before the others realised that there was a gentle tapping on the trapdoor. Ling followed him down and looked round, slightly warily.

'Why is it so dark?'

'It is not a trap,' Tsun said, nodding at Champa and Jigme who lit some mustard lamps.

'No, somehow I didn't think it was,' she said. 'I wouldn't be here if I thought it was, but I have learned to be careful.' She patted the leather holster on her belt and smiled at Tsun. Then she held out her hand and he shook it. He found it a very strange experience to be touching her again, while the two monks regarded her as being vulgar and rude in her directness. He saw the look of concern on her face as she noticed how much he had aged.

'I'm sorry, Tsun,' she whispered.

'What happened to you?' he asked, their voices low so that the others would not hear. 'I waited for months, then gave up believing.'

'I had a lot of difficulty when you couldn't be traced.'
'But how could they know?'
'The guard told them, when a little pressure was put on him.'
'I'm sorry, Ling . . .'
'Why?' she laughed. 'Anyway, you will have had a harder time.'
As Tsun showed her over to Pema's rug-covered divan on the far side of the room, he was struck by Ling's confident manner. She wore the good quality jacket and trousers of a senior cadre. With the passing of only a few years, her face with its regular, attractive features and beautiful smile, even with her severe glasses, had developed. Perhaps it was the confidence of position, he thought.
Samden brought them both tea. Tsun nodded in his direction. 'He did well to find you,' he said.
'Well, what is it you want of me, Tsun?' She made her tone deliberately businesslike.
'I've seen a considerable amount of the city, Ling, I can talk from first hand knowledge. Can you get it into the thick skulls of your choleric masters, cloistered behind their compound walls, that the Kundun, the Cabinet, and the Mimang have no more control over the people of Lhasa than they do! The great irony, Ling, is that it is the People's Liberation Army on the one hand, and the People on the other. You must have heard something of it?'
She nodded. 'But we have been ordered not to leave our quarters because of the danger of attack.'
'The Generals have been putting pressure on the Kundun and the other leaders, saying that the rising is evidence of their collusion in counter-revolutionary activities. The leaders no longer control events. Even the Kundun does not. He has asked the people to disperse. They've agreed, when they are satisfied that there is no longer any insistence that he go to the Tibet Military Area Command.'
'But Tsun . . .' Ling put her cup down. 'You are not going to tell me that your people have not announced independence, and have not been distributing arms?'
'No, of course not. But what can you expect? The fact remains that the Kundun and the Cabinet and the Mimang all know the likely outcome of the rising, just as much as you do. We want to avoid it.'
'How can I do anything?'
'At least you are a reliable means of communication. The Generals cut themselves off completely. It seems impossible to get the situation through to them.'

She drank her tea slowly. 'I'll do my best, Tsun.'

'Will they accept it? How will you explain your role as messenger?'

'I'll say that the Mimang Committee contacted me because I speak Tibetan. I have more contacts with the Tibetans than most of the cadres so it will not cause any surprise.'

'They could say that it is a deliberate ploy,' said Tsun.

'To get us to hold back?'

'Yes.'

'Yes, Tsun, they could,' she said thoughtfully. 'I'll try to convince them otherwise. What do you want them to do?'

'To hold off any attack. Not to believe immediately that if some young hotheads take a few pot shots, it is war.' He thought of Genyen and hoped she had been dissuaded from attacking the Han arms dump. 'And to establish a reliable means of communication.'

'You ask a lot! What can I say will be done at your end?'

'We are trying to stop the people from rising, Ling.' He paused. 'I have to say this honestly, in the belief that it will only strengthen, rather than weaken your case, but the crowds are unpredictable. I don't know if we have left it too late. If you can get a message to me, perhaps through Samden, I shall do all that I can to get the resistance to remove some of the barricades and machine gun posts as an indication that they don't want to fight, but to talk. I have already succeeded some way in this.'

She nodded. There seemed to be little else to say.

'What will you do, Tsun?'

'Help, while I can.'

She looked at him, frowning. 'If things get difficult, you could contact me again through Samden.'

Tsun smiled and looked at her for a few moments. 'Thank you, Ling, but do you think I am likely to?'

'No,' she gave a sad smile, '. . . not really.'

As she got up to go, Samden climbed up the ladder to open the trapdoor to the roof.

'You didn't come entirely over the roofs?' Tsun asked.

'No, but the roofs are safer than the streets, and I've got two bicycles for us a few streets on.'

Tsun gripped her hand in both of his.

'Ling, I beg you to take seriously what I ask. It is not just for me . . .'

'I will, Tsun, and I shall get a message back to you.'

'At the Norbulinka?'

She nodded.

'Well,' he chuckled. 'We should have nothing to worr you are as thorough as you were in trying to get hold of tl And you won, in the end.'

She looked down from the ladder, surprised. 'How?

'Well, you know it didn't get to the United Nation:

'Oh, that wasn't why we wanted it. No, it would h useful in giving us a complete list, in the signatures, of th resistance in Kham, and all those likely to cause troub

The trapdoor slammed shut.

Chapter Thirty-Four

The Norbulinka

The shadow of a crow passed over Tsun as he entered the stables to walk down the line of stalls and inspect the horses. Genyen nodded towards the brightly coloured wooden pillars, the capitals of which were picked out with shaded flowers. The superb wall frescoes were spattered with horse dung.

'Their stalls are painted like a temple,' she said. 'And all these horses have ever done is feed themselves.' She slapped one of the creatures on its well rounded rump. 'Tsun, these creatures will never get you to India.'

'Better a well fed horse than a starved one,' answered an elderly groom who was following them. 'And they are exercised every day.'

Genyen grunted in disbelief. Tsun stopped by one of the stalls. The horse was larger than the rest and had evidently been ridden regularly. As he considered choosing it, he noticed the look of discomfort on the groom's face.

'Rinposhay,' the man said, 'this is one of the horses that the Kundun rides.'

'For this journey,' Tsun said, thinking of the leather bag in his ambac containing the evidence from the National Assembly for the United Nations, 'it is suitable.'

'Rinposhay,' the groom fiddled nervously with the horse's halter. 'I shall have to speak with the Grand Chamberlain, Phala.'

The man bowed and sucked in his breath in deference. Tsun smiled slightly.

'Of course,' he said.

They watched the man walk away.

'How,' Genyen asked, 'are you going to escape?'

'The groom will take this horse, with the others, to the pasture beside the Kundun's dairy. Then later, I shall leave the Norbulinka dressed as a servant. The dairy is beyond the last checkpoint, and there I shall collect the horses.'

He looked at the row of saddles set on pegs along the wall. Some

were covered with brocade and had gold filigree work on the high pommel and shaped back. Others were a simple wooden framework over which could be thrown a rug, and amongst them, looking ridiculously small, were a few English saddles. He chose one of padded leather with a painted pommel and high back rest.

The groom had returned with permission for Tsun to take the horse he had chosen. Tsun showed him the saddle he was going to take.

'How are you going to smuggle that past the Han?' Genyen asked, pointing at the saddle.

Tsun smiled at her. 'The groom has to ride,' he said.

'Tsun,' Genyen said earnestly, 'I wish you would come with us. Soon my men will be leaving for the south . . .'

Tsun cut her short with a laugh. 'You know you will not leave here until the fighting forces you to leave, and I want to go now.'

They walked out of the stables and found that a crowd had gathered near the gates. They could hear a babble of anxious voices and some women were weeping. Immediately, the thought flashed through Tsun's mind that there had been news of the Kundun . . . But the crowd fell silent on seeing them, and parted slowly to let them through.

'It is . . . Tul-lok . . . he is . . . dead!' Karma, one of Tul-lok's men, spoke to no one in particular.

Tsun reached him in a single stride and grabbed him by the shoulders.

'*Dead!* What happened?'

The man swallowed hard, and rubbed the cold sweat from his face.

'We were at the Potala . . . we had an empty truck to get more weapons for the Norbulinka . . . Tul-lok wanted to walk back after the trucks were loaded, but there were Han patrols. One of them stopped to question us.' Tsun could feel the man's body shaking beneath his hands.

'We told them we had been to see relatives, but, you know the Han . . . they realised we were Khambas and they arrested us. Tul-lok drew his revolver . . .' Karma shook his head despairingly. 'I tried to stop him, but as he tried to fire the gun jammed and . . . they shot him!' There was a low moan from those nearby. 'I ran,' he continued, his voice now drained of emotion. 'They didn't try to stop me, not even when they realised who they . . . that they had killed the famous Tul-lok . . .'

'Karma,' Genyen's voice was only above a whisper. 'I cannot believe that he is . . . dead!'

Karma looked up and found Tsun gazing at him with a cold, penetrating stare. A terrible dread filled his stomach.

'I . . . I told you . . .' he said, as though in explanation. Genyen gave them both a puzzled glance. 'Yes,' Tsun said quietly, 'you have told us.' He turned and walked away.

When Genyen caught up with him, they walked in silence over the ornamental stone bridge to the island in the lake. At the end of the bridge, Genyen stopped and gripped the balustrade.

'Tsun . . .' her voice was empty, her face white, and she retched. Tears poured down her face into the slowly moving waters of the dark blue lake beneath. 'Oh . . . no . . .'

Tsun knew that her pain and sense of loss were as deep as his own. He touched her arm in silent sympathy and she grasped his hand and held it tightly as if it were her lifeline to hope.

The small pavilion on the island was simply but exquisitely furnished. A rug covered the day bed on the patio and jade teacups were set on a delicately carved and brilliantly painted table, among superb thankas and decorated woodwork and plants in cloisonné vases.

Genyen and Tsun sat on a rug in the shadow of the patio. The pavilion was for the use of the Kundun only, but in their grief they thought nothing of this. Genyen slowly turned her head, appreciating the extreme blessing of being in this inner sanctuary of the Holy One. Then she raised her hands to her face and wept, deep, tearing sobs which shook her whole body.

After a while, her sobbing ceased and she lowered her hands to look at Tsun. The deep sadness of his expression made the realisation of Tul-lok's death even more certain.

'Why . . . why?' she moaned.

Tsun heard in her cry all the anguish of the bereaved and grief-stricken through the ages. Any words would have sounded banal in the stark reality of death, which was not, in truth, reality, but to mortal, dust-covered eyes seemed so terribly true.

Genyen was stifling her sobs and forcing herself to hear the sigh of the wind and the birdsong. In the distance the turbulent sounds from the crowds outside the Norbulinka floated through the air.

'This is the last refuge, in this garden,' she said. 'And for how long?' She looked at Tsun. 'Tul-lok was good to me . . .' She began to weep again, quietly, 'Oh, Tsun . . .' She leaned her head against his arm and gazed up at the turquoise blue sky. 'Why do our lives have to be like leaves falling from a tree, to be blown by the wind, even into the lake? We come together, to part, to rejoin, then the final separation. Nothing happens as we want it to . . .' She uttered the despairing cry of mankind. 'If only . . . if only . . .'

'We make our destinies, Genyen, we choose our course, unconsciously or consciously, we choose, each one of us.'

Her eyes looked into his. Never had she felt so helpless. Tsun touched her tear-stained cheek with gentle fingers, then lightly kissed her on the forehead. She raised her head, her waiting lips parted . . . her arms held him, she pressed her lips to his . . . and amidst her grief flowed hope, as he gently kissed her, his hand tenderly stroking her head.

'Why did you leave me, Tsun?'

'You know . . .'

'I shall never know! I love you . . .' she hesitated. 'And you loved me.'

'I still do, Genyen, you know that,' he said bleakly.

She searched his face, through eyes hazy with tears.

'Then why?'

'Because I was haunted after meeting Dorje Rinposhay. He gave me a glimpse of something I could not forget . . .'

'You could have tried, you . . .'

'I did! Holy Tara, those last months, how I did! I even thought of being a lay follower of Dorje Rinposhay, I thought that would be enough, but it was not! I had to *know*, Genyen. I had to see. I told you then . . .'

'It made it no easier.'

'I know. But when we were together during those last few months, we fought and argued too much . . . it would not have lasted.'

'Why do you think we fought?' She flung her head back and stared at him with blazing eyes. 'I know I was as much to blame, it was not easy for me either, Tsun. Since my father died and I became leader of his clan, *I* had chosen my men, and like it or not, they came . . . except for you. I loved you, and yet I thought I could treat you like the others. Even during the wonderful time when I realised that you loved me and wanted me, when you took me in a way I would allow no other man, even then, after so many years, it was hard sometimes not to treat you like the others.'

'That was our karma.'

'If only it could have been longer.'

'I thought about you . . .' Tsun's lips were pressed on hers, evoking old memories. '. . . all those years . . .'

'And I,' Genyen looked at him eagerly. 'I have never stopped thinking and wishing, Tsun.' She rubbed her cheek against his, holding him tightly, wanting to absorb, be absorbed . . . 'Tsun, could we begin again?'

He stroked her hair caressingly.

'No . . .' he murmured.

'Why?' She pushed herself back. 'Because of your cursed vows? You should not be with me now . . . hypocrite!'

'No, Genyen, I am not. I have been given a task to perform by Dorje Rinposhay.'

'You could still become a layman,' she insisted.

'And you could give up fighting.'

Genyen hesitated and her eyes fell from his gaze.

A duck took off from the lake, skidding across the water with flapping wings before rising slowly into the air.

Genyen raised her eyes to his again. 'And if I did, Tsun? If we made a bargain, would you give up your vows?'

He shook his head sadly. 'It would not work.'

'Damn you!' Genyen muttered fiercely.

'We are both too committed,' said Tsun.

'Oh, *life*!' Genyen laughed emptily. 'You are a bloody way of life. Tul-lok knew about us.' Her eyes filled with tears. 'He really cared for me, even though he knew that when he held me in his arms I was wishing for you . . . damn life!' She struck her open hand with a balled fist. 'I wish I had never met you again. It has made it so hard . . .' She brushed the tears from her cheeks with her hand.

'I had already decided to settle for Tul-lok. He was more like you than any other man I have known. We were both in the resistance, neither of us knew how soon we would be killed . . . but life goes on . . . damned life goes on, even now.' She flung her head back and railed at the sky. 'If only I had been the one to die . . . I could have been spared this anguish.'

She started to retch again, choking on her sobs. Tsun took her by the arms and drew her close. Her head rested on his chest, his hand stroked her hair. Gradually, a wave of calmness flowed over her, the pain numbed, her mind was stilled, and her eyes followed the flurried movements of the ducks on the lake. Frightened by the noise from outside the walls, a number of them rose in a body to circle the Garden of Jewels and glide down again to the lake, feet outstretched to touch the cold water.

'I was waiting for the moment . . . the right moment,' Genyen murmured. 'It is so cruel . . .' She drew back from Tsun's arms, sniffed and wiped her hair from her damp cheek. 'If my men could see me now,' she said more firmly, 'a weeping, pregnant woman!'

Tsun stared at her in disbelief. '*Pregnant!*'

Genyen nodded. 'I was going to tell Tul-lok.' She gave a bleak smile. 'Me, of all people, pregnant!'

She stared for a few moments at the ducks. 'It was a great shock when I realised that I was expecting a child. I had never before considered myself in the role of a mother.'

'What will you do?'

'I shall do nothing,' she sighed. 'Probably the child and I will soon die, before it has time to be born . . .' She paused, instinctively waiting for Tsun's denial, but none came. She looked up at him. 'This really is the beginning of the end?'

'Yes,' Tsun nodded. 'Yes, Genyen, it is.'

'And you know what it means?'

'No, I only know what I believe. I cannot be certain.'

'Please tell me, let me hope.'

'I can tell you nothing that . . .'

'So there is no hope?'

'There is always hope. The prophecies tell of us coming through our period of darkness.'

'Tsun,' Genyen sounded desperate. 'I know that we have little time left. When will you leave? Tomorrow?'

'No, Genyen, I must go today.'

He hesitated, then spoke to her urgently.

'Last night I arranged the escape of my sister and my pupils. If they leave now, they can always return; if they stay, soon they will never be able to escape. Would you consider coming with me to India?'

Genyen laughed and withdrew her hand from his.

'What masters of our own destinies we are. Neither of us can do what we want. I cannot come now, Tsun, too many men rely on my leadership.'

She moved closer to him, so that their bodies touched. Her hands sought him, he yielded for a moment, then pushed her away.

'No Genyen! I have told you, I am too committed.'

She stared at him, her face flushed with desire.

'But not wholly, or you would not have held me . . .'

'We owe something to the love we share, nothing can change that, but you ask me to sacrifice too much.'

She glowered at him. 'So, you are not a man any more, Tsun?'

His eyes blazed. He raised a hand to hit her . . . then dropped it to his side. His shoulders sagged.

'I am sorry, Genyen. I am truly sorry. It is not easy, you should realise that, for it was you who gave me the aphrodisiac.'

Genyen's face whitened. 'You . . . you know?' she stammered, then a fearful thought struck her. 'Tsun, everything that has been said here . . .' She moved her hands as though the words were patterns woven in the air about them. 'Was it . . . was it only because of *that*?'

'No,' he answered gently. 'I have been sincere with you, Genyen.'

Both were suddenly conscious of a low pitched whistle. It filled the garden, and even as they realised what it was, the shell hit the lake and exploded. It showered the two of them with water, and a cloisonné vase beside Tsun was shattered by a shell splinter, while another splinter buried itself in the woodwork and the body of a duck, bloody and torn apart, landed on the patio. At the sound of another shell, they both flattened themselves on the floor, but it exploded in the marshland short of the Garden of Jewels. They waited a few minutes, then, cautiously, they both rose to their feet.

'At last!' Genyen said, almost with pleasure.

Tsun watched the blood from the duck trickle slowly past his feet. He was mourning a death.

'It had to come,' Genyen went on. 'And these few days have given us time to prepare. The Cathedral is a fortress. The Potala is armed, so is Chakpori and the Norbulinka.'

'We have neither the equipment nor the men.'

'We have the skill. We have the city. We have the gods, because we are right. Can you not *feel* victory, Tsun? It is in the very air!' She moved to leave. 'I must go to my men.'

'Yes,' said Tsun quietly, 'and I must find out what the Mimang Freedom Committee is doing.'

They left the patio and rapidly crossed the bridge. As they reached the other side, a group of Khamba irregulars, carrying a mortar gun and a Lewis machine gun, ran past them. Everywhere, the troops, Khambas, and Lhasa citizens were preparing for the siege. Caught up in the swiftly changing pattern of events, the two of them parted with only a brief word of farewell, Genyen to take up command of her men who were guarding one of the gates.

Tsun gazed after her for a moment, then pushed his way through the crowd towards the Kundun's modest two-storeyed palace. People were streaming along the paths leading to the small whitewashed building, gay with brightly painted window frames. None of them knew that at that moment, a few yards away, the plans of the Grand Chamberlain were being put into effect in the Consul's room.

Expressing doubt over the wisdom of such a move, but aware of the dangerous signs, the Kundun formally took the Government's advice and informed them of his decision to quit Lhasa and establish the Government in the south of Tibet, in Khamba-held territory.

As Tsun approached the veranda and entrance to the Kundun's apartments, it was so crowded that he decided to wait a while.

'Rinposhay!'

He turned to see Jettie forcing his way through the crowd towards him. The youth was wearing a rifle slung across his shoulder and an ammunition belt around his waist.

'It has begun?' Tsun asked quietly, and he knew then that any plea from Ling on their behalf would have been as effectual as trying to hold sand in a sieve. It had been too late.

'Yes, Rinposhay.' Jettie's voice shook a little. 'But I do not understand why the Han attack is not heavier. They have only fired two shells at the Norbulinka.'

'As a warning, perhaps?'

'Which has only served to bring destruction on themselves. Premier Sukkhang is having to try and dissuade the army from attacking the Han Headquarters.'

'And what of the Freedom Committee?'

'We were arranging, as you know, to dismantle some of our barricades as a sign of goodwill, but now we are arming every man that we can.'

'But there is no cover outside,' said Tsun. 'The Han will kill you all.'

'We are taking up positions within the Norbulinka, laying in stocks of food, and a cannon is being taken in . . . have you heard about the Jo-Khang?'

Tsun nodded. 'I gather the Cathedral has become a fortress.'

'It could withstand a siege of six weeks or more.'

Tsun thought his estimate rather exaggerated.

'Rinposhay,' said Jettie, 'it would be most helpful if you could stay here to find out any news, for I have to go to the main gate to see if the men are in position.'

'I will stay,' Tsun agreed, and watched Jettie stride away.

Then he noticed a group of middle-aged women pouring petrol into bottles from jerry cans. Their motherly appearance belied their intentions. He caught hold of the arm of a servant who was passing.

'I am Tsun, Abbot of Dorje Ri-gon,' he explained. 'And I wish to see the Grand Chamberlain, Phala.'

The man bowed respectfully. 'I can do nothing,' he said apologetically. 'The Grand Chamberlain is in audience with the Kundun.'

Tsun let him go, and waited. He saw a number of officials leaving the apartments. They were arguing among themselves and planning with representatives of the National Assembly, the Civil Service, the army, the Freedom Committee.

Tsun watched them leave, then sat down, cross legged, on a low divan, and amidst the noise and bustle, he meditated.

Few paid any attention to him. Some recognised him and wondered at his presence. One or two even crept close enough to touch their foreheads on the hem of his robe in order to bless themselves.

The Jo-Khang

Brass Nose staggered as he pushed the flower box into a gap in the fortifications being built around the parapet, beneath the gilded roofs of Tibet's most holy place, the Jo-Khang Cathedral. He rested his forehead on the box's edge and heard one of the geraniums, scarlet and blooming, snap. He was aware of his increasing weakness and realised that death could not be far away. It was only through a supreme effort of will that he kept himself going. Of all his body, only his brass nose was unaffected by the advanced stage of scurvy. His now toothless gums were blackened and bleeding in his disfigured face.

He thought of the labour camp, where he had learnt to overcome the fear of death, for death slept with him, and he knew that, some day, it would wake him. What he hated most was the lingering, the fear of incapacity. He was grateful for the uprising. He wanted Tibet to be free. But most of all, he wanted to forget himself in the fight, and whether Tibet was won or lost would not matter to him when it was over.

Standing on the highest roof of the sprawling building, Brass

Nose was in the shadow of its gilded pagoda roofs. The city's main street encircled this, the very heart and centre of the Holy City. Opposite him, across the street, relaxing on a sandbagged flat roof, were some Han soldiers. Some lay asleep, others talked together while they cleaned a machine gun.

Brass Nose took a pair of field glasses out of a case tied to his belt next to his sword, and focused them on the outskirts of the city. Han soldiers were digging trenches across the main road from the city to the Potala and the Western gate. Slowly he panned with the glasses until he could see the Han setting up howitzers at all the city exits. He would have to report his observations to the City Council who were organising the police, Khambas and thousands of Lhasa citizens, to withstand the siege on the Jo-Khang. They were erecting barricades of torn-up flagstones at the entrance to the streets leading to the square. Women were carrying in sacks of tsampa and dried carcasses, and drawing water from the Cathedral well to make up a ceaseless supply of tea. Refugee families, with a few possessions, were settling themselves into corners of the Cathedral. As Brass Nose walked unsteadily towards the ladder leading to the lower levels, he saw a machine gun being brought onto the roof. Men were struggling up the ladders with machine gun belts. Women, talking and laughing as they had at their looms, were making petrol bombs on another roof. With crashing cymbals and deep roaring trumpets a procession of monks picked their way through the seething crowd in the courtyard to the inner hall, to invoke the forces personified as deities to keep the nation in safety; if it was necessary to fight, to ensure that Tibet won.

The Norbulinka

A bulky shadow fell across Tsun and awareness of it brought his mind back to the level of life. He opened his eyes to see the maroon-robed figure of Phala, the Grand Chamberlain, standing before him. Tsun rose to his feet out of respect. Both men bowed to each other and offered felicity scarves in greeting.

'Rinposhay,' Phala spoke quickly and without the usual inconsequential courtesies, keeping his voice low so as not to be heard by the members of the Mimang and other officials who were keeping a polite distance from them.

'I want your word that you will keep absolutely secret what I am about to say.'

'You have it.'

'The Kundun is to escape within the hour!' He paused for a moment to let the enormity of his statement sink in. 'His Holiness plans to establish his Government in the south. We want you to come with us.'

'To reach India with the documents more quickly, it would be better if I travelled alone.'

'But you will be safer with us, the route will be well guarded, also . . .'

'Will you go to India?'

'It is a possibility.'

'Then what use is it for me to take the documents? For the world will see and hear the Kundun himself speak of the fate of Tibet.'

'It is not certain . . . nothing is certain. We must see what happens, but your knowledge of the Injis' language will be of great service to us.'

'Kusho,' Tsun said, 'give me time to consider.'

Phala drew in his breath sharply, and moved his feet impatiently.

'Rinposhay,' he insisted, 'what is there to consider? Only a few are fortunate to have this opportunity. We leave within the hour.'

'If I do not attend your apartments,' Tsun answered gently, 'it will be because I cannot accompany you.'

'Cannot!' Phala said angrily, but still keeping his voice low. 'Do you realise the chance I am offering you? You do realise what could happen in Lhasa?'

Tsun nodded. 'Yes, Kusho,' he said. 'But I have been elected a leader of the Mimang Committee and if it is necessary for me to take the documents as a petition to the United Nations, that would be a reason for me to leave the country. If not, the people will need whatever help they can get when . . .'

'If I tell you that your presence will help the Kundun escape, will that make any difference?'

'I shall think.'

'Thinking,' Phala said bitterly, 'is a luxury. Now is the time for action!'

A young man dressed in a layman's blue chuba passed them and entered the adjoining chapel to sit for a few moments in silent meditation. Tsun did not move, but he realised that he was in the presence of the Kundun.

The sentry stood rigidly to attention as the Grand Chamberlain approached out of the twilight. With him was a small group of soldiers. Phala indicated one unarmed soldier with a nod of his head. The sentry handed the young man a rifle as he had been instructed, and as he passed it to him, the soldier pressed something into his hand. The sentry looked down at the tiny fragment of clay. It had been broken from a tablet containing a relic, and such tablets were broken and eaten at critical moments in life.

The young soldier pulled his woollen cap down over his forehead and swung the scarf round the lower half of his face. The sentry looked up and his eyes met those of the Kundun. The sentry slowly raised the fragment of clay to his mouth as he watched the Kundun follow the Grand Chamberlain through the side door into a rising sand storm.

With the Kundun's party went the documents for the United Nations. Tsun was staying.

He meditated throughout the night. The following day the officials who remained at the Norbulinka talked with the Mimang leaders and tried to dissuade the Tibetans from being the first to attack. But even as they talked, the resistance fighters were distributing arms and fortifying positions within the Garden of Jewels. The crowd outside the gates grew larger, although many who camped there had little idea of what was happening. Fathers helped their children to fly kites on the strong breeze, while the women kept tea constantly brewing and passed on the latest rumours. Already it was being murmured that the Kundun had mysteriously disappeared.

A large contingent of Khambas and military had been dispatched south to delay any following Han. It was rumoured that the Han were suspicious, but they spent most of the day preparing their positions throughout the city. Many of the soldiers made themselves a nice sum by selling bullets to the Tibetans.

The routine of the Royal Household continued as if nothing had changed. The gardens were tended, the horses exercised and groomed. Those clerks not engaged in military duty worked over their ledgers and records.

Genyen traced Tsun to the chapel. She stood in the doorway, her back to the sun, right hand hitched in her bandolier, and casting a long shadow. For a long time her eyes were on Tsun while he sat, sunk in meditation, and she realised with dread how strong was the rival for his heart. Her eyes were moist as she turned away.

'Rinposhay,' Jettie spoke softly, half afraid of disturbing the lama's meditation, yet equally anxious to talk with him. 'Rinposhay. . . ?' he said again, slightly louder.

'Yes Jettie?' Tsun was looking up at him with ebony eyes, the eyes that so many found startling and uncomfortably penetrating.

'Rinposhay, the leaders of the Freedom Committee have asked me to come and talk to you. We have received reports that the Han have started to search the Indian, Nepalese and Bhutanese Consulates.'

'What did they say?'

'They all refused, so the Han warned them to leave their buildings.'

'So,' Tsun said quietly, 'they are going to shell us.'

There was a moment's silence.

'It must be,' Jettie said. 'But we shall win. The whole city is ready to rise.'

Tsun appeared not to hear. He looked anxiously at Jettie.

'Disperse the crowd around the Norbulinka, I beg you.'

'Rinposhay!' Jettie was astounded. 'You know we cannot!'

'They have no protection against shells. They will be slaughtered.'

'But the Kundun?'

'Dead men cannot protect the Kundun.'

At last, Jettie asked the question the Freedom Committee had deputed him to ask.

'Rinposhay, the Han must think that the Kundun has escaped or gone into hiding.'

Tsun looked at Jettie long and the youth saw a heaviness about his features, as the Abbot realised the sense of purpose everyone in the garden had gained, to defend the Norbulinka, to freely declare their wish for a free Tibet. Young clerks, looking slightly incongruous in their ankle-length chubas, manhandled a mortar on iron wheels across a flower bed.

'Whether the Kundun escapes,' he said slowly, 'will depend on the gods.'

Jettie accepted the ambiguity and smiled broadly as he followed the Abbot through the milling crowd in the garden. Members of the Kundun's personal guard, exchanging their olive green PLA tunic and trousers for their Tibetan uniforms, recognised Tsun and made way for him.

'Jettie, we *must* disperse the crowd.'

'But, Rinposhay, how?' Jettie had difficulty keeping up with the lama as he strode through the gardens, past clumps of half grown flowers now trodden underfoot by the hundreds of people preparing to fight. He caught sight of Genyen helping to break open some crates of 57mm recoilless rifles to distribute them to the government officials.

As they drew nearer, Tsun counted the number of bullets she was giving out with each rifle.

'Eight is not many, Genyen.'

She gave a wry smile. 'Some have less.'

She continued to hand out the rifles, but the officials hesitated to take them, disconcerted by her lack of courtesy. Tsun laughed and freed his right arm from his upper robe, indicating, with a gesture, that she should continue.

'Rinposhay, when will you be leaving?' she asked.

He turned and began slowly walking away. 'When it is time,' he said without expression.

Genyen followed him. 'You cannot leave it too long.'

He smiled at her anxiety. 'I know, Genyen, but don't worry.'

'Tonight when it's dark would be safest. The Han may be fearful of coming out of their holes, but during the day, they have most of Lhasa covered.' She chuckled. 'The Grand Chamberlain, Phala, has banned the use of torches at night. I had not thought of it. Makes for as good a target as a camp fire.'

Tsun nodded. 'Genyen, we must disperse the crowd.'

'Why?' There was a note in his voice that chilled her. 'How?'

They were standing at the main gates, and as they swung open to allow a unit of the Tibetan army to take up their positions, a roar went up from the crowd. As it subsided, Tsun turned to Genyen.

'Genyen, why did the Han fire two shells at the Jewel Garden?'

'As a warning.' She looked surprised at his question.

'If our only response is to arm people, inadequately, we ensure their destruction. We have nothing to match the Han weapons and you know it.'

'We all know that,' Genyen shouted angrily. 'But will they? Will they attack a whole city? It's the whole city which has risen, Tsun. You and I are Khambas. We have warrior blood in our veins, but these are the quiet folk of Lhasa. Out there, it's not just the men, it's women and children, who for days have been demanding their freedom, who have marched to the Consulates begging to be heard. Is our determination going to be less?'

Before he could reply, Jettie returned and asked both of them to accompany him and three other representatives to the palace. As they entered one of the reception rooms, they caught sight of the Kundun's private secretary. Who would think that the Kundun had gone, Tsun thought, when he was still to be seen around the gardens? A monk closed the doors behind them. Suddenly, in that pillared room, with its intricately carved and painted decoration and wide glazed windows, there was the silence of former times. The elderly lama official with the goitre sat waiting for them. He acknowledged Tsun with a slight movement of his head. They each made a full prostration before the empty throne of the Kundun and then took their seats, drawing their legs beneath them. The monk poured tea into cups which were set on the small tables before the representatives.

The old lama held up a sealed paper. 'This is from the Kundun,' he said. 'Which of you will read it?'

The group looked at one another and nodded for the elder, a Guild leader, to take the letter. His hands trembled as he broke the seal. He read slowly the Kundun's reluctant agreement to escape from the city in the hope that he would be able to negotiate a settlement with the Han from an area outside their control. He thanked all the Mimang leaders for their loyalty, and begged them to persuade the people to remain peaceful and not initiate violence.

When they came out of the two-storeyed villa, the group instinctively made its way to the main gate. The crowd was getting noisier and angrier.

'Will this convince them,' Tsun murmured, 'when they know that they need no longer protect the Kundun?'

'Dare we tell them, Rinposhay?' Jettie asked.

'He is nearly two days away,' Tsun urged.

'Already,' Genyen added, 'there are rumours of his escape.'

'The Han are searching already,' Jettie said. 'If they *knew* they would mount a massive search, and the people . . .'

'You mean they would try to follow him?'

Jettie nodded.

'It is true,' Tsun murmured.

'All those people, Tsun, have come to protect the Kundun,' said Genyen. 'The longer the Han are uncertain, the safer he will be.'

As they climbed the steps to the gilt-roofed balcony overlooking the main gate, one of the Mimang leaders whispered to Jettie. Tsun stepped onto the granite of the wall and caught sight of Jigme Taring, the Kundun's personal photographer, taking photographs of the crowd. His tall figure was well known, as was his closeness to the Kundun and the fact that he had received an English education. His presence at the Norbulinka would convince many that the Kundun also remained. Including the Han, thought Tsun.

Tsun's fingers dug into the soft earth of one of the dozens of flowerpots arranged on the balcony, its red-painted woodwork picked out in entwining, delicately shaded flowers. Hundreds of faces looked up to the balcony, intrigued, as if expecting yet another appeal to disperse. The chant for a free Tibet grew. At least, Tsun thought, smiling at the irony, Tibetans have proved able pupils of the Han in slogan shouting.

As his fingers reached into the soil, he looked down on thousands of men, women and children stretching out before him, camped in a human wall round the Norbulinka. The majority had armed themselves, with daggers, staves, or anything which would serve as a weapon. Members of the resistance and Tibetan army had set up machine gun posts on the approach road, at the outskirts of the crowd. Many of the people were settled into a domestic routine, cooking on hundreds of fires, brewing tea, playing with their children, trading, preparing their weapons.

Genyen glanced at Tsun. The waning sun glinted on the golden medallion on the wall. Confusion broke out amongst part of the crowd as the attempted couplings of three street dogs erupted into fighting.

'Even if we convinced them, Tsun . . .' Genyen murmured.

'It is too late.' Tsun finished the sentence.

As Tsun and Genyen came down from the main gate, Jettie approached them.

'The Han have machine guns at all the entrances to the city, with barricades, mortars and armoured cars.'

'Breaking us down into contained and more manageable groups.' Tsun scratched the back of his head. 'Is there any way into the city?'

'Yes,' Jettie said. 'Across the meadows and down the alleys on the outskirts of the city. But many of the meadows are under water.'

'The Linkor?'

'We've no news of that being barricaded, but it would be difficult. You have to pass close to some of the well-established Han positions.'

'Still, it is something. Patrols?'

'They are too frightened.' Genyen was feeding cartridges into a bandolier.

Jettie left to join one of the dozens of groups planning action.

'What are you going to do, Tsun?'

The Abbot laughed and helped her feed the bullets into the belt.

'The Kundun will be far more effective than I, Genyen. So I stay, and fight for peace.' He laughed as he held up the belt.

'You believe that the Kundun will have to leave the country, Tsun?'

He nodded. She looked at him for some moments then, lifting her hand, she physically brushed away her thoughts with a dismissive gesture.

'Always, Tsun, you see the darkness, the depth of the river we cross.' She laughed a bitter laugh. 'The monastery has tamed you.'

'You saw what happened when the Han shelled the Norbulinka.'

A group of carpenters sent to help defend the Norbulinka by their guild, looked doubtfully at Tsun.

'If you dig trenches it will protect us.'

With evident disbelief they began to dig. One, a young man, came up to him with a young woman who had a baby tucked into her chuba. As Tsun's attention was diverted, some of the carpenters slipped away.

'Rinposhay, could you advise us?' Tsun received their scarves, returning and blessing them.

'I could not leave my wife at home,' the young man continued. 'There was too much shooting.'

'But it will be worse here when the Han attack.'

The baby grumbled as the woman pulled her chuba closer round him.

'Do either of you know the south?'

'I do, my wife doesn't.'

'Then leave tonight. The army still has control of the ferry.'

'But I am to be here. I wish to protect the Kundun. All the carpenters are protecting the Kundun.' The man looked at Tsun anxiously.

'Then one won't make any difference,' Tsun said, looking at them both. 'The Han will be very suspicious, so if you meet them, pretend to be beggars. If you can, try and get a horse once you are across the river, but you will attract less attention on foot.'

The young woman bit her lip as the danger became more immediate and personal. The man looked at his wife and baby.

'I can walk, Rinposhay.' She looked at her husband.

Tsun took threads from a cloth pouch in his ambac and swiftly tied the knot while blowing on it and murmuring the invocation. He laid the threads on their necks in blessing and placed one lightly on the neck of the baby, catching the devotion in the parents' eyes. They bowed.

'Be deterred by nothing. Do as I ask. May the Triple Refuge be with you.' He turned away abruptly.

The Drebung Monastery

The clouds had rolled back and the stars in the massive night sky were bright enough to illuminate the white pile of buildings aptly called Drebung, 'the heap of rice', at the foot of the mountains surrounding the Vale of Lhasa. With an official complement of 10,000 monks, the Monastic University was divided into six colleges, with monks from all over Tibet, and some from Mongolia, Ladakh, Sikkim, Bhutan and Nepal.

Kesang stood in the shadow of a horse as he inspected a revolver and watched the amazing sight of hundreds of young monks noisily pouring down the narrow lanes of the monastery. Many had torches and hurricane lamps, brilliant and hard after the mustard lamps in the monastery rooms. Officials of the Government Arsenal and monastery were arranging the distribution to the monks of weapons from three carts. The Abbot watched. With the monks, he was convinced that they must defend the Religion with whatever was available.

'Rinposhay!' Senge barked at Rinchen's approach. The monk frowned as he saw Kesang handling the revolver. Senge and the horse were cautiously sniffing each other, the horse thoughtfully grinding its teeth. Kesang moved to put the revolver back in the cart.

'Rinposhay,' Rinchen's voice was heavy. I'd better take it.'

The boy held the revolver out to the steward. They walked in silence back to their room, with Senge running ahead, black and white mop tail gently wagging at the intriguing lanes of Drebung Monastic University.

The Norbulinka

The weak electric light bulb in its dirty white plastic shade cast a bleakness over the whitewashed room, dulling the brilliance of the thankas and shrine. Thirty of the men and women of the Mimang, National Assembly, Guilds and Government officials were crowded together on felt rugs round a map of Lhasa spread on the floor before them. A large brass teapot was warming on a brass brazier.

'I wonder what General Tan is telling Peking.'

Tsun nodded and took the proffered snuff. Clustered in groups, the men and women were discussing possible tactics.

'Rinposhay,' the monk, with his sparse beard, tapped snuff onto his thumbnail and inhaled. 'If you were Tan, and had been criticised by Peking for allowing the rebellion in the east to spread, would you want to report that you did not know where the Kundun was, and that the citizens of Lhasa were in open revolt against the Han occupation?'

'What will he do? He can't back down.' Genyen was cleaning her rifle, working the buttered rag up and down the barrel.

'No, but if he can, he'll want to end it quickly and quietly.' Tsun paused. 'Then he will make sure that it will never happen again.'

'You assume defeat, Rinposhay.'

'No, I was just thinking that perhaps the world *and* Peking should know the truth from us.'

'The radio station?' Genyen looked at Tsun.

He nodded. 'But it is one of the best guarded places in Lhasa.'

'The Rinposhay's right,' Genyen said. 'If we could capture it, it would be worth many, many weapons.'

The noisy conversation in the room faltered as the light bulb flickered and finally went out, but it was nothing unusual. Then, as someone went to get a hurricane lamp, the first shell hit the roof of the small house in the Norbulinka.

In a kaleidoscopic moment, Tsun saw Genyen's startled expression, the shrine tilting, the butter lamps cascading, wood and plaster exploding above him as he was hurled from his feet. The room shook with the explosion, and Tsun cried out at the impact of debris falling on him. Suddenly, he was caught up in a tangle of arms and legs and heard the shattering of glass.

As he struggled to free himself, he heard calls of warning and glimpsed flames licking up the shrine hangings that had been ignited by the spilt coal of the brazier.

Two of the men managed to hack the hangings down with their swords, while Tsun threw rugs onto the swiftly growing stain of fire on the polished floor, in an attempt to douse it.

'Genyen, where are you?' he called. Although the flames had died, he could see the brazier embers glowing amongst the debris.

'Everyone out of here,' he shouted. 'This place is going to burn.'

All around him there were groans and curses as people tried to free themselves and find their way through the rubble in the darkness. Tsun was suddenly aware of shuddering explosions outside the room, of a tide of screams and shouts from the people camped outside the wall of the Norbulinka.

The room shook as another shell exploded a few yards away. The shattering of glass in the darkness chilled Tsun; in the smoky blackness he could see the glint of sharp fragments. A sliver had embedded itself in a wooden pillar and quivered there for a few moments.

'Genyen?'

He heard her. 'Here, Tsun! Help me!'

'Where are you?' He tried to locate the voice.

'Over by the shrine, Rinposhay.' One of the Mimang leaders was struggling to release Genyen's legs from the toppled shrine.

Tsun helped lift the shrine off her. She cried out in pain and, as her legs emerged, Tsun saw that they were covered in blood; a great sliver of glass had torn into one leg and was embedded there.

'Kunjosum!' Genyen yelled with pain as Tsun tried to ease the glass out.

'Get it out,' she hissed.

The room shook, and the shrine toppled again with a splintering of wood and breaking glass as images, ritual instruments and scriptures tumbled into the darkness. Tsun heard Jettie's agitated voice as he and other men tried to ease the pain of an official who had been hit by flying glass.

Tsun staunched the flow of blood from Genyen's leg with a felicity scarf. It was a clean, deep cut to the bone, but it hadn't cut the tendon and as soon as Tsun had tied the crude bandage she was up and on her feet. They both knew that the wound needed washing out with a herbal solution, for the risk of infection was high, but the danger of infection was not of immediate concern.

Relentlessly, shells pounded the Norbulinka. One exploded close to the room they were in and masonry was blown across the room by the blast.

'Let's get out!' Tsun yelled. His words were lost in a mind-numbing flash and explosion.

Chapter Thirty-Five

The Drebung Monastery

Kesang watched from the window of a house in Drebung. The mountains of the wide Lhasa valley, shadows against the darkness, Lhasa itself and the Potala, some three miles distant, were completely hidden from sight by the mountain outcrops. But Kesang could glimpse in the darkness the sudden brilliant flashes, could hear, moments later, the deep rumbling of the steady barrage. His lips moved in invocation, his fingers fumbled the beads wound round his hands. Senge sat on the floor leaning against his legs. The dog looked up into the boy's face and Kesang felt a periodic tremor in his small body.

Usually at this time of night, the thousands of windows in the monastery were dark; the pattern of daily activity was set by the rising and setting of the sun. Kesang did not look down at the turmoil in the narrow lanes of Drebung where hundreds of monks, some with electric torches and hurricane lamps, were hurrying about, discussing the latest news or rumour. Many believed that the Kundun had escaped. Enough had been heard of happenings in other monasteries for them to decide either to arm themselves or plan their own flight to the south.

'You are going, Rinchen-la?'

The steward nodded. 'Come with us,' he said.

The monk chuckled. His face was heavily lined, his nose large and thick, and short grey hair encircled the back of his brown polished skull. 'I am too old now,' he said. The two men looked at each other for a few moments, both aware that they were beginning a critical journey of which they knew nothing. Silently they exchanged felicity scarves and the monk left.

The room was lit with two mustard lamps. The flames flickered wildly in the draught from the open windows, casting strange, dancing shadows on the walls. Rinchen removed his fourteen-foot long maroon robe, carefully folded it and looked for a few moments at the pile of rags.

He watched Kesang's silently moving lips. The boy's eyes no

longer looked out over the darkness, but were half closed in meditation.

'Rinposhay.' Kesang did not move. Then, his eyes opened, his lips became still. For a moment, he thought of his fading memories of his previous life, but without regret; his life was now, that was his karma, as it was Tsun's to be at the Norbulinka. It would be their karma, as Tsun had said, to meet again.

'Rinposhay . . . Kesang-la?'

'Yes, Rinchen-la.' The boy turned to the steward and stared in disbelief at his patched and ragged layman's chuba. Rinchen smiled and then joined in Kesang's uninhibited laughter. Senge, front legs flat on the floor, back legs straight, his tail in the air, barked vigorously at the noise.

'These are yours, Rinposhay.' Rinchen pointed to a dirt-encrusted, tattered sheepskin chuba and some rags.

Kesang did not ask why; he just changed, taking off his robes and, still laughing, began pulling on the filthy, battered boots he was to wear with the chuba. He tied it with a stained red cloth belt, the long curling wool of the sheepskin, which he wore next to his skin, bunching out at the edge. Senge ran round him, sniffing the wealth of history adhering to the skins. He sat and sniffed the boots for a few minutes, then was suddenly standing on his hind legs to sniff high up the coat. Kesang laughed and pushed the dog away. He put his soft sheepskin hat on his head and placed his hands on his hips, looking pugnacious.

Rinchen laughed.

'Your face is far too clean.'

Kesang ran over to the teapot brazier. Using his hat to protect his hand, he lifted one side of the brazier to slip his fingers round the inside of the base. They emerged covered in blackened soot which he rubbed liberally over his face.

He looked at Rinchen, and caught sight of the steward slipping the revolver into his chuba. Unsure whether Kesang had seen him, Rinchen smiled and felt guilty. Kesang rubbed his blackened hands on Senge, who looked troubled as his long white hair became grey and dirty.

'We need baskets of yak chips,' said Rinchen, pulling the straps of the tube-like baskets over Kesang's shoulders. 'And a stick.' He was looking round the room. 'I can have a bad leg,' he said.

As they both walked down the narrow lanes, sloping towards the valley floor, monks hurried past. One of them recognised Rinchen, and then realised that Kesang was with him. Their disguise aroused great interest, and impatiently Rinchen explained the reasons for their strange appearance. Senge began to dig vigorously at the base of a wall.

'It is too dangerous,' one of the monks said, 'just for the two of you. Let us get a message to the resistance and arrange an escort.'

Rinchen rejected the idea, his concern growing as other monks gathered round, intrigued by what was happening. Realising Rinchen's anxiety to get away, the monk bowed and presented Kesang, then the steward, with scarves. Kesang blessed them as he returned them, causing even more curiosity among the gathering onlookers.

'Kesang, quickly now.'

The boy was surprised to hear the steward use his personal name as, swinging his stick, he set off down the lane.

'Senge, quickly, come on!' Kesang picked the dog up and tucked him in his chuba.

Suddenly, one of the monks leaned over and pressed a small yellow cloth-covered package containing a relic into Kesang's ambac.

'It was given to me by my tutor,' he said. 'I hope it will help you.' Kesang mumbled his thanks and, holding the basket on his shoulder, made off after Rinchen.

They had been walking for nearly an hour through the barley fields, Senge keeping beside them. The dim lights of Drebung had faded from sight. The clouds hung low, even the starlight had vanished. In the blackness, they were able to use the occasional mani walls and chortens by the vaguely defined track, to give them direction. Kesang felt the cold eating into him.

From the darkness, they could hear the distant pounding of the Han artillery, as rhythmic and unceasing as their every step. Neither spoke. Neither could believe that anything could survive that onslaught. It was some two hours later when they heard the sound of engines moving slowly, obscuring the sound of the artillery. They stopped and listened. Any other sound was welcome.

'Han trucks!' Rinchen whispered. Kesang listened; somehow, a long time ago, he had heard that sound . . . the iron guns on wheels!

They walked on as the column of tanks followed the northern road at the foot of the mountains heading towards the Potala.

The clouds began to lift and Kesang could just make out in the distance the vague black shape of the Potala and, close to it, the five hundred-foot iron hill with the Tibetan Medical College. For a few moments, he looked and listened, and then ran to catch up with Rinchen. Ahead was the surging torrent of the Kyi-Chu river; silhouetted against it were the round shapes of five coracles, propped on end with poles to enable them to dry out. Others, like black domes, lay with their bottoms up on the low sandbank. Kesang picked up Senge and tucked him in his ambac as they approached the bank, looking for the campfire of the boatmen.

Kesang pointed at smoke coming from behind the shelter of three coracles leaning against one another.

'Limp, Rinchen,' he murmured. The steward dragged his right leg slightly, leaning on his stick as they moved towards the coracles. For a moment they could not make out who had stepped from behind the boat; the torchlight shone in their eyes. Then they caught sight of the olive-green uniform and the 75mm recoilless rifle in the other hand.

Rinchen bowed low, showed his tongue and began sucking in his breath with the exaggerated humility of a beggar.

'Kusho, we are looking for a boatman and a way across to our village. We have been visiting relatives.'

Unable to understand, the young Han soldier called to a colleague, who stepped out from behind the shelter of the coracles. He was slightly older than his companion and was smoking. With a combination of gestures and Tibetan phrases, he began asking Rinchen who he was and why he was there. Rinchen, partly in mime, told their story. Kesang was fascinated by the steward's change of character.

'You don't have to bow to us, old man,' said the soldier, and again, through gestures and strangled Tibetan phrases, explained that the PLA would free Tibetans like them from their own servility. His eye was caught by Senge looking out of Kesang's ambac and as he scratched the dog's head he disclaimed all knowledge of the boatmen. Kesang was aware of the younger soldier idly looking into their baskets with his torch. Giving Kesang a sweet, the older soldier advised them to return to their relatives.

'Better go back,' he finished.

Rinchen took Kesang by the hand.

The soldier was taken by the boy, he had impudence and a knowingness. He is no ordinary beggar child, he thought, and as the two walked away he called after them.

'Here!' He pressed some coins into Kesang's hand. 'We need

fuel,' and he led them over to the campfire, motioning Kesang to empty the yak chips from his basket. Rinchen's face tightened as Kesang deftly upturned the basket onto the ground and lifted it, leaving the yak chips in a neat pile.

The steward thanked the soldier profusely, and as they turned to go, both caught sight of the younger soldier pulling something out of the pile of yak chips with his bayonet.

'What's this?' The soldier with the cigarette caught the look of apprehension in Kesang's face. He put the cigarette in his mouth and, leaning against the coracle, placed his hand on the pistol at his waist. The soldier held up the reliquary box. It glittered in the flames of the camp fire. The other two soldiers in the patrol went over to look at it.

'It's mine,' Kesang said, looking at the corporal.

'Yours?' The corporal kept the cigarette between his teeth as he spoke and pulled a disbelieving face at the boy. Then, grabbing Kesang firmly by the arm, he motioned Rinchen to sit by the camp fire. As he came up to them, Kesang saw Rinchen's right hand move to his ambac. He was barely two feet from the corporal when, as he steadied himself on the stick and bent to sit, he pulled the trigger of the revolver in his ambac. Under the impact of the shot the corporal gasped, staggered and collapsed.

'Run, Kesang, run!' ordered Rinchen.

Blood was seeping swiftly into the olive-green tunic; one of the other soldiers grasped Rinchen. Balling his fist, Kesang drove it into the man's crotch. Senge hurled himself at the third soldier as he pulled the trigger of his rifle, sending a bullet skimming off Rinchen's arm. The youngest soldier sought the cover of the coracles.

'Run!' Rinchen yelled. Turning quickly, he stumbled over the second soldier, who was kneeling, gasping in pain as he clutched his private parts. He saw the man's hand reach towards his rifle on the ground, and for the second time that night, Rinchen pulled the trigger of his revolver.

Kesang looked back at the sound of the shot. Rinchen was pounding after him, the dog running between them.

'Run, Kesang!'

Gasping with exertion, Rinchen was close behind as they ran for the life-giving obscurity of darkness.

A single shot. A gasping groan. Kesang turned. Rinchen lay on his side. More shots. A bullet plucked at Kesang's chuba. He ran with the dog into the darkness, towards the mountains.

Chapter Thirty-Six

The Norbulinka

Crouching low, men came running through the trees with shovels.

'Dig!' Tsun shouted. 'With anything you've got. Dig deep enough to lie in. Then we've got a chance.'

No one had ever seen shelling before and few believed they would live through the night. Tsun helped up a man who had tripped and fallen, clutching two nine-inch shells. He was one of the tailors carrying shells from the Norbulinka to the three First World War guns which the Tibetan army had sited as close as possible to the army camp and artillery. They kept up a high level of fire, putting two Han guns out of action and drawing such fierce fire on themselves that they had to manhandle the guns to new positions. The tailors, and any man or woman willing to help, kept up the flow of ammunition, and anyone who was able urinated periodically onto the breech to keep it cool.

The wounded had been brought to one of the Norbulinka temples where Tibetan doctors worked swiftly. Genyen's injury had been washed with appropriate herbs and bound. She sat on a rug talking to a young man whose leg had been blown off at the knee. His hands gripped hers in a desperate appeal. For half an hour there had been a pause in the shelling. The Mimang leaders had agreed to Tsun's idea of digging as many trenches as possible, and anyone not engaged in defensive duties was helping with the work. It was so cold that their breath was freezing in the night air.

Tsun stood listening, counting the rhythm of the Howitzer shells, the acrid smoke and dust catching in his throat and making him cough. Figures appeared and disappeared, running, diving for cover, trying to find some means of counter-attack. He estimated the pause in the shelling and ran, only the feel of the gravel path beneath his feet giving him direction to the main gate. In the few moments' pause in the shelling, he heard the shouts and screams of the wounded, of the frightened, of the lost. The citizens of Lhasa had never seen or experienced an artillery barrage.

He heard the frightened snorting of the two horses just in time to avoid being trampled as they careered in terror across his path. The shelling continued, one falling close and catching Tsun in the blast; the heat reached his lungs as he was hit by a hail of earth, stones and branches from a willow torn up by the explosion. He managed to gulp enough air to prevent his lungs collapsing.

As the smoke cleared, the high granite wall of the Norbulinka loomed ahead. Dozens of soldiers, Khambas and ordinary Lhasa citizens were milling around the great wooden gates.

Tsun's foot caught under something yielding, sending him sprawling over a dead man. He put his hand on the body to help himself up; it came away covered in blood. He wiped his hand on his robe, and for a few seconds his consciousness was on the anonymous body, to aid his release and rebirth.

He forced his way past a group of soldiers on the steps leading to the ornate, gilt-roofed balcony above the gate. They were chiselling out mortar from between the granite blocks to make a machine gun port. Once on the balcony, he was amazed and relieved to see that the megaphones were still there, sitting on a low table at the back.

There was less smoke outside the wall, and Tsun realised both that the Han had been very careful with their siting, and why there was an almost continuous barrage. Most of the shells were falling within the wall, and were fired from the Han garrison to the north of the park, the PLA Headquarters on the far side of the Happy River to the south, and from the Shuktilinka, a small park built by the Han as a gift to the Kundun. During the past few days, hundreds of Han troops had been reinforcing it with sandbags and digging in artillery positions.

The vast crowd was aimlessly milling. Men, women and children, some even trying to make their way along the road to the Potala and the city, right in the line of fire. A number of shells were falling short. As some, in fear, turned back, others, armed with anything they could lay their hands on, even pieces of wood, were surging forward determined to have revenge.

'Get to the meadows, you'll be safe there,' Tsun bellowed through a megaphone.

'The Kundun is safe. He wants you to go to safety.'

Again and again he repeated the call, and as some heard and began to make for the meadows, others followed.

Later in the night, Jettie and another leader came to help Tsun. They found him caked in dirt and blood, his robes torn, his voice hoarse, unrelentingly shouting against the sound of the explosions.

Jettie picked up another megaphone and, in turn, they shouted the simple instructions, for the most part unheard; in horror they watched the slowness of the response and the terrible effect of the shells falling on the crowd, the shrapnel burst timed before it hit the ground to achieve the maximum kill.

Over 10,000 people were camped around the Norbulinka and inside were 1,000 defenders. Virtually none of their weapons could reach the Han positions. The only retaliation came from the five hundred-foot iron mountain, where some Tibetan Army troops had dug in with a cannon and were keeping up a steady rate of fire on the Shuktilinka.

Jettie's hands shook slightly on the megaphone. A nine-inch shell tore through the roof of the balcony. The three men looked up and threw themselves down as it hit the floor by Jettie, bounced and rolled towards him. Jettie's lips moved in silent prayer and his whole body shuddered as he lay beside the unexploded shell.

At dawn, the shelling stopped. In the spring sunlight, Tsun and Jettie looked out over the Norbulinka. All the buildings were damaged. In the silence that was no silence, they could hear the anxiety in hundreds of voices. The moans of pain, the weeping and, from directly beneath the balcony, a man's stifled, agonised groans. Amongst the tangled and broken groves of willow and poplar, their strings of prayer flags caught and twisted like some strange cats' cradle, lay the torn and mangled remains of men and horses. The whole park was pock-marked with craters.

The gates beneath the balcony swung open, and the crowd cheered as Genyen and a group of Khambas rode out with two pre-Second World War field guns harnessed to mules. Genyen looked up at Tsun and waved. Something held her attention and she pointed. Tsun and Jettie saw two Yun-5 bi-planes flying southwards, their slow manoeuvrability making them ideal for reconnaissance in the mountains.

A single shot ended the breathless groans of the man below.

New Lhasa

It was quiet at the radio station. It had gone off the air within hours of the uprising's beginning. It was an insignificant building, Tashi thought, as he wondered how long it would be before the light of the false dawn became the dawn. A corrugated iron hut close to the transport centre between the city and the Potala, its significance was underlined by the high concrete wall surrounding it, and by the trench dug a few yards back inside the wall.

Tashi and three young Khambas walked quietly across the grass towards the sandbagged heavy machine gun emplacement. In the distance, Tashi could hear the sound of firing and the occasional sharp explosion of a mortar. There was dew on the grass; it clung to the minstrel's boots. He made to scratch his cheek, but the rope around his wrists stopped him. The PLA men with them stopped. The soldier near Tashi did not speak Tibetan. He turned the young Khamba by the shoulders, and as he tapped his knees and pointed to the ground with his rifle, their eyes met. The troops at the radio station were seasoned men, not the youths who made up most of the PLA. In that moment of rapport, Tashi knew that the soldier also did not want to be there. He felt his waist-length pigtail being grabbed and painfully hacked off. He heard the safety catches, the murmured invocations of his compatriots, and as his shout, 'Tibet!' hit the air the bullets blasted him and the three Khambas in the backs of their heads.

The sun glinted on the metallic blue of the rifle barrels. The crowd of Tibetans gathered at the tall, metal chain-link gates were stunned into silence by the shots before they took up Tashi's cry. For a few moments all was quiet at the radio station.

Lhasa City

The two planes circled low over the city as they flew southwards, radioing back to the Military Area Command on the deposition of the 'rebel' forces. They were well established in the enormous squat turrets guarding each end of the Potala, and had already succeeded in repelling a Han infantry attack on the Palace. Beneath the Potala, at the village of Sho, Han infantry and tanks sealed off the main road into the city. Hundreds of civilians were protesting on both sides of the barricade. The pilots reported that the largest demonstration, with thousands of people, was at the open area in front of the Han Transport Centre. They had been gathering all morning, with banners and posters calling for a free Tibet, and although, so far, the demonstration had been peaceful, the pilots confirmed the potential danger. The transport compound was not heavily guarded and contained fuel supplies, trucks and jeeps. The radio station was close by and twice already had been unsuccessfully attacked. Such a crowd of growing size was too close to Han Headquarters. Four jeeps with mounted machine guns were sent to disperse it.

The pilots saw increased activity at the Jo-Khang Cathedral, with barricades being erected in the square. Their reports on the heavy concentration of Tibetan troops and Khamba irregulars at the river confirmed the growing suspicion that the Kundun had been smuggled out of Lhasa and into the mountains to the south, where the resistance had established a stronghold.

The pilots could make out little in the narrow lanes of the houses clustered around the Cathedral. Pema, Namgyal, Jigme and Champa, backs flat against a wall, watched the planes fly overhead. They had left their departure too late and found it impossible to reach Drebung. Pema was dressed in a thick serge chuba and felt boots, but her most significant rejection of the Han way of life was her hair. She had carefully unplaited her pigtails, letting her long hair fall loose.

The only noise in the narrow, muddy lane was the eager snuffling of two pigs nosing round the accumulated heaps of offal, and the sound of gunfire from all over the city, against a background of artillery bombardment of the Norbulinka and the Potala. Namgyal signalled to the others and as swiftly as possible they made their way down the lane, keeping close to the sloping, whitewashed walls. Almost every window displayed flowering plants in pots and gaily painted tins.

Pema saw four Han soldiers, bent low, running across one of the flat roofs. They disappeared, and the unnatural quiet of the lane made Pema uneasy; she felt sure that fighting would erupt at any moment.

Just as the group reached the end of the lane, one of the pigs cantered past, careering into Champa who stumbled and fell over the dark, heavy animal. As he brushed the evil smelling mud from his robe, a woman turned into the lane, followed by a little girl of around four years old. For a moment, the woman hesitated instinctively, fearing that they might be Han, then on seeing that the group were Tibetan, she walked towards them, leaning heavily to the left under the weight of her large leather water pail. The little girl ran bare footed towards Champa. Pema assessed the woman as being in her thirties; her chuba and rainbow-striped apron were dusty and creased. The two women smiled at one another. Pema looked back as she heard Champa's laughter. The little girl, in a tiny chuba, one hand in the crease of her bare bottom, was standing with knees bent, laughing uninhibitedly as the young monk tried to push his way through the pigs snuffling among a pile of rubbish at the narrow intersection.

'You!' Champa spun round at the sound of the Han voice. A few yards away, a Han patrol of some twenty men was walking towards him. The officer was covering him with a rifle. Pema, Jigme and Namgyal heard the shout and saw Champa's reaction while they were still a few yards behind him and out of sight of the patrol. The woman with the pail called softly from a doorway. She had just reached the door of her home as the patrol sighted Champa. Namgyal, Pema and Jigme quickly followed her and the child inside.

The bayonet dug through Champa's robe. He saw suspicion and acuteness in the officer's eyes. The patrol was nervous and kept glancing at the rooftops. A cluster of narrow prayer flags, hanging on six-foot poles at the corner of a house, rustled in the breeze. Whatever the officer was about to say to Champa was drowned in the screams and shouts of an army of women who suddenly appeared on the roofs on both sides of the narrow street. As they began bombarding the troops with large stones which had been stacked in readiness behind the parapets, Champa ran. Glancing back, he saw a soldier aiming his rifle at him and twisted and dodged as he ran.

'Champa.' He saw Jigme at the door of the woman's house and dashed for it, keeping low.

The women were skilled, working in two waves to maintain a constant rain of stones on the Han and giving them little opportunity to recover from the initial surprise. Three Han found cover in the doorways and opened fire, wounding three of the women and killing two. Their bodies pitched over the rooftops with the stones they were about to throw, whereupon eight Khambas appeared from one of the houses in the midst of the patrol and, working swiftly with their foot-long daggers, quickly eliminated them. No more firing was heard. In minutes one Khamba and eighteen Han soldiers lay dead.

Through the holes they had made in the rice paper-covered windows, Pema and Namgyal saw the killing of the remaining two soldiers, who had been severely battered by the stoning, as the patrol was quickly stripped of its weapons and ammunition. The women had melted away.

Jigme looked back from the doorway at Champa.

'Come on,' he beckoned as he disappeared into the street. When the others had thanked the woman and left the small house, they found Jigme waiting for them. The Khambas had disappeared and Jigme's chuba bulged with the automatic pistol and ammunition he had persuaded them to give him.

They kept to the streets on the edge of the city, where the fighting was not so intense. The shops were shuttered and most people seemed to be outside, demonstrating or fighting. From almost every rooftop, plumes of white incense smoke rose into the sky, as families invoked the aid of Chenresi, the Lord of Compassion.

They made slow progress as they exchanged news of the fighting and the latest rumours about the Kundun. The Guild of Masons had at last been able to get weapons: a rifle and fifty bullets for every two men. The news that the PLA rarely ventured into the streets, keeping instead to their fortified positions, infected them all with the general feeling of excitement and exhilaration. Hope of freeing the city, even the country, swept through Lhasa.

Fighting was intense in the Barkor, the main shopping street around the Jo-Khang. A number of shops had been heavily fortified by the Han, and there was a constant exchange of fire between them and the positions held by groups of citizens. Keeping low and close to the wall, Jigme led the group towards a side door of the four-storey Cathedral, in the heart of the city. A mortar shell exploded a few yards away as they ran for shelter.

The Norbulinka

The houses in the Norbulinka Park were being fortified and more machine gun ports knocked through the great granite wall surrounding it. Tsun had realised that the telegraph wires between the Han camps around the Norbulinka were still intact, and he was discussing with Jettie the quickest and easiest way of putting them out of action, when wild cheering from the crowd outside cut short their conversation; they hurried over to the main gate as it swung open.

A long-nosed truck drove slowly through the gate and into the Norbulinka. It was covered with people – in the truck itself, on the cab roof and on the running board.

'Tul-lok!' Tsun couldn't believe his eyes as his cousin climbed down from the cab. They clasped one another.

'I heard you were short of ammunition, so I brought some!'

'I thought you were dead!'

As they talked, Tul-lok was looking round the Norbulinka. Dozens of people lay where they had been killed. The gardens and grass had disappeared in shell holes. Mangled horses lay among uprooted and broken trees. Some of the small four-roomed officials' houses were gutted, their ruins still smoking. The

Kundun's small palace had had part of a wall blown away and the gilded, cylindrical 'Victorious Banners' of Buddhism hung crazily over the edge of the roof.

'I was just concussed,' Tul-lok said quietly as they walked towards the temple. 'Then I was at the Potala.'

'What happened?'

'We repelled two infantry attacks. They went on sending in the men to be mown down. It can't be long . . . where's Genyen?'

'She's gone with two field guns to the garrison to draw the fire of the Han.'

'She's mad!' Tul-lok looked at his cousin. 'Nothing could reach them from here. We were being pounded into the ground.'

They both saw in each other's eyes the dreadful truth of the situation. A few feet away lay the twisted remains of the golden Wheel of the Law from the portico of the temple; the roof above was blackened and partly falling in.

The two men stood by the doorway. Pillars leaned crazily, frescoes, thankas and hangings were covered in soot and dust. One end of a roof beam rested on the floor. Over a hundred severely wounded men lay in the dimly lit temple. Where possible, monks and laymen were removing shrapnel, stitching wounds and trying to prevent blood loss, with only the minimum of resources to help them, no anaesthetic and little to relieve pain. Many of the injured had severe abdominal and chest wounds, and knew they would eventually die. At the far end of the temple, before an image of Chenresi, his thousand arms extended to the suffering of mankind, sat a group of monks, their deep voices intoning mantras, their hands moving in an impressive dance reflecting their meditation, the energy awakened within expressed through every movement of their bodies.

South Tibet

The young man in the dark blue chuba and woollen balaclava urged his horse along the mountain track, so narrow that the party was strung out in single file. The clouds were low, and he polished his rain-spotted glasses on his sleeve, listening intently to the aircraft overhead. The cloud protected the Kundun's party from discovery.

Chapter Thirty-Seven

The Jo-Khang

Pema had had to borrow the striped apron, as they were usually only worn by married women. By holding it out, it could easily accommodate eight grenades. During the night, Lhasa City Council and Mimang leaders had decided to launch a pre-dawn attack on the main Han strongholds that encircled the Jo-Khang Cathedral and cut the city off from possible reinforcements from the Norbulinka. Guildsmen and volunteers were armed from the Government Arsenal in the Jo-Khang. For whether it was a family's wealth, a village's surplus grain or the State's arms, the monasteries, by tradition, were the safest depositories.

Throughout the night, Pema and dozens of other women threaded their way through the thousands of people camping in the enormous courtyards round which the Jo-Khang was built, carrying grenades, mortar shells and ammunition in their aprons. They all felt secure in the Jo-Khang, which had been built thirteen hundred years before, at the time of the country's conversion to Buddhism, by King Srong-Tsen Gampo, to house the superb image of the Buddha which had been brought to the King by his Han queen. Many of the refugees had sought safety within its walls, using the hundreds of chapels, four storeys deep, that surrounded the courtyards, adding their butter lamps and felicity scarves to those of past generations. Knowing that the Jo-Khang, the Temple of the Buddha, was not only the holiest place in the country, but revered by people throughout Central Asia, few had doubts about their safety.

Pema gasped as she slipped on a greasy flagstone, and a grenade bounced out of her apron. It rolled into a three-inch dip in a flagstone, worn away by generations of devotional prostrations. As she picked it up, Pema caught Champa's eye amongst the hundred or so monks meditating before the main shrine. He smiled at her, his fingers working steadily over the wooden beads of his rosary.

As she handed over the grenades, Pema saw Jigme talking to a familiar hunched figure. He turned, and a flame glinted in reflection from brass.

'Jigme-la, Brass Nose!'

But Jigme was gone before she could reach them. There was a quality about Brass Nose which Pema felt dissipated much of the impact of his appearance.

'Pema-la! Come quickly with me.' He led her up the steep steps to the first floor roof and pointed across the cobbled square to a large three-storeyed house set back from the corner of the square by a wooden fence. The night sky was clear of cloud and she could see how well fortified the house was, with trenches behind the fence, sandbagged mortar and machine gun positions on the ground and the flat roof. It was full of PLA troops. Dozens were sleeping on the roof.

As Pema watched and time went by, she wondered whether anything was going to happen, but a glance at Brass Nose was enough. He had the alert, still and patient attention of the hunter. Suddenly, the house erupted in flame and shooting. Jigme, with eleven other monks, had worked his way through the fence and hurled petrol bombs through the windows. As he threw another bomb, Han troops came charging out of the house, firing automatic rifles. A figure in blue amongst the olive-green uniforms caught his eye, and as he ran for cover he realised it was Ling.

The Norbulinka

The raven, a bird of the deities, usually so eager to be in at the kill, had flown away a few moments before the artillery bombardment of the Norbulinka was renewed, in the late afternoon. High up on the rough-hewn telegraph pole, Jettie worked on, cutting the telegraph lines and praying that a shell would not hit him. Of the thousands of people around the park, many had fled only to find the road to the city cut by Han barricades and tanks, and had been forced to return. Others had sought shelter in the meadows and hundreds were trying to reach the river to escape south. Thousands remained, convinced that they must resist whatever happened, even if only with a stick or a cooking knife. The willow and poplar groves lining the processional route to the Potala Palace had been decimated by shells and by the resistance who were lopping the trees to make barricades.

Against the unrelenting sound of artillery and mortar shells, and the agonised cries of the horses, Tsun heard frantic shouting, and suddenly, machine guns positioned along the wall were brought into action. The mortar on the balcony over the main gate began firing. Wave upon wave of Han infantry had been sent in to take the park. Many were mown down by the machine guns, but more took their place.

Standing amidst the smoking ruins of the stables, Tsun shot the first horse. A cluster of shells had hit the stable roof, bursting among the horses. Over a dozen lay maimed, stomachs torn open, legs ripped off, heads pulped by the shrapnel. Tsun knew he might be doing the same to men soon. He doubted whether anyone in the Norbulinka would survive.

As he ran back towards the temple, Howitzer shells were being steadily lobbed into the Norbulinka park. Tsun threw himself to the ground, yelling to the man in front of him, but the latter just stood, turning slowly. The shell hit the soft ground and burst, blasting an enormous crater and deluging them with earth, rocks and debris, but the man remained unharmed. Truly, Tsun thought, he must be protected by the gods. He got up and began walking towards the man. As he drew closer he recognised Jettie, heard his plaintive cry and saw the blackened face with a livid scar.

'Help me . . . I can't see . . . someone help me.'

'Jettie, it's Tsun. You must run.' Tsun took his arm to guide him and they both ran, stumbling, towards the temple. As they reached the doors, Tsun saw three men crouched arguing around someone on the ground. He was screaming. Tsun put out a restraining hand as he saw the pistol. One of the men looked at him. Tsun followed his glance to the wounded man. He lowered his hand. The pistol was fired.

Shelters had been made for the wounded from fallen beams leant against the granite walls of the small temple.

'I thought I was going to be trapped up that pole when I saw the troops coming,' Jettie chuckled, as Genyen bathed his face in the semi-darkness. 'And nobody bothered to look up. In all that fighting, nobody bothered to look up!'

'You have some good karma, Jettie.'

'I think perhaps,' he smiled without rancour, 'none of us has, Genyen.'

'Keep down!' Tul-lok put his hand on Tsun's shoulder. From a vantage point at the outer wall, heavily overhung and hidden by willow trees, Tsun and Tul-lok were able to see what was happening outside the Norbulinka. The crowd had either scattered, or was engaged in hand to hand combat with the Han. Tsun saw women and children hurling themselves with suicidal fury at the troops, mostly young conscripts. The Tibetans' seemingly insane actions only confirmed the Han distrust of the barbaric 'green brains'. Hundreds of people were trying to escape to the river, to the city, to Drebung and the farms of the vale, but they found themselves trapped in the Han encirclement. All around the wall lay the dead and dying. Tibetans, Han, men, women and children. Tsun ducked as bullets rang ricocheting off the granite walls. Leaves and bits of branches, nicked by flying bullets, fell from the overhanging trees onto the two men.

'We can't hold out much longer!' Tul-lok shouted. 'The main gate can't stand up to much more. I'm going to withdraw my men. More reconnaissance planes have been sighted and the PLA is moving south. We've got to try and slow them down while the Kundun has a chance to get his headquarters established.'

As they climbed down from the wall, back into the shell-torn Norbulinka, Tsun asked:

'What about the wounded?'

'What do we do, Tsun? I can take men who can walk, but no one else.'

Tsun nodded. 'And Genyen?'

Tul-lok grinned broadly. 'She's agreed to come with me. You must also come, cousin. With your background, if the Han capture you, you won't have a chance.'

Tsun did not reply as, keeping low, they made their way towards the temple.

'You know what will happen, Tsun. Don't give them that victory.' Tul-lok looked at his cousin. They stopped for a few minutes in the cover of the inner wall and Tsun offered Tul-lok some snuff. As Tul-lok took it, he was conscious that Tsun knew more about their journeys than he did.

'What do you see, cousin?' He paused, then continued irritably. 'Are we all to die?'

Tsun chuckled. 'No, but your journeying is not my journeying, cousin.'

'Kunjosum!' Tul-lok slapped the snuff bottle back into Tsun's hand.

Chapter Thirty-Eight

The Jo-Khang

The reactionaries have been routed. They are fleeing. The Dalai Lama is safe. There have been false rumours designed to give the enemies of the people a chance to seize power over you. You need not fear. Return to your homes in peace. No one who voluntarily gives up . . . The broadcast over the loudspeaker system ended abruptly as a machine gun burst smashed the speakers on the Jo-Khang square.

Hundreds of people were making their way across the square to the Jo-Khang Cathedral. News had just reached the thousands already in the square and Cathedral that a resistance group had successfully seized the Turquoise Bridge and the cinema from the Han. The city was no longer cut off.

'We've won, Namgyal-la!' Pema yelled. 'We've won!' She clasped the youth, pointing at the stream of people pouring over the bridge into the square to seek refuge in the Cathedral. Her delight reflected the euphoria of victory sweeping the square. Namgyal did not point out that the thousands coming to join them came for protection, not as reinforcements. They were standing with six women in the shadow of the Cabinet Office attached to the Cathedral. A few yards away, families were cooking their meals. Children ran back and forth collecting spent cartridge cases and comparing them, their parents chiding them if they got too close to the Han positions.

Namgyal started to edge along the wall, keeping to the deep shadow as he moved towards the PLA-held houses on the other side of the Barkor Square. He looked back at Pema and the women, each tightly holding a clay bottle of petrol.

'As soon as I've done,' he said, 'come in behind me, and then away as fast as you can.'

He edged his way up beside the Government building which projected into the street, using doorways and the shadow as cover. A few yards behind were Pema and the other women. As he neared the corner, he slipped a grenade from his ambac and fitted it into his sling. He pulled the pin, swung the sling round his head and launched the grenade. Before it exploded, he had pulled the pin off a second grenade and launched it, too. Within seconds of its impact, the women raced the few yards across the street, past Namgyal, and hurled the petrol bombs into the house. As Namgyal ran. Han troops were spilling out of the house, some aflame. He heard shots and turned to see two of the women sprawled in the street. As he reached the corner of the building, he saw Pema and the other women running after him. The Lhasa police opened up with machine gun fire on the Han troops, covering the women.

On reaching safety, they laughed with relief for a few moments, but it evaporated quickly. People in the square cheered, but they walked towards the Cathedral in silence, each wondering who would be the next to die. On the other side of the Government office, PLA troops returned the fire of the Lhasa police.

As they reached the Cathedral gates, two elderly women offered them tea, inviting them to join them. Namgyal and the women stood by the small brazier at the foot of the Cathedral steps, and the two old women filled their bowls.

'Today you have taken on good karma,' said one. Answering Namgyal's doubtful smile she went on, 'You have saved the Han from committing more evil actions and so creating some bad karma for themselves. You acted for the religion, for the country.'

Namgyal grinned, but he did not delude himself.

The Norbulinka

The monk was portly, quite bald, his head copper-tanned, but he moved quickly with a lightness of touch on the wounded man's arm. He looked up at Tsun.

'Put it in a sling, Rinposhay.' He moved on to the next man. Tsun had gathered new felicity scarves as bandages, and used one to form a sling. The man murmured thanks, if anything, more appreciative of the blessing of Tsun's attention than the actual help. His fingers moved over his wooden beads as he mumbled invocations. Two shells burst close to the temple wall, more plaster and beams fell from the roof. Tsun was aware of someone kneeling by him as he worked in the confined, crude shelter. He looked up and recognised one of the leaders of the Ragyapas, the disposers of the dead. He was a tall man, wearing a filthy patched chuba and a long earring in one ear, indicating that he was a man of substance. He rubbed his long, broad nose and Tsun found himself looking into unusually intelligent eyes.

'Rinposhay, may I speak with you? I am Tenzing.'

Tsun found it impossible to hear him above the noise of the shelling; he moved closer. As he did so, a shell exploded at the entrance to the temple, blowing the portico apart. The two men threw themselves to the floor as the entrance pillars toppled and dust and debris billowed into the temple.

They ran over to see if anyone was hurt. The entrance to the temple was a heap of rubble, much of the front wall having been blown in, but, miraculously, no one had been injured.

'Rinposhay, Tul-lok has told me of your wish to stay with the wounded. It would be better for you if you were a Ragyapa. The Han would not look for you with us.' He held out a neatly folded but disgustingly dirty chuba. Tsun looked at him for a moment, laughed, and slapped him on the shoulders.

'I am honoured to be asked to become a Ragyapa, and grateful.'

'Rinposhay! Rinposhay!' One of Genyen's men came stumbling across the fallen masonry at the door of the temple. His face was cut and bruised and he held an automatic pistol in his hand.

'Rinposhay, please come. It is Genyen!'

Tsun followed him outside. A group of Genyen's men were bent over her as she knelt, hunched, on the ground. Tul-lok was by her. He glanced wordlessly up at Tsun who realised the position, as he came close to Genyen and saw the great dark stain of blood directly in front of her. A bullet had sliced open her abdomen, she was holding her intestines in. Tsun saw that she was weeping as he knelt down beside her. She looked up suddenly, her face wet with tears and twisted in pain. A few yards away they could hear an argument about the shortage of ammunition. Genyen looked at Tsun for a few seconds, then at Tul-lok.

'Two Rinposhays,' she said quietly, through cracked lips. 'Perhaps it will make up for much.' She turned her head away. 'Bless me, please, then go.'

Tsun and Tul-lok looked at one another, touched her head in blessing, and as they stood up, heard her say firmly to one of her men:

'Now . . . shoot me!'

The man was appalled, his eyes full of fear. He raised his pistol slowly.

'I can't, Genyen . . . I can't! No . . .'

She raised her head quickly, anger in her eyes.

'Kunjosum! I'd shoot you, you child of a dog. We've done it for the others. Listen.' She jerked her head towards the fierce fighting at the main gate. 'Will you leave me for them?'

The man's hand trembled as he raised his pistol and fired at her chest. A single shot. Genyen gave a slight, gasping groan and collapsed. The man clutched his head, still shaking in denial, in protest at his action. Tul-lok and Tsun, stunned, looked down at her. The slight lines in the round, well-proportioned face relaxed, the forehead smoothed. He saw a tiny scratch on her cheek, the slight scar by the left temple where she'd been nicked by a bullet, a few long strands of black hair across the slightly opened mouth . . . Tul-lok gave a roar of angered grief, and ran. Tsun stooped and swiftly took the sheath and dagger from her belt. He walked back to the shattered temple, as, silently, he wept.

Chapter Thirty-Nine

The Jo-Khang

Pema, Namgyal and Jigme stood to one side of the central shrine in the Jo-Khang Cathedral, invoking the mantra of Chenresi. Champa was among the two hundred monks whose meditation was drawing to a close. As they fought for freedom with every weapon at their disposal, Pema, Namgyal and Jigme knew, like everyone else in the Cathedral, that their plight was part of their individual karma as well as part of the national karma; that countless causes had given effect to the country's battle for freedom from oppression, all deriving, initially, from the mind. So if it was meant to be, the meditation of the monks could be quite as effective as the bullets, probably more so.

Although Jigme had been to the Jo-Khang regularly since his arrival in Lhasa, neither Pema or Namgyal were particularly pious, and both were surprised at the profound effect they felt as they meditated at the holiest place in the country.

Behind a silver mesh screen stood the statue of the Lord Buddha as a youthful prince of the land which is now Nepal. Beneath the gilding, the crown and robes, was believed to be the oldest image of the Buddha in the world, said to have been created in his lifetime, a physical seal on the adoption of the Buddha's teaching as the national religion. Namgyal looked up at the slightly smiling, gilded face, and was aware of the man, the sage, who first set the wheel of his teachings spinning through the ages, and of the essence of the Buddha's enlightenment which the glittering majesty of the image palely reflected, for it was, he thought, an essence which was in all beings.

As Champa and the other monks made their final prostrations, Brass Nose walked slowly over to Pema, Namgyal and Jigme. He looked at the sunshine slanting through the open roof of the enormous main courtyard, in front of the central shrine, onto an array of asters, hollyhocks and rose bushes, all cultivated in pots in the centre of the yard. There were more people in the courtyard than he had ever seen, and he knew that the Cathedral could hold 10,000 for the great debates. While some spun prayer wheels, or prepared meals, others cleaned weapons. Against the massive frescoes depicting the life of the Buddha were stacked bales of brick tea, butter in yak-skin sacks, barley flour and pig carcasses, gutted and dried. The irony was not lost on him. Pema looked in amazement at a mouse which had settled on her foot and was scratching its ear. Laughing, the men teased her, making bets on how long it would stay. Suddenly, the mouse darted away. They looked up. Brass Nose greeted them and indicated that they should get out of earshot to the cloisters of shrines encircling the main courtyard.

'When you came I had no news of Samden. Now I have heard.'

'Where is he, Brass Nose?' Pema was surprised at the depth of her concern.

'Why isn't he with us?'

'He came secretly to the City Council to warn them that tanks will be brought in to crush the uprising tomorrow.'

'He still works for them!' Jigme shouted. 'He's still working for the Han!' Brass Nose's voice had an edge to it as he said:

'You know what would happen to him if it were found out that he spied for us?'

Jigme nodded.

'I only tell you so that Tsun Rinposhay can know the truth about Samden, of how he has helped us.'

'Brass Nose,' Pema asked slowly, 'they will use tanks against the Jo-Khang, won't they?'

He nodded.

'But all these people . . .' Champa murmured. 'We've got to get them out before the fighting starts.' Brass Nose automatically turned a prayer wheel which was set in the wall. 'But where can they go?' Jigme asked.

'To their houses, anywhere, a hole in the ground if need be, but they must get away . . .' Brass Nose had a coughing spasm. 'Samden had a message for you . . . He begs . . .'

The two monks laughed. Brass Nose didn't smile. 'He said you would laugh, but that I was to be sure to say that he *begs* you to leave this evening for the south.'

In the few moments' silence which followed, they all looked at one another. Pema brushed her hair out of her eyes and looked pleadingly at Brass Nose.

'How can we?' she said. 'How can we leave, Brass Nose, when there are all these . . .' She gestured towards the crowded courtyard.

'As it is getting dark, go across the square to the Turquoise Bridge and when you are out of range of the Han outpost, go over the old wall into the meadows and from there straight to the river. The ferry should be there.'

'The Han haven't captured it?' Champa asked.

'We've got as many troops as possible at the river to prevent the Han from getting across in pursuit of the Kundun.'

'But you don't know what we'll find?' Jigme frowned.

'You'll be in good company,' Brass Nose said quietly. 'Hundreds of others don't . . .' Then laughing, he slapped Jigme on the shoulder. 'Indeed, do any of us know? You must get as much food as you can carry, travel by night and be careful about lighting fires. You'll be all right,' he said, 'and you've got Namgyal on your side!' He ruffled the boy's hair with a startling show of affection, as he saw in Namgyal the boy of his youth, what he had been. 'He is a little Agu Tempa – he has the wit and cunning of a rogue and he is a wise rogue. Wise rogues survive anything. Look at me!' he laughed. 'Survived everything. I came here to die and here I am, still alive, and probably will be after all this is over.'

In the serious silence which lasted only a moment, he tapped his brass nose.

'If not, a vulture is in for a surprise when he reaches this one!'

Chapter Forty

The Jo-Khang

Brass Nose's eyes, but not his mind, were focused on the flame in the gold butter lamp. Dust from the shattered ceiling lay in the semi-liquid butter and a flake from one of the frescoes of the life of the Buddha fluttered uncertainly, fell into the flame and was burned. The flame danced wildly on the point of extinction as mortar shells were lobbed into the Cathedral. Brass Nose looked up at the colossal, gilded bronze figure of the coming Buddha. Seated, European fashion, ready to rise, the figure was dressed in brocades and silks and crowned with a gilded aureole reflecting the awakened wisdom of the Coming One. Brass Nose inclined his head and slowly offered a felicity scarf at the shrine. After a few minutes, he turned, stepped over the body of a monk and made his way through the milling crowds of refugees to a side door.

As the PLA infantry had surged into the square, mortars had opened up on the Cathedral. The resistance and Tibetan Army machine gun posts had devastated the Han approach, but always there were more. Neither they nor the Han had anticipated the retaliation of the thousands of refugees still camped in the Square and Cathedral. Disbelief at the attack on the Jo-Khang had become a rage of dreadful proportions, each individual swept up in the mood of the crowd, adding his own fury until neither Han nor Tibetan machine gunners could fire. No matter how many died, the crowd drew the infantry to itself, the two becoming a seething amalgam of vengeance, of fight for life.

For a moment, the commander of the Soviet Type-T-54 tank felt a sense of overwhelming panic as the tank entered the far end of the square and he saw the crowd. Slowly, the vehicle moved across the square. He slewed the turret round as the following two tanks came up behind. There was a moment's hesitation in the concentrated rage of the crowd. The commander of the lead tank decided to press home the advantage. 'Move into the square.' The tank picked up speed and lurched round on its steel tracks to face the Cathedral; all the time the commander kept his gun sighted on the Jo-Khang. The other tanks had only just begun to turn when they were engulfed by the crowd. The crews heard people scrambling onto the tanks, trying to get at them, faces full of hatred as they screamed and clawed at the driver's window slits; people clinging to the turret to stop its movement as the gunner repeatedly fired the machine guns at those on the front of the tank at point blank range. As the crews tried to free themselves by moving against the crowd, petrol bombs were thrown at the tanks, but they seemed impenetrable.

Brass Nose, however, had seen tanks before, and knew that they were not.

Praying that a bullet would not hit the petrol bomb in his ambac, Brass Nose bent low and, screened by the crowd, positioned himself as the first tank came towards him, jerking as its wheels spewed out the rocks and logs thrown into its tracks. He hurled the petrol bomb exactly on target. The external fuel tanks exploded in a mushroom of flame which swiftly spread. The two tanks following came to a halt, machine guns pouring bullets into the crowd. Someone stepped on Brass Nose's hand. He did not notice. He was dead.

A mortar shell bursting on a butter-greasy flagstone of the Cathedral sent dozens of mice scurrying for cover in the recesses of the Coming One's shrine, their pink feet running over a shaped and polished brass nose, wrapped in a tattered and grimy felicity scarf.

The Happy River

Pema, Jigme, Champa and Namgyal, with dozens of others, lay in the cover of the slight rise behind the broad, stony bank of the river. Others had tried to reach the coracles during the day. They lay dead along the bank. Three coracles remained, broken and torn; of the ferry, there was no sign.

None of them spoke as they looked the bare mile down river to the main PLA camp on the far side, beneath the dun coloured mountains surrounding the vale. Its searchlights swept the river and bank as it maintained a continuous bombardment in the direction of the Norbulinka and the surrounding fields. Even at that distance, with the moon and the searchlights, they could see the ruins of the Medical College on the Iron Hill, behind which lay the Norbulinka Park. Each was thinking of Tsun.

'What are we going to do?' Pema asked nobody in particular, for she knew that no one would answer. Behind them, only a quarter of a mile away, fires were raging in the city, but with dusk had come sporadic lulls in the shooting.

'Come on.' A well built man, keeping low, had run to the edge of the wide river. 'If we form a chain we can ford it here. 'Quickly!'

The sixty or so people who were crouched behind the rise, joined him.

'The current's far too dangerous,' someone said.

It was, but there was nothing else. Three of the strongest men were first in, then Jigme, followed by Pema, holding his hand, then Namgyal and Champa. The water was icy. Gradually, the human chain moved out from the bank.

Clutching onto one another, with each step they went deeper into the torrential river, unable to hear or see properly from the spume and vicious currents which pulled at them relentlessly. An elderly woman lost her footing and, before anyone realised what had happened, her frail hands lost their grip and she was borne away, disappearing beneath the water as she was dragged towards the Han camp. As the broken chain struggled to keep its foothold and rejoin hands, others lost their grip and were swept away.

'Look out for the horse!' The three leading men caught sight of the body of a horse being carried towards them. They could not move away from the narrow ford where they were already chest deep. The current changed suddenly and Pema knew she couldn't keep her foothold much longer. She felt the physical grasp of the current as her clothes were ripped from her.

The three leaders warded off the horse, but instead of being swept on, it swung into the human chain. Pema heard a slight, distant yell. She saw Namgyal's face only inches from hers as she and Champa clung to one of his hands, trying to drag him back, his whole body being pulled away by the river. She glimpsed his frightened expression, then he was gone.

Jigme and Champa helped Pema from the water, and they in turn helped those behind them. So many had been lost in the crossing. As they stumbled up the bank, their clothes ripped to rags, Champa tripped over a bloated body, crumpled up in a tattered chuba. The young man Tsun had advised to flee with his wife and child three days before.

Chapter Forty-One

The Norbulinka

It was in the afternoon of the 23rd March, twelve days after the crowds had first gathered round the Norbulinka to prevent the Kundun from going to the Han headquarters, that the last pockets of resistance realised that the PLA troops were being pulled off the streets. The mortars and Howitzers fell silent. The fires were left to burn themselves out. There was hardly any movement in the city. The living had either fled or remained barricaded in their homes. Stunned, waiting; praying at their family shrines, or preparing for flight. Some had few preparations to make for their short, final journey: a noose, or just to walk quietly into the river.

The dead and the dying lay by the hundred in the streets, the parks, on the river bank, at the Potala, the Iron Mountain, the Cathedral, the Norbulinka. The desolation was highlighted by the few whose grief had overcome their fear as they moved from body to body in their search, needing to know, yet dreading the answer. A young woman angrily flayed with her apron at a street dog as it gnawed at the heel of a dying man. In the Norbulinka, everyone had been arrested by the PLA and grouped according to their occupation and class before being temporarily imprisoned in the remaining secure buildings. The tall Han officer spoke good Tibetan as he looked at the group of twenty Ragyapas, including Tsun.

'You are disposers of the dead, you can help dispose of your dead. Begin outside the park.'

Tsun and the Ragyapas were marched through the shattered main gate of the Norbulinka. They saw that already a prisoner detail of monks were building pyres from the debris and wood of the barricades, and stacking bags of butter beside them, while others were collecting the corpses for burning. Tenzing and Tsun had some difficulty in carrying the first body, a woman in her twenties with one leg blown off.

'The shooting's stopped,' said Tenzing. Tsun frowned. He hadn't heard. Tenzing repeated his comment. There was much

Tsun had not heard since the shelling of the Norbulinka. He was beginning to realise that what he thought was something temporary, was not. His hearing had been permanently damaged by the noise of the shelling.

The silence of Lhasa was broken by the loudspeaker system which announced General Tan Kuan-san, Political Commissar of the PLA:

People of Lhasa. The Potala, the Jo-Khang, the Medical College, the Rammoche Temple, the Norbulinka, have been freed from the rebels by the People's Liberation Army and patriotic Tibetans of the Motherland. Many people have been duped by the serf-owning reactionaries and counter-revolutionaries, with the connivance of foreign imperialist agents. Lay down your arms, don't allow yourselves to be used by these enemies of the people who can only offer death. Give up your arms, you will not be blamed.

The derisive scepticism of those who were PLA prisoners was more muted than the rest of the population. But everyone paused to listen to a familiar voice.

I am Ngabo, Nagwang Jigme. You know I am a member of the Tibetan Government. The Kundun has not been killed, he has been abducted against his will by reactionaries. I am speaking for the Tibetan Government. An agreement has been reached with the Han authorities of the Central People's Government. All fighting must stop. This is the wish of the Tibetan Government.

As Tsun hauled the body of an old man onto the mound of corpses, he reflected that Tan, late in the day, had been astute enough to give the population enough hope, when they knew they were beaten, to make them grasp at the straw. To have the Kundun's escape confirmed, to have the possibility of an amnesty, had brought many onto their rooftops and to their doorways, holding felicity scarves as a sign of surrender. The resistance were pulling out of their few remaining positions to carry on the fight in the mountains to the south.

At dusk the cremation fires burned fiercely. Tsun, his greasy patched chuba, face and hands covered in blood, was staggering with exhaustion as he dragged another body towards the fire. Many of the monks had broken down, even some of the Ragyapas had, and they were used to dissecting bodies for the vultures. On three occasions, Tsun had been stopped from taking the body of a monk to the fire until it had been checked by a small group of senior officers and civilian cadres. As they came closer and Tsun saw them use a sponge and bucket of water to clean the face of yet another dead monk, he knew that the Han were unsure of what had happened to the Kundun, that they thought he might have been killed. As Tsun collected a body close to the group, one, in a blue civilian uniform, caught his eye. It was Samden. There was only the slightest of reactions on the face of each, a recognition of the shared anguish and the questions which could not be answered.

As the group moved on, Tsun folded the mangled body of the monk they had checked into its robe. Using it as a sack, he dragged the broken body across the road, his eyes searching the sky, longing for darkness to come when surely the Han would let them rest. In the distance, his eyes focused on the Potala and he realised that, for the first time, Han red flags were flying from the roof. Six hundred feet below, at the end of the ceremonial way from the Norbulinka, the Great Chorten with its gilded spire, which formed the Western Gate, was reduced to an anonymous heap of rubble.

. . . all beings will be sunk in hardship and fear and the nights will drag on slowly in suffering . . .

Epilogue: February, 1983

Even Tsun had found the night cripplingly cold, with the temperature dropping to 30 degrees below freezing, and his companion had suffered particularly badly. The morning, however, was beautifully crisp, the sky cloudless, and their chilled bodies gradually responded to the warmth of the sun. The woman had untied the plaid scarf round her hair; unlike most Han women, Tsun noticed, she had let it grow and left it unplaited. He was reminded again that beneath the disguise of dirt, maturity suited Ling. She had the confidence of position and experience but also, he thought, very unusually for one of the 'higher levels', humour.

They were following the military road, across the rolling hills at the foot of Chomolhari. In the brilliant sunlight the mountain glistened, finely etched against the deep blue sky. Ling was having great difficulty in breathing at the high altitude. Tsun took her arm, and they slowed the pace as he talked, gently calming her.

'I thought I'd got acclimatised,' she said breathlessly.

'I noticed you didn't come clutching a canvas oxygen bottle, like most of your compatriots,' he laughed.

She looked at him. 'I really don't think I could survive another night like last night.'

The wind's penetrating coldness had been as terrible as a knife, the pain was so excruciating, its moans and howls made it impossible to hear or even think clearly. Tsun was worried about her, too, and the coming night.

'We should reach a Han rest-house by nightfall,' he smiled. 'And the following day the border.'

But they would be hard pressed, he thought, to reach shelter for the night unless they could keep up a good pace. He held her arm as they walked slowly beside the military road. She noticed his other hand counting off the beads of a rosary, seeming not to pause even when talking.

'Tell me, Ling,' he said suddenly, 'why *are* you here? A ranking cadre, dressed as a beggarwoman? I expect you even go about in those curtained limousines in Lhasa and Peking, don't you?'

She laughed:

'Sometimes in Lhasa, but I never go to Peking.'

'All right, so you arrived at Phari yesterday having tracked me down with the warning that I am likely to be discovered and then you want to come with me to India.'

'I told you why.' She looked at him with a dry smile, which always left an uncertainty. 'Anyway, you are the lama, you should know.'

Her words came in gasps, but her breathing was more rhythmic and there was not the same strain in her voice.

'Because I am a lama?' he laughed.

'Because you are Tsun Rinposhay.'

'For a time I was, as for a time I had another name; neither are me, Ling.'

She was about to mock him for his pedantry when she saw from his face, just for a moment, that he was only speaking the truth. The man who was Tsun Rinposhay had travelled a very long way since he had been known by that name. He looked at her, and she realised to her embarrassment that she was blushing. Perhaps it was because she wanted him to believe her, she thought.

'As you say, Tsun, I have done well since the last time I saw you.'

They were walking very slowly, occasionally pausing to allow her to maintain her regular breathing, and as she talked she found her eyes held by the mountain of the lady goddess, as it subtly changed in the shifting sunlight.

'I am now a ranking cadre. But rank brings responsibility. Its privileges, its disillusions, mount. You know I believed in our policy. But I saw confidential documents which showed that it was expected at a very early stage that the people here would resist, that if there was general discontent, food had to be cut and work increased. It was the document an invader prepares when he knows the country under occupation is going to resist. It was true. I knew that it was the people and not counter-revolutionaries who were resisting. I must stop for a moment, Tsun.'

He looked at her, concerned, but she was pulling a packet of cigarettes out of her pocket.

'You remember how I used to be?' She flicked the lighter, masking it from the light breeze with her other hand. As she pulled at the cigarette she had a violent fit of coughing. She walked on, holding the cigarette.

'I believed, and it seemed to me that Tibetans didn't understand because they saw the benefits we were bringing as something too frightening and too threatening. It was as they are with swimming, mostly too frightened to let go of the bank.'

Tentatively, she drew again on the cigarette, but immediately started coughing. Irritably she threw the cigarette away, aware that they really should quicken their pace. She paused while she got into her stride with her breathing. Tsun watched her visibly begin to relax.

'More than anything, though, it was the attitude which quickly disillusioned me, changed me. How our cadres have made themselves the elite, occasionally as it is called, "returning to the lower levels". In that respect Mao was right to want to break the bureaucracy. I was really naive, I suppose. I began to see the manoeuvring, the reliance on patronage, the importance of building oneself securely into a faction, the use that was made of the whole movement, and if there were these struggles at this level, what about higher up? Mao regarded the people as "a blank sheet of paper". They were, I thought, the words of a poet, a visionary. But he wrote, screwed up the paper, and started on another sheet. You know that, when we first met, I could speak Tibetan. It was unusual. It is still unusual twenty-seven years later. It comes from the basic attitude that pervades everything here, that Tibetans are fundamentally untrustworthy, are barbarians. The Lhasa uprising convinced them of that. This was the only lesson they drew from that uprising and they' – she shrugged – '*We*, I suppose, act on that basis. You would think that with official policy being to encourage the cadres in Tibet to rectify their mistakes of the past, to learn Tibetan, I would be in a more sympathetic situation. In fact, I am a source of suspicion. I've been here too long, become too associated with Tibetans. But the Tibetans can never trust me as a senior cadre.'

It was almost as though she were talking to herself. She had never been able to articulate these thoughts before.

'Perhaps it is that which has convinced me that it is too late. Now there is fear on both sides. Such a wide gulf, basic prejudice and antipathy. I used to think that at the central level in Peking it was not fully understood what was going on, much it did not realise, but Peking knows enough now. It is the central government which in the long term wants Tibet sinified, so that there is a majority of Han and Tibetans become a minority in their own land.'

For a few moments they walked in silence. Tsun asked slowly:

'You have a husband, perhaps children?'

'No child. But yes, a husband. And of the right class background.' She smiled as though it was almost a surprise to herself. 'We had to serve in different areas for most of the time we were married, just seeing one another for a month each year. For the past three years I haven't heard from him. I don't blame him.'

Suddenly she felt embarrassed again.

'And what is there in coming with me?'

It surprised her that the answer was not really quite as straightforward as she said:

'I have been brought up on hatred, Tsun. Always there has been an enemy to be defeated, to be struggled against. You don't hate. You don't hate us. Maybe, I should find out why? Perhaps this is a chance to find out.'

She looked up at him, he smiled. 'Maybe.'

'Look!'

A marmot the size of a large cat was sitting upright watching them as they approached.

'We call them gomchens,' Tsun said. 'The hermits. Their burrows are like the hermit's cave.'

She started to change direction to bring them closer.

'Take care. They can give off the foulest smell!'

'Are you angry?' Ling asked quietly. 'Or bitter?'

'There has been more anger, more bitterness, Ling, than I would have believed possible. But unless its energy was transmuted it achieved nothing except to add to my suffering. I grieve though, Ling, I weep at the years, the families broken, lost to one another, the cruelty, the countless unknown individual tragedies. I grieve at the destruction of our freedom, our religion, our culture. I grieve at the ignorance of those who have caused our suffering and at the effect it will have on them. I grieve that we weep alone, that no one in the world hears us. But I know that our weeping, the weeping of thousands, each alone and isolated, is not without its effect. In that grief it has been my karma to have learnt and to see beyond it a different perspective.'

For a while they did not talk, Ling concentrating on quickening her pace.

'And it was just my letter to Kesang which, after all this time, told you where I was?'

Ling nodded.

Kesang's letter had been written nearly twelve months before, reaching him only two weeks ago. He had taken such care not to write anything compromising, mentioning nothing that could cause difficulties if the Han got hold of it, so that inevitably it raised dozens of questions in Tsun's mind. He knew the letter by heart.

March 1982

Dear Pa-la,

I do not know if this letter will find you, or indeed if you really are alive. Someone from Phari was describing his friend to me and it sounded as though it was you, who are as my own father. Every day since we were parted I have prayed that we should one day be reunited.

Of the others: Rinchen-la died while we were leaving for India and I have to tell you that, sadly, Pema-la also died.

Champa has made a good life at the new Drebung Monastery built by the refugees in South India and Jigme is now married with two small girls. He works with a craft centre. Tul-lok is with me and gives his time to meditations. He has told me of Genyen's death, but I know nothing of Samden.

The dreams came true, Pa-la. I have travelled to other lands in the iron birds. There are many there interested in the teaching. I work to pass on to our people the teachings of the Buddha and our traditions. Our endeavours are for the day when we shall all be together.

If it is indeed my Pa-la who reads this letter, do please send me a message through our friend and if it is not, then forgive me and pray in your heart, I beg, for a true 'awakening warrior'.

Kesang.

Tsun discovered that quite by chance Kesang had met in India a Nepalese trader with a permit from the Han to trade with the state shops in Phari. He had talked of his friend in Phari who gave him spiritual advice. It wasn't long, the trader had told Tsun, before Kesang was sure he knew the 'friend' and the trader agreed to bring Kesang's letter on his next visit to Phari. When he left he had taken Tsun's reply. It was this that had given Ling the clue to his identity.

'I am puzzled, Ling. I am sure there is no record of me as "Tsun" after the uprising and I was very careful in my letter, both about names and places. What did I forget?'

Ling laughed.

'The messenger! When he was asked who the letter was for, he said Dorje Rinposhay. There seemed no harm. When Public Security eventually checked back on his name, there was yours. They knew the man had come from Phari and there has been concern at persistent rumours of an underground community of monks in the area, and this set off the interest.'

'So there wasn't any certainty that it was me?'

'No. But when I heard about it I decided to find out.'

'What will happen now, do you think?'

'I hope that I have pre-empted any action in Phari. They have no reason not to believe my story, that allowing you one of the new passes for pilgrimage and my going with you in disguise would make you far more useful to us at present, when we need to know what is happening outside among the refugees, than would arresting you.'

They might change their minds, Tsun thought, if they knew about the appeal!

The stunted bush and grass covering the low, rolling hills around them, whispered gently in the breeze. Ling felt the sun's warmth sinking into her and they walked for a few moments just listening.

'Will the border guards have been alerted to our coming as pilgrims?' Tsun asked.

'No. The more people I involved the more constraints I put on myself.'

Tsun almost wished the guards did know. He would have quite liked any help she could give them to get through the border post, although with the passes there should not be any trouble. But it was no guarantee, he thought.

'I can see why your colleagues at the Public Security Office were attracted by your idea.'

Ling frowned, taking off her glasses and polishing them on the sleeve of her jacket.

'It is a means,' Tsun continued, 'of getting into the first Great Prayer Festival held since the uprising. Refugees from all over the world will be attending with the Kundun, so what better place to assess the situation of Tibet-in-exile, which with your knowledge of Tibetan you are more than well qualified to do? It could be difficult on your own, but you have me with you, virtually as a protector and guide, and if I were to be unco-operative there are always Namgyal and his family as hostages.'

Ling looked at him with wide, angry eyes.

'Do you really believe that?' Her voice was sharp.

'Perhaps not, Ling.' He smiled. 'But can you blame me for being aware of it?'

She shook her head, but did not speak.

They walked in silence. Ling longed for a cigarette, but as her breathing was settling down she did not dare risk it, promising herself one when they stopped to eat. Suddenly she realised that with a shift of sunlight another fold of the mountains had appeared. The stratified layers were clearly visible in the wedge of rock.

'Do you remember your telling me, Tsun, about the belief that Tibet was once under water?' He did not, but he nodded.

'Well, a few years ago, we had two scientific expeditions of geologists,' then, unsure if he knew what it meant, 'who study rocks and so on, working in Tibet. They found fossils here of creatures which lived at the bottom of the sea some 180 million years ago, and it seems that about 70 million years ago the Indian sub-continent and Asia moved towards one another and the Himalayas were thrust up. Even now, they are still growing and changing.'

There was a lightness and enthusiasm in her voice which he had not heard before, and she caught his smile, but felt no embarrassment.

Something made Tsun turn. In the distance, a bus was coming towards them along the curving road. There were no bus services, only for special journeys, but sometimes it was possible to hitch a ride on an army truck, so why not a bus? Tsun thought.

'Tsun, can we try and get a lift?'

He was beginning to feel very concerned that they might not make shelter by nightfall.

'Yes. But be careful, Ling. Pretend that you are too shy to talk. Your too excellent Chinese could arouse suspicion!'

She nodded and hastily took off her glasses. They kept walking, turning as the bus approached, trying to see who was in it. Tsun waved the bus down, knowing it was quite likely to ignore him. But it slowed as it approached and he saw it was full of Westerners.

The bus drove very slowly past them. Ling was beside herself with rage, hurling abuse and epithets which even Tsun had not heard before. He was laughing and they were about to continue walking when the bus stopped, and half-a-dozen of the Westerners crowded out of the bus. Ling looked at Tsun nervously. Some of the men were relieving themselves at the roadside, but two walked towards the shabbily dressed couple in their odd mixture of Tibetan and Chinese-cum-Western clothing.

'Can we give you a ride?' one of the men asked.

Tsun resisted the temptation to reply in English as the man explained in sign language. They both smiled and nodded acceptance.

'We are going to give our friends a lift.' It was said mainly for the benefit of the Han accompanying the journalists as they climbed aboard the dusty single-decker bus. As Tsun and Ling were being shown to one of the wooden slatted seats, a furious Han cadre rushed up the gangway from the back of the bus.

'Out, green brains. Out! There's been a mistake.'

The man was shouting at them in Chinese and, assuming as he spoke that they did not understand, began physically to manhandle them off the bus.

Tsun gripped his arm, saying, 'I understand you.' And turning abruptly from the startled man, just managed to prevent an enraged Ling from saying anything, as they walked towards the door.

'What are you doing?' The press-men intervened. 'We invited them aboard to give them a lift. They are old and going in the same direction as us. What's the harm?'

'It isn't allowed,' the Han official shouted.

'What isn't allowed?'

A second Han came up from the back to join his colleague.

'Picking up strangers on the road. It could be dangerous.'

Amid the roars of laughter which greeted this remark and the angry confusion of the officials, Tsun and Ling climbed off the bus.

'Look, they've gone,' one of the journalists shouted. 'We asked them on board. Are you going to insult our hospitality?'

'It isn't allowed,' the official screamed at the bus-load of angry journalists, shouting at the driver to get the bus started. One of the press-men leaned out of the window. Tsun looked up at him and the man was aware of a curious strength in the ebony eyes.

'Please come with us.' He indicated the coach. 'We are sorry.'

Tsun smiled at the journalist.

'Thank you for your kindness,' he said quietly and quickly in English, 'but it is better that we make our own way.'

They walked on. The bus started up, came up behind them, then slowed. Ling was torn between hope and anxiety. It had almost stopped and as it came abreast of them they could see the Han officials and journalists arguing over the driver. Suddenly he changed gear and the bus lurched on, gathering speed. In their laughter, Tsun and Ling forgot what had been and what was to come.

The intense dark blue of the sky reflected in the folds of the white chiselled mountains. At the summit of the mountain of the goddess lady, a spume of snow was swirled up by a storm.